By George R. R. Martin

A Song of Ice and Fire

Book One: A Game of Thrones
Book Two: A Clash of Kings
Book Three: A Storm of Swords
Book Four: A Feast for Crows
Book Five: A Dance with Dragons

Dying of the Light
Windhaven (with Lisa Tuttle)
Fevre Dream
The Armageddon Rag
Dead Man's Hand (with John J. Miller)

Short Story Collections

Dreamsongs: Volume I
Dreamsongs: Volume II
A Song for Lya and Other Stories
Songs of Stars and Shadows
Sandkings
Songs the Dead Men Sing
Nightflyers
Tuf Voyaging
Portraits of His Children
Quartet

Edited by George R. R. Martin

New Voices in Science Fiction, Volumes 1–4
The Science Fiction Weight Loss Book (with Isaac Asimov and Martin Harry Greenberg)
The John W. Campbell Awards, Volume 5
Night Visions 3
Wild Cards I–XXII

Co-edited with Gardner Dozois

Warriors I–III
Songs of the Dying Earth
Songs of Love and Death
Down These Strange Streets
Old Mars
Dangerous Women

By Gardner Dozois

Novels

Strangers
Nightmare Blue (with George Alec Effinger)
Hunter's Run (with George R. R. Martin and Daniel Abraham)

Short Story Collections

When the Great Days Come
Strange Days: Fabulous Journeys with Gardner Dozois
Geodesic Dreams
Morning Child and Other Stories
Slow Dancing Through Time
The Visible Man

Edited by Gardner Dozois

The Year's Best Science Fiction #1–30
The New Space Opera (with Jonathan Strahan)
The New Space Opera 2 (with Jonathan Strahan)
Modern Classics of Science Fiction
Modern Classics of Fantasy
The Good Old Stuff
The Good New Stuff
The "Magic Tales" series 1–37 (with Jack Dann)
Wizards (with Jack Dann)
The Dragon Book (with Jack Dann)
A Day in the Life
Another World

ROGUES

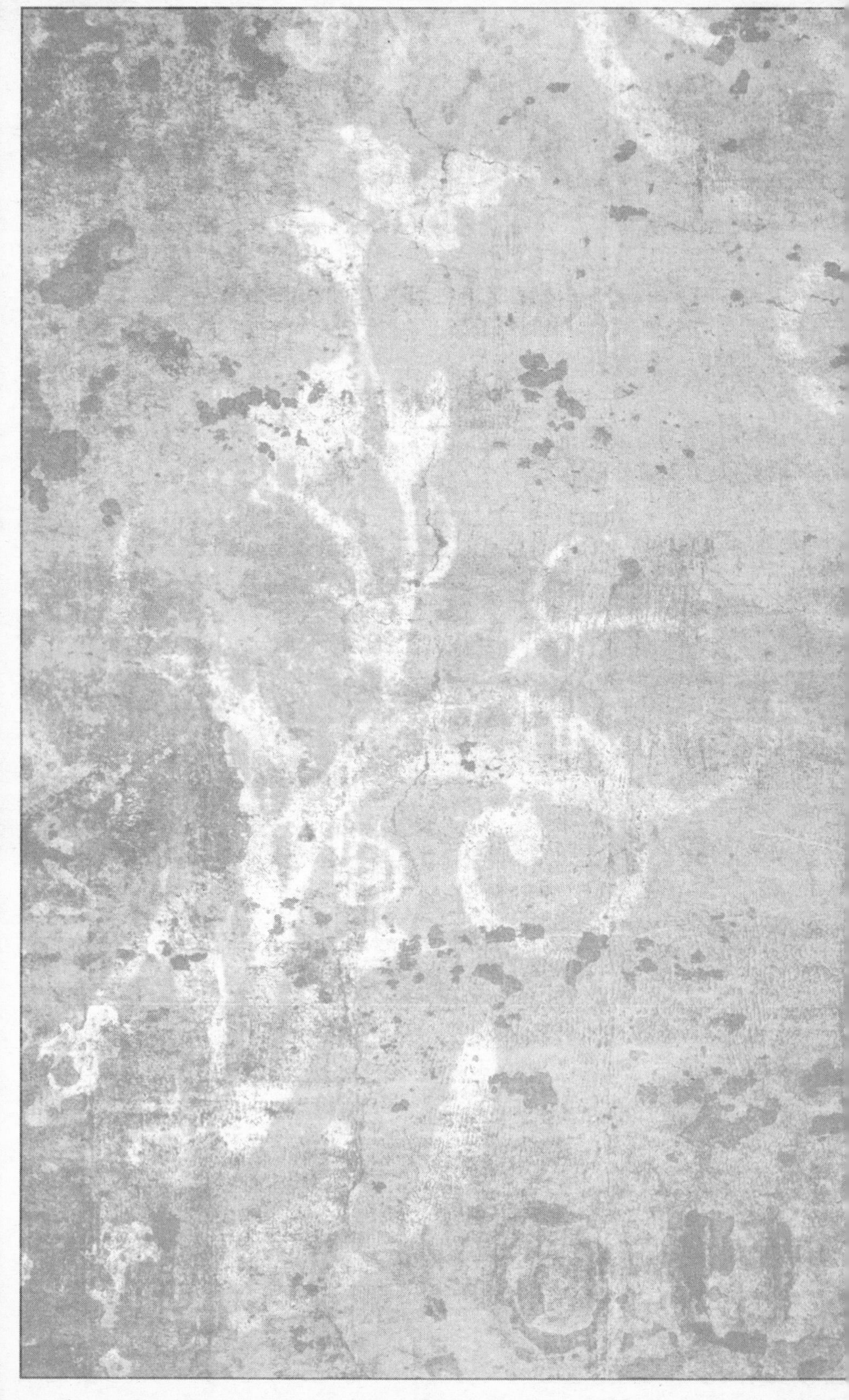

Edited by

George R. R. Martin

and Gardner Dozois

TITAN BOOKS

Rogues
Hardback edition ISBN: 9781783297191
Paperback edition ISBN: 9781783297405
E-book edition ISBN: 9781783297207

Published by Titan Books
A division of Titan Publishing Group Ltd.
144 Southwark Street, London, SE1 0UP

First edition August 2014
1 3 5 7 9 10 8 6 4 2

This edition published by arrangement with Bantam Books, an imprint of Random House, a division of Random House LLC, a Penguin Random House Company, New York.

www.titanbooks.com

Book design by Virginia Norey

A CIP catalogue record for this title is available from the British Library.

Printed and bound in Great Britain by CPI Group (UK) Ltd, Croydon, CR0 4YY

For
Joe and Gay Haldeman
Two Swashbuckling Rogues

Contents

Introduction

EVERYBODY LOVES A ROGUE

by George R. R. Martin

. . . though sometimes we live to regret it.

Scoundrels, con men, and scalawags. Ne'er-do-wells, thieves, cheats, and rascals. Bad boys and bad girls. Swindlers, seducers, deceivers, flimflam men, imposters, frauds, fakes, liars, cads, tricksters . . . they go by many names, and they turn up in stories of all sorts, in every genre under the sun, in myth and legend . . . and, oh, everywhere in history as well. They are the children of Loki, the brothers of Coyote. Sometimes they are heroes. Sometimes they are villains. More often they are something in between, grey characters . . . and grey has long been my favorite color. It is so much more interesting than black or white.

I guess I have always been partial to rogues. When I was a boy in the fifties, it sometimes seemed that half of prime-time television was sitcoms, and the other half was Westerns. My father loved Westerns, so growing up, I saw them all, an unending parade of strong-jawed sheriffs and frontier marshals, each more heroic than the last. Marshal Dillon was a rock, Wyatt Earp was brave, courageous, and bold (it said so right in the theme song), and the Lone Ranger, Hopalong Cassidy, Gene Autry, and Roy Rogers were heroic, noble, upstanding, the most perfect role models any lad could want . . . but none of them ever seemed quite real to me. My favorite Western heroes were the two who broke the mold: Paladin, who dressed in black (like a villain) when on the trail and like some sissified dandy when in San Francisco, "kept company" (ahem) with a different pretty woman every week, and hired out his services for money (heroes did not care about money); and the Maverick brothers (especially Bret), charming scoundrels who preferred the gambler's attire of black suit, string tie, and fancy waistcoat to the traditional marshal's garb of vest and badge and white hat, and were more likely to be found at a poker table than in a gunfight.

And, you know, when viewed today, *Maverick* and *Have Gun—Will Travel* hold up much better than the more traditional Westerns of their time. You can argue that they had better writing, better acting, and better directors than most of the other horse operas in the stable, and you would not be wrong . . . but I think the rogue factor has something to do with it as well.

But it's not just fans of old television Westerns who appreciate a good rogue. Truth is, this is a character archetype that cuts across all mediums and genres.

Clint Eastwood became a star by playing characters like Rowdy Yates, Dirty Harry, and the Man With No Name, rogues all. If instead he had been cast as Goody Yates, By-the-Book Billy, and the Man with Two Forms of Identification, no one would ever have heard of him. Now, it's true, when I was in college I knew a girl who preferred Ashley Wilkes, so noble and self-sacrificing, to that cad Rhett Butler, gambler, blockade-runner . . . but I think she's the only one. Every other woman I've ever met would take Rhett over Ashley in a hot minute, and let's not even talk about Frank Kennedy and Charles Wilkes. Harrison Ford comes across rather roguishly in every part he plays, but of course it all started with Han Solo and Indiana Jones. Is there anyone who truly prefers Luke Skywalker to Han Solo? Sure, Han is only in it for the money, he makes that plain right from the start . . . which makes it all the more thrilling when he returns at the end of *Star Wars* to put that rocket up Darth Vader's butt. (Oh, and he *DOES* shoot first in the cantina scene, no matter how George Lucas retcons that first movie.) And Indy . . . Indy is the very definition of rogue. Pulling out his gun to shoot that swordsman wasn't fair at all . . . but my, didn't we love him for it?

But it's not just television and film where rogues rule. Look at the books.

Consider epic fantasy.

Now, fantasy often gets characterized as a genre in which absolute good battles absolute evil, and certainly that sort of thing is plentiful, especially in the hands of the legions of Tolkien imitators with their endless dark lords, evil minions, and square-jawed heroes. But there is an older subgenre of fantasy that absolutely teems with rogues, called sword and sorcery. Conan of Cimmeria is sometimes characterized as a hero, but let us not forget, he was also a thief, a reaver, a pirate, a mercenary, and ultimately a usurper who installed himself on a stolen throne . . . and slept with every attractive woman he met along the way. Fafhrd and the Gray Mouser are even more roguish, albeit somewhat less successful. It is unlikely either one will end up a king. And then we have Jack Vance's thoroughly amoral (and thoroughly delightful) Cugel the Clever, whose scheming never quite seems to produce the desired results, but still . . .

Historical fiction has its share of dashing, devious, untrustworthy scalawags as well. The Three Musketeers certainly had their roguish qualities. (You cannot really buckle a swash without some.) Rhett Butler was as big a rogue in the novel as he was in the film. Michael Chabon gave us two splendid new rogues in Amram and Zelikman, the stars of his historical novella *Gentlemen of the Road,* and I for one hope we see a lot more of that pair. And of course there is George MacDonald Fraser's immortal Harry Flashman (that's *Sir Harry Paget Flashman* VC KCB KCIE to you, please), a character kinda sorta borrowed from *Tom Brown's Schooldays,* Thomas Hughes's classic British-boarding-school novel (sort of like Harry Potter without quidditch, magic, or girls). If you haven't read MacDonald's Flashman books (you can skip the Hughes, unless you're into Victorian moralizing), you have yet to meet one of literature's great rogues. I envy you the experience.

Westerns? Hell, the whole Wild West teemed with rogues. The outlaw hero is just as common as the outlaw villain, if not more so. Billy the Kid? Jesse James and his gang? Doc Holliday, rogue dentist *extraordinaire*? And if we may glance back at television once again—pay cable this time, though—we also have HBO's fabulous and much-lamented *Deadwood,* and the dastard at the center of it all, Al Swearengen. As played by Ian McShane, Swearengen completely stole that show from its putative hero, the sheriff. But then, rogues are good at stealing. It's one of the things that they do best.

What about the romance genre? Hoo. The rogue almost always gets the girl in a romance. These days the rogue IS the girl, oft as not, which can be even cooler. It is always nice to see conventions standing on their heads.

Mystery fiction has entire subgenres about rogues. Private eyes have always had that aspect to them; if they were straight-up, by-the-book, just-the-facts-ma'am sort of guys, they would be cops. They're not.

I could go on. Literary fiction, gothics, paranormal romance, chick lit, horror, cyberpunk, steampunk, urban fantasy, nurse novels, tragedy, comedy, erotica, thrillers, space opera, horse opera, sports stories, military fiction, ranch romances . . . every genre and subgenre has its rogues; as often as not they're the characters most cherished and best remembered.

All those genres are not represented in this anthology, alas . . . but there is part of me that wishes that they were. Maybe it's the rogue in me, the part of me that loves to color outside the lines, but the truth is, I don't have much respect for genre barriers. These days I am best known as a fantasy writer, but *Rogues* is not meant to be a fantasy anthology . . . though it does have some good fantasy in it. My co-editor, Gardner Dozois, edited a science-fiction magazine for a couple of decades, but *Rogues* is not a science-fiction anthology either . . . though it does feature some SF stories as good as anything you'll find in the monthly magazines.

Like *Warriors* and *Dangerous Women,* our previous crossgenre anthologies, *Rogues* is meant to cut across all genre lines. Our theme is universal, and Gardner and I both love good stories of all sorts, no matter what time, place, or genre they are set in, so we went out and invited well-known authors from the worlds of mystery, epic fantasy, sword and sorcery, urban fantasy, science fiction, romance, mainstream, mystery (cozy or hard-boiled), thriller, historical, romance, Western, noir, horror . . . you name it. Not all of them accepted, but many did, and the results are on the pages that follow. Our contributors make up an all-star lineup of award-winning and bestselling writers, representing a dozen different publishers and as many genres. We asked each of them for the same thing—a story about a rogue, full of deft twists, cunning plans, and reversals. No genre limits were imposed upon on any of our writers. Some chose to write in the genre they're best known for. Some decided to try something different.

In my introduction to *Warriors,* the first of our crossgenre anthologies, I talked about growing up in Bayonne, New Jersey, in the 1950s, a city without a single bookstore. I bought all my reading material at newsstands and the corner "candy shops," from wire spinner racks. The paperbacks on those spinner racks were not segregated by genre. Everything was jammed in together, a copy of this, two copies of that. You might find *The Brothers Karamazov* sandwiched between a nurse novel and the latest Mike Hammer yarn from Mickey Spillane. Dorothy Parker and Dorothy Sayers shared rack space with Ralph Ellison and J. D. Salinger. Max Brand rubbed up against Barbara Cartland. A. E. van Vogt, P. G. Wodehouse, and H. P. Lovecraft were crammed in with F. Scott Fitzgerald. Mysteries, Westerns, gothics, ghost stories, classics of English literature, the latest contemporary "literary" novels, and, of course, SF and fantasy and horror—you could find it all on that spinner rack, and ten thousand others like it.

I liked it that way. I still do. But in the decades since (too many decades, I fear), publishing has changed, chain bookstores have multiplied, the genre barriers have hardened. I think that's a pity. Books should broaden us, take us to places we have never been and show us things we've never seen, expand our horizons and our way of looking at the world. Limiting your reading to a single genre defeats that. It limits us, makes us smaller. It seemed to me, then as now, that there were good stories and bad stories, and that was the only distinction that truly mattered.

We think we have some good ones here. You will find rogues of every size, shape, and color in these pages, with a broad variety of settings, representing a healthy mix of different genres and subgenres. But you won't know *which* genres and subgenres until you've read them, for Gardner and I, in the tradition of that old wire spinner rack, have mixed them all up. Some of the tales herein were written by your favorite writers, we expect; others are by writers you may never have heard of (yet). It's our hope that by the time you finish *Rogues,* a few of the latter may have become the former.

Enjoy the read . . . but do be careful. Some of the gentlemen and lovely ladies in these pages are not entirely to be trusted.

ROGUES

Joe Abercrombie

Joe Abercrombie is one of the fastest-rising stars in fantasy today, acclaimed by readers and critics alike for his tough, spare, no-nonsense approach to the genre. He's probably best known for his *First Law* trilogy, the first novel of which, *The Blade Itself,* was published in 2006; it was followed in subsequent years by *Before They Are Hanged* and *Last Argument of Kings.* He's also written the stand-alone fantasy novels *Best Served Cold* and *The Heroes.* His most recent novel is *Red Country.* In addition to writing, Abercrombie is also a freelance film editor, and lives and works in London.

In the fast-paced thriller that follows, he takes us deep into the dirty, rank, melodious, and mazelike streets of Sipani, one of the world's most dangerous cities, for a deadly game of Button, Button, Who's Got the Button?

TOUGH TIMES ALL OVER

Joe Abercrombie

Damn, but she hated Sipani.

The bloody blinding fogs and the bloody slapping water and the bloody universal sickening stink of rot. The bloody parties and masques and revels. Fun, everyone having bloody fun, or at least pretending to. The bloody people were worst of all. Rogues every man, woman, and child. Liars and fools, the lot of them.

Carcolf hated Sipani. Yet here she was again. Who, then, she was forced to wonder, was the fool?

Braying laughter echoed from the mist ahead and she slipped into the shadows of a doorway, one hand tickling the grip of her sword. A good courier trusts no one, and Carcolf was the very best, but in Sipani, she trusted . . . less than no one.

Another gang of pleasure-seekers blundered from the murk, a man with a mask like a moon pointing at a woman who was so drunk she kept falling over on her high shoes. All of them laughing, one of them flapping his lace cuffs as though there never was a thing so funny as drinking so much you couldn't stand up. Carcolf rolled her eyes skyward and consoled herself with the thought that behind the masks they were hating it as much as she always did when she tried to have fun.

In the solitude of her doorway, Carcolf winced. Damn, but she needed a holiday. She was becoming a sour ass. Or, indeed, had become one and was getting worse. One of those people who held the entire world in contempt. Was she turning into her bloody father?

"Anything but that," she muttered.

The moment the revelers tottered off into the night, she ducked from her doorway and pressed on, neither too fast nor too slow, soft bootheels silent on the dewy cobbles, her unexceptional hood drawn down to an inconspicuous degree, the very image of a person with just the average amount to hide. Which, in Sipani, was quite a bit.

Over to the west somewhere, her armored carriage would be speeding down the wide lanes, wheels striking sparks as they clattered over the bridges, stunned bystanders leaping aside, driver's whip lashing at the foaming flanks of the horses, the dozen hired guards thundering after, streetlamps gleaming upon their dewy armor. Unless the Quarryman's people had already made their move, of course: the flutter of arrows, the scream of beasts and men, the crash of the wagon leaving the road, the clash of steel, and finally the great padlock blown from the strongbox with blasting powder, the choking smoke wafted aside by eager hands, and the lid flung back to reveal . . . nothing.

Carcolf allowed herself the smallest smile and patted the lump against her ribs. The item, stitched up safe in the lining of her coat.

She gathered herself, took a couple of steps, and sprang from the canal side, clearing three strides of oily water to the deck of a decaying barge, timbers creaking under her as she rolled and came smoothly up. To go around by the Fintine bridge was quite the detour, not to mention a well-traveled and well-watched way, but this boat was always tied here in the shadows, offering a shortcut. She had made sure of it. Carcolf left as little to chance as possible. In her experience, chance could be a real bastard.

A wizened face peered out from the gloom of the cabin, steam issuing from a battered kettle. "Who the hell are you?"

"Nobody." Carcolf gave a cheery salute. "Just passing through!" and she hopped from the rocking wood to the stones on the far side of the canal and was away into the mold-smelling mist. Just passing through. Straight to the docks to catch the tide and off on her merry way. Or her sour-assed one, at least. Wherever Carcolf went, she was nobody. Everywhere, always passing through.

Over to the east, that idiot Pombrine would be riding hard in the company of four paid retainers. He hardly looked much like her, what with the moustache and all, but swaddled in that ever-so-conspicuous embroidered cloak of hers, he did well enough for a double. He was a penniless pimp who smugly believed himself to be impersonating her so she could visit a lover, a lady of means who did not want their tryst made public. Carcolf sighed. If only. She consoled herself with the thought of Pombrine's shock when those bastards Deep and Shallow shot him from his saddle, expressed considerable surprise at the moustache, then rooted through his clothes with increasing frustration, and finally, no doubt, gutted his corpse only to find . . . nothing.

Carcolf patted that lump once again and pressed on with a spring in her step. Here went she, down the middle course, alone and on foot, along a carefully prepared route of back streets, of narrow ways, of unregarded shortcuts and forgotten stairs, through crumbling palaces and rotting tenements, gates left open by surreptitious arrangement and, later on, a short stretch of sewer that would bring her out right by the docks with an hour or two to spare.

After this job, she really had to take a holiday. She tongued at the inside of her lip, where a small but unreasonably painful ulcer had lately developed. All she did was work. A trip to Adua, maybe? Visit her brother, see her nieces? How old would they be now? Ugh. No. She remembered what a judgmental bitch her sister-in-law was. One of those people who met everything with a sneer. She reminded Carcolf of her father. Probably why her brother had married the bloody woman . . .

Music was drifting from somewhere as she ducked beneath a flaking archway. A violinist, either tuning up or of execrable quality. Neither would have surprised her. Papers flapped and rustled upon a wall sprouting with moss, ill-printed bills exhorting the faithful citizenry to rise up against the tyranny of the Snake of Talins. Carcolf snorted. Most of Sipani's citizens were more interested in falling over than rising up, and the rest were anything but faithful.

She twisted about to tug at the seat of her trousers, but it was hopeless. How much do you have to pay for a new suit of clothes before you avoid a chafing seam just in the worst place? She hopped along a narrow way beside a stagnant section of canal, long out of use, gloopy with algae and bobbing rubbish, plucking the offending fabric this way and that to no effect. Damn this fashion for tight trousers! Perhaps it was some kind of cosmic punishment for her paying the tailor with forged coins. But then Carcolf was considerably more moved by the concept of local profit than that of cosmic punishment, and therefore strove to avoid paying for anything wherever possible. It was practically a principle with her, and her father always said that a person should stick to their principles—

Bloody hell, she really was turning into her father.

"Ha!"

A ragged figure sprang from an archway, the faintest glimmer of steel showing. With an instinctive whimper, Carcolf stumbled back, fumbling her coat aside and drawing her own blade, sure that death had found her at last. The Quarryman one step ahead? Or was it Deep and Shallow, or Kurrikan's hirelings . . . but no one else showed themselves. Only this one man, swathed in a stained cloak, unkempt hair stuck to pale skin by the damp, a mildewed scarf masking the bottom part of his face, bloodshot eyes round and scared above.

"Stand and deliver!" he boomed, somewhat muffled by the scarf.

Carcolf raised her brows. "Who even says that?"

A slight pause, while the rotten waters slapped the stones beside them. "You're a woman?" There was an almost apologetic turn to the would-be robber's voice.

"If I am, will you not rob me?"

"Well . . . er . . ." The thief seemed to deflate somewhat, then drew himself up again. "Stand and deliver anyway!"

"Why?" asked Carcolf.

The point of the robber's sword drifted uncertainly. "Because I have a considerable debt to . . . that's none of your business!"

"No, I mean, why not just stab me and strip my corpse of valuables, rather than giving me the warning?"

Another pause. "I suppose . . . I hope to avoid violence? But I warn you I am entirely prepared for it!"

He was a bloody civilian. A mugger who had blundered upon her. A random encounter. Talk about chance being a bastard! For him, at least. "You, sir," she said, "are a shitty thief."

"I, madam, am a gentleman."

"You, sir, are a dead gentleman." Carcolf stepped forward, weighing her blade, a stride length of razor steel lent a ruthless gleam from a lamp in a window somewhere above. She could never be bothered to practice, but nonetheless she was far more than passable with a sword.

It would take a great deal more than this stick of gutter trash to get the better of her. "I will carve you like—"

The man darted forward with astonishing speed, there was a scrape of steel, and before Carcolf even thought of moving, the sword was twitched from her fingers and skittered across the greasy cobbles to plop into the canal.

"Ah," she said. That changed things. Plainly her attacker was not the bumpkin he appeared to be, at least when it came to swordplay. She should have known. Nothing in Sipani is ever quite as it appears.

"Hand over the money," he said.

"Delighted." Carcolf plucked out her purse and tossed it against the wall, hoping to slip past while he was distracted. Alas, he pricked it from the air with impressive dexterity and whisked his sword point back to prevent her escape. It tapped gently at the lump in her coat.

"What have you got . . . just there?"

From bad to much, much worse. "Nothing, nothing at all." Carcolf attempted to pass it off with a false chuckle, but that ship had sailed and she, sadly, was not aboard, any more than she was aboard the damn ship still rocking at the wharf for the voyage to Thond. She steered the glinting point away with one finger. "Now I have an extremely pressing engagement, so if—" There was a faint hiss as the sword slit her coat open.

Carcolf blinked. "Ow." There was a burning pain down her ribs. The sword had slit her open too. "Ow!" She subsided to her knees, deeply aggrieved, blood oozing between her fingers as she clutched them to her side.

"Oh . . . oh no. Sorry. I really . . . really didn't mean to cut you. Just wanted, you know . . ."

"Ow." The item, now slightly smeared with Carcolf's blood, dropped from the gashed pocket and tumbled across the cobbles. A slender package perhaps a foot long, wrapped in stained leather.

"I need a surgeon," gasped Carcolf, in her best I-am-a-helpless-woman voice. The Grand Duchess had always accused her of being overdramatic, but if you can't be dramatic at a time like that, when can you? It was likely she really did need a surgeon, after all, and there was a chance that the robber would lean down to help her and she could stab the bastard in the face with her knife. "Please, I beg you!"

He loitered, eyes wide, the whole thing plainly gone further than he had intended. But he edged closer only to reach for the package, the glinting point of his sword still leveled at her.

A different and even more desperate tack, then. She strove to keep the panic out of her voice. "Look, take the money, I wish you joy of it." Carcolf did not, in fact, wish him joy, she wished him rotten in his grave. "But we will both be far better off if you leave that package!"

His hand hovered. "Why, what's in it?"

"I don't know. I'm under orders not to open it!"

"Orders from who?"

Carcolf winced. "I don't know that either, but—"

Kurtis took the packet. Of course he did. He was an idiot, but not so much of an idiot as that. He snatched up the packet and ran. Of course he ran. When didn't he?

He tore down the alleyway, heart in mouth, jumped a burst barrel, caught his foot and went sprawling, almost impaled himself on his own drawn sword, slithered on his face through a slick of rubbish, scooping a mouthful of something faintly sweet and staggering up, spitting and cursing, snatching a scared glance over his shoulder—

There was no sign of pursuit. Only the mist, the endless mist, whipping and curling like a thing alive.

He slipped the packet, now somewhat slimy, into his ragged cloak and limped on, clutching at his bruised buttock and still struggling to spit that rotten-sweet taste from his mouth. Not that it was any worse than his breakfast had been. Better, if anything. You know a man by his breakfast, his fencing master always used to tell him.

He pulled up his damp hood with its faint smell of onions and despair, plucked the purse from his sword, and slid blade back into sheath as he slipped from the alley and insinuated himself among the crowds, that faint snap of hilt meeting clasp bringing back so many memories. Of training and tournaments, of bright futures and the adulation of the crowds. Fencing, my boy, that's the way to advance! Such knowledgeable audiences in Styria, they love their swordsmen there, you'll make a fortune! Better times, when he had not dressed in rags, or been thankful for the butcher's leftovers, or robbed people for a living. He grimaced. Robbed *women.* If you could call it a living. He stole another furtive glance over his shoulder. Could he have killed her? His skin prickled with horror. Just a scratch. Just a scratch, surely? But he had seen blood. Please, let it have been a scratch! He rubbed his face as though he could rub the memory away, but it was stuck fast. One by one, things he had never imagined, then told himself he would never do, then that he would never do again, had become his daily routine.

He checked once more that he wasn't followed, then slipped from the street and across the rotting courtyard, the faded faces of yesterday's heroes peering down at him from the newsbills. Up the piss-smelling stairway and around the dead plant. Out with his key, and he wrestled with the sticky lock.

"Damn it, fuck it, shit it—Gah!" The door came suddenly open and he blundered into the room, nearly fell again, turned and pushed it shut, and stood a moment in the smelly darkness, breathing hard.

Who would now believe he'd once fenced with the king? He'd lost. Of *course* he had. Lost everything, hadn't he? He'd lost two touches to nothing and been personally insulted while he lay in the dust but, still, he'd measured steels with His August Majesty. This very steel, he realized, as he set it against the wall beside the door. Notched, and tarnished, and even slightly bent toward the tip. The last twenty years had been almost as unkind to his sword as they had been to him. But perhaps today marked the turn in his fortunes.

He whipped his cloak off and tossed it into a corner, took out the packet to unwrap it and see what he had come by. He fumbled with the lamp in the darkness and finally produced some light, almost wincing as his miserable rooms came into view. The cracked glazing, the blistering plaster speckled with damp, the burst mattress spilling foul straw where he slept, the few sticks of warped furniture—

There was a man sitting in the only chair, at the only table. A big man in a big coat, skull shaved to greying stubble. He took a slow breath through his blunt nose and let a pair of dice tumble from his fist and across the stained tabletop.

"Six and two," he said. "Eight."

"Who the hell are you?" Kurtis's voice was squeaky with shock.

"The Quarryman sent me." He let the dice roll again. "Six and five."

"Does that mean I lose?" Kurtis glanced over toward his sword, trying and failing to seem nonchalant, wondering how fast he could get to it, draw it, strike—

"You lost already," said the big man, gently collecting the dice with the side of his hand. He finally looked up. His eyes were flat as those of a dead fish. Like the fishes on the stalls at the market. Dead and dark and sadly glistening. "Do you want to know what happens if you go for that sword?"

Kurtis wasn't a brave man. He never had been. It had taken all his courage to work up to surprising someone else; being surprised himself had knocked the fight right out of him. "No," he muttered, his shoulders sagging.

"Toss me that package," said the big man, and Kurtis did so. "And the purse."

It was as if all resistance had drained away. Kurtis had not the strength to attempt a ruse. He scarcely had the strength to stand. He tossed the stolen purse onto the table, and the big man worked it open with his fingertips and peered inside.

Kurtis gave a helpless, floppy motion of his hands. "I have nothing else worth taking."

"I know," the man said, as he stood. "I have checked." He stepped around the table and Kurtis cringed away, steadying himself against his cupboard. A cupboard containing nothing but cobwebs, as it went.

"Is the debt paid?" he asked in a very small voice.

"Do you think the debt is paid?"

They stood looking at one another. Kurtis swallowed. "When will the debt be paid?"

The big man shrugged his shoulders, which were almost one with his head. "When do you think the debt will be paid?"

Kurtis swallowed again, and he found his lip was trembling. "When the Quarryman says so?"

The big man raised one heavy brow a fraction, the hairless sliver of a scar through it. "Have you any questions . . . to which you do not know the answers?"

Kurtis dropped to his knees, his hands clasped, the big man's face faintly swimming through the tears in his aching eyes. He did not care about the shame of it. The Quarryman had taken the last of his pride many visits before. "Just leave me something," he whispered. "Just . . . something."

The man stared back at him with his dead fish eyes. "Why?"

Friendly took the sword too, but there was nothing else of value. "I will come back next week," he said.

It had not been meant as a threat, merely a statement of fact, and an obvious one at that, since it had always been the arrangement, but Kurtis dan Broya's head slowly dropped, and he began to shudder with sobs.

Friendly considered whether to try and comfort him but decided not to. He was often misinterpreted.

"You should, perhaps, not have borrowed the money." Then he left.

It always surprised him that people did not do the sums when they took a loan. Proportions, and time, and the action of interest, it was not so very difficult to fathom. But perhaps they were prone always to overestimate their income, to poison themselves by looking on the bright side. Happy chances would occur, and things would improve, and everything would turn out well, because they were special. Friendly had no illusions. He knew he was but one unexceptional cog in the elaborate workings of life. To him, facts were facts.

He walked, counting off the paces to the Quarryman's place. One hundred and five, one hundred and four, one hundred and three . . .

Strange how small the city was when you measured it out. All those people, and all their desires, and scores, and debts, packed into this narrow stretch of reclaimed swamp. By Friendly's reckoning, the swamp was well on the way to taking large sections of it back. He wondered if the world would be better when it did.

. . . seventy-six, seventy-five, seventy-four . . .

Friendly had picked up a shadow. Pickpocket, maybe. He took a careless look at a stall by the way and caught her out of the corner of his eye. A girl with dark hair gathered into a cap and a jacket too big for her. Hardly more than a child. Friendly took a few steps down a narrow snicket and turned, blocking the way, pushing back his coat to show the grips of four of his six weapons. His shadow rounded the corner, and he looked at her. Just looked. She first froze, then swallowed, then turned one way, then the other, then backed off and lost herself in the crowds. So that was the end of that episode.

. . . thirty-one, thirty, twenty-nine . . .

Sipani, and most especially its moist and fragrant Old Quarter, was full of thieves. They were a constant annoyance, like midges in summer. Also muggers, robbers, burglars, cutpurses, cutthroats, thugs, murderers, strong-arm men, spivs, swindlers, gamblers, bookies, moneylenders, rakes, beggars, tricksters, pimps, pawnshop owners, crooked merchants, not to mention accountants and lawyers. Lawyers were the worst of the crowd, as far as Friendly was concerned. Sometimes it seemed that no one in Sipani made anything, exactly. They all seemed to be working their hardest to rip it from someone else.

But then, Friendly supposed he was no better.

. . . four, three, two, one, and down the twelve steps, past the three guards, and through the double doors into the Quarryman's place.

It was hazy with smoke inside, confusing with the light of colored lamps, hot with breath and chafing skin, thick with the babble of hushed conversation, of secrets traded, reputations ruined, confidences betrayed. It was as all such places always are.

Two Northmen were wedged behind a table in the corner. One, with sharp teeth and long, lank hair, had tipped his chair all the way back and was slumped in it, smoking. The other had a bottle in one hand and a tiny book in the other, staring at it with brow well furrowed.

Most of the patrons Friendly knew by sight. Regulars. Some came to drink. Some to eat. Most of them fixed on the games of chance. The clatter of dice, the twitch and flap of the playing cards, the eyes of the hopeless glittering as the lucky wheel spun.

The games were not really the Quarryman's business, but the games made debts, and debts were the Quarryman's business. Up the twenty-three steps to the raised area, the guard with the tattoo on his face waving Friendly past.

Three of the other collectors were seated there, sharing a bottle. The smallest grinned at him and nodded, perhaps trying to plant the seeds of an alliance. The biggest puffed himself up and bristled, sensing competition. Friendly ignored them equally. He had long ago given up trying even to understand the unsolvable mathematics of human relationships, let alone to participate. Should that man do more than bristle, Friendly's cleaver would speak for him. That was a voice that cut short even the most tedious of arguments.

Mistress Borfero was a fleshy woman with dark curls spilling from beneath a purple cap, small eyeglasses that made her eyes seem large, and a smell about her of lamp oil. She haunted the anteroom before the Quarryman's office at a low desk stacked with ledgers. On Friendly's first day, she had gestured toward the ornate door behind her and said, "I am the Quarryman's right hand. He is never to be disturbed. *Never.* You speak to me."

Friendly, of course, knew as soon as he saw her mastery of the numbers in those books that there was no one in the office and that Borfero *was* the Quarryman, but she seemed so pleased with the deception that he was happy to play along. Friendly had never liked to rock boats unnecessarily. That's how people end up drowned. Besides, it somehow helped to imagine that the orders came from somewhere else, somewhere unknowable and irresistible. It was nice to have an attic in which to stack the blame. Friendly looked at the door of the Quarryman's office, wondering if there was an office, or if it opened on blank stones.

"What was today's take?" she asked, flipping open a ledger and dipping her pen. Straight to business without so much as a how do you do.

He greatly liked and admired that about her, though he would never have said so. His compliments had a way of causing offense.

Friendly slipped the coins out in stacks, then let them drop, one by one, in rattling rows by debtor and denomination. Mostly base metals, leavened with a sprinkling of silver.

Borfero sat forward, wrinkling her nose and pushing her eyeglasses up onto her forehead, eyes seeming now extra small without them.

"A sword, as well," said Friendly, leaning it up against the side of the desk.

"A disappointing harvest," she murmured.

"The soil is stony hereabouts."

"Too true." She dropped the eyeglasses back and started to scratch orderly figures in her ledger. "Tough times all over." She often said that. As though it stood as explanation and excuse for anything and everything.

"Kurtis dan Broya asked me when the debt would be paid."

She peered up, surprised by the question. "When the Quarryman says it's paid."

"That's what I told him."

"Good."

"You asked me to be on the lookout for . . . a package." Friendly placed it on the desk before her. "Broya had it."

It did not seem so very important. It was less than a foot long, wrapped in very ancient stained and balding animal skin, and with a letter, or perhaps a number, burned into it with a brand. But not a number that Friendly recognized.

Mistress Borfero snatched up the package, then immediately cursed herself for seeming too eager. She knew no one could be trusted in this business. That brought a rush of questions to her mind. Suspicions. How could that worthless Broya possibly have come by it? Was this some ruse? Was Friendly a plant of the Gurkish? Or perhaps of Carcolf's? A double bluff? There was no end to the webs that smug bitch spun. A triple bluff? But where was the angle? Where the advantage?

A quadruple bluff?

Friendly's face betrayed no trace of greed, no trace of ambition, no trace of anything. He was without doubt a strange fellow but came highly recommended. He seemed all business, and she liked that in a man, though she would never have said so. A manager must maintain a certain detachment.

Sometimes things are just what they seem. Borfero had seen strange chances enough in her life.

"This could be it," she mused, though, in fact, she was immediately sure. She was not a woman to waste time on possibilities.

Friendly nodded.

"You have done well," she said.

He nodded again.

"The Quarryman will want you to have a bonus." Be generous with your own people, she had always said, or others will be.

But generosity brought no response from Friendly.

"A woman, perhaps?"

He looked a little pained by that suggestion. "No."

"A man?"

And that one. "No."

"Husk? A bottle of—"

"No."

"There must be something."

He shrugged.

Mistress Borfero puffed out her cheeks. Everything she had she'd made by tickling out people's desires. She was not sure what to do with a person who had none. "Well, why don't you think about it?"

Friendly slowly nodded. "I will think."

"Did you see two Northmen drinking on your way in?"

"I saw two Northmen. One was reading a book."

"Really? A book?"

Friendly shrugged. "There are readers everywhere."

She swept through the place, noting the disappointing lack of wealthy custom and estimating just how dismal this evening's profits were likely to be. If one of the Northmen had been reading, he had given up. Deep was drinking some of her best wine straight from the bottle. Three others lay scattered, empty, beneath the table. Shallow was smoking a chagga pipe, the air thick with the stink of it. Borfero did not allow it normally, but she was obliged to make an exception for these two. Why the bank chose to employ such repugnant specimens she had not the slightest notion. But she supposed rich people need not explain themselves.

"Gentlemen," she said, insinuating herself into a chair.

"Where?" Shallow gave a croaky laugh. Deep slowly tipped his bottle up and eyed his brother over the neck with sour disdain.

Borfero continued in her business voice, soft and reasonable. "You said your . . . *employers* would be *most grateful* if I came upon . . . *that certain item* you mentioned."

The two Northmen perked up, both leaning forward as though drawn by the same string, Shallow's boot catching an empty bottle and sending it rolling in an arc across the floor.

"Greatly grateful," said Deep.

"And how much of my debt would their gratitude stretch around?"

"All of it."

Borfero felt her skin tingling. Freedom. Could it really be? In her pocket, even now? But she could not let the size of the stakes make her careless. The greater the payoff, the greater the caution. "My debt would be finished?"

Shallow leaned close, drawing the stem of his pipe across his stubbled throat. "Killed," he said.

"Murdered," growled his brother, suddenly no farther off on the other side.

She in no way enjoyed having those scarred and lumpen killers' physiognomies so near. Another few moments of their breath alone might have done for her. "Excellent," she squeaked, and slipped the package onto the table. "Then I shall cancel the interest payments forthwith. Do please convey my regards to . . . your employers."

"'Course." Shallow did not so much smile as show his sharp teeth. "Don't reckon your regards'll mean much to them, though."

"Don't take it personally, eh?" Deep did not smile. "Our employers just don't care much for regards."

Borfero took a sharp breath. "Tough times all over."

"Ain't they, though?" Deep stood, and swept the package up in one big paw.

The cool air caught Deep like a slap as they stepped out into the evening. Sipani, none too pleasant when it was still, had a decided spin to it of a sudden.

"I have to confess," he said, clearing his throat and spitting, "to being somewhat on the drunk side of drunk."

"Aye," said Shallow, burping as he squinted into the mist. At least that was clearing somewhat. As clear as it got in this murky hell of a place. "Probably not the bestest notion while at work, mind you."

"You're right." Deep held the baggage up to such light as there was. "But who expected this to just drop in our laps?"

"Not I, for one." Shallow frowned. "Or for . . . not one?"

"It was meant to be just a tipple," said Deep.

"One tipple does have a habit of making itself into several." Shallow wedged on that stupid bloody hat. "A little stroll over to the bank, then?"

"That hat makes you look a fucking dunce."

"You, brother, are obsessed with appearances."

Deep passed that off with a long hiss.

"They really going to score out that woman's debts, d'you think?"

"For now, maybe. But you know how they are. Once you owe, you always owe." Deep spat again, and, now that the alley was a tad steadier, tottered off with the baggage clutched tight in his hand. No chance he was putting it in a pocket where some little scab could lift it. Sipani was full of thieving bastards. He'd had his good socks stolen last time he was here, and worked up an unpleasant pair of blisters on the trip home. Who steals *socks*? Styrian bastards. He'd keep a good firm grip on it. Let the little fuckers try to take it *then.*

"Now who's the dunce?" Shallow called after him. "The bank's this way."

"Only we ain't going to the bank, *dunce,*" snapped Deep over his shoulder. "We're to toss it down a well in an old court just about the corner here."

Shallow hurried to catch up. "We are?"

"No, I just said it for the laugh, y'idiot."

"Why down a well?"

"Because that's how he wanted it done."

"Who wanted it done?"

"The boss."

"The little boss, or the big boss?"

Even drunk as Deep was, he felt the need to lower his voice. "The bald boss."

"Shit," breathed Shallow. "In person?"

"In person."

A short pause. "How was that?"

"It was even more than usually terrifying, thanks for reminding me."

A long pause, with just the sound of their boots on the wet cobbles. Then Shallow said, "We better hadn't do no fucking up of this."

"My heartfelt thanks," said Deep, "for that piercing insight. Fucking up is always to be avoided when and wherever possible, wouldn't you say?"

"Y'always aim to avoid it, of course you do, but sometimes you run into it anyway. What I'm saying here is, we'd best not run into it." Shallow dropped his voice to a whisper. "You know what the bald boss said last time."

"You don't have to whisper. He ain't here, is he?"

Shallow looked wildly around. "I don't know. Is he?"

"No, he ain't." Deep rubbed at his temples. One day he'd kill his brother, that was a foregone conclusion. "That's what I'm saying."

"What if he was, though? Best to always act like he might be."

"Can you shut your mouth just for a fucking *instant*?" Deep caught Shallow by the arm and stabbed the baggage in his face. "It's like talking to a bloody—" He was greatly surprised when a dark shape whisked between them and he found his hand was suddenly empty.

* * *

Kiam ran like her life depended on it. Which it did, o' course.

"Get after him, damn it!" She heard the two Northmen flapping and crashing and blundering down the alley behind, and nowhere near far enough behind for her taste.

"It's a girl, y'idiot!" Big and clumsy but fast they were coming, boots hammering and hands clutching, and if they once caught ahold of her . . .

"Who fucking cares? Get the thing back!" And her breath hissing and her heart pounding and her muscles burning as she ran.

She skittered around a corner, rag-wrapped feet sticking to the damp cobbles, the way wider, lamps and torches making muddy smears in the mist and people busy everywhere. She ducked and weaved, around them, between them, faces looming up and gone. The Blackside night market, stalls and shoppers and the cries of the traders, full of noise and smells and tight with bustle. Kiam slithered between the wheels of a wagon, limber as a ferret, plunged between buyer and seller in a shower of fruit, then slithered across a stall laden with slimy fish while the trader shouted and snatched at her, caught nothing but air. She stuck one foot in a basket and was off, kicking cockles across the street. Still she heard the yells and growls as the Northmen knocked folk flying in her wake, crashes as they flung the carts aside, as though a mindless storm were ripping apart the market behind her. She dived between the legs of a big man, rounded another corner, and took the greasy steps two at a time, along the narrow path by the slopping water, rats squeaking in the rubbish and the sounds of the Northmen now loud, louder, cursing her and each other. Her breath whooping and cutting in her chest, she ran desperate, water spattering and spraying around her with every echoing footfall.

"We've got her!" the voice so close at her heels. "Come here!"

She darted through that little hole in the rusted grate, a sharp tooth of metal leaving a burning cut down her arm, and for once she was plenty glad that Old Green never gave her enough to eat. She kicked her way back into the darkness, keeping low, lay there clutching the package and struggling to get her breath. Then they were there, one of the Northmen dragging at the grating, knuckles white with force, flecks of rust showering down as it shifted, and Kiam stared and wondered what those hands would do to her if they got their dirty nails into her skin.

The other one shoved his bearded face in the gap, a wicked-looking knife in his hand, not that someone you just robbed ever has a nice-looking knife. His eyes popped out at her and his scabbed lips curled back and he snarled, "Chuck us that baggage and we'll forget all about it. Chuck us it now!"

Kiam kicked away, the grate squealing as it bent. "You're fucking dead, you little piss! We'll find you, don't worry about that!" She slithered off, through the dust and rot, wriggled through a crack between crumbling walls. "We'll be coming for you!" echoed from behind her. Maybe they would be as well, but a thief can't spend too much time worrying about tomorrow. Today's shitty enough. She whipped her coat off and pulled it inside out to show the faded green lining, stuffed her cap in her pocket and shook her hair out long, then slipped onto the walkway beside the Fifth Canal, walking fast, head down.

A pleasure boat drifted past, all chatter and laughter and clinking of glass, people moving tall and lazy on board, strange as ghosts seen through that mist, and Kiam wondered what they'd done to deserve that life and what she'd done to deserve this, but there never were no easy answers to that question. As it took its pink lights away into the fog she heard the music of Hove's violin. Stood a moment in the shadows, listening, thinking how beautiful it sounded. She looked down at the package. Didn't look much for all this trouble. Didn't weigh much, even. But it weren't up to her what Old Green put a price on. She wiped her nose and walked along close to the wall, music getting louder, then she saw Hove's back and his bow moving, and she slipped behind him and let the package fall into his gaping pocket.

Hove didn't feel the drop, but he felt the three little taps on his back, and he felt the weight in his coat as he moved. He didn't see who made the drop and he didn't look. He just carried on fiddling, that Union march with which he'd opened every show during his time on the stage in Adua, or under the stage, at any rate, warming up the crowd for Lestek's big entrance. Before his wife died and everything went to shit. Those jaunty notes reminded him of times past, and he felt tears prickling in his sore eyes, so he switched to a melancholy minuet more suited to his mood, not that most folk around here could've told the difference. Sipani liked to present itself as a place of culture, but the majority were drunks and cheats and boorish thugs, or varying combinations thereof.

How had it come to this, eh? The usual refrain. He drifted across the street like he'd nothing in mind but a coin for his music, letting the notes spill out into the murk. Across past the pie stall, the fragrance of cheap meat making his stomach grumble, and he stopped playing to offer out his cap to the queue. There were no takers, no surprise, so he headed on down the road to Verscetti's, dancing in and out of the tables on the street and sawing out an Osprian waltz, grinning at the patrons who lounged there with a pipe or a bottle, twiddling thin glass stems between gloved fingertips, eyes leaking contempt through the slots in their mirror-crusted masks. Jervi was sat near the wall, as always, a woman in the chair opposite, hair piled high.

"A little music, darling?" Hove croaked out, leaning over her and letting his coat dangle near Jervi's lap.

Jervi slid something out of Hove's pocket, wrinkling his nose at the smell of the old soak, and said, "Fuck off, why don't you?" Hove moved on and took his horrible music with him, thank the Fates.

"What's going on down there?" Riseld lifted her mask for a moment to show that soft, round face, well powdered and fashionably bored.

There did indeed appear to be some manner of commotion up the street. Crashing, banging, shouting in Northern.

"Damn Northmen," he murmured. "Always causing trouble, they really should be kept on leads like dogs." Jervi removed his hat and tossed it on the table, the usual signal, then leaned back in his chair to hold the package inconspicuously low to the ground beside him. A distasteful business, but a man has to work. "Nothing you need concern yourself about, my dear."

She smiled at him in that unamused, uninterested way which, for some reason, he found irresistible.

"Shall we go to bed?" he asked, tossing a couple of coins down for the wine.

She sighed. "If we must."

And Jervi felt the package spirited away.

Sifkiss wriggled out from under the tables and strutted along, letting his stick rattle against the bars of the fence beside him, package swinging loose in the other. Maybe Old Green had said stay stealthy but that weren't Sifkiss' way anymore. A man has to work out his own style of doing things, and he was a full thirteen, weren't he? Soon enough now he'd be passing on to higher things. Working for Kurrikan maybe. Anyone could tell he was marked out special—he'd stole himself a tall hat that made him look quite the gent about town—and if they were dull enough to be entertaining any doubts, which some folk sadly were, he'd perched it at quite the jaunty angle besides. Jaunty as all hell.

Yes, everyone had their eyes on Sifkiss.

He checked he wasn't the slightest bit observed, then slipped through the dewy bushes and the crack in the wall behind, which honestly was getting to be a bit of a squeeze, into the basement of the old temple, a little light filtering down from upstairs.

Most of the children were out working. Just a couple of the younger lads playing with dice and a girl gnawing on a bone and Pens having a smoke and not even looking over, and that new one curled up in the corner and coughing. Sifkiss didn't like the sound o' those coughs. More'n likely he'd be dumping her off in the sewers a day or two hence but, hey, that meant a few more bits corpse money for him, didn't it? Most folk didn't like handling a corpse, but it didn't bother Sifkiss none. It's a hard rain don't wash someone a favor, as Old Green was always saying. She was way up there at the back, hunched over her old desk with one lamp burning, her long grey hair all greasy-slicked and her tongue pressed into her empty gums as she watched Sifkiss come up. Some smart-looking fellow was with her, had a waistcoat all silver leaves stitched on fancy, and Sifkiss put a jaunt on, thinking to impress.

"Get it, did yer?" asked Old Green.

"'Course,"said Sifkiss, with a toss of his head, caught his hat on a low beam, and cursed as he had to fumble it back on. He tossed the package sourly down on the tabletop.

"Get you gone, then," snapped Green.

Sifkiss looked surly, like he'd a mind to answer back. He was getting altogether too much mind, that boy, and Green had to show him the knobby-knuckled back of her hand 'fore he sloped off.

"So here you have it, as promised." She pointed to that leather bundle in the pool of lamplight on her old table, its top cracked and stained and its gilt all peeling, but still a fine old piece of furniture with plenty of years left. Like to Old Green in that respect, if she did think so herself.

"Seems a little luggage for such a lot of fuss," said Fallow, wrinkling his nose, and he tossed a purse onto the table with that lovely clink of money. Old Green clawed it up and clawed it open and straight off set to counting it.

"Where's your girl Kiam?" asked Fallow. "Where's little Kiam, eh?"

Old Green's shoulders stiffened but she kept counting. She could've counted through a storm at sea. "Out working."

"When's she getting back? I like her." Fallow came a bit closer, voice going hushed. "I could get a damn fine price for her."

"But she's my best earner!" said Green. "There's others you could take off my hands. How's about that lad Sifkiss?"

"What, the sour-face brought the luggage?"

"He's a good worker. Strong lad. Lots of grit. He'd pull a good oar on a galley, I'd say. Maybe a fighter, even."

Fallow snorted. "In a pit? That little shit? I don't think so. He'd need some whipping to pull an oar, I reckon."

"Well? They got whips, don't they?"

"Suppose they do. I'll take him if I must. Him and three others. I'm off to the market in Westport tomorrow week. You pick, but don't give me none o' your dross."

"I don't keep no dross," said Old Green.

"You got nothing but dross, you bloody old swindler. And what'll you tell the rest o' your brood, eh?" Fallow put on a silly la-di-da voice. "That they've gone off to be servants to gentry, or to live with the horses on a farm, or adopted by the fucking Emperor of Gurkhul or some such, eh?" Fallow chuckled, and Old Green had a sudden urge to make that knife of hers available, but she'd better sense these days, all learned the hard way.

"I tell 'em what I need to," she grunted, still working her fingers around the coins. Bloody fingers weren't half as quick as they once were.

"You do that, and I'll come back for Kiam another day, eh?" And Fallow winked at her.

"Whatever you want," said Green, "whatever you say." She was bloody well keeping Kiam, though. She couldn't save many, she wasn't fool enough to think that, but maybe she could save one, and on her dying day she could say she done that much. Probably no one would be listening, but she'd know. "It's all there. Package is yours."

Fallow picked up the luggage and was out of that stinking fucking place. Reminded him too much of prison. The smell of it. And the eyes of the children, all big and damp. He didn't mind buying and selling 'em, but he didn't want to see their eyes. Does the slaughterman want to look at the sheep's eyes? Maybe the slaughterman doesn't care. Maybe he gets used to it. Fallow cared too much, that's what it was. Too much heart.

His guards were lounging by the front door and he waved them over and set off, walking in the middle of the square they made.

"Successful meeting?" Grenti tossed over his shoulder.

"Not bad," grunted Fallow, in such a way as to discourage further conversation. *Do you want friends or money?* he'd once heard Kurrikan say, and the phrase had stuck with him.

Sadly, Grenti was by no means discouraged. “Going straight over to Kurrikan’s?”

“Yes,” said Fallow, sharply as he could.

But Grenti loved to flap his mouth. Most thugs do, in the end. All that time spent doing nothing, maybe. “Lovely house, though, ain’t it, Kurrikan’s? What do you call those columns on the front of it?”

“Pilasters,” grunted one of the other thugs.

“No, no, I know pilasters, no. I mean to say the name given to that particular style of architecture, with the vine leaves about the head there?”

“There?”

“No, no, that’s the masonry work, all dimpled with the chisel, it’s the overall design I’m discussing—hold up.”

For a moment, Fallow was mightily relieved at the interruption. Then he was concerned. A figure was occupying the fog just ahead. Occupying the hell out of it. The beggars and revelers and scum scattered round these parts had all slipped out of their way like soil around the plow ’til now. This one didn’t move. He was a tall bastard, tall as Fallow’s tallest guard, with a white coat on, hood up. Well, it wasn’t white no more. Nothing stayed white long in Sipani. It was grey with damp and black spattered about the hem.

“Get him out of the way,” he snapped.

“Get out of the fucking way!” roared Grenti.

“You are Fallow?” The man pulled his hood back.

“It’s a woman,” said Grenti. And indeed it was, for all her neck was thickly muscled, her jaw angular, and her red hair clipped close to her skull.

“I am Javre,” she said, raising her chin and smiling at them. “Lioness of Hoskopp.”

“Maybe she’s a mental,” said Grenti.

“Escaped from that madhouse up the way.”

“I did once escape from a madhouse,” said the woman. She had a weird accent; Fallow couldn’t place it. “Well . . . it was a prison for wizards. But some of them had gone mad. A fine distinction; most wizards are at least eccentric. That is beside the point, though. You have something I need."

"That so?" said Fallow, starting to grin. He was less worried now. One, she was a woman; two, she obviously was a mental.

"I know not how to convince you, for I lack the sweet words. It is a long-standing deficiency. But it would be best for us all if you gave it to me willingly."

"I'll give you something willingly," said Fallow, to sniggers from the others.

The woman didn't snigger. "It is a parcel, wrapped in leather, about . . ." She held up one big hand, thumb and forefinger stretched out. "Five times the length of your cock."

If she knew about the luggage, she was trouble. And Fallow had no sense of humor about his cock, to which none of the ointments had made the slightest difference. He stopped grinning. "Kill her."

She struck Grenti somewhere around the chest, or maybe she did; it was all a blur. His eyes popped wide and he made a strange whooping sound and stood there frozen, quivering on his tiptoes, sword halfway drawn.

The second guard—a Union man, big as a house—swung his mace at her, but it just caught her flapping coat. An instant later there was a surprised yelp and he was flying across the street upside down and crashing into the wall, tumbling down in a shower of dust, sheets of broken plaster dropping from the shattered brickwork on top of his limp body.

The third guard—a nimble-fingered Osprian—whipped out a throwing knife, but before he could loose it, the mace twittered through the air and bounced from his head. He dropped soundlessly, arms outstretched.

"They are called Anthiric columns." The woman put her forefinger against Grenti's forehead and gently pushed him over. He toppled and lay there on his side in the muck, still stiff, still trembling, still with eyes bulgingly focused on nothing.

"That was with one hand." She held up the other big fist, and had produced from somewhere a sheathed sword, gold glittering on the hilt. "Next I draw this sword, forged in the Old Time from the metal of a fallen star. Only six living people have seen the blade. You would find it extremely beautiful. Then I would kill you with it."

The last of the guards exchanged a brief glance with Fallow, then tossed his axe away and sprinted off.

"Huh," said the woman, with a slight wrinkling of disappointment about her red brows. "Just so you know, if you run I will catch you in . . ." She narrowed her eyes and pushed out her lips, looking Fallow appraisingly up and down. The way he might have appraised the children. He found he didn't like being looked at that way. "About four strides."

He ran.

She caught him in three, and he was suddenly on his face with a mouthful of dirty cobblestone and his arm twisted sharply behind his back.

"You've no idea who you're dealing with, you stupid bitch!" He struggled but her grip was iron, and he squealed with pain as his arm was twisted even more sharply.

"It is true, I am no high thinker." Her voice showed not the slightest strain. "I like simple things well-done and have no time to philosophize. Would you like to tell me where the parcel is, or shall I beat you until it falls out?"

"I work for Kurrikan!" he gasped out.

"I'm new in town. Names work no magic on me."

"We'll find you!"

She laughed. "Of course. I am no hider. I am Javre, First of the Fifteen. Javre, Knight Templar of the Golden Order. Javre, Breaker of Chains, Breaker of Oaths, Breaker of Faces." And here she gave him a blinding blow on the back of the head, which, he was pretty sure, broke his nose against the cobbles and filled the back of his mouth with the salt taste of blood. "To find me, you need only ask for Javre." She leaned over him, breath tickling at his ear. "It is once you find me that your difficulties begin. Now, where is that parcel?"

A pinching sensation began in Fallow's hand. Mildly painful to begin with, then more, and more, a white-hot burning up his arm that made him whimper like a dog. "Ah, ah, ah, inside pocket, inside pocket!"

"Very good." He felt hands rifling through his clothes, but could only lie limp, moaning as the jangling of his nerves gradually subsided. He craned his neck around to look up at her and curled back his lips. "I swear on my fucking front teeth—"

"Do you?" As her fingers found the hidden pocket and slid the package free. "That's rash."

Javre pressed finger against thumb and flicked Fallow's two front teeth out. A trick she had learned from an old man in Suljuk and, as with so many things in life, all in the wrist. She left him hunched in the road, struggling to cough them up.

"The next time we meet, I will have to show you the sword!" she called out as she strode away, wedging the package down behind her belt. Goddess, these Sipanese were weaklings. Was there no one to test her anymore?

She shook her sore hand out. Probably her fingernail would turn black and drop off, but it would grow back. Unlike Fallow's teeth. And it was scarcely the first fingernail she had lost. Including that memorable time she had lost the lot and toenails too in the tender care of the Prophet Khalul. Now, *there* had been a test. For a moment, she almost felt nostalgic for her interrogators. Certainly she felt nostalgic for the feeling of shoving their chief's face into his own brazier when she escaped. What a sizzle he had made!

But perhaps this Kurrikan would be outraged enough to send a decent class of killer after her. Then she could go after him. Hardly the great battles of yesteryear, but something to while away the evenings.

Until then, Javre walked, swift and steady, with her shoulders back. She loved to walk. With every stride, she felt her own strength. Every muscle utterly relaxed, yet ready to turn the next step in a split instant into mighty spring, sprightly roll, deadly strike. Without needing to look, she felt each person about her, judged their threat, predicted their attack, imagined her response, the air around her alive with calculated possibilities, the surroundings mapped, the distances known, all things of use noted. The sternest tests are those you do not see coming, so Javre was the weapon always sharpened, the weapon never sheathed, the answer to every question.

But no blade came darting from the dark. No arrow, no flash of fire, no squirt of poison. No pack of assassins burst from the shadows.

Sadly.

Only a pair of drunk Northmen wrestling outside Pombrine's place, one of them snarling something about the bald boss. She paid them no mind as she trotted up the steps, ignoring the several frowning guards, who were of a quality inferior even to Fallow's men, down the hallway, and into the central salon, complete with fake marble, cheap chandelier, and profoundly unarousing mosaic of a lumpy couple fucking horse-style. Evidently the evening rush had yet to begin. Whores of both sexes and one Javre was still not entirely sure about lounged bored upon the overwrought furniture.

Pombrine was busy admonishing one of his flock for overdressing, but looked up startled when she entered. "You're back already? What went wrong?"

Javre laughed full loud. "Everything." His eyes widened, and she laughed louder yet. "For them." And she took his wrist and pressed the parcel into his hand.

Pombrine gazed down at that unassuming lump of animal skin. "You did it?"

The woman thumped one heavy arm about his shoulders and gave them a squeeze. He gasped as his bones creaked. Without doubt she was of exceptional size, but even so the casual strength of it was hardly to be believed. "You do not know me. Yet. I am Javre, Lioness of Hoskopp." She looked down at him and he had an unpleasant and unfamiliar sensation of being a naughty child helpless in his mother's grasp. "When I agree to a challenge, I do not shirk it. But you will learn."

"I keenly anticipate my education." Pombrine wriggled free of the crushing weight of her arm. "You did not . . . open it?"

"You told me not to."

"Good. Good." He stared down, the smile half-formed on his face, hardly able to believe it could have been this easy.

"My payment, then."

"Of course." He reached for the purse.

She held up one callused hand. "I will take half in flesh."

"In flesh?"

"Isn't that what you peddle here?"

He raised his brows. "Half would be a great quantity of flesh."

"I get through it. And I mean to stay a while."

"Lucky us," he muttered.

"I'll take him."

"An excellent choice, I—"

"And him. And him. And her." Javre rubbed her rough palms together. "She can get the lads warmed up, I am not paying to wank anyone off myself."

"Naturally not."

"I am a woman of Thond, and have grand appetites."

"So I begin to see."

"And for the sun's sake, someone draw me a bath. I smell like a heated bitch already, I dread to imagine the stink afterward. I will have every tomcat in the city after me!" And she burst out laughing.

One of the men swallowed. The other looked at Pombrine with an expression faintly desperate as Javre herded them into the nearest room.

". . . you, remove your trousers. You, get the bandages off my tits. You would scarcely credit how tightly I have to strap this lot down to get anything done . . ."

The door snapped mercifully shut.

Pombrine seized Scalacay, his most trusted servant, by the shoulder and drew him close.

"Go to the Gurkish temple off the third canal with all haste, the one with the green marble pillars. Do you know it?"

"I do, master."

"Tell the priest who chants in the doorway that you have a message for Ishri. That Master Pombrine has the item she was asking after. For Ishri, do you understand?"

"For Ishri. Master Pombrine has the item."

"Then run to it!"

Scalacay dashed away, leaving Pombrine to hurry to his office with hardly less haste, the package clutched in one sweaty hand. He fumbled the door shut and turned the key, the five locks closing with a reassuring metallic clatter.

Only then did he allow himself to breathe. He placed the package reverently upon his desk. Now he had it, he felt the need to stretch out the moment of triumph. To weigh it down with the proper gravitas. He went to his drinks cabinet and unlocked it, took his grandfather's bottle of Shiznadze from the place of honor. That man had lived his whole life waiting for a moment worthy of opening that bottle. Pombrine smiled as he reached for the corkscrew, trimming away the lead from the neck.

How long had he worked to secure that cursed package? Circulating rumors of his business failings when in fact he had never been so successful. Placing himself in Carcolf's way again and again until finally they seemed to happen upon each other by chance. Wriggling himself into a position of trust while the idiot courier thought him a brainless stooge, clambering by minuscule degrees to a perch from which he could get his eager hands around the package, and then . . . unhappy fate! Carcolf had slipped free, the cursed bitch, leaving Pombrine with nothing but ruined hopes. But now . . . happy fate! The thuggery of that loathsome woman Javre had, by some fumbling miracle, succeeded where his genius had been so unfairly thwarted.

What did it matter how he had come by it, though? His smile grew wider as he eased the cork free. He had the package. He turned to gaze upon his prize again.

Pop! An arc of fizzy wine missed his glass and spurted across his Kadiri carpet. He stared openmouthed. The package was hanging in the air by a hook. Attached to the hook was a gossamer thread. The thread disappeared through a hole in the glass roof high above where he now saw a black shape spread-eagled.

Pombrine made a despairing lunge, bottle and glass tumbling to the floor and spraying wine, but the package slipped through his clutching fingers and was whisked smoothly upward out of his reach.

"Guards!" he roared, shaking his fist. "Thief!"

A moment later he realized, and his rage turned in a flash to withering horror.

Ishri would soon be on her way.

With a practiced jerk of her wrist, Shev twitched the parcel up and into her waiting glove.

"What an angler," she whispered as she thrust it into her pocket and was away across the steeply pitched roof, kneepads sticky with tar doing most of the work. Astride the ridge and she scuttled to the chimney, flicked the rope into the street below, was over the edge in a twinkling and swarming down. Don't think about the ground, never think about the ground. It's a nice place to be, but you wouldn't want to get there too quickly . . .

"What a climber," she whispered as she passed a large window, a garishly decorated and gloomily lit salon coming into view, and—

She gripped tight to the rope and stopped dead, gently swinging.

She really did have a pressing engagement with not being caught by Pombrine's guards, but within the room was one of those sights that one could not simply slide past. Four, possibly five, or even six naked bodies had formed, with most impressive athleticism, a kind of human sculpture—a grunting tangle of gently shifting limbs. While she was turning her head sideways to make sense of it, the lynchpin of the arrangement, who Shev took at first glance for a red-haired strongman, looked straight at her.

"Shevedieh?"

Decidedly not a man, but very definitely strong. Even with hair clipped close, there was no mistaking her.

"Javre? What the hell are you doing here?"

She raised a brow at the naked bodies entwined about her. "Is that not obvious?"

Shev was brought to her senses by the rattle of guards in the street below. "You never saw me!" And she slid down the rope, hemp hissing through her gloves, hit the ground hard, and sprinted off just as a group of men with weapons drawn came barreling around the corner.

"Stop, thief!"

"Get him!"

And, particularly shrill, Pombrine desperately wailing, "My package!"

Shev jerked the cord in the small of her back and felt the pouch split, the caltrops scattering in her wake, heard the shrieks as a couple of the guards went tumbling. Sore feet they'd have in the morning. But there were still more following.

"Cut him off!"

"Shoot him!"

She took a sharp left, heard the flatbow string an instant later, the twitter as the bolt glanced from the wall beside her and away into the night. She peeled off her gloves as she ran, one smoking from the friction, and flung them over her shoulder. A quick right, the route well planned in advance, of course, and she sprang up onto the tables outside Verscetti's, bounding from one to the next with great strides, sending cutlery and glassware flying, the patrons floundering up, tumbling in their shock, a ragged violinist flinging himself for cover.

"What a runner," she whispered, and leaped from the last table, over the clutching hands of a guard diving from her left and a reveler from her right, catching the little cord behind the sign that said *Verscetti's* as she fell and giving it a good tug.

There was a flash like lightning as she rolled, an almighty bang as she came up, the murky night at once illuminated, the frontages of the buildings ahead picked out white. There were screams and squeals and a volley of detonations. Behind her, she knew, blossoms of purple fire would be shooting across the street, showers of golden sparks, a display suitable for a baron's wedding.

"That Qohdam certainly can make fireworks," she whispered, resisting the temptation to stop and watch the show and instead slipping down a shadowy snicket, shooing away a mangy cat, scurrying on low for three dozen strides and ducking into the narrow garden, struggling to keep her quick breath quiet. She ripped open the packet she had secured among the roots of the dead willow, unfurling the white robe and wriggling into it, pulling up the cowl and waiting in the shadows, the big votive candle in one hand, ears sifting at the night.

"Shit," she muttered. As the last echoes of her fiery diversion faded she could hear, faintly, but coming closer, the calls of Pombrine's searching guards, doors rattling as they tried them one by one.

"Where did he go?"

"I think this way!"

"Bloody firework burned my hand! I'm really burned, you know!"

"My package!"

"Come on, come on," she muttered. To be caught by these idiots would be among the most embarrassing moments of her career. The time she'd been stuck in a marriage gown halfway up the side of the Mercers guildhall in Adua, with flowers in her hair but no underwear and a steadily growing crowd of onlookers below, would take some beating, but still. "Come on, come on, come—"

Now, from the other direction, she heard the chanting and grinned. The Sisters were always on time. She heard their feet now, the regular tramping blotting out the shouting of Pombrine's guards and the wailing of a woman temporarily deafened by the fireworks. Louder the feet, louder the heavenly song, and the procession passed the garden, the women all in white, all hooded, lit candles held stiffly before them, ghostly in the gloom as they marched by in unison.

"What a priestess," Shev whispered to herself, and threaded from the garden, jostling her way into the midst of the procession. She tipped her candle to the left, so its wick touched that of her neighbor. The woman frowned across and Shev winked back.

"Give a girl a light, would you?"

With a fizzle it caught, and she fell into step, adding her own joyous note to the chant as they processed down Caldiche Street and over the Fintine bridge, the masked revelers parting respectfully to let them through. Pombrine's place, and the increasingly frantic searching of his guards, and the furious growling of a pair of savagely arguing Northmen dwindled sedately into the mists behind.

It was dark by the time she slipped silently through her own open window, past the stirring drapes, and crept around her comfortable chair. Carcolf was asleep in it, one strand of yellow hair fluttering around her mouth as she breathed. She looked young with eyes closed and face relaxed, shorn of that habitual sneer she had for everything. Young and very beautiful. Bless this fashion for tight trousers! The candle cast a faint glow in the downy hairs on her cheek, and Shev felt a need to reach out and lay her palm upon that face, and stroke her lips with her thumb—

But, lover of risks though she was, that would have been too great a gamble. So instead she shouted, "Boo!"

Carcolf leaped up like a frog from boiling water, crashed into a table and nearly fell, lurched around, eyes wide. "Bloody hell," she muttered, taking a shuddering breath. "Do you have to do that?"

"Have to? No."

Carcolf pressed one hand to her chest. "I think you might have opened the stitches."

"You unbelievable baby." Shev pulled the robe over her head and tossed it away. "It barely broke the skin."

"The loss of your good opinion wounds me more deeply than any blade."

Shev unhooked the belts that held her thief's tools, unbuckled her climbing pads, and started to peel off her black clothes, acting as if it was nothing to her whether Carcolf watched or not. But she noted with some satisfaction that it was not until she was slipping on a clean gown that Carcolf finally spoke, and in a voice slightly hoarse besides.

"Well?"

"Well what?"

"It has always been a dream of mine to see a Sister of the White disrobe before my eyes, but I was rather wondering whether you found the—"

Shev tossed over the package and Carcolf snatched it smartly from the air.

* * *

"I knew I could rely on you." Carcolf felt a little dizzy with relief, not to mention more than a little tingly with desire. She had always had a weakness for dangerous women.

Bloody hell, she really was turning into her father . . .

"You were right," said Shev, dropping into the chair she had so recently frightened Carcolf out of. "Pombrine had it."

"I bloody knew it! That slime! So hard to find a good expendable decoy these days."

"It's as if you can't trust anyone."

"Still. No harm done, eh?" And Carcolf lifted up her shirt and ever so carefully slid the package into the uppermost of her two cash belts.

It was Shev's turn to watch, pretending not to as she poured herself a glass of wine. "What's in the parcel?" she asked.

"It's safer if I don't tell you."

"You've no idea, have you?"

"I'm under orders not to look," Carcolf was forced to admit.

"Don't you ever wonder, though? I mean, the more I'm ordered not to look, the more I want to." Shev sat forward, dark eyes glimmering in a profoundly bewitching way, and for an instant Carcolf's head was filled with an image of the pair of them rolling across the carpet together, laughing as they ripped the package apart between them.

She dismissed it with an effort. "A thief can wonder. A courier cannot."

"Could you be any more pompous?"

"It would require an effort."

Shev slurped at her wine. "Well, it's your package. I suppose."

"No, it isn't. That's the whole point."

"I think I preferred you when you were a criminal."

"Lies. You relish the opportunity to corrupt me."

"True enough." Shev wriggled down the chair so her long, brown legs slid out from the hem of her gown. "Why don't you stay a while?" One searching foot found Carcolf's ankle, and slid gently up the inside of her leg, and down, and up. "And be corrupted?"

Carcolf took an almost painful breath. "Damn, but I'd love to." The strength of the feeling surprised her and caught in her throat, and for the briefest moment she almost choked on it. For the briefest moment, she almost tossed the package out the window, and sank down before the chair, and took Shev's hand and shared tales she had never told from when she was a girl. For the briefest moment. Then she was Carcolf again, and she stepped smartly away and let Shev's foot clomp down on the boards. "But you know how it is, in my business. Have to catch the tide." And she snatched up her new coat and turned as she pulled it on, giving herself time to blink back any hint of tears.

"You should take a holiday."

"With every job I say so, and when every job ends, I find I get . . . twitchy." Carcolf sighed as she fastened the buttons. "I'm just not made for sitting still."

"Huh."

"Let's not pretend you're any different."

"Let's not pretend. I've been considering a move myself. Adua, perhaps, or back to the South—"

"I'd much rather you stayed," Carcolf found she had said, then tried to pass it off with a carefree wave. "Who else would get me out of messes when I come here? You're the one person in this whole damn city I trust." That was a complete lie, of course; she didn't trust Shev in the least. A good courier trusts no one, and Carcolf was the very best. But she was a great deal more comfortable with lies than with truth.

She could see in Shev's smile that she understood the whole situation perfectly. "So sweet." She caught Carcolf's wrist as she turned to leave with a grip that was not to be ignored. "My money?"

"How silly of me." Carcolf handed her the purse.

Without even looking inside, Shev said, "And the rest."

Carcolf sighed once more and tossed the other purse on the bed, gold flashing in the lamplight as coins spilled across the white sheet. "You'd be upset if I didn't try."

"Your care for my delicate feelings is touching. I dare say I'll see you next time you're here?" she asked, as Carcolf put her hand on the lock.

"I shall count the moments."

Just then she wanted a kiss more than anything, but she was not sure her resolve was strong enough for only one, so though it was a wrench, she blew a kiss instead and pulled the door to behind her. She slipped swiftly across the shadowed court and out the heavy gate onto the street, hoping it was a while before Shevedieh took a closer look at the coins inside the first purse. Perhaps a cosmic punishment was thus incurred, but it was worth it just for the thought of the look on her face.

The day had been a bloody fiasco, but she supposed it could have been a great deal worse. She still had ample time to make it to the ship before they lost the tide. Carcolf pulled up her hood, wincing at the pain from that freshly stitched scratch, and from that entirely unreasonable ulcer, and from that cursed chafing seam, then strode off through the misty night, neither too fast nor too slow, entirely inconspicuous.

Damn, but she hated Sipani!

Gillian Flynn

Gillian Flynn is the author of the #1 *New York Times* bestseller *Gone Girl*, the *New York Times* bestseller *Dark Places*, and *Sharp Objects*, which won two Dagger Awards. A former writer and critic for *Entertainment Weekly*, her work has been published in forty countries. She lives in Chicago with her family.

In the tense and twisty thriller that follows, she shows us that while it's always good to have professional ambitions, sometimes the career path can lead you into some very dangerous territory.

WHAT DO YOU DO?

Gillian Flynn

I didn't stop giving hand jobs because I wasn't good at it. I stopped giving hand jobs because I was the best at it.

For three years, I gave the best hand job in the tristate area. The key is to not overthink it. If you start worrying about technique, if you begin analyzing rhythm and pressure, you lose the essential nature of the act. You have to mentally prepare beforehand, and then you have to stop thinking and trust your body to take over.

Basically, it's like a golf swing.

I jacked men off six days a week, eight hours a day, with a break for lunch, and I was always fully booked. I took two weeks of vacation every year, and I never worked holidays, because holiday hand jobs are sad for everyone. So over three years, I'm estimating that comes to about 23,546 hand jobs. So don't listen to that bitch Shardelle when she says I quit because I didn't have the talent.

I quit because when you give 23,546 hand jobs over a three-year period, carpal tunnel syndrome is a very real thing.

I came to my occupation honestly. Maybe "naturally" is the better word. I've never done much honestly in my life. I was raised in the city by a one-eyed mother (the opening line of my memoir), and she was not a nice lady. She didn't have a drug problem or a drinking problem, but she did have a working problem. She was the laziest bitch I ever met. Twice a week, we'd hit the streets downtown and beg. But because my mom hated being upright, she wanted to be strategic about the whole thing. Get as much money in as little time possible, and then go home and eat Zebra Cakes and watch arbitration-based reality court TV on our broken mattress amongst the stains. (That's what I remember most about my childhood: stains. I couldn't tell you the color of my mom's eye, but I could tell you the stain on the shag carpet was a deep, soupy brown, and the stains on the ceiling were burnt orange and the stains on the wall were a vibrant hungover-piss yellow.)

My mom and I would dress the part. She had a pretty, faded cotton dress, threadbare but screaming of decency. She put me in whatever I'd grown out of. We'd sit on a bench and target the right people to beg off. It's a fairly simple scheme. First choice is an out-of-town church bus. In-town church people, they'll just send you to the church. Out of town, they usually have to help, especially a one-eyed lady with a sad-faced kid. Second choice is women in sets of two. (Solo women can dart away too quickly; a pack of women is too hard to wrangle.) Third choice is a single woman who has that open look. You know it: The same woman you stop to ask for directions or the time of day, that's the woman we ask for money. Also youngish men with beards or guitars. Don't stop men in suits: That cliché is right, they're all assholes. Also skip the thumb rings. I don't know what it is, but men with thumb rings never help.

The ones we picked? We didn't call them marks, or prey or victims. We called them Tonys, because my dad was named Tony and he could never say no to anyone (although I assume he said no to my mom at least once, when she asked him to stay).

Once you stop a Tony, you can figure out in two seconds which way to beg. Some want it over with fast, like a mugging. You blurt. "Weneedmoneyforfoodyouhaveanychange?" Some want to luxuriate in your misfortune. They'll only give you money if you give them something to feel better about, and the sadder your story, the better they feel about helping you, and the more money you get. I'm not blaming them. You go to the theater, you want to be entertained.

My mom had grown up on a farm downstate. Her own mother died in childbirth; her daddy grew soy and raised her when he wasn't too exhausted. She came up here for college, but her daddy got cancer, and the farm got sold, and ends stopped meeting, and she had to drop out. She worked as a waitress for three years, but then her little girl came along, and her little girl's daddy left, and before you knew it . . . she was one of them. The needy. She was not proud . . .

You get the idea. That was just the starter story. You can go from there. You can tell real quick if the person wants a scrappy, up-by-the-bootstraps tale: Then I was suddenly an honor-roll student at a distant charter school (I was, but the truth isn't the point here), and Mom just needed gas money to get me there (I actually took three buses on my own). Or if the person wants a damn-the-system story: Then I was immediately afflicted by some rare disease (named after whatever asshole my mom was dating—Todd-Tychon Syndrome, Gregory-Fisher Disease), and my health-care woes had left us broke.

My mom was sly but lazy. I was much more ambitious. I had lots of stamina and no pride. By the time I was thirteen, I was outbegging her by hundreds of dollars a day, and by the time I was sixteen, I'd left her and the stains and the TV—and, yes, high school—and struck out on my own. I'd go out each morning and beg for six hours. I knew who to approach and for how long and exactly what to say. I was never ashamed. What I did was purely transactional: You made someone feel good and they gave you money.

So you can see why the whole hand-job thing felt like a natural career progression.

Spiritual Palms (I didn't name the place, don't blame me) was in a tony neighborhood to the west of downtown. Tarot cards and crystal balls up front, illegal soft-core sex work in back. I'd answered an ad for a receptionist. It turned out "receptionist" meant "hooker." My boss Viveca is a former receptionist and current bona fide palm reader. (Although Viveca isn't her bona fide name, her bona fide name is Jennifer, but people don't believe Jennifers can tell the future; Jennifers can tell you which cute shoe to buy or what farmer's market to visit, but they should keep their hands off other people's futures.) Viveca employs a few fortune-tellers up front and runs a tidy little room in back. The room in back looks like a doctor's office: It has paper towels and disinfectant and an exam table. The girls froofed it up with scarves draped over lamps and potpourri and sequined pillows—all this stuff only girly-girls would possibly care about. I mean, if I were a guy, looking to pay a girl to wank me off, I wouldn't walk in the room and say, "My God, I smell hints of fresh strudel and nutmeg . . . quick, grab my dick!" I'd walk in a room and say very little, which is what most of them do.

He's unique, the man who comes in for a hand job. (And we only do hand jobs here, or at least I only do hand jobs—I have an arrest record for a few petty thefts, dumb stuff I did at eighteen, nineteen, twenty, that will ensure I never ever *ever* get a decent job, and so I don't need to pile a serious prostie bust on top of it.) A hand-job guy is a very different creature from a guy who wants a blow job or a guy who wants sex. Sure, for some men, a hand job is just a gateway sex act. But I had a lot of repeat customers: They will never want more than a hand job. They don't consider a hand job cheating. Or else they worry about disease, or else they never have the courage to ask for more. They tend to be tense, nervous married men, men with midlevel, mostly powerless jobs. I'm not judging, I'm just giving my assessment. They want you attractive but not slutty. For instance, in my real life I wear glasses, but I don't when I'm in back because it's distracting—they think you're going to pull a Sexy Librarian act on them, and it makes them tense while they wait for the first chords of a ZZ Top song and then they don't hear it and they get embarrassed for thinking that you were going to do Sexy Librarian and then they're distracted and the whole thing takes longer than anyone wants.

They want you friendly and pleasant but not weak. They don't want to feel like predators. They want this transactional. Service-oriented. So you exchange some polite conversation about the weather and a sports team they like. I usually try to find some sort of inside joke we can repeat each visit—an inside joke is like a symbol of friendship without having to do the work required of an actual friendship. So you say, *I see the strawberries are in season!* or *We need a bigger boat* (these are actual inside jokes I'm giving you), and then the ice is broken and they don't feel like they're scumbags because you're friends, and then the mood is set and you can get to it.

When people ask me that question that everyone asks: "What do you do?" I'd say, "I'm in customer service," which was true. To me, it's a nice day's work when you make a lot of people smile. I know that sounds too earnest, but it's true. I mean, I would rather be a librarian, but I worry about the job security. Books may be temporary; dicks are forever.

The problem was, my wrist was killing me. Barely thirty and I had the wrist of an octogenarian and an unsexy athletic brace to match. I took it off before jobs but that Velcro-rip sound made men a little edgy. One day, Viveca visited me in back. She's a heavy woman, like an octopus—lots of beads and ruffles and scarves floating around her, along with the big scent of cologne. She has hair dyed the color of fruit punch and insists it's real. (*Viveca: Grew up the youngest child in a working-class family; indulgent of people she likes; cries at commercials; multiple failed attempts to be a vegetarian.* Just my guess.)

"Are you clairvoyant, Nerdy?" she asked. She called me Nerdy because I wore glasses and read books and ate yogurt on my lunch break. I'm not really a nerd; I only aspire to be one. Because of the high-school-dropout thing, I'm a self-didact. (Not a dirty word, look it up.) I read constantly. I think. But I lack formal education. So I'm left with the feeling that I'm smarter than everyone around me but that if I ever got around really smart people—people who went to universities and drank wine and spoke Latin—that they'd be bored as hell by me. It's a lonely way to go through life. So I wear the name as a badge of honor. That someday I may not totally bore some really smart people. The question is: How do you find smart people?

"Clairvoyant? No."

"A seer? You ever had visions?"

"No." I thought the whole fortune-telling crap was *fer the berds,* as my mom would say. She really was from a farm downstate, that part was true.

Viveca stopped fiddling with one of her beads.

"Nerdy, I'm trying to help you here."

I got it. I'm not usually that slow, but my wrist was throbbing. That distracting kind of pain where all you can think about is how to stop the pain. Also, in my defense, Viveca usually only asks questions so she can talk—she doesn't really care about your answers.

"Whenever I meet someone, I have this immediate vision," I said, in her plummy, wise voice. "Of who they are and what they need. I can see it like a color, a halo, around them." This was all actually true but the last part.

"You see auras." She smiled. "I knew you did."

That's how I found out I was moving up front. I would read auras, which meant I needed zero training. "Just tell them what they want to hear," Viveca said. "Work 'em like a rib." And when people asked me: "What do you do?" I'd say, "I'm a vision specialist," or "I'm in therapeutic practices." Which was true.

The fortune-teller clients were almost all women, and the hand-job clients were obviously all men, so we ran the place like clockwork. It wasn't a big space: You had to get a guy in and settled in the back room, and make sure he was coming right before the woman was ushered into her appointment. You didn't want any orgasm yelps from the back when a lady was telling you how her marriage was coming apart. The new-puppy excuse only works once.

The whole thing was risky, in that Viveca's clients were mostly upper-middle class and lower-upper class. Being of these classes, they're easily offended. If sad, rich housewives don't want their fortunes told by a Jennifer, they definitely don't want them told by a diligent former sex worker with a bad wrist. Appearances are everything. These are not people who want to slum it. These are people whose primary purpose is to live in the city but feel like they're in the suburbs. Our front office looked like a Pottery Barn ad. I dressed accordingly, which is basically Funky Artist as approved of and packaged by J.Crew. Peasant blouses, that's the key.

The women who came in groups, they were frivolous, fancy, boozy, ready to have fun. The ones who came alone, though, they wanted to believe. They were desperate, and they didn't have good enough insurance for a therapist. Or they didn't know they were desperate enough to need a therapist. It was hard to feel sorry for them. I tried to because you don't want your mystic, the keeper of your future, to roll her eyes at you. But I mean, come on. Big house in the city, husbands who didn't beat them and helped with the kids, sometimes with careers but always with book clubs. And still they felt sad. That's what they always ended up saying: "But I'm just sad." Feeling sad means having too much time on your hands, usually. Really. I'm not a licensed therapist but usually it means too much time.

So I say things like, "A great passion is about to enter your life." Then you pick something you can make them do. You figure out what will make them feel good about themselves. Mentor a child, volunteer at a library, neuter some dogs, go green. You don't say it as a suggestion though, that's the key. You say it as a warning. "A great passion is about to enter your life . . . you must tread carefully or it will eclipse everything else that matters to you!"

I'm not saying it's always that easy, but it's often that easy. People want passion. People want a sense of purpose. And when they get those things, then they come back to you because you predicted their future, and it was good.

Susan Burke was different. She seemed smarter from the second I saw her. I entered the room one rainy April morning, fresh from a hand-job client. I still kept a few, my longtime favorites, and so I had just been assisting a sweet dorky rich guy who called himself Michael Audley (I say "called" because I assume a rich guy wouldn't give me his real name). Mike Audley: *Overshadowed by jock brother; came into his own in college; extremely brainy but not smug about it; compulsive jogger.* Just my guess. The only thing I really knew about Mike was he loved books. He recommended books with the fervor I've always craved as an aspiring nerd: with urgency and camaraderie. You *have* to read this! Pretty soon we had our own private (occasionally sticky) book club. He was big into "Classic Stories of the Supernatural" and he wanted me to be too ("You are a psychic after all," he said with a smile). So that day we discussed the themes of loneliness and need in *The Haunting of Hill House,* he came, I sani-wiped myself and grabbed his loaner for next time: *The Woman in White.* ("You *have* to read this! It's one of the all-time best.")

Then I tousled my hair to look more intuitive, straightened my peasant blouse, tucked the book under my arm, and ran out to the main room. Not quite clockwork: I was thirty-seven seconds late. Susan Burke was waiting; she shook my hand with a nervous, birdy up and down, and the repetitive motion made me wince. I dropped my book and we banged heads picking it up. Definitely not what you want from your psychic: a Three Stooges bit.

I motioned her to a seat. I put on my wise voice and asked her why she was here. That's the easiest way to tell people what they want: Ask them what they want.

Susan Burke was silent for a few beats. Then: "My life is falling apart," she murmured. She was extremely pretty but so wary and nervous you didn't realize she was pretty until you looked hard at her. Looked past the glasses to the bright blue eyes. Imagined the dull blond hair de-stringed. She was clearly rich. Her handbag was too plain to be anything but incredibly expensive. Her dress was mousy but well made. In fact, it could be the dress wasn't mousy—she just wore it that way. *Smart but not creative,* I thought. *Conformist. Lives in fear of saying or doing the wrong thing. Lacks confidence. Probably browbeaten by her parents, and now browbeaten by her husband. Husband has temper—her whole goal each day is to get to the end without a blowup. Sad. She'll be one of the sad ones.*

Susan Burke began sobbing then. She sobbed for a minute and a half. I was going to give her two minutes before I interrupted, but she stopped on her own.

"I don't know why I'm here," she said. She pulled a pastel handkerchief from her bag but didn't use it. "This is crazy. It just keeps getting worse."

I gave her my best *there, there* without touching her. "What's going on in your life?"

She wiped her eyes and stared at me a beat. Blinked. "Don't you know?"

Then she gave me a smile. Sense of humor. Unexpected.

"So how do we do this?" she asked, tucking herself in again. She massaged a spot near the nape of her neck. "How does this work?"

"I'm a psychological intuitive," I began. "Do you know what that means?"

"You can read people well."

"Yes, to a degree, but my powers are much stronger than just a hunch. All my senses play a part. I can feel vibrations coming off people. I can see auras. I can smell despair, or dishonesty, or depression. It's a gift I've had since I was a small child. My mother was a deeply depressed, unbalanced woman. A dark blue haze followed her. When she was near me, my skin plinked—like someone was playing a piano—and she smelled of despair, which presents itself to me as the scent of bread."

"Bread?" she said.

"That was just her scent, of a desperate soul." I needed to pick a new *eau de sad girl.* Not dying leaves, too obvious, but something earthy. Mushrooms? No, inelegant.

"Bread, that is so strange," she said.

People usually asked what their scent or aura was. It was their first step to committing to the game. Susan shifted uncomfortably. "I don't mean to be rude," she said. "But . . . I think this isn't for me."

I waited her out. Empathetic silence is one of the most underused weapons in the world.

"OK," Susan said. She tucked her hair behind both ears—thick diamond-scattered wedding bands flashing like the Milky Way—and looked ten years younger. I could picture her as a kid, a bookworm maybe, pretty but shy. Demanding parents. Straight As, always. "So what do you read off me?"

"There's something going on in your house."

"I already told you that." I could feel the desperation coming off her: to believe in me.

"No, you told me your life was falling apart. I'm saying it's something to do with your house. You have a husband, I sense a lot of discord: I see you surrounded by a sick green, like an egg yolk gone bad. Swirls of a healthy vibrant turquoise on the outer edges. That tells me you had something good and it went very bad. Yes?"

Obviously this was an easy guess, but I liked my color arrangement; it felt right.

She glared at me. I was hitting on something close to the bone.

"I feel the same vibrations off you as my mother: those sharp, high piano plinks. You're desperate, you're in exquisite pain. You're not sleeping."

The mention of insomnia was always risky but usually paid off. People in pain don't generally sleep well. Insomniacs are exquisitely grateful for people to recognize their weariness.

"No, no, I sleep eight hours," Susan said.

"It's not a genuine sleep. You have unsettling dreams. Maybe not nightmares, maybe you don't even remember them, but you wake up feeling worn, achy."

See, you can rescue most bad guesses. This woman was in her forties; people in their forties usually wake up feeling achy. I know that from commercials.

"You store the anxiety in your neck," I continued. "Also, you smell of peonies. A child. You have a child?"

If she didn't have a child, then I just say, "But you *want* one." And she can deny it—*I've never, ever even thought about having kids*—and I can insist, and pretty soon she leaves thinking it because very few women decide not to procreate without some doubts. It's an easy thought to seed. Except this one's smart.

"Yes. Well, two. A son and a stepson."

Stepson, go with the stepson.

"Something is wrong in your house. Is it your stepson?"

She stood up, fumbled through her well-constructed bag.

"How much do I owe you?"

I got one thing wrong. I thought I'd never see her again. But four days later Susan Burke was back. ("Can *things* have auras?" she asked. "Like, objects. Or a house?") And then three days later ("Do you believe in evil spirits? Is there such a thing, do you think?") and then the next day.

I was right about her, mostly. Overbearing, demanding parents, straight As, Ivy League, a degree that had something to do with business. I asked her the question: What do you do? She explained and explained about downsizing and restructuring and client intersects, and when I frowned, she got impatient and said, "I define and eliminate problems." Things with her husband were OK except when it came to the stepson. The Burkes had moved into the city the year before, and that's when the kid went from troubled to troubling.

"Miles was never a sweet boy," she said. "I'm the only mom he's known—I've been with his dad since he was six. But he's always been cold. Introverted. He's just empty. I hate myself for saying that. I mean, introverted is fine. But in the past year, since the move . . . he's changed. Become more aggressive. He's so angry. So dark. Threatening. He scares me."

The kid was fifteen, and had just been forcibly relocated from the suburbs into the city where he didn't know anyone, and he was already an awkward, nerdy kid. Of course he was angry. That would have been helpful, my saying that, but I didn't. I seized an opportunity.

I'd been trying to move into the domestic aura-cleansing business. Basically when someone moves into a new home, they call you. You wander around the house burning sage and sprinkling salt and murmuring a lot. Fresh start, wipe away any lingering bad energy from previous owners. Now that people were moving back into the heart of the city, into all the old historic houses, it seemed like a boom industry waiting to happen. A hundred-year-old house, that's a lot of leftover vibes.

"Susan, have you considered that the house is affecting your son's behavior?"

Susan leaned in, her eyes wide. "Yes! Yes, I do. Is that crazy? That's why . . . why I came back. Because . . . there was blood on my wall."

"Blood?"

She leaned in and I could smell the mint masking sour breath. "Last week. I didn't want to say anything . . . I thought you'd think I was crazy. But it was there. One long trickle from the floor to the ceiling. Am I . . . am I crazy?"

I met her at the house the next week. Driving up her street in my trusty hatchback, I thought, *rust.* Not blood. Something from the walls, the roof. Who knew what old houses were built of? Who knew what could leak out after a hundred years? The question was how to play it. I really wasn't interested in getting into exorcism, demonology church shit. I don't think that's what Susan wanted either. But she did invite me to her house, and women like that don't invite over women like me unless they want something. Comfort. I would breeze over the "blood trickle," find an explanation for it, and yet still insist the house could use a cleansing.

Repeated cleansings. We had yet to discuss money. Twelve visits for $2,000 seemed like a good price point. Spread them out, one a month, over a year, and give the stepson time to sort himself out, get adjusted to the new school, the new kids. Then he's cured and I'm the hero, and pretty soon Susan is referring all her rich, nervous friends to me. I could go into business for myself, and when people asked me, "What do you do?" I'd say, *I'm an entrepreneur* in that haughty way entrepreneurs had. Maybe Susan and I would become friends. Maybe she'd invite me to a book club. I'd sit by a fire and nibble on Brie and say, *I'm a small business owner, an entrepreneur, if you will.* I parked, got out of the car, and took a big breath of optimistic spring air.

But then I spotted Susan's house. I actually stopped and stared. Then I shivered.

It was different from the rest.

It lurked. It was the only remaining Victorian house in a long row of boxy new construction, and maybe that's why it seemed alive, calculating. The mansion's front was all elaborate, carved stonework, dizzying in its detail: flowers and filigrees, dainty rods and swooping ribbons. Two life-sized angels framed the doorway, their arms reaching upward, their faces fascinated by something I couldn't see.

I watched the house. It watched me back through long, baleful windows so tall a child could stand in the sill. And one was. I could see the length of his thin body: gray trousers, black sweater, a maroon tie perfectly knotted at the neck. A thicket of dark hair covering his eyes. Then, a sudden blur, and he'd hopped down and disappeared behind the heavy brocade drapes.

The steps to the mansion were steep and long. My heart was thumping by the time I reached the top, passed the awestruck angels, reached the door, and rang the bell. As I waited I read the inscription carved in the stone near my feet.

carterhook manor
established 1893
patrick carterhook

The carving was in a severe Victorian cursive, the two juicy o's dissected by a feathery curlicue. It made me want to protect my belly.

Susan opened the door with red eyes.

"Welcome to Carterhook Manor," she said, fake grandeur. She caught me staring—Susan never looked good when I saw her, but she hadn't even pretended to brush her hair, and a foul, acrid odor came off her. (Not "despair" or "depression," just bad breath and body odor.) She shrugged limply. "I've finally stopped sleeping."

The inside of the house was nothing like the outside. The interior had been gutted and now looked like every other rich person's house. It made me feel immediately more cheerful. I could cleanse *this* place: the tasteful recessed lights, the granite counters and stainless-steel appliances, the new, freakishly smooth wood paneling, wall upon wall of Botoxed oak.

"Let's start with the blood trickle," I suggested.

We climbed to the second floor. There were two more above it. The stairwell was open, and I peered up through the banisters to see a face peering down at me from the top floor. Black hair and eyes, set against the porcelain skin of an antique doll. Miles. He stared at me for a solemn moment, then disappeared again. That kid matched the original house perfectly.

Susan pulled down a tasteful print on the landing, so I could see the full wall.

"Here, it was right here." She pointed from the ceiling to the floor.

I pretended to examine it closely, but there was nothing really to see. She'd scrubbed it down completely; I could still smell the bleach.

"I can help you," I said. "There is a tremendous feeling of pain, right here. Throughout the whole house, but definitely here. I can help you."

"The house creaks all night long," she said. "I mean, it almost moans. It shouldn't. Everything inside is new. Miles's door slams at strange times. And he . . . he's getting worse. It's like something has settled on him. A darkness he carries on his back. Like an insect shell. He scuttles. Like a beetle. I'd move, that's how scared I am, I'd move, but we don't have the money. Anymore. We spent so much on this house, and then almost that much renovating, and . . . my husband won't let me anyway. He says Miles is just going through growing pains. And that I'm a nervous, silly woman."

"I can help you," I said.

"Let me give you the whole tour," she replied.

We walked down the long, narrow hall. The house was naturally dark. You moved away from a window and the gloom descended. Susan flipped on lights as we walked.

"Miles turns them off," she said. "Then I turn them back on. When I ask him to keep them on, he pretends he has no idea what I'm talking about. Here's our den," she said. She opened a door to reveal a cavernous room with a fireplace and wall-to-wall bookshelves.

"It's a *library,*" I gasped. They had to own a thousand books, easy. Thick, impressive, smart-people books. How do you keep a thousand books in one room and then call the room a den?

I stepped inside. I shivered dramatically. "Do you feel this? Do you feel the . . . heaviness here?"

"I hate this room." She nodded.

"I'll need to pay extra attention to this room," I said. I'd park myself in it for an hour at a time and just read, read whatever I wanted.

We went back into the hall, which was now dark again. Susan sighed and began flipping on lights. I could hear a patter of feet upstairs, running manically up and down the hallway. We passed a closed door to my right. Susan knocked at it—*Jack, it's me.* A shuffle of a chair being pushed back, a snick of a lock, and then the door was opened by another child, younger than Miles by several years. He looked like his mother. He smiled at Susan like he hadn't seen her in a year.

"Hi, Momma," he said. He wrapped his arms around her. "I missed you."

"This is Jack, he's seven," she said. She ruffled his hair.

"Momma has to go do a little work with her friend here," Susan said, kneeling to his eye level. "Finish your reading and then I'll make a snack."

"Do I lock the door?" Jack asked.

"Yes, always lock your door, sweetheart."

We started walking again as we heard the snick of the lock behind us.

"Why the lock?"

"Miles doesn't like his brother."

She must have felt my frown: No teenager likes his kid brother.

"You should see what Miles did to the babysitter he didn't like. It's one of the reasons we don't have money. Medical bills." She turned to me sharply. "I shouldn't have said that. It wasn't . . . major. Possibly an accident. I don't know anymore, actually. Maybe I am just goddam crazy."

Her laugh was raw. She swiped at an eye.

We walked to the end of the hallway, where another door was locked.

"I'd show you Miles's room, but I don't have a key," she said simply. "Also, I'm too scared."

She forced another laugh. It wasn't convincing; it didn't have enough energy to even pose as a laugh. We went up to the next floor, which was a series of rooms, wallpapered and painted, with fine-boned Victorian furniture arranged haphazardly. One room held only a litterbox. "For our cat, Wilkie," Susan said. "Luckiest cat in the world: his own room for his own crap."

"You'll find a use for the space."

"He's actually a sweet cat," she said. "Almost twenty years old."

I smiled like that was interesting and good.

"We obviously have more room than we need," Susan said. "I think we thought, there might be another . . . maybe adopt, but I wouldn't bring another child into this house. So instead we live in a very expensive storage facility. My husband does like his antiques." I could picture him, this uptight, snooty husband. A man who bought antiques but didn't find them himself. Probably had some classy decorator woman in horn-rims doing the actual work. She probably bought those books for him too. I heard you could do that—buy books by the yard, turn them into furniture. People are dumb. I'll never get over how dumb people are.

We climbed some more. The top floor was just a large attic space with a few old steamer trunks all along the walls.

"Aren't the trunks stupid?" she whispered. "He says it gives the place a little authenticity. He didn't like the renovation."

So the house had been a compromise: The husband wanted vintage, Susan wanted new, so they thought this outside/inside split might settle things. But the Burkes ended up more resentful than satisfied. Millions of dollars later, and neither of them were happy. Money is wasted on the rich.

We went down the back stairs, cramped and dizzying, like an animal's burrow, and ended up in the gaping, gleaming modern kitchen.

Miles sat at the kitchen island, waiting. Susan started when she saw him.

He was small for his age. Pale face and pointy chin, and black eyes that reflected twitchily, like a spider's. Assessing. *Extremely bright but hates school,* I thought. *Never gets enough attention—even if he got all of Susan's attention it still wouldn't be enough. Mean-spirited. Self-centered.*

"Hi, Momma," he said. His face was transformed, a bright, goofy smile cracking through it. "I missed you." *Sweet-natured, loving Jack.* He was doing a perfect version of his little brother. Miles went to hug Susan, and as he walked, he assumed Jack's slump-shouldered, childish posture. He wrapped his arms around her, nuzzled into her. Susan watched me over his head, her cheeks flush, her lips tight as if she smelled something nasty. Miles gazed up at her. "Why won't you hug me?"

She gave him a brief hug. Miles released her as if he were scalded.

"I heard what you told her," he said. "About Jack. About the babysitter. About everything. You're such a bitch."

Susan flinched. Miles turned to me.

"I really hope you leave and don't come back. For your own good." He smiled at both of us. "This is a family matter. Don't you think, Momma?"

Then he was clattering in his heavy leather shoes up the back stairway again, leaning heavily forward. He did scuttle as if he bore an insect's shell, shiny and hard.

Susan looked at the floor, took a breath, and looked up. "I want your help."

"What does your husband say about all this?"

"We don't talk about it. Miles is his kid. He raised him. Anytime I say anything remotely critical, he says I'm crazy. He says I'm crazy a lot. A haunted house. Maybe I am. Anyway, he travels all the time; he won't even know you're here."

"I can help you," I said. "Shall we talk pricing very quickly?"

She agreed to the money, but not the timeline: "I can't wait a year for Miles to get better; he may kill us all before then." She gave that desperate burp of a laugh. I agreed to come twice a week.

Mostly I came during the day, when the kids were at school and Susan was at work. I did cleanse the house, in that I washed it. I lit my sage and sprinkled my sea salt. I boiled my lavender and rosemary, and I wiped down that house, walls and floors. And then I sat in the library and read. Also, I nosed around. I could find a zillion photos of grinning-sunshine Jack, a few old ones of pouty Miles, a couple of somber Susan and none of her husband. I felt sorry for Susan. An angry stepson and a husband who was always away, no wonder she let her mind go to dark places.

And yet. And yet, I felt it too: the house. Not necessarily malevolent, but . . . mindful. I could feel it studying me, does that makes sense? It crowded me. One day, I was wiping down the floorboards, and suffered a sudden, slicing pain in my middle finger—as if I'd been bitten—and when I pulled it away, I was bleeding. I wrapped my finger tightly in one of my spare rags and watched the blood seep through. And I felt like something in the house was pleased.

I began dreading. I made myself fight the dread. *You are the one who made this whole thing up,* I told myself. *So cut it out.*

Six weeks in, and I was boiling my lavender in the kitchen one morning—Susan off to work, the kids at school—when I felt a presence behind me. I turned to find Miles in his school uniform, examining me, a small smirk on his face. He was holding my copy of *The Turn of the Screw.*

"You like ghost stories?" He smiled.

He'd been through my purse.

"Why are you at home, Miles?"

"I've been studying you. You're interesting. You know something bad is going to happen, right? I'm curious."

He moved closer, I moved away. He stood next to the pot of boiling water. His cheeks flushed from the heat.

"I'm trying to help, Miles."

"But you agree? You feel it? Evil?"

"I feel it."

He stared into the pot of water. Traced a finger on its edge, then snatched the finger away, pink. He assessed me with his shining black spider eyes.

"You don't look how I thought you'd look. Up close. I thought you'd be . . . *sexy.*" He said the word ironically, and I knew what he meant: Halloween fortune-teller sexy. Lip gloss and big hair and hoop earrings. "You look like a babysitter."

I stepped farther back from him. He hurt the last babysitter.

"Are you trying to scare me, Miles?"

I wished I could reach the stove, turn off the burner.

"I'm trying to help you," he said reasonably. "I don't want you around her. If you come back, you will die. I don't want to say more than that. But I've warned you."

He turned away and left the room. When I heard him hit the front stairs, I poured the scalding water down the drain, then ran to the dining room to grab my purse, my keys. I needed to leave. When I picked up my purse, a foul, sweet heat hit my nostrils. He'd vomited inside—all over my keys and wallet and phone. I couldn't bear to pick up the keys, touch that sickness.

Susan banged through the door, frantic.

"Is he here? Are you OK?" she said. "School called, said Miles never showed. He must have walked in the front door and straight out the back. He doesn't like it that you're here. Did he say anything to you?"

A loud smash came from upstairs. A wail. We ran up the stairs. In the hallway, hanging from a ceiling hook, was a tiny, primitive figure made of cloth. A face drawn in magic marker. A noose made from red thread. Screaming came from Miles's room at the end of the hall. *Nonoooooooo, you bitch, you bitch!*

We stood outside the door.

"Do you want to talk to him?" I asked.

"No," she said.

She turned back down the hall in tears. Plucked the figure from the light fixture.

"I thought this was me at first," Susan said, handing it to me. "But I don't have brown hair."

"I think it's me," I said.

"I'm so tired of being afraid," she murmured.

"I know."

"You don't," she said. "But you will."

Susan went to her room. I went to work. I swear I worked. I washed the house, every inch of wall and floor, with rosemary and lavender. I smudged the sage and said my magical words that were gibberish as Miles screamed and Susan cried in the rooms above me. Then I dumped everything from my vomit-smeared purse into the kitchen sink and ran water over it until it was clean.

As I was unlocking my car in the dusk, an older woman, well powdered and plump-cheeked, called out to me from down the block. She scurried over in the mist, a little smile on her face.

"I just want to thank you for what you are doing for this family," she said. "For helping little Miles. Thank you." And then she put her fingers to her lips and pantomimed locking them, and scurried away again before I could tell her I was doing absolutely nothing to help this family.

A week later, as I was killing time in my tiny apartment (one bedroom, fourteen books), I noticed something new. A stain, like a rusty tidal pool on the wall by my bed. It reminded me of my mother. Of my old life. All the transactions—this for that, that for this—and none of it had made any difference until now. Once the transaction was complete, my mind was a blank, awaiting the next transaction. But Susan Burke and her family, they stuck with me. Susan Burke and her family and that house.

I opened up my ancient laptop and did a search: Patrick Carterhook. A whir and a grind and finally up came a link to an article from a university English Department: Victorian True Crime: The Grisly Tale of the Patrick Carterhook Family.

> The year is 1893, and department-store magnate Patrick Carterhook moves into his splendid Gilded Age mansion in the heart of the city with his lovely wife, Margaret, and their two sons, Robert and Chester. Robert was a troubled boy, much given to bullying schoolmates and harming neighborhood pets. At age twelve, he burnt down one of his father's warehouses and remained on scene to watch the wreckage. He endlessly tormented his quiet younger brother. By age fourteen, Robert proved unable to control himself. The Carterhooks chose to keep him away from society: In 1895 they locked him inside the mansion. He was never again to set foot outdoors. Robert steadily grew more violent in his gloomy, gilded prison. He smeared his family's belongings with his own excrement and vomit. A nursemaid was sent to the hospital with unexplained bruises; she never returned. The cook, too, fled one winter morning. Rumors had it that she'd suffered third-degree burns from boiling water in a "kitchen mishap."
>
> No one knows exactly what went on in that house the night of January 7, 1897, but the bloody results are indisputable. Patrick Carterhook was discovered stabbed to death in his bed; his body was pocked with 117 knife wounds. Patrick's wife, Margaret, was found struck down by an ax—still in her back—as she was fleeing up the stairs to the attic, and young Chester, age ten, was found drowned in a bathtub. Robert hanged himself from a beam in his room. He had apparently dressed up for the occasion: he wore a blue Sunday suit, covered in his parents' blood. It was still wet from drowning his little brother.

Beneath the story was a blurry ancient photo of the Carterhooks. Four formal unsmiling faces peering out from layers of Victorian ruffles. A slender man in his forties with an artfully pointed beard; a blond, petite woman with sad, piercing eyes so light they looked white. Two boys, the younger blond like his mother; the elder dark-haired, black-eyed with a slight smirk and his head tilted at a knowing angle. Miles. The elder boy looked like Miles. Not a perfect match, but the essence was exact: the smugness, the superiority, the threat.

Miles.

If you remove the bloody floorboards and water-stained tiles; if you destroy the beams that held Robert Carterhook's body, and you tear down the walls that absorbed the screams, do you take down the house? Can it be haunted if the actual guts—its internal organs—have been removed? Or does the nastiness linger in the air? That night I dreamt of a small figure opening the door to Susan's room, creeping across the floor as she slept, and standing calmly over her with a gleaming butcher knife borrowed from her million-dollar kitchen. The room smelled of sage and lavender.

I slept into the afternoon and woke in the darkness, in the middle of a thunderstorm. I stared at the ceiling until the sun set, then got dressed and drove over to Carterhook Manor. I left my useless herbs behind.

Susan opened the door with wet eyes. Her pale faced glowed from the gloom of the house.

"You *are* psychic," she whispered. "I was going to call you. It's gotten worse, it's not stopping," she said. She collapsed onto a sofa.

"Are Miles and Jack here?"

She nodded and pointed a finger up. "Miles told me last night, quite calmly, that he was going to kill us," she said. "And I actually worry . . . because . . . Wilkie . . ." She was crying again. "Oh, God."

A cat padded slowly into the room. Ribby and worn, an old tomcat. Susan pointed to it.

"Look what he did . . . to poor Wilkie!"

I looked again. At the cat's back haunches was only a frayed tuft of fur. Miles had cut off the cat's tail.

"Susan, do you have a laptop? I need to show you something."

She led me up to the library, and over to the Victorian desk that was clearly her husband's. She clicked a switch and the fireplace whooshed on. She hit a key and the laptop glowed. I showed Susan the Web site and the story of the Carterhooks. I could feel her warm breath on my neck as she read.

I pointed at the photo: "Does Robert Carterhook remind you of anyone?"

Susan nodded as if in a trance. "What does it mean?"

The rain spattered at the black windowpanes. I longed for a bright blue day. The heaviness of the house was unbearable.

"Susan, I like you. I don't like many people. I want the best for your family. And I don't think it's me."

"What do you mean?"

"I mean, you need someone to *help* you. I can't help. There is something wrong with this house. I think you should leave. I don't care what your husband says."

"But if we leave . . . Miles is still with us."

"Yes."

"Then . . . he'll be cured? If he leaves this house?"

"Susan, I don't know."

"What are you saying?"

"I'm saying you need more than me to fix this. I'm not qualified. I can't fix it. I think you need to leave tonight. Go to a hotel. Two rooms. Lock the adjoining door. And then . . . we'll figure it out. But all I can really do for you is be your friend."

Susan stood dizzily, holding her throat. She pushed back from me, murmured *excuse me,* and disappeared out the door. I waited. My wrist was throbbing again. I glanced around the book-filled room. No parties here for me. No referrals to rich, nervous friends. I was ruining my big chance; I gave her an answer she didn't want. But I felt, for once, decent. Not telling-myself-I-am decent, but just decent.

I saw Susan flicker past the door heading down the stairs. Then Miles swooped immediately after her.

"Susan!" I yelled. I stood up but I couldn't will myself to go outside the room. I heard murmuring. Urgent or angry. Then nothing. Silence. And still nothing. *Go out there.* But I was too afraid to go alone into that dark hallway.

"Susan!"

A child who terrorized his little brother and threatened his stepmom. Who told me calmly that I would die. A kid who cut the tail off the family pet. A house that attacked and manipulated its own inhabitants. A house that had already seen four deaths and wanted more. *Stay calm.* The hallway was still dark. No sign of Susan. I stood. I began walking to the door.

Miles suddenly appeared in the doorway, stiff and upright, in his school uniform, as always. He was blocking my exit.

"I told you not to ever come back here, and you came back—you came back again and again," he said. Reasonable. Like he was talking to a child being punished. "You know you're going to die, right?"

"Where's your stepmom, Miles?" I backed away. He walked toward me. He was a small kid, but he scared me. "What did you do with Susan?"

"You're still not understanding, are you?" he said. "Tonight is when we die."

"I'm sorry, Miles, I didn't mean to upset you."

He laughed then, his eyes crinkling up. Complete mirth.

"No, you misunderstand me. She's going to *kill you. Susan* is going to kill you and me. Look around this room. Do you think you're here by accident? Look closely. Look at the books closely."

I had looked at the books closely. Every time I cleansed in here, I looked at all the books, I coveted them. I pictured stealing one or two for my little book club with . . .

With Mike. My favorite client. Every book I ever read with Mike over the past few years was here. *The Woman in White, The Turn of the Screw, The Haunting of Hill House.* I'd congratulated myself when I'd seen them—how clever I was to have read so many of these fancy-people library books. But I wasn't a well-read bookworm; I was just a dumb whore in the right library. Miles pulled out a photo from the desk drawer, a wedding photo. The summer sunset behind the bride and groom left them backlit, shrouded. Susan was gorgeous, a luscious, lively version of the woman I knew. The groom? I barely recognized the face, but I definitely knew the dick. I had been giving hand jobs to Susan's husband for two years.

Miles was watching me, his eyes squinting, a comedian waiting for the audience to get the joke.

"She's going to kill you, and I'm pretty sure she's going to kill me too," he said.

"What do you mean?"

"She's calling 911 downstairs right now. She told me to stall you. When she comes up, she's going to shoot you, and she's going to tell the cops one of two things. One: You are a con artist who claims she has psychic powers in order to prey on the emotionally vulnerable. You told Susan you could help her mentally unstable son—and she trusted you—but instead, all you've been doing is coming into the house and stealing from her. When she confronted you, you became violent, you shot me, she shot you in self-defense."

"I don't like that one. What's the other option?"

"You actually are legit. You really did believe that the house was haunting me. But it turned out I'm not haunted, I'm just a run-of-the-mill teen sociopath. You pushed me too hard, I killed you. She and I struggled with the gun, she shot me in self-defense."

"Why would she want to kill you?"

"She doesn't like me, she never has. I'm not her son. She tried to pack me off to my mom, but my mom has zero interest. Then she tried to ship me to boarding school but my dad said no. She definitely would like me dead. It's just how she is. It's how she makes her living: She defines and eliminates problems. She's practical in an evil way."

"But she seems so—"

"Mousy? No, she's not. She wanted you to think that. She's a beautiful, successful executive. She's a goddam overdog. But you needed to feel like you were preying on someone weaker than you. That you had the upper hand. I mean, am I wrong? Isn't that your whole business? Manipulating the manipulatable?"

My mom and I played that game for a decade: dressing and acting the part of people to be pitied. I didn't see it coming the other way.

"She wants to kill me . . . because of your dad?"

"Susan Burke had the perfect marriage, and you ruined it. My dad's gone. He left."

"I'm sure a few . . . liaisons is not the reason your dad left."

"It's the reason she has chosen to believe in. It's the problem she has defined and plans to eliminate."

"Does your dad know . . . I'm here?"

"Not yet—he really does travel all the time. But once my dad learns we're dead, hears Susan's story? Once she tells him about being so scared, and coming across the business card for the psychic in his copy of *Rebecca,* and desperately asking her to help . . . imagine that guilt. His kid is dead because he wanted a hand job. His wife was forced to defend her family and *kill* because he got a hand job. That horror and guilt—he'll never be able to make it up to her. Which is the point."

"That's how she found me? My business card?"

"Susan found the card. She thought it was odd. Fishy. My dad loves ghost stories, but he's the world's biggest skeptic—he'd never see a palm reader. Unless . . . she wasn't really a palm reader. She followed him. She made an appointment. And then you walked in from the backroom with his copy of *The Woman in White,* and she knew."

"She confides in you."

"At first I took it as a compliment," he said. "Then I realized she's trying to distract me. She told me about her plan to kill you so I wouldn't realize I was going to die too."

"Why not just shoot me in an alley one night?"

"Then my dad feels no pain. And if she's seen? No. She wanted to kill you here, where it looked like she was the victim. It's actually the easiest way to do it. So she made up that haunted-house story to lure you here. Carterhook Manor, so *scary.*"

"But the Carterhooks? I read about them online."

"The Carterhooks are a fiction. I mean, they existed, I guess, but they didn't die like you read."

"I read about them!"

"You read about them because she wrote about them. It's the Internet. Do you know how easy it is to make a Web page? And then make some links to it, and then have people find it and believe it and add it to their Web pages? It's tremendously easy. Especially for someone like Susan."

"That photo, it looked like—"

"Ever been to a flea market—shoebox after shoebox of those old photos, buck apiece. It's not hard to find a kid that might look like me. Especially if you have a person who is willing to believe. A sucker. Like you."

"The bleeding wall?"

"She just told you that. Sets the mood. She knew you liked ghost stories. She wanted you to come, and to believe. She likes to fuck with people. She wanted you to befriend her, be worried about her, and then—bam!—have that moment of shock when you realized you were going to die, and you'd been scared of the wrong thing. Your *senses* betrayed you."

He smirked at me.

"Who cut off your cat's tail?"

"It's a manx, dummy, they have no tails. Can I answer any other questions on the road? I'd rather not wait here to die."

"You want to come with me?"

"Let's see: leave with you or stay here and die. Yeah, I'd like to come with you. She's probably done with her call. She's probably at the bottom of the stairs. I already hooked up the fire ladder in my room."

Susan's heels clattered across the living room, toward the stairs. Two floors below and moving fast. Calling my name.

"Please take me with you," he said. "Please. Just until my dad gets home. Please, I'm scared."

"What about Jack?"

"She likes Jack. She only wants us gone."

Susan's footsteps one floor down, climbing.

We took the fire escape. It was quite dramatic.

We were in my car, driving away before I realized I didn't know where the hell I was driving. Miles's pale face reflected passing headlights like a sickly moon. Raindrops glided from his forehead down his cheeks and off his chin.

"Call your dad," I said.

"My dad's in Africa."

The rain was clattering against my tinny rooftop. Susan Burke (that magnificent con artist!) had infused me with such a fear of the house, I'd been insensible. Now I could think: A successful woman marries a rich man. They have a baby who's a real charmer. The life is good except for one thing: the weirdo stepson. I believed her when she said Miles had always been cold to her. I'm sure she was always cold to Miles. I'm sure she tried to get rid of him from the start. Someone as calculating as Susan Burke wouldn't want to raise the oddball, awkward kid of another woman. Susan and Mike muddle along, but soon her cruelty toward his firstborn infects their relationship. He turns away from her. Her touch chills him. He comes to see me. And keeps seeing me. We have just enough in common, with the books, he can trick himself into thinking it's a relationship of some sort. Things with Susan continue to disintegrate. He moves out. He leaves Miles behind because he's traveling overseas—as soon as he returns, he'll make arrangements. (This was pure guess, but the Mike I knew, who giggled when he came, he seemed like a guy who'd retrieve his kid.) Unfortunately, Susan discovers his secret and blames me for the destruction of her marriage. Imagine the rage, that a lowdown woman like me was *handling* her husband. And now she was stuck with a creepy kid she hated and a house she didn't like. How to solve the problem? She begins to plot. She lures me in. Miles warns me in his elliptical way, toying with me, enjoying the game for a bit. Susan tells the neighbors something vague—that I'm here to help poor little Miles—so that when the truth comes out—that I'm a former hooker and current grifter—she will seem wretched, pitiful, pathetic. And I will seem ruinous. It's the perfect way to commit murder.

Miles looked over at me with his huge moon face and smiled.

"You know you're basically now a kidnapper," he said.

"I guess we need to go to the police."

"We need to go to Chattanooga, Tennessee," he said, somewhat impatiently, as if I were backing out of a long-standing plan. "Bloodwillow is there this year. It's always overseas—this is the first time it's been in the United States since 1978."

"I have no idea what you're talking about."

"It's only the biggest supernatural convention in the world. Susan said I couldn't go. So you can take me. I thought you'd be happy—you love ghost stories. You can hit the highway if you take a left at the third light up there."

"I'm not taking you to Chattanooga."

"You'd better take me. I'm in charge now."

"You are delusional, little boy."

"And you are a thief and a kidnapper."

"I'm neither."

"Susan didn't call 911 because she was about to kill you." He laughed. "She called 911 because I told her I caught you stealing. She's been missing jewelry, you see." He patted the pockets of his blazer. I heard a jangle inside.

"By now she has come back upstairs and found her troubled stepson kidnapped by a fortune-telling hooker-thief. So we'll have to lie low for a few days. Which is fine, Bloodwillow doesn't start till Thursday."

"Susan wanted to kill me because she found out about me and your dad."

"You can say *hand job,* you know," he said. "It doesn't offend me."

"Susan found out."

"Susan found out nothing. She's an incredibly intelligent idiot. I figured it out. I borrow my dad's books all the time. *I* found your business card, *I* found your notes in the margins. *I* went to your place of work and figured it out. Part of what Susan said is true: She does think I'm weird. When we moved here—after I told her I didn't want to; I was very clear that I didn't want to—I started making things happen, in the house. Just to screw with her. *I* made up that Web site. Me. *I* made up the story of the Carterhooks. *I* sent her to you, just to see if she would finally freakin' figure it out and leave. She didn't, she fell for your bullshit."

"So Susan was telling the truth, about all the scary things in the house. You really did threaten to kill your brother?"

"It says more about her that she believed me than it does about me that I said it."

"You really did throw your sitter down the stairs?"

"Please, she fell. I'm not violent, I'm just smart."

"That day, with the vomit in my purse and the fit you had upstairs and the doll hanging from the light?"

"The vomit was me because you weren't listening to me. You weren't leaving. The doll too. Also the razor-blade tip in the floorboard that sliced your finger. That's actually an idea inspired by ancient Roman warfare. Have you ever read—"

"No. The screaming you did? You sounded so furious."

"Oh, that was real. Susan had cut up my credit card and left it on my desk. She was trying to wall me in. But then I realized you were my way out of that stupid house. I need a grown-up to do anything, really: drive a car, get a hotel room. I'm too little for my age. I'm fifteen but I look like I'm twelve. I need someone like you to really get around. All I had to do was get you to take me out of the house, and you were done. Because you know you're not going to show up at the cops. I assume someone like you has a criminal record."

Miles was right. People like me didn't go to the police, ever, because it never turned out well for us.

"Turn left up here to catch the freeway," he said.

I turned left.

I took in his story, turned it over, and inspected it. *Wait, wait.*

"Wait. Susan said you cut off your cat's tail. You told me it was a manx . . ."

He smiled then.

"Ha! Good point. So someone's lying to you. I guess you'll have to decide which story to believe. Do you want to believe Susan is a nutjob or that I'm a nutjob? Which would make you feel more comfortable? At first, I thought it'd be better if you thought Susan was the crazy—that you'd be sympathetic to my plight, and we'd be friends. Road-trip buddies. But then I thought: Maybe it's better if you think I'm the evil one. Maybe then you're more likely to understand I'm in charge here . . . what do you think?"

We drove in silence as I viewed my options.

Miles interrupted me. "I mean, I really think it's a win-win-win here. If Susan is the nutjob and she wants us gone, we're gone."

"What will she tell your dad when he gets home?"

"That depends on what story you want to believe."

"Is your dad really even in Africa?"

"I don't think my dad is a factor you need to worry about in your decision-making."

"OK, so what if you're the nutjob, Miles? Your mom will have the cops on us."

"Pull over at that parking lot, the church."

I looked him up and down for a weapon. I didn't want to be a body dumped in an abandoned church lot.

"Just do it, OK?" Miles snapped.

I pulled into a shuttered church parking lot just off the highway entrance. Miles leapt out in the rain and ran up the stairs and under the eaves. He pulled his cell from his blazer and made a call, his back to me. He was on the phone for a minute. Then he smashed the phone to the ground, stomped on it a few times, and ran back to the car. He smelled disturbingly springlike.

"OK, I just called my nervous little stepmom. I told her you freaked me out, I'm sick of the house and all her weirdness—her habit of bringing in such unsavory people—and so I ran off and I'm staying at my dad's place. He just got back from Africa and so I'll stay there. She never calls my dad."

And he smashed the phone so I couldn't see if he really called Susan or if he was just playacting again.

"And what will you tell your dad?"

"Let's just remember that when you have two parents who hate each other and are always working or traveling and would like you out of their lives anyway, you can say a lot of things. You have a lot of room to work with. So you really don't need to worry. Get to the highway and then there's a motel about three hours on. Cable TV and a restaurant."

I got on the highway. The kid was sharper at fifteen than I was at twice his age. I was starting to think this whole going legit, thinking-of-others, benevolent thing was *fer the berds.* I was starting to think this kid might be a good partner. This tiny teen needed a grown-up to move in the world, and there was nothing a con girl could use more than a kid. "What do you do?" people would ask, and I'd say, "I'm a mom." Think of what I could get away with, the scams I could pull, if people thought I was a sweet little *mom.*

Plus that Bloodwillow convention sounded really cool.

We pulled into the motel three hours later, just as Miles had projected. We got adjoining rooms.

"Sleep tight," Miles said. "Don't leave in the night, or I'll call the cops and go back to the kidnap story. I promise that's the last time I'll threaten you, I don't want to be an asshole. But we've *got* to get to Chattanooga! We're going to have so much fun, I swear. I can't believe I'm going. I've wanted to go since I was a kid!" He did a strange little dance of excitement and went into his room.

The kid was kind of likable. Also a possible sociopath, but very likable. I had a good feeling about him. I was going with a smart kid to a place where everyone wanted to talk about books. I was finally going to leave town for the first time in my life, and I had the whole new "mommy" angle to work. I decided not to worry: I may never know the truth about the happenings at Carterhook Manor (how's that for a great line?). But I was either screwed or not screwed, so I chose to believe I wasn't. I had convinced so many people of so many things over my life, but this would be my greatest feat: convincing myself what I was doing was reasonable. Not decent, but reasonable.

I got in bed and watched the door of the adjoining room. Checked the lock. Turned off the light. Stared at the ceiling. Stared at the adjoining door.

Pulled the dresser in front of the door.

Nothing to worry about at all.

Matthew Hughes

Matthew Hughes was born in Liverpool, England, but has spent most of his adult life in Canada. He worked as a journalist, as staff speechwriter for the Canadian Ministers of Justice and Environment, and as a freelance corporate and political speechwriter in British Columbia before settling down to write fiction full-time. Clearly strongly influenced by Jack Vance, as an author Hughes has made his reputation detailing the adventures of rogues like Old Earth's master criminal, Luff Imbry, who lives in the era just before that of *The Dying Earth*, in a series of novels and novellas that include *Fools Errant, Fool Me Twice, Black Brillion, Majestrum, Hespira, The Spiral Labyrinth, Template, Quartet and Triptych, The Yellow Cabochon, The Other,* and *The Commons,* and short-story collections *The Gist Hunter and Other Stories, 9 Tales of Henghis Hapthorn,* and *The Meaning of Luff and Other Stories.* His most recent books are the novels in his urban fantasy trilogy, To Hell and Back: *The Damned Busters, Costume Not Included,* and *Hell to Pay.* He also writes crime fiction as Matt Hughes and media tie-in novels as Hugh Matthews.

For a down-on-his-luck thief on the run through a danger-haunted forest with only a few coins in his purse, finding a valuable magical object may be a stroke of luck. Or maybe *not.*

THE INN OF THE SEVEN BLESSINGS

Matthew Hughes

The thief Raffalon was sleeping away the noonday heat behind some bracken a short distance from the forest road when the noise of the struggle awakened him. He rolled over onto his stomach, quietly drawing his knife in case of need. Then he lay still and tried to see through the interlayered branches.

Figures scuffled, voices spoke indistinctly, the syllables both sibilant and guttural. A muffled cry, as of a man with a hand over his mouth, was followed by the sharp *crack* of hardwood meeting a human cranium.

Raffalon had no intention of offering assistance. The voices he had heard were those of the Vandaayo, whose border was not far away. Vandaayo warriors left their land only for ritual purposes, and then always in groups of six, and never without their hooks and nets and cudgels. Their seasonal festivals centered on the consumption of manflesh, and if Raffalon had attempted to intervene in the harvesting now taking place on the other side of the thicket, the only result would have been to add a bonus to the part-men's larder.

He waited until the poor captive had been trussed, slung, and carried away, then waited a little longer—the Vandaayo might assume that where they found one fool in a forest they might find another. Only when he heard birds and small beasts resuming their interrupted business did he rise and creep toward the road.

He found it empty, except for the possessions of the unfortunate traveler who was now being marched east into Vandaayoland. He examined the scattered goods: a scuffed leather satchel, a water bottle, a staff whose wood was palm-polished smooth at its upper end. With small expectation, he squatted and sorted through the satchel's contents, finding only a shirt of indifferent quality, a fire-starting kit inferior to his own, and a carved oblong of wood about the size of his hand.

He studied the carvings. They formed a frieze of human and animal figures, connecting to each other in manners that some would have called obscene, but which to Raffalon's sophisticated eye were merely anatomically unlikely. In a lozenge at the center of the display was a deeply incised ideogram that the thief found difficult to keep in focus.

That difficulty caused Raffalon's mouth to widen in pleasure. The object had magical properties. It would surely command some value in the bazaar at Port Thayes, less than a day's march in the direction he was headed. Thaumaturges came thick on the ground there. He turned the item over, to see what if anything was on the other side. As he did so, something faintly shifted inside.

A box, he thought. *Better.* He rotated the thing and examined it from several angles, but found no seams or hinges or apparent means of opening it. *Even better, a puzzle box.*

The day was improving. For Raffalon, it had begun with a flight into the forest in the cold dawn, with only two copper coins in his wallet and a half loaf of stale bread in his tucker bag. There had been a disagreement with a farmer as to the ultimate fate of a chicken the thief had found in a flimsy barnyard coop. Now it was midafternoon, and, though the chicken had remained in its pen, the bread had been eaten as he marched. He still had the coins and had acquired a box that was valuable in its own right and might contain who knew what?

The satchel could also be useful. He slung its strap over his shoulder after throwing away the shirt, which was too large and smelled of unwashed body. He uncorked the bottle and sniffed its contents, hoping for wine or arrack but being disappointed to find only water. Still, he tucked it into the leather bag, and, after a moment, decided not to take the staff as well, even though there were steep slopes ahead, the land rising before the road descended into the river valley of Thayes—he was better with a knife if he had time to draw it.

As he walked on, he studied the box and noticed a worn spot on one corner. He pushed it. Nothing happened. He rubbed it, again without result. He tried sliding it, this way and that. He heard a tiny *click* from within. A sliver of wood moved aside, revealing a pin-sized hole beneath.

Raffalon had no pin, but he had the knife and a whole forest made of wood. He whittled a twig down to the right size, inserted it into the hole, and pushed. A plug of wood on the opposite side of the box popped out. When the thief applied pressure here and there, suddenly the carved side of the box slid sideways a small distance and revealed itself to be the top of the container that moved on a hidden hinge.

Inside was a lining of plush purple cloth, with a hollowed space in the middle in which rested a carved wooden figurine the size of his thumb. It had the likeness of a small, rotund personage, bald and probably male, with head inclined indulgently and mouth formed into an indulgent grin. Raffalon took the carving out, the better to examine it.

When his fingertips touched the smooth wood, a faint tingling passed along the digits, into his palm and through his arm, growing stronger as it progressed. Alarmed, he instinctively sought to fling the thing away from him but found that his fingers and arm refused to obey him. Meanwhile, the tingling sensation, now grown into a full-body tremor, reached its crescendo. For several moments, the thief stood, vibrating, in the middle of the forest road. His eyes rolled up into his head and his breathing stopped, his knees locked, and it seemed as if a strong wind passed through his skull from left to right.

Abruptly, the sensations ended and he had control of his body again—except when he tried once more to throw the carving from him. His arm obeyed him, but his hand did not. The treacherous extremity closed tightly around the smooth wood and all of Raffalon's considerable will would not cause it to open.

Meanwhile, he heard a voice: *We had better move. When the Vandaayo are ahunting, it does not do to lollygag.*

Without much hope, the thief spun around. But there was no one there. The words had formed in his mind, without the involvement of his ears. His hand now opened and he addressed the object nestled comfortably in his palm. "What are you?"

It is a long story, said the voice that spoke in a place where he was accustomed to hear only his own. *And I lack the energy to tell it.*

Raffalon agreed with the sentiments about lollygagging. He set off again in the direction of Port Thayes, his gaze sweeping left and right as far up the forest track as he could see. But he had taken only two or three steps when his legs stopped, and he found himself turning around and returning the way he'd come.

The other way, said the voice. *We have to rescue Fulferin.* In Raffalon's mind, an image appeared: a tall, lanky man in leather clothing, with a long-jawed face and eyes that seemed fixed on some faraway vista. The thief shook his head to drive the unwanted image away—rescuing mooncalves was not on his itinerary—but he struggled without success to regain control of his lower limbs.

The voice in his head said, *You waste energy that you will need when we catch up to the Vandaayo.* Another image blossomed on his inner screen: of half a dozen hunch-shouldered Vandaayo warriors, their heads bald, their ears and teeth equally pointed, their skins mottled in light and dark green. They jogged along a forest trail, two of them carrying a long, netted bundle slung between a pole.

He did not try to dispel the vision but examined it with some interest. He knew no one who had ever had an unobscured view of the Vandaayo; invariably, those who saw them clearly and up close—as opposed to a brief glimpse at a distance before the perceiver wisely turned tail and sped away—saw very little thereafter, except presumably the butcher's slab set up next to the communal cauldron.

Raffalon knew what everyone knew: that they were a species created by Olverion the Epitome, an overweening thaumaturge of a bygone age who had meant the part-men to be a torment to his enemies. Unfortunately, the sorcerer had misjudged some element of the formative process, and his had been the first human flesh his creations had tasted.

Strenuous and repeated efforts by the surrounding communities had managed to confine the anthropophagi to the wild valley that had been Olverion's domain. But all attempts to enter the deep-chasmed vale and eliminate the monsters once and forever had ended in bloody tatters: the thaumaturge had not stinted in instilling his creatures with a talent for warfare and an unalloyed genius for ambush.

Eventually, an undeclared truce established itself, the terms of which were that the local barons would not lead their levies into the valley so long as the Vandaayo left their towns and villages unmolested. The part-men could snatch their festive meat only from the road that passed through the forest on the west of the valley, and the trail that led over the mountains to the northeast. The locals knew the times of the year when the Vandaayo were on the prowl and avoided the thoroughfares in those seasons. Wanderers and drifters of the likes of Raffalon the thief and Fulferin the god's man were welcome to take their chances.

The image of the anthropophagi faded from Raffalon's mind as his legs marched him to the spot where the victim had been taken. Without pause, he turned away from the forest road and plunged through some bushes, almost immediately finding himself on a game trail. He saw deer scat but also the splay-footed tracks of the Vandaayo, instantly recognizable by the webbing and the pointed impression made in the soft earth by the downcurved talon on the great toe.

The tracks led toward Vandaayoland. Raffalon also saw droplets of blood on a bush beside the trail. No sooner had he registered these details than he was striding along in pursuit.

Within the confines of his skull, he said, "Wait! We must find a quiet place and discuss this business!"

His pace did not slacken, but the voice in his mind said, *What is there to discuss?*

"Whether it will succeed if you fail to gain my cooperation!"

The man had the sense that the deity was thinking about it. *Fairly said. It would drain my energy less. Let us find a spot out of view.*

The trail led them through a quiet glade bisected by a meandering stream. The thief saw a thick-strand willow, and said, "Here will do." He ducked beneath the willow withes and sat on one of the gnarled roots, peered through the green screen until he was sure he was the clearing's only occupant. Then he addressed the little piece of carved wood in his hand and repeated his original question: "What are you?"

Less than I was, less than I shall be.

Raffalon groaned. In his experience, entities that spoke in such a high-toned manner tended to have an acute regard for themselves that was inversely matched by a lack of concern for the comfort of those who minioned for them—indeed, even for their continued existence.

On the other hand, his captor's determination to rescue the unfortunate Fulferin betokened some capacity for consideration of others' needs. Perhaps terms could be negotiated. He put the proposition to the piece of wood.

I see no need for terms, said the voice, its tone maddeningly calm. *Fulferin is in need of rescue. You are between engagements. One is a high imperative, the other mere vacancy.*

"Who says I am between engagements?"

I have access, said the voice, *to the vaults of your memory, not to mention the contents of your character.* It took on a distant tone. *Which scarcely bear mentioning. Fulferin stands in a better category.*

"Fulferin," said the thief, "hangs in a Vandaayo net, and soon will be simmering in a pot—not a category aspired to by men of stature."

His legs straightened and he found himself stepping outside of the willow. "Wait!" he said. "You've already lost one beast of burden to the Vandaayo. If you lose me, do you think you can seize one of the man-eaters to—"

Fulferin, said the voice, *is no beast of burden. He is a devotee, a disciple. He knows the rite that will restore my name.*

"And yet he is on his way to dine with the Vandaayo. Which tells me that at least one of you was in too great a hurry."

His legs stopped moving. *You have a point,* said the voice. *Speak on.*

"Is Fulferin necessary?" said the thief. "If it is only transport you require . . ."

Fulferin is indispensable. Only he is versed in the ritual.

"So I must rescue him from the Vandaayo?"

I have said that it is an imperative.

"Why? For what do I risk my life?"

For matters beyond your ken. Issues sublime and surpassing.

"God business," Raffalon guessed. "You're some kind of worn-out deity, probably reduced to a single devotee. And you're not even able to keep him out of the stewpot."

Fulferin must not stew.

"What can you do to prevent it?"

Send you.

"But I am unwilling."

A problem I must work around.

"Which brings us back to the question of terms."

Raffalon sensed from the silence in his head that the entity was considering the matter. Then he heard, *Speak on, but hurry.*

He said, "You want your devotee rescued. I want to live."

Fair enough. I will endeavor to keep you alive.

The thief's legs started moving again. "Wait!" he said. "Mere survival is not enough!"

You do not value your own existence?

"I already had it before I met you. If I am to risk it on your behalf, that is surely worth some compensation."

Again he had the sense that the other was weighing the matter. Then he heard, *What had you in mind?*

"Wealth—great wealth—is always welcome."

I have no command over gross physicality, said the voice, *only over certain attributes of individuals as they relate to the flow of phenomenality.*

"You mean you can't deliver heaps of precious goods?"

Not even small quantities.

The thief thought, then said, "What 'attributes of individuals' can you alter? Strength of ten men, ability to fly, impermeability to pointed weapons? All of those would be useful."

Alas, none are within my ambit.

Raffalon realized it might be better to come at the question from the supply side. "What exactly can you offer?"

My powers, said the deity, *are in the realm of probabilities.*

"You mean you make the unlikely likely?"

Say rather that I can adjust the odds, as they affect a selected person.

Raffalon brightened. "So you could fix it so that I could win the Zagothian communal lottery?"

I will be honest, said the voice. *In my present condition, I could at best reduce the odds from millions-to-one against to thousands-to-one.*

"But still against?"

Yes.

"So, essentially, you're a god of luck but only in small things?"

At present, my potency is reduced. Fulferin is going to assist me in restoring my powers.

"If he survives," said the thief. Then a thought occurred. "You weren't very lucky for him."

He had not invoked my help. He acted from . . . I suppose I must call it enthusiasm. Besides, I must conserve my strength. The box assists, by acting as an insulator.

Raffalon thought briefly, then said, "I will summarize. You wish me to risk my life, in circumstances in which a bad outcome would be particularly grisly and painful. In return, you will make sure that, along the way, I do not stub my toe or lose my comb."

In a close-run contest, I can tip the balance in your favor.

"Me against a half dozen hungry Vandaayo does not meet my definition of close-run."

These are, said the deity, *the only terms I can offer.*

"You control my body. Can you not at least alter it?" Raffalon touched his prominent nose. "Perhaps make some part smaller?" He clutched another organ. "Or make this more prodigious?"

I control only certain interstices within your cerebrum. They generate a field that I can enhance.

"And only," said the thief, remembering, "when my flesh touches your image."

No. Once I alter them they remain altered for all time.

"I suppose it's something," the thief said. "Still, it is not the best bargain I have ever made."

It is the best I can offer. On the other hand, I do not need to offer it. I can compel you, as long as your flesh touches my portal.

"Portal?"

"The wooden eidolon."

"I see." Raffalon brushed aside the willow withes and stepped into the clearing, crossed to the trail. He saw more spots of blood, presumably Fulferin's. "If your devotee survives and completes the ritual you spoke of, your powers will increase?"

Oh, yes. Manyfold.

"What, then, of the Zagothian lottery?"

You would win something.

"Every time I bought a ticket?"

Every time.

The man stepped onto the trail. "And this small luck would apply to my other endeavors?" He could think of past occasions when a slight nod from a god of fortune would have been useful, including one desperate flight that had led only to a lengthy term on the contemplarium's treadmill.

You would have to rescue Fulferin so that he can fulfill the requirements of the rite.

"Then that," said Raffalon, "must be our bargain." He pointed his still-prominent nose in the direction of Vandaayoland and followed the trail. After a few steps, he said, "Perhaps you would be more comfortable traveling in your plush-lined box?"

No. You might then decide not to keep our bargain.

Their mission having been successful, the Vandaayo did not set themselves a grueling pace. Nor did they watch their back trail, the chances of anyone's wishing to be on the same path as six of their ilk being far too slim to warrant even a glance over a green-mottled shoulder. So it was that, toward late afternoon, as Raffalon descended a slope into a narrow valley, he saw through the trees a motion in the greenery on the other side of the declivity. The part-men marched steadily up an incline that zigzagged up and out of the valley. At one switchback in the trail, the thief saw the band pause and transfer their pole-slung burden from one pair of bearers to another.

Raffalon had a rough idea how far it was to Vandaayoland and did not think that the man-snatchers could cross the border before nightfall. He thought it probable that they would stop before dark; this part of the forest had become uninhabited after Olverion's final misjudgment and the large predatory beasts that now roamed free had no compunctions against dining on wereflesh.

He closed the distance between them until he could hear their grunts and panting breath ahead of him, a turn or two in the trail. As dusk began to settle, he heard different sounds and crept forward to find that the path crossed another in a clearing. Here the Vandaayo had stopped and were now gathering wood for a fire and bracken for sleeping pads. Fulferin, still wrapped in the net that had captured him and trussed to a pole, lay inert beside the track.

Raffalon established himself behind a tree and observed as the partmen built themselves a good fire. They settled themselves around it, squatting or sitting cross-legged in a circle. They had been carrying capacious leather pouches from which they now drew gobbets of rank-smelling meat and bottles of fired clay. The sounds of tearing flesh and gurgling liquids were added to the crackle of the flames, followed by grunts and belches and the occasional growl when one Vandaayo paid too much attention to another's victuals.

Dusk became darkness. At a sound from the other trail, the partmen became alert. They put down their uneaten meals and stood up, watchful. A moment later, they relaxed, though only slightly, as a second party of Vandaayo emerged from the forest, carrying their own pole-slung contribution to the ritual feast.

Greetings were exchanged—or at least that was what Raffalon thought the spate of grunting signaled. But he noted that the two groups did not mix, and that the party he had been following did not lapse into complete relaxation as the newcomers began gathering fuel for a second fire and leaves for their own beds. Indeed, two of the first arrivals left the communal blaze and went to squat beside poor Fulferin, while the other party put their own captive as far from the new camp as the clearing's size would allow.

The last light was now fading from the leafy canopy above the thief's head. He watched the proceedings as the newcomers made their own rough supper and the two groups settled for the night, each arranging its sleeping positions on the far side of its fire from the others, so that between the two hearths was a wide space of trampled grass that was clearly no-Vandaayo's-land.

"Hmm," the thief said to himself. After watching a little longer, he withdrew deeper into the forest, out of pointy earshot, and spoke softly to the small deity. "I am going to need both hands."

He felt the hand that held the deity rise and find its way to the open neck of his tunic. A moment later, the little piece of wood tumbled down to rest against his stomach. The voice in his head said, *As long as some part of me touches some part of you, I will remain in control.*

The thief's curiosity was piqued. "Are you actually within the wood?"

I am where I am. The eidolon opens a . . . conduit between there and here. Now, please get on with the rescue.

Raffalon shrugged and went farther back along the trail until he came to a place where he had crossed a small watercourse. He knelt and put his hand into the water, feeling along the stream bottom, and found what he needed. He rose and looked about. Fifty paces away, a lofty, well-leafed tree arched over the stream. He went to it, fished in his wallet, and drew out a stout knotted cord connected to a grapple. He threw this up into the branches and, luck being with him, it caught securely on the first cast.

He left the cord hanging and returned to the edge of the clearing, Fulferin's wallet heavier by the weight of several pebbles, ranging in size from the width of his thumbnail to almost the breadth of his fist.

Staying within the tree line, he circled stealthily around the clearing until he found a tree that would best suit his purposes. He climbed until he found a comfortable crutch between two branches with a good view of the two camps. Then he composed himself to wait.

Night eased itself down over the clearing. The Vandaayo fires burned low and were refreshed. Then they burned down again. By now, all of the anthropophagi were curled or sprawled on the grass, save for one from each group. Raffalon noted that these sentries did not face the outer darkness and whatever threats might lurk there. They kept an eye on one another.

He waited until he saw one rise and go to fetch a new log for its fire. As the hunched figure bent to pick up the length of wood, the thief whispered to the deity, "A little luck would assist us now," and lobbed a pebble out into the darkness. The missile arced across the dark air and he heard a satisfying *snick* as it connected with the Vandaayo's hairless pate.

"Ow!" said the injured sentry, adding a stream of gobbling gutturals directed at its opposite number. The other group's sentry peered across the open space and, though it could not ascertain the cause of the other's pain, it recognized an occasion for mirth.

The head-struck sentry went back to its position, tossing the new log onto the fire. It squatted, rubbing its injury, and stared through slitted eyes at its counterpart, muttering what Raffalon took to be dire vows of retribution.

The thief waited until the second sentry saw that it was time for fresh fuel. As it stooped to lift a log from its group's supply, he tossed another stone. He heard the same noise of impact as with the first, a similar cry of pain that was met with a hoot and jeers from the other side of the clearing.

The newly injured Vandaayo stalked to the edge of the open ground between the fires and addressed several remarks to the mocker, accompanied by juts of jaw and shakes of fists. The recipient of these attentions replied with words and gestures of its own, including the revelation of naked green buttocks and the sound of their cheeks being slapped by hard hands.

It was while the thief's first Vandaayo target was thus bent over with its back turned to the second that Raffalon sped another pebble—this one larger—on its way through the darkness. It landed with a solid *crack!* on the butt-slapper's head, bringing a new howl of rage and pain.

The freshly wounded Vandaayo spun around and charged across the neutral zone, its hand reaching for a cudgel thrust through a strap that circled its waist. Its opposite number drew its own weapon, a club ground from gray stone, and, bellowing its own war cry, rushed to meet the assault. They came together in the middle of the clearing and went at each other with all the fervor and indifferent coordination—compensated for by great strength—for which Vandaayo warriors were renowned.

The noise and tumult awoke the others, who sat up or got to their feet, blinking and staring about. Raffalon launched several missiles in rapid succession, including his largest. Aided by the luck of the small god, each found a target among one of the two clusters of sleep-fuddled part-men. One rock came down with sufficient force as to lay out the leader of the six that had snatched Fulferin. When his fellows saw their superior stretched out on the ground and their sentry doing battle, they took up their weapons and, ululating, charged the foe. The enemy, smarting from their own hurts, raced to meet them.

Raffalon descended lightly from the tree and turned to skirt the clearing to where Fulferin lay bound. But his legs disobeyed him and turned in the opposite direction. At the same time, the voice in his head said, *We may need something to delay pursuit,* while an image appeared of himself and the rescued devotee fleeing along a trail while some hapless and ill-defined person was left behind for the pursuing Vandaayo to squabble over.

"You are a cruel god," he whispered as he headed for the other captive.

I am, by nature, a kindly sort of god, came the answer, *dispensing what small blessings are within my power. But now I do as I must.*

Raffalon made no further comment but skulked along the edge of the clearing until he came to the recumbent form wrapped in a stout net that had been snugged tightly with braided leather cords. He found his knife and cut through the restraints, whispering, "Hush! Here is a rescue. Rise and follow me in silence."

He could not see the figure clearly, this far from the fire, but he recognized the motion of a nod and heard a grunt. He set off around the clearing toward where Fulferin lay, aware of the released captive slipping through the bushes behind him. He found the god's man awake and struggling against his bonds, muttering something that sounded like a cantrip.

"Easy," he whispered. "I will cut you loose and we will flee while they are busy battering each other."

"Hurry!" said the bound man. "I see only six left standing."

Raffalon worked with his knife, looking up to see that the fight was indeed reaching its conclusion. Two Vandaayo of Fulferin's group were standing back-to-back, surrounded by four of the opposition. It was only a matter of time before matters were settled and the victors came to see what prize they had won.

"This way," he said, as Fulferin rose to his feet. Though both captives must have been stiff and cramped from their confinement, they came along after him as he skirted the rest of the clearing to find the trail back toward the forest road. As they plunged back into the darkness of the night forest, he could hear grunts and impacts. Moments later, the ugly sound of Vandaayo crowing triumph came to his ears, and he said over his shoulder, "Faster!"

They reached the little brook where he had chosen the stones and he turned to lead them upstream to the knotted rope.

"Climb!" he said to Fulferin. The god's man had recovered his strength because he swarmed up the rope like a well-conditioned acrobat. Raffalon turned to the indistinct figure of the second captive, and said, "Now you."

But this one, though smaller, was in poorer condition and struggled to make the climb. Now the thief heard new sounds from the Vandaayo camp, howls of anger and outrage. He reached out in the darkness and seized the other's torso in both hands, intending to supply extra lift. The effort was successful and the person, now able to apply feet as well as hands to the knotted cord, began to ascend.

He waited until the feet had passed above his head, then he took hold of the hemp and followed, fretting at the slowness of the climber above as the slap of Vandaayo footsteps came from the direction of the clearing. He came up onto the branch around which the grapple had snagged the rope, and said to the figures beside him, "Higher, quickly but quietly."

He heard the rustle of their ascent while he freed the grapple and drew up the rope. Then he turned and silently climbed into the tree's sheltering canopy, finding two blobs of darkness against the slight shimmer of the foliage, sitting on stout branches, their backs against the trunk.

"Absolute silence," he whispered as he found a perch for himself and froze. Through the leaves, he could see the glow of torches. The Vandaayo were coming along the stream, bending over to sniff at either bank. They passed beneath without looking up.

Time passed, then the searchers came back, shoulders slumped, addressing one another in tones that Raffalon took to be accusatory. One shoved another so that its torch fell into the stream with a hiss. Grumbling, they went downstream to the trail and back to the shambles of their camp.

"We will wait," said Raffalon, softly, "until daylight, then find our way back to the road to Port Thayes."

"Agreed," said Fulferin.

"I, too," said the second rescued. Raffalon was not surprised to hear the tones of a young woman. His hands, earlier moving over her torso as he helped her up the rope, had encountered two parts of her that, though smaller than he preferred, were inarguably female.

"I will take first watch," he said. He listened to their breathing settle and thought that if he had to abandon anyone to the Vandaayo, he would prefer to leave Fulferin behind.

The little god read his thoughts. The voice said, *I must do as I must.*

At first light, they heard the Vandaayo moving off but waited in the tree until midmorning. They descended and made a thin breakfast of water from the stream, then set off up the watercourse. The part-men would be anxious to replenish their stolen larder, Raffalon told the others. Trails and tracks were their preferred settings for ambush. Besides, the sound of the moving water would disguise the noise of their movements.

They walked in silence and single file for a time. Then the thief felt a tug on his sleeve. Fulferin said, "That is my satchel slung across your shoulder."

"Opinions are divided on that matter," said Raffalon. "I found it abandoned, which entitles—" but even as he spoke, he saw that his treacherous hands were unslipping the strap and handing the leather bag to the other man.

Fulferin threw open the cover flap and delved into the satchel. He came out with the puzzle box then issued a yelp of unhappy surprise as he saw its secrets exposed and its velvet-lined inner compartment empty.

He looked a sharp question at his rescuer, but the voice in Raffalon's head was already saying, *Give me to him.* The thief complied without reluctance, glad to be his own man again, but he watched Fulferin carefully as the little sculpture changed hands. Actually, he noted that hands were not equally employed on both sides: the lanky man did not touch the wood but instead held out the box so that Raffalon could snug the eidolon into its former place. Then he carefully slid the cover back into position and restored the hidden locks.

Raffalon heard the other man's sigh of relief. While Fulferin slung the satchel's strap over his own shoulder, the thief studied the man he had saved. He was interested to compare the reality before him with the image the little god had put into his mind. They did not match. Physically, Fulferin was as advertised, tall and spare, with long spatulate fingers and knobby protrusions at knee and elbow. But the face was different. Raffalon had been shown a wide-eyed visionary; the visage he now saw was that of a man who calculated closely and went whichever way his sums dictated.

The exchange had been watched by the young woman, whose manner indicated that she found little to choose between the two men and, despite having been rescued by one of them, would not have gladly elected to spend time with either. For his part, Fulferin ignored her, all his concern fixed on the box and its contents.

Raffalon studied the woman as frankly as she had him. She was well past girlhood, but not matronly, sharp of eye and even sharper of nose, with a thin-lipped mouth that easily fell into a mocking twist. She was dressed better than a farmer's girl though not so richly as a merchant's daughter. When his gaze rose again to her face, their eyes met. He said, "I am Raffalon, already known to you as a man of resource and valor. He is Fulferin, a god's devotee. What is your name and station?"

"Erminia," she said. "My father is an innkeeper—the Gray Bird at Fosseth."

"How did you come to be taken by the part-men?"

"My father sent me to pick morels for the Reeve's banquet."

Raffalon's brow wrinkled. "When the Vandaayo were ahunting?"

The corners of her mouth drew down. "The inn's license comes up for renewal next month. My father weighs the value of his possessions by his own scale."

"We should get on," Fulferin said, clutching the satchel to his chest. His chin indicated the stream. "Where does this lead?"

The thief shrugged. "I have seen maps. It parallels the forest road. Somewhere ahead it flows through an old estate that was abandoned after Olverion's slight miscalculation. If we can find it, it would be a good place to stay under cover until we are sure the Vandaayo have gone home."

"I must get to Port Thayes as soon as I can."

Raffalon gestured eloquently at the thickets that lined the stream on either side. Fulferin subsided, but the thief saw a flicker of calculation in those definitely-not-otherworldly eyes and surmised that the same thought about having someone to leave for the anthropophagi had just crossed Fulferin's mind. The god's man gestured in a way that invited his rescuer to lead them on.

An hour's more walking brought them to a weir that cut across the stream at a place that must have been the beginning of a stretch of rapids before the barrier was put in place. When they scrambled up they saw that the weir had created a long and narrow lake. On one of its shores, surrounded by weed-choked gardens and orchards of unpruned fruit trees, stood a moldering agglomeration of vine-draped stone walls, spiral towers, cupolas, colonnades, peristyles, and arcades.

They explored and found that one of the towers had been built with defense in mind—probably some generations ago when the Vandaayo were only an inchoate nuisance. It had a stout door and hinges so well greased that they had not rusted. In the basement, the stored food had long since rotted, but the wine in one of the butts was still potable.

Erminia said that she would gather fruit from the orchards if someone would come and keep watch. Raffalon volunteered. Fulferin said that he would climb to the highest point of the tower and stand sentry, calling out if he spied any Vandaayo coming their way. The thief doubted that the god's man would make so much as a squeak, and when he and the woman reached the fruit trees he climbed the highest and kept a lookout.

Erminia found apples, persimmons, karbas, and blood-eyes, wrapping them up in her shawl. She called up to Raffalon, who climbed down to rejoin her. The thief thought this might be an opportune moment to test the extent of the young woman's gratitude for his having delivered her from the Vandaayo cooking pot. She was not his type, but she was here.

A moment later, face smarting from a hard-handed slap and hip aching from a knee that he had avoided just in time, he understood that Erminia drew sharply defined limits. Angered, he briefly considered enlisting Fulferin's help in mounting a concerted assault on the innkeeper's daughter's virtue. But the thought of any cooperative endeavor with the god's devotee gave him more qualms than did the concept of forcing her acquiescence.

He showed Erminia two palms in token of surrender and accompanied her back to the tower, where they bolted the door and climbed the spiral staircase to the top apartment. Here they found Fulferin, not on the alert but at ease amid the dust, sprawled on a grimy divan, drinking from a wineskin he had filled from the ample supply downstairs.

The windows were glassless, but the season was mild. Raffalon cleared a table and Erminia spread her harvest on it. They found chairs and Fulferin came to join them, bringing the wine. The young woman went to rummage in a sideboard and came back to the table with a stout cook's knife. But instead of using it to cut the fruit, she showed the point to each of the men in a meaningful way, then tucked the blade into her kirtle.

They ate in silence, passing the wineskin around. The liquid had a tinge of the vinegar to it but was otherwise drinkable. Finally, his stomach full and his blood warmed by the wine, the thief pushed himself back from the table and regarded the god's man.

Fulferin looked back with an expression that said he did not invite the curiosity of strangers. Raffalon ignored the implied rebuff, and said, "Your god made an arrangement with me. Having rescued you, I am sure you will want to help him honor it."

The worldly eyes narrowed. "What arrangement?"

"He is a god of luck in small things. He said that, if I aided you, he would henceforward bless me with his intervention. I believe his influence has already served me, and it will grow even stronger once you have revived his powers."

Fulferin shrugged. The matter clearly did not engage his interest.

Erminia said, "What is this god talk?"

Fulferin seemed disinclined to answer. Raffalon succinctly described the series of events that had brought them all together. He saw no profit in disclosing the god's willingness to sacrifice her.

The woman leaned forward, her heavy brows downdrawn. "What is this rite that will restore the god's strength? And what, by the way, *is* his name?"

Raffalon realized that the question had not come up and turned to Fulferin, his face forming an interrogative. Again, the god's man showed no inclination to continue the conversation, but when pressed, he said, "Gods who do not hear their names from worshippers gradually forget them. It is akin to falling into a deep sleep, from which it is difficult for them to wake."

"So the rite will wake him up?"

The god's man shrugged. "I am no expert."

When the thief questioned him further, he displayed annoyance and made gestures that said the inquisition was an affront.

"Why this reluctance?" Erminia said. "Are you not this god's devotee, dedicated to restoring his powers? Speak!"

But Fulferin did not. Instead, with a gesture of irritation, he rose from the table, taking his satchel and its precious contents with him, and went up the small flight of stairs that ended in a door that opened onto the flat roof.

Raffalon watched him go and was prey to dark thoughts. Fulferin was not the man the god thought he was. He remembered how careful the fellow had been not to touch the idol, which would have given the deity access to his innermost thoughts.

The thief made a thoughtful sound in the back of his throat. His gaze slid sideways toward Erminia. The woman, sitting with her chin in her hands and her elbows on the table, had also watched Fulferin depart.

Now she threw a look Raffalon's way, tilting her head and moving her mouth in a way that said she knew something.

"What?" he said. "What do you know?"

But now her face said she was keeping the information to herself.

Raffalon grunted. "Next time I rescue people from the Vandaayo's cauldron, I mean to be more choosy."

That won him a short laugh from Erminia, but the sound lacked humor. She took a final apple and went to sit in one of the open windows, where she could keep an eye on one of the approaches to the estate. Raffalon took the embrasure opposite. As the day wore on, one or the other would come back to the table for a swallow of wine or a piece of fruit, but otherwise they kept their separate vigils.

At nightfall, Fulferin came down from the roof. They did not seek to light a fire, the windows being unblockable. Raffalon said he would take the first watch. Erminia said she would take the second. Fulferin shrugged and lay on the floor, his satchel for a pillow.

After three hours without incident, Raffalon woke the woman—carefully, because she slept with her knife to hand—and disposed himself to sleep. Fulferin snored loudly in a corner, but it had been a long day following a short night's sleep, and that in a tree. The thief soon fell into oblivion.

He awoke in the full light of morning to find Erminia shaking him. "Get up!" she said. "The bastard has betrayed us!"

He sprang to his feet and followed her to a window. The sun was a good handsbreadth above the forest canopy. Below, in a leaf-strewn, flagstoned courtyard, a fire smoldered, sending a tall column of gray smoke into the still air. Of Fulferin, there was no sign.

"The Vandaayo will have seen the smoke," said the woman. "We have to get out of here!"

Raffalon was already moving toward the staircase. He picked up his wallet along the way, then went leaping down the stairs, Erminia close on his heels. At the ground floor, he found the stout door open, its lock crammed with mud.

Outside, the thief hopefully kicked aside the smoldering fire, then went to an ornately perforated garden wall and peered through one of the openings. Across the lake he could see motion in the tree line. In a moment, it had resolved into the shapes of the Vandaayo. They plunged into the water, trusting in the amphibian strands of their ancestry to sustain them. It would not take them long to cross the distance.

"Run!" he said.

"If we're lucky," he said to the woman as they pounded along a trail that he thought would lead back to the road to Port Thayes, "Fulferin went this way, and we'll catch up to him."

"And then?" she said, panting as she strove to keep up.

"Between the two of us, we overpower him and leave him to do for us what he intended us to do for him."

"Leave him for the Vandaayo? Agreed."

The trail was hard-packed and showed no tracks. But Raffalon caught sight of an overturned pebble, its reversed side darker than the others around it. A little while farther on, he spied a thread snagged on a thorn. The influence of the god of small luck was still with him.

They came to a wider stream, crossed by stepping-stones. As they slowed to navigate their passage, Erminia said, "I know something about Fulferin that he does not know I know."

"What?" said the thief. "And how?"

"He has come through Fosseth and stopped at our inn."

"He didn't recognize you."

"I am mostly consigned to the kitchen, scrubbing pots and scraping plates while my sister, Elfrey—she of the blond hair and balloonish breasts and pneumatic hips that draw all eyes—she waits on the customers. Father reckons it good for business."

Raffalon extended a hand to help her cross a wide gap where the current ran strong between the stones. "What do you know of Fulferin?"

"He is no more than a hedge sorcerer, if that." She leapt over, daintily. "I doubt he knows more than a handful of minor spells, but he is in service to Bolbek, who calls himself the Potence, a powerful thaumaturge in Port Thayes."

"Why does Bolbek send him through Fosseth?"

"It is on the old road to the ruins of Itharios."

The man knew of the place, a tumble of broken walls and upheaved pavements, devastated in an earthquake millennia ago. "So?" he said.

"Fulferin delves in the old fanes, seeking out effigies of foregone gods. These he delivers to his master. Though sometimes they dig together."

"To restore their powers?"

They had crossed over now. She shook her head. "It involves powers, to be sure, but from what I heard them whispering when once they both stopped at the Gray Bird, the thaumaturge uses the gods the way a spider uses a fly."

"Ah," said Raffalon. Having been once incarcerated and treated in ways he had not enjoyed, he had since tended to come down on the side of flies and to reject the claims of spiders. "He has fooled the god," he said.

"I suppose," she said, "that even deities are disposed to believe what they want to believe, especially when they are desperate to survive. And when a powerful mage cloaks his assistant's true nature."

The man remembered the image of an innocent Fulferin that the god had put up on the screen in his mind. "Hmm," he said, then, "we had better move on."

They continued along the trail, making good time. The thief always seemed to place his foot in just the right place for maximum traction. Bushes did not impede his passage. He wondered if his luck would actually put barriers in their quarry's way and decided that it could not. But it might be enough to keep him out of the Vandaayo's reach. He wondered if he was also lucky to have found Erminia; she was turning out to be a useful companion.

He came across another upturned pebble and paused to examine it. The exposed bottom was still wet even though the sun was now well up and the day warming. He said to the woman, "He has slowed down. By now, he thinks the Vandaayo have us and is no longer hurrying."

"He struck me as the kind who expects matters to arrange themselves to his convenience," she said.

They went quickly but quietly now. The country was more up and down than level and soon they found themselves traversing a ridge. Through the trees, Raffalon saw a flicker of movement ahead. He stopped and peered forward, and in a moment he was sure. "There he is."

"He's long-legged," Erminia said. "If he hears us coming, he may well outrun us."

The man took a moment to appreciate that scrubbing pots had not diminished this woman's ability to focus on what mattered. Meanwhile, he was scanning the woods around them, seeking an opportunity for advantage.

Ahead of them, the ridge and the trail made a leisurely curve to the right. If, swiftly and silently, he could cut across the bight, he might come out on the track ahead of the sauntering Fulferin.

"There," he said, pointing. A tall tree had recently fallen, crashing through what would otherwise have been an impenetrable thicket. They pushed through the bushes, scaled the tree's exposed root mass, and now they were on a clear, straight course. They ducked low and ran fast.

The fallen trunk was branchless for a long stretch and when they encountered its first foliage, they dropped down onto an open space carpeted in moss and lichens. It followed what must have once been the course of a spring-fed stream, now dried up, that led through a low tunnel of overarching branches and ended up behind a screen of a single flowered bush, only a few paces from the trail.

The man and the woman arrived just in time to see knob-kneed Fulferin come striding along at an easy pace. There was no time to plan a strategy. They simply leapt from concealment and threw themselves on their betrayer. Raffalon took him high, and Erminia low, and between them they conclusively toppled the tall man to the ground. By another bit of luck, the thief's knees landed square on the god stealer's midriff, driving the air from him in a great *whoof*.

Raffalon dug in his wallet and came out with a length of cord. With Erminia's help, he flipped the recumbent, gasping man over and quickly bound him at wrist and ankle. Then they turned him again so that he was sitting with his back against a bank of earth. The woman tore a strip from Fulferin's shirt and gagged him well, lest he speak a spell to do them mischief.

While she was doing this, Raffalon said, "If you had merely abandoned us, I could be more forgiving. But lighting a fire to draw the Vandaayo?" He left the consequences unsaid.

Erminia was more forthright. She delivered a substantial kick to Fulferin's ribs. To Raffalon, she said, "Let us go."

The bound man was making facial signs that he wished to tell them something. Raffalon stooped, removed the gag, but held his knife to the betrayer's throat. The thaumaturge's assistant said, "My master will pay you well if you help me deliver what I am bringing him." When his captors made no particular response, he went on: "This item will complete a project of great importance to him."

Raffalon hefted the man's satchel. "I'll be sure to tell him that you were thinking of him till the end," he said.

A sly look occupied Fulferin's face. "But you do not know who he is!"

"I didn't," said the thief, then nodded at the woman. "Until she told me." He reapplied the gag, then turned and looked back along the curve of the ridge, where mottled green shapes were bustling along the trail. "We'll be on our way now."

The house of Bolbek the Potence was in the upper reaches of Port Thayes, which occupied a hillside that ran down to the river port. It was built of an unlikely combination of black iron panels and hemispheres of cerulean blue crystal. To discourage the uninvited, it was fenced by a tall hedge of semisentient ravenous vine, the plant's thorn-bedecked catch-creepers constantly probing for flesh scent.

Raffalon and Erminia approached the single entrance, a narrow, wooden archway that pierced the hedge. As they neared the opening, the air turned cold and something vaporous hovered indistinctly in the gap. "My master," it said, "expects no visitors."

"Say to your master," Raffalon said, holding up the carved box, "that something he *is* expecting has arrived."

The apparition issued a sigh and faded in the direction of the manse.

The man and woman waited, batting away the hedge's mindless inquiries, until the gatekeeper once more semicoalesced in the air before them. "Follow," it said.

The vines shrank back and the ghost led them along a path of luminous flagstones to a pair of tall double doors in each of which was carved a great contorted face. It was only when they reached the portals that Raffalon, seeing the wooden features move as the faces turned his way, realized that the panels were a pair of forest elementals enthralled by the thaumaturge to guard his entrance.

The doors opened at the ghost's further approach; the man and woman stepped into the foyer, a place clearly intended to disorient the senses. The thief closed his eyes against the onset of dizziness, and said, "We will not endure ill treatment. We will leave now." He turned and groped blindly toward the doors, finding Erminia's hand and leading her behind him. Eyes downcast, she demurely followed.

"Wait," said a commanding voice. The thief's giddiness abruptly ceased. Raffalon reopened his eyes and saw that they had been joined by a short, wide-bellied man clad in a blood-red robe figured in black runes and a tall hat of complexly folded cloth and leather. His expression was impassive. He said, "What have you brought me?"

Raffalon reached into his wallet and brought forth the puzzle box.

Bolbek's eyes showed a glint of avarice. "What of Fulferin?" he said.

"He accepted an invitation to dinner," said the thief. "In Vandaayoland."

The thaumaturge's face showed a brief reaction that might have been regret. Then he said, "And in the box?"

"Fulferin said it was a god of small luck," said Raffalon. He smiled a knowing smile and added, "so to speak."

The greedy glint in Bolbek's eyes became a steady gleam. "Bring it to my workroom," he said.

Raffalon stood still. "First, we must settle the issue of price."

Bolbek named a number. Raffalon doubled it. The mage gestured to show that chaffering was beneath him, and said, "Agreed. Bring it." He turned and exited by a door that appeared in the wall as he approached it.

The thief was concerned. Sometimes those who agreed too easily to an extortionate price did so because they had no expectation of having to pay it. As he and Erminia followed the thaumaturge, he was alert for sudden departures from his plan.

The room they entered was of indeterminate size and shape. The walls appeared to recede or advance depending on whether they were viewed directly or peripherally, nor could the angles where they met floor or ceiling be depended on to remain static. Raffalon saw shelves and sideboards on which stood several items he would have liked to examine more closely. Indeed, he would have liked to take them away for a leisurely valuation, followed by a quick resale.

But Bolbek gave him no time. The thaumaturge bustled his way across the stone floor to a curtained alcove. He pulled back the heavy brocaded cloth to reveal a work in progress in two parts. One was a cylindrical container of white gold, on whose sides were drawn in shining metal a string of characters the thief could not decipher, though he had the sense that one of them replicated the unreadable symbol on the puzzle box. The ideograms must be a cantrip of considerable power, he thought, seeing them glow rhythmically against the gold, like a slowly beating heart.

The second part of the project was man-shaped—indeed, shaped very much like the man who had made it. It was a wire framework fashioned from gold and electrum, connected to the cylinder by thick, braided cables of silver. The framework was made in two halves, hinged so that the thaumaturge could open it and then stand within, completely enclosed by whatever energies the cylinder would presumably generate.

Bolbek cast an eye over the double apparatus. Apparently satisfied, he turned to Raffalon. "The box," he said.

"The price," said the thief.

A flash of irritation animated the mage's bland features, then he spoke two words and made a complex motion of one hand. A leather pouch appeared in the air before the thief, then fell to the floor with a sound that said it was well filled with Port Thayes double mools.

Raffalon handed over the box and stooped to pick up the purse. Then he turned away, as if to examine the contents in private. As he did so, he reached into a fold of his garment, out of Bolbek's line of sight. His hand closed on something concealed there. Now he tucked the coins away while sending a meaningful glance Erminia's way.

The woman, who had so far been at pains not to draw attention to herself, began to drift toward one of the sideboards. She fixed her eyes on a glass-topped jar full of blue liquid in which swam a short-limbed homunculus with enormous eyes of lambent yellow.

Meanwhile, the thaumaturge had set the box on a small table next to the cylinder of white gold. He moved briskly to take from a drawer in the table a pair of gloves that he now pulled on up to his elbows. They were of a shimmering, scaly leather, iridescent in the room's diffuse light, as if they contained rainbows.

With clear evidence of excitement, Bolbek now turned to the box. He found the entry point on one end and slid aside the little piece of worn wood. Then he took a pin from the drawer and inserted it into the hole. His former lifeless expression had transformed into a mask of intensity and his breath came sharp and fast.

Raffalon heard the *click* as the box unlocked. He looked to Erminia. The woman had reached the sideboard. She now turned so that her elbow struck the jar. It wobbled and almost toppled, the lid coming free and blue ichor splashing out, with a harsh sound of glass on glass.

Bolbek's head snapped her way. "Idiot! Get away from—" he began, but at that moment, Raffalon swiftly brought the little effigy of the luck god from concealment and touched it to the bare flesh of the thaumaturge's neck. Instantly, the mage stiffened. Cords stood out in his throat and his eyes bulged. His lips writhed as he struggled to speak a syllable. To be sure he didn't, Raffalon pinched the man's lips together.

The thief was impressed at how long the spell-slinger was able to resist the god's power; his own enthrallment had been almost instantaneous. But finally the struggle ended. Bolbek's body relaxed, though his eyes spoke of inner misery.

"All well?" the thief said. He kept the idol pressed against the man's neck.

"I am still examining the contents of the memory," said the god through the thaumaturge's vocal apparatus. "Remarkable."

Erminia came forward. "What would this have done to you?" she said, indicating the apparatus.

"Dissolved me, taken my power, infused it into Bolbek." A moment's pause. "The cylinder already contains six imprisoned deities. My entry would have allowed this fellow to take the final step to leach us of our energies. Then the mana would have been transferred to the cage, to be incorporated into his own being."

"He would have become a god?" said the thief.

"No. The procedure would have failed. They always do. But he would have had a very interesting few moments before the cataclysm obliterated him, his house, and the neighborhood."

Raffalon examined Bolbek's eyes, saw rage and despair. "And yet, somehow," he said, "I do not think that he would thank us for intervening."

"He would not," said the god within the thaumaturge. "You had better bind him well, including his fingers. And gag him thoroughly. He knows spells that need only a single syllable, and he is resolved to use them on you."

"There's a wizard's gratitude for you," said Erminia. She went and found cords, chains, and cloth, then set about rendering Bolbek harmless. She even tied his toes together. When he was comprehensively immobilized, Raffalon removed the effigy from contact with the mage's skin and set the little god on the table. "Now what?" he said.

The deity spoke in his mind again. *I studied his plans for the apparatus,* it said. *If you carefully unscrew the lid, the prisoners will be released.*

The thief said, "They are liable to be angry, and perhaps indiscriminate in how they express themselves."

I will see that they do you no harm. Indeed, I believe they will see that they owe the two of you whatever rewards are in their power.

Raffalon relayed this information to Erminia and suggested that she come and stand close to him. When she had done so, he reached for the cylinder's top and slowly rotated it. Fine threads showed, and the white gold squeaked faintly as it unwound.

Then came the last turn, and the top of the cylinder flew into the air, knocking the man's hand aside. A coruscating fount of force, in several colors and of an intensity too bright to be even squinted at, shot up to the ceiling. The air of the room was filled with overpowering scents, rushing winds, claps of near thunder, and waves of pressure that made the thief's ears hurt.

Invisible hands seized Raffalon and Erminia in a crushing grip and raised them high above the floor. The thief had but a moment to think that he was about to be dashed against the flagstones. Then as quickly as they had been taken up, they were gently lowered again.

I regret, said a different voice. *Potho has explained that you have been our deliverers, not our captors.*

"Potho?" Raffalon and Erminia said together.

It is my name, said the voice the thief recognized as the luck god's. But now he sounded delighted. *Mithron recognized me, as I did him. We are the divine equivalent of cousins.*

"Mithron?"

Now the other voice spoke. *A god of those who race horses,* it said. *Potho and I were often invoked together.*

The luck god made other introductions: Iteran, who presided over crossroads; Belseren, whose province was health and vigor; Samiravi, a goddess of erotic fulfillment; Fhazzant, who looked after license inspectors and tax collectors; Tewks, who, if properly propitiated, could fulfill heart's desire.

We are all grateful to you, said Potho. *And each of us has bestowed upon you both what blessings are within our purview, now that we all know our names and our powers are restored.*

"You mean I can count on a good day at the races?"

Always, said Mithron.

Raffalon mentally itemized his other gains. He would never be ambushed at street corners. He would never sicken or tire, nor be embarrassed or unfulfilled in moments of intimacy. What benefits he would accrue from the patron of tax collectors he could not at first imagine.

They will leave you unmolested, said a new voice he assumed to be Fhazzant's.

"I thank you all," he said and made a formal gesture of gratitude.

"As do I," said Erminia, although at first Raffalon did not recognize the musical voice as hers. He turned to her and saw that Samiravi had been at work. The young woman's eyes were now not quite so close together, nor her nose so long and pointed. Her lips had become fuller and a hairy mole on her chin was gone. Her upper and lower garments had filled out. She glowed with health and erotic promise.

From the way she was looking at him, it seemed that he, too, had been reordered and improved. He felt his nose and found it handsomely reshaped, while a surreptitious hand slipped into a pants pocket quietly determined that his initial inquiry about prodigiousness had been remembered and fully answered as well.

"I thank Tewks, most particularly," he said.

Now, said Potho, *we will say farewell. We have business with this prideful sorcerer.*

Mithron added, *We have dismissed all his familiars and frighteners. If, on the way out, you see anything you like, feel free to take it with you.*

Fhazzant's voice said, *He will have no further need of his goods.*

Raffalon repeated the gesture of gratitude. Erminia offered a graceful curtsy, then said with a ravishing smile, "I've never been able to do that right before."

Together, they left the thaumaturge's workroom, where the winds had once more begun to roar. Throughout the mansion, doors slammed open, locked coffers popped their lids, and cupboard doors swung wide.

Sometime later, their pockets full, bearing between them a densely packed trunk, they were making their way down one of Port Thayes's better boulevards, seeking a place to stay. Erminia said, "I have been thinking. If we built an inn at a crossroads, near a good racecourse . . ." She paused for thought, then went on, "And if I served the customers and you ran a few games of chance, perhaps set up a tote . . ."

Raffalon said, "We would have no troubles with overzealous officials."

"It could work," she said. "Of course, you and I would have to be personally compatible."

"There is a hotel across the way," the thief said. "We could take a room for the night and see."

He was surprised, but pleased, when she forthrightly expressed approval of his proposal.

Later that night, having discovered that they were indeed wonderfully compatible, she threw a sated arm across his chest, and said, "To be a success, an inn needs a good name."

He said, "With luck, I'm sure I'll think of one."

Joe R. Lansdale

Prolific Texas writer Joe R. Lansdale has won the Edgar Award, the British Fantasy Award, the American Horror Award, the American Mystery Award, the International Crime Writer's Award, and nine Bram Stoker Awards. Although perhaps best known for horror/thrillers such as *The Nightrunners, Bubba Ho-Tep, The Bottoms, The God of the Razor,* and *The Drive-In,* he also writes the popular Hap Collins and Leonard Pine mystery series—*Savage Season, Mucho Mojo, The Two-Bear Mambo, Bad Chili, Rumble Tumble, Captains Outrageous*—as well as Western novels such as *The Magic Wagon,* and totally unclassifiable cross-genre novels such as *Zeppelins West, The Drive-In,* and *The Drive-In 2: Not Just One of Them Sequels.* His other novels include *Dead in the West, The Big Blow, Sunset and Sawdust, Act of Love, Freezer Burn, Waltz of Shadows,* and *Leather Maiden.* He has also contributed novels to series such as *Batman* and *Tarzan.* His many short stories have been collected in *By Bizarre Hands, Sanctified and Chicken-Fried, The Best of Joe R. Lansdale, The Shadows, Kith and Kin, The Long Ones, Stories by Mama Lansdale's Youngest Boy, Bestsellers Guaranteed, On the Far Side of the Cadillac Desert with Dead Folks, Electric Gumbo, Writer of the Purple Rage, Fist Full of Stories, Bumper Crop, The Good, the Bad, and the Indifferent, Selected Stories by Joe R. Lansdale, For a Few Stories More, Mad Dog Summer: And Other Stories, The King and Other Stories, Deadman's Road, High Cotton: The Collected Stories of Joe R. Lansdale,* and an omnibus, *Flaming Zeppelins: The Adventures of Ned the Seal.* As editor, he has produced the anthologies *The Best of the West, Retro Pulp Tales, Son of Retro Pulp Tales* (with Keith Lansdale), *Razored Saddles* (with Pat LoBrutto), *Dark at Heart: All New Tales of Dark Suspense* (with wife, Karen Lansdale), *The Horror Hall of Fame: The Stoker Winners,* and the Robert E. Howard tribute anthology, *Cross Plains Universe* (with Scott A. Cupp).

An anthology in tribute to Lansdale's work is *Lords of the Razor.* His most recent books are two new Hap and Leonard novels, *Vanilla Ride* and *Devil Red,* as well as the short novels *Hyenas* and *Dead Aim,* the novels *Edge of Dark Water* and *The Thicket,* two new anthologies—*The Urban Fantasy Anthology* (edited with Peter S. Beagle), and *Crucified Dreams*—and three new collections, *Shadows West* (with John L. Lansdale), *Trapped in the Saturday Matinee,* and *Bleeding Shadows.* He lives with his family in Nacogdoches, Texas.

Here he sends two of his most popular characters, Hap and Leonard, on a gritty, perilous quest to rescue a Damsel in Distress—although not the kind you usually meet in fairy tales.

BENT TWIG

A Hap and Leonard Adventure

Joe R. Lansdale

When I got in from work that night, Brett, my redhead, was sitting at the kitchen table. She didn't have a shift that week at the hospital, so I was surprised to see her up and about. It was 2:00 A.M. I had finished up being a night watchman at the dog-food plant, hoping my buddy Leonard would be back soon from Michigan, where he had gone after someone in some case he had hired out to do for our friend Marvin and the detective agency Marvin owned. We did freelance work like that from time to time.

There was no job for me in this one, and since Leonard was without a job at all and needed the money more than I did, he hired on. I had a temporary at the dog-food plant. It was okay, but mostly boring. The most exciting thing I had done was chase some rats I had caught in the feed-storage room, nibbling on some bags of dog food, stealing chow out of some hound's mouth, so to speak. Those rats knew not to mess with me.

I kept hoping Marvin would have something for me so I could quit, but so far, nothing. I did have that week's paycheck from the dog-food plant in my wallet, though.

"What are you doing up?" I asked.

"Worrying," she said.

I sat down at the table with her.

"We have enough money, right?"

"We got plenty for a change. It's Tillie."

"Oh, shit," I said.

"It's not like before," Brett said. What she meant was a little of column A, a little of column B.

Column A was where she got in with a biker club at the local poke and got hauled off to be a prostitute, partly on purpose, as it was her profession, and partly against her will because they didn't plan to pay her. We had rescued her from that, me, Brett, and Leonard. She had then gone off and gotten into a series of domestic problems over in Tyler, but those were the sort of things Brett got her out of, or at least managed to avert catastrophe for a while. Every time Brett mentioned Tillie it meant she would be packing a bag, putting her job on hold, and going off for a few days to straighten some stupid thing out that never should have happened in the first place. Since she was Brett's daughter, I tried to care about her. But she didn't like me and I didn't like her. But I did love Brett, so I tried to be as supportive as possible, but Brett knew how I felt.

"You have to go for a few days?" I asked.

"May be more to it."

"How's that?"

"She's missing."

"Wouldn't be the first time she took a powder for a while. You know how she is. Goes off without a word, comes back without one, unless she needs money or a tornado got the double-wide."

"It's not all her fault."

"Brett, baby. Don't give me the stuff about how you weren't a good mother."

"I wasn't."

"You were young yourself, and I don't think you did all that bad. You had some circumstances, and you did what you could for her. She's mostly a mess of her choosing."

"Maybe."

"But you're not convinced."

"It doesn't matter. She's my daughter."

"You got me there," I said.

"I got a call from a friend of hers. You don't know her. Her name is Monica, and she's all right. I think she's got a better head on her shoulders than Tillie. I met her when I was there last. I think she's been a pretty good guide for my girl. Fact is, I sort of thought Tillie was getting it together, and I've been keeping in touch with Monica about it. She called to say they were supposed to go to a movie, a girl's night out. Only Tillie didn't show. Didn't call. And now it's three days later. Monica said when she got over being mad, she got into being worried. Says the guy Tillie lives with, that he could be the problem. He used to run whores, and Tillie could easily fall back into that life. I mean . . . Well, there's a bit of a drug problem with the guy, and Tillie, sometimes. He could have gotten tough with Tillie. He might be trying to make some money off of her, or he might have gotten into something bad and Tillie got dragged with him."

"Monica think he's holding her at home?"

"Maybe worse."

"I thought he was supposed to be all right."

"Me too," she said. "But lately, not so much. At first, he was a kind of Prince Charming, an ex-druggie who was doing good, then all of a sudden he didn't want her out of the house, didn't want her contacting anyone. Didn't want her seeing Monica. But Monica thinks it's because he was choosing who he wanted Tillie to see."

"Prostitution," I said.

Brett nodded. "Yeah, it's how those kind of guys play. Like they care about you, or they got some of the same problems they're kicking, and the next thing Tillie knows she's on the nose candy again and is selling her ass, and then pretty soon she's not getting any money from the sell. He gets it all."

"The pimp gets it all, keeps her drugged, and keeps the money flowing in."

"Yeah," Brett said. "Exactly. It's happened to her before, and you know that, so—"

"You're thinking it could happen again."

"Yeah," she said. "I am."

"'Course it doesn't matter, and it may not have been planned. He may have just fallen off the wagon and grabbed her as he fell. After he got the prize he wanted, he didn't want to share it or show it around."

"He liked showing her around at first, all right," Brett said. "He liked her to dress sexy, and then if anyone looked, he was mad. She was for him, and yet he wanted to parade her and not have anyone look at the parade. Later on, he wanted to bring people to the parade. Maybe when his drug habit got bad. I don't know. I don't care. I just want to know she's safe."

"And you want me to check it out?"

"I want us to check it out."

"Let me drive back to the dog-food plant and quit with prejudice first."

"Short notice," Brett said.

"I know," I said. "But then so was this."

It felt odd going off to see about something like this without Leonard. I liked having him around in these kinds of circumstances. He helped strengthen my backbone. I liked to think I was already pretty firm in that area, but it never hurt to have your brother from another mother there to keep you feeling confident.

Tillie lived just outside of Tyler, between there and Bullock, a little burg outside of the city. Tyler wasn't up there with Dallas and Houston, but it was a big town, or small city, depending on how you liked your labels. A hundred thousand or so, with lots of traffic, illegal immigrants, and college students. The immigrants they liked to hire to get work done cheap, then use them for every scapegoat situation possible, forgetting they wouldn't even be there to blame for what they did and for what they didn't do, if they weren't offered the jobs in the first place.

When we got to Tillie's house we found two cars in the carport. Brett said, "That's Tillie's and Robert's cars. Both cars are here."

I went over and knocked on the front door, but no one answered. It's hard to explain, but sometimes you knock, you know someone's inside, and other times it has a hollow feel, like you're tapping on a sun-bleached skull, thinking a brain that isn't inside of it anymore is going to wake up. And sometimes you're just full of shit and whoever is inside is hiding. I remember my mother doing that from time to time when a bill collector came around. I always wondered if they knew we were inside, hiding out on paying the rent we hadn't earned yet but would pay, hiding out from paying a car payment, hoping they wouldn't haul the car away.

I went around back and knocked but got the same lack of response. I walked around the house with Brett and we looked in windows when there was a window to look in. Most were covered with blinds or curtains, but the kitchen window at the back had the curtains pulled back, and we could see inside by cupping our hands around our faces and pressing them against the glass. There was nothing to see, though.

Finally we went back out to my car. We leaned on the hood.

I said, "You want me to get inside?"

"I don't know," she said. "I called the police yesterday, well, it was the sheriff's department, but they wouldn't do anything."

"Not twenty-four hours?" I said.

"Actually, it has been. Over. But the thing is, they've dealt with her before." I didn't know all the details on that, but I figured as much. Tillie tended to get in trouble, run off from time to time, so they weren't quick on using manpower to chase a sometime prostitute and drug user and full-time pain in the ass.

"Okay," I said. "Going to make an executive decision. I'm going to break in."

There were houses around, but no activity, and I didn't see anyone parting the curtains for a peek, so I got a lock-picking kit out of the glove box that I use with the agency from time to time, went around back, and got to it. I'm not that good a lock picker, and to tell the truth, it's seldom like on TV, least for me. It always takes a while. This door was easy though, so it only took me about five minutes, and then me and Brett were inside.

Brett called out. "Tillie. Robert. It's Mom."

No one answered. Her words bounced off the wall.

"Hang by the door," I said.

I went through the house, looked in all the rooms. There was no one handy, but in the living room a chair and a coffee table were turned over, some drink of some kind spilled on the floor and gone sticky, a broken glass nearby. I went back and told Brett what I had seen.

"Maybe now we can get the law interested," I said.

Outside, out back, I saw there was a thin trail of blood drops. I hadn't noticed it before, but now, coming out of the house and with the sun just right, I could see it. It looked like someone had dropped rubies of assorted size in the grass. I said, "Brett, honey. Go out to the car and sit behind the wheel. Here are the keys in case you need to leave. And if you do, leave. Don't worry about me."

"Bullshit," she said. "We'll get the gun out of the glove box."

I have a conceal carry permit, but I seldom carry the gun. Fact is, I don't like the idea of one, but in my line of work—and I don't just mean watchman at the dog-food plant—stuff sometimes requires one.

We went and got the pistol out of the glove box, an old-style revolver, and walked after the blood drops.

It trailed into the woods, and then we didn't see much of it anymore. We went along the trail a bit more, and I saw where something had been pulled into the bushes, mashing them down. We went up in there and found a body lying on the ground. It was lying facedown. I shouldn't have moved the body, but I nudged it with my foot so as to turn it over. The face looking up at me was that of a young man and it had eyes full of ants and the victim's nose was flattened and scraped where it had been dragged along the ground. There was a bullet hole in the chest, or so I assumed. I had seen a few of them, and it had been delivered right through the shirt pocket. I could see there was another one in his right side. I figured one shot had wounded him, he had made a break for it, and whoever shot him caught up with him and shot him again, then dragged him in the bushes. I also noted the man had tattoos up and down both arms, and not very good ones. They looked as if they had been put there by a drunk trying to write in Sanskrit and hieroglyphics. Either that or a cellmate.

Brett was standing right there with me. She said, "That's him."

"Meaning Robert, Tillie's boyfriend."

"Yeah," she said, and started looking around. Me too. I sort of expected to find her daughter's body, but we didn't. We even went back to the house and walked through it without handling anything but the doorknob, just in case we had missed Tillie on first pass, stuffed under a bed, in a closet, or a freezer. They didn't have a freezer and she wasn't under the bed or in a closet.

I put my pistol back in the glove box of the car and called 911.

What they sent out was a young guy wearing an oversized pair of pants and a badge as shiny as a child's Christmas dreams. He had a gun on his hip that was large enough to make me think he might have been expecting elephants to give him trouble. He had on a cowboy hat that seemed too tall, the brim too wide. He looked like someone playing shoot-'em-up. He told me he was a deputy.

There was another guy with him, older, sitting on the passenger side of the car. The young guy got out and the old guy didn't. He just opened the door and sat there. He looked like a man waiting for retirement and not sure he'd make it. He might have been forty, but there was something in his face that made him seem older. He had a smaller gun on his hip. I could see that clearly, and he had a cowboy hat on his knee.

The younger man listened to us make our statement. He looked interested and wrote some stuff down on a notepad. I told him I had a gun in my glove box and I had a permit, just so things wouldn't get dicey in case they found it later. After a time, the older man got out of the car and came over. He said, "You get it all down, Olford?"

"Yes, sir," said the deputy.

I saw then that the guy in front of us had a badge that said SHERIFF on it. It looked very much like those kind of badges we used to buy as kids, ones that came with a cap gun and no caps. You had to buy those separate.

He asked us some of the same questions, just to see if we'd trip up, I figure. He didn't look at me much when I answered. He studied Brett constantly. I didn't blame him. She looked fine, as always. Long red hair tumbling over her shoulders, great body kept firm through exercise, and the kind of face that would make Wonder Woman beat herself in the head with a hammer.

"Walk with me," said the sheriff to me.

"I'm coming too," Brett said. "I'm no shrinking violet."

"I bet you aren't," said the sheriff. "Olford, you go sit in the car and get your notes straight."

"They're straight, Sheriff," Olford said.

"Go sit in the car anyway," he said.

We walked along a ways. The sheriff, who we learned was named Nathan Hews, said, "Olford is the mayor's boy. Whatcha gonna do?"

"Did he get his uniform from Goodwill?" I asked.

"Don't be disrespectful," the sheriff said. "He stole that off a wash line."

We came to the body. I said, "I turned him over."

"Not supposed to do that," Sheriff Hews said.

"I know. But I checked to see if he was alive."

"When they look like this, facedown or faceup, you got to know they're dead."

"Maybe," I said.

"You know something," the sheriff said. "You called things in, said who you two were, so I made some calls, checked some things out. The chief over in LaBorde, he said you're a real pain in the ass. That you usually run with a black guy named Leonard."

"Yep, that's me," I said. "I mean, I run with a black guy named Leonard. I don't know about the pain-in-the-ass part."

"I think you do," he said. "Chief told me some things."

"Blabbermouth," I said.

When we finished looking at the body, we walked back to the car. The sheriff had Olford get a camera out of their car and go out and take some pictures.

"We don't have a real team," he said. "There's me, Olford, one other deputy, and a dispatcher. Sometimes we get free doughnuts, though."

"That's keeping in form," I said.

"You betcha," he said. He looked at Brett. "You seem to be holding up well, considering your daughter is missing and a man is dead."

He was still playing us, trying to see if we had anything to do with the business that had gone down.

"Trust me," Brett said. "I'm worried sick."

We had to stay at a motel for a couple of hours before the sheriff showed up with a lack of information. "We didn't find your daughter," he said to Brett. "That could be good news."

"Could be," Brett said. What the sheriff had missed in his absence was Brett's breaking down and crying, but he could probably notice the red in her eyes. She listened to what he had to say and went into the bathroom and closed the door.

He said to me, "Listen, I'm going to square with you. Going to tell you what you probably have already figured. I'm a one-horse sheriff in a one-horse town with two deputies who are working their first murder case. They're more suited to chasing down renegade cats and dogs and figuring out who stole whose graham crackers at the nursery school. If we had one. I'm not telling you to go off on your own, and there's bigger law can be brought into this. But if I was you, from what I know about you, I'd tell you on the sly, which is what I'm doing now, just in case you don't get it, to do some looking on your own."

I nodded, said, "You got any idea where I should start?"

"I said I was a one-horse sheriff, but I once upon a time did some city work. I came here so I'd see fewer bodies. So far, I've seen fewer. This is the first murder that isn't a suicide I've seen in five years. The dead man is Robert Austin, he was wanted for some shit. The girl, your woman's daughter, word was she did some business, if you know what I mean."

"That word is probably good," I said.

"This guy, Robert, sold drugs and sold her. Town like this, people who used her services . . . Well, everyone knows. Everyone here knows the size of their neighbor's turds and can tell one's stink from the other. Thing is, Robert, he was most likely selling drugs for Buster Smith. Buster runs a Gospel Opry show over in Marvel Creek."

"I was born there," I said.

"Then you know the place. Used to be tough as a doorstop and sharp as a razor. All that booze out there on Hell's half mile. Now it's a town known for antiques and all the tonks are gone. The Gospel Opry, well, they say that's a cover for old Buster. Marvel Creek sees him as a pious businessman. Me, I see him as a man gives real Christians like me a bad name."

"All right," I said.

"He's about fifty, with slicked-back hair and a very cool manner. Wears awful plaid sports jackets all the time. I've met him a time or two, when I was over that way. I even went to the Opry once. Good entertainment. But the word kept drifting back about him, and though it's rumor, I've come to believe it. He's an operator living a simple life on the surface, putting himself in a squeaky-clean front while he does the bad stuff out the back door. He's got everyone that matters over there in his pocket.

"Another thing, there's a guy named Kevin Crisper hangs out at the Go-Mart here, sits on a bench out front. It's his bench. He works his drug deals there, and rumor is, though we can't prove it, he works for Buster. I keep a watch on him, but so far I haven't caught him doing what he shouldn't be doing. He has a guy or two to help him out. They all got a few snags on their arrest sheet, but nothing that keeps them anywhere behind bars. I mean, I know what they're doing, and I can't prove it. I can't do to them what needs to be done. Thing is, though, Kevin Crisper does sales of drugs and gets a percentage. Buster gets the lion's share because he provides the goods. At least the dope. Tillie, and I want to say this before your girlfriend comes back, she was a self-operator, but word was she was getting pretty deep in the drugs and that maybe she didn't know if she was about to shit or go blind. She was down in the dead zone with one brain cell or two for a life preserver, and that was it. Robert, he might have been farming her out through this Kevin. Probably was. And Tillie, like I said, she might as well have been a blow-up sex doll, way her mind was messed up."

"And you know all this and couldn't do nothing?" I said.

"That's right," he said. "Isn't that nice? Listen here, chief in LaBorde said you were smarter than you looked, so I'm thinking what I said before. There's stuff you can do I can't. Law and all. But, you get caught doing it, I didn't tell you to do it, and you say I did, I'll call you a big fat liar. I'll even arrest you. How's that for modern law enforcement?"

"I can live with it," I said.

It took some doing, but I finally talked Brett into letting me take her home. I called Leonard on my cell, but he didn't answer his. I left him a message. I drove over to downtown Bullock, which was a cross street, and went over to the Go-Mart and found Kevin Crisper. He was a man in his forties trying to look thirty. He had similar tattoos to Robert. Kevin looked like a man who had been soaked down wet and overheated in a microwave. Skin like that was last seen on Tutankhamen's mummy. That said, he had muscular arms, the kind of muscles some people are born with, long and stringy and deceptively strong.

I walked over to him, said, "I hear you can sell me some things."

"Some things?" he said. "What kind of things? I look like I got something to sell? Pots and pans. Maybe gloves or shoes?"

"I was told you had some entertainments. Guy named Robert told me. You are Kevin, right?"

"Yeah, that's me." Kevin lifted his head, said, "When did Robert tell you that?"

I backdated the time, just in case Kevin had some idea when Robert bit the big one. I added, "He said there's a girl that could do me some favors, you know. For some money."

"You heard all that, huh?"

"I did."

"He didn't offer just to take care of you himself?"

"He said he worked for you and that I should talk to you."

"That's funny he should say that," he said.

"Look, you got the goods or you don't. I got money. I want some services. I'd like to party with a girl and I'd like to make myself right. You know where I'm coming from."

He nodded. "Say I know how to get this girl, the stuff you want to get right, you think I'd have it on me? Think I got that girl's pussy in my back pocket along with a sack of blow?"

"That would be handy if you did."

"Listen here, tell you what. I like Robert, and since he sent you, I got a place where you can come for the stuff and the girl. We don't use a motel. There ain't but one and everyone knows everyone."

"So where is this place?"

"You going to be around tonight?"

"Could be."

"You want some leg and some head-twister, then you got to be around."

"Head-twister?"

"Stuff I'm selling. It's a mixture. You take this stuff your dick gets hard, your head gets high, and you'll have so much fun you'll drive over and slap your mama."

"That right?"

"Way I hear. 'Course, I don't sample that shit myself."

"That's not much of a selling point," I said.

"Oh, it's not that. I sample the girl, of course, but the rest of it, that's product, man. You dip into your own product, especially with it being available, you can get in Dutch pretty quick."

He gave me a time and an address. I thanked him and tried to look excited. I drove over to the one café and parked out front and sat behind the wheel and called Leonard again. I had some idea that the Michigan thing was near wrapped up, that he ought to be driving back down and in Texas by now, but it appeared it had taken more time than expected because I got the same thing. No answer. I left him a detailed message, even told him where I was supposed to be and at what time. I gave him the same directions Kevin had given me. I went in the café and had some coffee and a sandwich. I figured I might want to be fortified. I bought a sack lunch and an axe handle at the feed store and put it in the car, and then I drove out to where I was supposed to meet Kevin. Only thing was I was four hours early.

* * *

I tried Leonard a few more times, leaving the same directions, but whatever he was up to, it didn't involve having his phone on. The location Kevin gave me was not deep in the woods, but it was out of town, which would of course suit his kind of services. But since I didn't think Tillie, possibly the only lady working the grid, so to speak, was truly available, and since I knew Robert was dead as a pair of posthole diggers, and had a suspicion Kevin knew it as well, I thought I wouldn't rely on his hospitality to bring Tillie straight to me. Me and Brett and Leonard had rescued her once before, a few years back, from something stupid she had gotten herself into that sounded a lot like this, and frankly, there was a part of me that wanted to leave her to it. I couldn't do that because she was Brett's daughter. That was the big part. The other part was I was me. I seem to be one of those guys who would help a rabid dog across the street if I thought it were confused on directions.

I thought over the directions I had been given, then varied from them. I found a little road to go down, a hunting trail, and then a little path off of it. I parked there and hoped no one found my car and decided they'd like to hot-wire it and drive it off, or for that matter, just vandalize it. I got my pistol out of the glove box and stuck it in the pants at the base of my spine, and pulled my shirt over it. I got the food I had bought extra at the café, a hamburger and fries and a canned Diet Coke, tucked the axe handle under my arm, and walked to where I understood the meeting place to be.

When I could see the house, which seemed pretty rickety and set off partly in the woods, I was pretty sure my suspicions were confirmed. Anyone coming here expecting pussy and drugs was a dumb-ass. I wasn't actually expecting either, but I was a dumb-ass, because here I was. I went to the house and checked the door. It was locked. I went around back. The door there was locked too, but it was thin. I thought that would be my surprise entrance, kicking the door down. I could do it now, and wait on him, but if he came around back, or that was his preferred way of entering, the joke could be on me.

I walked off in the woods to the left of the place and found a tumbled-down tree to sit on. I had my supper, which was all right if you had no taste buds and your stomach was made of cast iron. I only ate a few of the french fries, being as how they were greasy enough to give a garden statue the shits. I drank the Diet Coke and ate the burger. The meat seemed suspicious, but I was already hungry. I always got hungry when I thought I might kill someone or get killed myself.

As it grew dark, mosquitoes came out and buzzed around, and a few bit me. I wondered if they were carrying the West Nile virus, or maybe something worse. I slapped at them. I caught a chigger on its way up my pant leg, heading for my balls; I felt proud to have rescued them.

After a while I saw Kevin drive up and park and go inside the house. I saw a light go on. He didn't have Tillie with him. He didn't seem to have anything with him. He was early too. I thought I would wait a few minutes then surprise him. I looked at my watch. I'd give him a few minutes to feel secure, then I'd surprise him. 'Course, if he had a gun, which he would have, the surprise would be on me. 'Course, I had one too, but when guns come into play, anything can happen.

I thought about this, and I thought about that, and then I thought I felt something cold at the base of my skull, and since this was the dead of summer, even if it was just now dark, I knew it wasn't a cold breeze.

It was a gun barrel.

I can't explain how much like a dick I felt. Here I was putting the sneak on them, and they had put the sneak on me. I turned around slowly. A short fat man with a face that looked like it had been used for missile targeting, it had so many pocks, was smiling about $15,000 of much-needed dental work at me.

"I could shoot you, you know," he said.

"Yep," I said.

"What we're gonna do, is we're gonna walk up there and see Kevin. Stand up first."

I stood up, leaving the axe handle on the log. He patted me down with one hand and found my pistol and stuck it in one of his baggy pants pockets. He picked up the axe handle with his free hand and tapped my shoulder with it.

"Walk on up to the house," he said.

I was getting old, I figured. Any other time I would have been prepared. Or so I told myself. I had thought I was being smart getting there early, but they had put the sneak on me, putting moon-crater face in the woods to wait, and Kevin to come up like a staked goat.

"There's a road behind the woods here, dickhead," said Moon Crater. "I come up on that, then through the woods. I hid out and waited. I thought I might have to do some serious sneaking, but you picked a spot not that far from me. It was easy, man. Kevin said he thought you thought you were a smart guy, but you're not really so smart, are you?"

"I have to agree with that," I said.

In the house Kevin was waiting. He said, "No snatch or juice for you, huh? 'Course, that isn't what you were coming for, were you? I didn't like your looks from the start."

"You ain't got no mirrors at your house?"

Moon Crater whacked me across the back of the legs with the axe handle hard enough I went to my knees.

"I got a suspicion you got some other reason to see me. I got a suspicion you might be looking for Tillie or Robert. I got to tell you, I think you know Robert's dead."

"You got me," I said. "I know he's dead. What about Tillie?"

"She's all right, but she won't be long," Kevin said. "Mr. Smith likes to get all the juice out of a product before he lets it go. He gets her hotwired enough on something or another, he can sell her out until there's nothing to sell, you know. She then gets a hot shot, looks like an accident. They find her in a ditch somewhere with toadstools growing out of her ass."

"Robert didn't look like an accident."

"He proved more of a problem. Things got out of hand. You see, he was dipping, him and the cunt. We don't like dippers, unless maybe it's with chips and dip."

Kevin and Moon Crater liked that. Both of them laughed. I figured they didn't get out much.

"Get him in the chair," Kevin said.

They were ready for me. The chair was arranged in the middle of the floor. I did have a nice view through a window when Kevin moved out from in front of it, which he did from time to time. I could tell he lied about sampling his product. He had some of it in him right then, and it was giving him a nervous twitch. They put me in the chair and Moon Crater tied my legs and arms to it with rope while Kevin held Moon Crater's gun on me. When I was good and tied, Kevin said, "Now you got to tell me what you're up to."

"You can take a running leap up a donkey's ass," I said.

"Oh, that's not nice," Kevin said. "Jubil, hold this gun."

Jubil, aka Moon Crater, took the pistol. Kevin picked up my axe handle. I knew I was going to regret having brought that. He swung it hard against my shins. The pain jumped from my leg to my spine to the base of my brain. For a moment I thought I was going to be sick to my stomach and black out.

"That's got to hurt," Kevin said.

"You think," I said. It wasn't much, and it wasn't good, but it was something, even if it sounded as if it were coming from a very small man under a pillow in the corner.

Kevin went over and put the axe handle by the front door. He reached in his pocket and took out a long pocketknife. He flipped it open.

"This house was left to me by my old grandma. It's not much, but I come here now and then for things. And I got a sentimental spot for it, even if it is starting to go bad. That being the case, what I want to say is, I don't want to bloody it up, I don't have to. So, for your sake and mine, you should talk."

"I talk, you're just going to let me go?" I said.

"Sure," Kevin said.

"Bullshit," I said.

"Okay, you're right. I'm gonna kill you. But I can make it quick, a cut throat. Nasty to think about, but it gets over quick. Bleeds out good. Robert, I ended up having to shoot him a couple of times. Not so good. He was in pain right up until that last bullet. You, I can make you last a long time with this here knife."

"So my choice is I talk and you cut my throat, or I don't talk and you cut on me a while till I do?"

"That's it," he said.

Right then, by the window, I saw Leonard's head go by. I stalled. I said, "So what would you like to know? I might have some answers, long as it doesn't involve math problems."

"Okay. First, who the fuck are you?"

I said, "I'm a census collector."

"That's going to get you cut," Kevin said. "I'm going to have to take an ear."

"Before you do," I said, "I really need to tell you something."

"What would that be?" Kevin said.

"Hell is coming," I said.

At that moment the door burst open, propelled forward by Leonard's foot. Leonard spied the axe handle, and he had it in his free hand before you could say, "My, is that an axe handle?"

Leonard said, striding forward, "Queer, roughhouse nigger, coming through."

He stepped forward quick and caught Moon Crater in the teeth with a left-handed swing of the handle. It knocked Moon Crater to the floor, sending the gun spinning away from him.

The light caught the black gleam of Leonard's close-shaved head, and it danced in his eyes, it danced along the length of the brand-new axe handle. The axe handle cut through the air like a hot knife through butter. When Kevin met the wood there was a sound like someone's slapping a belt on a leather couch, and then there were teeth and there was enough blood flying out of Kevin's mouth I was sure Grandma's house was ruined. It splattered on the wall and on the window, teeth clattered on the floor.

Kevin hit the floor on his belly, dropped the knife. He tried to crawl for it, but Leonard stomped his hand and the axe handle came down again. This time it was a sound more like someone chopping the neck off a turkey with a meat cleaver.

Kevin didn't move after that lick, but just for good measure, Leonard hit him again. He went over then to Moon Crater, who was trying to get up, and kicked him in the mouth. That dental work Moon Crater already needed was going to cost a lot more now.

When Kevin came awake, he was strapped to the chair where I had been. Leonard was nearby, leaning on the axe handle. I was squatted down in front of Kevin. Moon Crater was still stretched out on the floor. If he wasn't dead or in a coma, he probably down deep in some part of his being wished he was.

"Howdy," I said.

"Fuck you," Kevin said, but it was hard to be sure if that was actually what he said. He was spitting up blood.

"If you leave here," I said, "and it's possible, you might want to pick up your teeth, not confusing them with the gems that were in Jubil's mouth. You might want to put them in a glass of water and freeze them. I hear they can do wonders with knocked-out teeth now."

"Who are you?" he asked.

"My name is Hap, and this is my brother, Leonard. But you two have already met."

"Glad to make your fucking acquaintance," he said.

I stood up, turned to Leonard. "I didn't think you were coming."

"I was on my way home when you called. Started driving back two days ago, but I was in a blind spot for the phone. Bottomland. I got your message a little late."

"Not too late, though."

I turned back to Kevin. "Kevin," I said, "you and me, we got to talk, and I got to get some answers, and if I like them, I'm not even going to cut your throat."

They told us Tillie had been taken by the Gospel Opry guy, Buster Smith, and that Kevin and Moon Crater had helped him take her. She was in an old theater. I knew the theater. I was from Marvel Creek, and when I was growing up I went to many movies there. They had a stage at that theater, a movie screen behind it. They had kid shows and they brought out clowns and jugglers and special entertainment. It was awful and I was always glad when they got off the stage and turned off the light, leaving me with the roaches and a movie.

Leonard didn't want to leave them with their car, and he decided he didn't want to fuck it up. He wanted to fuck them up. I don't like that sort of thing, but, hey, what you gonna do? They started it.

Leonard put them in the trunk of his car, and I followed in mine after he dropped me off. We took them into the river bottoms. Leonard let them out of the trunk. They got out, though neither felt well. Leonard had really laid that axe handle on them. He said, "Thing I'm going to do is break both your legs. One apiece."

"No need in that, Leonard," I said.

"I know. I just want to do it."

"Look now," said Kevin. "Listen to your friend. We just work for that dickhead. We're out of it. We hope you get the girl back."

"Oh, we'll get her back if she's to be gotten back," Leonard said. "But here's the thing. You were going to kill my friend. Had I not showed up, you would have. So which leg?"

Kevin and Moon Crater looked at me.

"He's sort of got his mind made up," I said. "And you were going to kill me."

"But we'll die out here if our legs are broke," Moon Crater said.

"Don't be so goddamn dramatic," Leonard said. "You'll still be able to crawl, maybe find a stick to support yourself or something. Really, it's not our problem."

"Which leg?" Leonard said. "Or I choose."

"Left," Kevin said. Moon Crater didn't choose. "But—"

Before Kevin could protest again, Leonard swung that axe handle. It whistled and caught the man on the side of the knee, which is where it's the weakest. I heard a sound like someone's breaking a rack of pool balls. Kevin screamed and went down holding his knee.

"One," Leonard said.

Moon Crater made a break for it. I owed Leonard one, so I chased Moon Crater down and grabbed him by the shoulder and spun him around and threw a right cross into his face, and his face took it. He fell down. Before he could get up Leonard was there with the axe handle. I think it took about three whacks for Leonard to catch him good; I don't really remember. I looked away. But I think it was the right leg.

We drove Leonard's car to a church lot, which struck us as ironic, and I drove us in mine over to Marvel Creek. I said, "What if those guys get out of the woods and call? Warn Buster."

"It's miles to their car," Leonard said. "It's miles to No Enterprise. They got broke legs. Besides, it was you didn't want me to kill them. Up to me, they'd be in the Sabine River somewhere with fish nibbling on them."

"You are cold, man," I said.

"Absolutely," Leonard said.

We thought we'd stake out the Gospel Opry, but when we drove by, there was action there. A big crowd. Leonard said, "They're loading them inside. What is it? Nine? Ten o'clock? I didn't know Jesus stayed up this late."

"True. He's usually early to bed and early to rise."

I got my gun and put it under my shirt in the small of my back. We left the axe handle in the backseat with its memories. As we walked up, we saw the crowd was growing.

I said to an old man on a cane, "What's up?"

"The Gospel Opry usually. Talent show tonight, though. Y'all don't know about it?"

"No," I said. "We don't."

"It's more fun than a barrel of monkeys. There's people who sing and dance and do comedy. Good clean fun." He looked at Leonard. "You'll be able to get in, son. I remember when your color couldn't."

"My, how times have changed," Leonard said.

I glanced around and saw a line going through another door, off to the side. I said to the old man, "Who are they?"

"The talent. They signed up to perform."

Leonard said, "Come on, Hap."

We got in line at the talent door.

"More fun than a barrel of monkeys," I said, "and they let your kind in, Leonard."

"Well, suh, I sho' is beholding to some peckerwoods for that. Sho' is."

Inside there was a little man at a desk. He wore a bad wig. He asked us our name. We gave him our first names. Leonard said we were a singing act.

The little man couldn't find us on the roster, of course.

"We were set," I said. "We called ahead and everything. They think we're the bee's knees over in Overton."

"Overton is so small you can throw a rock across it," the man said.

"Yep, but we're still big there," I said.

He thought about it a moment, said, "Look here. There's a couple of guys who play bagpipes that canceled. Laundry lost their kilts or some such something. I'll give you their spot. You didn't get registered, but it'll work out. So you sing?"

"Like fucking birds," Leonard said.

The man looked at him, grinned slowly. Jesus didn't seem to always be at his house. He waved us inside, and we went.

"A singing group?" I said.

"The bee's knees," Leonard said.

Way it worked is we were guided backstage. There were a lot of acts there. One old man had on what looked like a sergeant's uniform. He was potbellied, bald, and looked as if he should have been on oxygen. He had a ventriloquist dummy with him. It was dressed up like a private, with a field cap and everything. I got to tell you, I seriously hate me some ventriloquist dummies. When I was a kid, late at night, I caught an old movie titled *Dead of Night,* an anthology film. One of the sections was about a man and a ventriloquist dummy that takes over his life. It scared the living dog shit out of me. I see a block of wood that might be carved into a ventriloquist dummy I get nervous. And this dummy looked as if the rats and someone with an ice pick had been at him.

"How long you been doing this?" I said.

He wheezed a moment before answering. "I used to make real

money at it. No one will have me now, except these talent shows, some kids' parties. I don't do as well as I once did. They got the goddamn Internet now. Oh, you boys won't tell on me, will you? They like us to watch our language."

"We won't say a fucking word," Leonard said.

The old man laughed. He leaned in close. "Neither of you boys got a drink, do you?"

We admitted that we didn't.

"That's all right, then. Just wondering." He shook the doll a little, causing dust to stir up. "Private Johnson is getting worn-out. My wife took a knife to him once, and used him to beat me over the head. It did some damage to him and me. I fart, it blacks me out and I wake up wearing a tutu."

He barked then at his joke, and then he carried on. "I haven't had the money to get him fixed. I act like the one eyelid he's got that droops is just part of the act. It adds character."

"Sure it does," I said. "You'll knock them dead."

I hoped he didn't knock himself dead. He was red-faced and breathing heavy and looked as if he might blow a major hose at any moment. Maybe his talk about farting and blacking out wasn't just a joke.

We all stood there in line, looking out at the stage. There were some dance acts going on out there. The band sounded like cows dying. The dancers moved like they had wooden legs. Next a young, beak-nosed man who played a fiddle so bad it sounded like he was sawing on a log did his act. It was the kind of noise that made your asshole pucker.

"The sisters will win this thing," said the old man. "I ain't seen them yet, but they'll probably show soon. Those dried-up-cunt bitches. They enter ever' week and win the five hundred dollars. It's those damn hymns. It gets the Jesus going in folks, and they feel like they got to vote for them. Shit, I'm up."

The old man waddled out with that horrible doll, picked up a stool on the way out. His act was so painful I thought I might use a curtain rope to hang myself, but at the same time I admired the old bastard. He wasn't a quitter. He wheezed and tried to throw his voice, but by the end of his act the dummy looked healthier than he did.

He came back with his doll and stool. He sat on the stool. "I tried to hit a high note there, when Private sang 'Boogie Woogie Bugle Boy,' and I damn near shit on myself. I think one of my rib bones moved."

"You did fine," I said.

"I did fine about fifty years ago and it was a spring morning and I had just knocked off a piece of ass. I did fine then. Least that's how I like to remember it. Might have been a hot afternoon in the dead of summer and it might have been a stump-broke cow."

"Just sit there and rest," I said.

"You're all right," he said to me. "Sure you haven't a drink?"

"Sure," I said.

There was another dance troupe onstage, and a guy with some bowling pins he was going to juggle was next in line. Leonard and I glanced around, trying to take in the place. It didn't look like a joint where a prostitute would be kept, or in this case made to go for free until she was used up. It didn't look like a place where someone sold drugs. It looked like a place full of bad entertainment. That's what made it a good hideout, of course, but I wasn't convinced.

I noticed that the acts that finished were ushered along a certain path, and that there were two guys on either side of a dark stairway. They didn't look like church deacons, but I decided to call them that in my mind. I left Leonard and walked over to the stairway, looked up it. I said, "What's up there?"

One of the men stepped forward, said, "That's private, sir."

I went back to Leonard. I said, "There's a whole nuther floor up there."

"There's a stairway on the other side of the stage too," he said. "You can see it from here. It's got bookends on either side of it too."

I looked. Sure enough. Two more guys. If the two near us were not church deacons, those two were not in the choir. Upstairs could have just been a storage place for hymn books, but I doubted it.

"Buster don't work the brothers," Leonard said. "All white thugs."

"It may not seem that long ago to them that your kind couldn't come in, and it may be they liked it like that."

"That really isn't true," Leonard said. "They did come in here, and you know it."

"They did janitor work," I said, "and they used to come up the stairs at the back and sat up there in the balcony."

"Nigger money was good as any," Leonard said. "I know. I sat up there in the balcony once and spat on a white boy's head."

"You did not," I said.

"No, but now and again I like to dream."

We were whispering a game plan when all of a sudden the little fellow that had signed us in came over. He said, "The Honey Girls are sick."

"Who?" I said.

"The gospel singers I told you about," said the old ventriloquist, who had come over. "Their adult diapers probably got bunched up and they couldn't make it. Or they heard that young girl come on and sing and left. I know they were here. I seen them, the smug assholes."

"That'll be enough," said the little man.

"Sorry," said the ventriloquist, and he waddled back to his stool.

I had my mind on other things, and hadn't even noticed the young girl, not really. But in the back of my mind I sort of remembered her doing a Patsy Cline number, and not badly at all.

"Honey Sisters say they got sick," said the little man.

"Both of them?" Leonard said.

"It hit them sudden, so you two are on next."

"Oh," I said.

Leonard grabbed my elbow. "Come on, I still remember 'The Old Rugged Cross.'"

"You're yanking me," I said. "We're really going out there?"

"I sing in the shower," Leonard said. "I do all right."

"Oh, hell," I said.

Well, we went out there, and I knew that old tune too. I am an atheist, but I like a good gospel tune now and again. We didn't have any music, but there was the house band and they knew the tune, sort of, though I didn't remember it with a tuba solo. We started out with it. Leonard was good, actually; he sounded way all right. I sort of chimed in when he lifted a hand to me, but after a few lines I forgot the words, so I started singing nonsense. An old lady in the front row in a wheelchair said, "Get the hook."

Leonard finished out while I snapped my fingers and tried to look cool. I think had I had sunglasses I could have pulled it off.

When we finished, or more less quit, they were glad to see us go. Someone even threw a wadded-up paper cup at me. Fuckers missed.

When we exited on the other side, Leonard said, "Damn, Hap. You fucked it up. We could have won that prize money. Or I could have."

"I didn't make us out as a duet, since we have never sung together even once. I never intended to go out there."

"I've always wanted to do that."

"You sounded all right," I said, "but don't be thinking of it as a second job."

"As for you," Leonard said, "you don't be thinking of it at all. Now, let's see if we can find Tillie."

"If she's alive," I said.

"She's alive, they are going to pay for it. If she's dead, they're going to pay for it, and then pay a dividend."

I didn't even like Tillie, but I sure liked Brett. Brett called her a bent twig. She'd say, "Hap, she's a bent twig, but she's not broken. She can weather the storm and come out on the other side."

She was pretty much still in the storm as far as I was concerned, but if the information we had was right, she didn't deserve this; this was even worse than what should happen to politicians. We headed toward the staircase on the side where we exited, near the choirboys. A man over there pointed us toward an exit. He was a chubby guy in a faded, purple leisure suit old enough to belong in a museum. He said, "That was bad, boys. Real bad."

We ignored him and headed for the staircase.

"Not over there," he said, and he grabbed my sleeve. I shook him loose and kept going. I had a feeling that most everyone here had no idea what was going on upstairs, no idea that the man who ran the Gospel Opry was about as reverent and kind as the business end of a hatchet.

"Those guys don't kid," said the man who had grabbed my sleeve. He was talking about the two boys at the stairs. They stepped out, one toward me, one toward Leonard.

The choirboy on my side said, "You don't come this way."

I kicked him in the balls and he bent a little and I hit him with a right hook. He went against the wall and came off of it mad. I hit him again, a straight right to the jaw. He went to one knee and tried to draw a pistol from under his coat. I pulled mine and hit him in the head with it. He went to his hands and knees, and I hit him again. He kind of bent his elbows like he had failed to do a push-up and lay on the floor. It was then that I noticed my leg where Kevin had hit me with the axe handle was really aching. I noticed this because I was going to kick him again and decided against it.

I looked over at Leonard. His man was already unconscious at the base of the stairs. I think he took him out with one good punch. I rolled my man over and took his gun. I had one in either hand now. I went up the stairs behind Leonard. Back onstage I heard laughter. Someone had finally succeeded at something. A joke maybe.

When I got to the top of the stairs, Leonard had taken an automatic off of the man he had hit and he had it at the ready. I turned and looked down, wondering if the deacons across the way knew what we were up to. If they didn't, they would soon. I figured the man who grabbed my sleeve would tell them. He might not know what really went on here, but he knew who he worked for.

Of course, if we were wrong, and what we expected was not at the top of the stairs, was really a bingo parlor, we would have a lot of explaining to do. For that matter, we could have a lot of explaining to do anyway.

The deacons figured it out. They came running across the stage in the middle of a dance number with a man and a woman in a horse suit. The man was the back end, the horse's ass. I knew this because I came back down the stairs when I heard running. It gave me a view of the stage. The deacons knocked the horse over and the man and woman spilled out of it. The couple said some words you wouldn't expect to hear at a Gospel Opry. God probably made a big black mark in their book right then.

The deacons didn't have guns drawn, and they almost ran right over me they were coming so fast. When they saw my revolver, as well as the automatic I had taken off one of the choirboys, they stopped up short. They froze like ice cubes.

I said, "Do you really want to get dead?"

One man shook his head and started to run across the stage again, past the horse that had been put together again. A tinny trumpet was playing somewhere and a piano. The horse was dancing. That goddamn tuba was hitting some random notes; that guy, he ought to be put down in the ground with that tuba.

The other deacon, the one that didn't run, put his hands up. He said, "You got to at least take my gun, so I can say I was unarmed."

"That'll work," I said. "But pull it easy."

He did, squatted down and put it on the floor and backed up. "I got no beef," he said.

"That's good," I said, "because I am in one shitty mood."

He backed out and went across the stage, walking fast. The couple in the horse suit just quit then. The woman pulled off the horse's head and tossed it into the audience. I hoped she hit the old woman in the wheelchair who said to get the hook.

I picked up his gun, a little nine, and went up the stairs again. Leonard was waiting.

"Stop to go to the bathroom?" he asked.

"I was disarming a gentleman."

Leonard pointed with his handgun. "There's one door. Shall we see what's on the other side? Lady or the tiger."

"I think we might get both," I said.

We moved quickly down the hall and Leonard kicked at the door and it swung back and came loose, hanging on one hinge, and then it came loose and fell. It was a toilet. It was empty.

"They were guarding a bathroom?" Leonard said. "Really."

There was probably some way to get across, but we didn't see it right away, and we were in a bit of a hurry. We put the guns in our waistbands, under our shirts, went down the stairs and behind the stage. The Gospel Opry folks were not deterred. The action, such as it was, was still going on. It was some kind of comedy act. When we got to the other side, we passed the man and the woman who had been wearing the horse outfit. They gave us the hard eye.

"Were you two part of the disruption?" said the woman.

"No, ma'am," I said, and kept going. We went up the stairs where the deacons had been. We pulled out our guns. There were two doors along the hallway.

"I'll take one, you take the other," Leonard said.

We chose a door, nodded at each other, and stomp-kicked them. My door went back completely off the hinges, old as it was. I could hear Leonard still kicking as I went through.

There was a bed in the room and a little light to the right, and there was a row of four chairs on that side, and I'm dying if I'm lying, there were four men in those chairs, and the one closest to the light was reading a newspaper. It was like they were in a barbershop waiting their turn. Tillie was on the bed, and a nude man was on her, his naked ass bobbing like a basketball. Tillie wasn't there, really. She was in some other zone. She had her eyes open, but they might as well have been closed. She looked skeletal. My guess is she hadn't been fed in a while, outside of what was in a needle. She looked a lot like Brett, if Brett were a concentration-camp survivor, and that disturbed me even more.

The four men stood up. They were all dressed, though one had taken off his shoes and placed them under his chair. One of them was wearing a police uniform and had his hand on the pistol in his belt. He was out for a little on-duty nookie and a bit of blow it seemed.

By then, Leonard had come through the door. The cop pulled his pistol and I shot him. I hit him in the arm and he fell down on the floor and started going around in circles like Curly of the Three Stooges. He was yelling, "Don't shoot me no more, don't shoot me no more."

Blood was all over the place.

The other three men acted as if to run, but Leonard resorted to foul language that had to do with their mothers. They sat back down, as if still waiting their turn. Their mothers be damned.

I said, "Where's dickhead? Buster?"

Nobody said anything.

"He asked you a question," Leonard said. "You don't say, and we find him, we're going to shoot all your toes off. And then your dick."

By this time the man in the bed had got off Tillie and was standing beside the bed with one hand over his pecker.

Leonard said, "I had a turkey neck like that, I'd keep it covered too. Fact is, I'm an expert on dicks, and that is an ugly one."

"He does know dicks," I said.

The man in the police uniform had quit spinning and had stuck his head up under a chair. He said, "I'm hit. I'm hit."

"No shit," I said.

I went over and saw that Tillie was breathing hard. I pulled the blanket at the end of the bed over her. I looked at the naked man with his hand over his privates and I just went berserk. I don't know what happened to me, but I just couldn't stand to think people like this existed, that they could sit in chairs and wait their turns to top some drugged girl. I kicked the naked man in the balls and hit him in the head with the pistol, and then I went after the other three, but not before I kicked the police officer on the floor once and heeled his gun under the bed. I started hitting those three guys with the pistols, one in either hand. I was hitting so fast I looked like Shiva. They tried to run for it, but each time they did Leonard kicked them back into play, and I just went to work. I felt wrong. I felt savage. I felt awful, and yet, I felt right.

It didn't take long before all of them were bleeding. Two were on the floor. One had fallen back into his chair. The naked man on the floor wasn't moving. He was lying on his side and had thrown up all over the place, and the air was thick with the stench of vomit.

"Okay," Leonard said. He walked over and put his gun against the shoeless man's nose. He was the one who had sat back down. "Where is Buster?"

The man didn't answer. He didn't need to. A door opened at the far end and two men came in. One had a shotgun. He cut down with it, but we were already moving. I dropped to the floor behind the bed, and Leonard leaped through the door he had kicked down, landed out in the hallway. From under the bed I could see the man's legs, and I shot at them, three times in rapid succession. I hit him somewhere because he yelped and fell down. I shot him again, this time in the top of the head, cracking it apart like a big walnut. The other man had a handgun and he had been firing it all this time. So far he had hit the bed, killed the barefoot man in the chair behind me, and had put some holes in the wall.

From under the bed I saw Leonard's feet as he came through the other door, the one I had kicked down, and then he was on that bastard. I got to my feet and started around, tripped over the policeman who had, without me seeing him, started crawling toward the open doorway.

"Stay," I said, as if speaking to a dog.

He stopped crawling.

By the time I got around to Leonard he had already taken the man down. Somehow the man had shot himself in the foot. I kicked him in the head, just to let him know I was in the game, and then Leonard reached down and took the man's pistol. Considering this guy's aim it was probably best to have left him with it. In time he would have shot himself again, maybe in the head.

"You stick," I said to Leonard.

"All right, but I hear too much gunfire, I'm coming. Right after I kill the lot of them."

I went through the door the two had come through, and by now I could hear yelling down below in the auditorium. The gunfire had roused things up, and was probably more exciting than anything they had seen tonight.

When I got into the room upstairs I saw that it was well tricked out for an old building. Lots of modern furniture, including a big couch. It was pushed back from the wall and I could see feet sticking out from behind it. I walked over there and laid my guns on the coffee table and grabbed the man by the ankles and pulled him out face-first. He tried to hang on to the floor, but this only resulted in his dragging his nails across it. He was a long lean man in a plaid sports coat with hair the color of black shoe polish. I said, "You Buster Smith?"

He said, "No."

I got his wallet out of his back pocket and looked at his driver's license. "Yes, you are," I said. "I bet you always got caught when you played hide-and-go-seek as a kid."

He got to one knee. "I did, actually."

I went over and got my guns, said, "I wouldn't try anything. I shoot you, then Leonard will shoot everyone else, and we'll have a hard time explaining things. But you'll be dead."

We didn't go to jail.

That's the important part. Let me tell you why. So when it was done and everyone was hauled in, including me and Leonard, they waltzed us into the police chief. This is after interrogations, searches, a rubber glove up the asshole, just in case we were hiding hand grenades. He was a nice-looking guy with his black hair cut close to his head and one ear that stood out more than the other, as if it were signaling for a turn. He sat behind a big mahogany desk. There was a little sign on the desk that read: POLICE CHIEF.

"Well now, Hap Collins," he said.

I recognized him. A little older. Still fit. James Dell. We had gone to school together.

"It's been a while," he said. "What I remember best about you is I don't like you."

"It's a big club," Leonard said. "Hap even has a newsletter."

"Me and Jim dated the same girl," I said.

"Not at the same time," Jim said.

"He dated her last," I said.

"That's right. And I married her."

"So, you won," I said.

"Way I like to see it," James said. "You boys raised some hell. And you shot people. And you hit people. And Hap, you killed a guy. I also got word there's two boys with broken legs over in No Enterprise. They gave themselves up to the sheriff over there."

"Nice guy," I said.

"One of the men you shot was a police officer," said James.

"I know. He was waiting in line to rape a young woman. How is she, by the way?"

"Hospital. Touch-and-go for a while. But she made it. Apparently she's no stranger to drugs, so maybe she had some tolerance. Hadn't eaten in days. Buster Smith, we talked to him. He came apart like a fresh biscuit. He was only tough when his money worked for him. That cop, by the way, he was the police chief."

"Oh," Leonard said. "Then, what are you?"

"The new police chief. I should also mention that the mayor is the one that caught a stray bullet and is as dead as an old bean can."

"Mayor. Police chief. We had quite a night," I said.

To make this part of the story short, we had to stay in the jail till our friend Marvin Hanson could get us a lawyer, and then we got out, and then we got no-billed, in spite of the fact we had hunted the bastard down and caused quite a ruckus. The former police chief was dead, by our hand, and the mayor was on the deceased list as well, by a stray slug, and the others who had been in the row of chairs were all prominent citizens. It was best to take it easy on us, let them cover their own dirt in their own way.

Thing was simply this: the crime being done to Tillie was so bad they let us pretty much skate on self-defense. Hell, after all, it is Texas.

Brett and I climbed into bed and she lay in the crook of my arm.

"Tillie is going to be out of the hospital tomorrow," Brett said.

She had spent about three months in there. She had been in a bad way. I had to say this for the kid, she was tough as yesterday's fajita meat.

"I have to go get her, then," Brett said.

"All right," I said.

"I know you don't like her."

"Correct."

"You didn't have to do what you did."

"Yes, I did."

"For me?"

"You and her."

"But you don't like her."

"I don't like a lot of things," I said, "but you love her. You think she's a bent twig, and maybe you're right. No one deserves that."

"But she sets herself up for it, right?"

"Yeah," I said. "She does. I don't think she'll ever change. Sometime soon, she doesn't, she's going to be dead. She picks men like ducks pick June bugs. At random."

"I know. I tried to be a good mother."

"I know that too, so don't start on how you failed. You did what you could."

"I did set her father's head on fire," Brett said.

"Yes, you did," I said. "But by all accounts, he had it coming."

"He did, you know."

"Never doubted it."

"I love you, Hap."

"And I love you, Brett."

"Want to lose five minutes out of your life the hard way?" she said.

I laughed. "Now, that's not nice."

She laughed, rolled over, and turned off the light. And then she was very nice.

Michael Swanwick

Michael Swanwick made his debut in 1980, and in the thirty-four years that have followed has established himself as one of SF's most prolific and consistently excellent writers at short lengths, as well as one of the premier novelists of his generation. He has won the Theodore Sturgeon Award and the *Asimov's* Readers Award poll. In 1991, his novel *Stations of the Tide* won him a Nebula Award as well, and in 1996 he won the World Fantasy Award for his story "Radio Waves." He's won the Hugo Award five times between 1999 and 2004, for his stories "The Very Pulse of the Machine," "Scherzo with Tyrannosaur," "The Dog Said Bow-Wow," "Slow Life," and "Legions in Time." His other books include the novels *In the Drift, Vacuum Flowers, The Iron Dragon's Daughter, Jack Faust, Bones of the Earth,* and *The Dragons of Babel.* His short fiction has been assembled in *Gravity's Angels, A Geography of Unknown Lands, Slow Dancing Through Time, Moon Dogs, Puck Aleshire's Abecedary, Tales of Old Earth, Cigar-Box Faust and Other Miniatures, Michael Swanwick's Field Guide to the Mesozoic Megafauna,* and *The Periodic Table of SF.* His most recent books are a massive retrospective collection, *The Best of Michael Swanwick,* and a new novel, *Dancing with Bears.* Swanwick lives in Philadelphia with his wife, Marianne Porter. He has a Web site at: www.michaelswanwick.com and maintains a blog at www.floggingbabel.blogspot.com.

Here he takes his famous rogues Darger and Surplus, con men extraordinaire, to a surreal Post-Utopian New Orleans full of pygmy mastodons, sea serpents, and lots and *lots* of zombies, where they learn that making money—literally—may be easy, but hanging on to it and staying alive is very, very hard.

TAWNY PETTICOATS

Michael Swanwick

The independent port city and (some said) pirate haven of New Orleans was home to many a strange sight. It was a place where sea serpents hauled ships past fields worked by zombie laborers to docks where cargo was loaded into wooden wagons to be pulled through streets of crushed oyster shells by teams of pygmy mastodons as small as Percheron horses. So none thought it particularly noteworthy when, for three days, an endless line of young women waited in the hallway outside a luxury suite in the Maison Fema for the opportunity to raise their skirts or open their blouses to display a tattooed thigh, breast, or buttock to two judges who sat on twin chairs watching solemnly, asked a few questions, thanked them for their time, and then showed them out.

The women had come in response to a handbill, posted throughout several parishes, that read:

SEEKING AN HEIRESS

ARE YOU . . .

A YOUNG WOMAN BETWEEN THE AGES OF 18 AND 21?

FATHERLESS?

TATTOOED FROM BIRTH ON AN INTIMATE PART OF YOUR BODY?

IF SO, YOU MAY BE ENTITLED TO GREAT RICHES

INQUIRE DAYTIMES, SUITE 1, MAISON FEMA

"You'd think I'd be tired of this by now," Darger commented during a brief break in the ritual. "And yet I am not."

"The infinite variety of ways in which women can be beautiful is indeed amazing," Surplus agreed. "As is the eagerness of so many to display that beauty." He opened the door. "Next."

A woman strode into the room, trailing smoke from a cheroot. She was dauntingly tall—six feet and a hand, if an inch—and her dress, trimmed with silver lace, was the same shade of golden brown as her skin. Surplus indicated a crystal ashtray on the sideboard and, with a gracious nod of thanks, she stubbed out her cigar.

"Your name?" Darger said after Surplus had regained his chair.

"My real name, you mean, or my stage name?"

"Why, whichever you please."

"I'll give you the real one, then." The young woman doffed her hat and tugged off her gloves. She laid them neatly together on the sideboard. "It's Tawnymoor Petticoats. You can call me Tawny."

"Tell us something about yourself, Tawny," Surplus said.

"I was born a carny and worked forty-milers all my life," Tawny said, unbuttoning her blouse. "Most recently, I was in the sideshow as the Sleeping Beauty Made Immortal By Utopian Technology But Doomed Never To Awaken. I lay in a glass coffin covered by nothing but my own hair and a strategically placed hand, while the audience tried to figure out if I was alive or not. I've got good breath control." She folded the blouse and set it down by her gloves and hat. "Jake—my husband—was the barker. He'd size up the audience and when he saw a ripe mark, he'd catch 'im on the way out and whisper that for a couple of banknotes it could be arranged to spend some private time with me. Then he'd go out back and peer in through a slit in the canvas."

Tawny stepped out of her skirt and set it atop the blouse. She began unlacing her petticoats. "When the mark had his trousers off and was about to climb in the coffin, Jake would come roaring out, bellowing that he was only supposed to look—not to take advantage of my vulnerable condition." Placing her underthings atop the skirt, she undid her garters and proceeded to roll down her stockings. "That was usually good for the contents of his wallet."

"You were working the badger game, you mean?" Surplus asked cautiously.

"Mostly, I just lay there. But I was ready to rear up and coldcock the sumbidge if he got out of hand. And we worked other scams too. The pigeon drop, the fiddle game, the rip deal, you name it."

Totally naked now, the young woman lifted her great masses of black curls with both hands, exposing the back of her neck. "Then one night the mark was halfway into the coffin—and no Jake. So I opened my eyes real sudden and screamed in the bastard's face. Over he went, hit his head on the floor, and I didn't wait to find out if he was unconscious or dead. I stole his jacket and went looking for my husband. Turns out Jake had run off with the Snake Woman. She dumped him two weeks later and he wanted me to take him back, but I wasn't having none of that." She turned around slowly, so that Darger and Surplus could examine every inch of her undeniably admirable flesh.

Darger cleared his throat. "Um . . . you don't appear to have a tattoo."

"Yeah, I saw through that one right away. Talked to some of the girls you'd interviewed and they said you'd asked them lots of questions about themselves but hadn't molested them in any way. Not all of 'em were happy with that last bit. Particularly after they'd gone to all the trouble of getting themselves inked. So, putting two and four together, I figured you were running a scam requiring a female partner with quick wits and larcenous proclivities."

Tawny Petticoats put her hands on her hips and smiled. "Well? Do I get the job?"

Grinning like a dog—which was not surprising, for his source genome was entirely canine—Surplus stood, extending a paw. But Darger quickly got between him and the young woman, saying, "If you will pardon us for just a moment, Ms. Petticoats, my friend and I must consult for a moment in the back room. You may use the time to dress yourself."

When the two males were secluded, Darger whispered furiously, "Thank God I was able to stop you! You were about to enlist that young woman into our conspiracy."

"Well, and why not?" Surplus murmured equally quietly. "We were looking for a woman of striking appearance, not overly bound to conventional morality, and possessed of the self-confidence, initiative, and inventiveness a good swindler requires. Tawny comes up aces on all counts."

"Working with an amateur is one thing—but this woman is a professional. She will sleep with both of us, turn us against each other, and in the end abscond with the swag, leaving us with nothing but embarrassment and regret for all our efforts."

"That is a sexist and, if I may dare say so, ungallant slander upon the fair sex, and I am astonished to hear it coming from your mouth."

Darger shook his head sadly. "It is not all women but all female confidence tricksters I abjure. I speak from sad—and repeated—experience."

"Well, if you insist on doing without this blameless young creature," Surplus said, folding his arms, "then I insist on your doing without me."

"My dear sir!"

"I must be true to my principles."

Further argumentation, Darger saw, would be useless. So, putting the best possible appearance on things, he emerged from the back room to say, "You have the job, my dear." From a jacket pocket he produced a silver-filigreed vinaigrette and, unscrewing its cap, extracted from it a single pill. "Swallow this and you'll have the tattoo we require by morning. You'll want to run it past your pharmacist first, of course, to verify—"

"Oh, I trust you. If y'all had just been after tail, you wouldn't've waited for me. Some of those gals was sharp lookers for sure." Tawny swallowed the pill. "So what's the dodge?"

"We're going to work the black-money scam," Surplus said.

"Oh, I have always wanted a shot at running that one!" With a whoop, Tawny threw her arms about them both.

Though his fingers itched to do so, Darger was very careful not to check to see if his wallet was still there.

The next day, ten crates of black money—actually, rectangles of scrap parchment dyed black in distant Vicksburg—were carried into the hotel by zombie laborers and then, at Surplus's direction, piled against the outside of Tawny's door so that, hers being the central room of the suite, the only way to enter or leave it was through his or Darger's rooms. Then, leaving the lady to see to her dress and makeup, her new partners set out to speak to their respective marks.

Darger began at the city's busy docklands.

The office of the speculator Jean-Nagin Lafitte were tastefully opulent and dominated by a *Mauisaurus* skull, decorated with scrimshaw filigree chased in silver. "Duke" Lafitte, as he styled himself, or "Pirate" Lafitte, as he was universally known, was a slim, handsome man with olive skin, long and flowing hair, and a mustache so thin it might have been drawn on with an eyebrow pencil. Where other men of wealth might carry a cane, he affected a coiled whip, which he wore on his belt.

"Renting an ingot of silver!" he exclaimed. "I never heard of such a thing."

"It is a simple enough proposition," Darger said. "Silver serves as a catalyst for a certain bioindustrial process, the precise nature of which I am not at liberty to divulge to you. The scheme involves converting bar silver to a colloidal slurry which, when the process is complete, will be recovered and melted back into bar form. You would lose nothing. Further, we will only tie up your wealth for, oh, let us say ten days to be on the safe side. In return for which we are prepared to offer you a 10 percent return on your investment. A very tidy profit for no risk at all."

A small and ruthless smile played upon the speculator's lips. "There is the risk of your simply taking the silver and absconding with it."

"That is an outrageous implication, and from a man I respected less highly than I do you, I would not put up with it. However"—Darger gestured out the window at the busy warehouses and transshipment buildings—"I understand that you own half of everything we see. Lend my consortium a building in which to perform our operation and then place as many guards as you like around that building. We will bring in our apparatus and you will bring in the silver. Deal?"

For a brief moment, Pirate Lafitte hesitated. Then, "Done!" he snapped, and offered his hand. "For 15 percent. Plus rental of the building."

They shook, and Darger said, "You will have no objection to having the ingot tested by a reputable assayer."

In the French Quarter, meanwhile, Surplus was having an almost identical conversation with a slight and acerbic woman, clad in a severe black dress, who was not only the mayor of New Orleans but also the proprietress of its largest and most notorious brothel. Behind her, alert and unspeaking, stood two uniformed ape-men from the Canadian Northwest, both with the expressions of baffled anger common to beasts that have been elevated almost but not quite to human intelligence. "An assayist?" she demanded. "Is my word not good enough for you? And if it is not, should we be doing business at all?"

"The answer to all three of your questions, Madam-Mayor Tresjolie, is yes," Surplus said amiably. "The assay is for your own protection. As you doubtless know, silver is routinely adulterated with other metals. When we are done with the silver, the slurry will be melted down and recast into an ingot. Certainly, you will want to know that the bar returned to you is of equal worth to the bar you rented out."

"Hmmm." They were sitting in the lobby of the madam-mayor's *maison de tolérance,* she in a flaring wicker chair whose similarity to a throne could not possibly be unintentional, and Surplus in a wooden folding chair facing her. Because it was still early afternoon, the facility was not open for business. But messengers and government flunkies came and went. Now one such whispered in Madam-Mayor Tresjolie's ear. She waved him away. "Seventeen and a half percent, take it or leave it."

"I'll take it."

"Good," Tresjolie said. "I have business with the zombie master now. Move your chair alongside mine and stay to watch. If we are to do business, you will find this salubrious."

A round and cheerful man entered the public room, followed by half a dozen zombies. Surplus studied these with interest. Though their eyes were dull, their faces were stiff, and there was an unhealthy sheen to their skin, they looked in no way like the rotting corpses of Utopian legend. Rather, they looked like day laborers who had been worked into a state of complete exhaustion. Which doubtless was the case.

"Good morning!" said the jolly man, rubbing his hands briskly together. "I have brought this week's coffle of debtors who, having served their time, are now eligible for forgiveness and manumission."

"I had wondered at the source of your involuntary labor force," Surplus said. "They are unfortunates who fell into arrears, then?"

"Exactly so," said the zombie master. "New Orleans does not engage in the barbarous and expensive practice of funding debtors prisons. Instead, debt-criminals are chemically rendered incapable of independent thought and put to work until they have paid off their debt to society. Which today's happy fellows have done." With a roguish wink, he added, "You may want to keep this in mind before running up too great a line of credit at the rooms upstairs. Are you ready to begin, Madam-Mayor Tresjolie?"

"You may proceed, Master Bones."

Master Bones gestured imperiously and the first zombie shuffled forward. "Through profligacy you fell into debt," he said, "and through honest labor you have earned your way out. Open your mouth."

The pallid creature obeyed. Master Bones produced a spoon and dipped into a saltcellar on a nearby table. He dumped the salt into the man's mouth. "Now swallow."

By gradual degrees, a remarkable transformation came over the man. He straightened and looked about him with tentative alertness. "I . . ." he said. "I remember now. Is my . . . is my wife . . . ?"

"Silence," the zombie master said. "The ceremony is not yet complete." The Canadian guardsmen had shifted position to defend their mistress should the disoriented ex-zombie attack her.

"You are hereby declared a free citizen of New Orleans again, and indebted to no man," Tresjolie said solemnly. "Go and overspend no more." She extended a leg and lifted her skirts above her ankle. "You may now kiss my foot."

* * *

"So did you ask Tresjolie for a line of credit at her sporting house?" Tawny asked when Surplus reported his adventure to his confederates.

"Certainly not!" Surplus exclaimed. "I told her instead that it has always been my ambition to own a small but select private brothel, one dedicated solely to my own personal use. A harem, if you will, but one peopled by a rotating staff of well-paid employees. I suggested I might shortly be in a position to commission her to find an appropriate hotel and create such an institution for me."

"What did she say?"

"She told me that she doubted I was aware of exactly how expensive such an operation would be."

"And you said to her?"

"That I didn't think money would be a problem," Surplus said airily. "Because I expected to come into a great deal of it very soon."

Tawny crowed with delight. "Oh, you boys are such fun!"

"In unrelated news," Darger said, "your new dress has come."

"I saw it when it first arrived." Tawny made a face. "It is not calculated to show off my body to its best advantage—or to any advantage at all, come to that."

"It is indeed aggressively modest," Darger agreed. "However, your character is demure and inexperienced. To her innocent eyes, New Orleans is a terribly wicked place, indeed a cesspool of carnality and related sins. Therefore, she needs to be protected at all times by unrevealing apparel and stalwart men of the highest moral character."

"Further," Surplus amplified, "she is the weak point in our plans, for whoever has possession of her tattoo and knows its meaning can dispense with us entirely by kidnapping her off the street."

"Oh!" Tawny said in a small voice, clearly intended to arouse the protective instincts of any man nearby.

Surplus took an instinctive step toward her, and then caught himself. He grinned like the carnivore he was. "You'll do."

The third meeting with a potential investor took place that evening in a dimly lit club in a run-down parish on the fringe of the French Quarter—

for the entertainment was, in the public mind, far too louche for even that notoriously open-minded neighborhood. Pallid waitresses moved lifelessly between the small tables, taking orders and delivering drinks while a small brass-and-drums jazz ensemble played appropriately sleazy music to accompany the stage show.

"I see that you are no aficionado of live sex displays," the zombie master Jeremy Bones said. The light from the candle sconce on the table made the beads of sweat on his face shine like luminous drops of rain.

"The artistic success of such displays depends entirely on the degree to which they agree with one's own sexual proclivities," Darger replied. "I confess that mine lie elsewhere. But never mind that. Returning to the subject at hand: The terms are agreeable to you, then?"

"They are. I am unclear, however, as to why you insist the assay be performed at the Bank of San Francisco, when New Orleans has several fine financial institutions of its own."

"All of which are owned in part by you, Madam-Mayor Tresjolie, and Duke Lafitte."

"Pirate Lafitte, you mean. An assay is an assay and a bank is a bank. Why should it matter to you which one is employed?"

"Earlier today, you brought six zombies to the mayor to be freed. Assuming this is a typical week, that would be roughly three hundred zombies per year. Yet all the menial work in the city has been handed over to zombies and there still remain tens of thousands at work in the plantations that line the river."

"Many of those who fall into debt draw multiyear sentences."

"I asked around and discovered that Lafitte's ships import some two hundred prisoners a week from municipalities and territories all the way up the Mississippi to St. Louis."

A small smile played on the fat man's face. "It is true that many government bodies find it cheaper to pay us to deal with their troublemakers than to build prisons for them."

"Madam-Mayor Tresjolie condemns these unfortunates into the city's penal system, you pay her by body count, and after they have been zombified you lease them out for menial labor at prices that employers find irresistible. Those who enter your service rarely leave it."

"If a government official or family member presents me with papers proving that somebody's debt to society has been paid off, I am invariably happy to free them. I grant you that few ever come to me with such documentation. But I am always available to those who do. Exactly what is your objection to this arrangement?"

"Objection?" Darger said in surprise. "I have no objection. This is your system and as an outsider I have no say in it. I am merely explaining the reason why I wished to use an independent bank for the assay."

"Which is?"

"Simply that, happy though I am to deal with you three individually, collectively I find you far too shrewd." Darger turned to stare at the stage, where naked zombies coupled joylessly. Near the front, a spectator removed several banknotes from his wallet and tapped them meaningfully on his table. One of the lifeless waitresses picked up the money and led him through a curtain at the back of the room. "Acting together, I suspect you would swallow me and my partners in a single gulp."

"Oh, there is no fear of that," Master Bones said. "We three only act collectively when there is serious profit in the offing. Your little enterprise—whatever it is—hardly qualifies."

"I am relieved to hear it."

The next day, the three conspirators made three distinct trips to the Assay Office at the New Orleans branch of the Bank of San Francisco. On the first trip, one of Madam-Mayor Tresjolie's green-jacketed zombie bodyguards opened a lockbox, withdrew a silver ingot, and placed it on the workbench. Then, to the astonishment of both the mayor and the assayist, Surplus directed his own hired zombies to hoist several heavy leather bags to the bench as well, and with the aid of his colleagues began pulling out drills, scales, acids, reagents, and other tools and supplies and setting them in working order.

The affronted assayist opened his mouth to object, but—"I'm sure you won't mind if we provide our own equipment," Darger said suavely. "We are strangers here, and while nobody questions the probity of San Francisco's most prestigious financial concern, it is only good business to take proper precautions."

As he was talking, Tawny and Surplus both reached for the scales at once, collided, and it almost sent them flying. Faces turned and hands reached out to catch them. But, in the fact, it was Surplus who saved the apparatus from disaster.

"Oops," Tawny said, coloring prettily.

Swiftly, the assayist performed his tests. At their conclusion, he looked up from the ingot. "The finding is .925," he said. "Sterling standard."

With an absent nod, Madam-Mayor Tresjolie acknowledged his judgment. Then she said, "The girl. How much do you want for her?"

As one, Darger and Surplus turned. Then they subtly shifted position so that one stood to either side of Tawny. "Ms. Petticoats is our ward," Darger said, "and therefore, it goes without saying, not for sale. Also, yours is not an entirely reputable business for so innocent a child as she."

"Innocence is in high demand at my establishment. I'll give you the silver ingot. To keep. Do with it as you wish."

"Believe me, madam. In not so very long, I shall consider silver ingots to be so much petty cash."

Master Bones watched the assay, including even the chaotic assembly of the trio's equipment, with a beatific smile. Yet all the while, his attention kept straying to Tawny. Finally, he pursed his lips and said, "There might be a place in my club for your young friend. If you'd consider leasing her to me for, oh, let's say a year, I'd gladly forgo my 20 percent profit on this deal." Turning to Tawny, he said, "Do not worry, my sweet. Under the influence of the zombie drugs you will feel nothing, and afterwards you will remember nothing. It will be as if none of it ever happened. Further, since you'd be paid a commission on each commercial encounter performed, you'd emerge with a respectable sum being held in trust for you."

Ignoring Tawny's glare of outrage, Darger suavely said, "In strictest confidence, sir, we have already turned down a far better offer for her than yours today. But my partner and I would not part with our dear companion for any amount of money. She is to us a treasure beyond price."

"I'm ready," the assayist said. "Where do you wish me to drill?"

Darger airily waved a finger over the ingot and then, seemingly at random, touched a spot at the exact center of the bar. "Right there."

"I understand that on the street they call me the Pirate," Jean-Nagin Lafitte said with quiet intensity. "This, however, is an insolence I will not tolerate to my face. Yes, I do chance to share a name with the legendary freebooter. But you will find that I have never committed an illegal act in my life."

"Nor do you today, sir!" Darger cried. "This is a strictly legitimate business arrangement."

"So I presume or I would not be here. Nevertheless, you can understand why I must take offense at having you and your clumsy confederates question the quality of my silver."

"Say no more, sir! We are all gentlemen here—save, of course, for Ms. Petticoats who is a gently reared Christian orphan. If my word is good enough for you, then your word is good enough for me. We may dispose of the assay." Darger coughed discreetly. "However, just for my own legal protection, in the absence of an assay, I shall require a notarized statement from you declaring that you will be satisfied with whatever quality of silver we return to you."

Pirate Lafitte's stare would have melted iron. But it failed to wilt Darger's pleasant smile. At last, he said, "Very well, run the assay."

Negligently, Darger spun a finger in the air. Down it came on the exact center of the bar. "There."

While the assayist was working, Pirate Lafitte said, "I was wondering if your Ms. Petticoats might be available to—"

"She is not for sale!" Darger said briskly. "Not for sale, not for rent, not for barter, not available for acquisition on any terms whatsoever. Period."

Looking irritated, Pirate Lafitte said, "I was *going* to ask if she might be interested in going hunting with me tomorrow. There is some interesting game to be found in the bayous."

"Nor is she available for social occasions." Darger turned to the assayist. "Well, sir?"

"Standard sterling," the man said. "Yet again."

"I expected no less."

For the sake of appearances, after the assays were complete, the three swindlers sent the zombies with their lab equipment back to Maison Fema and went out to supper together. Following which, they took a genteel stroll about town. Tawny, who had been confined to her room while negotiations took place, was particularly glad of the latter. But it was with relief that Darger, Surplus, and Tawny saw the heavy bags waiting for them on the sitting-room table of their suite. "Who shall do the honors?" Darger asked.

"The lady, of course," Surplus said with a little bow.

Tawny curtsied and then, pushing aside a hidden latch at the bottom of one of the bags, slid out a silver ingot. From another bag, she slid out a second. Then, from a third, a third. A sigh of relief went up from all three conspirators at the sight of the silver glimmering in the lanternlight.

"That was right smartly done, when you changed the fake bars for the real ones," Tawny said.

Darger politely demurred. "No, it was the distraction that made the trick possible, and in this regard you were both exemplary. Even the assayist, who was present all three times you almost sent the equipment to the floor, suspected nothing."

"But tell me something," Tawny said. "Why did you make the substitution before the assay, rather than after? The other way around, you wouldn't have needed to have that little plug of silver in the middle for the sample to be drawn from. Just a silver-plated lead bar."

"We are dealing with suspicious people. This way, they first had the ingots confirmed as genuine and then saw that we came nowhere near them afterwards. The ingots are in a safety-deposit box in a reputable bank, so to their minds there is not the least risk. All is on the up-and-up."

"But we're not going to stop here, are we?" Tawny asked anxiously. "I do so want to work the black-money scam."

"Have no fear, my lovely," Surplus said, "this is only the beginning. But it serves as a kind of insurance policy for us. Even should the scheme go bad, we have already turned a solid profit." He poured brandy into three small glasses and handed them around. "To whom shall we drink?"

"To Madam-Mayor Tresjolie!" Darger said.

They drank, and then Tawny said, "What do you make of her? Professionally, I mean."

"She is far shrewder than she would have you think," Surplus replied. "But, as you are doubtless aware, the self-consciously shrewd are always the easiest to mislead." He poured a second glass. "To Master Bones!"

They drank. Tawny said, "And of him?"

"He is more problematic," Darger said. "A soft man with a brutal streak underneath his softness. In some ways he hardly seems human."

"Perhaps he has been sampling his own product?" Surplus suggested.

"Puffer-fish extract, you mean? No. His mind is active enough. But I catch not the least glimmer of empathy from him. I suspect that he's been associating with zombies so long that he's come to think we're all like them."

The final toast inevitably went to Pirate Lafitte.

"I think he's cute," Tawny said. "Only maybe you don't agree?"

"He is a fraud and a poseur," Darger replied. "A scoundrel who passes himself off as a gentleman, and a manipulator of the legal system who insists he is the most honest of citizens. Consequently, I like him quite a bit. I believe that he is a man we can do business with. Mark my words, when the three of them come to see us tomorrow, it will be at his instigation."

For a time they talked business. Then Surplus broke out a deck of cards. They played euchre and canasta and poker, and because they played for matches, nobody objected when the game turned into a competition to see how deftly the cards could be dealt from the bottom of the deck or flicked out of the sleeve into one's hand. Nor was there any particular outcry when in one memorable hand, eleven aces were laid on the table at once.

At last Darger said, "Look at the time! It will be a long day tomorrow," and they each went to their respective rooms.

That night, as Darger was drifting off to sleep, he heard the door connecting his room with Tawny's quietly open and shut. There was a rustle of sheets as she slipped into his bed. Then the warmth of Tawny's naked body pressed against his own, and her hand closed about his most private part. Abruptly, he was wide-awake.

"What on earth do you think you're doing?" he whispered fiercely.

Unexpectedly, Tawny released her hold on Darger and punched him hard in his shoulder. "Oh, it's so easy for you," she retorted, equally quietly. "It's so easy for men! That hideous old woman tried to buy me. That awful little man wanted you to let him drug me. And God only knows what intentions Pirate Lafitte holds. You'll notice they all made their propositions to you. Not a one of them said a word to me." Hot tears fell on Darger's chest. "All my life I have had male protectors—and needed them too. My daddy, until I ran away. My first husband, until he got eaten by giant crabs. Then various boyfriends and finally that creep Jake."

"You have nothing to worry about. Surplus and I have never abandoned a confederate, nor shall we ever. Our reputation is spotless in this regard."

"I tell myself that, and daytimes I'm fine with it. But at night . . . well, this past week has been the longest I ever went without a man's body to comfort me."

"Yes, but surely you understand . . ."

Tawny drew herself up. Even in the dim half-light of the moon through the window she was a magnificent sight. Then she leaned down to kiss Darger's cheek and murmured into his ear, "I've never had to beg a man before, but . . . Please?"

Darger considered himself a moral man. But there was only so much temptation a man could resist without losing all respect for himself.

The next morning, Darger awoke alone. He thought of the events of last night and smiled. He thought of their implications and scowled. Then he went down to the dining room for breakfast.

"What comes next?" Tawny asked, after they had fortified themselves with chicory coffee, beignets, and sliced baconfruit.

"We have planted suspicions in the minds of our three backers that there is more profit to be had than we are offering to share," Surplus said. "We have given them a glimpse of our mysterious young ward and suggested that she is key to the enterprise. We have presented them with a puzzle to which they can think of no solution. On reflection, they can only conclude that the sole reason we have the upper hand is that we can play them off of one another." He popped the last of his beignet into his mouth. "So sooner or later they will unite and demand of us an explanation."

"In the meantime . . ." Darger said.

"I know, I know. Back to my dreary old room to play solitaire and read the sort of uplifting literature appropriate to a modest young virgin."

"It's important to stay in character," Surplus said.

"I understand that. Next time, however, please make me something that doesn't need to be stored in the dark, like a sack of potatoes. The niece of a Spanish prisoner, perhaps. Or a socialite heiress. Or even a harlot."

"You are a Woman of Mystery," Darger said. "Which is a time-honored and some would say enviable role to play."

Thus it was that when Darger and Surplus left Maison Fema—at precisely ten o'clock, as they had made it their invariant habit—they were not entirely astonished to find their three benefactors all in a group, waiting for them. A brusque exchange of threats and outrage later, and protesting every step of the way, they led their marks to their suite.

The three bedrooms all opened off of a sunny common room. Given the room's elegant appointments, the crates of black paper that had been stacked in front of Tawny Petticoats's door looked glaringly out of place.

Gesturing their guests to chairs, Darger adopted an air of resignation and said, "In order to adequately explain our enterprise, we must go back two generations to a time before San Francisco became the financial center of North America. The visionary leaders of that great city-state determined to found a new economy upon uncounterfeitable banknotes, and to this end employed the greatest bacterial engraver of his age, Phineas Whipsnade McGonigle."

"That is an unlikely name," Madam-Mayor Tresjolie sniffed.

"It was of course his *nom de gravure,* assumed to protect him from kidnappers and the like," Surplus explained. "In private life, he was known as Magnus Norton."

"Go on."

Darger resumed his narrative. "The results you know. Norton crafted one hundred and thirteen different bacteria which, as part of their natural functions, lay down layer upon layer of multicolored ink in delicate arabesques so intricate as to be the despair of coin-clippers and paperhangers everywhere. This, combined with their impeccable monetary policies, has made the San Francisco dollar the common currency of the hundred nations of North America. Alas for them, there was one weak point in their enterprise—Norton himself.

"Norton secretly created his own printing vats, employing the bacteria he himself had created, and proceeded to mass-produce banknotes that were not only indistinguishable from the genuine item but for all intents and purposes *were* the genuine item. He created enough of them to make himself the wealthiest man on the continent.

"Unfortunately for that great man, he tried to underpay his paper supplier, precipitating an argument that ended with his being arrested by the San Francisco authorities."

Pirate Lafitte raised an elegant forefinger. "How do you know all this?" he asked.

"My colleague and I are journalists," Darger said. Seeing his audience's expressions, he raised both hands. "Not of the muckraking variety, I hasten to assure you! Corruption is a necessary and time-honored concomitant of any functioning government, which we support wholeheartedly. No, we write profiles of public figures, lavishing praise in direct proportion to their private generosity; human-interest stories of heroic boys rescuing heiresses from fires and of kittens swallowed by crocodiles and yet miraculously passing through their alimentary systems unharmed; and of course amusing looks back at the forgotten histories of local scoundrels whom the passage of time has rendered unthreatening."

"It was this last that led us to Norton's story," Surplus elucidated.

"Indeed. We discovered that by a quirk of San Francisco's labyrinthine banking regulations, Norton's monetary creations could neither be destroyed nor distributed as valid currency. So to prevent their misuse, the banknotes were subjected to another biolithographic process whereby they were deeply impregnated with black ink so cunningly composed that no known process could bleach it from the bills without destroying the paper in the process.

"Now, here's where our tale gets interesting. Norton was, you'll recall, incomparable in his craft. Naturally, the city fathers were reluctant to forgo his services. So, rather than have him languish in an ordinary prison, they walled and fortified a mansion, equipped it with a laboratory and all the resources he required, and put him to work.

"Imagine how Norton felt! One moment he was on the brink of realizing vast wealth, and the next he was a virtual slave. So long as he cooperated, he was given fine foods, wine, even conjugal visits with his wife . . . But, comfortable though his prison was, he could never leave it. He was, however, a cunning man and though he could not engineer his escape, he managed to devise a means of revenge: If he could not have vast wealth, then his descendants would. Someday, the provenance of the black paper would be forgotten and it would be put up for public auction as eventually occurs to all the useless lumber a bureaucracy acquires. His children or grandchildren or great-great-grandchildren would acquire it and, utilizing an ingenious method of his own devising, convert it back into working currency and so make themselves rich beyond Croesus."

"The ancients had a saying," Surplus interjected. "'If you want to make God laugh, tell him your plans.' The decades passed, Norton died, and the black paper stayed in storage. By the time we began our researches, his family was apparently extinct. He had three children: a daughter who was not interested in men, a son who died young, and another son who never wed. The second son, however, traveled about in his early adulthood, and in the same neglected cache of family papers where we discovered Norton's plans, we found evidence that he was paying child support for a female bastard he had sired here some twenty years ago. So, utilizing an understanding of the city bureaucracy which Norton's wife and children lacked, we bribed the appropriate official to sell us the crates of seemingly worthless paper and came to New Orleans. Where we found Tawny Petticoats."

"This explains nothing," Madam-Mayor Tresjolie said.

Darger sighed heavily. "We had hoped you would be satisfied with a partial explanation. Now I see that it is all or nothing. Here before you are the crates of blackened banknotes." A plank had been removed from one of the topmost crates. He reached in to seize a handful of black paper rectangles, fanned them for all to see, and then put them back. "My colleague and I will now introduce you to our young charge."

Swiftly, Darger and Surplus unstacked the crates before the doorway, placing them to either side. Then Surplus rapped on the door. "Ms. Petticoats? Are you decent? We have visitors to see you."

The door opened. Tawny's large brown eyes peered apprehensively from the gloom. "Come in," she said in a little voice.

They all shuffled inside. Tawny looked first at Darger and then at Surplus. When they would not meet her eyes, she ducked her head, blushing. "I guess I know what y'all came here to see. Only . . . must I? Must I really?"

"Yes, child, you must," Surplus said gruffly.

Tawny tightened her mouth and raised her chin, staring straight ahead of herself like the captain of a schooner sailing into treacherous waters. Reaching around her back, she began unbuttoning her dress.

"Magnus Norton designed what no other man could have—a microorganism that would eat the black ink permeating the banknotes without damaging the other inks in any way. Simply place the notes in the proper liquid nutrient, add powdered silver as a catalyst, and within a week there will be nothing but perfect San Francisco money and a slurry of silver," Darger said. "However, he still faced the problem of passing the information of how to create the organism to his family. In a manner, moreover, robust enough to survive what he knew would be decades of neglect."

Tawny had unbuttoned her dress. Now, placing a hand upon her bosom to hold the dress in place, she drew one arm from its sleeve. Then, switching hands, she drew out the other. "Now?" she said.

Surplus nodded.

With tiny, doll-like steps, Tawny turned to face the wall. Then she lowered her dress so that they could see her naked back. On it was a large tattoo in seven bright colors, of three concentric circles. Each circle was made of a great number of short, near-parallel lines, all radiant from the unmarked skin at the tattoo's center. Anyone who could read a gene map could easily use it to create the organism it described.

Master Bones, who had not spoken before now, said, "That's an *E. coli,* isn't it?"

"A variant on it, yes, sir. Norton wrote this tattoo into his own genome and then sired three children upon his wife, believing they would have many more in their turn. But fate is a fickle lady, and Ms. Petticoats is the last of her line. She, however, will suffice." He turned to Tawny. "You may clothe yourself again. Our guests have had their curiosities satisfied, and now they will leave."

Darger led the group back to the front room, closing the door firmly behind him. "Now," he said. "You have learned what you came to learn. At the cost, I might mention, of violently depriving an innocent maiden of her modesty."

"That is a swinish thing to say!" Pirate Lafitte snapped.

In the silence that followed his outburst, all could hear Tawny Petticoats in the next room, sobbing her heart out.

"Your work here is done," Darger said, "and I just ask you to leave."

Now that Tawny Petticoats was no longer a secret, there was nothing for the three conspirators to do but wait for the equipment they had supposedly sent for upriver—and for their marks to each separately approach them with very large bribes to buy their process and the crates of black paper away from them. As simple logic stipulated that they inevitably must.

The very next day, after the morning mail had brought two notes proposing meetings, the trio went out for breakfast at a sidewalk café. They had just finished and were beginning their second cups of coffee when Tawny looked over Darger's shoulder and exclaimed, "Oh, merciful God in heaven! It's Jake." Then, seeing her companions' incomprehension, she added, "My husband! He's talking to Pirate Lafitte. They're coming this way."

"Keep smiling," Darger murmured. "Feign unconcern. Surplus, you know what to do."

It took a count of ten for the interlopers to reach their table.

"Jake!" Surplus exclaimed in evident surprise, beginning to rise from his chair.

"Come for his pay, no doubt." Darger drew from his pocket the wad of bills—one of large denomination on the outside, a great many singles beneath—which any sensible businessman carried with him at all times and, turning, said, "The madam-mayor wishes you to know—"

He found himself confronted by a stranger who could only be Tawny's Jake and Pirate Lafitte, whose face was contorted with astonishment.

Darger hastily thrust the wad of bills back into his pocket. "Wishes you to know," he repeated, "that, ah, anytime you wish to try out her establishment, she will gladly offer you a 10 percent discount on all goods and services, alcohol excepted. It is a courtesy she has newly decided to extend, out of respect for your employer, to all his new hires."

Lafitte turned, grabbed Jake by the shirtfront, and shook him as a mastiff might a rat. "I understand now," he said through gritted teeth. "The honorable brothel-keeper wished to deal me out of a rich opportunity, and so she sent you to me with a cock-and-bull story about this virtuous and inoffensive young woman."

"Honest, boss, I ain't got the slightest idea what this . . . this . . . foreigner is talking about. It's honest info I'm peddling here. I heard it on the street that my filthy bitch of a—"

With a roar of rage, Pirate Lafitte punched Jake so hard he fell sprawling in the street. Then he pulled the whip from his belt and proceeded to lay into the man so savagely that by the time he was done, his shirt and vest were damp with sweat.

Breathing heavily from exertion, he touched his hat to Darger and Surplus. "Sirs. We shall talk later, at a time when my passions are not so excited. This afternoon, five o'clock, at my office. I have a proposition to put to you." Then, to Tawny: "Miss Petticoats, I apologize that you had to see this."

He strode off.

"Oh!" Tawny breathed. "He beat Jake within an inch of his worthless life. It was the most romantic thing I've ever seen."

"A horsewhipping? Romantic?" Darger said.

Tawny favored him with a superior look. "You don't much understand the workings of a woman's heart, do you?"

"Apparently not," Darger said. "And it begins to appear that I never shall." Out in the street, Jake was painfully pulling himself up and trying to stand. "Excuse me."

Darger went over to the battered and bleeding man and helped him to his feet. Then, talking quietly, he opened his billfold and thrust several notes into the man's hand.

"What did you give him?" Tawny asked, when he was back inside.

"A stern warning not to interfere with us again. Also, seventeen dollars. A sum insulting enough to guarantee that, despite his injuries, he will take his increasingly implausible story to Master Bones, and then to the madam-mayor."

Tawny grabbed Darger and Surplus and hugged them both at once. "Oh, you boys are so good to me. I just love you both to pieces and back."

"It begins to look, however," Surplus said, "like we have been stood up. According to Madam-Mayor Tresjolie's note, she should have been here by now. Which is, if I may use such language, damnably peculiar."

"Something must have come up." Darger squinted up at the sky. "Tresjolie isn't here and it's about time for the meeting with Master Bones. You should stay here, in case the madam-mayor shows up. I'll see what the zombie master has to say."

"And I," Tawny said, "will go back to my room to adjust my dress."

"Adjust?" Surplus asked.

"It needs to be a little tighter and to show just a smidge more bosom."

Alarmed, Darger said, "Your character is a modest and innocent thing."

"She is a modest and innocent thing who secretly wishes a worldly cad would teach her all those wicked deeds she has heard about but cannot quite imagine. I have played this role before, gentlemen. Trust me, it is not innocence per se that men like Pirate Lafitte are drawn to but the tantalizing possibility of corrupting that innocence."

Then she was gone.

"A most remarkable young lady, our Ms. Petticoats," Surplus said.

Darger scowled.

After Darger left, Surplus leaned back in his chair for some casual people-watching. He had not been at it long when he noticed that a remarkably pretty woman at a table at the far end of the café kept glancing his way. When he returned her gaze, she blushed and looked quickly away.

From long experience, Surplus understood what such looks meant. Leaving money on the table to pay for the breakfasts, he strolled over to introduce himself to the lady. She seemed not unreceptive to his attentions and, after a remarkably short conversation, invited him to her room in a nearby hotel. Feigning surprise, Surplus accepted.

What happened there had occurred many times before in his eventful life. But that didn't make it any less delightful.

On leaving the hotel, however, Surplus was alarmed to find himself abruptly seized and firmly held by two red-furred, seven-foot-tall uniformed Canadian ape-men.

"I see you have been entertaining yourself with one of the local sluts," Madam-Mayor Tresjolie said. She looked even less benevolent than usual.

"That is a harsh characterization of a lady who, for all I know, may be of high moral character. Also, I must ask you why I am being held captive like this."

"In due time. First, tell me whether your encounter was a commercial one or not."

"I thought not when we were in the throes of it. But afterward, she showed me her union card and informed me that as a matter of policy she was required to charge not only by the hour but by the position. I was, of course, astonished."

"What did you do then?"

"I paid, of course," Surplus said indignantly. "I am no scab!"

"The woman with whom you coupled, however, was not a registered member of the International Sisterhood of Trollops, Demimondaines, and Back-Alley Doxies and her card was a forgery. Which means that while nobody objects to your noncommercial sexual activities, by paying her you were engaged in a union-busting activity—and *that,* sir, is against the law."

"Obviously, you set me up. Otherwise, you could have known none of this."

"That is neither here nor there. What is relevant is that you have three things that I want—the girl with the birthmark, the crates of money, and the knowledge of how to use the one to render the other negotiable."

"I understand now. Doubtless, madam-mayor, you seek to bribe me. I assure you that no amount of money—"

"Money?" The madam-mayor's laugh was short and harsh. "I am offering you something far more precious: your conscious mind." She produced a hypodermic needle. "People think the zombification formula consists entirely of extract of puffer fish. But in fact atropine, datura, and a dozen other drugs are involved, all blended in a manner guaranteed to make the experience very unpleasant indeed."

"Threats will not work on me."

"Not yet. But after you've had a taste of what otherwise lies before you, I'm sure you'll come around. In a week or so, I'll haul you back from the fields. Then we can negotiate."

Madam-Mayor Tresjolie's simian thugs held Surplus firmly, struggle though he did. She raised the syringe to his neck. There was a sharp sting.

The world went away.

Darger, meanwhile, had rented a megatherium, complete with howdah and zombie mahout, and ridden it to the endless rows of zombie barns, pens, and feeding sheds at the edge of town. There, Master Bones showed him the chest-high troughs that were filled with swill every morning and evening, and the rows of tin spoons the sad creatures used to feed themselves. "When each of my pretties has fed, the spoon is set aside to be washed and sterilized before it is used again," Master Bones said. "Every precaution is taken to ensure they do not pass diseases from one to another."

"Commendably humane, sir. To say nothing of its being good business practice."

"You understand me well." They passed outside, where a pair of zombies, one male and the other female, both in exceptional condition and perfectly matched in height and color of hair and skin, waited with umbrellas. As they strolled to the pens, the two walked a pace behind them, shading them from the sun. "Tell me, Mr. Darger. What do you suppose the ratio of zombies to citizens is in New Orleans?"

Darger considered. "About even?"

"There are six zombies for every fully functioning human in the city. It seems a smaller number since most are employed as field hands and the like and so are rarely seen in the streets. But I could flood the city with them, should I wish."

"Why on earth should you?"

Rather than answer the question, Master Bones said, "You have something I want."

"I fancy I know what it is. But I assure you that no amount of money could buy from me what is by definition a greater amount of money. So we have nothing to discuss."

"Oh, I believe that we do." Master Bones indicated the nearest of the pens, in which stood a bull of prodigious size and obvious strength. It was darkly colored with pale laddering along its spine, and its horns were long and sharp. "This is a Eurasian aurochs, the ancestor of our modern domestic cattle. It went extinct in seventeenth-century Poland and was resurrected less than a hundred years ago. Because of its ferocity, it is impractical as a meat animal, but I keep a small breeding herd for export to the Republic of Baja and other Mexican states where bullfighting remains popular. Bastardo here is a particularly bellicose example of his kind.

"Now consider the contents of the adjoining pen." The pen was overcrammed with zombie laborers and reeked to high heaven. The zombies stood motionless, staring at nothing. "They don't look very strong, do they? Individually, they're not. But there is strength in numbers." Going to the fence, Master Bones slapped a zombie on the shoulder and said, "Open the gate between your pen and the next."

Then, when the gate was opened, Master Bones made his hands into a megaphone and shouted, "Everyone! Kill the aurochs. Now."

With neither enthusiasm nor reluctance, the human contents of one pen flowed into the next, converging upon the great beast. With an angry bellow, Bastardo trampled several under its hooves. The others kept coming. His head dipped to impale a body on its horns, then rose to fling a slash of red and a freshly made corpse in the air. Still the zombies kept coming.

That strong head fell and rose, again and again. More bodies flew. But now there were zombies clinging to the bull's back and flanks and legs, hindering its movements. A note of fear entered the beast's great voice. By now, there were bodies heaped on top of bodies on top of his, enough that his legs buckled under their weight. Fists hammered at his sides and hands wrenched at his horns. He struggled upward, almost rose, and then fell beneath the crushing sea of bodies.

Master Bones began giggling when the aurochs went down for the first time. His mirth grew greater and his eyes filled with tears of laughter and once or twice he snorted, so tremendous was his amusement at the spectacle.

A high-pitched squeal of pain went up from the aurochs . . . and then all was silence, save for the sound of fists pounding upon the beast's carcass.

Wiping his tears away on his sleeve, Master Bones raised his voice again: "Very good. Well done. Thank you. Stop. Return to your pen. Yes, that's right." He turned his back on the bloodied carcass and the several bodies of zombies that lay motionless on the dirt, and said to Darger, "I believe in being direct. Give me the money and the girl by this time tomorrow or you and your partner will be as extinct as the aurochs ever was. There is no power as terrifying as that of a mob—and I control the greatest mob there ever was."

"Sir!" Darger said. "The necessary equipment has not yet arrived from the Socialist Utopia of Minneapolis! There is no way I can . . ."

"Then I'll give you four days to think it over." A leering smile split the zombie master's pasty face. "While you're deciding, I will leave you with these two zombies to use as you wish. They will do anything you tell them to. They are capable of following quite complex orders, though they do not consciously understand them." To the zombies, he said, "You have heard this man's voice. Obey him. But if he tries to leave New Orleans, kill him. Will you do that?"

"If he leaves . . . kill . . . him."

"Yasss."

Something was wrong.

Something was wrong, but Surplus could not put his finger on exactly what it was. He couldn't concentrate. His thoughts were all in a jumble and he could not find words with which to order them. It was as if he had forgotten how to think. Meanwhile, his body moved without his particularly willing it to do so. It did not occur to him that it should behave otherwise. Still, he knew that something was wrong.

The sun set, the sun rose. It made no difference to him.

His body labored systematically, cutting sugarcane with a machete. This work it performed without his involvement, steadily and continuously. Blisters arose on the pads of his paws, swelled, and popped. He did not care. Someone had told him to work and so he had and so he would until the time came to stop. All the world was a fog to him, but his arms knew to swing and his legs to carry him forward to the next plant.

Nevertheless, the sensation of wrongness endured. Surplus felt stunned, the way an ox that had just been poleaxed might feel, or the sole survivor of some overwhelming catastrophe. Something terrible had happened, and it was imperative that he do something about it.

If only he knew what.

A trumpet sounded in the distance, and without fuss all about him the other laborers ceased their work. As did he. Without hurry he joined their chill company in the slow trek back to the feeding sheds.

Perhaps he slept, perhaps he did not. Morning came and Surplus was jostled to the feeding trough where he swallowed ten spoonsful of swill, as a zombie overseer directed him. Along with many others, he was given a machete and walked to the fields. There he was put to work again.

Hours passed.

There was a clop-clopping of hooves and the creaking of wagon wheels, and a buckboard drawn by a brace of pygmy mastodons pulled up alongside Surplus. He kept working. Somebody leaped down from the wagon and wrested the machete from his hand. "Open your mouth," a voice said.

He had been told by . . . somebody . . . not to obey the orders of any strangers. But this voice sounded familiar, though he could not have said why. Slowly his mouth opened. Something was placed within it. "Now shut and swallow."

His mouth did so.

His vision swam and he almost fell. Deep, deep within his mind, a spark of light blossomed. It was a glowing ember amid the ashes of a dead fire. But it grew and brightened, larger and more, until it felt like the sun rising within him. The external world came into focus, and with it the awareness that he, Surplus, had an identity distinct from the rest of existence. He realized first that his throat itched and the inside of his mouth was as parched and dry as the Sahara. Then that somebody he knew stood before him. Finally, that this person was his friend and colleague Aubrey Darger.

"How long have I . . . ?" Surplus could not bring himself to complete the sentence.

"More than one day. Less than two. When you failed to return to our hotel, Tawny and I were naturally alarmed and set out in search of you. New Orleans being a city prone to gossip, and there being only one anthropomorphized dog in town, the cause of your disappearance was easily determined. But learning that you had been sent to labor in the sugarcane fields did not narrow the search greatly for there are literally hundreds of square miles of fields. Luckily, Tawny knew where such blue-collar laborers as would have heard of the appearance of a dog-headed zombie congregated, and from them we learned at last of your whereabouts."

"I . . . see." Focusing his thoughts on practical matters, Surplus said, "Madam-Mayor Tresjolie, as you may have surmised, had no intention of buying our crates of black paper from us. What of our other marks?"

"The interview with the Pirate Lafitte went well. Tawny played him like a trout. That with Master Bones was considerably less successful. However, we talked Lafitte up to a price high enough to bankrupt him and make all three of us wealthy. Tawny is accompanying him to the bank right now, to make certain he doesn't come to his senses at the last minute. He is quite besotted with her and in her presence cannot seem to think straight."

"You sound less disapproving of the girl than you were."

Twisting his mouth in the near grimace he habitually assumed when forced to admit to having made a misjudgment, Darger said, "Tawny grows on one, I find. She makes a splendid addition to the team."

"That's good," Surplus said. Now at last he noticed that in the back of the buckboard two zombies sat motionless atop a pile of sacks. "What's all that you have in the wagon?"

"Salt. A great deal of it."

In the final feeding shed, Surplus kicked over the trough, spilling swill on the ground. Then, at his command, Darger's zombies righted the trough and filled it with salt. Darger, meanwhile, took a can of paint and drew a rough map of New Orleans on the wall. He drew three arrows to Madam-Mayor Tresjolie's brothel, Jean-Nagin Lafitte's waterfront office, and the club where Master Jeremy Bones presided every evening. Finally, he wrote block letter captions for each arrow:

> THE MAN WHO TRANSPORTED YOU HERE
> THE WOMAN WHO PUT YOU HERE
> THE MAN WHO KEPT YOU HERE

Above it all, he wrote the day's date.

"There," Darger said when he was done. Turning to his zombies, he said, "You were told to do as I commanded."

"Yass," the male said lifelessly.

"We must," the female said, "oh bey."

"Here is a feeding spoon for both of you. When the zombie laborers return to the barn, you are to feed each of them a spoonful of salt. Salt. Here in the trough. Take a spoonful of salt. Tell them to open their mouths. Put in the salt. Then tell them to swallow. Can you do that?"

"Yass."

"Salt. Swall oh."

"When everyone else is fed," Surplus said, "be sure to take a spoonful of salt yourselves—each of you."

"Salt."

"Yass."

Soon, the zombies would come to feed and discover salt in their mouths instead of swill. Miraculously, their minds would uncloud. In shed after shed, they would read what Darger had written. Those who had spent years and even decades longer than they were sentenced to would feel justifiably outraged. After which, they could be expected to collectively take appropriate action.

"The sun is setting," Darger said. In the distance, he could see zombies plodding in from the fields. "We have just enough time to get back to our rooms and accept Pirate Lafitte's bribe before the rioting begins."

But when they got back to Maison Fema, their suite was lightless and Tawny Petticoats was nowhere to be seen. Nor was Pirate Lafitte.

The crates of black paper, having served their purpose, had not been restacked in front of Tawny's bedroom door. Hastily lighting an oil lamp, Darger threw open the door. In the middle of her carefully made bed was a note. He picked it up and read it out loud:

Dear Boys,

I know you do not beleive in love at first site because you are both Synics. But Jean-Nagin and I are Kindrid Spirits and meant to be together. I told him so Bold a man as he should not be in Trade, esp. as he has his own ships banks and docks and he agrees. So he is to be a Pirate in fact as well as name and I am his Pirate Queen.

I am sorry about the Black Mony scam but a girl can't start a new life by cheating her Hubby that is no way to be

Love,
Tawny Petticoats

P.S. You boys are both so much fun.

"Tell me," Darger said after a long silence. "Did Tawny sleep with you?"

Surplus looked startled. Then he placed paw upon chest and forthrightly, though without quite looking Darger in the eye, said, "Upon my word, she did not. You don't mean that she . . .?"

"No. No, of course not."

There was another awkward silence.

"Well, then," Darger said. "Much as I predicted, we are left with nothing for all our labors."

"You forget the silver ingots," Surplus said.

"It is hardly worth bothering to . . ."

But Surplus was already on his knees, groping in the shadows beneath Tawny's bed. He pulled out three leather cases and from them extracted three ingots.

"Those are obviously . . ."

Whipping out his pocketknife, Surplus scratched each ingot, one after the other. The first was merely plated lead. The other two were solid silver. Darger explosively let out his breath in relief.

"A toast!" Surplus cried, rising to his feet. "To women, God bless 'em. Constant, faithful, and unfailingly honest! Paragons, sir, of virtue in every respect."

In the distance could be heard the sound of a window breaking. "I'll drink to that," Darger replied. "But just a sip and then we really must flee. We have, I suspect, a conflagration to avoid."

David W. Ball

A former pilot, sarcophagus maker, and businessman, David W. Ball has traveled to more than sixty countries on six continents, crossed the Sahara Desert four times in the course of researching his novel *Empires of Sand,* and explored the Andes in a Volkswagen bus. Other research trips have taken him to China, Istanbul, Algeria, and Malta. He's driven a taxi in New York City, installed telecommunications equipment in Cameroon, renovated old Victorian houses in Denver, and pumped gasoline in the Grand Tetons. His bestselling novels include the extensively researched historical epics *Ironfire* and the aforementioned *Empires of Sand,* and the contemporary thriller *China Run.* He lives with his family on a small farm in Colorado, where, after a writing hiatus of nearly a decade, he is back at work, growing tall tales.

They say that beauty is in the eye of the beholder, but the desire to *possess* beauty, particularly when it's worth a great deal of cash, can bring you up against some very unsavory characters indeed . . .

PROVENANCE

David W. Ball

The letter arrived at the Wolff Gallery in New York with the usual catalogs and gallery announcements. It was marked "Personal," so Max's secretary left it on his desk, unopened.

Max slit the envelope with his good hand and removed a note, handwritten but neat. "Dear Mr. Max Wolff," it said. "I hear you know a lot about fancy paintings and can sell them sometimes. I have one that I'm not sure is worth much, but thought you ought to take a look and if you are ok with it we could maybe do some business. On the quiet, of course. If you are interested, please send a note at the post office box below. Sincerely, L.M."

Then Max saw the photograph. He blinked, disbelieving. He felt a fullness in his chest, a surge of pleasure and shock and sadness. He swept aside the clutter of papers on his desk and set the photo on the blotter. He opened a drawer and felt for the magnifying glass, then bent close to the desk.

The photograph had been taken in poor light by an amateur, but that didn't make any difference. Max *knew* this painting, as any student of art history would know it. It was a beautiful and cursed creation, the work of a madman.

And it had been missing since the Second World War.

He straightened up, eyes watering. He felt light-headed and fumbled in his vest for one of his pills.

Max did not hear his secretary say good night, did not realize that dusk had turned to dark, as his mind churned through the sweep of its history, of Nazis and the Stasis, of arms dealers and Roman Catholic cardinals. So much violence and corruption in its past. He knew clearly then what must be the next stop in its long and troubled journey.

His good hand trembling, Max Wolff picked up the phone.

* * *

On a Sunday morning two weeks later Max waited for a client in a private study just off the sanctuary of the Risen Savior Church in Colorado Springs.

He sat in an overstuffed chair that nearly swallowed his small frame. Despite the sound-deadened walls he could hear the thunder and feel the building shake as four thousand impassioned souls in the sanctuary next door stomped and clapped and laughed and cried and sang, as the service rose to a crescendo.

The Reverend Joe Cooley Barber was in the business of saving souls, and business was brisk. With charisma, looks, and a voice born for a microphone, he had created an empire that spanned forty-seven countries on six continents. His Sunday Believers program, a folksy mix of parable and gospel, was simulcast in sixty-eight languages. He had seventeen books in print, all perennial best sellers. His media division sold CDs, videos, and T-shirts, every product carrying a Risen Savior hologram to thwart counterfeits.

He employed nearly a thousand people and had almost as many accountants and MBAs working for him as there were members of his choir: precisely 229, a number chosen from a revelation he'd had at a low point in his life when—drunk, destitute, and desperate—he dropped his Bible and it fell open to page 229 of the New Testament. On that page he read the second verse of the third epistle of John: "Prosper and be in health, even as thy soul prospereth." Joe Cooley chose to give the word "prosper" its modern meaning, and from this passage sprang his signature refrain: "God wants us wealthy."

He was not the first of the prosperity preachers, but he was the best ("a bit more satin than Satan," he liked to say), and he lived what he preached: he owned a Gulfstream jet, a small fleet of cars including an Aston Martin and a Bentley, and what he liked to describe as "a modest little horse farm in Kentucky" where he raised Thoroughbreds. "I am not an end-of-times preacher," he said. "I am a best-of-times preacher."

With such success came controversy. For every dollar he took in from ministry, Joe Cooley Barber earned five from offshore corporations, all cloaked behind an impenetrable web of ownership. Amid allegations that a mere thirty cents of every dollar went toward missionary work, half a dozen investigations had been launched by the IRS, the Justice Department, and various congressional committees. A defiant Joe Cooley Barber was fond of pointing out that not one shred of evidence of wrongdoing had ever been proven against him. "I am just a simple God-fearing humanitarian," he said. He had fed tens of thousands of hungry souls throughout Asia and Africa. Millions of Risen Savior malaria pills saved babies in Bangladesh and Botswana. Annual missions taught modern agricultural techniques to farmers in Malawi and Tanzania, providing tractors and seed to help the multitudes help themselves. He built churches in Zambia and opened new schools in Zaire.

"A plague of pissants," was the way he privately described the prosecutors and politicians who hounded him. Yet he relished their attention and prospered from it. The more they complained, the more the money poured in. "Your dollars pave the road to your salvation," Joe Cooley preached to the television cameras. "Your dollars are God's judgment on our ministry."

"Max, my friend!" Joe Cooley said, wiping the sweat from his forehead as he fairly burst into the room half an hour later. "I'm sorry to keep you."

"Not at all," Max said. "Quite a production. I've never seen you work before."

Joe Cooley gave a broad smile. "You Jewish?"

"No."

"Then why aren't you here every week?"

"It would be a long commute. Perhaps if you sent your jet."

"No need!" Joe Cooley went into the private bathroom to freshen up. "I'm as close as your television dial." He emerged, wiping his hands. "But now, to business. I could hardly believe your call." He lowered his voice a little. "Can it be? A *Caravaggio*?"

Max nodded. "There are perhaps ninety of his paintings in the world. I thought of you the moment it came into my hands."

"I take it this one is off the radar?"

"Definitely one for your private collection," Max said. "If you want it, that is."

"Let's go to the studio," the preacher said, extending a hand to help Max up. The art dealer picked up his cane. His right hand was gnarled, the fingers crabbed and crippled. He slung the briefcase strap over his shoulder and picked up a large leather portfolio.

Joe Cooley's eyes widened. "Tell me you don't have it right there in that case," he said. "What balls!"

"Hardly," Max said. "It is well packed, and your men have been with me the whole way. Besides, I don't look much like a mark. I once carried $5 million across Manhattan in this briefcase. All anyone tried to do was help me cross the street."

"I'm not so trusting," Joe Cooley said, "but I see your point." Max was in his early seventies, standing just over five feet tall. He always wore a gray fedora. Years spent in study, sifting through historical records and peering at art, had made his eyes so bad that the thick lenses of his glasses distorted his features. He looked like a kindly old bookkeeper. Despite all that, Joe Cooley knew he was a tough negotiator with shrewd business sense. Max ran a highly respected art gallery and was a regular at Christie's and Sotheby's. His most lucrative business, however, was done in the netherworlds of commerce, a world in which men who shunned publicity bought and sold art, or used it in lieu of cash to leverage large purchases of drugs or arms. Max could find the paintings and arrange the deals.

They climbed in a golf cart for the ride across the complex. Risen Savior occupied a seventy-acre campus near the Garden of the Gods. Along with the church there were foundation offices, the broadcasting studio, a Christian college, and a museum. As the cart whisked them through statuary gardens and past contemplation pools, Joe Cooley returned the waves and the shouted greetings of parishioners who were enjoying the sunny day.

The museum was Joe Cooley Barber's pride and joy. He loved beautiful things, things that shouted out the glory of God. He believed there was no greater homage to the Almighty than to collect images that glorified Him and His holy word. Its galleries brimmed with religious art from every age: stained glass, Greek icons, illustrated manuscripts and early Christian scrolls, a Giotto, several Rembrandts, a Rubens, and an El Greco. Then there were Joe Cooley's own oil paintings, mostly depictions of biblical prosperity tales, of Job and Solomon. To Max they stood out like pustules on the gallery walls, but they were among the most popular exhibits.

They entered Joe Cooley's hideaway, a combination studio and study, with picture windows overlooking the grounds. Besides a large conference table there were workbenches, easels, and bookshelves filled with rare Bibles and rich leather volumes.

Max set the portfolio on the table, undid the snaps, and removed the inner case. The painting rested snugly in a bed of soft white cotton. Max laid back the cloth, gently lifted the painting, and set it on the easel. He stepped to the wall and flipped a switch, bathing the work in soft light.

The young shepherd David, sword in one hand, was lifting the bloody head of Goliath, the Philistine warrior. Goliath's face was frozen in death, eyes and mouth open, forehead gashed, blood dripping from his severed neck. Joe Cooley Barber stared in silent awe, transfixed. "It's smaller than I imagined," he said quietly. "And darker."

Max removed several thick binders from his briefcase. "I've brought documentation on the provenance, of course," he said, setting them out on the table, then extracting folders which appeared to contain clippings, books, and handwritten notes.

Joe Cooley knew Max didn't need the notes; those were for him. "My friend the professor begins," he said. "Better have a drink. Whisky? Wine?"

"Just water." The preacher poured whisky for himself and water for Max, and pulled up a chair.

"His work could be quite gruesome—beheadings, like this one. Assassinations, betrayals, martyrdoms, all caught at the instant of perfect revelation. It was his gift, capturing that moment. He painted this scene at least four times over the course of his career, each representing a progression in his maturity, expressed in the two faces," Max said. "This was probably the second version, in which there is pride in David's expression, but also deep humility—the triumph of the kingdom of heaven over the forces of Satan."

Max ran his crippled hand just above the canvas, lovingly following Caravaggio's lines, picturing the artist at work. "So sure of himself he rarely used sketches, like other artists. He painted directly from life. He left *pentimenti,* sharp creases in the paint—you can see traces here, and here. Such genius, do you see?—and all of it done so quickly that some said his work flowed as if from the hand of God. And the light! Look how the flesh runs to shadow, blood red runs to black, light runs to darkness and to death. Such mastery of light—or of the darkness, depending upon your point of view."

"Light, of course," said Joe Cooley Barber. "I've never seen you quite this worked up over a painting."

Max smiled sheepishly. "There are not many paintings like this one, or many painters. His work was new and brilliant, but so raw that it often shocked his patrons in the Church, who complained of his vulgarity and sacrilege. He used whores for his models and dressed the Virgin Mary in a low-cut gown. He put warts on saints and gave them dirty fingernails. The Church establishment found him intolerable. They preferred perfection in their saints."

"So does the U.S. Senate," Joe Cooley muttered, sipping his whisky.

"His life was just as raw as his work. He was a tortured soul. Some think his madness came from lead poisoning, from his paints, others that he was simply tormented by his own genius. Whatever the cause, he lived hard, dueling and drinking. He whored and gambled and was hauled in and out of court. He assaulted a waiter for bad service and stabbed a lawyer in a fight over a prostitute. He murdered a police official, was tortured, and escaped. Another man would have languished in prison for any of that, but while Caravaggio had detractors in the Church, he had powerful protectors as well, this one among them."

Max had marked a page in an art-history book, and opened it to a portrait of an ascetic-looking cleric. "This is Scipione Borghese, a nephew of Pope Paul V—the pope who ordered Galileo to abandon his heretical notions about our solar system. Paul elevated Borghese to the position of Cardinal Nephew, a position of immense power. He was brilliant, ruthless, and unprincipled. Besides being the de facto head of the Vatican government, he held multiple offices and titles that made him rich beyond measure. He bullied men and threatened their souls. He imposed taxes and acquired estates—whole villages—through extortion and papal edicts. He had an extensive collection of pornography, and his homosexuality scandalized the Church."

Joe Cooley could not suppress a snicker of delight. "Somehow that Church has always known how to grow real scoundrels," he said.

"Yes, but for all his faults, he was a great patron of the arts. He used his wealth to build a magnificent villa to display the works of Raphael, Titian, Bernini—and Caravaggio, for a time his favorite."

"A man after my own heart, I guess," Joe Cooley said. "Except for the boys, of course. All things for the glory of God."

Max turned to another file. "As for our painting here, the Church owned it first," he said. "Or, more precisely, was the first to steal it. Borghese had begun to collect art aggressively and was learning to use the tools of his power. Giuseppe Cesari was a prominent artist who had an important collection of more than a hundred paintings, including several by Caravaggio, who had worked in his studio as a young man. Borghese learned that Cesari also had a collection of arquebuses. Cesari was harmless, the guns just a hobby, but they were illegal. Borghese had Cesari arrested, his possessions confiscated. He was sentenced to death. That sentence was eventually lifted, but not until Cesari agreed to donate his paintings to the apostolic chamber. Several months later, the pope gave the entire lot to the Cardinal Nephew.

"About this same time, Caravaggio killed a man he thought cheated him at tennis and fled Rome with a price on his head. He spent the rest of his life running, hoping Borghese could arrange a papal pardon. While he was a fugitive, he did some of his best work. In Malta he painted for the Knights of St. John, becoming a Knight himself, until the Order imprisoned him for fighting. He escaped, but in Naples he was attacked and badly wounded, likely by assassins in the pay of the Knights. He made his way back toward Rome. His pardon had been granted, but he died of fever before he heard." Max shook his head. "He was only thirty-eight. Imagine what he could have done with another twenty years."

Max slid a ledger across the table. "As for our painting, Borghese only parted with it because he owned another version, sent to him by Caravaggio from exile. He included this one as part of a bribe to a Polish count named Krasinski. There were three other paintings—an Annibale Carracci, a Reni, and a Lanfranco—and an exquisite jeweled reliquary. We have cross-checked the list with Count Krasinski's household ledgers. On his death the count bequeathed the items to his brother, who had just been appointed by the king as bishop of Stawicki. As you can see here, the items are included in a church inventory from 1685." Max fished a paper out of the stack. "This is in Polish, of course, but I've circled the items for you.

"The paintings and reliquary stayed safe and anonymous in that church for nearly three hundred years, surviving fires and insurrections. For most of that time Caravaggio was a forgotten man, all but lost to history until the twentieth century, when scholars began to appreciate what a giant he was."

Joe Cooley stood. "Time for another drink. Sure you won't have something stronger?"

"Just a bit more water. There is a great deal more to cover."

Max opened a thick file of yellowed documents and newspaper clippings. On top was a black-and-white photograph of a German officer. Max slid it across the table.

"SS," Joe Cooley commented. "Handsome devil."

Max nodded. "Walter Beck. This photograph was taken just after his promotion to colonel, a year before the end of the war."

Joe Cooley studied the long, angular face and intelligent eyes. "Perfect German officer," he said. "Cold bastard, by the look of him."

Max pulled a clipping from the folder, a copy of a birth announcement from the Berlin papers. "He was the oldest son of Otto Beck, a prominent German art dealer. Beck's was one of Berlin's oldest galleries, started by Otto's grandfather as an artist's supply shop, selling oils, stretchers, and canvas. The artists were always poor, so Beck's sometimes traded supplies for their work. Otto's father began selling the paintings. Business flourished and by 1900 Beck's occupied a large two-story building. The family lived on the upper floor, while the rest of the building was devoted to a gallery and workshops where Beck's craftsmen restored and repaired paintings. Artists, collectors, and curators brought damaged works from all over Europe.

"Walter worked for his father for a few years. He had a good head for business but no particular love of art. He was young and ambitious and got swept up in the socialist fever of the thirties. He joined the Nazi party. His father disapproved but Walter didn't care. He read the political climate and he understood Hitler. He moved quickly up the ranks, and his training in his father's gallery landed him a position with the *Sonderauftrag Linz.*"

"English, Max."

"It means 'Special Operation Linz,' a secret project of Hitler's. He was a frustrated artist, of course, and thought most of Europe's art was his by right. He was obsessed with building a museum in Linz, a city he was going to remake into the cultural capital of Europe after the war. Before the war his agents toured museums, galleries, and private collections throughout Europe, compiling exhaustive lists of the most important artworks. The result was a guide to what Hitler's armies were to confiscate—to loot—the instant German forces overran an area. Beck helped compile that guide, which is how he came to know where our painting was hidden.

"Beck should have spent the war in Paris, where all the best art was, but he was an arrogant man and made the mistake of getting into an argument with Alfred Rosenberg himself. Rosenberg was the Nazis' ideologue, one of the most powerful men in Germany, and Beck found himself reassigned to the eastern front. He was an excellent officer, but even by SS standards he was exceptionally cruel. Russia, Czechoslovakia, Poland—Beck managed to make himself one of the most wanted criminals of the war."

There were more yellowed clippings, most in languages Joe Cooley did not recognize—eastern European, he thought, and some in Hebrew. Most carried the same photograph. He could not read the captions, but he was looking at a hunted man.

* * *

The German column pulled to a halt on a ridge near the ancient village of Stawicki. There were five troop carriers, two tanks, and various smaller vehicles, the ragtag remnants of a routed army that had banded together in retreat. SS Colonel Walter Beck emerged from an open staff car carrying a pair of field glasses. He stretched his legs, then calmly trained the glasses on the distant road behind them. The Russians were not in view. Thanks to the mines laid by Beck's men, they would probably be another few hours, giving him time for the present business. Beck knew the war was hopelessly lost and that he would soon be hunted by men who would not forget. Surrender would mean execution. He would run, but first needed to acquire the means to ensure the hunters would never find him.

He turned his attention to the village. From outward appearances, this war had somehow passed the village by. He could see the steeple of the old church, and beyond that the clock tower of the town hall; everything seeming at peace. He could send his men to find what he sought, but the villagers would long ago have carefully hidden their precious treasure. He did not have time for games of hide-and-seek.

"Bring the village priest, and the mayor and his family," he said to a lieutenant.

"At once, *Standartenführer.*"

"And twenty-five villagers," Beck added.

As the officer set off with a truck, an aide set up a portable table and chair. Beck sat down with a bottle of wine and turned his face toward the sun, enjoying its warming glow.

The truck soon snaked its way back up the road, halting near Beck, who sipped his wine as soldiers barked orders, prodding the villagers out of the truck. There were only women, children, and old men. The priest, the mayor, and the mayor's wife, daughter, and child were brought before the colonel. The mayor was a heavyset man with florid cheeks, the priest old, lean, and cross.

"I must protest," the mayor began. "We are noncombat—" A soldier struck him in the stomach with the butt of his rifle. The mayor fell to his knees and bent over, gasping and retching.

"There is no need for unpleasantness," Beck said, "if you do as I say. I merely require several items from your church."

"Our church has already been stripped bare," said the priest. "There is nothing of value left."

"Quite the contrary," Beck said. "Carracci and Caravaggio. Reni. Lanfranco." He smiled. "Does my memory serve? All gifts of Count Krasinski to his brother the bishop." A flicker in the priest's expression was all the confirmation Beck needed.

"Excellency," the mayor blurted, his face bright red, "those paintings were all taken away before the war, to Gdynia. Yes, to Gdyn . . ." He couldn't catch his breath.

"Help me, here, Father," Beck said to the priest. "Surely you recall. Behind a false wall in the crypt, or beneath a carefully laid pile of rubble? No doubt a search will turn them up. Most likely near the reliquary, I suspect." He sipped his wine. "Which, by the way, I shall require as well, although you can keep its contents—a finger of Saint Barnabas, I believe? Or a rib of Hedwig or the hair of Casimir or the toe of Sarkander? Forgive me, I cannot recall that detail, but I would not dream of removing such a precious relic from your devotions." He looked at his watch. "I have very little time, I'm afraid. The Bolsheviks are pressing."

"We cannot give what we do not possess," said the priest.

"Very well." Beck stood, dropped his leather gloves on the table, unsnapped his holster and removed his Luger. He picked an old man from the crowd and shot him. A woman fell to her knees beside him, shrieking in grief as his body twitched in death. Beck shot her as well. Villagers screamed. Beck's soldiers stood fast around them, weapons at the ready.

"Well, Father?" Beck asked. "What are you prepared to sacrifice to protect a few paintings? What is the going price in your church for oil and canvas, for a few baubles? A dozen lives? Everyone here? Or will you martyr a whole village?"

The priest closed his eyes, crossed himself, and bowed his head in prayer. Beck raised the Luger to his temple. The priest flinched at the touch of the hot metal but kept praying. Beck considered the possibility that only the priest knew where to find what he wanted. He returned his pistol to its holster and turned to the mayor, still on his knees. "You have not introduced me to your family," he said, stepping forward to the young woman and her baby who stood behind him. "Your lovely daughter, I presume?" The mayor's fat cheeks quivered with fear. His daughter gasped and shrank back, clutching her baby tightly. Beck reached for the child and pried it from her grasp. The baby began to cry.

"Please, no," she pleaded quietly, tears streaking her cheeks. Beck cooed at the baby. "What a lovely child," he said. "You must be so proud." Playfully bouncing it up and down, he walked to the edge of the escarpment, its slope scarred with jagged rocks.

He tossed the baby into the air, as an uncle would do. The baby's cry rose in pitch.

The mother moaned and slumped. "Father, tell them," she pleaded with the priest.

Beck tossed the child higher, her cry now searing. A woman fainted; another screamed. "Yes, Father," Beck said as the child soared. "Tell me."

The priest prayed.

Beck tossed the baby again, harder. She wailed angrily.

"I beg of you," the mayor's daughter said, crawling toward Beck on her hands and knees. "Do not hurt my baby." A soldier stepped in her way.

The child flew higher, and then higher still, both mother and child now crying hysterically.

"Jerzy, please! For the love of God, give him what he wants!" The mayor's wife pleaded with her husband.

Beck nearly missed, catching the baby roughly with one hand. She wiggled and kicked in his grasp, howling angrily. "This is really quite difficult," Beck said. "I don't believe I can catch her next time." He began again, but the mayor had had enough. "Yes! We'll show you!"

"No!" the priest snapped. "Be silent!"

The mayor ignored him, appealing to Beck. "If we do as you say, you will leave our village in peace? You will let us all go?"

"I want nothing more of you. You have my word."

A dozen soldiers accompanied the mayor and the priest back to the village in one of the trucks. Beck returned the child to her mother's care and sat again, sunning himself. Forty minutes later, just as the lieutenant reported sighting the advancing Russians, the truck bounced back up the rutted road, carrying its precious cargo.

The priest watched sullenly as Beck examined the reliquary, an exquisite ivory-and-gold casket that glistened with rubies and pearls, and then each of the paintings, everything precisely as Beck expected.

When everything had been safely loaded Beck took his seat in the back of his staff car. "You are free to go," he said to the mayor. "You'd better hide quickly, before your new Russian masters arrive. I have heard they have no love for the Poles."

The column's engines roared to life as the villagers collected their dead and started down the hill.

Beck's lieutenant approached. "At your command, *Standartenführer,* I am ready to carry out our orders." The guns of the waiting Panzers were trained on the village, to follow the scorched-earth orders of the German high command.

"It would be unforgivable to destroy such a picturesque village," said Beck. "Centuries of history should not be rubble. We shall leave Stawicki for the Russians to enjoy." He nodded toward the departing villagers. "Only our friends there," he said. "Nothing more."

As Beck's car pulled away canvas sides dropped from one of the troop trucks. With a great roar the machine guns inside opened fire.

Half an hour later, the screaming had stopped and the dust and smoke had settled. In the field before the village, there was only the sound of the approaching Russian column to break the silence.

Joe Cooley Barber set down the photograph of a stone memorial in front of the church in Stawicki, erected in memory of the villagers murdered during the war. "My God," he said softly. "I thought they only did that to Jews." He picked up a clipping from a South American newspaper, with Beck's picture. "So Beck escaped with the painting to South America?"

"It wasn't as simple as that. It took me time and a great many sources to piece the story together. U.S. Army reports, CIA documents, journalists' reports, that sort of thing. And then these."

Max leafed through a stack of copies of microfilm records, white on black and very difficult to read. "In the 1970s we found—or should I say the Stasi, the East German secret police, found—a collection of papers buried in a basement in Berlin, in what was the Soviet sector. The papers were part of the secret Stasi archives until after the fall of the Berlin wall, when they were released along with thousands of other documents. There was a journal, kept by Walter Beck's younger brother Heinrich, who was just young enough to miss the shooting war. This is a copy."

"It's in German," Joe Cooley said. "Can't anybody write in English?"

"There's a translation on the back."

Business was always good at Beck's. After the Great War proud old Germans sold family heirlooms to keep up with ruinous inflation. In the 1930s it was not only paintings but silverware and jewelry, the trade rising along with the Nazis. Even Jews could sell their valuables at Beck's, at least until Kristallnacht in 1938, when it became too dangerous to deal with them. Otto Beck did not cheat the Jews but knew that he was often the beneficiary of their persecution. By 1940 it was wartime again and business prospered as never before, as officers returning from various fronts brought looted art to sell—paintings and tapestries, gold and silver. Beck's paid top prices. Limousines arrived and departed, carrying a constant stream of government ministers and staff officers. Hitler's own art dealers bought there. Goering was a regular. Otto Beck sold them what they wanted while privately mocking the Nazi taste in art. "Matisse and van Gogh, Kandinsky and Klee—*mein Gott,* the world for his taking, and the Führer prefers hunters and dumplings," he said to his young son.

Heinrich cared nothing for the guns and games of war that fascinated most boys his age. He loved the art that moved through Beck's. He accompanied his father on a business trip to Paris when he was only eight, and Otto Beck could not extract him from the Louvre.

From the time he was old enough to hold a brush, Heinrich devoted every spare moment to painting. He was a careful craftsman and displayed solid talent if not brilliance. One of his father's workers told him he could improve his technique by copying the works he admired. Heinrich's favorites were the Baroques. After half a dozen attempts, he produced an extraordinary Velázquez; except for the fresh paint and the craquelure—the age cracks in the painting—even the most knowledgeable restorers who worked for his father could hardly tell which was the master's and which the boy's. Had the war not intervened, Heinrich Beck might well have become a successful artist.

He learned all aspects of his father's business, helping the artisans repair the traces of war on paintings passing through the gallery—boot marks and deep scratches, neat bullet holes and ragged edges left by knives that hacked priceless canvases from old frames, all mute testament to a war he did not see.

As Allied bombs began to bring the war closer, Otto moved his family and his inventory to the basement. The workshops were stacked floor to ceiling with frames and canvases, and the family slept on cots in a small room. The heavy floor beams rumbled and shook from distant bombs, but business went on.

The gallery's clientele grew more desperate with each passing week, trying to finance escapes or buy new identities, or simply trying to survive. Rivers of art and silverware and cash flowed in and out of Beck's through the winter of 1944–45.

"The war is coming close," one entry read. "Our house smells of oil paint, mother's cooking, and fear."

Late one night in the spring of 1945, Heinrich looked up from his workbench to see a man standing in the shadows. He knew instantly whom it was. "Walter!"

Otto emerged from the back, where he had been working on the accounts. They had seen Walter only once since the war's beginning, in 1941 as the Nazi high command prepared to open an eastern front. Then he had worn the black of the SS; now he wore civilian clothes. He was gaunt and his face was hard and he smelled of cigarettes and alcohol.

"Walter?" Otto said. "Are you all right?"

"I have some things you will keep safe for me."

"Where are you going?" Otto Beck asked his son. Walter said nothing, stepping aside for two men carrying a wooden crate.

"I asked you a question, Walter," Otto said, irritated. Otto Beck was head of his house and SS or not, Walter was his son. "Where are you—"

Walter slapped him viciously, knocking him down. *"Arschloch!"* he snarled. "Make certain this case is safe. Do you understand?" Otto was too stunned to reply.

Heinrich nodded for his father. "Yes, I heard you," he said in a small voice. "We'll take care of it. I promise."

Walter turned and started up the steps. Bravely, Heinrich followed. "Walter, wait! Are you a general now? What did you do in the war? Were you ever shot? Do you know how close the Russians are? Are you hungry?"

Walter Beck stepped into the night and ducked into the back of a waiting car. It sped off as Heinrich's other questions died on his lips.

Otto Beck's mouth was bleeding, his cheek bruised. Heinrich helped him up onto a chair and ran to get water and a cloth. Otto waved him away, his eyes on the empty stairs, his mind on his wife, who was sleeping. "Don't tell her he was here," he said. Otto Beck never spoke of Walter again.

The crate was hidden away below the basement with Otto's most valuable paintings, in a vault that was lined with metal to keep it dry. It remained there until after the war, long after the Russians had come looking for Walter. Russian reprisals against former SS were terrible, especially for those like Walter Beck, who had made their reputation in the east.

One day Russian troops smashed their way into the building. Otto had just enough time to shove his son into the lower basement and close the trapdoor. The Russians beat Otto to death and shot his wife. They tore apart the shop, but they were drunk and not very good at what they did and never found the trapdoor beneath which Heinrich trembled with his treasures. For three months they peed on priceless canvases and drank vodka while Heinrich hid beneath the floor, listening to their balalaika and living on jam and stale bread and a drum of water that tasted of diesel, only emerging when they were asleep or out on patrol.

"My God," Joe Cooley said. "How does a boy live through that?"

"He was luckier than most," Max said. "He was alive."

After the Russians left, Heinrich resumed his father's business under the new reality of life in East Berlin. As the years passed and Heinrich heard nothing from Walter, he assumed his brother was dead or a prisoner of the Soviets, which amounted to the same thing. But one day a man came to the gallery with a letter from Walter, instructing Heinrich to give his crate to the man carrying the letter.

"Heinrich only kept his journal for a few months after that," Max said. "The last entry was made just two days before the Stasi raided the gallery. It is possible they were aware of his black-market dealings. We have no further word of Heinrich. He disappeared."

Max paused, taking a drink. He took off his glasses and rubbed his eyes. "Walter also disappeared, but he had a great deal of help, from some very surprising sources." He picked up the next document, a declassified U.S. Army report, and continued the story.

Walter Beck was captured by American forces as he made his way toward northern Italy. His papers identified him as Horst Schmidt, a Wehrmacht chaplain. His interrogation by an army lieutenant had just commenced when Beck, desperately ill, collapsed in a faint from a lucky but severe case of flu and was carried unconscious to the infirmary. After his recovery, a paperwork mistake sent him directly into the general camp population of POWs without further questioning. He never had to bare his arm, on which the SS blood-group tattoo would have betrayed his identity. After the general release of prisoners he spent the next three years working in an olive grove on a farm owned by a friend of the SS, part of an underground network devoted to helping ex-Nazis elude detection. One day he received a packet with Red Cross identity papers and an Argentine landing permit, provided through the efforts of Alois Hudal, an Austrian bishop at the Vatican.

In May 1948 he boarded a Croatian freighter bound for Buenos Aires, where he was welcomed into a community of German fugitives among Argentine Catholics. He was given a laborer's job in a saddle factory, but introductions made by his contacts soon led to work for the Perón government, which needed officers like Beck to train the military. Beck also found himself sought out by the American CIA, which paid him to provide a steady stream of hearsay and gossip about men he had known in his ancestral home, in what was now East Berlin, in exchange for which they kept his identity a secret. Beck was soon living opulently, happy to serve both masters. He married an heiress and thought his future secure.

After a decade or so things began to fray. The Americans grew bored with gossip and their money dried up. And then an Israeli team kidnapped Adolf Eichmann, who lived quite near Beck.

Argentina was no longer safe. He needed money. He left his wife without saying good-bye and went deep underground, hiding in a basement flat belonging to a sympathetic Argentine diplomat. He used his network to send a man to his father's gallery in Berlin, to collect the case he'd left there in 1945. The crate traveled to Argentina in a diplomatic shipment, a costly but common method used by the Nazis to transport contraband out of Europe.

Beck had the reliquary broken down, the gold melted, and the jewels mounted and sold. He also disposed of several of his paintings, modern works by Picasso and Chagall, highly marketable at the time.

He made his way to Paraguay, whose president, Alfredo Stroessner, had long provided another safe haven for Nazis. Beck lived in Asunción for nearly a decade, making regular payments for protection but growing more uncomfortable as the corruption of Stroessner's government spiraled out of control. Men with so little personal honor would sell him for a pittance to the Jews, who were not letting go of a long-ago war. Josef Mengele was in country, one of the most high-profile targets alive.

One day Beck noticed two young men watching him at a café. They appeared not to know each other, one on a bicycle, another reading a paper, but to his growing paranoia they might as well have been wearing Stars of David. They followed him but he lost them. He did not return home but collected his valuables from their hiding place and fled to La Paz.

"This brings us to Victor Maslov," Max said. He pulled a thick stack of clippings from a file. "He figured prominently in a series of articles in the *New York Times* about international arms dealers."

Victor Maslov had scrapped his way up from nothing, starting work for a cousin who had acquired a World War II–era American bomber and converted it to carry freight. The cousin was no businessman but Maslov was. He learned to fly and soon was ferrying black-market goods to Croatia and Yugoslavia, Greece, and Hungary. He dealt mostly in wheat and flour at first, then beer and whisky, willing to make dangerous night landings as he built a network of partners in Europe and Africa. He soon had two more planes, graduating to small arms along with the whisky, then abandoning whisky altogether and selling nothing but arms. As regional conflicts grew so did his capabilities. His fleet eventually included an Ilyushin-76 aircraft big enough to ferry tanks.

He bought from America and Europe and sold in every corner of the world, meticulous with the end-user certificates he needed to keep the business legitimate under international law. His was a world of killers and despots, and one did not survive in that world without being ruthless and shrewd. Wherever he operated men died, whether as victims of the weapons he sold or from the hidden workings of his enterprise. He was a master of the grey world of the international arms trade, protected by powerful interests in every country. Governments condemned him at the same time they did business with him.

The press dubbed him the Merchant of Death. News magazines ran full-color spreads of the destruction caused by his weapons, sometimes in the same issue in which they ran features about his private life. One of the world's most eligible bachelors, he had homes in Los Angeles and Paris, a liking for high-stakes gambling, and impeccable taste in clothing and women. He had one genuine passion: he loved fine art. He collected it, studied it, was moved by it. He was self-taught, spending time in galleries and museums the world over. His acquisitions came from established auction houses and dealers and from less legitimate sources. Not only did he love art, he sometimes used it as currency in cases where a government's financial controls hindered a particular transaction.

In 1981 Maslov was in Bolivia to negotiate a large arms deal with General Luis García Meza, the brutal new Bolivian president. A bizarre alliance of characters had swept Meza to power in 1980, including the Roberto Suarez drug cartel and a group of Nazis and young neofascists led by Klaus Barbie, a member of the Gestapo known as the Butcher of Lyon.

Maslov disliked dealing with drug-financed clients because they attracted the attention of the American DEA, which Maslov feared more than the drug lords. They at least operated ethically, but the agency had used vile means to bring down more than one of his competitors. He was glad of their misfortune but had no desire to join their numbers.

Maslov was in the Palacio Quemado in La Paz on the final day of a difficult negotiation, in the course of which he had sized up Meza as an untrustworthy fool who would hold power no more than six months. Meza had placed a sizable order but wanted more weaponry than he could afford, particularly semiautomatic weapons and grenade launchers. He was still $8 million short of Maslov's price. Meza had little hard currency and offered drugs instead, seeming genuinely surprised when Maslov laughed out loud at the notion, then compounding the humor by suggesting that Maslov extend credit. Exasperated, Maslov had excused himself to let Meza confer with his advisers.

That was when, almost absently, he noticed the Caravaggio.

He nearly strode right by it, a dark painting in a dark corner, propped casually with a half dozen others against a wall dominated by the gilded-gaudy portraits of Bolivian dictators and generals, which in turn were dwarfed by a twenty-foot painting of Simón Bolívar astride his horse, victorious on the battlefield.

The painting was unsigned, but Maslov knew the artist almost as surely as he knew his own face in the mirror. All of the paintings propped against the wall were valuable, but only one truly mattered to him.

Maslov returned to his meeting. "As you might know, Excellency, I am something of an art enthusiast. I see four or five pieces there that might interest me. Perhaps we could make an arrangement that would solve your cash-flow difficulties?"

"We can do nothing with those, at least not yet. They belong to a new supporter. A friend of Barbie's, a Colonel Beck. We are at a stalemate. His estimation of their value is, I'm afraid, quite inflated."

"If I am not overstepping, what does Colonel Beck want?"

"What they all want," Meza said contemptuously. "A diplomatic passport and money. He claims the paintings are worth eight million. Our expert placed their value at no more than four."

Maslov knew their expert, the director of the national museum, a man who'd spent a lifetime acquiring portraits of generals and their horses. He had to be a fool of considerable accomplishment to have missed this, but he had.

"Your expert is wrong," Maslov said.

"Perhaps, but no matter. We have summoned a specialist from Paris to settle the difference."

Maslov shrugged. "Suit yourself, but I'll give you Beck's eight. However, I leave tonight. The offer is good only if we conclude the arrangement now, at this moment. If so you'll have your weapons—the entire order—before the week is out."

Meza could barely conceal his surprise, but he saw the opportunity to up the ante. "Unfortunately, my friend, it is not so easily done. The offer is very generous, but the paintings are not an outright gift. Colonel Beck wants cash out of the deal."

"How much?"

Beck had asked for $2 million. "Three million," Meza said.

"Why don't you throw him in prison and keep it yourself?"

"His German friends continue to provide us support. We cannot alienate them. Besides, these are not the last of his assets. We may need him again."

"Very well," said Maslov. "I'll pay the colonel myself."

"But . . ." Meza fumbled for words, outmaneuvered.

"I insist," said Maslov, rising to leave. "Do we have a deal?"

That night Caravaggio, Velázquez, Picasso, Braque, and a few others accompanied Victor Maslov to Los Angeles. From the aircraft he made a call to General Torrelio, the minister of the interior who was seeking to overthrow the young Meza dictatorship. Maslov did not often betray a client, but he knew not to back a loser. General Torrelio was delighted to receive details of the impending shipment and promptly wired $2 million to Maslov as the discounted price for the weapons. Maslov knew the money came from the DEA, which sweetened the deal. A week later, the promised arms shipment arrived at a remote airstrip near La Paz. Torrelio's men ambushed Meza's troops and took possession of the cargo Maslov had sold to Meza. It was the beginning of the end of the young Meza dictatorship.

A Bolivian colonel delivered a message to Walter Beck, arranging a meeting at which he would be paid for the paintings and given his new passport. Beck appeared punctually, secure in the knowledge that the Bolivian generals did not betray their benefactors.

Eighteen hours later, an unconscious Walter Beck was carried off a plane in Tel Aviv and bundled into the back of a battered van. His captors did not care to repeat the spectacle of an Eichmann trial. Beck awakened naked in the Negev desert, in a tiny dark cell with a dirt floor and a slit for a window. He bloodied his hands pounding on the walls, calling for help from men who did not hear him. It was hellish hot. "Water!" he screamed. "Animals!"

In Bolivia, word leaked that the Israelis had abducted Beck. The Israelis denied it. Of course, everyone assumed they were lying.

Max closed the folder on Walter Beck and Victor Maslov. "That's just about it," he said.

"Just about," Joe Cooley said. "But there's the obvious question—how did a man like Victor Maslov part with a painting like this? How did it get to you?"

"A petty thief, a man named Lonnie. One of the most interesting clients I've worked with in thirty years. He sent me a letter." Max found yet another magazine clipping, this one featuring his own picture.

"Remember this?"

It was Max's gift that he was able to read people. He had been wrong on occasion, but not often, and the trepidation he'd felt about Lonnie Mack contacting him out of the blue being a disguise for some sting or fraud had dissipated the instant they met. By the end of the meeting he was as certain as he'd ever been of anything that Lonnie Mack was the genuine article. Sometimes it was that way in the art world: a Rembrandt discovered at a rummage sale, a Braque in Aunt Sally's attic. And then a man like Lonnie, a petty thief who accidentally stumbled into the mother lode.

Lonnie was skinny, nervous, and polite, worried whether he could trust Max, at first saying that it was a friend who had actually stolen the painting but quickly giving up that pretense.

"So I can trust you, I mean, even if it was stolen? I mean, not that I did, or anything. I just know someone."

Max waved his hands. "Please, Mr. Mack, tell me. If I can't help you, I'll tell you that, too. There are many possibilities with something like this—including returning it to the owner, or their insurance company, for a reward. That can be done anonymously."

"Really?" Lonnie's eyes lit at that. "OK then. See, I'm a termite man, you know?"

"I beg your pardon?"

"Termites, you know. Bugs."

"Ah." Max raised his eyebrows. He did not understand.

"My brother Frank has a company. We kill drywood termites. They do a lot of damage, you know? They'd go through this place of yours in about a week. The only way you can get them is gas."

"Gas?"

"Yeah. Sulfuryl fluoride. We have to wrap it up in tarps—the whole house. Takes three days. I'm the one does the alarm systems, so we can clear the house and secure it. Well, I always tell the owners to change their codes after we finish, but I've taken a course, you know? I can fix the box so I can still get in, even after they've changed it.

"I check out the house and see what there is to boost later on. We gas the termites, take off the tarps, and that's that. Then a few weeks or months later, I get back in and help myself. I never get greedy or nothin', just stuff that's easy to get rid of."

"That's not risky?"

"Nah, that's the easy part. On the way out I set the alarm, and then just break a window or door. Alarm goes off, police show up, bam. Burglar, they think."

Max was amused. "And this is how you came across this painting? A . . . termite job?"

Lonnie nodded eagerly. "What a place, you know? Some kind of international businessman or something. I never met him. Always traveling, they said, real hotshot. I only met his man, this guy who said he was a curator. I didn't know what that was until he told me; he took care of the stuff. Boy, did that place have stuff. Marble statues like in a museum, and bronze in the halls, paintings everywhere, and antique furniture. Fact is, I really didn't like it much, you know? I figured the termites might actually improve things, but you don't say that to a customer.

"We looked around and boy, there were termites. You can tell by their feces. They leave little piles, you know? You see those piles, that's your house, coming down.

"He was all worried about the paintings. I told him it was probably one of the frames that brought the termites in in the first place, from Bora-Bora or somewhere, and that the gas would hurt them, wouldn't hurt nothing except food and dogs and like that. He said he couldn't take any chances, though, so he went to all the trouble to get the pictures out of their frames.

"He called an armored-car company to pick everything up, and that's when I got lucky. My guys were setting up, you know, tarps everywhere, plastic and all, and these guys are crating up the pictures, very white-glove deal. Big waste of time, but it's not my money, OK? Must have been a hundred crates, all over the place, but I didn't care, I was just noticing they had a pretty good set of copper pots and pans in the kitchen.

"They finished up and signed their papers, and the armored cars left, and I had to see everyone out, see, it's my job and I have to be very careful so nobody gets gassed. And that's when I saw they missed a crate. It was half-covered by some of our plastic already and they just missed it, you know?

"I didn't even know what was in it, but I knew I could take it and nobody would ever be the wiser, because they signed the papers and all, and if they ever noticed, they'd figure it was the armored-car guys, and some insurance company would pay. I don't like insurance companies much, you know? So I took it."

Lonnie shrugged. "Easy as that, but I have to say I was pretty disappointed when I got the crate open. A bejillion bucks' worth of stuff in that house, and all I managed to get was an old painting. A pretty gross one at that. Kid holding up a guy's head, blood everywhere. Definitely not something to hang next to your TV, you know?

"I thought about just throwing it out, or even taking it back and leaving it in the hallway, and no one would ever know. Hell, I couldn't do nothin' with a painting. The only painting I'd ever boosted was a velvet one. They said it was done for Elvis Presley, you know? Or was it by him, maybe? Anyway, I got eight hundred bucks for it, so I was pretty happy.

"So I didn't know what else to do, I just nailed it up in the shed. Then one day Della—she's my girlfriend, she works in a beauty salon, and like five years later, she brought home one of those magazines the customers look at, and there was a story about a lost painting. The picture was a lot like mine, only hanging in Italy or something. I knew mine was old, too, so . . . well? I just thought it might be the real deal. So I brought it home and showed Della, and we put it up over the dinette."

"So that's how you found me," Max said. In thirty years there had been only one public blemish on the Wolff Gallery. The story had been sensational, involving famous clients and alleging that Wolff had sold a stolen painting on the black market. Max had done that very thing many times, but not in the instance alleged in the article. Nothing had come of it except for a libel suit, which Max won, and the publicity, which had not been altogether a bad thing. The story had run in the same issue as that about the lost Caravaggio.

"That's right," Lonnie nodded proudly. "I read the article. So, Mr. Max Wolff, do you think you can help me?"

Joe Cooley laughed out loud. "Imagine that," he said. "A Caravaggio, hanging in a trailer. Next to the spaghetti sauce."

Max smiled. "I actually think Caravaggio himself might have approved."

He closed the file and patted it. "So there you have it. Quite a simple provenance, really. A curse heaped upon a damnation, one of the scholars said. A mirror of its maker, perhaps." He gave a little shrug. "Or just a beautiful painting. So, tell me. You are satisfied?"

"I was satisfied, my friend Max, the moment you told me I might buy this at all," he said. "But I am curious. Why *did* you come to me? Why not give the painting back to Maslov?"

"Simple economics. I know Victor Maslov quite well. He would pay me a finder's fee. Generous, no doubt, but a mere reward. You, on the other hand, will pay me more—still only a fraction of its true worth, but a great deal more—and of course you will never display the painting in public, any more than Victor himself could. If you did, you would face an embarrassing and endless succession of lawsuits as the painting's former owners tried to recover what at one time belonged to them. No publicity, no trouble. The painting will satisfy your vanity—forgive me, but is it not true? And you will treat it well and leave the question of its ownership to your heirs. As for Victor, he is a realist. I have always treated him fairly. I value him as a client, but I owe him nothing. He lost a painting, I found one. I am neither the thief nor Victor's police. I am just a simple art dealer."

Joe Cooley Barber laughed at that. "Simple indeed," he said, shaking his head. "It's good enough for me."

"I think I'll have a glass of wine now," Max said. Joe Cooley poured him one, and a double whisky for himself. He picked up the phone and reached his business manager, who called their banker. New York, the Bahamas, the Caymans; the money moved at light speed as Max nursed his wine, lost in thought. When he received confirmation from his own banker he stood and Joe Cooley helped him with his things.

"Done, then," Max said.

"As quickly as that," Joe Cooley Barber said. "The good Lord is smiling, that this troubled painting has found a home in a blessed place at last. A golden new entry in the provenance."

The private jet lifted off, giving Max a glorious view of the sun setting over Pikes Peak. He felt a great calmness, and slept peacefully on the flight. Once back in his Manhattan study he telephoned Lonnie Mack, who ecstatically received the news that he would receive half a million dollars for a painting he had nearly tossed out. "You'll have the money tomorrow," Max said. "But I must remind you that you must not say anything about this to anyone."

"Are you kidding?" Lonnie said, hurt, his euphoria briefly tempered by Max's caution. "I never talk about my jobs."

"Of course not," Max said. "Just being cautious. Tell me where you'd like to meet. Somewhere safe. You choose."

Lonnie thought for a moment, then gave him an address. Max heard him whooping for joy as they hung up.

Max made another call. "Victor? Max. Quite well, thank you. I have wonderful news. I've recovered your painting. Yes, the Caravaggio."

He smiled at Maslov's reaction. Of all his clients, Victor Maslov loved his art the best. "Yes, quite certain. It's in good shape, considering it's been hanging in a storage shed for a few years. It had spaghetti stains, believe it or not, but no lasting damage. I've had it cleaned in my studio. It's as good as new. I'm looking into David's eyes right now." He lightly touched the shepherd's cheek. "Such a powerful work, my friend. The triumph of good over evil."

Max gave Maslov brief details about how he'd recovered the painting. "Yes," he laughed. "As easy as that. It was just a lucky call, that's all.

He's a good kid, Victor. I promised him half a million—a modest fee, I think, even though he took the painting. Yes, good. You'll take care of that for me? Just a moment, I've already lost the paper." He patted his pockets, then realized the paper was still sitting on the table. He read off the address. "Yes, that's right."

"There's the matter of your finder's fee," Maslov said. "I was thinking five million."

"Please, Victor. You're a good client, but that is too generous."

"The painting is worth many times that to me. I thought it was lost forever. I thought my curator took it." Victor laughed. "All this time, a termite man." Max knew that Victor's curator had died in an automobile accident not long after the theft.

"I'll be happy to take your money once the painting is safely back in your hands," Max said. "For now you just need to send someone for it." He couldn't resist a gentle jab. "Someone competent, please. It wouldn't do to lose it again."

The next day, as promised, Lonnie Mack received his cash, neat stacks of bills in an aluminum briefcase delivered by a man he didn't know. Lonnie had never seen so much money. He took it home to Della with a bottle of expensive champagne, and they began planning a trip to Las Vegas.

That night the local TV news stations led with a story of a fiery explosion in a trailer park, the result of an apparent propane leak. News helicopters captured dramatic footage of the flames and smoke from the blast, which leveled half a dozen homes and left an unknown number of dead.

It was the part of the business Max enjoyed least. One could not have Lonnie concocting stories for the press, any more than one could have him showing up on the doorstep in a year, looking for more money.

Accompanied by two bodyguards, Victor Maslov's new curator picked up the Caravaggio in person, fairly bubbling with enthusiasm when he saw it. A few days later Victor wired the finder's fee to Max, less the money that had gone up in smoke with Lonnie.

Now Max had only to decide what to do with the original Caravaggio, still sitting in his office.

* * *

There were, of course, a few details he'd left out of Joe Cooley's provenance—particularly about Heinrich Beck, Walter's younger brother. His journal had ended with a Stasi raid, but not his story.

The Russians who killed his parents had billeted in Beck's building for several months, while he remained hidden in the vault below the basement. He emerged only at night to forage for food and water, at rare moments of safety.

Beneath the trapdoor his father had built, Heinrich filled those lonely months with painting. Though surrounded by beautiful art, he had no new canvas on which to work, so he painted over some of the works he liked least, trying his hand at new ideas, then scraping canvases clean to start again. He also worked at his copies, learning to mimic brushstrokes and color and depth. It pleased him how good his copies were, and how much the process taught him. Among the originals, of course, were those in his brother's case. The more Heinrich studied the Caravaggio, the more he admired it. He made six copies in all but kept only two, reusing the other canvases. He knew the two copies were the best he'd ever done.

The Russians eventually abandoned the gallery and he emerged from his hiding hole. Life in postwar Berlin was difficult, but Heinrich was a survivor. Art remained easy to work with and was better than currency if one knew how and had the connections, and of course Heinrich had both. He still had scores of paintings from the cellars that had survived with him, and he began trading. For a long time his business was conducted mostly in secret, buying from the nameless and selling to the faceless, servicing newly humbled Germans who denied the past and bowed now to Russian masters, as they set about learning the new subtleties of festering Bolshevik corruption.

It was not long before it occurred to Heinrich to sell his own copies as well. It was easy, particularly among the new elite classes who had money but knew nothing whatever of art. Heinrich knew his father would have been appalled, but his father was dead and he was not, and that truth made for the only rules that mattered. He painted new copies and traded and bribed and survived as the war began to recede and Berlin rebuilt and the radio ran hot with a new cold war.

Walter's icy note, demanding that he give the crate to the emissary, prompted Heinrich to do what he did. He reacted impulsively, from anger—for shame at what Walter had done to the family name, for parents dead because of Walter's past, for a note that merely demanded obedience, asking nothing about him or his parents.

He sent his brother one of the copies, sure that Walter would never know the difference.

The Stasi raid told him how wrong he had been. They had come at night after the gallery closed and he was alone. They were not only Stasi but former SS, and they had known what they were looking for. They asked him where the original painting was hidden. The more he denied any knowledge, the more they beat him. "You are a fool," one said. "Your brother left a mark on all his paintings. It was missing from the one you sent."

Heinrich did not give up the painting. He decided he would die before he would do that. They nearly obliged him, beating him savagely.

They helped themselves to a fortune in other works, loading canvases into the back of their truck, taking everything they could carry. Before leaving, one of the men untied his right arm and forced it out over the workbench. "Your brother told us not to kill you," he said as Heinrich struggled fiercely. "He did tell us, however, to make certain you never fooled him again." Using a ball-peen hammer, the other man carefully smashed the bones of Heinrich's right hand, and then each of the fingers, one by one.

Heinrich Beck never wrote another word in his journal, and never painted again. It took him two years, but eventually he was able to buy the passport of a dead German youth named Max Wolff and bribe his way out of East Berlin, the Caravaggio and one copy rolled up with some of his own paintings. The U.S. customs agent glanced at a few of the canvases and waved the lot through, as the amateur work of a second-rate student.

Now Max considered what to do with the original. He was an old man, running out of time. Perhaps he ought to think about a legacy. He considered bequeathing it to the village of Stawicki, where it had spent more than three centuries, but that seemed so . . . profitless.

He leafed through his old telephone messages, and found one from a newly wealthy Chinese collector who was looking for precious art. Something important, he had said. Something spectacular. He was going to build a museum.

Carrie Vaughn

New York Times best seller Carrie Vaughn is the author of a wildly popular series of novels detailing the adventures of Kitty Norville, a radio personality who also happens to be a werewolf, and who runs a late-night call-in radio advice show for supernatural creatures. The eleventh and twelfth Kitty novels, *Kitty Rocks the House* and *Kitty in the Underworld,* were released in 2013. Her other novels include the Young Adult books *Voices of Dragons* and *Steel;* a fantasy, *Discord's Apple;* and the superhero novel *After the Golden Age.* Vaughn's short work has appeared in *Lightspeed, Asimov's Science Fiction, Subterranean, Wild Cards: Inside Straight, Realms of Fantasy, Jim Baen's Universe, Paradox, Strange Horizons, Weird Tales, All-Star Zeppelin Adventure Stories,* and elsewhere. Some of her short stories are collected in *Straying from the Path* and in *Kitty's Greatest Hits.* She lives in Colorado. Coming up is *Dreams of the Golden Age,* a sequel to her superhero novel, and more books in the Kitty series.

Even rogues need a place to drink and relax, like the Blue Moon Club in the suspenseful story that follows, although being *in* a place where rogues drink and relax, you'd be well-advised to watch your back—even if you're a rogue yourself.

ROARING TWENTIES

Carrie Vaughn

The good thing about Blue Moon is that it's invisible, so it never gets raided. Bad thing is, being invisible makes it hard to find for the rest of us. You have to have a little magic of your own, which Madame M does, and finding places that aren't there is never much of a problem for her.

Madame M has the car drop us off at the corner of Fifth and Pine, and she sends the driver away. I follow her down a damp sidewalk along brick buildings. It's early enough that the streets are crowded, cars and people jammed up on their way to somewhere else, no one much looking around. A few wheezing horns honk, and the orange from the streetlights make polished steel and frowning faces seem like they're lit with embers. I shrug my mink more firmly over my shoulders. Madame M's has slipped down to her elbows, showing off the smooth skin of her back. We look like sisters, walking side by side, in step.

The alley she turns down looks like any other alley, and that passage leads to another, until we're alone with the trash cans and a yowling cat, under iron fire escapes and a sky threatening rain. She knocks on a solid brick wall, blocks from any door or window, and I'm not surprised when a slot opens at head height. She leans in to whisper a word, and the door opens. Either a door painted to look like bricks or the wall itself swinging out; I can't tell and it doesn't really matter.

The music of a three-piece combo playing jazz drifts in from down the hall, and it sounds like heaven.

The doorman, a gorilla of a guy in a brown suit that must be tailored to fit those shoulders, looks us over and nods his approval. He's got a little something else, extra fur around the collar, on his hands and tufting off his ears. When he smiles, he shows fang, and his eyes glint golden. He's some kind of thing, far be it from me to guess what. I walk on by without meeting his gaze. A coat check girl who seems normal enough, but who knows, takes our furs, and I tip her well. A clean-cut, scrubbed, and polished waiter guides us into the club proper. There's a table just opened up, of course, a table always opens up for Madame M. I order soda water for us both, and the waiter looks at me funny because why come to a place like this if you're not into booze? The booze here is good, top-shelf, smuggled in, not cooked up in some unsavory backwoods tub. Maybe later, I tell him, and he scurries off.

We're near the dance floor, in the middle of everything, and the place is full. The band is a white guy on piano, and two black guys on bass and drums, and a microphone stand means someone might sing later, but for now they're playing something with a bit of a kick, and couples are dancing on a tiny floor down front. At first glance it's a normal crowd on a normal night, flappers and fine women in evening gowns, men in suits and even a few tuxes. Looking closer I see the odd fang and claw, the glimmer of a fae wing, a bit of horn under slicked-back hair, other bits and pieces I might guess at, but I'd likely be wrong. These folk aren't drawing attention to themselves, so I won't either, because then they might start looking too closely at me and Madame M.

Doorways lead to back rooms where you can find cards and craps and whatever else you might fancy. One doorway is covered by a shimmering beaded curtain, and through them and the cigarette-smoke haze beyond I can just make out a grand lady holding court at a sofa and coffee table, surrounded by men in suits and women dolled up like paintings. The scene is vague, as if I'm seeing it through etched glass.

Madame M wants to talk to Gigi, the woman behind the beaded curtain, who runs the place, and I think it's a bad idea, but I'm not going to argue because M's smarter about these things than I am. The back-and-forth and the deals, the secrets and the swindles. The things I'm smart about: watching her back and seeing trouble a minute before it happens.

It's just the two of us in a den where the gamblers and bootleggers are the least of it. There are people here who'll drink your blood dry if you let them, others who'll tear out your throat, and a few who'll buy your soul, even knowing how little some souls around here are worth. M and I do all right, her tricks and my eyes keeping us safe. A couple of molls out on the town, that's what we look like, in our colored silk and fringe, bare shoulders and knees, dresses that swish and show off our hips when we kick our heels and shimmy our legs. Sequins and feathers over bobbed hair. They think we're easy prey, and they'll be wrong.

The drinks arrive more quickly than I expect because I think the waiter is on the other side of the room taking someone else's order. But no, he's right here, polished as ever, smiling as he transfers glasses from tray to table. The music plays on, and M sips.

"Something bad's coming," she murmurs.

I'm looking out. A card game's going in the corner. Nearby, a gangster's foot soldier is trying to impress his girl, both of them leaning over their tiny round table while he shows her the gold band on his watch. Her lips are smiling, but her eyes are hungry. She's trying to get something out of him. A dozen small intrigues are brewing. Mostly, though, people are here to have a good time, to drink some good booze and revel in the feeling of getting away with something bad.

"Raid?" I answer. "A takeover? Is Rocco finally moving in on Margolis?" Anthony Margolis is the one presiding over the card game. He's here playing to show he isn't worried about Rocco or anyone else.

"No, this is bigger. Everything goes to hell."

With her I can't tell if that's a metaphor. "This one of your dreams?"

"Visions," she says. Takes a sip, leaves a print of red lipstick on the glass.

"The future?"

"It is."

"What do you want me to do?"

"Same as always: Keep your eyes open and invest in liquor."

She's thinking out loud, and it makes me nervous. More nervous. I nod to the beaded curtain. "She's gotta know you're here."

"She's going to make me ask," M says.

"That's what we're here for, yeah?"

"Let's just pretend like we're here for a good time." She leans back, stretching through her back, and puts one arm over the back of my chair. I draw a cigarette out of my clutch, light it, offer it to her. Her gloved and jeweled hand takes it, she draws a long breath from it and lets out a cloud of smoke, her mouth open and lazy. Her foot taps along with the music.

Her pretending to have a good time looks like the real thing. She could make a living doing anything she put her mind to, but she's ended up in a place like this for a reason. So have I.

The place smells of alcohol and sawdust. Nothing is off in the rhythm, waiters and drinks flowing from bar to tables and back, a cigarette girl making the rounds. The card game in the corner is accompanied by a lot of nervous laughter, men pretending like the grand they just lost doesn't matter while sweat drips onto their collars. If any trouble is going to happen, it'll come from them, one of the jokers taking issue with another, then tipping over the table and starting a fistfight. The gorilla by the door would have made them leave their guns, so that's one thing I don't have to worry about. M and I can take cover easy enough from a fistfight. Bullets, not so much. Being invisible can't always save you from getting shot in a cross fire.

Third song in, halfway through my drink, a guy stumbles in from outside, gaping like a fish out of water, which he is, and I wonder what he said to get past the gorilla. He must have something, a charm or an aura, first to find the place and another to make himself look like he belongs. Now he stands at the entrance, gazing around, eyes wide like he didn't expect it to work, and now that it has, he doesn't quite know what to do. He wears a nondescript brown suit, belatedly takes off his fedora. He's clean-cut and square-jawed, and he has a gun in a shoulder holster under the jacket. He must have had a spell to hide that, too, because the gorilla should have spotted it.

Everything in Blue Moon pauses for a half a breath because some kind of balance has shifted and everyone feels it. The piano muffs a chord, and a string on the bass twangs. The guy looks back at all the eyes on him before straightening an extra inch and scowling.

Then it all goes back to what it had been a second ago as if nothing happened.

I watch the band, keep the new guy in view out of the corner of my eye, and lean into M like I'm telling a joke. "I think we've got ourselves a Fed."

She's too polite to turn and stare but does raise an eyebrow. "How'd he get in?"

"I don't know. He's armed."

"Maybe he's just here to have a good time, like everyone else."

The Fed looks like a hunter who's found himself a prize. Casual-like, he leans on the bar. Doesn't flag the bartender, doesn't ask for anything, just watches, staring hungrily at all that bootlegged liquor sitting on the shelf, wondering how big a raid this would really be if he could pull off a raid. The bartender ignores him, wiping down the counter cool as ice and pretending he doesn't have a Fed breathing down his neck. A minute later, the Fed flags the waiter, who shows him to a table in back, and my neck itches because I can't see him anymore but I feel him staring straight at me.

Guy knew enough to get in here, he'll figure out soon enough who the people with the power are, and the problem of getting M out of here in one piece when trouble starts gets a lot more complicated.

M puts a hand on my arm, pats it once. A signal to calm down. I listen to the music, watch the dancers on the floor, and try to remember that we're supposed to look like we're having fun.

The cigarette girl walks past our table for the fourth time, eyeing me and M but not saying a word. Cute kid in satin shorts and a bustier, dark hair done up under a little hat. She's one of those girls with legs up to here and too much makeup painted on, but that's the style and she knows how to wear it. She slinks deftly between the tables, maneuvering her box in front of her, counting out change and never missing a beat, like she's been doing this a while. Still manages to smile.

The fifth time she walks past, not offering cigarettes but still catching my eye, I raise my hand for her to stop. She seems grateful when she does, a bit of a sigh expanding the spangles of her neckline.

"Pack of cigarettes," I say. "There's something else you want to ask, isn't there?"

She looks back and forth between us, which tells me she knows us by reputation but doesn't know which of us is Madame M, and which of us is just that sidekick Pauline. I nod at M, indicating that she's the one the girl ought to talk to.

"What's the problem, dear?" M asks. "Quickly."

I pretend to dig in my clutch for an elusive bill, making her wait, giving her as much time as she needs.

She screws up her expression and says, "I'm stuck. I mean, we're both stuck. I mean—" She lowers her voice to the barest whisper. I can barely hear, but M doesn't even have to lean forward. "—I mean, I gotta get out of here, and I gotta take my guy with me."

"Your guy?"

"One of Anthony's boys." Her eyes dart to the card game in the corner, and I spot her guy right off, one of the heavies standing guard, medium-size and baby-faced, in a cheap suit. He's got his hands deep in his trouser pockets and he's sweating harder than any of them. He keeps glancing over here, lips trembling like he wants to say something.

"We've saved up the money to get to California, to go straight. But we don't need Anthony or . . . or her coming after us." She doesn't have to gesture to the woman behind the beaded curtain. "I . . . we . . . we can pay you." She looks worried, like she knows exactly what she's really saying, what the price of M's help might really be.

M regards her, a sly smile on her face. I've got my hand on a bill; I can only keep digging around in my clutch for so long.

"Your bosses don't approve, I take it? Of you kids ditching your gainful employment—your *families*—to run off? Regular Romeo and Juliet story?"

The cigarette girl bites her lip. It shouldn't be too tough a problem, not the kind of problem a person would usually bring to M. But she knows Anthony, and even more than that she knows Gigi, and the problem isn't so simple as all that. I watch M; even I don't know what she's going to say.

She stubs out her last cigarette and takes another from the pack I just bought. "I think we can manage something. But pay attention—you won't get a second chance."

The girl nods quickly. "And how much—"

"I'll ask for something, when I think of the right thing. But for now . . . Pauline?"

My hand already in the bag, I scrounge around a second and find the empty matchbox I know she's asking for.

M says, "I need a hair from you and a hair from him. It'll help me keep track of you. Can you do that?"

She already has, it turns out, reaching into the back of her white glove and drawing out the two thin strands, twined together. M seems impressed that she's come prepared—she knows exactly what she's asking for.

I offer the girl the dollar bill I've dug out of my clutch, which hides her slipping the hairs to me. I put the hair in the box and hand the box to M. Transaction complete, the girl dons her professional cherry-lipped smile again and bounces off.

"You going to ask for their firstborn?" I say to M, raising a brow.

She grimaces. "What would I do with a kid?"

So now I have to look out for the girl and her beau, and wonder what it is exactly M has planned for them. Should be fun to watch. M will decide when she makes a move, and all I can do is wait for her to give the sign.

The combo takes a break, comes back, and a singer, a beautiful round black woman in a rose-sequined gown, her hair twisted up and pinned with a silk magnolia, steps on stage and adjusts the microphone stand.

M pushes her tumbler away and stands from the table.

"I'm going to be brazen. I'm going to get a message to Gigi," she says, nodding at the bartender.

I glance at the bartender, who hasn't looked up, who's been pouring drinks and sodas all night, shaking cocktails and dropping cherries into tumblers like clockwork. When no one's around he just wipes down the surface, over and over.

"Think it'll work?"

"Maybe if I look desperate, Gigi'll talk to me."

I don't say that M already looks a little bit desperate. "I'll hold down the fort."

She tosses me a grin. I watch her slink to the bar, hips sashaying under her dress, causing the beads and sequins to flash. Her brown hair in a perfect bob, not a strand of hair out of place, her skin that perfect flawless ivory. People assume she keeps up her looks with magic, but she doesn't. It's all her, just her. She isn't so vain that she'd waste her magic on something as trite as looking good.

The woman at the microphone sings, her voice as rich and sweet as I knew it would be, the kind of jazz too hot for the clubs you can just walk into off the street. I sit back in my chair, sip my soda water, and pay attention. Watch the people who are watching M, wondering what angle she's working.

Behind the beaded curtain, the smoke and shadows haven't changed. Gigi must know we're here, but she must not care.

Back to the card game. The poor young goon keeps glancing toward the worried cigarette girl, who circulates and does good business, smiling enough that most people don't notice the crease in her brow. She's smarter than her beau because she doesn't dare look back at him. The boy doesn't give himself away because anyone can forgive him for staring at a long-legged girl all night. I try to think of how M will make good on her promise to help them out. She might just send them a couple of train tickets and a bit of a spell to make them invisible, or at least make it so no one sees them. That'd be the simple thing.

On the other hand, I bet there's a way to do the whole thing without magic. If there is, that's what M will do, just to show that it can be done, to show that she doesn't rely too much on the tricks she's known for. To keep people guessing. A distraction and a threat. That's all she'd need to get those kids out of town. And I hope once they get where they're going, they settle down for good and have kids and all the rest, and realize forever how lucky they are.

The back of my neck is still itching where the Fed's been watching me this whole time. Me, not M, or he would have wandered over to the bar where she's leaning in to talk to the bartender. I can't see the Fed, but I'm not surprised when he arrives at our table, pulls out M's chair, and sits. I don't even flinch.

"Mind if I join you?"

I smirk at him. The pack of cigarettes we bought from the girl is still there, so I pick it up and hold it out. "Cigarette?"

The Fed takes one and keeps his gaze on me. I strike a match and offer a light because it's only polite. Then I wait for him to say something. He seems content to watch, and my job is to let him. I can wait all night, as long as that beauty at the microphone keeps singing.

"I know who you are," he says finally.

"Oh?"

"I think we can help each other." He leans back, acting cool, and turns his gaze to the singer. "Say I wanted to move in, and I wanted a partner—"

"I give you the key to the place, you make sure I don't get swept up in the raid, maybe slip me something under the table, especially if you keep me in your pocket?"

Right up till that moment, he thought he had me fooled. "Well. That's putting it bluntly."

"I thought I'd save time."

"This place is going down one way or another, but having help will make it easier, and you look like a woman who knows what's what."

He's talking to the wrong woman, he's gotta know that. Maybe he thinks I want to move up, that I'm tired of being hired help. Which tells me something about how he sees the world.

"Flatterer," I say, my eyes half-lidded.

"It's a sweet little setup here, I have to admit," the Fed says. He scans the room, the players and dancers, and I'm pretty sure he doesn't see the horns tucked under feathered headbands or the tails curled under trousers. He pauses a moment at the card game in the corner before landing back on the singer. He never seems to notice the beaded curtain. "To think it's been slipping past us all this time." He snubs out his cigarette.

"Can I ask you a question?" I say, studying him with honest curiosity. He waves a hand for me to continue. "How'd you get in here? Guy like you, with such a clean suit and clean hands, shouldn't have been able to find the door, but here you are."

"Give me a little credit. We've had our eye on this place for a long time."

He's bluffing. Half-lidded, he got himself a few tricks and trinkets, maybe strong-armed some low-level fortune-teller into helping him out. Or maybe, heaven help him, he found a book of spells and worked it out on his own. Like handing a guy a loaded gun without showing him how it works.

I can't write him off because nothing in Blue Moon will keep the bullets in that gun from killing if he decides to shoot.

"What exactly are you looking for from me, Mr. Clean Suit?"

"How about you just keep quiet for now and not warn anyone I'm here?" he says. Like I'd have to warn anyone. "If you have anything else for me, we could work out a deal."

"I'll think it over, let you know."

"Thanks for the cigarette," he says, and leaves my table to return to his own, and I get the feeling he thinks I might really help him if he just sticks around long enough.

M leans on the bar for a respectable few minutes before returning, a sway in her hips, her smile wry. She's brought a couple of fresh sodas.

"You made a friend," she says.

"I believe we have ourselves a crusader with a stick of dynamite and no idea what to do with it," I say. "We might think about being on our way. Take care of our Romeo and Juliet, then wander out while we can. Give the word, I can start a diversion—"

"No, I still have to talk to Gigi."

I knew that's what she'd say. "So what did the bartender say?"

"Not a damn thing. He's a zombie."

Gigi's got herself a zombie bartender? I chuckle. "Cute. So a shot of whiskey's a shot of whiskey, nothing skimmed off the top and nothing extra for the band." I glance over, and sure enough, the bartender's standing in the same place, wiping down the surface, back and forth, over and over. His skin is gray, his expression slack.

"She'll talk to me, I just have to wait her out."

"Not a thing you can do about it if she doesn't want to talk to you."

She's got her chin in her hands and is looking hard at the beaded curtain. We wait, and I have to resist an urge to look over my shoulder at the Fed, who's still sitting there, watching, waiting.

The singer's finished her latest song, a slow sad piece about how he done her wrong, and she keeps coming back, like the girls always seem to do in these songs. People listen to the songs and think they'd never do that, they'd never go back to a guy who treated them bad. Then they do, because they're different. Their love is different, like it is for everybody, and it's hard to stay away when you're in love, and you're sure he'll change, so you keep going back. Unless you have someone in your life who sits you down and says, "Don't." Like M did for me.

A rare thing, having someone like that in your life.

Gigi's not going to talk to M, I'm sure of it, and we're going to sit here all night, and I'm sure now the Fed's going to do something stupid because if he'd been smart, he'd have cased the joint then left to make a plan to come back with more muscle. He's painted a target on himself. I can get M out through a back door. You need a little magic to get into Blue Moon, and it helps to have a little magic to get out, but I'll charge straight out if I have to. Lack of subtlety, that's how you beat magic.

"He's got you worked up," M says.

My back is stiff, and I keep glancing over my shoulder out of the corner of my eye. Not doing a good job of pretending to have a good time.

She continues, "He's harmless. He's got no trap to spring, and he's too proud to leave without a trophy."

"I'm worried about what happens when he pulls out that gun."

"Pauline, relax. I'm more worried about Gigi than I am about some guy in a government suit."

The scene behind the beaded curtain hasn't changed. Gigi is back there, holding court, not paying any attention to M at all. I ought to trust Madame M. She's so rarely wrong. But she's not seeing the big picture right now.

I think I have a plan for getting rid of the Fed.

"You trust me?" I say to M, who furrows her brow at me.

"Sure. What are you thinking of?"

"It'll just take a minute."

"That's not what I asked."

But I'm already gone. Looking around casual-like, dodging past that fast-moving waiter, my gaze falls on the Fed. I look thoughtful, interested. He's been watching me like I'd hoped, and I give him a sweet smile. There's a chair at the table, tilted out, just waiting for me. Let him think he made the invitation and planned the whole thing himself.

"Mind if I sit?"

He gestures to the chair and I fold myself into it, demurely crossing my ankles. I reach into my clutch for a pack of cigarettes, but not the pack we bought from the girl—another one that I save for emergencies.

"Another cigarette?" I offer, and he takes one, and I helpfully light a match for him.

He takes a long, slow drag, and what he blows out doesn't smell quite like tobacco, but he doesn't notice. "You look like you have something to say."

"Just some advice," I say. "The thing is, you're talking to the wrong woman if you think you'll get anything from me or my friend."

His expression turns skeptical, his brow furrowed. He thought he had the place figured out. "I know who you two are. Madame M and Pauline, the two dames who aren't what they seem. You think you're under the radar, but you've left fingerprints on a lot of business in this town."

"Fingerprints don't mean we're holding the bag. We leave that to the fancy people." We don't have a place like Blue Moon of our own, or a gang like Anthony's, for a reason. We keep moving because it makes us a harder target to hit.

"Then what fancy people should I be talking to?"

"The deal still stands? I help you, you'll let me know when I should get out, before anything happens?" I even bat my eyes at him.

He taps off the ash and takes another long drag. "Of course. I'll keep you out of it for sure."

Doesn't even matter if I believe him. "You really want to know what's going on here and who you need to deal with, you gotta talk to her." I nod to the stage.

He frowns. "The singer?"

"That's right. Quite a front, huh? She stands up there, keeps an eye on the whole place, and no one ever realizes she isn't just working for tips."

"That's very interesting."

"You bet it is."

I'm about to stand and leave when he leans in close. His breath smells of what he's been smoking, sweet and sour and just a bit wrong. "Can I get you a drink? Show my appreciation?"

"Thanks, but I've got my drink. Soda water. I'm a law-abiding citizen, just like you."

"Well, then. You keep your nose clean, hear?"

I can't punch him, not yet. If this works, I won't have to.

Heading back to my table, I pause, because the scene has shifted. Not paying attention, I missed the moment the cigarette girl disappeared. The cigarette girl's beau is sweating buckets, and his boss is going to notice, especially when the lunk can't stop looking at the door and is fidgeting like he wants to run out. M is over by the door talking to the gorilla and trying to catch my eye. Her frown shows it's serious, and I've missed her cue. She raises an annoyed eyebrow. Past time for that distraction. I understand her plan, the need for a long fuse and a slow burn. That means I probably still have time to get started.

I put on a smile and walk on over to the card game.

Anthony sees me. He's likely been watching both M and me just as hard as we've been watching him. Maybe not *just* as hard. But I doubt he'll have any idea what we're up to. What we're *really* up to, I mean. We're those two crazy witches, and who knows what a broad's looking for when she starts scheming, right?

I touch the shoulder of the player across from Anthony. The guy shivers and licks his lips, and he won't be good for anything for the rest of the game. I focus on Anthony.

"Got room for one more, Mr. Margolis?" I ask, sweetly as I know how.

"Pauline. Doll," Anthony says, opening his arms, a gesture of false generosity. "How much would it take to hire you away from that broad?"

He thinks he's being clever. He thinks he's putting me in my place, and M too, for all that. I know what he sees, what he thinks he sees.

"Oh, honey, you know you can't afford me," I say, as if I'm really sorry.

"But Madame over there can?"

"You gotta understand, we're like sisters."

He shakes his head like he thinks it's a pity. "Harry, deal the lady in, why don't you?" He makes a sign and the men at the table shift their places, and the cigarette girl's beau brings over an extra chair. I know what the stake is, two grand, and I draw the bundle of bills out of my clutch and put it on the table. The players pretend not to be surprised.

The one called Harry, who's got a thin moustache and a suit so blue it's almost purple, deals me in, and we play cards. Harry's a local guy who's completely honest because if he weren't, nobody would play in Anthony's game. People play in Anthony's games because they think they can get rich off him, but the secret is that Anthony's actually a pretty good player. He doesn't play with his pride is the thing and can fold when he has to.

The dealer deals, I sweep up my hand and play. I've done this enough it's reflex, habit. The cards are going to do what they do, I just have to keep up the rhythm.

First order of business is to break even, because two G's is worth something no matter what you have. And it's a matter of saving face, and making sure the boys don't think they pulled one over on the doll. So we play poker, and I earn back what I put in, and after that I'm not playing to lose, but I'm not exactly playing to win, either. I'm playing to bide time, watching Anthony watch me because he thinks I'm up to something, while I'm also watching the kid, M, and the Fed. And the beaded curtain, just in case. M's about to mess up her pretty club, surely Gigi will notice and put her foot down.

M is by the bar again, looking more relaxed than she did a minute ago, so maybe I'm not too late with this. Maybe it'll all work out and we won't have to run out in a rain of bullets. People might wonder why M's not surrounded by men hoping to make time with the beautiful doll who's all on her own. I think maybe she's decided not to let them see her.

Two of the guys at the card game know about M and know, therefore, that they can't discount me. But two of the guys figure I'm the rube. They have a very bad time of it but stick it out because of pride. Who's the rube, then?

I lose a hand, win a hand, and the players chalk it up to luck because it's easier than admitting a woman can actually play. I don't win too much, so they don't get angry. They start bantering again, not forgetting I'm there so much as not taking me seriously.

"Tommy, you okay there?" Anthony studies his young heavy, who's been tugging at his collar. He's going to blow the whole thing if he's not careful, and I realize why the girl needed help to pull this off. All I can do at the moment is glance at him with a bit of sympathy, then study my cards.

Tommy looks back, rabbit-eyed. "It's a little warm in here, sir."

"You're not feeling faint, are you? Tell me you're not feeling faint."

"No, no sir!"

"Good."

And now Anthony's on edge, and this could all fall to pieces. It isn't too late to walk away, if I can warn M . . .

The Fed, still smoking the cigarette I gave him, is looking green around the gills, and in a fit of agitation pushes away from the table and squares his gaze on the card game. On *me.* Like he knows I lied, or that the cigarette I gave him isn't really tobacco. He starts toward the table, and he's got to know better than to approach Anthony. Or maybe he doesn't, after all that smoking . . .

I have to stay cool and not jump up in a panic, which isn't easy. I just have to look like I don't have a clue.

"What's this clown want?" Anthony grumbles, and all his boys go stiff, perking up like hunting dogs at a duck pond.

And just then the singer hits a high note, crazy high, rattling the glasses on the tables and setting my heart pounding. We all can't help but look on in admiration as she holds that note with full lungs, arms wide, eyes closed, and head tipped back, like she's singing the world into being.

The Fed stops, listens, drifts to a table close to the stage, sinks into the chair like he's caught in quicksand. The singer's voice falls back into the chorus and she smiles sweetly at her brand-new greatest admirer.

I catch M winking at the singer. Yeah, M always knows what she's doing.

The game continues. Anthony's boys relax a notch, except for the cigarette girl's guy, who's still watching the door, and Anthony just shakes his head. Not too much longer after that, M touches her earring, adjusts her headband, and strokes the plume across her hair. Time to light the fuse. So I slip a couple of extra aces into my hand. Which I fold. When the hand ends, the dealer sweeps up the cards, shuffles, and deals them out again.

No one ever thinks to accuse me of palming cards, because where the hell would I hide them in this outfit, with all this bare skin?

"Boys," I say, gathering the rest of my winnings, arranging them neatly, fastidiously, "I want to thank you for a lovely time of it, but I've got to go. I hope you're not offended." I blush and bat my eyes, and they can't argue because I haven't done anything to offend them. I haven't cleaned them out. I haven't damaged their pride too terribly much.

"Pauline. Darling. You are welcome at my table anytime." Anthony spreads his arms like he always does. I lean in and kiss his cheek, and his compatriots at the table glare bullets at him. Smiling sweetly over my shoulder, I return to Madame M.

"Well, I was starting to wonder if we could pull this off," she says.

I scowl. "Whatever do you mean?"

"Doesn't matter, we're both on the same page now."

"You'll thank me for putting the whammy on the Fed, just wait."

She nods at the card game. "About five minutes, before they figure it out?"

"About."

"I'm going to go powder my nose. Hold down the fort?"

"I always do."

In about five minutes, right when we called it, the first of the players shouts, "Hey, what are you trying to pull?" Loud enough that everyone in Blue Moon looks over.

"What do you mean, what am I trying to pull, what are *you* trying to pull?"

"You can't have three aces, because I have three aces!"

"Boys, boys!" Anthony hollers, but it's too late. Anthony follows the rules, so they've left their guns outside, but that doesn't stop one of the players from tipping over the table when another guy takes a swing at him. Cards and chips and bills go flying, then skitter across the floor. The bodyguards and hangers-on rush in, trying to protect Anthony, who's already taken one on the jaw.

All except Tommy, who's smarter than he looks because he's gotten out of the way. M moves to his side and whispers in his ear. He follows her to the front of the club, and I might have been the only one to see them go.

I move to the back of the club and try to be invisible, but I'm not as good at it as M is. A dancer screams as the fight spills onto the floor, and the band is back, playing in an only partially effective distraction. A couple of guys look on eagerly, crack their knuckles, and smile wide enough to show inhuman fangs. They'd enjoy a fight, and they'd win, oh yes.

I know better than to ask for trouble, so I sit on the bar, out of the way. But I have to move when the zombie bartender starts wiping down the surface around me.

M joins me, and we're watching the proceedings, along with a few other creatures of the night. I've got a bottle in hand, an empty that the zombie bartender missed, just in case.

"Everything cool?" I ask M, and she smiles, and I imagine the cigarette girl and Tommy are on a bus for the coast. Good luck to them.

"Nice bit of entertainment," she observes, and I beam.

The Fed only has eyes for the singer and doesn't seem to notice the whole place falling into an uproar around him. The singer has moved to sit at the edge of his table, still crooning, and twining a strand of his hair around her finger. She's somehow gotten a drink in her hand and offers it to the Fed, who takes a grateful, enamored sip. We won't have to worry about him for the rest of the evening.

"You know she's a siren, yeah?" M says, watching this play out.

"I sure do," I say.

She grins. "And that I wouldn't trust that drink as far as I could spit it?"

"Oh, I know." The Fed's sipping down his bootleg whiskey like he's in heaven and thinking the siren's singing just for him.

"He wasn't going to cause any trouble, you know," she says. "Not tonight, anyway."

"No, I didn't know." She just shakes her head.

One of the heavies slams up against the bar, and I crack the bottle over his head because it's a classic move and I can't resist. The bottle breaks, pieces of glass rain down like bells, and the lunk of a guy slides to the floor, unconscious. Very satisfying.

There's a wrestling mob in the middle of Blue Moon now, accompanied by otherworldly growls, and a few more people seem to be sporting fur than did before, and some of those fangs might be dripping blood now, and it's a bit more than I'd anticipated, and I'm thinking it's time to get M out of here.

Then, a glass chiming like the sound of icicles rings over it all. The sound should be subtle, but it's rattling, and the whole place pauses, time stopping. The fistfights cease, the punches stop landing, chairs are raised over heads but don't come down, and everyone turns to the beaded curtain. A woman stands there, pushing back the strings of beads with an ebony cigarette holder, studying the place through long lashes. She's wearing a red silk dress like a second skin, her hip cocked out, arms crossed, and she's got a thing about her, like once you see her you can't look past her. And once she sees you, you're trapped because she knows everything about you and there's nothing you can do about it.

And everyone, even the singer, even Anthony, even me, looks away, chagrined, knowing we've stepped out of bounds. Everyone looks away but the Fed, who's put his face down on the table and seems to be weeping, and M, who looks right back at her.

It's all over. At some signal, the gorilla bouncer and a couple of his buddies wade in and start throwing people out, including Anthony and his boys. The gangster is shouting that he doesn't know what happened and he had nothing to do with it, but it doesn't matter. He never even notices that his kid Tommy is gone. When he does notice, he might even figure out that me and M had something to do with it. But he won't be able to do a thing about it. Besides, there's a hundred kids where Tommy came from and revenge isn't good for business.

Once the trouble is gone, the waiters rush in to sweep up glass and set tables upright, and I realize why I've had such a hard time keeping track—there are three, identical triplets or something else. They move in a coordinated routine without speaking, like they can read one another's minds, zipping through the place, so efficient because they can do triple the work. How do you like that?

Across the tables and past the waiters cleaning up broken glasses and spilled drinks, the woman in red meets M's gaze, and a long moment passes. I hold my breath and wait, heart thudding, because I don't know what's going to happen, how this is going to play out, who's going to look away first and what it'll mean. All M wants to know: Will Gigi talk to her? Gigi isn't giving anything away.

Gigi looks behind her, to a handful of people who troop out of the back room as she holds the curtain aside. Men in suits, but none of them are goons, they're all fine businessmen in tailored jackets, expensive handkerchiefs peeping out of front pockets, rosebuds nestled on lapels. On their arms walk beautiful women with perfectly painted faces, flappers in short dresses and ropes of pearls, walking on high heels, looking bored and superior. Kept, I think, not hired, because they cling a little too desperately to their beaus' arms, as if they might fall off if they're not careful. And this, I think, is why M is self-employed.

We're not kept. We work for our place, and we do not have to cling.

Then the woman in red, Gigi, nods, and M nods back, and at the same time they turn away, the one retreating back behind the curtain, M looking around for her chair. Right around us, the chairs and tables are knocked over, and we stand there like a couple of rowboats gone adrift. I wave to a waiter, who runs over and sets a table and a couple of chairs upright, wipes them down, and even finds a little vase of silk flowers to put in the middle of it.

We sink down into the chairs at our table and lean close to talk.

"What's it mean?" I say.

"I don't know."

"She going to talk to you or not?"

"I don't know." She says it calmly, like it doesn't matter, and maybe it doesn't. This was a long shot to start with.

"She's playing with you, making you wait. She thinks she's better than you, and this is how she proves it."

"If she has to prove it, she knows she ain't."

"How long are we waiting?" I'm impatient. We've been here too long already, and I have this vision of Anthony and his boys, or his remaining boys rather, waiting outside for us, to give us one of those little talks. M's got her tricks and we'll walk away, but Anthony's got his tricks too, and I worry that one of these days M's won't be enough. I have to see that day before it comes, and I worry that I won't.

"A little while longer," she says. "I thought you liked her." She nods at the singer, who's back, and M is right, the woman is beautiful and her voice is ringing, and couples are back to dancing on the floor like nothing's wrong because fights break out all the time in a place like this, it's part of the reason people come here. I also notice: The Fed is gone, probably thrown out with the rest of the mob. I hope he's too trashed to remember Blue Moon or any of the rest of us.

We've been here too long.

"It's just one beautiful girl on one night," I say. "I'm worried about you."

"I'm fine." She frowns, and I raise my brow at her. "I thought I was looking after you," she says.

"That's right, you are."

A waiter comes over. Either the first or one of his brothers, I can't guess. I don't know if it's a trick, if there's a reason for it, some con Gigi runs where she needs a set of identical triplets waiting tables, but it wouldn't surprise me. I spend a few minutes thinking about it and what I would do with identical triplets working for me. M would have some ideas if I ask her about it.

But the waiter is talking to M, and I cock my ear to listen.

"She'll see you now, in the back, if you'll come with me."

M turns to give me a look like "I told you so" and moves to push back from the table. I pick up my clutch and do likewise, when the waiter says, wincing apologetically, "I am sorry, it's only Madame who may come with me."

How do you like that? I try to plan out the next few moments because there's no way I'm letting M walk into that room without me.

"Pauline is my best friend in the world," M says, clearly shocked and offended. "We don't go anywhere apart. We're like sisters!"

Not much like, I think, but that's too long a story to tell. But M doesn't have to tell the story because she's batting her eyes at the guy, who's clearly ready to fold. "Please, it won't hurt a thing, I just know it."

The poor kid sighs. He knows he's being duped but what can he do? "All right, all right. Both of you, come with me."

We pass through the beaded curtain, bits of glass chiming around us, bending the soft light into colors. The music outside is suddenly distant, like we're in a whole other building or a whole other world.

Gigi lies back on a red velvet sofa, her smooth legs tucked up next to her. She frowns. "I only wish to speak to Madame." Her tone is light, observational, but the waiter wilts.

M launches in, "Oh, let Pauline stay. I promise you she won't hurt a fly." And butter wouldn't melt in her mouth, I swear to God.

Arching a skeptical brow, Gigi taps ash off the cigarette in the end of the holder. "Peas in a pod, you are. Fine. Let them both in."

She has no bodyguards, no goons to watch for hidden guns or break up fights before they start. Rather, she doesn't have the usual kind, apart from the gorilla at the door. Here in her sanctum, she doesn't need the men in suits with shoulder holsters tucked under their jackets. She's got other eyes looking out for her. I don't know what exactly would happen to someone who tried something back here, but I'm not going to be the one who tests it.

Gigi turns the cigarette holder to a straight-backed padded chair across from a little round table in front of her, an arrangement designed for serious meetings, for two people staring at each other, reading each other while they make deals. M folds into this chair like a pro, crossing her ankles, leaning forward like she's about to tell a secret. I put myself in a sofa tucked off to the side and pretend to study my nails.

The room is set up like a parlor, with the chairs and sofas collected around the table, cabinets against the walls holding cut-crystal decanters sparkling with amber liquids. Tiffany lamps give off soft yellow light, so that the dark brocade wallpaper seems painted with shadows. Looking into this room from outside, the place is shrouded, the beaded curtain and cigarette smoke fogging the view. Looking out, though, the bar, tables, dance floor, and band are all clear. I can see straight back to the entryway and the main door and the gorilla standing guard. Doesn't seem like I should be able to, it doesn't seem quite right, but there it is and I try not to question it too much. The mist in the air might be as exotic as opium, but I'm pretty sure it's only tobacco. She might try to dope her associates, but never herself.

The woman in red starts, which is only right because it's her place. "Well, my dear, how are we going to do this little dance?"

"You know what's coming," M says, to the point, not playing the game or doing the dance, and I can't tell if Gigi is surprised by this. She doesn't twitch a muscle, not even to blink, and the cigarette holder never trembles. Smoke flows straight up from its end to the ceiling.

A moment passes; we wait for Gigi to agree or disagree. She doesn't. "And?"

"I'm aiming to circle the wagons. Safety in numbers. We're stronger together than we are apart. We always have been."

"What's in it for me?" she asks. The cliché is beneath her. I can't help but think she's gone soft. Not soft, not in the way she treats people or runs her business. But soft in that she's comfortable. She knows what she's got and she's keeping hold of it. She's not thinking ahead because she thinks that she's got it as good as it can get. M isn't going to get the answer she wants at the end of the meeting.

"Safety," M says without hesitation. "Longevity. Peace."

"Those are very abstract words."

M says, "We can pool resources, double protections around us and ours, and the vultures—like Anthony Margolis and that Fed—won't be able to touch us. How'd that Fed even get in here tonight, hmm? It isn't like you, Gigi, to let a crack open up in your armor."

Gigi tries not to fidget, but her legs straighten and recross, and she looks at M with such contempt. "He's nothing. Didn't take much to take care of him, did it?" She looks at me, her smile cruel.

How hard it is to keep quiet. I bite my tongue and try to watch every square inch of the room for the thing that will leap out and bite us.

There's a phonograph in the corner, sitting on a little mahogany table. Its scalloped bell is turned out to the room, like it should be, but there's no record on the platter, and no needle on the arm, which means it's doing something else other than playing records. The skin on my neck crawls a bit, thinking of what else it might be doing.

"This thing that's coming," M says, trying one more time. "It's not magical. It's not the vampires or the sirens or anything. It's economic. It's the businessmen, the bankers and stockbrokers and money people who'll bring it all down. People like you, who think you're safe, and that nothing's ever going to change. What'll you do, Gigi, when everything changes?"

"Why are you so worried about me?" Gigi says, as if amazed.

"Why not?"

"I can take care of myself. You should take care of *yourself,* instead of worrying about people who don't need your help." She takes another drag on the cigarette, lets it out in a cloud through her round mouth. Just like M might do. M studies the woman in red for a long moment, and Gigi won't notice the sadness there because she isn't looking. She leans over to tap off her ashes into a glass dish.

Then suddenly she looks up, concerned for no reason that I can see. M hasn't done anything different, and I haven't moved an inch. But she's looking over M's shoulder, through the beaded curtain to the dining room, which is silent. The band's stopped playing, voices have stopped humming, not even glasses clink against each other, and now I'm worried too. I don't need any extra sense to tell that the whole pattern of the place has changed, and it's got to be worse than I think for Gigi to be looking like that.

There's a gunshot, a body falling to the floor with a thud.

M rushes to the curtain to see, and I follow, ready to push her back into safety. It should be me walking first into the trouble, and why does she always have to see what's happening? Gigi pauses a moment to pull back the slit panel of her skirt and retrieve the pistol held in a garter, and that's when I know it's bad, worse than bad.

M pushes back the curtains and we all see the tableau as it happens, the five or ten guys in suits and fedoras pulled low over their heads storming into the place, all armed and ready for battle like soldiers in the Great War. Some with tommy guns, some with shotguns, one guy with a revolver. All led by him, the arrogant Fed who's got his raid, just like he promised. Must have sobered up after he got thrown out—and he remembered, too bad. Must have stuck wax in his ears to get past the siren, and sure enough, I see them all with cotton sticking out of their ears. Had to hand it to the guy, he might not have held all the cards but he was figuring out the game all the same. But he should have waited until he had the whole thing figured out, and not just part of it. Footsteps pound, a woman screams.

The gorilla manning the door is lying dead on the floor, and the Fed must be using silver bullets to be able to kill him. That's why no one's taken him out.

"Everybody freeze!" the Fed hollers.

It's like some scene out of a moving picture, and I imagine everyone's getting shot and dying, reaching up, trembling dramatically as the bullets hit them, collapsing in ways that no one ever does in life but people in the pictures must think looks good. Can't see the blood splatter in the pictures, or maybe they just haven't figured out how to fake that yet.

I grab M's arm to pull her out of the way, just as Gigi pushes past us, maybe to get a better look. I don't care if she gets shot, but I have to get M out of here.

Everyone's staring, frozen just like the Fed asked. Gigi and all her people all stare, the band and singer, and even the zombie bartender, because this isn't supposed to happen. Blue Moon is supposed to be safe, and if Feds can raid the place that's supposed to be invisible, then what else can they do? It's like a little bit of magic going out of the world.

M puts her hand over mine, smiles at me, with an unspoken command: Wait. She's crazy, or she's got a plan, and because it's M, it's got to be a plan, so I wait.

"Everybody, down on the floor! Flat on the floor! This is a raid!" He sounds so pleased, like he's won a battle. His men spread out through the room.

From across the room, the Fed looks right at me like I've done him some specific wrong. He's too far away for me to reach, for me to do anything but frown at him. I've got all kinds of thoughts, though, about snatching that gun right out of his hand and maybe kicking in his kneecaps. I clench my hands and glare, for all the good it does.

M leans close to Gigi and says, "Didn't see this coming, did you?"

"Did you?" Gigi spits back.

M looks at me, and I smile.

She walks past Gigi onto the dance floor. Now all gazes fall on her. She has drawn every last bit of attention just by moving, and I want to scream, because here and now attention isn't a good thing—every Fed in the place turns his gun to her, and fingers move to triggers. But she knows what she's doing, she always knows.

Raising her arm, she makes a gesture, fingers bent in a pattern that looks simple but no one could ever replicate. Looking right at the Fed, she waves her other arm to encompass them all, and it's like the air goes thin and sound fails. There's a pop in my ears, like sinuses clearing after a bad cold, and the Fed's rage-filled snarl freezes. Trigger fingers are still, the gunmen stand still, and no one even blinks. They are more still than stone because the stillness of stone is natural, and this is something else.

The others in the room, the band and singer, the waiters and patrons and gangsters look at one another as if confirming this is a dream, and brush themselves off like they've been in a storm. They start moving around, studying the gunmen, who are nothing more than obliging statues.

"I'm just doing what the guy asked." M brushes her hands like she's wiping off dust, but I know they're spotless. The Fed can't do a damn thing now, when she walks up to him and starts patting down his jacket and trouser pockets. I can almost see the protest in his watering eyes, though.

It's the jacket's inside pocket where she finds the spell book, a drab little thing with a red cover, worn edges, and a broken spine, like it's been sitting in some attic for a century or two, just like you'd expect an old lost spell book to look. M scans the first couple of pages, smirks.

"That's what I thought," she says. "You had talent, to get this far. You could have made something of yourself. But you thought you could pick this up and aim it like a gun. Well, it doesn't work like that. Pauline?"

I step forward at her call. She hands me the book, and I put it in my clutch. We'll get rid of it later.

"You can clean this up?" Madame M asks Gigi.

Gigi purses her lips. She might be thinking a million things and won't say any of them. She might be shocked at what M could do on Gigi's own territory, but she won't show it. Even after this, Gigi still doesn't know how much power M really has. She so rarely shows off.

"Yeah. Sure. I'll clean 'em up and throw 'em out." She nods, and the triplet waiters go around to all the goons, depriving them of their weapons. However much we all might want to make the whole crowd of them disappear, most likely Gigi will just obfuscate their memories and throw them in some far-off alley where they can't bother her anymore. She'll find a new guard for the door.

"Remember what I said," M adds. "Call me if you change your mind."

Gigi wears her sneer like a mask. "I'll do that."

M's got on a sad look and might stand there all night, but I touch her arm and point her to the door. I don't know what to think about Gigi except maybe to feel sorry for her. To have someone like M around wanting to help and to snub her like that.

Gigi calls after us one last time. "M. Don't get in too much trouble."

"You too, Gigi."

And that's that. I take one last look over my shoulder to the beautiful singer, who's singing again, trying to get back to normal, crooning about how wonderful it is to dance in the arms of your man. It's got to be near dawn, closing time. She's singing to a near-empty room, the only ones still around are the waiters and the zombie bartender, who's still got that rag in his hand, wiping.

We retrieve our furs from the coat check girl, a new guard—also thick as a barrel, with odd fur around his ears—opens the door to let us outside, and we're back on the street, next to a dirty brick wall, and the glow from a distant streetlight makes our shadows long. She keeps walking. The car ought to be around here somewhere. It'll find us when she wants it to find us. Meanwhile, she's in a mood to walk, and I stay at her side.

"You got a bottle of whiskey in that thing?" M asks, nodding at my clutch.

"Probably. Might have to go digging around for it." The clutch is no bigger than my two hands put together, but it's got everything in it because that's what it's designed for. Cigarettes, cash and poker chips, a pretty little Derringer for emergencies that no one will ever find unless I want them to, a handful of bus tokens, an extra pair of stockings, a spool of thread, and a lipstick. And now an odd little book of spells. Maybe I can find a bottle of whiskey.

"Never mind." She gives a deep sigh. "I knew it was a long shot. Oh well."

"She doesn't know what she's doing," I say.

"Not our problem. Not anymore."

We walk for maybe half a mile, and I might be tough and M might be magic, but my shoes aren't built for this and I'm getting sore. But I'll stay right with her. The sky is gray, the sun's coming up.

We pause when we hear singing, gruff and out of tune. It's around the next corner, and I can't help it, I have to go look. And there he is: The Fed's lying in the gutter, no jacket, his shirt torn open. His shoulder holster is hanging lopsided, and he's got a revolver in his hand, waving it around in what might be despair. Gigi took their guns—but he must have had one hidden, under a trouser leg maybe. So the Fed's standing here, gun in his hand, lost as a puppy and trying to figure out where his life went, and who to blame.

I put myself in front of M like I always do in my imagination in this scenario. This isn't too rough. We can get away, get out of his sight before he even knows we're here, and I press back against M, urging her to turn around.

Too late, though, because the Fed sees us, and his arm suddenly becomes steady, and scrambling to his feet, he levels the weapon.

He's got us in his sights and the gun is real. No back door to escape out of. I can hear M breathing hard behind me, and I don't know if she has any tricks for this.

"What—what *happened* in there?" He's gesturing with the gun, like it's an extension of his arm.

I can feel sweat freezing on my skin under the silk of my dress. "I don't even know what you think you saw."

"Yes, you do, you saw everything, you saw it all! I don't even remember! What am I supposed to tell the director?"

He can shoot me and say it was my fault. Sure he can. Can't come back from his raid empty-handed, and I think how silly, that it all comes down to this, getting held up in a back alley by some drunk-ass Fed.

I step forward and grab the gun out of his hand, all in one smooth movement that he doesn't see coming. The weapon comes loose from his hand like a plucked flower, and he collapses into a sob, leaking tears and snot, hands over his face. He slumps to the sidewalk.

We stand looking down at him. I'm holding this weapon that I don't want. But I'm relieved, M is safe, and all is well. Sprawled on the concrete, he starts singing his mashed-up song again, and this time I can hear what it is, or what it's supposed to be: the one the siren at Blue Moon sang, about the guy who done her wrong.

I empty the bullets from the chamber into my clutch and drop the gun on the sidewalk. I say, "You think we should help him? Call the cops or something?"

"He's not going anywhere. They'll find him soon enough. Come on, Pauline."

She loops her arm around mine and we walk away. The car pulls up to the curb ahead of us, right on schedule, and the driver gets out to open the door for us. Time to go home, wash the paint off my face and roll into bed.

"I wonder sometimes how it all could have come out different," M says. "With Gigi, I mean."

"I don't think you could have said anything—"

"Not here, not now," she says, turning inward, thoughtful, and I can't guess what webs she's spinning, what plans she's making, or past plans she's picking apart for the flaws. "I'm talking ten, twenty years ago. Did all this happen because I took her doll, or because she stole my licorice? Or because Mama loved her best, or me best? I don't know who Mama loved best, or if she loved either of us at all. Probably doesn't matter one little bit."

I don't say anything because what can I say? I've never gotten the whole story about M and Gigi's mama, probably because I haven't asked. And I won't. I don't want or need to know because it wouldn't change a thing.

"I imagine it doesn't," I say. "You and your sister have done most of this your own damn selves."

M smiles, squeezes my arm. "I'm a lucky woman to have you walking by my side."

"Oh, I don't know about that. I thought I was lucky that you put up with me at all."

"The two of us make the best damn gang in this city, you know that? No matter what comes, we'll be okay." She doesn't sound certain.

"Yes, ma'am," I say firmly. "We will."

Scott Lynch

Fantasy novelist Scott Lynch is best known for his *Gentleman Bastard* sequence, about a thief and con man in a dangerous fantasy world, which consists of *The Lies of Locke Lamora,* which was a finalist for both the World Fantasy Award and the British Fantasy Society Award, *Red Seas Under Red Skies,* and *The Republic of Thieves.* He also runs an online serialization of a novel, *Queen of the Iron Sands,* on his Web site, www.scottlynch.us. He lives in New Richmond, Wisconsin, but spends several months of the year in Massachusetts with his partner, SF/F writer Elizabeth Bear.

Here he takes us to a beleaguered city, torn by a war among wizards and under assault from deadly magic raining from the sky, where a desperate group of thieves and rogues must steal something that's impossible to steal—and are running out of time to steal it before forfeiting their lives.

A YEAR AND A DAY IN OLD THERADANE

Scott Lynch

1. *Wizard Weather*

It was raining when Amarelle Parathis went out just after sunset to find a drink, and there was strange magic in the rain. It came down in pale lavenders and coppers and reds, soft lines like liquid dusk that turned to luminescent mist on the warm pavement. The air itself felt like champagne bubbles breaking against the skin. Over the dark shapes of distant rooftops, blue-white lightning blazed, and stuttering thunder chased it. Amarelle would have sworn she heard screams mixed in with the thunder.

The gods-damned wizards were at it again.

Well, she had a thirst, and an appointment, and odd rain wasn't even close to the worst thing that had ever fallen on her from the skies over Theradane. As she walked, Amarelle dripped flickering colors that had no names. She cut a ghostly trail through fog that drifted like the murk beneath a pink-and-orange sea. As usual when the wizards were particularly bad, she didn't have much company. The Street of Pale Savants was deserted. Shopkeepers stared forlornly from behind their windows on the Avenue of Seven Angles.

This had been her favorite sort of night, once. Heavy weather to drive witnesses from the streets. Thunder to cover the noise of feet creeping over rooftops. These days it was just lonely, unpredictable, and dangerous.

A double arc of silvery lights marked the Tanglewing Canal Bridge, the last between her and her destination. The lights burned within lamps held by rain-stained white marble statues of shackled, hooded figures. Amarelle kept her eyes fixed on her feet as she crossed the bridge. She knew the plaques beneath the statues by heart. The first two on the left, for example:

BOLAR KUSS
TRAITOR
NOW I SERVE THERADANE ALWAYS

CAMIRA THOLAR
MURDERESS
NOW I SERVE THERADANE ALWAYS

The statues themselves didn't trouble her, or even the lights. So what if the city lit some of its streets and bridges with the unshriven souls of convicts, bound forever into melodramatic sculptures with fatuous plaques? No, the trouble was how those unquiet spirits whispered to passersby.

Look upon me, beating heart, and witness the price of my broken oaths.

"Fuck off, Bolar," muttered Amarelle. "I'm not plotting to overthrow the Parliament of Strife."

Take warning, while your blood is still warm, and behold the eternal price of my greed and slaughter!

"I don't have a family to poison, Camira."

Amarelle, whispered the last statue on the left. *It ought to be you up here, you faithless bitch.*

Amarelle stared at that last inscription, just as she promised herself she wouldn't every time she came this way.

SCAVIUS OF SHADOW STREET
THIEF
NOW I SERVE THERADANE ALWAYS

"I never turned my back on you," Amarelle whispered. "I paid for sanctuary. We all did. We begged you to get out of the game with us, but you didn't listen. You blew it."

You bent your knees to my killers before my flesh was even cold.

"We all bought ourselves a little piece of the city, Scav. That was the plan. You just did it the hard way."

Someday you will share this vigil with me.

"I'm done with all that now. Light your bridge and leave me alone."

There was no having a reasonable conversation with the dead. Amarelle kept moving. She only came this way when she wanted a drink, and by the time she got off the bridge she always needed at least two.

Thunder rolled through the canyons of the streets. A building was on fire somewhere to the east, smoldering unnatural purple. Flights of screeching bat-winged beasts filled the sky between the flames and the low, glowing clouds. Some of them tangled and fought, with naked claws and barbed spears and clay jars of explosive fog. The objectives the creatures contended for were known only to gods and sorcerers.

Gods-damned wizards and their stupid feuds. Too bad they ran the city. Too bad Amarelle needed their protection.

2. The Furnished Belly of the Beast

The Sign of the Fallen Fire lay on the west side of Tanglewing Street. Was, more accurately, the entire west side of Tanglewing Street. No room for anything else beside the cathedral of coiled bones knocked down fifteen centuries before, back when wild dragons occasionally took offense at the growing size of Theradane and paid it a visit. This one had settled so artistically in death, some long-forgotten entrepreneur had scraped out flesh and scales and roofed the steel-hard bones right where they lay.

Amarelle went in through the dragon's mouth, shook burnt orange rain from her hair, and watched wisps of luminous steam curl up from the carpet where the droplets landed. The bouncers lounging against eight-foot serrated fangs all nodded to her.

The tavern had doors where the dragon had once had tonsils. Those doors smelled good credit and opened smoothly.

The Neck was for dining and the Tail was for gambling. The Arms offered rooms for sleeping or not sleeping, as the renters preferred. Amarelle's business was in the Gullet, the drinking cavern under the dead beast's ribs and spine, where one hundred thousand bottles gleamed on racks and shelves behind the central bar.

Goldclaw Grask, the floor manager, was an ebony-scaled goblin in a dapper suit woven from actual Bank of Theradane notes. He had one in a different denomination for every night of the week; tonight he wore fifties.

"Amarelle Parathis, the Duchess Unseen," he cried. "I see you just fine!"

"That one certainly never gets old, Grask."

"I'm counting glasses and silverware after you leave tonight."

"I'm retired and loving it," said Amarelle. She'd pulled three jobs at the Sign of the Fallen Fire in her working days. Certainly none for silverware. "Is Sophara on bar tonight?"

"Of course," said Grask. "It's the seventeenth. Same night of the month your little crew always gets together and pretends it's just an accident. Those of you that aren't lighting the streets, that is."

Amarelle glared. The goblin rustled over, reached up, took her left hand, and flicked his tongue contritely against her knuckles.

"I'm sorry," he said. "I didn't mean to be an asshole. I know, you paid the tithe, you're an honest sheep living under the bombardment like the rest of us. Look, Sophara's waving. Have one on me."

Sophara Miris had mismatched eyes and skin the color of rosewood, fine aquamarine hair and the hands of a streetside card sharp. When she'd paid her sanctuary tithe to the Parliament of Strife, she'd been wanted on 312 distinct felony charges in eighteen cities. These days she was senior mage-mixologist at the Sign of the Fallen Fire, and she already had Amarelle's first drink half-finished.

"Evening, stranger." Sophara scrawled orders on a slate and handed it to one of the libationarians, whose encyclopedic knowledge of the contents and locations of all the bottles kept the bar running. "Do you remember when we used to be interesting people?"

"I think being alive and at liberty is pretty damn interesting," said Amarelle. "Your wife planning on dropping in tonight?"

"Any minute now," said Sophara, stirring equal parts liquor and illusion into a multilayered concoction. "The self-made man's holding a booth for us. I'm mixing you a Rise and Fall of Empires, but I heard Grask. You want two of these? Or something else?"

"You feel like making me a Peril on the Sea?" said Amarelle.

"Yours to command. Why don't you take a seat? I'll be over when the drinks are ready."

Ten dozen booths and suspended balconies filled the Gullet, each carefully spaced and curtained to allow a sense of intimate privacy in the midst of grand spectacle. Lightning, visible through skylights between the ribs, crackled overhead as Amarelle crossed the floor. Her people had a usual place for their usual night, and Shraplin was holding the table.

Shraplin Self-Made, a softly whirring concatenation of wires and gears, wore a tattered vermilion cloak embroidered with silver threads. His sculpted brass face had black gemstone eyes and a permanent ghost of a smile. A former foundry drudge, he'd taken advantage of the old Theradane law that a sentient automaton owned its own head and the thoughts therein. Over the course of fifteen years, he'd carefully stolen cogs and screws and bolts and wires and gradually replaced every inch of himself from the neck down until not a speck of his original body remained, and he was able to walk away from the perpetual magical indenture attached to it. Not long after that he'd found klepto-kindred spirits in Amarelle Parathis's crew.

"Looking wet, boss," he said. "What's coming down out there?"

"Weird water," said Amarelle, taking a place beside him. "Pretty, actually. And don't call me boss."

"Certain patterns engrave themselves on my ruminatory discs, boss." Shraplin poured a touch of viscous black slime from a glass into a port on his neck. "Parliament's really going at it tonight. When I got here purple fire was falling on the High Barrens."

"That's one advantage of living in our prosperous thaumatocracy." Amarelle sighed. "Always something interesting exploding nearby. Hey, here are our girls."

Sophara Miris had one hand under a tray of drinks and the other around Brandwin Miris's waist. Brandwin had frosted lavender skin that was no magical affectation and thick amber spectacles over golden eyes. Brandwin, armorer, artificer, and physician to automatons, had the death sentence in three principalities for supplying the devices that had so frequently allowed the Duchess Unseen's crew to evade boring entanglements in local judicial systems. The only object she'd ever personally stolen in her life was the heart of the crew's magician.

"Shraplin, my toy," said Brandwin. She touched fingertips with the automaton before sitting down. "Valves valving and pipes piping?"

"Fighting fit and free of rust," said Shraplin. "And your own metabolic processes and needs?"

"Well attended to," said Sophara with a smirk. "Shall we get this meeting of the Retired Folks' Commiseration and Inebriation Society rolling? Here's something phlegmatic and sanguine for you, Shraplin."

She handed over another tumbler of black ooze. The artificial man had no use for alcohol, so he kept a private reserve of human temperaments magically distilled into asphaltum lacquer behind the bar.

"A Black Lamps of Her Eyes for me," said Sophara. "A Tower of the Elephant for the gorgeous artificer. And for you, Your Grace, a Peril on the Sea and a Rise and Fall of Empires."

Amarelle hefted the latter, a thick glass containing nine horizontal layers of rose-tinted liquors, each layer inhabited by a moving landscape. These varied from fallow hills and fields at the bottom to great cities in the middle layers to a ruin-dotted waste on high, topped by clouds of foam.

"Anyone heard from Jade?" she said.

"Same as always," said Shraplin. "Regards, and don't wait up."

"Regards and don't wait up," muttered Amarelle. She looked around the table, saw mismatched eyes and shaded eyes and cold black stones fixed on her in expectation. As always. So be it. She raised her glass, and they did likewise.

"Here's a toast," she said. "We did it and lived. We put ourselves in prison to stay out of prison. To absent friends, gone where no words nor treasure of ours can restore amends. We did it and lived. To the chains we refused and the ones that snared us anyway. We did it and lived."

She slammed the drink back, poured layers of foaming history down her throat. She didn't usually do this sort of thing to herself without dinner to cushion the impact, but hell, it seemed that kind of night. Lightning flashed above the skylights.

"Did you have a few on your way over here, boss?" said Shraplin.

"The Duchess is dead." Amarelle set her empty glass down firmly. "Long live the Duchess. Now, do I have to go through the sham of pulling my cards out and dealing them, or would you all prefer to just pile your money neatly in the center of the table for me?"

"Oh, honey," said Brandwin. "We're not using your deck. It knows more tricks than a show dog."

"I'll handicap myself," said Amarelle. She lifted the Peril on the Sea, admired the aquamarine waves topped with vanilla whitecaps, and in two gulps added it to the ball of fast-spreading warmth in her stomach. "There's some magic I can appreciate. So, are we playing cards or having a staring contest? Next round's on me!"

3. *Cheating Hands*

"Next round's on me," said Amarelle an hour and a half later. The table was a mess of cards, banknotes, and empty glasses.

"Next round's IN you, boss," said Shraplin. "You're three ahead of the rest of us."

"Seems fair. What the hell did I just drink, anyway?"

"A little something I call the Amoral Instrument," said Sophara. Her eyes were shining. "I'm not allowed to make it for customers. Kind of curious to see what happens to you, in fact."

"Water off a duck's back," said Amarelle, though the room had more soft edges than she remembered and her cards were not entirely cooperating with her plan to hold them steady. "This is a mess. A mess! Shraplin, you're probably sober-esque. How many cards in a standard deck?"

"Sixty, boss."

"How many cards presently visible in our hands or on the table?"

"Seventy-eight."

"That's ridiculous," said Amarelle. "Who's not cheating? We should be pushing ninety. Who's not cheating?"

"I solemnly affirm that I haven't had an honest hand since we started," said Brandwin.

"Magician," said Sophara, tapping her cards against her breast. "Enough said."

"I'm wearing my cheating hands, boss," said Shraplin. He wiggled his fingers in blurry silver arcs.

"This is sad." Amarelle reached behind her left ear, conjured a seventy-ninth card out of her black ringlets, and added it to the pattern on the table. "We really are getting old and decrepit."

Fresh lightning tore the sky, painting the room in gray-white pulses. Thunder exploded just overhead; the skylights rattled in their frames and even the great bone-rafters seemed to shake. Some of the other drinkers stirred and muttered.

"Fucking wizards," said Amarelle. "Present company excepted, of course."

"Why would I except present company?" said Brandwin, tangling the fingers of one hand in Sophara's hair and gracefully palming an eightieth card onto the table with her other.

"It's been terrible all week," said Sophara. "I think it's Ivovandas, over in the High Barrens. Her and some rival I haven't identified, spitting fire and rain and flying things all over the damn place. The parasol sellers have been making a killing with those new leather-and-chainmail models."

"Someone ought to stroll up there and politely ask them to give it a rest." Shraplin's gleaming head rotated slowly until he was peering at Amarelle. "Someone famous, maybe. Someone colorful and respected. Someone with a dangerous reputation."

"Better to say nothing and be thought a fool," said Amarelle, "than to interfere in the business of wizards and remove all doubt. Who needs a fresh round? Next one's still on me. I plan on having all your money when we call it a night, anyway."

4. The Trouble with Glass Ceilings

The thunder and lightning were continuous for the next hour. Flapping, howling things bounced off the roof at regular intervals. Half the patrons in the Gullet cleared out, pursued by the cajoling of Goldclaw Grask.

"The Sign of the Fallen Fire has stood for fifteen centuries!" he cried. "This is the safest place in all of Theradane! You really want to be out in the streets on a night like this? Have you considered our fine rooms in the Arms?"

There was a high-pitched sound of shattering glass. Something large and wet and dead hit the floor next to the bar, followed by a shower of skylight fragments and glowing rain. Grask squawked for a house magician to unmake the mess while the exodus quickened around him.

"Ahhh, nice to be off duty." Sophara sipped unsteadily from a tumbler of something blue and uncomplicated. The bar had cut her off from casting her own spells into drinks.

"You know," said Amarelle, slowly, "maybe someone really should go up there to the High Barrens and tell that old witchy bitch to put a leash on her pets."

The room, through her eyes, had grown softer and softer as the noisy night wore on and had now moved into a decidedly impressionist phase. Goldclaw Grask was a bright smear chasing other bright smears across the floor, and even the cards on the table were no longer holding still long enough for Amarelle to track their value.

"Hey," she said, "Sophara, you're a citizen in good standing. Why don't we get you made a member of Parliament so you can make these idiots stop?"

"Oh, brilliant! Well, first I'd need to steal or invent a really good youth-binding," said the magician, "something better than the three-in-five I'm working now, so I can ripen my practice for a century or two. You might find this timeline inconvenient for your purposes."

"Then you'd need to find an external power locus to kick up your juice," said Brandwin.

"Yes," said Sophara, "and harness it without any other hazard-class sorcerers noticing. Oh, and I'd also need to go *completely out of my ever-fucking head*! You have to be a dead-eyed dirty-souled maniac to want to spend your extended life trading punches with other maniacs. Once you've seized that power, there's no getting off the merry-go-round. You fight like hell just to hold on or you get shoved off."

"Splat!" said Brandwin.

"Not my idea of a playground," said Sophara, finishing her drink and slamming the empty glass down emphatically.

An instant later there was a horrendous shattering crash. A half ton of dark-winged something, its matted fur rain-wet and reeking, plunged through the skylight directly overhead and obliterated their table. A confused blur of motion and noise attended the crash, and Amarelle found herself on the floor with a dull ache between her breasts.

Some dutiful, stubborn fraction of her awareness kicked its way to the surface of the alcoholic ocean in her mind, and there clutched at straws until it had pieced together the true sequence of events. Shraplin, of course—the nimble automaton had shoved her aside before diving across the table to get Sophara and Brandwin clear.

"Hey," said Amarelle, sitting up, "you're not drunk at all!"

"That was part of my cheating, boss." The automaton had been very nearly fast enough, very nearly. Sophara and Brandwin were safe, but his left leg was pinned under the fallen creature and the table.

"Oh, you best of all possible automatons! Your poor foot!" Brandwin crawled over to him and kissed the top of his brass head.

"I've got three spares at home," said Shraplin.

"That tears it," muttered Amarelle, wobbling and weaving back to her feet. "Nobody drops a gods-damned gargoyle on my friends!"

"I think it's a byakhee," said Brandwin, poking at the beast. It had membranous wings and a spear protruding from what might have been its neck. It smelled like old cheese washed in gangrene and graveyard dew.

"I think it's a vorpilax, love," said Sophara. She drunkenly assisted her wife in pulling Shraplin out from under the thing. "Consider the bilateral symmetry."

"I don't care what it is," said Amarelle, fumbling into her long black coat. "Nobody drops one on my card game or my crew. I'm going to find out where this Ivovandas lives and give her a piece of my mind."

"Haste makes corpses, boss," said Shraplin, shaking coils and widgets from the wreckage of his foot. "I was just having fun with you earlier."

"Stupid damn commerce-murdering wizards!" Goldclaw Grask arrived at last, with a gaggle of bartenders and waiters in train. "Sophara! Are you hurt? What about the rest of you? Shraplin! That looks expensive. Tell me it's not expensive!"

"I can soon be restored to prime functionality," said Shraplin. "But what if I suggested that tonight is an excellent night for you to tear up our bill?"

"I, uh, well, if that wouldn't get you in trouble," said the goblin, directing waiters with mops toward the growing puddle of pastel-colored rainwater and gray ichor under the beast.

"If you give it to us freely," said Sophara, "it's not theft, and none of us break our terms of sanctuary. And Shraplin is right, Amarelle. You can't just go berate a member of the Parliament of Strife! Even if you could safely cross the High Barrens in the middle of this mess—"

"Of course I can." Amarelle stood up nearly straight and, after a few false starts, approximately squared her shoulders. "I'm not some marshmallow-muscled tourist, I'm the Duchess Unseen! I stole the sound of the sunrise and the tears of a shark. I borrowed a book from the library of Hazar and didn't return it. I crossed the Labyrinth of the Death Spiders in Moraska TWICE—"

"I know," said Sophara. "I was there."

". . . and then I went back and stole all the Death Spiders!"

"That was ten years and an awful lot of strong drinks ago," said Sophara. "Come on, darling, I mixed most of the drinks myself. Don't scare us like this, Amarelle. You're drunk and retired. Go home."

"This smelly thing could have killed all of us," said Amarelle.

"Well, thanks to a little luck and a lot of Shraplin, it didn't. Come on, Amarelle. Promise us you won't do anything stupid tonight. Will you *promise* us?"

5. *Removing All Doubt*

The High Barrens, east of Tanglewing Street, were empty of inhabitants and full of nasty surprises from the battle in progress. Amarelle kept out of the open, moving from shadowed arch to garden wall to darkened doorway, stumbling frequently. The world had a fragile liquid quality, running at the edges and spinning on previously unrevealed axes. She was not drunk enough to forget that she had to take extra care and still far too drunk to realize that she ought to be fleeing the way she'd come.

The High Barrens had once been a neighborhood of mansions and topiary wonders and public fountains, but the coming of the wizard Ivovandas had sent the former inhabitants packing. The arguments of the Parliament of Strife had blasted holes in the cobblestones, cracked and dried the fountains, and sundered the mansions like unloved toy houses. The purple fire from before was still smoldering in a tall ruined shell of wood and brick. Amarelle sidestepped the street-rivers of melted lead that had once been the building's roof.

It wasn't difficult to find the manse of Ivovandas, the only lit and tended structure in the neighborhood, guarded by smooth walls, glowing ideograms, and rustling red-green hedges with the skeletons of many birds and small animals scattered in their undergrowth. A path of interlocked alabaster stones, gleaming with internal light, led forty curving yards to a golden front door.

Convenient. That guaranteed a security gauntlet.

The screams of terrible flying things high above made concentration even more difficult, but Amarelle applied three decades of experience to the path and was not disappointed. Four trapped stones she avoided by intuition, two by dumb drunken luck. The gravity-orientation reversal was a trick she'd seen before; she cartwheeled (sloppily) over the dangerous patch and the magic pushed her headfirst back to the ground rather than helplessly into the sky. She never even felt the silvery call of the tasteful hypnotic toad sculptures on the lawn, as she was too inebriated to meet their eyes and trigger the effect.

When she reached the front door, the golden surface rippled like a molten pool and a sculpted arm emerged clutching a knocker ring. Amarelle flicked a collapsible baton out of her coat and used it to tap the ring against the door while she stood aside. There was a brief pause after the darts had hissed through empty air, and then a voice boomed:

"WHO COMES UNBIDDEN TO THE DOOR OF THE SUPREME SPELLWRIGHT IVOVANDAS OF THE HONORABLE PARLIAMENT OF THERADANE? SPEAK, WORM!"

"I don't take shit from doors," said Amarelle. "I'm flattering your mistress by knocking. Tell her a citizen of Theradane is here to give her a frank and unexpurgated opinion on how terrible her aim is."

"YOUR ATTITUDE IS UNDERSTANDABLE AND NONETHELESS THOROUGHLY OFFENSIVE. ARCS OF ELECTRODYNAMIC FORCE WILL NOW BE APPLIED TO THE LOBES OF YOUR BRAIN UNTIL THEY ARE SCALDED PULP. TO RECEIVE THIS PRONOUNCEMENT IN THE FORM OF UNIVERSAL PICTOGRAMS, SCREAM ONCE. TO REQUEST MORE RAPID SENSORY OBLIVION, SCREAM TWICE AND WAIT TO SEE WHAT HAPPENS."

"The name is Amarelle Parathis, also known as the Duchess Unseen. Your mistress's stupid feuds are turning a fine old town into a shitsack misery farm and ruining my card games. Are you going to open up, or do I find a window?"

"AMARELLE PARATHIS," said the door. A moment passed. "YOUR NAME IS NOT UNKNOWN. YOU PURCHASED SANCTUARY FROM THE PARLIAMENT OF THERADANE TWO YEARS AND FOUR MONTHS AGO."

"Attadoor," said Amarelle.

"THE MISTRESS WILL RECEIVE YOU."

The sculpted hand holding the knocker withdrew into the liquid surface of the door. A dozen others burst forth, grabbing Amarelle by the throat, arms, legs, and hair. They pulled her off her feet and into the rippling golden surface, which solidified an instant later and retained no trace of her passage.

6. The Cabinet of Golden Hands

Amarelle awoke, thoroughly comfortable but stripped of all her weapons and wearing someone else's silk nightgown.

She was in a doorless chamber, in a feather bed floating gently on a pool of liquid gold that covered the entire floor, or perhaps was the entire floor. Ruby shafts of illumination fell from etched glass skylights, and when Amarelle threw back her covers they dissolved into wisps of aromatic steam.

Something bubbled and churned beneath the golden pool. A small hemisphere rose from the surface, continued rising, became a tall, narrow, humanoid shape. The liquid drained away smoothly, revealing a dove-pale albino woman with flawless auric eyes and hair composed of a thousand golden butterflies, all fluttering elegantly at random.

"Good afternoon, Amarelle," said the wizard Ivovandas. Her feet didn't quite touch the surface of the pool as she drifted toward the bed. "I trust you slept well. You were magnificent last night!"

"Was I? I don't remember . . . uh, that is, I remember some of it . . . am I wearing your clothes?"

"Yes."

"Shouldn't I have a hangover?"

"I took it while you slept," said Ivovandas. "I have a collection of bottled maladies. Your hangover was due to be the stuff of legends. Here be dragons! And by 'here,' I mean directly behind your eyeballs, probably for the rest of the week. I'll find another head to slip it into, someday. Possibly I'll let you have it back if you fail me."

"Fail you? What?" Amarelle leapt to her feet, which sank awkwardly into the mattress. "You have me confused with someone who knows what's going on. Start with how I was magnificent."

"I've never been so extensively insulted! In my own foyer, no less, before we even adjourned to the study. You offered penetratingly savage elucidation of all my character flaws, most of them imaginary, and then you gave me the firmest possible directions on how I and my peers were to order our affairs henceforth, for the convenience of you and your friends."

"I, uh, recall some of that, I think."

"I am curious about a crucial point, citizen Parathis. When you purchased sanctuary from the Parliament of Theradane, you were instructed that personal threats against the members of said Parliament could be grounds for summary revocation of sanctuary privileges, were you not?"

"I . . . recall something with that flavor . . . in the paperwork . . . possibly on the back somewhere . . . maybe in the margins?"

"You will agree that your statements last night certainly qualified as personal threats?"

"My statements?"

Smiling, Ivovandas produced a humming blue crystal and used it to project a crisp, solid image into the air beside the bed. It was Amarelle, black-coated and soaked with steaming magic rain, gesturing with clutching hands as she raved:

"And another thing, you venomous milk-faced thundercunt! NOBODY drops a dead vorpilax on my friends, NOBODY! What you fling at the other members of your pointy-hatted circle jerk is your business, but the next time you trifle with the lives of uninvolved citizens, you'd better lock your doors, put on your thickest steel corset, and hire a food taster, you catch my meaning?"

The image vanished.

"Damn," said Amarelle. "I've always thought of myself as basically a happy drunk."

"I'm 310 years old," said Ivovandas, "and I learned some new words last night! Oh, we were having such fun, until I found myself personally threatened."

"Yes. So it would seem. And how were you thinking we might, ah, proceed in this matter?"

"Ordinarily," said Ivovandas, "I'd magically redirect the outflow of your lower intestine into your lungs, which would be my little way of saying that your sanctuary privileges had been revoked. However, those skills of yours, and that reputation . . . I have a contract suited to such a contractor. Why don't you get dressed and meet me in the study?"

A powerful force struck Amarelle from behind, knocking her off the bed, headfirst into the golden pool. Rather than swimming down she found herself floating up, rising directly through the floor of Ivovandas's study, a large room full of bookshelves, scrollcases, and lacquered basilisk-skin paneling. Amarelle was suddenly wearing her own clothes again.

On the wall was an oil painting of the bedroom Amarelle had just left, complete with a masterful rendering of Ivovandas floating above the golden pool. As Amarelle watched, the painted figure grew larger and larger within the frame, then pushed her arms and head out of it, and with a twist and a jump at last floated free in the middle of the study.

"Now," said Ivovandas, "to put it simply, there is an object within Theradane I expect you to secure. Whether or not your friends help you is of no concern to me. As an added incentive, if you deliver this thing to me quietly and successfully, you will calm a great deal of the, ah, public disagreement between myself and a certain parliamentary peer."

"But the terms of my sanctuary!" said Amarelle. "You got part of my tithe! You know how it works. I can't steal within the boundaries of Theradane."

"Well, you can't threaten me either," said Ivovandas. "And that's a moot point now, so what have you got to lose?"

"An eternity not spent as a streetlamp."

"Admirable long-term thinking," said Ivovandas. "But I do believe if you scrutinize your situation, you'll see that you're up a certain proverbial creek, and I am the only provisioner of paddles willing to sell you one."

Amarelle paced, hands shoved sullenly into her coat pockets. She and her crew needed the security of Theradane; they had grown too famous, blown too much cover, taken too many interesting keepsakes from the rich and powerful in too many other places. Theradane's system was simplicity itself. Pay a vast sum to the Parliament of Strife, retire to Theradane, and don't practice any of the habits that got you in trouble outside the city. Ever.

"Have some heart, Amarelle. It's not precisely *illegal* for me to coax a master criminal back into operations within the city limits, but I can't imagine my peers would let the matter pass unremarked if they ever found out about it. Do as I ask, and I'll gladly smash my little blue crystal. We'll both walk away smiling, in harmonious equipoise."

"What do you want me to secure for you?"

Ivovandas opened a tall cabinet set against the right-hand wall. Inside was a blank tapestry surrounded on all sides by disembodied golden hands not unlike the ones that had hauled Amarelle across the threshold. The hands leapt to life, flicking across the tapestry with golden needles and black thread. Lines appeared on the surface, lines that rapidly became clear to Amarelle as the districts of Theradane and their landmarks: the High Barrens, the Sign of the Fallen Fire, the Deadlight Downs, and a hundred others, stitch by stitch.

When the map was complete, one hand stitched in a final thread of summer-fire crimson, glowing somewhere in the northeastern part of the city.

"Prosperity Street," said Ivovandas. "In Fortune's Gate, near the Old Parliament."

"I've been there," said Amarelle. "What do you want?"

"Prosperity Street. In Fortune's Gate. Near the Old Parliament."

"I heard you the first time," said Amarelle. "But what do you . . . oh, *no.* You did not. You did *not* just imply that implication!"

"I want you to steal Prosperity Street," said Ivovandas. "The whole street. The entire length of it. Every last brick and stone. It must cease to exist. It must be removed from Theradane."

"That street is three hundred yards long, at the heart of a district so important and money-soaked that even you lunatics don't blast it in your little wars, and it's trafficked at every hour of every day!"

"It would therefore be to your advantage to remove it without attracting notice," said Ivovandas. "But that's your business, one way or the other, and I won't presume to give you instruction in your own narrow specialty."

"It. Is. A. STREET."

"And you're Amarelle Parathis. Weren't you shouting something last night about how you'd stolen the sound of the sunrise?"

"On the right day of the year," said Amarelle, "on the peak of the proper mountain, and with a great deal of help from some dwarfs and more copper pipe than I can—damn it, it was very complicated!"

"You stole tears from a shark."

"If you can figure out how to identify a melancholy shark, you're halfway home in that business."

"Incidentally, what *did* you do with the Death Spiders of Moraska once you'd taken them?"

"I mailed them back to the various temples of the spider-priests who'd been annoying me. Let's just say that confinement left the spiders agitated *and* hungry, and that the cult now has very firm rules concerning shipping crates with ventilation holes. Also, I mailed the crates postage *due.*"

"Charming!" cried Ivovandas. "Well, you strike me as just the sort of woman to steal a street."

"I suppose my only other alternative is a pedestal engraved 'Now I Serve Theradane Always.'"

"That, or some more private and personal doom," said Ivovandas. "But you have, in the main, apprehended the salient features of your choices."

"Why a street?" said Amarelle. "Before I proceed, let's be candid, or something resembling it. Why do you want this street removed, and how will doing so calm down the fighting between you and your . . . oh. Oh, hell, it's a locus, isn't it?"

"Yes," said Ivovandas. Her predatory grin revealed teeth engraved with hair-fine lines of gold in arcane patterns. "Prosperity Street is the external power locus of the wizard Jarrow, my most unbeloved colleague. It's how he finds the wherewithal to prolong this tedious contest of summoned creatures and weather. Without it, I could flatten him in an afternoon and be home in time for tea."

"Forgive me if this is a touchy subject, but I thought the nature of these loci was about the most-closely-guarded secret you and your . . . colleagues possess."

"Jarrow has been indiscreet," said Ivovandas. "But then, he understands the knowledge alone is useless if it can't be coupled to a course of action. A street is quite a thing to dispose of, and the question of how to do so absolutely *stymied* me until you came calling with your devious head so full of drunken outrage. Shall we go to contract?"

The cabinet of golden hands unstitched the map of Theradane, and in its place embroidered a number of paragraphs in neat, even script. Amarelle peered closely at them. They were surprisingly straightforward, describing a trade of one (1) street for one (1) blue crystal to be smashed, but then . . .

"What the hell's this?" she said. "A deadline? A year and a day?"

"It's the traditional span for this sort of arrangement," said Ivovandas. "And surely you can see the sense in it. I prefer Jarrow defanged fairly soon, not five or ten or some nebulous and ever-changing number of years from now. I require you working with determination and focus. And you require some incentive other than simple destruction for failure, so there it all is."

"A year and a day," said Amarelle, "and I deliver the street or surrender my citizenship and worldly wealth to permanent indenture in your service."

"It would be a comfortable and exciting life," said Ivovandas. "But you can avoid it if you're as clever as I hope you are."

"And what if I were to quietly report this arrangement to the wizard Jarrow and see if he could do better for me?"

"A worthwhile contemplation of treacherous entanglement symmetrical to my own! I salute your spirit, but must remind you that Jarrow possesses no blue crystal, nor do you or he possess the faintest notion of where my external locus resides. You must decide for yourself which of us would make the easier target. If you wish to be ruled by wisdom, you'll reach into your pockets now."

Amarelle did, and found that a quill and an ink bottle had somehow appeared therein.

"One street," she said. "For one crystal. One year and one day."

"It's all there in plain black thread," said Ivovandas. "Will you sign?"

Amarelle stared at the contract and ground her teeth, a habit her mother had always sternly cautioned her against. At last, she uncapped the bottle of ink and wet the quill.

7. Another Unexpected Change of Clothing

The usual tumult of wizardly contention had abated. Even Ivovandas and Jarrow seemed to be taking a rest from their labors when Amarelle walked out of the High Barrens under a peach-colored afternoon haze. All the clocks in the city sounded three, refuting and echoing and interrupting one another, the actual ringing of the hour taking somewhere north of two and a half minutes due to the fact that clocks in Theradane were traditionally mis-synchronized to confuse malicious spirits.

Amarelle's thoughts were an electric whirl of anxiety and calculation. She hailed a mechanavipede and was soon speeding over the rooftops of the city in a swaying chair tethered beneath the straining wings of a flock of mechanical sparrows. There was simply nowhere else to go for help; she would have to heave herself before her friends like jetsam washed up on a beach.

Sophara and Brandwin lived in a narrow, crooked house on Shankvile Street, a house they'd secured at an excellent price due to the fact that it sometimes had five stories and sometimes six. Where the sixth occasionally wandered off to was unknown, but while it politely declined their questions about its business it also had the courtesy to ask none concerning theirs. Amarelle had the mechanavipede heave her off into a certain third-floor window that served as a friends-only portal for urgent business.

The ladies of the house were in, and by a welcome stroke of luck so was Shraplin. Brandwin was fussing with the pistons of his replacement left foot, while Sophara sprawled full-length on a velvet hammock wearing smoked glasses and an ice-white beret that exuded analgesic mist in a halo about her head.

"How is it that you're not covered in vomit and begging for death?" said Sophara. "How is it that you consumed three times your own weight in liquor and I've got sole custody of the hangover?"

"I had an unexpected benefactor, Soph. Can you secure this chamber for sensitive conversation?"

"The whole house is reasonably safe," groaned the magician, rolling off the hammock with minimal grace and dignity. "Now, if you want me to weave a deeper silence, give me a minute to gather my marbles. Wait . . ."

She pulled her smoked glasses off and peered coldly at Amarelle. Stepping carefully around the mess of specialized tools and mechanical gewgaws littering the carpet, she approached, sniffing the air.

"Something wrong, dearest?" said Brandwin.

"Shhhh," said Sophara. She rubbed her eyes in the manner of the freshly awake, then reached out, moved Amarelle's left coat lapel aside, and pulled a gleaming gold thread out of the black wool.

"You," she said, arching her aquamarine eyebrows at Amarelle, "have been seeing another wizard."

Sophara clapped her hands and an eerie hush fell upon the room. The faint sounds of the city outside were utterly banished.

"Ivovandas," said Amarelle. "I ran off and did something stupid last night. In my defense, I would just like to say that I was angry, and you were the one mixing the drinks."

"You unfailingly omnibothersome bitch," said Sophara. "Well, this little thread would allow Ivovandas to eavesdrop, if not for my counterspell and certain fundamental confusions worked into the stones of this house. And where there's obvious chicanery, there's something lurking behind it. Take the rest of your clothes off."

"What?"

"Do it now, Amarelle!" Sophara retrieved a silver-engraved casket from a far corner of the room, clicked it open, and made urgent motions while Amarelle shed her coat.

"You see how direct she is?" Brandwin squeezed a tiny bellows to pressurize a tube of glowing green oil within Shraplin's leg. "We'd never have gotten anywhere if she'd waited for me to make the first move."

"You keep your eyes on your work," said Sophara. "I'll do the looking for both of us and give you details later."

"I sometimes think that 'friend' is just a word I use for all the people I haven't murdered yet," said Amarelle, hopping and twirling out of her boots, leggings, belts, vest, blouse, sharp implements, silk ropes, smoke capsules, and smallclothes. When the last stitch was discarded, Sophara slammed the casket shut and muttered spells over the lock.

As a decided afterthought, smiling and taking her time, she eventually fetched Amarelle a black silk dressing robe embroidered with blue-white astronomical charts.

"It seems to be my day to try on everyone else's clothes," she muttered.

"I'm sorry about your things," said Sophara. "I should be able to sweep them for further tricks, but Ivovandas is so far outside my weight class, it might take days."

"Never let a wizard get their hands on your clothes," said Brandwin. "At least not until she promises to move in with you. It ought to be safe to talk now."

"I'm not entirely sure how to say this," said Amarelle, "but the concise version is that I'm temporarily unretired."

She told the whole story, pausing only to answer Sophara's excited questions about the defenses and décor of Ivovandas's manse.

"That's a hell of a thing, boss," said Shraplin when Amarelle finished. The clocks within the house started chiming five and didn't finish for some time. The city clocks were still sealed beyond Sophara's silence. "I thought we were up against it when that shark-tears job landed on us. But a street!"

"I wonder how Jarrow figured out it was a locus." Sophara adjusted the analgesic hat, which had done her much good over the long course of Amarelle's story. "I wonder how he harnessed it without anyone's interfering!"

"Keep it relevant, dreamer." Brandwin massaged her wife's legs. "The pertinent question is, how are we going to pull it off?"

"I only came for advice," said Amarelle hastily. "This is all my fault, and nobody else needs to risk their sanctuary because I got drunk and sassed a wizard."

"Let me enlighten you, boss," said Shraplin. "If you don't want me to follow you around being helpful, you must be planning to smash my head right now."

"Amarelle, you *can't* keep us out in the cold now! This mischief is too delicious," said Sophara. "And it's clearly not prudent to let you wander off on your own."

"I'm grateful," said Amarelle, "but I feel responsible for your safety."

"The Parliament of Strife craps destruction on its own city at random, boss." Shraplin spread his hands. "How much more unsafe can we get? Frankly, two and a half quiet years is adequate to my taste."

"Yes," said Sophara. "Hang your delicate feelings, Amarelle, you know we won't let you . . . oh, wait. You foxy bag of tits and sugar! You didn't come here just for advice! You put your noble face on so we'd pledge ourselves without the pleasure of seeing you beg!"

"And you fell for it." Amarelle grinned. "So it's agreed, we're all out of retirement and we're stealing a street. If anyone cares to let me know how the hell that's supposed to work, the suggestion box is open."

8. *The Cheap Shot*

They spent the first two days in measurement and surveillance. Prosperity Street was three hundred and seventeen yards long running north–south, an average of ten yards wide. Nine major avenues and fifteen alleys bisected it. One hundred and six businesses and residences opened onto it, one of which was a wine bar serving distillations of such quality that a third day was lost to hangovers and remonstrations.

They struck on the evening of the fourth day, as warm mist curled lazily from the sewers and streetlamps gleamed like pearls in folds of gray gauze. The clocks began chiming eleven, a process that often lasted until it was nearly time for them to begin striking twelve.

A purple-skinned woman in the coveralls of a municipal functionary calmly tinkered with the signpost at the intersection of Prosperity and Magdamar. She placed the wooden shingle marked PROSPERITY S in a sack and tipped her hat to a drunk, semicurious goblin. Brandwin emptied three intersections of PROSPERITY S signs before the clocks settled down.

At the intersection of Prosperity and Ninefingers, a polite brass-headed drudge painted over every visible PROSPERITY S with an opaque black varnish. Two blocks north, a mechanavipede flying unusually low with a cargo of one dark-haired woman crashed into a signpost, an accident that would be repeated six times. At the legendarily confusing seven-way intersection where the various Goblin Markets joined Prosperity, a sorceress disguised as a cat's shadow muttered quiet spells of alphabetic nullification, wiping every relevant signpost like a slate.

They had to remove forty-six shingles or signposts and deface the placards of sixteen businesses that happened to be named after the street. Lastly, they arranged to tip a carboy of strong vitriol over a ceremonial spot in the pavement where PROSPERITY STREET was set in iron letters. When those had become PRCLGILV SLGFLL, they gave the mess a quick splash of water and hurried away to dispose of their coveralls, paints, and stolen city property.

The next day, Ivovandas was less than impressed.

"Nothing happened." Her gold eyes gleamed dangerously and her butterflies were still. "Not one femto-scintilla of deviation or dampening in the potency of Jarrow's locus. Though there were quite a few confused travelers and tourists. You need to steal the street, Amarelle, not vandalize its ornaments."

"I didn't expect it to be that easy," said Amarelle. "I just thought we ought to eliminate the simplest approach first. Never lay an Archduke on the table when a two will do."

"The map is not the territory." Ivovandas gestured and transported Amarelle to the front lawn of her manse, where the hypnotic toad sculptures nearly cost her even more lost time.

9. Brute Force

Their next approach took eleven days to plan and arrange, including two days lost to a battle between Parliament wizards in the western sectors that collapsed the Temple-Bridge of the God of Hidden Names.

The street signs had been restored at the intersection of Prosperity and Languinar, the southernmost limit of Prosperity Street. The sunrise sky was just creeping over the edge of the city in orange-and-scarlet striations, and the clocks were or were not chiming seven. A caravan of reinforced cargo coaches drawn by armored horses halted on Languinar, preparing to turn north. The signs hanging from the coaches read:

Nusbarq Desisko and Sons
Hazardous Animal Transport

As the caravan moved into traffic, a woman in a flaming-red dress riding a mecharabbit hopped rudely into the path of the lead carriage, triggering an unlikely but picturesque chain of disasters. Carriage after carriage toppled, wheel after wheel flew from its hub, horse team after horse team ran neighing into traffic as their emergency releases snapped. The side of the first toppled carriage exploded outward, and a furry, snarling beast came bounding out of the wreckage.

"RUN," cried someone, who happened to be the woman in the red dress. "IT'S A SPRING-HEELED WEREJACKAL!"

A heartbeat later her damaged mecharabbit exploded, enveloping her in a cloud of steam and sparks. The red dress was reversible and Amarelle had practiced swapping it around by touch. Three seconds later she ran from the cloud of steam dressed in a black-hooded robe. Shraplin, not at all encumbered by seventy-five pounds of fur, leather, and wooden claws, merrily activated the reinforced shock-absorbing leg coils Brandwin had cobbled together for him. He went leaping and howling across the crowd, turning alarm into panic and flight.

Twenty-two unplanned carriage or mechanavipede collisions took place in the next half minute, locking traffic up for two blocks north of the initial accident. Amarelle didn't have time to count them as she hurried north in Shraplin's wake.

Another curiously defective carriage in the Nusbarq Desisko caravan cracked open, exposing its cargo of man-sized hives to the open air and noise. Thousands of Polychromatic Reek-Bees, scintillating in every color of the rainbow and fearful for the safety of their queens, flew forth to spew defensive stink-nectar on everything within buzzing distance. The faintest edge of that scent followed Amarelle north, and she regretted having eaten breakfast. Hundreds of people would be burning their clothes before the day was through.

All along the length of Prosperity Street, aural spells prepared in advance by Sophara began to erupt. Bold, authoritative voices ordered traffic to halt, passersby to run, shops to close, citizens to pray for deliverance. They screamed about werejackals, basilisks, reek-bees, Cradlerobber Wasps, rabid vorpilax, and the plague. They ordered constables and able-bodied citizens to use barrels and carriages as makeshift riot barricades at the major intersections, which some of them did.

Amarelle reached the alley after Ninefingers Way and found the package she'd stashed behind a rotten crate the night before. Soon she emerged from the alley in the uniform of a Theradane constable, captain's bars shining on her collar, steel truncheon gleaming. She issued useless and contradictory orders, fomented panic, pushed shopkeepers into their stores and ordered them to bar their doors. When she met actual constables, she jabbed them with the narcotic prong concealed on the end of her truncheon. Their unconscious bodies, easily mistaken for dead, added a piquant verisimilitude to the raging disquiet.

At the northern end of Prosperity Street, a constabulary riot wagon commanded by a pair of uniformed women experienced another improbable accident when it came into contact with the open fire of a careless street fondue vendor. Brandwin and Sophara threw their helmets aside and ran screaming, infecting dozens of citizens with disoriented panic even before the rockets and canisters inside the wagon began to explode. For nearly half an hour pinkish white arcs of sneezing powder, soporific smoke, and eye-scalding pepper dust rained on Prosperity Street.

Eventually, two Parliament wizards had to grudgingly intervene to help the constables and bucket brigades restore order. The offices of Nusbarq Desisko and Sons were found to be empty and their records missing, presumably carried with them when they fled the city. The spring-heeled werejackal was never located and was assumed taken as a pet by some wizard or another.

"What do you mean, nothing happened?" Amarelle paced furiously in Ivovandas's study the following day, having explained herself to the wizard, who had half listened while consulting a grimoire that occasionally moaned and laughed to itself. "We closed the full length of Prosperity Street down for more than three hours! We stole the street from everyone on it in a very meaningful sense! The traffic didn't flow, the riot barriers were up, not a scrap of commerce took place anywhere—"

"Amarelle," said the wizard, not taking her eyes from her book, "I applaud your adoption of a more dynamic approach to the problem, but I'm afraid it simply didn't do anything. Not the merest hint of any diminishment to Jarrow's arcane resources. I do wish it were otherwise. Mind the hypnotic toads, as I've strengthened their enchantments substantially." She snapped her fingers, and Amarelle was back on the lawn.

10. The Typographic Method

Sophara directed the next phase of their operations, resigning her place as mage-mixologist indefinitely.

"It was mostly for easy access to the bar, anyway," she said. "And they'd kiss my heels to have me back anytime."

A studious, eye-straining month and a half followed. Sophara labored over spell board, abacus, grimoire, and journal, working in four languages and several forms of thaumaturgical notation that made Amarelle's eyes burn.

"I keep telling you not to look at them!" said Sophara as she adjusted the analgesic beret on Amarelle's head. "You haven't got the proper optical geometry! You and Brandwin! You're worse than cats."

Brandwin prowled libraries and civic archives. Amarelle broke into seventeen major private collections. Shraplin applied his tireless mechanical perception to the task of rapidly sifting thousands of pages in thousands of books. A vast pile of notes grew in Brandwin and Sophara's house, along with an inelegant but thorough master list of scrolls, pamphlets, tomes, and records.

"Any guide to the city," chanted Amarelle, for the formula had become a sort of mantra. "Any notes of any traveler, any records of tax or residence, any mentions of repairs, any journals or recollections. Have we ever done anything *less* sane? How can we possibly expect to locate every single written reference to Prosperity Street in every single document in existence?"

"We can't," said Sophara. "But if my calculations are anywhere near correct, and if this can work at all, we only need to change a certain critical percentage of those records, especially in the official municipal archives."

Shraplin and Brandwin cut panels of wood down to precise replicas of the forty-six street signs and the sixteen business placards they had previously tried to steal. They scraped, sanded, varnished, and engraved, making only one small change to each facsimile.

"I have the key," said Brandwin, emerging from her incense-filled workroom one night, bleary-eyed and cooing at a small white moth perched atop her left index finger. "I call it the Adjustment Moth. It's a very complex and efficient little spell I can cast on anything about this size."

"And what will they do?" said Amarelle.

"They'll become iterating work-enhancers," said Sophara. "It'd take us years to manually adjust all the records we're after. Enchanted with my spell to guide and empower them, we can send these little darlings out to do almost all of the work for us in one night."

"How many do we need?" said Shraplin.

Nine nights later, from carefully selected points around the city, they loosed 3,449 of Sophara's Adjustment Moths, each of which fluttered into the darkness and thence into libraries, archives, shop cupboards, private studies, and bedside cabinets. The 2,625 Adjustment Moths that were not eaten by bats or appropriated as cat toys located a total of 617,451 references to the name "Prosperity Street" and made one crucial change to each physical text. By sunrise they were all dead of exhaustion.

Amarelle and her crew replaced the forty-six street signs and sixteen business placards under cover of darkness, then pried up one of the (restored) ceremonial iron letters sunk into the pavement. PROSPERIT STREET, the survivors said. PROSPERIT, read the signs and placards.

"Prosperit Street" read the name of the place in every guidebook, private journal, lease, assize, and tax record in the city, save for a few in magically guarded sanctums of the Parliament of Strife.

Overnight, Prosperity Street had been replaced by its very close cousin, Prosperit Street.

"Amarelle," said Ivovandas, sipping daintily at a cup of molten gold she'd heated in a desk-side crucible, "I sympathize with your agitation at the failure of so original and far-ranging a scheme, but I really must stress the necessity of abandoning these fruitlessly metaphysical approaches. Don't steal the street's name, or its business, or its final 'Y.' Steal the street, wholly and physically!"

Amarelle groaned. "Back to the lawn?"

"Back to the lawn, my dear!"

11. After Amarelle, the Deluge

Twenty-seven days later, one of the natural storms of summer blew in from the west, a churning shroud of dark clouds looking for a brawl. As usual, the wizards of Parliament preserved their individual territories and let the rest of Theradane fend for itself. It was therefore theoretically plausible that the elevated aqueduct that crossed Prosperity Street just north of Limping Matron Lane would choose that night to break under the strain.

Prosperity Street was already contending with plugs of debris clogging its sewer grates (these plugs granted unusual thickness and persistence by the spells of Sophara Miris) and with its own valleylike position at the foot of several more elevated neighborhoods. The foaming rush from the broken aqueduct turned a boot-soaking stream into a rather more alarming waist-high river.

Amarelle and her crew lurked in artificial shadows on a high rooftop, dutifully watching to ensure that no one, particularly children and goblins, suffered more than a soaking from the flood. The city hydromancers would eventually show up to set things right, but they were no doubt having a busy night.

"This is still a touch metaphysical, if you ask me," said Sophara.

"It's something of a hybrid approach," said Amarelle. "After all, how can it be a street if it's been physically turned into a canal?"

12. No

"No," said Ivovandas. Amarelle was returned to the lawn.

13. Instructive Measures

Half a year gone. Despite vandalism, riot, werejackals, clerical errors, and flood, Prosperity Street was more worthy of its name than ever. Amarelle strolled the pavement, feeling the autumn sun on her face, admiring the pale bronze leaves of Prayer-trees as they tumbled about in little clouds, inscribed with calligraphic benedictions for anyone whose path they crossed.

There was a stir in the crowds around her, a new cacophony of shouting and muttering and horse hooves and creaking wheels. Traffic parted to the north, making way for a rumbling coach, half again as high and wide as anything on the street. It was black as death's asshole, windowless, trimmed with engraved silver and inlaid nacre. It had no horses and no driver; each of its four wheels was a circular steel cage in which a slavering red-eyed ghoul ran on four limbs, creating a forward impetus.

The singular coach moaned on its suspension as it swerved and lurched to a halt beside Amarelle. The ghouls leered at her, unbreathing, their flesh crisply necrotic like rice paper pressed over old oozing wounds. The black door flew open and a footstep fell into place. A velvet curtain still fluttered in the entrance to the coach, concealing whatever lay inside. A voice called out, cold as chloroform and old shame.

"Don't you know an invitation when you see one, citizen Parathis?"

Running from wizards in broad daylight without preparation was not a skill Amarelle had ever cultivated, so she stepped boldly into the carriage, ducking her head.

She was startled to find herself in a warm gray space at least forty yards on a side, with a gently curving ceiling lit by floating silver lights. A vast mechanical apparatus was ticking and pulsing and shifting in the middle of the room, something along the lines of an orrery, but in place of moons and planets the thin arms held likenesses of men and women, likenesses carved with exaggerated features and comical flaws. Amarelle recognized one of them as Ivovandas by the gold eyes and butterfly hair.

There were thirteen figures, and they moved in complex interlocking patterns around a model of the city of Theradane.

The carriage door slammed shut behind her. There was no sensation of motion other than the almost-hypnotic sway and swing of the wizard-orrery.

"My peers," said the cold voice, coming now from behind her. "Like celestial bodies, transiting in their orbits, exerting their influences. Like celestial bodies, not particularly difficult to track or predict in their motions."

Amarelle turned and gasped. The man was short and lithe, his skin like ebony, his hair scrapped down to a reddish stubble. There was a scar on his chin and another on his jawline, each of them familiar to her fingers and lips. Only the eyes were wrong; they were poisoner's eyes, dead as glass.

"You have no fucking right to that face," said Amarelle, fighting not to shout.

"Scavius of Shadow Street, isn't it? Or more like 'wasn't it?' Came with you to Theradane, but we never got his sanctuary money. Blew it in some dramatic gesture, I recall."

"He got drunk and lost it all on a dice throw," she said, wetting her lips and forcing herself to say, "Jarrow."

"Pleased to meet you, Amarelle Parathis." The man wore a simple black jacket and breeches. He extended a hand, which she didn't take. "Lost it all on one throw? That was stupid."

"I'm not unacquainted with drunken mistakes myself," said Amarelle.

"And then he went and did something even more stupid," said Jarrow. "Earned a criminal's apotheosis. Transfigured into a streetlamp."

"Please . . . take some other form."

"No." Jarrow scratched his head, shook a finger at her. "That's a fine starting point for the discussion I really brought you here for, Amarelle. Let's talk about behavior that might get someone transfigured into a street decoration."

"I'm retired."

"Sure, kid. Look, there's a very old saying in my family: 'Once is happenstance. Twice is coincidence. Three times is another wizard fucking with you.' You never spent much time near Prosperity Street before, did you? Your apartments are on Hellendal. South of Tanglewing Street. Right?"

"About the location of my apartments, of course."

"You've got iron in your spine, Amarelle, and I'm not here to prolong this or embarrass you. I'm just suggesting, to the room, if you like, that it would be a shame if any more unusual phenomena befell a part of Theradane that is of particular sentimental value to me. This is what your sanctuary money gets you. This is me being kind. Are you pretending to listen, or are you listening?"

"I'm listening."

"Here's a little something to further sharpen your hearing." A burlap sack appeared in Jarrow's hands and he threw it to her. It weighed about ten pounds, and the contents rattled. "The usual verification that I'm serious. You know how it works. Anyhow, in the best of all possible worlds, we never have to have a conversation like this again. What world do you want to live in, Amarelle Parathis?"

The air grew cold. The lights dimmed and receded into the corners of the room, vanishing like stars behind clouds. Amarelle's stomach tumbled, and then her boots were on pavement, the sound of traffic was all around her, and Prayer-tree leaves brushed her face.

The sun was high and warm, and the black coach was nowhere in sight.

Amarelle shook the sack open and cursed as Shraplin's head tumbled out. The edges of the pipes running out of his neck were burnt and bent.

"I don't know what to say, boss." His voice was steady but weak. "I'm embarrassed. I got jumped last night."

"What the hell did they do?"

"Nothing technically illegal, boss. They left my head, the contents intact. As for the rest, let's just say I don't expect to see it again."

"I'm sorry, Shraplin. I'll get you to Brandwin. I'm so sorry."

"Quit apologizing, boss." Something whirred and clunked behind the automaton's eyes, and he gave a garbled moan. "But I have to say, my reverence for these high-level wizard types is speeding in what you might call a southerly direction."

"We need more help," whispered Amarelle. "If we're going to put the boot to this mess, I think it's high time we got the whole band back together."

14. The Unretirement of Jadetongue Squirn

She was tall for a goblin, not that that meant anything to most other species. Her scales were like black glass, her eyes like the sudden plunge to blue depths beyond a continental shelf. Her pointed ears were pierced with silver rings, some of which held writing quills she could reach up and seize at leisure.

They all went together to see her in her shadowed cloister at the Theradane Ministry of Finance and Provision, a place that stank of steady habits, respectability, and workers who'd died at their desks with empty in-boxes. She was not best pleased to receive them.

"We're not what we were!" Jade hissed when Amarelle had finished telling most of the story, safely inside the goblin's office and Sophara's soundproof bubble. "Look at you! Look at the messes you've made! And look at me. How can I possibly help you? I'm an ink-stained functionary these days. I scribe ordinances and design engravings for banknotes."

Amarelle stared at her, biting her lip. Jadetongue Squirn had been jailed six times and escaped six times. You could walk nearly around the world by setting foot only in nations that still sought her for trial. Smuggler, negotiator, procurer of bizarre supplies, she was also the finest forger Amarelle had ever met, capable of memorizing signatures at a glance and reproducing them with either hand.

"We've missed you at our drinking nights," said Brandwin. "You were always welcome. You were always *wanted.*"

"I don't belong anymore." Jade's voice was flat and she clung to her desk as though it could be a wall between herself and her old comrades. "I'm like a hermit crab that's pulled an office over itself. Maybe the rest of you were only kidding yourselves about retiring, but I'm the real thing. I haven't been coming out to see you because you'd expect Jade-tongue Squirn, not this timid little person who wears her clothes."

"We're like a hand with a missing finger," said Amarelle. "We've got half a year to make three hundred yards of street vanish and we need that slick green brain of yours. You said it yourself—look at what a mess we've made so far! Look what Jarrow did to Shraplin."

Amarelle reached into a leather satchel. The automaton's head bounced on Jadetongue's desk a moment later, and she made a rattling noise in her throat.

"Ha-ha! The look on your face!" said Shraplin.

"How about the look on *yours,* duncebucket?" she growled. "I ought to stuff you in a drawer for scaring me like that!"

"You see now why we have to have you back," said Amarelle. "Shrap-lin's the warning. Our next shot has to be for keeps."

"Three funny bitches and a smart-ass automaton sans ass," said Jade. "You think you can just walk in here, tug on my heartstrings, and snatch me out of my sad retirement?"

"Yes," said Amarelle.

"We're still not what we were." She put a scaly hand on Shraplin's face, then spun him like a top. "I'm definitely not what I was. But what the hell. Maybe you're right, about needing help, at least."

"So, are you going to take a leave of absence or something?" said Shraplin, when he'd stopped saying "Whaaaaargabaarrrrrgggh!"

"A leave of absence? Are you sure you didn't damage the contents of your head?" Jadetongue glanced around at all the members of the crew. "Sweethearts, softskins, thimblewits, if you're determined to see this thing through, the municipal bureaucracy of Theradane is the *last* asset you want to toss carelessly over your shoulder!"

15. Honest Business

"I haven't asked you for anything to assist us in this whole affair," said Amarelle. "Not once. Now that needs to change."

"I'm not averse in theory to small favors," said Ivovandas, "given that the potential reward for your ultimate success is so personally tantalizing. But do understand, most of my magical resources are currently committed. Nor will I do anything overt enough to harden Jarrow's suspicions. He has the same authority to kill you outright that I do if he can prove your violation of your sanctuary terms to our peers."

"We're starting a business," said Amarelle. "The High Barrens Reclamation Consortium. We need you to sign on as the principal stakeholder."

"Why?"

"Because nobody can sue you." Amarelle pulled a packet of paper out of her coat and set it on Ivovandas's desk. "We need a couple of wagons and about a dozen workers. We'll provide those. We're going to excavate wrecked mansions in the High Barrens on days when you and Jarrow aren't blasting at each other."

"Again, why?"

"There are some things we need to take," said Amarelle with a smile, "and some things we need to hide. If we do it in our names, the heirs of all the families that ran like hell when you settled here and started shooting at other wizards will line up in court to stop us. If you're the one in charge, they can't do a damned thing."

"I will examine these papers," said Ivovandas. "I will have them returned to you if I deem the arrangement suitable."

Amarelle found herself on the lawn. But three days later, the papers appeared in her apartments, signed and notarized. The High Barrens Reclamation Consortium went to work.

The Parliament of Strife ruled Theradane absolutely but were profoundly disinterested in the mundane business of cleaning the streets and sorting the paperwork. That much they left to their city's strangely feudal and secretive bureaucracy, who were essentially free to do as they pleased so long as the hedges were trimmed and the damage from the continual wizard feuding was repaired. Jade worked efficiently from within this edifice. She pushed through all the requisite paperwork, forged or purchased the essential permits, swept all the mandated delays and hearings under the rug, and then stepped on the rug.

Brandwin hired their crew, a dozen stout men and women. They were paid the going wage for their work, that much again for the occasional danger of proximity to Ivovandas's battles, and a triple portion for keeping their mouths shut. For a week or two they excavated carefully in the wreckage of once-mighty houses, concealing whatever they took from the ruins beneath tarps on their wagons.

Next, Brandwin and Shraplin spent a week refurbishing a trio of wagons as mobile vending carts. They extended wooden skirts around them to the ground, installed folding awnings and sturdy roofs, carved signs, and painted them attractively. One of the wagons was kitted out as a book stall, the other two as food carts.

The labyrinth of bribes and permits needed to launch this sort of venture was even more daunting than the one that had preceded the excavation company. Jade outdid herself, weaving blackmail and intimidation into a tapestry of efficient palm-greasing. Whether the permit placards that hung from the vending carts were genuine articles or perfect copies was ultimately irrelevant. No procedural complication survived first contact with Jade's attention.

With four months remaining, Amarelle and Sophara went into legitimate business for themselves. Amarelle peddled books on Prosperity Street until noon, while Sophara plied her precision sorcery for appreciative breakfast crowds on Galban Street. She cooked frosted walnut cakes into the shape of unicorns and cockatrices, caused fresh fruit to squeeze itself into juice glasses, and made her figs and dates give rude speeches while her customers tried to eat them and laugh at the same time. In the afternoon, she and Amarelle switched places.

Some days, Brandwin would operate the third vending cart, offering sweets and beer, but for some time she was absorbed in a number of demanding modifications to Shraplin's body and limbs. These modifications remained hidden in the darkness of her workshop; Shraplin never went out in public wearing anything but one of his ordinary bodies.

One bright day on Prosperity Street, a stray breeze blew one of Amarelle's books open and fluttered its pages. She moved to close it and was startled to find a detailed grayscale engraving of Scavius's face staring up at her from the top page.

"Amarelle," said the illustration. "You seem to have an unexpected literary sideline."

"Can't practice my former trade," she said through gritted teeth. "Money's getting tight."

"So you're exploring new avenues, eh? New avenues? Not even a smile? Well, fine, have it your way. I ought to snuff you, you realize. I don't know who or what prompted the weirdness of the previous few months—"

Amarelle fanned the pages of the book vindictively. The illustration flashed past on each one, and continued talking smoothly when Amarelle gave up.

". . . but the wisest and cleverest thing would be to turn your bones to molten glass and take no chances. Alas, I need evidence of wrongdoing. Can't just blast sanctuary tithers. People might stop giving us large piles of treasure for the privilege."

"My business partners and I are engaged in boring, legitimate commerce," said Amarelle.

"I know. I've been peeking up your skirts, as it were. Very boring. I thought we ought to have a final word, though. A little reminder that you should stay boring, or I can think of one story that won't have a happy ending."

The book slammed itself shut. Amarelle exhaled slowly, rubbed her eyes, and went back to work.

On the days wore, on the legitimate business went. The women began to move their vending carts more frequently, investing some of their profits in small mechanical equines to make this work easier.

With three months left in the contract, the carts that moved up and down Prosperity Street began to cross paths with carts from elsewhere in the city in a complicated dance that always ended with an unmarked High Barrens Reclamation Consortium wagon paying a quiet evening visit to one of the mansions they were excavating.

Another two months passed, and there was no spot on Prosperity Street that Amarelle or Sophara or Brandwin had not staked out at least temporarily, no merchant they hadn't come to know by name, no constable they hadn't thoroughly pacified with free food, good beer, and occasional gifts of books.

Three days before the contract was due to expire, a loud explosion shook the north end of Prosperity Street, breaking windows and knocking pedestrians to the curb. A mansion in a private court was found burning, already collapsing into itself. A huge black coach lay wrecked in the drive, its ghoul-cage wheels torn open, its roof smashed, its insides revealing nothing but well-upholstered seats and a carpeted floor.

The next day, Amarelle Parathis was politely summoned to the manse of the wizard Ivovandas.

16. Bottled Malady

"Am I satisfied? Satisfaction is a palliative," said Ivovandas, gold-threaded teeth blazing with reflected light, butterflies fluttering furiously. "Satisfaction is mild wine. Satisfaction is a tiny fraction of what I feel. Delight and fulfillment pounding in my breast like triumphant chords! Seventy years of unprofitable disdain from this face-changing reprobate, and now his misery is mine to contemplate at leisure."

"I'm so pleased you were able to crush him," said Amarelle. "Did you manage to get home in time for your tea afterward?"

The golden wizard ignored her and kept staring at the glass cylinder on her desk. It was six inches tall and half as wide, capped with a ground-glass stopper and sealed with wax the color of dried blood. Inside it was wretched Jarrow, shrunken to a suitable proportion and clad in rags. He had reverted (or been forced into) the shape of a cadaverous pale man with a silver-black beard.

"Jarrow." She sighed. "Jarrow. Oh, the laws of proportion and symmetry are restored to operation between us; my sustained pleasure balanced accurately against your lingering discomfort and demise."

"So obviously," said Amarelle, "you consider me to have stolen Prosperity Street in accordance with the contract?"

Jarrow pounded furiously against the glass.

"Oh, obviously, dear Amarelle, you've acquitted yourself splendidly! Yet the street is still there, is it not? Still carrying traffic, still hosting commerce. Before I retrieve your blue crystal, are you of a mind to indulge my former colleague and I with an explanation?"

"Delighted," said Amarelle. "After all our other approaches failed, we decided to try the painstakingly literal. Prosperity Street is roughly 3,170 square yards of brick and stone surface. The question we asked ourselves was: Who *really* looks at each brick and each stone?"

"Certainly not poor Jarrow," said Ivovandas, "else he'd not find his bottle about to join my collection."

"We resolved to physically steal every single square yard of Prosperity Street, every brick and stone," said Amarelle. "Which yielded three problems. First, how to do so without anyone's noticing the noise and tumult of our work? Second, how to do so without anyone's objecting to the stripped and uneven mess made of the street in our wake? Third, how to provide the physical labor to handle the sheer volume and tedium of the task?

"To answer the second point first, we used the High Barrens Restoration Consortium. They carefully fished through the mansions you two have destroyed in your feud to provide us with all the bricks and stones we could ever need.

"A large hollow space was constructed beneath each of our vending carts, which we first plied up and down assorted city streets, not just Prosperity, for an *interminable* length of time to allay suspicion that they were directly aimed at Jarrow's locus."

Jarrow banged his head repeatedly against the inside of his prison.

"Eventually we felt it was safe to proceed with our real business. The rest you must surely have guessed by now. The labor was provided by Shraplin, an automaton, whose meeting with Jarrow left him very eager to bear any trouble or tedium in the cause of his revenge. Shraplin utilized tool-arms custom-forged for him by Brandwin Miris to dig up the bricks and stones of the actual street, and to lay in their place the bricks and stones taken from the High Barrens mansions. At night, the detritus he'd scraped up by day was dumped into the ruins of those same mansions. As for why nobody ever heard Shraplin scraping or pounding away beneath our carts, all I can say is that our magician is highly adept at the production of soundproof barriers to fit any space or need.

"All that was left to do," said Amarelle, stretching and yawning, "was to spend the months necessary to carefully position our carts over every square foot of Prosperity Street. Nobody ever noticed that when we moved on, the patches of street beneath us had changed subtly from the hour or two before. Eventually, we pried up the last brick that was genuinely important, and Jarrow's locus became just another city lane."

"Help me!" Jarrow cried, his voice high and faint as a whisper in the wind. "Get me away from her! I can be him for you! I can be Scavius! I can be anyone you want!"

"Enough from you, I think." Ivovandas slid his prison lovingly into a desk drawer, still smiling. She curled her fingers, and a familiar blue crystal appeared within them.

"You have suffered quite tenaciously for this," said Ivovandas. "I give it to you now as my half of our bargain, fairly begun and fairly concluded."

Amarelle took the glowing crystal and crushed it beneath her heel.

"Is that the end of it?" she said. "All restored to harmonious equipoise? I go on my way and leave you to your next few years of conversation with Jarrow?"

"In a manner of speaking," said Ivovandas. "While I have dutifully disposed of the crystal recording from last year's intemperate drunken visitation, I have just now secured an even more entertaining one in which you confess at length to crimes carried out in Theradane and implicate several of your friends by name."

"Yes," said Amarelle. "I did rather expect something like this. I figured that since I was likely to eat more treachery, I might as well have an appreciative audience first."

"I am the *most* appreciative audience! Oh, we could be so good for one another! Consider, Amarelle, the very reasonable bounds of my desires and expectations. I fancy myself fairly adept at identifying the loci in use by my colleagues. With Jarrow removed, there will be a rebalancing of the alliances in our Parliament. There will be new testing and new struggles. I shall be watching very, very carefully, and inevitably I expect to have another target for you and your friends to secure on my behalf."

"You want to use us to knock off the Parliament of Strife, locus by locus," said Amarelle. "Until it's something more like the Parliament of Ivovandas."

"It might not happen in your lifetime," said the wizard. "But substantial progress could be at hand! In the meantime, I'll be quite content to let you remain at liberty in the city, enjoying your sanctuary, doing as you please. So long as you and your friends come when I call. Doubt not that I shall call."

17. The Work Ahead

Amarelle met them afterward on the Tanglewing Bridge, in the pleasant purple light of fading sunset. The city was quiet, the High Barrens peaceful, no fires falling from the clouds or screeching things sinking claws into one another.

They gathered in an arc in front of Scavius's statue. Sophara muttered and gestured with her fingers.

"We're in the bubble," she said. "Nobody can hear us, or even see us unless I . . . shut *up,* Scavius, I know you can hear us. You're a special case. How did it go down, Amarelle?"

"It went down like we expected," said Amarelle. "*Exactly* like we expected."

"I told you those kinds of sorcerers are all reflexively treacherous bags of nuts," said Sophara. "What's her game?"

"She wants us on an unpaid retainer so she can dig up the loci of more of her colleagues and send us after them."

"Sounds like a good way to kill some time, boss." Shraplin wound a crank on his chest, resynchronizing some mechanism that had picked up a slight rattle. "I could stand to knock over a few more of those assholes. She'd save us a lot of work if she identified the loci for us."

"Couldn't agree more," said Sophara. "Now hold still."

She ran her fingers through Amarelle's hair, and after a few moments of searching carefully plucked out a single curling black strand.

"There's my little spy," said Sophara. "I'm glad you brought me that one Ivovandas planted on you, Am. I never would have learned how to make these things so subtle if I hadn't been able to pry that one apart."

"Do you think it will tell you enough?" said Brandwin.

"I honestly doubt it." Sophara slipped the hair into a wallet and smiled. "But it'll give me a good look at everything Amarelle was allowed to see, and that's much better than nothing. If we can identify her patterns and her habits, the bitch will eventually start painting clues for us as to the location of her own locus."

"Splat!" said Brandwin.

"Yeah," said Sophara. "And that's definitely my idea of a playground."

"I should be able to get some messages out of the city," said Jadetongue. "Some of the people we've got howling for our blood hate the Parliament of Strife even more. If we could make arrangements with them before we knock those wizards down, I'd bet we could buy our way back into the world. Theradane sanctuary in reverse, at least in a few places."

"I like the way you people think," said Amarelle. "Ivovandas as a stalking horse, and once we've got the goods on her we dump her ass in the river. Her and all her friends. Who's got the wine?"

Jade held out the bottle, something carnelian and bioluminescent and expensive. They passed it around, and even Shraplin dashed a ceremonial swig against his chin. Amarelle turned with the half-empty bottle and faced Scavius's statue.

"Here it is, you asshole. I guess we're not as retired as we might have thought. Five thieves going to war against the Parliament of Strife. Insane. The kind of odds you always loved best. Will you try to think better of us? And if you can't, will you at least keep a few pedestals warm? We might have a future as streetlamps after all. Have one on us."

She smashed the bottle against his plaque, and they watched the glowing, fizzing wine run down the marble. After a few moments, Sophara and Brandwin walked away arm in arm, north toward Tanglewing Street. Shraplin followed, then Jade.

Amarelle alone remained in the white light of whatever was left of Scavius. What he whispered to her then, she kept to herself.

She ran to catch up with the others.

"Hey," said Jade. "Glad you're back! You coming to the Sign of the Fallen Fire with us? We're going to have a game."

"Yeah," said Amarelle, and the air of Theradane tasted better than it had in months. "Hell *yeah,* we're going to have a game!"

Bradley Denton

World Fantasy Award and John W. Campbell Memorial Award–winner Bradley Denton was born in 1958, grew up in Kansas, and took an M.A. in creative writing from the University of Kansas. He sold his first story in 1984, and soon became a regular contributor to *The Magazine of Fantasy and Science Fiction*. His first novel, *Wrack and Roll*, was published in 1986, and was followed by *Lunatics*, *Buddy Holly Is Alive and Well on Ganymede*, *Blackburn*, and *Laughin' Boy*. He's perhaps best known for his series of *Blackburn* stories and novels about an eccentric serial killer, but he won the John W. Campbell Memorial Award for his novel *Buddy Holly Is Alive and Well on Ganymede*, and his two-volume collection *A Conflagration Artist* and *The Calvin Coolidge Home for Dead Comedians* won the World Fantasy Award as the year's Best Collection. His stories have also been collected in *One Day Closer to Death: Eight Stabs at Immortality*. He lives in Austin, Texas.

In the wry, fast-paced comic thriller that follows, we learn that it's not the instrument—it's the music.

BAD BRASS

Bradley Denton

1. Lost in the Woods

With only a fragment of moon above, and surrounded by the twisted limbs of live oaks and Texas cedars, I wasn't worried that the five thieves in the crooked house might spot me. For one thing, I was forty yards away in the woods. For another, it was late on Saturday night—1:30 A.M. Sunday morning, really—and my targets were seventeen-year-olds who were oblivious to anything that wasn't on their smartphones or in their pants.

As far as I could tell, the most dangerous thing about them was the Hank Williams III country punk that blasted out every time the front door opened. These kids were poor excuses for crime kingpins, which was one reason I liked the idea of taking their ill-gotten gains. I doubted it would be much trouble for me, and maybe it'd be a learning experience for them. Win-win. Besides, if my ex-wife called me to come teach again next week, and if any of these kids happened to be in my class, then ace substitute Matthew Marx would have the pleasure of seeing the hangdog expressions on their pimply faces.

At the moment, though, I thought I needed a better look. Besides the scrap of moon, the available light consisted of off-white beams stabbing from the house windows and a custard-yellow glow from a bulb on the front porch. Not bad. But I had been watching with my folding binoculars for almost forty-five minutes, and I had realized I was too far away to have a good view when the money changed hands. Especially if it happened inside. I needed to be sure I could tell which kid took the cash—and whether that kid kept it, split it with the others, or stashed it.

I also wanted to see how much they collected. There wasn't much point in tailing a teenager for a lousy hundred bucks . . . or in burglarizing this dump later if there was nothing inside but empty beer cans and Cheetos bags. I had been in that situation before, and I had been bitten by a previously undetected Chihuahua for my trouble. Then the Chihuahua had only sold for twenty bucks, which hadn't been enough to cover my pain and suffering. I hoped he had ended up in a stir-fry.

That misadventure had taught me that appearances could be deceiving. The Chihuahua's house had been a minimansion occupied by successful marijuana importers, yet it had yielded next to bupkis. This rural house with the crooked frame, in contrast, was little more than an oversized Dogpatch shack. It had once been a spiffy guest cabin on the third-largest ranch in Kingman County, but now it was old, ugly, and warped. Yet it might contain a heart of gold.

I had swiped the directions here from a smartphone belonging to a Kingman High football star named Donny. In the hallway before one of my classes, I had heard him brag to a friend about his off-season criminal enterprises. That was the advantage of being an old dude at a high school, and a substitute old dude at that. Unless I stood right in front of them and yelled in their faces, the kids didn't even see me. And they ignored the school rule against phone use during class. So I could eavesdrop, or walk past their desks and read their texts, as if I were a ghost.

Once I had the directions, some persistent Googling had revealed that the crooked house plus five acres currently belonged to the bidnissman-father of another high-school kid named Jared. I hadn't laid eyes on that one at school, but I had figured out which one he was from my vantage point in the woods. Assuming Facebook photos didn't lie.

It didn't look as if Jared's daddy was interested in mowing or other upkeep for this little country retreat. No doubt he'd bought the place as an investment before the latest real-estate bust. So now his seventeen-year-old heir had a clubhouse. And since the next occupied home was a half mile away, the club might as well indulge in some illegal activity.

I was pretty sure no hard drugs were involved, so I doubted that I needed to worry about assault weapons. Sure, this was Texas, so there might be a few shotguns or deer rifles inside. But I wasn't too scared of anything that needed to be cocked between rounds.

I didn't have a gun myself. I never do. Guns are a crutch for those who aren't in good enough shape to run. I did have my Swiss Army knife, but that was just in case I needed a compact burglary tool.

And I didn't think I would. So far, these kids didn't seem bright enough to lock their doors.

2. Defective Merchandise

At 1:55 A.M. by my watch, a pair of headlights came toward the crooked house from the county road to the north, bouncing along the dirt-and-gravel driveway just east of my hiding place. I crouched behind a live-oak trunk until a grimy, rust-spotted white van with no side or rear windows passed by. This looked promising.

The van drove past a PT Cruiser, a Honda Civic, and a Ford pickup that were all parked in the grass on the other side of the driveway. It pulled off a wide patch of dirt at the end into the weed-tangled front yard, then backed up until its rear bumper was almost touching the porch steps. The rear doors opened.

On the porch, a skinny guy with shaggy brown hair—Jared—and a tall girl with long, straight blond hair had been making out on an old sofa beside the front door. Now they jumped up. Jared opened the door to wave at someone inside, and Hank Williams III fell silent. I could hear crickets and cicadas again, but the voices from the porch were just a mumble.

I closed my binoculars flat. No one would be looking in my direction now that the van had arrived. I jammed the binoculars into the back pocket of my black jeans, then zipped up my black sweatshirt and flipped up the hood. Late April in Central Texas, even in the middle of the night, was too warm for this ensemble. And the sports eye black I had smeared over my face made me itch. But sometimes comfort had to be sacrificed for style.

I left the trees and angled fifteen yards across the driveway in a low scuttle, ducking behind the PT Cruiser. I paused a moment, then made my way to the Civic. My knees didn't hurt enough to slow me down, but I could still feel them more than I would have liked. At my checkup right after the move from Chicago, my new Texas doctor had said I was in decent shape "for a forty-three-year-old who smokes, drinks, and already has a touch of osteoarthritis." This from a seventy-year-old G.P. with peanut-butter breath and a gut like a beach ball. I might not have minded if he hadn't gone on to ask if I wanted to do something about my thinning hair. "At least mine's still brown," I'd said. "Tick-tock," he'd replied. My kind of guy.

I stopped in a crouch behind the left-front fender of the Civic, holding my breath. I could hear hi-how-ya-doin' chatter from the porch. But under that, there were soft voices from the bed of the Ford pickup on the other side of the Honda.

"What's happening?" It was the whisper of a teenage girl.

"They're about to make an offer," a male whisper answered. "Don't worry. Tyler's got this."

"Shouldn't you be up there, too, Donny?"

"Naw, it's cool. Come on, Marisa. Kiss me again."

"Marisa" was a name I recognized from a few days before, when I'd subbed a college-prep comp-and-lit class. She had been a tiny, dark-haired young woman with huge brown eyes and a hint of a Tejano accent. She had said some perceptive things about D. H. Lawrence's "The Rocking-Horse Winner." I had been impressed enough to remember her.

But as it turned out, she was just another teenage criminal. It was disappointing because I hadn't expected any of the kids involved in the theft to be smart. Sure, these particular thieves had been smart enough to get in and out of Kingman Rural High School at night without being picked up on security video—but there were only three working cameras, and two of them were aimed at the main entrance. It wouldn't take any valedictorians to avoid them.

When I heard the wet sounds of Marisa and Donny gnawing at each other's faces, I crept to the Civic's rear fender and looked around it. I was within ten yards of the house now, and my angle was straight toward the west side of the porch. There wasn't even a railing. If the kids and their buyers stayed where they were, I would see the whole deal.

In the pickup bed, Donny was doing his best to turn his make-out session with Marisa into something more. But Marisa was disengaging every few moments to rise up and watch the proceedings on the porch. I was amused. But I had to watch the porch, too.

Three Caucasian high-schoolers—Jared and the girl from the couch, plus Donny's football buddy Tyler—stood with their backs to the open front door. Tyler was a lumpy-nosed, stubble-headed bruiser in blue jeans and a Toby Keith T-shirt who was destined for a career in either the NFL or the liquor-store-holdup industry. He hadn't had jack to say about "The Rocking-Horse Winner."

Two adult dudes stood with their backs to the van. One was a pink-faced, grizzled white guy wearing a NASCAR cap who could have been a less-beefy, much-older clone of Tyler. He looked about sixty-five or seventy, but some of that might have been due to hard living. I thought I recognized him as a long-ago skunkweed associate of my old man's, but I couldn't be sure.

The other guy was a slim, fair-skinned hombre with a grim expression and gunmetal-gray eyes. He looked to be in his mid-thirties. He was wearing a white cowboy hat, a gold-paisley-embroidered red jacket over a black shirt with white-pearl buttons, a gold bolo tie and wristwatch, crisp black slacks, and pointy-toed red rodeo boots. Here was another man who knew that comfort sometimes had to be sacrificed for style. Or maybe he had just come from a gig.

NASCAR-Cap Guy was talking. "—appreciate the offer, but we'd prefer to evaluate the goods out here. Carlos and I can drink our own beer, know what I mean?"

Tyler grinned and stuck out his hand toward the man in the cowboy hat. "Carlos, is it? I'm looking forward to earning your business."

I winced. Tyler was doing an imitation of an appliance-store salesman. It was not good.

Carlos didn't like it, either. His eyes narrowed, and his shoulders twitched. He did not extend a hand to meet Tyler's.

NASCAR-Cap Guy gave a forced chuckle. "Uh, 'Carlos' ain't his real name. I'm just calling him that for the purposes of this transaction. And you should call me Mr. Anthony, as I told you on the phone, on account of I'm your respected elder. Now, let's get on with it."

Yup, this was the guy I remembered from when I was a kid. Bobby Anthony. Daddy had called him Bobby Tone. He had gone to the pokey for a while. And my mama had not liked him even a little bit.

Tyler dropped his hand. The scowl on his face said that Carlos and Bobby Tone had disrespected him, and he was offended.

I winced again. *Bad move, Tyler. These guys might pull your spine out through your nose.*

Fortunately, the scowl passed in an instant, and Tyler turned into Willy Loman again. "Well, sure, of course! Let's get on with it! Jared, you want to bring 'em out?"

Jared looked confused. "All at once?"

"Kaylee can help." Tyler nodded toward the blond girl, who was looking down at her feet and brushing her hair from her eyes.

Now Carlos cleared his throat and spoke. He was dressed like a *banda* musician and standing on a porch in Texas, but his voice sounded as if it belonged to an Anglo news anchor in Connecticut.

"As I understand it," he said, "you have three different models available. I suggest you bring them out one at a time, so I can evaluate them individually."

Tyler and Jared stared dumbly, and Kaylee continued looking at her feet. Then Bobby Tone barked at them. "Goddamn, boys, what you waitin' for?"

Tyler flicked a hand at Jared, and Jared hurried into the house. Kaylee scuffed her flip-flops, but otherwise didn't move.

In the bed of the Ford, Donny grunted. I looked up and saw that Marisa had been watching the porch with her arms propped on the sidewall of the pickup bed. But now Donny was trying to pull her back down.

"Donny, no!" Marisa said, no longer whispering.

Donny grunted again and kept pulling. Marisa vanished downward, and I had the sick feeling that I might have to do something. Which would be really stupid of me.

"Donny! *Basta ya!*" This was accompanied by the sound of flesh being smacked. I guessed it was Donny's face. And I relaxed a little.

On the porch, Carlos glanced toward the Ford. Which was pretty close to glancing toward me. I held my breath.

But Carlos didn't let his gaze linger. He turned back toward Tyler, checked his wristwatch, and muttered something about amateurs.

Marisa rose up to look over the sidewall again.

Donny stood, hissed "Screw this," and jumped to the ground. Then he stomped to the porch.

"'Bye," Marisa whispered. Her back was toward me, but I had the sense that she was smiling.

I smiled too. Then I looked toward the porch again.

Tyler scowled again as Donny hopped onto the porch. "You need something, bro?"

"Yeah, but I ain't gettin' it."

Bobby Tone cleared his throat. "If you boys could put your love lives on hold until we're done, we'd appreciate it."

Then Jared came back outside, lugging a trapezoidal black-plastic case that was almost as big as he was. He flopped it onto the concrete porch with a thud, and Tyler squatted down to snap open the latches.

"Feast your eyes on this, gentlemen," he said.

The top of the case swung up so I couldn't see what lay inside. But I could see the sour expression on Carlos.

"Uh, no good?" Bobby asked.

Carlos gave one slow, grim shake of his head.

"Mucho asso sucko," he said. He still sounded like he was from Connecticut.

Bobby Tone took one step forward, put a work-boot-clad foot against the case, and kicked it off the porch. When it hit the ground, the big white bell of a sousaphone tumbled out, rolling a few feet in my direction before it came to rest facing the porch. The coiled white tubing of the rest of the instrument fell from the case, and then the case flopped over on top of it.

"Hey!" Donny yelled. "What the hell?"

Carlos regarded Donny and Tyler with a dark glare.

"Fiberglass," Carlos said. His voice was a growl.

He reached behind his back, under the jacket, and came out with a revolver so big that it looked as if it belonged in a cartoon.

Then he cocked it and blasted away at the sousaphone bell.

He was a good shot, too.

3. Bull-shiit!

I ducked behind the Civic's left-rear tire. The movement might give me away, but it was better than catching a pellet. Carlos fired five rounds in all, each one making a noise like a half stick of dynamite. I recognized the sound: .410 Magnum shotgun shells.

When the last echo had died away and my humming ears could make out the voices of shouting teenagers, I risked a look around the Civic's bumper again. The sousaphone bell now sported five golf-ball-sized holes and a peppering of smaller wounds. The grass around it was dusted with white-fiberglass snow.

While Bobby Tone reamed his ears with his pinky, Carlos flipped out the cylinder of the big revolver and dumped the empty shotgun shells. Then he reached into his jacket, brought out five more shells, and reloaded.

"This firearm," Carlos said, snapping the cylinder back into place, "is called the Judge. And the Judge doesn't like fiberglass." He looked sidelong at Bobby Tone. "Didn't you tell them the Judge wouldn't like fiberglass?"

Bobby nodded. "I mentioned that low-quality instruments would not be considered."

Tyler stabbed a finger toward the ventilated bell. "That's a King! It's a four-thousand-dollar horn!"

"If you say so," Bobby Tone said. "This ain't my area of expertise. I'm just the middleman."

Carlos tucked the Judge behind his back again. "So, children," he said. "What else do you have?"

While Tyler, Donny, and Jared conferred in a nervous huddle and Kaylee sat down on the tattered couch again, I glanced at the Ford. I didn't think any of the shotgun pellets had pinged the truck, but I guessed Marisa had gotten a good scare. And sure enough, she was out of sight. I assumed she had flattened on the floor of the pickup bed.

Good. A smart kid like Marisa needed to be scared away from dodgy crap. Otherwise she might wind up in a hoodie with eye black all over her face, crouching in the weeds somewhere.

Up on the porch, Jared was dragging another big black case outside. This time, when Tyler opened it, I saw a gold-lacquered brass bell gleaming inside.

Carlos pursed his lips. "This appears to be acceptable," he said. "But let's find out."

In a few smooth motions, Carlos had the sousaphone out of its case with the bell attached. He dropped the circular tubing over his head and onto his shoulders, then placed his fingers on the valve keys and his lips to the mouthpiece.

A fast, booming scale burst forth and made the Civic's bumper rattle. I could feel it in my chest, too. It wasn't as sharp as the sound the Judge had made, but it penetrated deeper. I was impressed.

Carlos stopped after thirty seconds, removed and disassembled the instrument, and replaced it in its case. He snapped the case shut, then stood up and looked at Bobby Tone.

"Twenty-two hundred," he said.

Donny made a noise like a burro kicked in the balls, and Tyler exclaimed, "Bull-shiit!"

Carlos turned away and stared off into the night.

Bobby Tone extended his hands toward the boys, palms turned upward. "He says twenty-two hundred, it's twenty-two hundred."

"Aw, Jesus," Tyler said. His appliance-store-salesman voice had morphed into a whine. "That's a Conn. It sells for eight thousand new, and it's only, like, four months old. It ain't even been marched. You gotta give us at least four thousand. Especially since y'all shot up the King."

Carlos remained stock-still.

Bobby Tone raised an eyebrow. "Boys, take it or leave it. And if you leave it, he will not be making another offer."

Tyler and Donny both cussed. But Jared just looked at Kaylee, who was sitting on the couch with her hair in her face, staring down at her knees.

I saw her nod.

Then Jared and Tyler exchanged a look, and Tyler gave an exasperated groan.

"If we gotta, we gotta," he said.

Carlos turned to face them and reached behind his back again. The boys flinched. But this time Carlos brought out a leather wallet the size of a small notebook. He opened it as if it were the Bible, counted out twenty-two bills, and handed them to Bobby Tone. Then he tucked the wallet back with the Judge.

Bobby peeled two bills from the stack and extended the rest toward Tyler.

"Dude, you're shorting us," Tyler whined.

Bobby Tone frowned. "Nope. My finder's fee is 10 percent. So you still owe me twenty bucks."

Tyler took the stack of hundreds and stuffed it into his back pocket.

"Now," Carlos said, "did you save the best for last?"

Donny jerked a thumb at Jared, and Jared went inside.

"We did, sir," Tyler said. The kid was doing his best to regain his composure. "This one is about three years old, but it's in perfect shape. A new one would run you 15 K."

Carlos raised an eyebrow. "Sousaphones don't often cost that much."

Tyler grinned as Jared dragged out the third case and set it on the porch beside the second.

"That's because this sucker ain't a sousaphone," he said. He squatted, unsnapped the latches, and flipped open the lid with a flourish. "According to my band-geek colleagues, this right here is a Gronitz concert tuba. It's the Kingman High band teacher's pride and joy since he convinced some rich San Antonio asshole to donate it. But Mr. Garrett's loss can be your gain."

That made my teeth grit. Up to now, I had held out some hope that David Garrett might be part of the sousaphone-stealing conspiracy. After all, he was a low-paid teacher with access to high-cost instruments. But there was no sign of him here, and Tyler seemed amused by his potential discomfort.

Nuts. I hadn't even been introduced to Garrett yet, but I was pretty sure he was sleeping with my ex. It would have made me happy if he were a criminal. All I'd seen for sure in the five weeks I'd been back in Kingman was that he was talented, handsome, popular, and drove an almost-new Nissan Maxima. Also, he was African-American, which gave him some heritage in common with Elizabeth. Of course, I knew that my European genes weren't the reason our marriage had cratered. But then, I had wished I were black ever since I'd seen Freddie King play at the Armadillo in Austin when I was six. My father had shown me a few good things besides how to pick a lock.

Carlos leaned over, looked into the case, then gave a sigh.

"No," he said. "No, I don't think so."

Tyler stood up bug-eyed. "Are you kidding? This thing is pristine."

"And look at all that metal!" Donny said. "There's more than in three sousaphones!"

Carlos looked into the case again. "This would be fine as a recording instrument, or for a symphony—but these are not my markets. I think you may have been misled by the fact that in Mexico, a sousaphone is simply called a tuba." He gave Donny a disdainful glance. "As for the amount of metal, I assume you think I am in the scrap business. I am not." He looked into the case a third time. "Eight hundred."

Then Carlos turned away and stared into the night again.

This time Donny was the one who yelled: "Bull-shiit! Bu-ull-SHIIT!"

Bobby Tone held out his hands. "Boys, you got ten seconds."

I watched as Tyler and Donny stomped and cussed some more. Then, as before, Jared looked at Kaylee, whose face was still hidden in her hair. She was picking at a piece of dead skin on her ankle. But she gave Jared another nod, and Jared passed it on to Tyler.

Tyler groaned and held out his hand.

As before, Carlos turned around, produced the big wallet, pulled out some bills, and handed them to Bobby Tone.

Bobby thumbed the top bill away and tucked it into his pocket. "Now you don't owe me twenty anymore." He handed Tyler the remaining seven hundred.

Tyler, as sullen as a neutered bulldog, stuffed it into his back pocket with the rest. The pocket bulged now, but that only seemed to make him sadder.

I would do what I could to relieve him of that burden. Twenty-seven hundred wasn't a huge payday. But I'd often settled for less.

Carlos turned to Bobby Tone. "If there's nothing else, we should be going."

Bobby pointed at the house. "Y'all got anything else in there?"

"Naw, that's all we could grab," Donny said. "Kingman only has one other sousaphone anyway, and it's old and beat-up."

"In that case," Bobby Tone said, "you might want to expand to other school districts. Carlos tells me we can use trumpets and trombones, too. But those won't bring as much. If you want the big money, grab more sousaphones."

Carlos made a dismissive gesture toward the blasted bell in the grass. His upper lip curled.

"But remember," he said. "No fiberglass."

There was a moment of silence. Then Bobby Tone kicked the lid of the tuba case closed. "All right, boys, load 'em up."

Jared began to lean down toward the instrument cases. But Donny stepped in front of him. "I got it, clarinet-boy."

Donny squatted and snapped the latches on the tuba case, then lugged it to the van and tossed it in. It landed with a bang.

"Take it easy!" Bobby Tone said.

Donny looked pissed. "Aw, it's fine. It's only worth seven hundred." He kicked the left-rear van door, which slammed shut with another bang.

"Now, that's just rude," Bobby Tone said. Carlos glared.

Donny ignored them and reached for the sousaphone case.

At which point the van's engine turned over. Then it bellowed, and the van spun away from the porch, its rear tires flinging dirt and grass, its right-rear door flapping. It fishtailed onto the dirt apron at the end of the driveway and blasted toward the county road.

As the van roared past me, I caught a glimpse of the driver.

Marisa.

I glanced back at the porch, expecting that Carlos would bring out the Judge again. But Carlos just stood there looking bemused while the other males on the porch hollered. Meanwhile, Kaylee had brushed her hair away from one eye and was watching the van make its getaway.

I watched it, too. Its lights came on as it squealed onto the blacktop road, and it roared away to the east. Its right-rear taillight winked as the open door swung over it and then swung back again. Then both taillights vanished among the live oaks, and the roar dwindled to a distant whine.

Up on the porch, the yelling and cussing dwindled as well. When it fell to silence, Carlos spoke. For the first time, he sounded as if he could be from Texas.

"Damn," he said. "Whose girlfriend just jacked my tuba?"

4. Not a Pervert

I had no idea why Marisa had done it. Maybe she was mad at Donny for stomping off when she'd refused to put out. But for a smart kid, stealing the van seemed a stupid way of expressing her displeasure. Seeing as how Carlos and the Judge might decide to shoot up more than a fiberglass sousaphone bell.

Fortunately, Carlos didn't seem to care about the van, and not much about the tuba. He just seemed happy that he still had the brass sousaphone.

Bobby Tone, however, was perturbed. I listened as he instructed Tyler to return the money for the tuba, plus another five hundred for the van.

"I stole that shitbox for the sole purpose of this transaction," he said. "So it ain't about the vehicle per se. It's the principle. You invite a person to a business meeting, that person has a reasonable expectation of leaving in the same vehicle in which he arrived."

The boys glanced at Kaylee, who gave a slight nod. Her hair fell over her face again.

Tyler, his shoulders hunched in misery, reached into his back pocket and pulled out the wad of bills. He counted off twelve and gave them back to Bobby Tone. Then Bobby counted off eight and extended them toward Carlos.

Carlos held up a hand. "No, you keep the finder's fee."

Bobby Tone peeled off a bill and handed over the rest. "That's why I appreciate our association, Carlos."

Carlos produced his wallet and tucked the bills inside. "You did your part." Now he gave Tyler a cold stare. "But you'll give me that hundred, *pendejo.*" The Spanish word didn't sound natural coming from him. He put the emphasis on the first syllable instead of the second. "Then you'll drive Mr. Anthony, me, and my sousaphone to our cars, which are parked in Kingman. And if I ever do business with you again, you'll make sure the transaction proceeds in a more professional manner. *Comprende?*"

This time Tyler didn't look to Jared or Kaylee. He just nodded, then handed Carlos another hundred.

I suppressed an urge to moan. Now the Kingman High sousaphone-stealing ring was left with a mere fourteen hundred. Plus some shot-gunned fiberglass.

And I wasn't going to go after the cash on Bobby Tone and Carlos. I just wanted to steal candy from babies for a change. Especially after the Christmas mess in Chicago involving the Santa-with-a-Sig-Sauer. That payoff had financed my move back to Texas, but it still hadn't been worth the near violation of Rule Number One: Don't get killed.

Okay, so fourteen hundred wasn't much. But it was something. And I had invested too much time to just let it go. So I had to stop pondering Marisa's theft of the van. It wasn't relevant to the goal.

Kaylee stood and took the remaining cash from Tyler's hand. She didn't speak, and she didn't look up. She just smoothly . . . *took* it as she walked by. Tyler blinked and looked startled, but he didn't say boo. Then Kaylee and Jared went into the house, closing the door behind them.

"All right, youngsters," Bobby Tone said, slapping his hands together. "Time for me and Carlos to vacate Romper Room. Who's drivin'?"

Donny mumbled and gestured toward the Ford pickup.

I eased away from the Civic's rear bumper and moved up to the front end. Once there, I paused and listened long enough to hear the plastic-on-concrete scrape of the sousaphone case being picked up. Then, taking a quick breath, I scuttled past the Ford's front end to the back corner of the crooked house. I squatted there, out of sight of the parked cars, with my back against the peeling wooden siding.

A glance around the corner revealed Tyler coming off the porch with the sousaphone case, followed by Donny, Bobby Tone, and Carlos.

"Hey, where's Marisa?" Tyler asked as he hefted the sousaphone into the pickup bed. He wasn't too bright.

"Gone," Donny said.

Tyler climbed into the pickup bed with the instrument, and the other three got in front. When Donny started the engine, I ducked back around the corner before the headlights came on. Then I looked again while the Ford backed past the blasted fiberglass bell, shifted gears, and headed out to the road.

When it was gone, I remained still for a few minutes and listened. I heard Jared's and Kaylee's muffled voices inside the house, and no one else's. I was pretty sure they were alone. I had watched the place for hours, and I had seen all of the vehicles arrive. The Ford was Donny's, and Tyler had ridden shotgun. The Honda was Jared's. And Kaylee had driven the PT Cruiser with Marisa as a passenger. I wondered how their friendship would evolve now that Marisa had screwed up what appeared to be Kaylee's deal. And then I quashed that thought because, again, it wasn't relevant to my goal.

I crept around to the south side of the house, following Jared's and Kaylee's voices. As I passed the concrete stoop on the east, I saw that the back door was standing open. There was a wooden screen door over it, but there was no latch or hook. I wouldn't need my Swiss Army knife.

Once I was on the south side, I paused in the weeds under the second window. Like the back door, it was open but covered with a screen. A soft glow inside was accompanied by rustling noises, but the voices had fallen silent. It sounded as if Jared and Kaylee were going further than Donny and Marisa had gone.

As the sounds became rhythmic, I risked standing up far enough to look inside. I ignored the teenagers on the bed and scanned their clothes on the floor. The light from the lamp on the battered chest of drawers wasn't great, but it was good enough for me to spot Kaylee's white shorts in the doorway. The folded cash was visible in one of the pockets.

In the movies, a lone thief is often portrayed as an elegant schemer. But in the actual process of stealing, especially when stealing from other crooks, cleverness matters less than luck. Down and dirty gets the money.

I went back the way I had come, gingerly pulled open the screen door, and slipped inside.

The rest was easy. In a crouch, I passed through a small utility room and kitchen, entered the hallway, and followed the lamplight to the open bedroom door. Jared and Kaylee were busy, and it would have taken a hand grenade to distract them. So I snagged the shorts and crept back the other way until I was on the stoop. Thirty seconds, in and out.

Once I had eased the screen door closed, I removed the cash from the left rear pocket of Kaylee's shorts and transferred it to my jeans. Then I found her smartphone in the right rear pocket. And now that I had the cash, I decided to allow myself some curiosity. I tapped the screen and it came to life, displaying the last text message Kaylee had seen before taking off her clothes.

GLAD U R OK, it read. ALL OK W ME 2. NO HAY PROBLEMA.

The sender was identified as MRSA.

Maybe Marisa hadn't screwed up Kaylee's deal after all. Maybe they had been working on something together.

I didn't know what kind of deal took twenty-two hundred bucks and turned it into fourteen hundred. But whatever it had been, these kids now had nothing other than the bitter lesson that crime doesn't pay.

Not enough, anyhow.

No longer worried about making a little noise, I jogged between the

Honda and the PT Cruiser, across the driveway, and back into the trees. From there, with the aid of my trusty penlight, I would make my way along a few deer trails back to the side road where I'd parked my Toyota Corolla.

I left Kaylee's phone and shorts on the stoop. I was glad there hadn't been any underwear inside the shorts. That would have made me feel creepy.

As it was, I could tell myself that even though I was a lowlife, I wasn't a pervert. I would cling to that.

That, and fourteen hundred dollars swiped from a gang of teenage sousaphone thieves.

5. No Puns Allowed

When I arrived at Kingman Rural High School on Monday morning, feeling like a fraud in khakis and a blue sport shirt, I encountered a sixtyish sheriff's deputy just inside the front doors. He was blocky and big-nosed, and he occupied the center of the brick-and-tile foyer like a monument to local law enforcement. He was wearing aviator sunglasses with his deerskin-colored uniform and Stetson, and he was chewing gum with slow menace. The holster for the .357 revolver on his hip was unsnapped, and there was nothing else on the gunbelt except a handcuff holster. I hadn't seen a cop carry a weapon other than a semiauto since I was a kid, and most were also adorned with radios, Tasers, collapsible clubs, mace canisters, and all sorts of other toys. But this guy was old-school.

I didn't recognize him, even though I'd grown up in Kingman County, which meant that despite his age, he was new around here. So I decided to have a chat. Whenever possible, I like to be on friendly terms with potential problems.

"Some kinda trouble, chief?" I asked as kids poured into the building around us. I had to raise my voice to be heard over the yammering teenagers.

The deputy didn't look at me as he answered. "Break-in and theft last Friday night. School property stolen."

I cocked my head like a confused spaniel. "How's standing here on Monday morning gonna help that?"

The deputy's eyebrows pinched closer by a few millimeters. "Just doing what I can." He looked at me over the top of the sunglasses. "I told the sheriff I suspect students. So her idea is the culprits will see me and get nervous. And nervous kids tell tales. In theory."

I glanced around at the rushing influx of tall and short, fat and skinny, white, black, and brown teenagers. Half of them were staring down at their phones as they flowed past, and the other half were either engrossed in conversation or rolling their eyes at us.

"Well, good luck with that," I said.

The deputy pushed up his sunglasses. "I'm well aware that these little bastards aren't intimidated by a fat old man. But as I say, I'm doing what I can. And I get to have my second cup of coffee when the bell rings." He glanced at the clock on the wall behind him. "Thirteen minutes."

I nodded toward the unsnapped holster. "Just be careful you don't shoot any of the little bastards in the meantime, hoss."

One of his eyebrows rose. "So far, you've called me 'chief' and 'hoss.' I suspect sarcasm. So if I shoot anybody, it's gonna be you."

I checked my wristwatch. "I'll take a rain check on that, colonel. The principal wants to see me, and as you've pointed out, I only have thirteen minutes to the bell."

"That's a shame," the deputy said. "I've been so enjoying your company."

"Name's Matthew Marx, by the way." I stuck out my hand. "Substitute teacher par excellence. Pleased to make your acquaintance, Deputy—"

I looked at the name on the rectangular tag over his badge.

"'Beeswax'?" I asked.

He didn't extend his hand. "As in none of yours."

"But we have something in common, *jefe.* Our names both end in 'x.'"

His face was like a big-nosed rock. "Ain't no such thing as alphabet brothers."

So I turned my attempted handshake into a salute and then moved into the main hallway, weaving through the throng until the brick wall to my left turned into glass panels. I cut across the hall, stopping twice to avoid kids who wouldn't look up from their phones, and then opened the door to the school office.

Lester, the office manager—he didn't like being called the secretary—was leaning on the long counter that split the room between his workspace and the waiting area. Lester was a retired history teacher and coach who had taken this job, he claimed, because his wife had threatened to stab him with her garden shears if he stayed home. At the moment, Lester had his bald head in his hands, propping his ruddy lump of a face in the steam from a jumbo travel mug. His necktie was slung over the shoulder of his plaid shirt so it didn't hang down into the mug.

"She's with a student," Lester said without looking up. His voice was like gravel in a blender. "So just stand there and don't say nothin'. I'm hungover like a mother."

I leaned on the counter, too, facing him. "Did your mother get hungover a lot, Lester?"

"If you'd met my daddy, you wouldn't ask. Now shuddup."

I clucked my tongue. "Boy, everyone's in a mood this morning. Deputy Beeswax out there nearly bit my head off, too."

"That's Ernest," Lester said. "'Beeswax' is what they called him in the Houston P.D. Dunno why. Now he's a Kingman deputy, which is his idea of semiretirement. The sheriff must agree, because Ernest showed up here this morning driving his own car. Now, it's a nice new Chrysler, but it ain't got a police radio or a prisoner cage or even a shotgun rack. So I think Ernest's plan is to stand at the entrance in the morning and afternoon, looking vicious, and read Louis L'Amour paperbacks in the parking lot in between. Maybe catch a few winks. I reckon his driver's seat reclines."

"Maybe I'll stick a firecracker in his tailpipe," I said. "Like I used to."

Lester's eyes widened, and he let out a low whistle. "No, you don't want to do that. I played football with him at Southwest Texas back in the Cretaceous period, and I saw him break a linebacker's neck with a fair hit. Guy wound up driving a ButterKrust delivery truck he had to turn by blowin' into a straw."

The inner-office door at the far end of the counter opened, and a small, dark-haired girl in jeans and a bright red KINGMAN COUGAR BAND T-shirt stepped out. She juggled a blue backpack from one hand to the other and closed the door behind her, then looked at me. It was Marisa.

Her eyebrows rose. "Oh, hi, Mr. Marx." Her Tejano accent was downright musical. "Are you teaching our comp-and-lit class again today?"

"I, uh, dunno," I said. I was discombobulated. The last time I had seen this girl, she had been stealing a van with a tuba in the back. "I assume Eliz—uh, Ms. Owens will tell me where to go."

At the counter, Lester made a choking noise.

Marisa smiled. She probably knew "Ms. Owens" and I had been married in the distant past. In fact, it had only been six years since Elizabeth had divorced me and I'd bugged out to Chicago. But to a seventeen-year-old, that would seem like ancient history. I wished it seemed that way to me, too.

"Well, I hope we have you again," Marisa said. "I liked that D. H. Lawrence story. Mr. Morris would have made us write about 'The Cask of Amontillado' for the tenth time."

"Poe you," I said.

Marisa frowned. "Huh?"

The inner-office door opened again, and my ex-wife stood there in all of her tall, smooth-skinned, blue-pantsuited glory. Her hair was tied back, emphasizing her high forehead, dark eyes, and perfect cheekbones. It would have been nice if she'd let herself fall apart after we'd split, but no such luck.

"As I've told you before, Mr. Marx," Elizabeth said, "no one likes puns. And I won't tolerate them at Kingman Rural High." She glanced at Marisa. "Don't be late, now. They'll need you to unlock the cabinets."

Marisa said, "Yes, ma'am," and started for the exit. She nodded to me. "See you later, Mr. Marx."

I watched her as she went into the hall, and I saw what was silk-screened on the back of her band T-shirt.

In bold block letters, it said BAD ASS. But in a stylized scrawl, the letters "BR" were inserted before "ASS."

BAD BRASS.

6. *Sparks and Wildfires*

I turned to Elizabeth. "If I'd worn a shirt like that back when I was a student here, I would've been suspended. After Lester here had smacked me upside the head."

Lester snorted. "Well, it woulda been *you.*"

Elizabeth shrugged. "We've had one parent complain. Then that parent found out the shirts were gifts from our anonymous San Antonio band benefactor. When donations are the only way a school can maintain its music program, people find they can put up with a little vulgarity."

"Even the Baptists?" I asked.

"Especially the Baptists. They embrace the fact that we're all sinners. Come on in, Mr. Marx."

I followed Elizabeth into her office and closed the door behind me as I heard Lester mutter, "*Mister* Marx?"

"You know," I said as Elizabeth sat down behind her desk, "you might as well use my first name. Everyone knows we used to bump uglies."

Elizabeth gave me a thin smile and gestured at the two black-vinyl chairs on my side of the desk. "Speak for yourself, Matt."

I sat down sideways in one of the chairs and propped my feet on the other. "I love it when we banter, Lizbeth. That's how I know the spark is still there."

"This is Texas. Sparks start wildfires and ruin hundreds of lives."

"You're exaggerating," I said. "At most, we only ruined *my* life. You, on the other hand, are running one of the twenty or thirty finest high schools between Conroe and Nacogdoches. How many badass students you got now, anyway? About 666?"

Her smile flatlined. "I take it you still think of Kingman as 'Satan's cornhole.' But I'm grateful you brought me here. I was scared to death of any part of Texas that wasn't Austin, but Kingman showed me there are good people everywhere." She gave an annoyed sigh that I remembered well. "Why'd you come back, Matt? Your parents are gone, and I'm a thorn in your side. And you can't be happy in that tiny apartment over the hardware store."

"*Casa de Kingman Bolt and Supply* is temporary," I said. "Regardless of living quarters, though, this is where I grew up. It's home. But I can't idealize it because I know what's under all the rocks. Such as the fact that this county harbors more than its fair share of plain old-fashioned racism. You know how many people said unkind things about our marriage?"

Actually, what I had heard most people say was that I wasn't good enough for her. I could go to UT, make the Dean's List, and get a master's in education, but I would always be a third-generation delinquent to the older folks. They weren't wrong, of course, but it was still unkind of them to comment on it.

Elizabeth gave a short laugh. "If I let a few garden-variety racists drive me off, I couldn't live *any*where." Then she frowned. "But if I couldn't have this job, I'd go where I could. Which brings me to something I've been wanting to tell you." She leaned forward. "Maybe you're thinking if you watch and wait, a space will open up so you can join the Kingman faculty again. But that won't happen anytime soon. Whereas you could go full-time right now in, say, Dallas. Or Fort Worth, or Oklahoma City." Her eyebrows rose. "Or Canada. If you liked Chicago, you'd love Canada. Snow. Ice. Moose. All sorts of things you can't have here."

I made a face. "Naw. Some of those people speak French. I have a hard enough time with Spanish." I checked my watch. "Bell's gonna ring. Where do you need me? Which you could have told me in voice mail, by the way. If you didn't want to banter."

"I didn't tell you because I wasn't sure," Elizabeth said. "But I knew we'd have a few teachers calling in sick. That happens toward the end of the term as they realize they haven't burned through their sick leave yet. I thought one of them might be Morris again, in which case you could continue doing some actual English teaching. Except he's here after all."

"Too bad. Some of those kids verged on being bright."

"I know." She looked down at her desk. When she spoke again, her voice was quieter. "However, someone I didn't expect to bail . . . did. He sent an 'I can't come in' text this morning with no explanation. And now he isn't answering texts or phone calls, either."

I waited. Given the way Elizabeth was talking, it wasn't hard to guess who the culprit was. But I wanted her to say it.

"It's the band instructor," Elizabeth said. "David Garrett."

I swung my feet down. "You mean the guy you've been riding like a rodeo bull?"

It didn't faze her. "That's a gross mischaracterization," she said. "And no one else knows. So don't say anything."

I gave a chuckle that came out a little bitter. "Hell, Lester probably has tiny red X's on his calendar to mark the mornings when you and Mr. Garrett happen to arrive within five minutes of each other. This is a small town, Lizbeth. If the high-school principal is playing the slide trombone with the duke of the band dorks, I'm not the only one who's noticed."

Now Elizabeth gave me a look that could have cut glass.

"All I need to hear from you," she said, "is whether you'll take symphonic band for first hour, then kill an hour, then cover two back-to-back history classes. Ms. Conley left a Gettysburg DVD she says will be fine for both. After that, you can go home with a half day's pay. Or you can take two study halls this afternoon. Final exams start in a week, and a few real teachers could use the planning periods."

I tried to give her back the same stare she was giving me. But she was a whole lot better at it. "First of all, I don't know nothin' 'bout teaching no band. Second, kudos on the 'real teachers' shot. Third . . ." If only my weekend adventure had been more profitable. I could use the full eighty bucks. "Okay. I can do the afternoon, too."

Elizabeth regained her leader-of-the-pack composure. "Don't worry about the band. That's why Marisa was here. She's only a junior, but even the seniors respect her. So does David. I gave her a key to the instrument cabinets, and she'll be running the rehearsal. All you have to do is make sure no one disrupts it. The spring concert is this Friday, and they have to play well. The bake sale and barbecue are right after, and people buy more cookies if they like the show. Our benefactor has provided some nice instruments and T-shirts, but we still need gas money to get the band to football games and district competitions next year."

"You think your, uh, Mr. Garrett will be back by Friday?" I asked. "I mean, it's worrisome that he wouldn't say why he skipped today, don't you think? Ditto the fact that he's gone out of cell-phone range?"

These were neither nice nor helpful questions for me to ask. But then, I wasn't as nice or helpful a guy as I had once been.

This time, Elizabeth stayed cool. "David has a brother in some sort of difficulty. He hasn't volunteered details, and I haven't asked. But I think that's why he's absent. In any case, he won't let down the band. In fact, he was here yesterday, on a Sunday. We both were, installing new padlocks on the instrument cabinets. David paid for them out of his own pocket, by the way." She took a breath. "And now I'm asking myself why you should care."

"Hey, I just want to help out if I can," I said. "I'm pretty sure I could learn how to conduct by Friday."

"Ah. I'll keep that in mind." She was ready for me to leave.

But I wasn't. "Speaking of new padlocks, the deputy out front told me about the instrument theft." He hadn't, exactly. But it was only a small lie. "That gonna be a problem for my class today?"

Elizabeth shook her head. "No. In fact, one of the stolen instruments—the tuba—has been returned. It magically appeared on the cafeteria loading dock yesterday morning. I guess the thief realized the *banda* black market doesn't want sit-down instruments. When you mash polka, cumbia, ranchera, and pop together, nobody sits. Especially not the bass-horn players."

I knew it had to be Marisa who had returned the tuba although I didn't know why. And I had already figured, even before seeing how Carlos had been dressed, that the sousaphones had been stolen for resale to *banda* players—maybe in Texas, maybe in Mexico. Who the hell else would want them? "That's why I prefer electric blues. You can sit or stand, you don't have to pucker or blow, and you don't drip spit all over the place. Unless you're a drummer. Plus you don't have to take orders from bass players."

Now Elizabeth gave me a small but genuine smile. "I remember," she said. Then she stood, stepped to the door, and put her hand on the knob. "As it happens, we have a pretty good bass-horn player here in our little school band. You'll see." The bell rang, and she opened the door. "Now you're late."

I stood up, looked at her, and had a pang. "I'll bet Annie would have played something." The words were out before I knew I was saying them.

Elizabeth closed her eyes, and I wished I had bitten off my tongue instead of thinking out loud.

Then her eyes were open again, and we were back in the present.

She opened the door. "The band room is in the new annex, away from the other classrooms. Just this side of the hallway exit to the rear parking lot. Go down the hallway between the cafeteria and the gym, and then—"

I stepped past her. "I'll just follow the sound of puppies being kicked."

Elizabeth closed the door behind me, and I strode past the counter where Lester was still leaning over his coffee.

"You able to hear all of that?" I asked.

He gave me a bleary look. "I have to find my entertainment somewhere. It's not like I get to stay home and watch the soaps with my wife. She'd stab me."

"I don't blame her, Lester."

"Nobody does."

I hit the outer office door and stepped into the now-empty hallway. I would have been feeling pretty good if I had only left Elizabeth's office a minute sooner. After all, spending time with Elizabeth always made me feel good. The key was to keep it short.

But then, some things tend to be self-limiting.

7. *Cetacean Flatulence*

Marisa was short and slight, and the Gronitz tuba looked bigger than she was. When she held it propped on her lap in playing position, all I could see was a tangle of brass with a pair of feet in white sneakers.

But from the top row of the terraced band room, she bellowed orders and counted off time like a drill sergeant. And just as Elizabeth had said, the other kids respected her.

There were only fifty-six of them, but that was the biggest band Kingman had ever had. And they were good. Especially Marisa. She even took the solo on "Stars and Stripes Forever" that you usually hear played by a piccolo. And every note from the tuba was rapid-fire, articulate, and perfect.

Well, to be honest, every note sounded like a whale fart to me. But it was a rapid-fire, articulate, and perfect whale fart.

I was impressed. Also puzzled. The kid obviously loved playing in this rinky-dink high-school band. So how could she be part of the sousaphone-stealing ring that had ripped it off? Had she regretted it since she had brought back the tuba? Or had she only brought back the tuba because she had realized she wouldn't have a decent horn to play otherwise?

Her co-conspirators and their buyer knew what she'd done. And their buyer packed a stupid-huge pistol loaded with shotgun shells. Which he wasn't afraid to use. Regardless of her reasons, shouldn't that have made Marisa think twice about returning the Gronitz?

None of those questions should have mattered to me. Marisa was a little crook, so I had stolen from her and her little-crook friends because stealing from crooks was what I did. Her motives weren't my problem. Nor were her consequences.

But sitting in on the band rehearsal made it tough to quash my curiosity. Two of Marisa's fellow gangsters were here with her. Kaylee, wearing another BAD BRASS T-shirt and playing trumpet, was seated one level down from Marisa. And Jared was on the bottom level, to the left of the conductor's stool where I was perched. He was one of eight clarinet players, seated in the first chair. I assumed that meant he was hot stuff.

When I had come into the room at the top of the period, the first thing I had seen was the back of Jared's KINGMAN COUGAR BAND T-shirt. It read WICKED WOOD.

"Guess it ain't bragging if it's true," I had said.

Jared's response had been, "Huh?"

Now, as the period wound down and "Stars and Stripes Forever" ended with a huge whale fart from the entire band, I rubbed my ears and pondered how to spend my upcoming free hour. Not the teacher's lounge, where substitutes were treated like chicken-pox carriers and naps were impossible. The janitor's closets smelled funny. And my Toyota didn't have reclining seats like Deputy Beeswax's Chrysler. So the band instructor's office, marked by a door and a blind-covered window in the rehearsal room's south wall, was my first choice.

Besides, what I really wanted was a chance to rummage through David Garrett's desk. Maybe "Know your enemy" didn't quite apply, but "Know your replacement" did.

Of course, the door might be locked. Which wouldn't stop me. But I would have to wait until the kids were gone.

When the last note had stopped reverberating, Marisa stood with the tuba propped on her left hip, leaning far to the right for balance. "All right, let's make sure Mr. Garrett doesn't cancel the show!" she yelled. "Woodwinds, don't leave your cruddy old reeds on the floor! Brass, mop up your spit! Percussion, get out of the way! If your instrument stays here, pack it up fast. Three minutes!"

She leaned down to the tuba mouthpiece and played seven quick notes: *Shave-and-a-hair-cut, two-bits!*

Not a single student looked toward me for confirmation but began following Marisa's orders with case-snapping clatter. I just stayed where

I was and kept watching Marisa, Kaylee, and Jared. None of them looked guilty or nervous as a result of their criminal weekend. But then, I supposed I didn't either.

Nor did they look upset or depressed because their payoff had been stolen. That bugged me.

As the kids finished packing up, Kaylee and Jared joined Marisa at the north wall, which was dominated by a huge five-door oak cabinet. Trombones, French horns, baritone horns, and a few trumpets went inside, and Marisa and her friends locked the doors with the brand-new padlocks. The tuba went in last. After that, Kaylee and Jared followed the other kids out through the room's big double doors, and Marisa threaded her way through the folding chairs to pick up her backpack. She paused beside my conductor's stool on her way to the exit.

"Thanks for babysitting us," she said. "Will I see you in English class later?"

"Afraid not. I'm a babysitter all day long. But getting a paycheck for doing nothing is . . ." I swept my hand in a gesture taking in the entire room. "How should I put it in this setting? Doing nothing is . . . my forte?"

Marisa gave me a sardonic grin. "A musical pun. Very clever, Mr. Marx. But don't let Ms. Owens hear it."

She began to step away, and I decided to try something.

"I'm curious," I said. "How'd you get the thieves to bring back the Gronitz?"

She stopped and frowned. "What makes you think I'd have anything to do with that?"

"You're the only tubist in the band," I said. "So if I'd swiped a tuba, you're who I'd hit up for ransom."

Marisa took two steps toward the exit. "That wouldn't work. I'm broke."

I tried something else. "So who do you think took the horns?"

Marisa looked back at me and she didn't blink. "There's no telling. You never know who might be a thief."

She pivoted, looking more like a ballerina than a tuba player, and was gone.

8. Teeny-Purple-Bikini Good

I went to the doorway and watched until Marisa vanished around the corner toward the cafeteria. Now there was no one else in the annex hallway. I stepped back into the band room and pulled the double doors closed.

Then I tried the door to the band director's office and found that it was indeed locked. So I pulled two paper clips from my pocket and was inside in twenty seconds, closing the door behind me and relocking it. A switch set into the cinder-block wall turned on a pair of fluorescent bulbs, and they illuminated a jam-packed space that was barely ten by ten. That would have been without the filing cabinets, stacked boxes, desk, and industrial-strength office chair.

I sat in the chair and tried the center desk drawer. It was locked, too, which made me happy.

It took about a minute. Pretty slow for a desk drawer, but I had time. I also wasn't searching for anything in particular. But if I happened to run across something that would make Garrett look bad, I wouldn't mind. I had a fantasy that involved anonymously sending Elizabeth proof that she was making a terrible mistake.

At first, I didn't see anything in the drawer worth locking up. Pens, dimes and pennies, clarinet and saxophone reeds. A pink eraser, a broken conductor's baton. A few brass-instrument mouthpieces.

But underneath all of that was a spiral notebook. I pulled it out, opened it, and found a jumble of scribbled comments about ranking the woodwind section. It was as thrilling as a driver's-license test.

Then two business-sized envelopes fell from the notebook's back pages. They weren't sealed, so I opened them.

Okay, I would have opened them anyway.

The first envelope contained a stack of five photographs that had been produced on a home printer from digital pictures. They were of Elizabeth, and they were naughty.

Well, not really. But they weren't safe for school, either. Even Baptists had their limits when it came to how kids saw the principal. Or how much of her. The pictures had been taken on a summer day at the beach in Galveston, and Elizabeth had looked good. Teeny-purple-bikini good. Teenage-boys-would-scan-and-post-these-on-the-Internet good.

I was annoyed. Did Garrett really have to print these out and bring them to work? Couldn't he last eight hours without glimpsing Elizabeth's belly button? Hell, I'd been holding out for six years, and I was doing all right. More or less.

I tucked the purple-bikini photos back into their envelope, having decided against scanning them myself. I knew where to find them again.

Then I opened the second envelope. It contained just one photograph, but this one was much older. It had been taken with an actual film camera and developed and printed at an actual photo lab. That was how old it was.

It was of David Garrett at high-school age, standing in front of a large ranch-style house with another dude who was a few years younger. Teenage David was grinning for the camera and holding—or more accurately, wearing—a gleaming brass sousaphone. He'd been handsome then, too, and probably talented and popular despite being a band geek. So I still wanted to reach back in time and slap him.

Except for that urge, though, I was more interested in the other guy.

He was white. He and David were both wearing blue jeans and Jimi Hendrix T-shirts. The T-shirts were different colors, but the boys still looked as if their clothes had been purchased for them by the same person at the same store.

It took me a minute although it shouldn't have. Maybe the other guy's dark blond hair threw me since I hadn't seen it before. But then I recognized him, too. He wasn't wearing a red jacket or a cowboy hat, but his gray eyes and grim expression hadn't changed much.

In the photo, he had a fiberglass sousaphone on his shoulders. Maybe, since he didn't have the shiny brass one, that accounted for his expression.

He was the *banda* buyer from Saturday night. The dude with the humongous pistol he called the Judge.

He was Carlos.

9. *A Weak Embouchure*

I was still looking at the photo of Garrett and Carlos when I heard the double doors in the band room open.

I glanced to my right. The office door was closed and locked, and the blinds over the window were drawn. Whoever was out there couldn't see inside. They might not even be able to see that the light was on. So I just stayed quiet and listened.

"Make it quick, Donny." It was Marisa. "I don't want to be too late. I can get away with six or seven minutes, but not ten."

"So why'd you drag me down here?" Donny asked. "And where's Mr. Marx? You said he subbed. But we didn't pass him in the hall."

"I guess he went to the back lot to smoke a cigarette," Marisa said. "Or whatever. He's gone, and so is everyone else. There's no class in the annex this period, which makes this the safest place to talk. So what do you want? And why couldn't you just text me?"

To the back lot to smoke a cigarette? That struck me as presumptuous. I didn't smoke. Not cigarettes, anyway, and not at school.

"What's my problem?" Donny's voice cracked. "Are you kidding? You stole Mr. Anthony's van, you brought back the tuba, and you left the van in a ditch. So I had to drive those dudes back to town. Now Kaylee claims she doesn't have the money from the Conn. And you haven't answered my texts since you took off."

Marisa's response was cool and steady. "First of all, it isn't Mr. Anthony's van. He stole it, and stealing something from someone who stole it himself isn't really stealing. Second of all, Kaylee warned you guys not to show the buyers anything but the sousaphones. She and I both could have told you they'd lowball the tuba before you even stole it if you'd let us know you were going to do it."

"I couldn't say anything before we did it!" Donny said. "Besides, Mr. Anthony didn't tell us *not* to get the tuba. But at least the tuba didn't make Carlos mad. That was a sousaphone. And then running off with the van made Mr. Anthony mad. That was you!"

Marisa muttered something in Spanish that I couldn't make out, and then she said, "I don't understand these fiberglass snobs. But as for what I did—well, I couldn't let them buy a Gronitz so cheap. It wasn't right."

"But Kaylee nodded!"

"That wasn't a signal to take the deal. Mr. Anthony is Kaylee's second cousin or third uncle or something, and she says he's worked the shady side of Kingman County since before our mamas were born. She could tell from the way he acted that they had offered the best deal they were going to offer. That's all she meant."

This time, when Donny spoke, his voice was lower and darker. "Well, she was wrong. Tyler got a text from Mr. Anthony before first period. Turns out Carlos will give us a good price for the tuba after all, if we bring it back tonight. Twenty-five hundred."

There was a pause before Marisa spoke again. *"No me digas!"*

"I'm serious," Donny said. "And listen, Kaylee has to bring the fourteen hundred and hand it over to Tyler. Then, when we get the twenty-five hundred to add to it, we'll give you guys a share. But we can't trust Kaylee to hold it anymore. Tyler says if she doesn't show up with it, he's gonna beat the shit out of Jared. Like a serious beatdown, broken bones and teeth. He wants to make Kaylee watch. Then he says he'll e-mail her dad and tell him she and Jared have been hooking up, so the old man will cut off her college fund. We heard he's sending her to Baylor, but only if she's a virgin. Is that his rule or Baylor's, do you think?"

"I'm sure I don't know," Marisa said. "But I know somebody broke into the house and took the money while Kaylee and Jared were asleep. They didn't even know it was gone until Kaylee's mom called and woke them up. And they found Kaylee's phone on the back porch."

Donny wasn't buying it. "How do we know they didn't make up that story so they could keep the money?"

Marisa was indignant. "How do we know it wasn't you and Tyler who came back and took it?"

This part of the situation was my doing, and it had the potential to become ugly. But it wouldn't have happened if the kids hadn't been larcenous little punks. So I didn't feel too bad about it.

"You'll have to take my word for it," Donny said. His tone shifted to a ridiculous coo that he probably thought sounded seductive. "I wouldn't shit you, Marisa. I like you too much. That's why I wanted to bring you in on this. But Kaylee and Jared were your idea, so if they ripped us off, it's your fault."

Marisa gave a sharp laugh. "You didn't bring me in because you like me. You brought me in because you and Tyler didn't know how much the horns were worth. But Kaylee's the one who knew how to read Mr. Anthony. And Jared is a package deal with Kaylee. So if you don't want band geeks around next time, then next time don't steal band instruments."

I pictured Donny giving a shrug. "We thought it'd be easy. And honest to God, Marisa, I wanted you to have a share. I knew you'd have to play that twenty-year-old junk sousaphone after we took the good ones, so I felt bad. I really like you . . ."

A moment later, I heard the sound of flesh being smacked, just as I had on Saturday night.

"You know what?" Marisa said. "We're not going out anymore. You have a weak embouchure. And I should know. I play brass."

Donny grunted. "Okay, so you're good for something. You get to take that tuba home to practice, right?"

"No. When I practice with the Gronitz, I do it here. And Mr. Garrett is usually around."

"But not today," Donny said. "So no one would stop you from taking it. Not even that deputy out front. And Ms. Owens must have given you the cabinet key. So take the tuba home this afternoon, and we'll sell it tonight."

Marisa was not on board. "Then I'll be the first one they interrogate."

"No problem," Donny said. "You'll be catching a ride with Kaylee in that stupid little PT Cruiser, right? Just say it was stolen from her car when you guys stopped for a Coke or something. I'll even bust out one of her windows for you."

"You're so sweet, Donny."

"Let me prove it."

"Like you said, I'll have to take your word for it."

Donny grunted again. "Okay, whatever. Meet us at Jared's ranch tonight at 11:30. If you have to sneak out past your mom, do it. Kaylee and Jared need to bring the fourteen hundred—"

"They don't have it."

"—and you need to bring the tuba. Don't be late."

"This is a mistake," Marisa said. "Don't you remember how cheap that Carlos guy was? What makes you think he'll pay twenty-five hundred for a horn he didn't even want a day and a half ago?"

"All I know," Donny said, "is what Mr. Anthony told Tyler. He said if we mess up again, Carlos will hunt us down and use that giant pistol to blast us some extra assholes."

This time when Marisa spoke, her voice was quiet. *"Quizás sí, quizás no,"* she said. "But I guess we don't want to find out." She took a quick, audible breath, and then her voice was normal again. "All right, I'll figure something out. Now we'd better get to class. You go first."

"Huh? Why?"

"So no one sees us coming out of the annex together. If the tuba's going to disappear again, we don't want anyone saying they saw us together near the band room. You're not in the band. I play the tuba. See the problem?"

"Oh. Okay." One of the double doors to the hallway creaked. "Don't forget—11:30. Get there early if you can."

The door clunked shut, and then I listened for Marisa to go out, too.

Instead, I heard her fumbling with her backpack. And then I heard her speak again.

"I'm leaving voice mail so you know nobody else is texting with my phone," she said. "You were right. They want the Gronitz. So I'll bring it. Tonight, 11:30. Jared's country place. But they want the money, too, and we don't have it. So don't leave us hanging, or it'll all go to *mierda.*"

There was a soft snap, and then one of the double doors opened again. After that, silence.

I took one last look at the photo of the teenage Garrett and Carlos. Except for the fact that they had divergent skin tones and were holding different instruments, they sure looked a lot alike.

Then I replaced the photo in its envelope, tucked both envelopes into the notebook, and put everything back the way I'd found it. I made sure to lock the drawer.

I had some time now, but I wasn't going to get a nap after all. Instead, I would think about how I was going to spend my evening.

It might be worth twenty-five hundred bucks to me. I had a lavish lifestyle over the hardware store to maintain.

10. The Fluffy Bunny Land Solution

By 10:00 P.M., I was in the woods northwest of the crooked house again, once more wearing my dark clothes and full-face eye black. I was aware of the extra lump in my back pocket and feeling stupid for having it.

The house was dark, and there were no vehicles parked along the driveway. So I decided to begin my vigil at the same vantage point where I'd started on Saturday. I was early. But I had the complete recorded works of Otis Rush on a thumb-sized mp3 player. So I was good.

Or I would have been, if I hadn't fallen asleep. That was what I got for skipping a nap at school.

I awoke to "Crosscut Saw" in my earbuds, with the right side of my face mashed against a live-oak trunk and the itch of ants crawling up my shins. I yanked out the earbuds, jammed them into my jeans pocket with the mp3 player, then slapped at my legs until I couldn't feel anything crawling anymore. My watch said 11:15.

Across the driveway, illuminated by the weak moonlight and a dull lemon glow from the crooked house, sat Donny's pickup, Jared's Honda, and Kaylee's PT Cruiser. The sounds of their arrivals had been masked by Otis in my ears. I wondered how they were all getting along since the missing fourteen hundred couldn't have rematerialized—unless the band geeks had raided their parents' cookie jars.

Then a set of headlights stabbed into the driveway. At least, I thought, I had awakened in time for the arrival of Bobby Anthony and Carlos.

But the almost-new Maxima that cruised past my position wasn't bringing Bobby Tone and Carlos, although it did have two occupants. I couldn't get a good look at the driver, but I knew the car belonged to David Garrett, Kingman High band director and amateur purple-bikini photographer. So it was a reasonable bet that he was driving. And the passenger, whose face was just illuminated enough for me to see, was Principal Elizabeth Owens, dedicated educator and amateur purple-bikini model.

Whatever this meant, and whatever the result might be, there was almost no chance it would make me happy. But at least I was wide-awake now.

The Maxima pulled off the driveway between the PT Cruiser and the house. Garrett and Elizabeth got out. They were both wearing jeans and T-shirts, as if on a weekend painting project. They stepped onto the front porch and went inside without pausing. I couldn't tell whether the door was unlocked or whether one of the kids let them in. But there was no Hank Williams III playing in there tonight.

It looked as if the crooked house's windows had been opened to let in a little of the muggy April air. And since there was no one on the porch, I didn't have to be as stealthy as I had been on Saturday night. So less than two minutes after Garrett and Elizabeth walked into the house, I was crouched under a front-room window on the north wall.

I had caught a glimpse inside as I had scuttled up from the woods, so I knew that Donny, Tyler, Kaylee, Jared, and Marisa were all in there with Garrett and Elizabeth. The band kids had looked relaxed and were staying quiet, so I had the impression that they were fine with the new arrivals. But Donny and Tyler were upset. They were doing a lot of cussing and whining. And it was easy to understand why. The principal and her boyfriend were ruining the whole operation.

"This is the way it's going to be, boys," Elizabeth said. "If the two missing instruments are returned, we won't press charges."

It sounded odd to me. Letting punks off the hook was not the Texas way. Elizabeth was from Austin, which is the Fluffy Bunny Land of the Lone Star State—but even she wouldn't just say "Oh, well, kids will be kids" in the face of grand larceny.

"Somebody ratted!" Tyler said. He was trying to sound like a gangster, just as he had tried to sound like a salesman two days earlier. He wasn't any better at it. "Donny, it was your goddamn girlfriend!"

I heard the scrape of a chair on floorboards, and then David Garrett spoke. His voice was deep, strong, and commanding. I liked him less than ever.

"Sit down, Tyler," Garrett said. "Back in the day, I had to make a choice, and I chose band over football. But I still know how to hit."

The chair scraped again, but with less volume.

"That's better. First of all," Garrett continued, "there were no rats. Rats would have told the sheriff instead of coming to me. But I would have known what was going on anyway because I saw Donny's pickup driving through town at 3:00 A.M. Sunday with you and a sousaphone case in the back. And when I spoke with my musicians and they described your buyer, I knew who he was. So I asked some friends to let that person know that a Corpus Christi *banda* with a recording contract was in the market for an actual tuba. And sure enough, you got the word. So here we are."

My guess was that Garrett really had seen Donny's pickup hauling the sousaphone . . . while he'd been driving back to his place after spending most of Saturday night at Elizabeth's. It wouldn't do to drive to church from the principal's house on Sunday morning, now, would it? Even if everyone already knew you were sleeping with her.

But the part about rats not being rats if they tell the teacher instead of the cops was a little dicey. On the other hand, maybe ratting on the gang wasn't really ratting if you were never really a member of the gang in the first place.

Besides, I knew something that Tyler and Donny, team players, couldn't grasp: The only way to guarantee a "No Leaks" policy is to work alone.

"Here's what needs to happen." Elizabeth again. "Before the buyers arrive, Donny and Tyler will take the tuba out to the porch. We want the buyers to see it when they pull up, with people they recognize. We want them out of their vehicle and on the porch. Then the two of you can come back inside. At which point Mr. Garrett will deal with them."

"Like how?" Tyler asked. "Make a citizen's arrest or something?"

"Nobody's getting arrested," Garrett said. "There's no need, because we're going to put everything right. I just need to talk with the buyers to make that happen. One of them in particular."

Now Marisa spoke up. "The Gronitz doesn't have to come out of its case, does it? These guys won't be careful with it."

"The boys can just open the lid," Garrett said. "The buyers might get nervous and take off if they don't see it. And if that happens, we really will have to get the sheriff involved to recover the Conn sousaphone. Which won't work out well for anyone. It's bad enough that the King is damaged. But it's just the bell, and we'll see about having that replaced."

There was silence for a few seconds. Then Donny said, "Uh, the guy named Carlos shot the King just because he was surprised by the fiberglass. So if he gets surprised again, he might start shooting again."

Garrett made a noise between a grunt and a groan. "Don't worry. He won't hurt anyone. He probably borrowed the gun to look tough."

I heard a rumble and rattle from the county road, and I looked back to see another pair of headlights turning into the long driveway.

It was tuba-time again.

11. You Will Not Take My Tuba

I scrambled to the north and got between the PT Cruiser and the Honda. Then I watched as a battered, dirt-smeared Plymouth minivan rattled past. It pulled onto the apron at the end of the driveway, then backed up to the porch just as the white van had done two days earlier. No doubt this decrepit old rust bucket had been stolen just for tonight's purpose, too.

I still had a scrap of hope that I might find a chance to steal more dirty money, although it was looking problematic. Garrett had set up a false sale, and no money was going to change hands. On the other hand, Bobby Tone and Carlos were supposed to be arriving with twenty-five hundred in cash on them. So as long as I was here, it was worth sticking around to see how this played out. Based on the photo I'd found in Garrett's desk, he and Carlos had a possibly contentious history. So maybe the shock of their reunion would make Carlos drop his wallet. Or at least his guard.

Besides, like Lester, I wasn't able to watch soap operas. My hardware-store apartment didn't have cable.

I tucked in beside the PT Cruiser's rear bumper and watched as Tyler and Donny came out of the crooked house's front door and closed it behind them. Donny had the tuba case, and he set it on the porch as the minivan's engine fell silent and Bobby Tone and Carlos emerged from the vehicle. I noticed that everyone was dressed almost exactly as they had been dressed on Saturday night. It was as if they had specific uniforms for the exchange of hot brass. Carlos was even wearing his cowboy hat.

Donny bent down, opened the tuba case, and began to lift the instrument from it. Bobby Tone and Carlos stepped up to the porch, and Bobby Tone opened the minivan's hatchback.

Then the front door opened again, and Marisa burst out in apparent violation of Garrett and Elizabeth's plan. She shoved Donny away from the case and closed it over the Gronitz.

"This instrument," she said, "is no longer for sale."

At that, Carlos darted in front of Marisa, grabbed the case, and flung it into the minivan. Then Bobby Tone slammed down the hatchback as Carlos reached behind his back and brought out the Judge. I tensed.

"Since you have attempted to renege," Carlos said, "we will be changing our terms. The price is now five hundred dollars."

I had a feeling that the price had really been five hundred dollars all along.

Bobby Tone gave the kids a snaggle-toothed grin. "Same situation as before. Take it or leave it. But if you leave it, Carlos and I might be taking it anyhow."

Then, finally, David Garrett stepped onto the porch.

"Everyone under the age of thirty, back into the house," he said.

Donny and Tyler complied, but Marisa stood her ground, glaring at Bobby Tone and Carlos.

"No tomarás mi tuba," she said.

You didn't have to know Spanish to know what she was saying. If Bobby and Carlos tried to leave with the Gronitz, they were going to have ninety pounds of Bad-Brass wildcat on their backs.

I liked that kid.

But Carlos was looking past Marisa. He and Garrett had locked stares like a couple of angry chickens.

"Tell your *student* that I don't speak Spanish," Carlos said. He said the word "student" as if spitting out a mouthful of bat guano.

"Marisa, you should go inside," Garrett said.

"They've got the Gronitz," Marisa said.

"They won't take it. Go on in with Ms. Owens and the others, and I'll get this straightened out."

Marisa took a few slow steps backward, keeping her gaze fixed on Carlos. Then she turned and went inside. Garrett closed the door behind her.

I relaxed a little.

Garrett sighed. "Charlie, I don't know what you think you're doing with that silly-ass pistol. It looks like something Yosemite Sam might carry."

Carlos/Charlie glowered. "You always did want to be Bugs Bunny." The Judge remained hanging at his side, but his hand twitched.

Bobby Tone cleared his throat. "Uh, Carlos, I have the sense that this situation has transformed into something other than a business transaction. And since you seem to harbor some personal animosity toward this gentleman, I'm going to ask you to return the Judge. A firearm can be useful for making a point, which is why I was happy to lend it. But business should never involve personal animosity." He held out a hand.

I almost let out a whistle. The Bobby Anthony I had known when I was a kid had carried a .25-caliber pistol in his back pocket and a shotgun behind the seat of his International Harvester. So perhaps I should have guessed that in his old age, he had decided to combine the two. And I also should have guessed that a man who spoke and dressed like Carlos wasn't really a Judge kind of guy.

Carlos/Charlie had a pained expression, as if a dance partner had drilled a heel into the arch of his foot. But then he flipped the Judge to hold it by the barrel and extended it to Bobby Tone.

Bobby took it, turned the cylinder while squinting at the shells, then tucked it into his waistband. He nodded at Garrett. "Go ahead and straighten out whatever you have to straighten out. Then maybe I'll have a further proposition. This has been a complicated enterprise, but I've invested too much time and energy to walk away now."

I felt the same way. It was almost as if Bobby Tone and I were cut from the same bolt of cloth. He'd gone to jail and I'd gone to UT, but there are those who would argue there's not much difference.

Garrett took a step toward Carlos/Charlie, who took a step back and almost fell off the porch. Garrett stopped and shook his head.

"Look, Charlie," he said, "I'm not mad about your taking the money. I don't know how you got the PIN number, but it's okay. I was just glad to know you were back in Texas. I didn't think you were ever coming home."

Now I was a little envious of Charlie. As far as I could tell, nobody was glad *I* had come home. And I hadn't even broken into anyone's bank account.

"I had to," Charlie said darkly. "California isn't what it was. Texas is where the music I want to play is happening now. I'm starting my own *banda,* David. I've been in Baja with the real guys, learning to play the real songs."

"Really? Say something in Spanish, Charlie."

Charlie's chest puffed out. "*No.* How's that? See, as long as you're not the singer, the real *banda* guys don't care what words you're able to say. It's about what notes you're able to play. So now, while you're tucked away in your school in the sticks, teaching scales and marches, I'll be making music in the real world for real people." He pointed a thumb at himself. "No more second-chair fiberglass for me."

Now Garrett was pissed. "So you're going to skim from Mom's bequest and buy and sell instruments ripped off from schools? Instruments that Mom's money helped pay for in the first place?"

"Mom left that money to help *musicians,*" Charlie said. "Not just school bands. And you were supposed to consult me. But you did it all yourself. So I'm expressing my disagreement."

Bobby Tone interjected. "Hold on, now. Are y'all saying that the two of you have the same mother? I find that chromatically unlikely."

I almost spoke up to tell him he was being rude, then decided that would be rude as well.

Garrett gave Bobby a quick glance. "Not your business," he said. Then he looked back at Charlie. "You're really going to get what you want by stealing from kids?"

Charlie's upper lip warped into a sneer. "Just from kids who don't care. If they did, they wouldn't be selling their school's brass."

"It's not the band kids," Garrett said. "They tried to call me as soon as they found out what was going on. But I—I had my phone turned off. So they did what they thought best. And they didn't call the sheriff because they didn't want their friends to go to jail, for which you should be grateful."

"New girlfriend?" Charlie asked. "That's usually what it means if someone needs you and you've found something better to do."

Oh yeah. These guys were brothers.

"What I'm telling you is, the band kids didn't steal anything," Garrett said. "The only thing they did wrong was try to protect a couple of white-trash jocks."

There were shouts of protest from inside the house. Donny and Tyler both objected to the characterization. As a member of that tribe myself, though, I felt the term was accurate.

Bobby Tone cleared his throat. "Excuse me, sir, but that's a term I, too, find offensive."

This time Garrett didn't even look at him. "Tell me you've never used an equivalent term for black people and I'll apologize."

Bobby scratched his jaw. "Point taken," he said. "But we're getting off topic. Have you boys got your shit straight enough so we can complete our transaction?"

Garrett turned on him. "Don't you get it? There isn't going to be a transaction. You and Charlie are going to remove the Gronitz tuba from your car, and then you're going to return the Conn sousaphone. You'll also provide money for a new bell for the King. In exchange, nobody's going to jail."

"And what am I supposed to do then?" Charlie asked.

Garrett turned back to him. "You're my brother. So come stay with me. Return as much of the money as you've still got. We'll figure it out from there."

Charlie gave a short, sardonic snort. "On your terms," he said. "With no *banda* for me."

"Like I said, we'll figure it out."

Bobby Tone stepped in between them, clucked his tongue, and pulled the Judge from his waistband.

"What I'm hearing," he said, "is that whatever the two of y'all decide to do, I'm gettin' nothing. Not from a purchase today, and not from resales down the line. And I was being so careful not to be greedy, too, since this was a new line of business for me. I was happy just to be a facilitator and to be paid accordingly."

Garrett eyed the gun. "I'll give you seventy-six dollars for your trouble. That's all I have on me."

Bobby kept the Judge pointing downward, but he cocked it.

"Seventy-six bucks?" he said. "Man with a charitable bank account and all? No, I'll need at least a thousand to release the tuba from the custody of this minivan." He paused and scratched his jaw with his free hand again. "Actually, I'll need the thousand just to walk away without shooting you. And I'd have to shoot both of you, so no one could accuse me of racial bias. One thousand dollars. And then y'all can do whatever you like with the tuba and the sousaphones and the glass fuckin' harmonicas and whatever else you got."

Charlie looked at him. "You know I only have five hundred tonight. There isn't a thousand dollars on this porch."

Bobby Tone raised the pistol. "Then one of you needs to go get it."

"Or you could have five hundred and seventy-six dollars right now," Garrett said.

Bobby didn't seem to hear the offer. He began swiveling the barrel of the Judge back and forth, pointing it first at Charlie and then at Garrett.

"Eeny," he said. "Meeny. Miney. Moe."

Then the front door opened, and Elizabeth stepped out. She had her cell phone in her hand, and she looked straight at Bobby Tone.

"Do you want the sheriff out here?" she asked.

Garrett groaned. "Elizabeth, no—"

Bobby stopped swiveling the Judge, and he lowered it a bit. But he gave Elizabeth a wry look. "Ma'am, nobody from the sheriff's office could be out here in less than thirty minutes. And if you were to make me worry that you'd accuse me of wrongdoing, why, I could just shoot all of you to prevent that."

I tensed again. Bobby Tone didn't know I was there. So if my knees cooperated, I might be able to be on him before he could react. Or I might not. I prepared to flip a mental coin.

At that moment, I heard the crunch of tires coming from the driveway again.

Well, good. I had been wondering how this situation could get any more complicated. Now I was about to find out.

12. Everybody's Beeswax

No one on the porch seemed to hear what I heard. They were all wrapped up in their four-way Texican standoff.

A slow, black Chrysler 300 came idling up the driveway past my hiding place. Its lights were off. And except for the soft crunch of its tires, it was almost silent.

I had a premonition that this new development meant the Judge was going to express its opinion again.

So as the car idled past me, I came out in a crouch and tucked in behind its rear bumper. Maybe, if I got close enough, I could at least try to jump onto the porch and shield Elizabeth.

Then someone—Carlos/Charlie, I thought—finally spotted the Chrysler and yelled. So I was ready when the car came to a halt, and I didn't whack my head on the trunk.

I looked around the glowing left brake light just as the Chrysler's headlights came on, flooding the porch. Bobby Tone, Charlie, Garrett, and Elizabeth all winced in the glare.

Then the driver's door opened, and the driver stepped out. He kept the open door between himself and the porch.

"Everybody just stay right like you are," he said in a deep, phlegmy voice. "I suspect I'm gonna have to arrest somebody. But let me get a look so we can figure out who."

It was Ernest, also known as Deputy Beeswax. At some point after I had encountered him that morning, he had apparently decided he ought to do more than stand around. But he had just made a tactical error.

The first shot from the Judge took out the Chrysler's left headlight. Its roar was still rattling in my skull as I jumped forward, grabbed Ernest by his gunbelt, and shoved him into the car facedown on the front seat. His deputy hat fell to the floorboards, exposing a scalp the color and texture of a bathroom scrub brush in the blue glow from the dash.

Up on the porch, everyone was shouting and the front door was slamming.

"Get the hell off me!" Ernest yelled into the passenger-seat cushion. "Whoever you are, you're interfering with an officer of the law."

I held Ernest down with a forearm across his neck and a knee on his rump. "I don't think you're even on duty," I growled, trying to disguise my voice. I was going for something between Winston Churchill and Batman. "This isn't a squad car. There's no radio."

"I got one in the glove box," Ernest said. "All I got to do is turn it on. And it don't matter if I'm on duty or not. All I need is a reason to believe a crime is in progress. Getting a headlight shot out and your knee up my ass both qualify."

The Judge exploded again, and I heard the other headlight shatter. I glanced up through the windshield and saw that the porch light and the lights in the crooked house had been turned off, too.

"Listen, Deputy," I said. "I'm an innocent passerby, but I happen to know the only things at stake here are a few band instruments. Nothing worth getting shot over."

Ernest tried to shake me loose. "I agree," he said. "So let me up so I can shoot back."

That struck me as a bad option. Bobby Tone hadn't hit anything but headlights. But if Ernest returned fire, somebody might get killed. And it might be me.

Bobby Tone shouted from the porch. "Hey! I'm guessing y'all are associated with these kids, and that you don't know your heads from your taints any better than they do. My suggestion is you get that vehicle off the driveway so I have a clear exit. I'll give you—oh, two minutes. That sounds generous to me. That sound generous to y'all?"

"That's fine!" I bellowed.

Ernest increased his efforts to dislodge me, but I held firm.

"Listen here," he said, panting. "As long as we have two minutes, Mr. Innocent Passerby, I want you to understand something. I've been a Texas law officer for forty years, and there are rules I'm bound to follow. One of those rules says if a suspect discharges a firearm in my direction, I, by God, discharge one right back."

I groped for Ernest's .357 with my free hand. "I respect that," I said. "But all of my own rules are devoted to self-preservation. So I'm gonna work with that."

Sure enough, the strap over the grip of Ernest's .357 was still unsnapped. The pistol slid into my hand as slick as a pumpkin seed.

"I dunno what you think you're gonna do now," Ernest said. "That ain't loaded with nothin' but empty cartridges."

I was baffled. "Why on earth would you do that?"

Ernest managed a chuckle that came out more like a grunt. "I'm semiretired in Kingman County. I generally find that the intimidation factor of a pistol works just fine without actual bullets. Besides, this way, some asshole grabs my gun, joke's on him."

"That's funny, all right," I said. "Almost as funny as a deputy approaching what he thinks is a crime in progress without live cartridges or backup."

"There's crimes, and there's crimes," Ernest said. "I observed a scrawny old redneck and some guy dressed like Roy Rogers driving a scabrous minivan with a WOMEN FOR OBAMA bumper sticker. Looked suspicious, so I followed. And now you've implied that in addition to stealing a twenty-four-dollar Plymouth, they're involved in a recent case of grand theft tuba. But until now, neither situation would have seemed to call for live ammo. What should I have hoped to shoot, a sousaphone?"

"You wouldn't be the first," I said. "But I guess that line about a Texas lawman always firing back was bullshit."

Ernest tried to swing his left fist back at me, but human arms don't bend that way. "I don't want to kill anyone over a decrepit mommy-mobile or an oversized bugle," he said, "but I'm not a fanatic. I've got live rounds handy. But I ain't telling you where."

"The glove box," I said. "With the radio."

Ernest grunted again. "Just let me up, genius."

I chucked the .357 backward as far as I could, and I heard it hit the ground past the other cars. Then I felt along Ernest's belt and found his handcuff holster. And after thirty seconds of struggle, I managed to get his wrists cuffed behind his back.

"I'm gonna tell you something in the interest of fairness," Ernest said then. "If I find out who you are, you're gonna have to run until you hit ocean. At which point you will want to start swimming for Cuba."

The Chrysler was still idling. I sat up on Ernest's lower legs, waved at the silhouettes on the dark porch, and threw the car into reverse without trying to close the open door. It would have hit Ernest's feet.

I punched the gas, and the car lurched backward, switchbacking like a panicked squirrel, the open door flapping. When we were past Donny's pickup, I cranked the wheel to the left, and the Chrysler bounced into the rough grass along the east side of the driveway. Ernest cussed as we hit bump after bump, and I finally stomped the brakes so that we came to rest about twenty yards off the driveway, near the eastern tree line. Then I killed the engine and threw the keys into the night.

"You have bashed up my brand-new car's oil pan and exhaust system," Ernest said. "So once you've swum to Cuba, you better keep doing the crawl all the way to the goddamn Canary Islands."

I got out without answering, tucked Ernest's feet inside, and closed the door. I felt bad about the damage, but none of it had been my fault. So I didn't think it was fair of Ernest to blame it on me, especially since he had ruined my own evening.

I scuttled along the tree line back toward the crooked house. I had realized there was no more money here for me. But before I ran back across the driveway and made my way to my Toyota, I wanted to be sure Elizabeth and the band kids were all right. Screw the rest of them. They were all crooks, except for Garrett. And he was Elizabeth's boyfriend, so screw him, too.

I was about halfway back when, up at the porch, the Plymouth minivan spun its tires. Then its lights came on, and it clattered up the driveway toward the road at high speed. There was a lot of yelling from the crooked house as this happened, and I assumed that Bobby Tone was cutting his losses and taking off with the tuba.

I paused to watch as the minivan sped past my position, and there was just enough light for me to see that once again, the Gronitz's getaway driver was Marisa.

"Man," I said aloud. "She really loves that tuba."

The minivan reached the road and rattled away. And I was just about to turn back toward the crooked house when I heard a metallic click a few yards to my left.

It sounded a whole lot like a pistol being cocked.

13. Meet the Boyfriend

As I turned, a sudden flashlight beam caught me full in the face.

"Whoever you are," David Garrett's voice said, low and angry, "you have just created more problems than you could possibly—"

He stopped. The bright disc of the flashlight moved in closer.

Then Garrett spoke again.

"Are you seriously wearing blackface?" he asked.

I decided to fight fire with fire. "Are you seriously pointing a gun at me?"

He lowered the flashlight.

"I'm not pointing it," he said. "I'm just holding it. I found it on the ground over there."

I could see it now, in his left hand, pointing at the ground. But I had heard him cock it, so I knew he wasn't "just" holding it. Or at least he didn't think he was. If Ernest hadn't lied to me, there weren't any live rounds.

Garrett's face became clearer as my eyes adjusted, and I could see that he was peering at me with a puzzled frown.

"Do I know you?" he asked.

I'd only seen Garrett at a distance at school, and I doubted that he'd noticed me at all. There was a chance he'd seen me in some of Elizabeth's photos, but those were all more than six years old. So maybe aging, plus the full-face sports black and bad light, would keep him from recognizing me.

When I answered him this time, I used the same Churchill/Batman voice I'd used with Ernest.

"No," I said. "But I'm on your side."

His frown deepened. "What the hell side is that?"

"The side that gets your brass back and keeps everyone out of jail. Without getting anyone shot."

"What's any of that to you?" he asked.

"Let's assume I'm a concerned parent."

"One who runs around in the dark wearing blackface?"

"All right," I said. "A concerned parent with a hobby."

Garrett shook his head. "I get sent out here by a hick with a giant handgun, and I find a lurker dressed like a ninja. While I'm doing that, one of my students drives off in a stolen minivan to keep the hick from taking our tuba. My estranged brother has become a black-market sousaphone smuggler to get back at me for a crappy adolescence. My girlfriend doesn't want her students in trouble with the law, so we're making deals with the gang who couldn't shoot straight instead of calling the sheriff. And now I have to go back and report that I've found a concerned parent in blackface, but that I still don't have the money the hick is demanding for his time and trouble." He sighed. "I moved to a rural school district because I wanted a simpler life. Jesus."

"Where'd you teach before?" I asked.

"Chicago. Twelve years. Just came here two years ago."

The universe was full of coincidences. "Never been to Chicago," I lied. "But I hear it's nice. Low sousaphone-theft rate." I held up my hands. "I'm going to reach into my back pocket now. Don't get excited."

Garrett hefted the .357, but didn't aim it at me. That was nice of him.

I pulled the stack of fourteen one-hundred-dollar bills from my back pocket. I unfolded it, took four bills off the top, and put them back in my pocket. Then I extended the other ten toward Garrett.

"If you give this to the gentleman on the porch," I said, "he'll go away. Although you might have to give him a ride. The rest of it—getting back your instruments, punishing larcenous students, resolving sibling rivalries, and all that horseshit—that's your problem."

Garrett stared at the cash. "You playing Robin Hood or something? How dirty's this money, anyway?"

It annoyed me that he wouldn't just shut up and take the dough. "It's as clean as any you're going to get. And this offer expires in about five seconds, bubba."

He took it. "Okay. Thanks, I guess."

I knew Elizabeth and the kids would be all right now. So I turned and started for the driveway.

"Hey!" Garrett said. "Hold it. Whoever you are, I think you'd better stay."

I paused, glanced back, and saw that he had raised the .357.

I gave him a big smile, and I hoped the moonlight was strong enough for him to see my teeth.

"In the first place," I said, "that pistol's got nothing in it but brass. In the second place, you're going to have to rescue the deputy sheriff I handcuffed in that Chrysler. Oh, and you're going to want to blame everything that's happened on the mysterious stranger who cuffed him. Maybe you can spread a little blame onto the boys who stole the instruments in the first place, if you're careful about it. But if you tell the deputy about the hick, the hick will see to it that your brother and all the kids go to jail with him. I know the guy, so you can trust me on that. Got it?"

Garrett lowered the .357. "Got it." He looked down at the pistol. "I thought this thing felt a little light. But I don't know much about guns. I'm a schoolteacher. And a musician."

"So at least you're rich." I pointed at the crooked house. "Go pay the man and get him out of here. Then look after the deputy."

"I can handle them," Garrett said. "It's my damn brother who's going to be a problem. We had the same mother, but she never could make us get along."

I shrugged. "People tend to be less trouble when they get what they want. I overheard some of your conversation, and I gather he wants something called *banda.* So give him *banda.*" I turned away again. "But no fiberglass."

Then I jogged across the driveway into the woods where I'd started the evening. This time, Garrett didn't say anything to stop me, and it was a good thing. I'd had a stupid, altruistic impulse, and now I was pissed off about it.

I didn't like the feeling. So I tried to convince myself that the whole mess had been worth the four hundred dollars I was walking away with.

But instead, I only managed to convince myself that being a nice guy is a big pain in the ass.

14. Old Friends in Need

I wasn't in a hurry, and I took my time getting through the woods. After about fifteen minutes, I emerged onto the side road where I had parked my Toyota. It was hidden in a shallow ditch under the low canopy of a huge live oak, almost invisible. So at least I had done one thing right tonight.

"Hold up there, friend."

The voice was behind me, and I recognized it.

I turned with my hands held out to my sides. Bobby Tone stood at the edge of the road. The barrel of the Judge gleamed even in the weak moonlight.

"I sure am glad I caught up with you," Bobby said. "See, now that

I've been paid, I need a ride. I didn't want to bother the others on account of there turned out to be a deputy sheriff on the premises. So I thought it best to depart immediately."

"I see," I said. "And you knew I was here because—?"

"Oh, that band-teacher fellow mentioned you. And sure enough, here you are." Bobby Tone took a step closer and peered at me. "My goodness, is that little Matty Marx? I ain't seen you since your daddy and me moved our last load of East Texas Canna-Bliss. That's been a few years." He made a "tsk-tsk" sound. "I was sorry to hear he passed, by the way. I was a guest of the state at the time, or I would've gone to the funeral. Lord rest him, though, and your mama, too."

I lowered my hands. "Thank you, Bobby."

"And while we're on the topic," he said, "I want to say I was also sorry to hear about your baby girl. Terrible thing, that sudden infant syndrome business. No fault of yours or the missus, and nobody thinks it was. But it seems the loss took a toll on your marriage, and I was sorry to hear about that as well. I, for one, happen to approve of interracial unions."

I looked at Bobby Tone's eyes. I didn't think I saw any compassion there. But I wanted to believe there was.

"I appreciate the condolences," I said. "But you don't mind my saying so, you could probably lower that big-ass hand cannon now."

He took another step closer. "Well, if it's all the same to you," he said. "I'll wait 'til you drop me off in town."

Which was what I'd figured. "Let's go," I said.

As I started the Toyota's engine and the lights came on, Bobby Tone waggled the barrel of the Judge at me.

"Son, I thought I was imagining things," he said, "but you've got your face done up in black, haven't you?"

"I don't want to talk about it," I said.

Bobby cleared his throat. "Well, it's highly inappropriate, I'll have you know. And since we'll have a little time here as we drive, I'll explain why. Then, once we've reached our destination, I'll require a good-faith demonstration that you've received and accepted my message of understanding and tolerance."

I looked at him. "How much?" I asked.

"Depends on how much you got," Bobby Tone said. He faced forward and tapped the Judge on the Toyota's windshield. "Come on now, son. I parked my new truck behind the propane dealership. I can't wait for you to see it. It's a big old silver Dodge Ram, and I'm just tickled to death with it."

I pulled the Toyota onto the dirt road and began my drive back to empty pockets.

15. It's the Music, Not the Instrument

Elizabeth didn't call me to school for the rest of the week. But I went to the spring concert Friday evening, even though it was three bucks to get in. I was curious to see how the sousaphone gangsters were doing.

I don't know what I expected. Marisa, Kaylee, and Jared were in their places along with the rest of the band, and they played well. As far as I could tell. The Kingman Rural High gymnasium had terrible acoustics, especially from my perch at the top of the bleachers. But David Garrett seemed pleased with his players, and so did the crowd of parents and grandparents. Many bows were taken, and there was even an encore: "Stars and Stripes Forever."

I had the strong sense that it was a setup.

Marisa's tuba solo was amazing, though. Even in the echoey gym. I don't know how she made each whale-fart note sound better in there than it had in the band room. But she did.

When the encore was over and Garrett and the band had received their applause, Elizabeth stepped out from her seat in the front row and faced the crowd.

"Once more for the Cougar Band!" she cried, and everyone applauded and whooped again. "Now, for those of you who can stick around, the annual bake sale and barbecue dinner will take place in the faculty parking lot, just through the rear doors. And I'm told that some members of the band will have a surprise for us."

I stayed where I was as the band packed up and everyone else filtered down from the bleachers. Almost all of them went out the back, so apparently the bake sale really was a big deal. But I wasn't planning to stay. I was just waiting for everyone to clear out of my way so I could climb down and head for the front doors.

Then I noticed that the band kids were placing their packed-up instruments next to the folded bleachers on the far side of the gym. And standing next to the growing pile of instruments were Donny, Tyler, and Deputy Beeswax.

This, I had to check out.

As the last of the band kids dropped off their cases, I came down and crossed the gym. Ernest's head moved ever so slightly in my direction.

"Attention, gentlemen," Ernest said as I approached. The boys pressed their backs against the folded bleachers and stared at a point somewhere on the distant ceiling.

"Deputy," I said, extending my hand as I came near. "Haven't seen you since Monday morning, so I thought I'd say hello."

Once again, Ernest did not acknowledge my hand. "Are you someone I should remember?"

I gave up on the handshake. "Probably not. I'm Matthew Marx. Both our names end in 'x,' which makes us alphabet buddies."

Ernest tilted his head downward to give me a baleful stare over the top of his sunglasses. "No such thing," he said. "Now, is there something I can help you with? I have a chore to attend to."

"I can see that," I said. "Did these boys volunteer to help the band with their equipment?"

Ernest nodded. "Indeed they did. And then they're going to do anything else I ask them to do for the foreseeable future, including shine my shoes and execute a few automotive repairs. They have volunteered to perform these and other tasks to serve as shining examples to all young men in the Kingman community who wish to continue to breathe free and have a snowball's chance of playing football next season. Isn't that right, gentlemen?"

"Sir," Donny and Tyler said in unison. "Yes, sir."

I couldn't help grinning. And I wished I had heard the conversation after Garrett had freed Ernest from the handcuffs. At some point, though, Donny and Tyler had been presented with a choice of penance or arrest. I wasn't sure they were going to conclude they'd made the right choice.

"Something funny, Mr. Marx?" Ernest asked.

I shook my head. "No, sir. I just wanted to say howdy."

"I see." Ernest pushed up his glasses. "Well, you probably don't want to say anything further. You're starting to sound familiar."

Once again, I gave him a salute. Then I turned away and started for the front doors.

But I saw Elizabeth and Garrett standing at one of the back doors. And Elizabeth was gesturing for me to come over.

I didn't see any way out of it. So I went.

"I don't think the two of you have officially met," Elizabeth said. She was speaking rapidly, the way she did on those rare occasions when she was feeling nervous. "Matthew Marx, this is David Garrett. David, Matt and I used to be married."

Garrett and I shook hands. "I used to be married, too," he said.

"But not to Elizabeth."

"I wasn't that lucky."

I looked at Elizabeth. "How's the banter so far?"

She looked upward as if praying for strength. Then she said, "Okay, that's out of the way. And now I need a piece of cake. David?"

"You go on," he said. "I'd like to have a quick private word with Mr. Marx."

Elizabeth's eyes widened. "Oh, that's such a bad idea."

"I promise to play nice," Garrett said.

I gave him my best this-smile-really-means-up-yours smile. "I will if he will."

Elizabeth raised her hands in surrender. "There's a deputy sheriff right over there. Just sayin'." She went outside.

"Okay," Garrett said then. "Even without the blackface, I recognize you."

"I figured."

"And I can only assume the reason you were out there was because you were stalking Elizabeth and me. You followed us there."

It hadn't occurred to me that Garrett would jump to that conclusion. I even opened my mouth to tell him he was wrong—and then realized I might as well let him think that.

"It was stupid," I said. "And it'll never happen again."

"Better not," Garrett said. "I'm going to let it go this time because you helped me out. But I'm not paying back the thousand bucks, mainly because I can't. For one thing, I've got my brother living with me now. People seem to think I'm rich, but I'm just the trustee for my mom's estate. What I have of my own is schoolteacher money, which means I for damn sure don't have an extra thousand. And I'm sorry about that."

"Don't be," I said. "It was my choice." *And it was your mom's money.*

Garrett nodded. "All right. I won't say anything to Elizabeth about your being there the other night. And you and I are starting from scratch." He held out his hand again.

We shook hands again for the briefest of moments, both hating it. Then he pushed open the door and gestured outside. "You joining the party?"

I was about to decline. Then I looked at the crowd and the tables of food in the small rear parking lot. And I saw Bobby Anthony at the cookie table. He was wearing a "Guns & Ammo" gimme cap and an "I ♥ Rodeo" T-shirt under a washed-out denim jacket.

So I nodded to Garrett and stepped outside. I glanced back long enough to see him join Elizabeth at a table full of cakes.

I followed Bobby Tone to the edge of the crowd. He saw me coming and stopped under a light pole, leaning against it and pulling the plastic wrap from a paper plate of oatmeal cookies. He took a bite of one as I came near.

"You know," he said, "most folks zero in on the chocolate-chip ones. But I say there ain't nothin' like a good oatmeal cookie. It's all wholesome and brown-sugary, you know?" He held the plate out toward me. "Go on, Matty. It's on me."

I took one and had a taste. "It's good," I said. "Not four hundred dollars good. But not bad."

Bobby gave me his snaggle-toothed grin. "Now, if I thought for a second that you'd earned that four hundred dollars through honest work, I might feel bad. But I know who raised you. I personally don't believe in hell, though, so I think he's enjoying an oatmeal cookie and a reefer at the right hand of my Lord. Even as we speak."

"That's a special heaven you have there, Bobby." I glanced around. "A special earth, too, where you can walk among people you've messed with and know they won't touch you."

He nodded and polished off his cookie. "My Lord is merciful," he said, pointing skyward. "That's why I know your little girl is up there, too. So remember, Matty. When something precious is stolen from you, you can't steal it back. Not from anyone in heaven or on earth. Don't even try."

I turned to head back toward the food tables. "I'll see you around, Bobby," I said.

"Not if I see you first, Matty."

There was a commotion across the lot at the cafeteria loading dock, and as I crossed in that direction, David Garrett's brother Charlie came out onto the dock dressed as he had been dressed at the crooked house. He was followed by a dozen band kids with instruments, with every kid dressed just like him. I saw Kaylee with her trumpet, Jared with his clarinet . . . and Marisa carrying a white-fiberglass sousaphone with five ragged holes in the bell.

Down at ground level, Garrett whistled to get the crowd's attention, and Elizabeth raised her hands.

"Here's the surprise I promised," she said. "Ladies and gentlemen, for the first time ever—*Banda de Pumas*!"

Charlie raised his arms and brought them down like twin axes. Then *Banda de Pumas* blasted out three of the loudest, brassiest, bass-horn-and-drum-heavy Mexican tunes ever heard in Kingman County. They had put the whole thing together in four days, but they looked and sounded as if they'd been doing it for years. Kaylee even sang on the second number, but it was in Spanish, so I had no idea what it was about. But I knew Marisa's sousaphone was dominant and perfect, and I knew *Banda de Pumas* would be sticking around.

Just before the final number, Charlie disappeared for a moment and reappeared with the brass Conn sousaphone on his shoulders. Then he and Marisa played harmonizing bass lines, which I hadn't even known was possible.

After that, the *banda* members vanished back inside. All except Marisa, who stepped down from the dock so the audience members could stuff fives, tens, and twenties into her sousaphone bell.

I searched my pockets and came up with two crumpled ones. I had been thinking about a slice of brisket, which smelled pretty good. But what the hell. So when the mob around Marisa thinned, I stepped up and added my bills.

"I assume this is all going to a good cause," I said.

Marisa nodded. "*Sí.* Mr. Garrett's brother Carlos is going to manage the *banda,* and anything we make after expenses will go to a scholarship fund." She touched the collar of her red jacket. "The outfits were donated by our benefactor, so we didn't waste any money there. And if you come to our next gig, I promise we'll know more than three songs."

"Y'all sounded swell," I said. I reached out and touched one of the ragged holes in the sousaphone bell. "Despite a defective tuba made out of fiberglass."

Marisa gave me a bright smile.

"Es la música," she said. *"No el instrumento."*

I looked around and saw no one else within fifteen feet.

"You knew I'd be there with the money Monday night, didn't you?" I said. "You must have spotted me Saturday as you drove off in the van. And you knew I was in Garrett's office when you brought Donny to the band room Monday morning."

Instead of answering, she pressed her lips to the sousaphone mouthpiece and played seven quick, low notes.

Shave-and-a-hair-cut, two-bits!

Then she spun away, once again like a ballerina. No mean feat while wearing a sousaphone.

"I knew you were smart when you made D. H. Lawrence your bitch," I called after her. I got a few sharp looks from some of the parents in my vicinity, but I didn't care.

Then I went to the gymnasium door and ran into Lester coming out. He had a stunning brunette woman on his arm who was a full head taller and at least thirty years younger than he was.

"Any barbecue left, *Mister* Marx?" Lester asked. "My lovely spouse insists upon some brisket. So I got to get her fed in a big goddamn hurry."

The stunning brunette smiled. It was dazzling. "Otherwise," she said in the sweetest of voices, "I'm going to stab him."

I told them that my share was still there, and I stepped aside and held the door for them. As I did, I looked back toward the loading dock and saw Garrett and Elizabeth talking and laughing. I thought about going over to say good night. But then I went on through the gym, into the foyer, and out to the main parking lot.

The week had not turned out as I'd hoped. I had done much better in much tougher circumstances in Chicago, so I wasn't sure why I'd had so much trouble in my own hometown. Maybe I could only thrive someplace where I wasn't comfortable. Like Chicago.

But as I slid into my Toyota, I looked across the Kingman Rural High parking lot . . . and there, at the gray edge of the artificial light, saw Bobby Tone handing his plastic-covered plate of oatmeal cookies to a chubby guy with a ponytail. Simultaneously, the chubby guy handed Bobby something that Bobby tucked into his denim jacket. I noticed then that the plate of cookies looked bulkier than it had before.

Bobby Tone watched the chubby guy climb into an SUV and drive off. Then Bobby climbed into his big silver Dodge Ram and drove off as well.

It occurred to me that I still didn't know where he was living these days. And since he was an old friend of the family, that didn't seem right.

No, I wasn't going back to Chicago or anywhere else for a while. I was curious about too many new developments in the land of my birth. Things like Lester's unlikely marriage to his possibly violent showgirl wife. Things like Donny's and Tyler's indentured servitude to Deputy Beeswax. Things like whether Kaylee would choose Jared or Baylor. Things like Marisa's burgeoning *banda* career.

And of course I should at least stick around long enough to see if Elizabeth needed me to teach on Monday.

Besides, I hadn't liked it when Bobby Tone had told me I couldn't steal anything back. I didn't think that was his call.

I waited until the Dodge's taillights were almost out of sight out on the highway. And then I started up my Toyota, flipped on my headlights, and followed Bobby Tone into Kingman.

I didn't know what he had slipped into his jacket.

But I knew it was going to be mine.

Cherie Priest

Cherie Priest is probably best known for her steampunk *Clockwork Century* series, consisting of the novels *Boneshaker, Clementine, Dreadnought, Ganymede,* and, most recently, *The Inexplicables,* as well as the chapbook novella *Tanglefoot,* but she has also written the Southern Gothic *Eden Moore* series, consisting of *Four and Twenty Blackbirds, Wings to the Kingdom,* and *Not Flesh Nor Feathers,* and the urban fantasy *Cheshire Red Reports* series, consisting of *Bloodshot* and *Hellbent*. She's also written the stand-alone novels *Dreadful Skin, Fathom,* and *Those Who Went Remain There Still.* Her latest is a new novel, *Fiddlehead.* She lives in Chattanooga, Tennessee.

Sometimes, when things get tight, a bad man is the best one to have on your side. And the worse things get, the badder that man needs to be . . .

HEAVY METAL

Cherie Priest

Kilgore Jones wrestled free from the Eldorado and kicked the driver's door shut. It bounced and swung back open again, so he gave it a shove with his hip. The old car rocked back and forth, creaking in protest, but this time the latch caught and held—mostly for its own good. The Jolly Roger was a big car, but its driver was a big man.

It wouldn't be a real bold stretch to say he was six and a half feet tall, and a good carnival guesser might put his bulk at a quarter ton. Bald of head and fancy of facial hair, he boasted a carpet of impressive brown muttonchops that shone red in the sun, and a pair of mirrored aviator glasses. Everything else he wore was black. If you asked him why, he'd straight-faced tell you it was slimming.

His wardrobe notwithstanding, Kilgore threw a globe-shaped shadow on the ground—a one-man eclipse as he walked across a set of ruts that passed for parking spaces.

The old hoist house loomed before him: a nineteenth-century behemoth built for work and not beauty. It was red brick with a green roof, and easily the size of the grand old church in Chattanooga where he was no longer welcome—because a pastor singing about Satan made sense, but a layman going on about monsters was just plain silly.

As he approached, he saw patched-up places where new brick filled in old windows, doors, and shafts. He noted the remains of white paint around the main door and its entry platform, all of it lead, most of it peeling and fluttering in a cold, sharp November breeze.

Gravel crunched beneath his feet, and the wind yanked at his coat. The sun was vivid and white against a crisp blue sky without any clouds, but there wasn't much warmth to go around. The Smokies were not yet brittle like they would be in another month, but he could smell it coming.

"Hello?" Kilgore called. The word went wild, echoing against the hoist-house walls and adjacent boiler rooms, banging off the time shack and the bit-building across the way, rattling against last century's mining equipment abandoned on the end of the track. "Anybody here? Miss Huesman?"

He scaled the steps of the entry platform and stood on the wood-slat landing—gazing toward the cavernous interior. Inside he saw pumpkins, leftover from a Halloween fund-raiser, if the banner could be believed. They were laid out on pallets with discount signs scrawled by hand in thick red marker. Even the largest, a gourd advertised as a seventy-pounder, looked tiny beneath the vast, gabled ceiling strewn with crisscrossing tracks that toted great tubs of ore back before Kilgore's grandparents were born.

Wind whistled through the rafters above, scattering dead leaves and ruffling the fat little birds who huddled on the hauling lines.

"Hello?" he tried again. "Anyone here?"

"Hello?" someone called back, then added more, but he couldn't make it out. The voice came from deep inside, past the pumpkins on their pallets and back against the far wall . . . behind a door that might lead to an office.

He headed toward the sound of the speaker.

". . . sorry if you're here about Rich. He's gone home for the day—and I think he took the money pouch for the pumpkins. But if you want one, and you have exact change, I'll see what I can do. All the proceeds go to support the museum . . ."

The door banged open, forced that way by the shoulder of a woman whose arms were full of miscellany: files, papers, magazines from the first Bush era, and a messenger bag from which peeked the sleek shape of a tablet. She paused. Or more precisely, she froze. Whatever she'd been expecting, Kilgore Jones wasn't it.

"Can . . . can I help you?" she asked. She shifted her weight and deposited her armload of stuff onto an old telephone seat that languished against the wall.

She was young, lanky, and tall. Long blond hair, shiny and well kept. Wearing an oversized cardigan over a black tee shirt for a band Kilgore didn't recognize, and that was saying something. Her dark jeans were dusted with Ducktown, Tennessee's, ubiquitous red dirt in the shape of handprints. Her own, he assumed.

He pushed his sunglasses onto the top of his head. "Miss Huesman?"

"Yes? I mean, *yes.*" She nodded, finding some relief in hearing her own name. "I'm Bethany. No one calls me Miss Huesman outside the university. And you are . . . ?"

Now he stepped forward, hand outstretched. "Kilgore Jones. Jennifer Andrews told you I was coming, I think?"

Bethany's stiff fight-or-flight stance softened. "Yes! You're the guy who worked with Pastor Martin on Sand Mountain, back in the day. And you're . . . you're The Heavy? Well, Jenn *did* say . . ." She extended her hand to take his and shook it. Her fingers were small and cold, and they sported a cute assortment of shiny silver rings.

Kilgore smiled, and hoped it was disarming. At his size, putting people at ease took extra work, so he'd learned to watch all of his language. "Let me guess: She said that when you saw me, you'd know why people call me that."

She blushed, or maybe it was only the chill hitting her cheeks. "More or less. I'm sorry, I didn't mean to be rude. Any friend of Pastor Martin's . . ." Her voice trailed off and her gaze swept the hoist house, scanning the vast interior as if making sure they were alone. "Jenn said the pastor wouldn't come. Why do you think that is?"

Kilgore should've said something about Sand Mountain. After all, she'd brought it up first.

He kept his mouth shut anyway. She deserved the truth, but it wouldn't do her any good. "I couldn't say, but I'm here to help if I can. If you've got a few minutes, I'd like to ask you a few questions."

"Okay, but can we go someplace a little warmer to talk?"

"What do you have in mind?"

"Just up the hill," she indicated with a toss of her head. "The museum's closed, but I have a key—and they have a heater." She retrieved her messenger bag but left everything else where it was sitting. "We can walk it, no problem. Even with the wind, it's so close that it'd be crazy to drive."

He was inclined to disagree with her, but he restrained himself. "All right. Can I help you carry anything?"

"Naw," she said dismissively, yanking the office door. It closed with a sticky squeak. "This stuff'll be fine where it is. There's nothing worth stealing, and nobody to take it. Not since . . ." She paused, and changed her mind. "Not anymore. But I'll tell you about that when I've got a cup of coffee in my hand."

The hill was blessedly short, but not so short that he didn't wish for the Jolly Roger to help him scale it. He hated hills. Counted them among his archest of enemies. But at the top waited the museum, a squat, single-story building that was too modern to match the old buildings, but too new to call vintage. Its roof sloped unevenly above cheap white siding, fronted by a gravel lot that might've held half a dozen cars if you stacked them right.

Kilgore pulled a bandanna out of his pocket and wiped his forehead, never mind the breeze. "Museum doesn't see a lot of traffic, does it?"

"Why would you say that?" she asked, digging keys out of her bag and unlocking the door.

"The parking lot says they don't expect much company."

She looked over her shoulder. "Oh. Yeah, I guess you're right. Come to think of it, I've never seen more than three or four cars up here. And one of those usually belongs to Ammaw Pete."

"Ammaw Pete? The volunteer coordinator?"

The door swung open. Bethany reached inside and flipped on a light, though the day was still bright enough they almost didn't need it. "How did you know?"

"I called this morning before I came out, and she's the one who answered the phone. Seems like an . . . interesting lady."

"*Interesting.* That's her. She volunteers here most days. Other than that, she's retired." Bethany tossed her bag onto the counter and led the way to an understocked and overdirty kitchenette.

She rummaged for the Folgers, scooped out a filter's worth, and fidgeted around the small, cold space while the coffee brewed and the freshly rebooted heater took the frost out of their breath. It had its work cut out for it; the building had the cheap, temporary feel of a trailer, and the walls were thinner than sandwich cheese. It hadn't been closed up more than a couple of hours, but all the warmth had bled out already.

She dug her fingernails into the cup, leaving small half-moons in the smooth white surface. The heater hummed loudly and the coffee oozed warm curls of steam.

Bethany cleared her throat.

"I know how crazy this sounds . . . but Adam and Greg are dead. I don't know why it took them, and I don't know if I'm next. There's . . . there's a lot I don't understand, about what happened. About this place. About that *thing.*"

Kilgore prompted, "Is this your first time in Ducktown?"

She nodded. "If it weren't for the program, I never would've heard of the place. The ecology department at UTK has been involved in the cleanup here for ten or twelve years now—monitoring it and making recommendations. I've gone through the files and casebooks; it's fascinating stuff, if you're that kind of nerd. And if I weren't, I'd be doing my grad work in something else." She added a soft, quick laugh that was meant to sound light but only sounded strange.

"All right. And to be clear, it was you, Adam Frye, and Greg Malcolm on this trip, correct?"

"That's right. I took point because they were first-years, and I'm only a semester away from finishing my master's. The bulk of my research was geared toward the mountaintop removals. You know—the coal companies to the north and east of here. But the Burra Burra Mine is a legend, and the destruction it caused in the copper basin is virtually unique in scope; so even though it wasn't my cup of tea, when the field assignment came up, I threw my hat in the ring. It sounded like a good idea at the time."

"Famous last words." Kilgore poured himself another cup and slipped the carafe back onto the burner. "Now tell me, when did you first arrive?"

"A week and a half ago. We were staying at a Holiday Inn Express out by the highway. The university put us up, gave us a little per diem, the whole nine yards. We were supposed to check the soil pH levels across a mapped grid and catalog the plant creep along the preserved area."

He frowned. "Preserved area?"

"It's a stretch of the old red dirt—the blighted turf left from the sulfur dioxide—where nothing grows and nothing lives. The government's restoration campaign left this one section unreclaimed. I heard they did it as a reminder, but I bet they just ran out of funding."

Kilgore knew about the dead red dirt, but he hadn't realized there was any of it left. He'd seen the old pictures from the EPA reports, and a big spread in *LIFE* magazine from decades ago, before the cleanup. Fifty square miles of lifeless landscape, nothing but poisonous red hills as far as the eye could see. Except for the smattering of houses, churches, and the central hub of the mine facility, it'd looked like the surface of Mars.

Bethany continued, intermittently raising her eyes to see if he was listening. "It looks normal now, like the trees have been here forever, and we're surrounded by regular old forests; but it took years of planning—adding new species of acid-resistant grasses to anchor the turf, and planting specially imported trees. They brought in plants that could filter toxins with their roots and flora that would give these hills a fighting chance at recovery. Eventually." She waved her hand in the general direction of the valley. "It worked. But they left this one stupid patch of the old red dirt, down by the water. That's what we were sent to examine. That, and the water itself, down in the crater."

His ears perked. "Where *is* the crater? If this museum's on the old mine site, it must be nearby . . . ?"

"It's on the other side of the parking lot. You know what? Forget this coffee. It's terrible." She rose suddenly and tossed the cooled contents of her cup into the nearby sink. "Come on. I'll show you."

Out the door she went, past a wooden rack stuffed with local-attraction brochures—for a relative value of "local." He tagged along in her wake.

She was nearly at a run. She wanted to get this over with.

Her boots crunched and scuffed across the unpaved lot, and she paused beside a big metal cage that had once lowered miners three thousand feet down the shaft in search of copper. She turned then, and her hair billowed wildly as the wind rushed up the crest behind her. She raised her voice to be heard, almost shouting as she pointed off to the north.

"That's where the plant used to be, right over there—facing the hoist house, on the ridge's natural peak! Used to be, they had a set of tracks that ran ore buckets overhead between them!" She turned around, and now her hair was a halo, vast and golden, wilder than Medusa's. It looked for all the world like she stood at the edge of a cliff and was prepared to jump.

She said something else but Kilgore couldn't hear her; she was speaking into the wind and the words were lost. But when he joined her, he understood.

More quietly now, she told him, "The mine caved in years ago, but by then, they weren't digging copper hardly at all: They made more money on sulfuric acid, generated from sulfur dioxide as part of the smelting process—you know, the same stuff that denuded this whole corner of the Smokies. But anyway, there it is. There's the lake where my friends drowned."

Beyond the miner cage, all the way down the far side of the sharp, ragged ridge, waited a great crater full of bright blue water surrounded by stiff green trees. It looked like someone'd pulled a plug and the landscape had sloughed down the drain, leaving only this cerulean pool, shimmering at the very bottom of the world.

Kilgore resisted the urge to call the scene "beautiful." Instead he drew Bethany back away from the edge, stepping down out of the wind.

When they were standing again in the gravel lot, she said, "That's where they died. Adam first—two days after we got here. A freak accident, that's what they said. He fell in and . . . forgot how to swim, or some bullshit like that."

"Did they send his body back home? I don't expect they have the facilities out here for an autopsy."

"Yeah, he's home by now. Greg, though—he died two days after that, and he's at the Copper Basin Medical Facility, unless they released his body and no one told me, which is possible. Nobody out here tells me a damn thing. Ammaw Pete thinks I'm an uppity little city bitch, like Knoxville is New York, and I'm carpetbagging for the ages. She doesn't know I heard her say it, but she probably wouldn't care if she did." She looked at Kilgore with something new in her eyes, something cunning. "Maybe they'll talk to *you*."

"I try my best to be a sociable man . . . but in my experience, people open up faster to a pretty woman like you than a guy like me."

She shrugged. "Not here. They don't like me. They don't trust me. They put me in the same category as the lawyers and environmentalists who closed down the mine and put the whole town out of work. If you're not *for* the copper, you're against it. Like all the *life* we're bringing back to this place isn't worth a damn thing."

Kilgore Jones made noises of polite protest, but she didn't respond. She only stared over the ridge, toward that bright blue hole in the pale red dirt, surrounded by all the defiant trees, roots clinging to the steep crater walls, twisted and anchored and still alive—like a big "fuck you" to history.

But she still hadn't said what he needed to hear, so he prodded her again, friendly but firm. "Tell me what you saw that night, when Greg went under."

Slowly, she nodded. Not to him, but herself. "Something came up, almost out of the water but not quite. It whispered to Greg," she said, hardly any louder than the whisper she described. "It called him. *Lured* him. And when he wouldn't follow it, it grabbed him—and it dragged him right into the lake."

"Describe it—the thing you saw."

"I . . . I can't."

"You'd better, because I'm shit when it comes to mind reading. *Bethany*," he said, urgently if not impatiently. "You sent for help. Now *talk* to me."

She swallowed and crossed her arms over her stomach, drawing her oversized sweater tighter around her body. "It looked like a man, but it wasn't. It looked like a miner—one of the old miners, from the eighteen hundreds. But not exactly." Her eyebrows crunched together. "Do you think it was a ghost?"

This was more comfortable turf for Kilgore, if not for the grad student. "Ghosts are mostly made of memories and imagination—their own, and everyone else's. Once in a blue moon one'll have the strength to make a ripple in the real world, but I've never heard of one tough enough to drown a grown man."

She burrowed her hands deeply into her sleeves, then stuffed them under her arms. "This thing . . . whatever it was, it wasn't a memory. It was really *there.* So if it wasn't a ghost, what *was* it?"

"I don't know yet." He didn't give her any guesses because they'd only frighten her. He needed more information, and that meant he needed a local. All his polite protests aside, Bethany wasn't one, and everyone in the county knew it.

Kilgore wasn't local either, and Chattanooga wasn't any more rural than Knoxville—but there was more to being local than your starting address.

He left Bethany on the museum steps. He shook her hand and made her promise to be in touch and stay away from the crater. She agreed to these terms, but he didn't know how much that meant. Her abject horror at watching her fellow student drown might be nothing compared to the siren song of an otherworldly creature, or even her simple curiosity.

Siren.

The word floated to the surface of his brain and refused to sink back down. He made a mental note of it because there was no sense in denying the overlap. Sirens were water elementals, of a fashion; they called, lured, and killed—though they usually came in a prettier package than that of an old miner. "There's a first time for everything. Then again," he mumbled, as he yanked the Eldorado's bum door and settled back inside the car, "it talked to Greg, and Greg didn't listen. So it resorted to force."

He gazed up at the silver crucifix that hung from the rearview mirror, trembling and bobbing like a pendulum. It'd been a gift, from someone who wouldn't speak to him anymore—a man he'd come to view as a father, at the third church that threw him out. The last church. The one he drove past sometimes, still not quite finished with that argument but knowing better than to go inside.

They'd disinvited him, like he was some kind of goddamned vampire who knew better than to cross the threshold.

He stayed away anyhow. He knew where he wasn't wanted, and no amount of wishing or praying would change that. Apparently.

He sighed because he sure could've used the help right about now; but he sucked it up, withdrew his small notebook from his pocket, and added what he'd learned. Then he flipped to the back page—where two addresses were written down: One was the local watering hole, a joint that went by the uninspiring legend of "Ed's," and the other belonged to the woman either named or called "Ammaw Pete," who volunteered at the museum and allegedly didn't think much of poor Miss Huesman.

His watch said it was too early to bother with the bar; he wouldn't find anyone useful to chat up. But Mrs. Pete? It wasn't even suppertime yet, and she'd said he could swing by before nightfall. She knew to expect him but he would've liked to call first, as a matter of manners . . . but by her own admission, she didn't have a phone. She took all her messages out of the museum's line and appeared perfectly content with that arrangement.

Kilgore Jones did have a phone, but it was a POS without a GPS. He consoled himself with the knowledge that by the grace of God, Ducktown had made it onto Google Maps, and therefore a stash of home-produced printouts gave him an idea of what the area looked like.

Ammaw Pete lived within spitting distance of the mine—walking distance for someone more hiking inclined than Kilgore—but it took him fully twenty minutes to find his way to her driveway via the Eldorado. Her road was neither marked nor paved, and he stumbled upon it only after the process of elimination ruled out four other identical roads. How anybody got their mail delivered was a mystery to him, but small towns and out-of-the-way places all had their methods. When everyone knows everyone, things don't often go lost or missing. And that made the situation with the UTK ecology students all the stranger.

Or then again, maybe it didn't. Those kids were outsiders, and the community didn't feel obligated to look out for them. They went missing more easily than the mail.

He engaged the parking brake and the car lurched hard, then settled with its customary squeaking.

Ammaw Pete's place was an early craftsman in good repair, with a yard that didn't get as much love as the hanging flower baskets on the porch. The baskets were emptied of everything but the purple and pink petunias; everything else had died for the season, and these would too, probably before Thanksgiving. But for now they gave the white house with its gray roof a pop of color that said somebody lived there, and somebody cared about the place.

Kilgore tried the steps and found them true, then knocked upon a red-painted door.

Behind the door, he heard a television mumbling what sounded like the local news; a chair squealed, a board creaked, and then a set of footsteps stopped long enough for an eyeball to appear in the small window that served as a peephole.

The door didn't open. "Who's there?"

He assumed his most polite pose, hands folded in front of himself, slight stoop to minimize his prodigious height. "Pardon me, ma'am—but I'm looking for Ammaw Pete. Would that be you?"

"What's it to you?"

"I'm Kilgore Jones. We spoke on the phone this morning," he told her.

"That's right, I recall. You're a big son of a bitch, aren't you?"

"That's what they tell me."

"What is it you do again? You're not with the po-po, I remember that much."

"I'm a machine-shop worker from Chattanooga."

The eyeball narrowed. "And investigator of the occasional drowning . . . ?"

"Not the drowning, ma'am. The thing what caused it."

He heard a click, the twist of an old knob, and the scrape of a door being drawn back an inch. "You've got my attention, big man. Don't waste it." She opened the door enough to reveal herself. Small and old, but not elderly yet. Silver-haired and bright-eyed, in a tidy blue dress and gray slippers. "You ain't a feeler, are you?"

"No, ma'am. I don't detect anything I can't see."

"You're a fighter, then. Got to be one or the other." She sighed and tossed the door open all the way with a flick of her wrist. "I guess you'd better come inside."

Withdrawing to make room for him, she turned and sauntered through a cluttered home that was not the least bit dirty or unorganized—only filled to capacity with whatever things moved her magpie of a soul. Here there were stacks of Time-Life books on the Civil War and the Old West, and over there, that series from the eighties about unexplained phenomena; figurines from nearby and faraway lands alike; rows of bells from assorted tourist traps; spoons with small emblems identifying them as collector's pieces; photos of loved ones framed and arranged across all but a few square inches of wall space; a batch of prettily organized teakettles and pot holders; a latticework of diverse coffee mugs hung on the walls around the cabinets; handmade afghans with bright colors and unfortunate patterns; curtains sewn from bedsheets; Christmasy villages with ice-skaters and post offices and train stations awaiting the next month with flickering lights and cheerful miniature residents, pets, vehicles—plus wreaths on every door.

"I'll put the kettle on and you can have a seat."

Of *course* she'd put the kettle on. Kilgore would never escape an old Southern woman's home without tea, same as he'd never settle down to a young Southern woman's company without coffee, now that he thought about it. It was like nobody could talk without something to sip for distraction.

But they'd done the same thing at the old First Baptist, hadn't they? If not potlucks then communions, and that's why they called it a Fellowship Hall.

Ammaw, whose name he'd first misheard as "Grandma," gestured at the dining-room table, a well-varnished and rough-hewn piece that someone must've made for her. None of the pretty little chairs matched, and none of them looked like they'd hold Kilgore without protest and structural failure.

He was prepared to suggest that perhaps they could sit outside on the porch, but then he spied a cedar bench that probably belonged in a garden—but in Ammaw's kitchen it was piled with folded hand towels and a stack of cast-iron skillets nested together. "You think perhaps I could just . . . clear off that bench? We'll both be happier if I don't break anything."

She coughed the laugh of an octogenarian smoker, but her age wasn't so advanced and Kilgore didn't see any cigarettes. "Do what you gotta."

It wasn't just her laugh, he realized. Her words were offered up with that same ragged edge that sounded like more than age peeking through. While he gently adjusted her décor, he said, "I hope I haven't intruded on you, particularly not if you've been feeling poorly."

"Poorly?" She paused at the stove and shot him a look. "Oh, the cough, you mean? Hardly even a rattle, and I guess you ain't been in town too long, or you'd have heard it by now. All us old folks who grew up here . . . we all got the *voice.*"

"I'm sorry to hear that."

"Why? It don't hurt, and I don't mind. Makes you feel like part of a tribe," she informed him, and she hauled a box of tea bags from a cabinet, then yanked two mugs off the wall. For herself she chose a soft pink jobbie with a nicely shaped handle. For him, Tweety Bird sitting in a bathtub. "Once upon a time, Ducktown and Copperhill had a big tribe between 'em. The mine took good care of its workers," she insisted, her cough to the contrary. "Now it's gone, and so are most of us. It's just the way of things."

"But the land's come back real nicely," he said, accepting a measure of steaming water and dipping his tea bag, prompting it to steep. "So there's that."

"There's that, yes. And there's snakes, and there's rats and bugs, too. Didn't used to have any of that nonsense, but here they come, creeping back. None of them worth the trouble of those goddamn trees. We *liked* our red dirt, I'll have you to know . . ." She eyed him over the edge of the mug. "But you're not here for tea or bitchin'. You want to talk about the crater, and what sleeps inside it."

He didn't like the way she phrased it. It offered up too many suggestions, too many implications. He wondered how much she really knew, so he asked outright. "Yes, ma'am. And you've worked the museum longer than anyone, besides being local to boot. I figure you're the best person to ask."

"How much do you know already?"

"Only what Bethany Huesman thinks she saw."

Ammaw Pete made a derisive noise that flicked at the surface of her tea. "That girl. Thinks she knows so much. She didn't tell me she saw anything. Didn't tell the sheriff either."

"She said you don't like her any. Thinks it's because she's an out-of-towner."

"It's because she tried to order a skinny half-caff something-something at a gas station on the edge of town, and acted snotty when she couldn't have anything but old-fashioned drip," she snapped. But Kilgore figured they were saying the same thing. "So she didn't say a damn thing to me . . . but she'll talk to you. All right then, so she saw something, did she?"

"Something shaped like one of the old miners, rising up from the water. It dragged her friend down into the crater and drowned him."

"Shaped like one of the miners?" she echoed pensively, and gave it a question mark. "Well, sometimes these things take the shape they're called by. They show us what we expect to see." She closed her eyes and breathed deeply over her mug, taking the steam and smiling at it, but her smile verged on the grim. "Them things that were here before us . . . before the mine. Before the Indians. They'll be here still, when the last of us are gone."

"You think that'll make them happy? The last of us being gone?"

"I don't know. They belong to the land."

Kilgore frowned. "But the ecology students from UTK are here for the land too—they're putting it back in order. You'd think any resident haints or elements would be glad to see them."

"Ducktown don't want 'em here. Whatever's at the bottom of the lake don't want 'em here. The whole world ain't made of hippies and sunshine, big man. It's a balance, you know—and here in the basin, it's always been about the metal. There's the earth that holds the copper, the things that *draw* the copper, and things that *work* the copper. A *balance.*"

"Yeah, well, this place hasn't been in *balance* for 150 years, and those kids shouldn't have to risk their lives to put it back."

"Why not?" she asked with a wink, but there was a gleam of something hard behind the flutter of her lid. He feigned astonishment, but she waved it away. "No, now. You know I'm only teasing. Whatever that little ol' Nick might be, it shouldn't be left to grow there. Shouldn't let it fester. You'd better take it out and deal with it."

"How?"

"Beats me. But if it's nasty enough to kill people, a good talking-to won't do it. Not from *you,* anyway."

He considered this. "Thank you," he finally said, his lips pausing on the rim at the top of Tweety's head. "You've given me plenty to think about."

He finished his tea, thanked the woman again, and retreated to his hotel to get ready for the night's work. He'd booked a room in the same Holiday Inn Express the grad students used, not by any great design but because there was nothing else for miles.

Down the corridor on the way to his room, he ran into Bethany—who was barefoot and holding an ice bucket. "Hi there!" she chirped, and he said "hello" in return, adjusting the backpack he toted as luggage. Then she added, "I don't know why I'm surprised to see you here. Can't imagine where else you'd crash."

"This is close and clean. It'll be fine for the night."

"Is that how long you're staying? Just overnight?"

"Depends. We'll see what happens."

She shuddered and clutched her ice bucket. "You sure you'll be okay?"

"I always am."

She laughed nervously, and he wondered if she ever laughed any other way. "I guess nobody bothers *you,* not very often."

"No, ma'am, they do *not.*"

They said their good-nights and he went alone to his room. He flipped on the light to reveal nothing at all outstanding but nothing offensive either: a bed with an ugly comforter, a tiny stack of sample-sized toiletries, and a sink with a chipped faucet head.

He wondered what Bethany would've thought if he'd blurted out the things he kept close to his chest—if he'd said that no, nobody bothered him too often but when they did, they did it for keeps. Anyone who's ever watched a prison movie knows you take down the biggest man first; and the monsters knew it too. So far he'd escaped those greetings with only a few scars to show for it, but they were ugly scars, and they reminded him daily of those who hadn't been so lucky.

The nothings out there . . . they were worse than the nobodies.

Sometimes the nothings bit and fought, screamed and spewed poison or fire. Nothings could change their shapes and shift their bones, and sometimes, only a Bible and brute force could put them down.

Kilgore's Bible was a small red leather-bound thing, thumbed into softness with onionskin pages that flapped, fluttered, and stuck together. He didn't read it much anymore. Didn't need to. Knew it forward and backward, just like the devil. But he kept it on his person because once it'd deflected a swipe of claws that would've otherwise opened his chest instead of leaving him looking like he'd passed out facedown on a barbecue grill.

And that made it lucky.

In the absence of mortal assistance, he'd take what luck he could get. He'd rather have Pastor Martin by his side, but that ship had sailed, hadn't it?

So when night came, he tucked the Good Book into his pocket, smashed up against his battered notebook—a worn thing filled with thoughts and research on the case, scribblings and small, carefully drawn images that might or might not mean anything to him later on. An hour or two of potting around on the Internet had given him a name, or at least a direction. It was only a starting point, but it was better than nothing.

Back into his car he climbed. He tossed his pack onto the passenger's seat, and in doing so, he winged the silver cross that hung from the rearview mirror. It swung back and forth, smacking the glass with a loud *crack.* He grabbed the holy trinket and steadied it. He held it an extra moment or two, then said, "Fuck it," pulled it off the mirror and slung it around his neck. He didn't have a church, but he had his faith. And he had the trusty old Jolly Roger, which started on the first try.

Out past what few streetlights and corner stores Ducktown boasted, the car's headlights cut a bold path through the pitch-black, middle-of-nowhere murk.

He wasn't more than a couple of miles from the mine, but there were few signs to guide the way and little in the way of civilized lighting; the stars were so damn bright overhead, and the trees loomed so tall, so close together on every side of the service road that would take him down to the crater lake.

He watched those trees as he drove, hunting for something that might live there and hide behind them. Some hint of the old balance. Some kind of resurrection.

When he hit a low-slung bar across the road, the headlights shone bright on a big-ass NO TRESPASSING sign. The high beams glinted off the rest of the message, which stopped just short of promising that anyone who drove any farther would be shot on sight and fed to the bears for fun. Probably because there weren't any bears.

He left the car to inspect the situation in person. The hip-high gate across the road wore the sign like a badge, but Kilgore couldn't find a shit to give, and nothing but a rusted padlock on an old chain held the whole thing together. A pair of swift kicks with his steel-toed work boots made short work of the matter, and one more kick sent the gate swinging back into the trees, where it dragged itself to a halt and leaned off-kilter against a raggedy evergreen.

It almost wasn't worth the effort to clear the way. The dirt road ran out another hundred yards down the line, petering into a wide patch that gave a vehicle enough room to turn around, but that was about it.

With some creative steering, he maneuvered the car into an about-face so he could hit the ground running if conditions called for it later. Then he parked, pulled the brake, and left the door open so the dome light would stay on while he checked his supplies.

A plastic ketchup squirt bottle full of holy water. A well-worn gris-gris he'd had made in New Orleans, the year before The Storm. Flashlight and extra batteries, and a head-mounted lamp he'd borrowed from a buddy who was a mechanic. An old silver cake knife because sometimes silver meant something, but it was expensive—so he took it where he found it.

A loaded nine-millimeter because you never know.

He patted his chest and felt the reassuring bulk of the notebook and the Bible. Tucked the gun into his waistband, up front where it'd be easier to reach even though the cold metal on his belly gave him a full-body shiver. He donned the headband with the LED light on it, and felt ridiculous but his hands were free, and that was more important than dignity in the dark.

Everything else he stashed in his trench-coat pockets.

He closed the car door and the light went out. He flipped the switch on his headlamp, and it came on, illuminating the woods without quite the vigorous panache of the Eldorado's beams; but outside what passed for town, a little light went a long way.

For a moment he stood still and listened. He didn't hear much. It almost bothered him, but then he remembered Ammaw Pete grousing about how all the critters were only just coming back, and then he supposed it wasn't quite so unsettling. There weren't any crickets to fiddle their legs in the grass. No mice to rustle in the leaves, or squirrels to build nests high above. Nothing and no one, except whatever waited in the crater.

Kilgore had a pretty good sense of direction—almost an uncanny one, or so his mother used to tell people. He could feel it in his head, the tug of the crater's location. The smell of its water wafted up through the trees, an unpleasant stink of bottom-pocket pennies and stagnation.

The service road had gotten him close.

He sniffed, wiped his nose on his forearm's sleeve, and started marching.

The grade grew steeper as he proceeded; with every step, the ground dropped away more sharply beneath him. He slipped and skidded, catching himself on the vegetation or—on one particularly unpleasant stumble—his own hands.

And then he reached the clearing that surrounded the water—a ring of red dirt that held back the trees, or maybe the trees just didn't want to dip their roots into that questionable pond. It was a creepy little beach, angled and naked, with all the grimy allure of a bathtub ring.

Unmoving except for the pivot of his neck, the big man surveyed the scene and still, he heard nothing. But he felt something, and he didn't like it: the prickling, unhappy sense that he was being watched.

He fished out his notebook. The brightness of his headlamp washed out the pages and made it tough to read, but he squinted and forced his own words to appear.

"You took two boys." He said it quietly. Like the light, a little sound went a long way. "They were here to help the basin, and you killed them."

A ripple scattered the calm surface of the night-blackened pool. He heard it, the soft rush of water in motion, the ripple of a solitary wind chime playing its only note.

"Ammaw Pete said something that got me thinking: She said a good talking-to wouldn't stop you, not if it came from *me.* So I wondered if there was anyone you might obey. Everything's afraid of something, but you've been living the high life up in here, haven't you?"

The water moved again. From the edge of his vision, Kilgore saw it, the shifting lines of something traveling below the surface but not yet rising.

"She called you a little ol' Nick, and that's not just an expression. She meant you're a little ol' devil, but I doubt you qualify for the title. A devil could leave the water and wreak more . . . *interesting* havoc someplace else. And you can't, can you?"

He lifted his gaze without lifting his head. The offset glare of the light showed him a shape that was round and bald, a head not unlike his own. Eyes rising just far enough to break the waterline and see what motherfucker was doing all this taunting.

Kilgore fought back a shudder and returned his eyes to the notebook, to the word he'd written down. "Not sure how to pronounce this," he admitted. "And it might be the wrong name anyhow, but it's a pretty coincidence all the same, so I'm going to call you *Kupfernickel.*"

The eyes in the water were blacker than the sky above or the water below. They were so black that the darkness spilled out in an ambient glow of evil.

Kilgore met the thing's glare. "That word . . . does it mean anything to you?"

A low, burbling sneer blew bubbles in the lake. And then, so softly that it could scarcely be understood, the creature replied.

Silly sprites.

"Silly sprites," Kilgore repeated, too surprised to say anything else until he'd checked the notebook again. Often these things couldn't speak—or if they could, they found it hard to make themselves understood. This one's voice was clear, though it sounded like it came from miles and miles underground. "But they're dangerous, aren't they? And tied to metal . . . like the metal here at the Burra Burra Mine, sort of."

German miners of old complained about copper that was bedeviled and could not be smelted. They didn't know that the metal wasn't copper at all, but nickel arsenide; they couldn't get copper out of it because there wasn't any copper *in* it.

"You're not so different from that, *Kupfernickel.* One thing pretending to be another. You're no elemental—no creature of *life,* that's for damn sure."

Your word means nothing. You mean nothing. There is no life here.

"You ought to be a small thing, a cold spot. A patch where grass won't grow. But the pollution from the mine let you outgrow your britches."

I am stronger than you know, it hissed, and it lifted itself, crawling toward the bank, and toward Kilgore with a deliberate slowness that showed off its fearsome, knock-kneed, and razor-sharp shape.

"No," he insisted, and he did not back away, calling its bluff. "If you had any strength of your own, you wouldn't be wearing the skin of a dead man. You haven't got enough substance. Not enough life." He looked up quickly, scanning the woods with the white-bright beam that shot from his forehead. The tree line appeared impenetrable and unbroken, a row of trunks divided with stripes of darkness. It felt like a cage.

The creature fussed some moist complaint, but it stopped its progression from the water and remained thighs-deep in the glassy lake. It scanned the tree line too, seeking whatever Kilgore might be hunting; but seeing nothing, it sneered afresh.

You know little and understand less than that.

"Then come up out of that water. Get out here and teach me a lesson, eh, Nick?"

The creature hesitated, then lunged—and retreated, as if it'd changed its mind.

But Kilgore knew a fake-out when he saw one. "You can't, can you?"

Can, it insisted.

"Show me."

But the thing watched the trees again, seeking some response that Kilgore couldn't see. It cowered in the water, stuck in a pose between menace and retreat. The thing wore loose-fitting clothes—the homespun and overalls of a miner a hundred years ago, in boots and gloves, and the smudge of candle soot around its empty eyes. Sopping and stark, its clothing clung wetly to its skin-and-bones form, showing off the crooks and bends of something made of little more than gristle and myth.

"Come on out and take a swing at me if you think you're so tough. I've smacked the shit out of bigger things, and I'll smack it out of *you.*"

The coal-black eyes squinted, and tendrils of pitch-colored smoke oozed from the sockets. *You fear the water.*

"You fear the land," he countered.

I fear nothing.

"Then why do you watch the trees?"

It scowled and dipped, its joints creaking and bowing, as it adjusted itself in the water. The smoke that poured from its blank, deep eyes likewise spilled from the corners of its mouth when it spoke. *I fear no trees.*

"And I ain't afraid of the dark, but I know what's *in* it."

Kilgore checked his distance from the water's edge: a good thirty feet. Far enough that even with a lunge, the creature probably couldn't grab him. Even so, to be on the safe side . . . he sidled back another yard or two, never taking his eyes off the two smoking craters in the creature's shriveled-apple face.

His notebook slipped, but he caught it. He held it up to the light of his headlamp and began to read.

"By the standing stone and twisted tree, thee we invoke—where gather thy own." He cleared his throat, and ignored the splash and hiss from the creature that still stood in the water. "Mighty Lord of the woods and animals, hunter and hunted, I call to you."

None shall answer! There is no life here!

"Hear me, and come once more to this, your sacred home. Keeper of the mighty gates of winter, watcher of the living land," he breathed, and it might've been his imagination that something flickered in the trees beyond the edge of his headlamp's glare.

None remain to hear you!

"You'd best fucking pray that's the case," Kilgore growled. "In the name of Jesus, of the Father, Son, and Holy Spirit . . ."

Hear yourself, you coward, the creature spit. *Singing to the crucified king and calling the old gods with the same breath.*

He shook his head. He'd heard it before, from holier things and people by far. "God of Creation, send Your angels. Send them in a shape this motherfucker will *know,* and lend them Your Almighty power."

Your God has no angels for the likes of me. No swords. No choirs.

There, back toward the Eldorado, he saw it this time for certain: moving between the gnarled greenery like a stream flowing past rocks, one moment slow, one moment lightning-fast, shifting in some strange spot between the worlds. "And He shall give His angels charge over thee." He repeated his favorite bit from the red-bound book. "To keep thee in all thy ways."

Nowhere did it specify what those angels would look like or how they'd do any of the promised keeping.

You cannot have it both ways. Old ways and new gods.

"One God," he corrected. "Just the one—old, new, and always. But He's got a very diverse workforce."

And one thing was certain, sometimes things took the names they were called by. They assumed the shapes that were best believed. He didn't know how it worked, or why. He didn't understand the mechanisms of the Law, but he suspected that no one on earth ever had—or ever could. All he knew was that God was on his side. He believed it harder than he believed his own name.

Your Christ has no power here!

"You're wrong about that and everything else," he said—and he might've said more but a vivid white light sparked, quivered, and blasted out from the tree line. It all but blinded Kilgore, who still had the good sense to keep one watering eye on the creature, though he backed away farther. One arm up, shielding himself from the sudden illumination.

The supernova cast shadows of trunks sharper than prison bars, flinging the shapes across the crater lake and around the hole where a mine once worked, and up the ridge around it—past the miners' cage that split the light into lace, and all along the determined sprouts that clung to the piss-poor dirt, red as the face of Mars.

"There is life here yet!" he gasped, his breath sucked out of him by that divine, demanding illumination.

Between his fingers, around the edges of the fierce brilliance that was colder than November, he saw a four-legged shape, each limb as narrow as a sapling; there stood a barrel-chested trunk and a proud head capped with a crown as wide as Kilgore's outstretched arms. Or not a crown at all—antlers, then, if that's what they were.

This thing had names as well as antlers, though Kilgore could not bring himself to call any of the common ones. Not for prayer or entreaty, for it was too close to blasphemy. Even if he knew what his own God called this thing, it wouldn't be a word for lips like his to pronounce.

He inhaled, exhaled. Forced himself to breathe through the rapture of this piercing light that cut through the copper basin and everything in it.

"Tubal-cain," was the best he could muster in salutation. A name for the horned guardian from the mighty red book. He gagged on a small laugh, remembering a tidbit of lore he'd almost forgotten. "You were a metalsmith, praise Jesus! I see Your patterns, Lord. I see You turn the wheel . . ."

The great stag shifted. Its shape wavered between wafer-thin projection and flesh and blood, but it held and it glared down at the creature in the lake—which cringed against the light.

The creature struggled in place, a fly in molasses. It fumed and reared, lunging backward and going nowhere . . . no, going forward, toward the shining thing in the trees. Dragged up, kicking and fighting from the water until it was free and suspended, angry and dripping and swearing in a tongue no living man has ever understood. Shrinking and withering like the grass once withered and the trees once wilted where they stood.

"Take him away!" he gasped, not quite laughing anymore, too winded to do anything but wheeze. And as the miner-shaped creature rose up, wriggling and dying, sailing reluctantly toward the woods, Kilgore felt a pressure in his chest like a hand squeezing. The pressure crushed hard, and he wiped at his eyes but saw only the searing afterburn of the light from the trees . . . and then he saw stars.

And then he saw nothing, not even the ever-present light.

Not anymore.

Not until it crept back, a flicker here and there. A pixel at a time, that charred patchwork of vision, gleaming around the edges from all the cones and rods adjusting to the light that wasn't there.

The stars came back, but this time they were above him. He blinked. Real stars. Not the ones that snowed across his vision when the light went away.

He was lying on his back, and a sharp jabbing sensation in his side suggested that someone was poking him with a stick.

"Ow . . ." he mumbled, then swiped at the stick.

The stick was held by Ammaw Pete, who also hefted an oversized flashlight with a big 9-volt battery exposed on its underside. To her credit, she didn't aim it at his face. She aimed it at the ground beside him, illuminating his headlamp—which had fallen off and ceased to function.

"Wake up, big man. You're done here."

"Done . . . here? I didn't . . ." He rose slowly, ratcheting himself up with his elbows. "I didn't do anything."

The frown on her face suggested she might argue, but she only said, "Whatever. Get yourself together. I found your car up the hill there, but your battery'll need a jump. There's more than one kind of life, you know, and I'll want a ride home."

"You walked here?"

She shined the light in his face this time, and he winced. "Of course I walked. How else was I supposed to follow that light? Drive through the trees? Not sure what kind of car you think I got, and I don't ride a bicycle. Never did learn. It ain't natural, running around on two wheels like that."

"Pretty sure it's . . . pretty natural," he argued with a grin. She offered him a hand for the sake of show, but he pushed himself to his feet without her assistance. "Is that how you found me? You followed the light?"

"Better than the star of Bethlehem."

He was only half-serious when he said, "Hush your mouth, ma'am."

"Oh, sure. You can ask the pagan holdouts for a handout, but I can't tease a bit about astrology. Fine. You big fat hypocrite."

He dusted himself off and felt around for any broken bits. All in all, he felt pretty good. Tired, but good. "I'm a big fat lot of things, but that's not one of them."

"Well then, maybe you're only confused. Whoa now," she said, and stepped in to steady him. It worked, mostly because he didn't want to fall down on top of her. "Take a moment if you need it."

"Not sure what's wrong with me," he muttered. "I didn't *do* anything. I asked for help, and it came. That's all."

She patted his arm. "No, darling. That wasn't all. You were right," she told him, guiding him by the crook of his arm, back up the hill toward the Jolly Roger. "There was life in this place. A lot of life. *Your* life. And my Old Man," she said with a wink. "He borrowed a bit to make his point. You did a good job, calling him back."

Kilgore frowned down at the small woman with the fierce grip on the meat of his arm. She carried on, straight ahead.

"I knew if I asked you outright, you'd never do it. Not in a million years. Bless Him, He's got the time, but you and I *don't.*"

And as they walked, the flicker in her eyes didn't come from the flashlight, or the moon.

Daniel Abraham

Daniel Abraham lives with his family in Albuquerque, New Mexico, where he is Director of Technical Support at a local Internet service provider. Starting off his career in short fiction, he made sales to *Asimov's Science Fiction, SCI FICTION, The Magazine of Fantasy & Science Fiction, Realms of Fantasy, The Infinite Matrix, Vanishing Acts, The Silver Web, Bones of the World, The Dark, Wild Cards,* and elsewhere, some of which appeared in his first collection, *Leviathan Wept and Other Stories.* Turning to novels, he made several sales in rapid succession, including the books of *The Long Price Quartet,* which consists of *A Shadow in Summer, A Betrayal in Winter, An Autumn War,* and *The Price of Spring.* He's also written *The Dagger and the Coin* series, which consists of *The Dragon's Path, The King's Blood,* and *The Tyrant's Law.* He also wrote *Hunter's Run,* a collaborative novel with George R. R. Martin and Gardner Dozois, as M. L. N. Hanover, wrote the four-volume paranormal romance series *Black Sun's Daughter,* and with Ty Franck, writing as James S. A. Corey, the space-opera *Expanse* novels, consisting (so far) of *Leviathan Wakes, Caliban's War,* and *Abaddon's Gate.*

In the worst of bad neighborhoods, where life is cheap and usually it's everyone for himself, it's good to find a friend whom you can count on—and sometimes they're to be found in the most unexpected of places . . .

THE MEANING OF LOVE

Daniel Abraham

The name Sovereign North Bank referred to a strip of land along the river Taunis *within* the great city of Nevripal, but not *of* it. It existed first as an accident of politics. When, centuries before, the wizards of the Hanish Empire sued for peace after the War of Ten Emperors, the lands surrounding the slow, dark river were ceded to the Council of Nestripon, but an exception was made for the Hanish winter palace and its grounds, which were the favorites of the Empress. In a sentimental gesture of good faith that often follows wars between monarchs who are also family, the land remained technically within the Hanish Empire, though no official or citizen remained there. The mayor and burghers of Nevripal, not sharing the familial fondness for their defeated enemies, declared that the Sovereign North Bank was, in essence, its own problem. With no Hanish to oversee it and no Nestripon willing to take responsibility, it became that rarest of all places: an autonomous zone where the law protected and enforced lawlessness.

Over the ages since, the north bank had become a curiosity. The detritus of a dozen cultures found their way there, or were forced to it when there was no other refuge. The sluggish, dark waters of the Taunis carried barges and rafts to the muddy shores. Criminals and debtors fled to it, refugees of wars national and domestic, the addicted and the poverty-lost. And like the vast and mindless organism that it was, the Sovereign North Bank grew.

That there were no magistrates did not mean there were no planners, no architects, no geniuses or madmen. Rather it meant there was no restraint to those who lived there and invented. Over the decades, the press of humanity and desperation drove the buildings higher. One story and then another rose up, built from whatever came to hand with the unofficial motto *Good enough is good enough.* Towers leaned and swayed and sometimes collapsed, grinding the men and women within them to blood and pulp, only to be rebuilt by the survivors or the next wave of refugees. Walkways of rope and wood were hoisted between the buildings until it was said a native of the place could cross from the boundary wall on the north to the sluggish waters at the south without ever touching ground. Shit and piss and trash were thrown from windows to the distant street until rain came to wash them away, and like plants in rich soil, the unstable, unreliable buildings rose, driven by the deep human desire to be the one least shat upon. The streets, such as they were, grew darker and narrower and sometimes disappeared altogether under plank-and-tar awnings that redefined them as homes and shacks.

As with any community, there were landmarks and centers all through it. The Temple at the root of the city that was said to be part of the original Hanish palace. The Water Market, built out over the river itself, where men and women exchanged trinkets and junk with the focus and ferocity of gem merchants. The opium dens against the wall where men slept themselves to death under strings of pale beads long since yellowed to amber by their smokes. There were neighborhoods and demarcations invisible to the untrained eye, but named by the natives: the Salt, Hafner's Choke, Jimtown.

Two miles long, a mile and a half wide at its greatest, the Sovereign North Bank was home and hovel to fifty thousand people. What little order there was came from the crime lords for whom it was a refuge from the magistrates. What little food there was came from houses of charity in Nevripal whenever the gentry of the greater city felt magnanimous, or was stolen from the river traffic or fished from the filthy waters. The residents of the city-without-citizens ranged from squalid and starving babies who shat their brief lives away in the shadows to the dark-robed holy men in the Temple, from rail-thin addicts half-mad from longing and hunger to masters of crime and violence whose penthouses looked across the river at the lights of the respectable world like reflections in a tarnished mirror.

And in the depths of the city, not too near the wall nor too close to the river, neither at the exalted and uncertain heights nor drowned in the trash and offal that choked the lowest streets, there was a small room with a tin brazier under a thick clay-pipe chimney, filled with two ancient, stained mattresses. On one mattress lay Prince Steppan Homrey, fugitive heir of Lyria. On the other, Asa, who was secretly in love with him.

Despite the lateness of the hour, neither was sleeping.

"I *love* her," the prince said, his arm thrown over his brow and manly tears beading in the corners of his eyes. He was ten days past his twenty-third naming day, and the older of the pair by half a year. "I love her, and she is going to be sold to the workhouse."

A half dozen possible replies wrestled in Asa's mind—*You've seen her once, and from a distance* and *Better the workhouse than here* and *You may be confusing love for a different kind of longing*—until a diplomatic victor came out on top.

"I'm sorry."

"You should have seen her. She was like dawn on a winter morning."

"Frosted over, you mean?"

"No," the prince said. "She was pure and pale, and she shone like the horizon when it is almost too bright to look upon."

"Ah."

"I asked her name from a boy there. Zelanie, daughter of Jost. I would swear she has royal blood. If you'd seen her, you'd know what I mean. The way she held herself was like seeing a queen at her coronation. Everything around her was made bright just because she was close to it. I was meant to find her. I see that now. Whatever plan the gods have for me, I was meant to find her. And so I must have been meant to save her. You should have seen her father. He had the face of a butcher."

Asa shifted. The mattress rustled and settled.

"You think I'm a fool," the prince said. His eyes were red with weeping, and his face a mask of melancholy. Asa sighed.

"I think you're being hunted by a stepmother who'd like nothing better than to see you facedown in a river. Your father is the prisoner of a Kyrean wizard, if he's not dead. Half the people in your home country think you're a murderer and the other half think you're a fool. You've got a full plate without taking on anything else."

"This isn't something I asked for," he said. "You see that, don't you?"

Asa's whole life had been spent in and out of the Sovereign North Bank, working as a petty thief, an acolyte of the gods, a grifter, a broker of information, and—like the city itself—an avatar and embodiment of whatever-needs-doing-gets-done. Becoming the unofficial protector of a political fugitive wasn't the wise thing either, but it had happened.

Steppan had just arrived when they met the winter before, the fine stitching and well-carded wool of his supposedly unobtrusive cloak making him stand out like blood on a wedding dress. He'd worn a scowl that had been equal parts moral outrage at the misery around him and masculine self-pity, and he'd lost the coins carefully stitched into his sleeve within the first half day of coming down the wall. Even the priests would have thought twice before putting their fates with his, but here he was, months later, his hair longer and shaggy at the nape, his clothes the yellow-brown that everything washed in the Taunis eventually became, and staring across the room with tear-stained eyes like a puppy that had lost its boy. He hadn't shaved in a month, and his black whiskers shone like they'd been oiled. He was the very image of not-something-I-asked-for, and so Asa had to allow him the point.

"Where was she, again?"

"I saw her on the walk beside the one building that looks like it's stooping. With the four pillars."

"I know the one. And this was two days ago?"

Prince Steppan nodded, then he rolled over and propped himself up on his elbows. "Will you find her for me? Will you carry her a message from me?"

"No, I will under no circumstances start announcing you to anyone I'm not utterly certain of. But I'll look into the situation. See what there is to be seen. Zelanie, daughter of Jost? That, then."

Asa knew the place. The building was the old tower with roots in the stables of the Hanish Emperor's palace and a long history of minor collapse. A family living there was likely desperate enough to sell their adult children into the workhouses. Traffic in slaves was prohibited in Nevripal, but Sovereign North Bank wasn't Nevripal. Asa knew of two places where legitimate businessmen met to make trades like that without technically breaking the law. And in truth, it wasn't the worst thing a father could do with his daughter.

"Thank you for this, my friend," the prince said. "I love her."

You'd mentioned that, Asa thought bitterly but didn't say.

When the sun first started brightening the eastern skies, Asa was already walking across the rope bridges between the buildings. The air stank of smoke and sewage, but no more so than usual. The sounds of voices came from bare windows and the streets below: shouting and cursing but also singing and laughter. Men and women in dark cloaks squeezed past each other on bridges no wider across than a single handspan, backs and bellies rubbing against each other in a way that would have been intimate if it hadn't been routine. Every week or two, a bridge would collapse, spilling two or three people down through the filthy air, smashing their bodies through whatever roof lay below them. But then, more died from the flux and no one was doing anything about that either. The bridges would be rebuilt if enough people cared and had the rope to spare, or they wouldn't. The paths of the city would shift and change like a slow river uneasy in its banks. It was part of what Asa loved about the city. But only part.

The old tower looked sad in the yellow light of morning. It leaned a degree to the east, and windows spotted its sides, knocked through the walls wherever convenience demanded until they looked like an architectural pox. Asa took a ladder and then a stairway made from driftwood logs nailed to the outside of the building, and emerged in the yard Steppan had described. Four massive pillars rose up from the ground, tall and proud as trees, and overshadowed. A few dozen men and women slept in the muck or made a show of waking up. At the far end, three boys played a game of chase with a dog no one had eaten yet.

"Looking for a man named Jost. Daughter's Zelanie," Asa said, touching a man's shoulder. A head shake and a shrug, and then the same question again of the next person, and then on and on, one after another, until movements and words became rote. When, near midday, a woman nodded and pointed, she nodded and pointed toward the river. Asa cursed. That wasn't a good sign.

The men from the workhouses were set up on the westernmost quay. They had well-fed faces and laughter that was made cruel by its context the way a gem could be made ugly by being set in tin. The pens weren't finished yet, but a pair of local boys were hammering the walls in place, building the corral for their less fortunate compatriots. The workhouse overseer stood smoking a pipe at the waterside, looking out over the sullen gyre where the river shaved off a bit of its current. His desk was a plank between two piles of bricks with a purple cloth over it to make it seem respectable. A line of men and woman waited for the trades to begin. One of them was a tired-looking man perhaps twice the prince's age with a pale-skinned girl at his side.

"Jost?" Asa asked, coming near.

The man looked over, and his daughter a moment later.

"Here," the man said.

Asa smiled. "Then this would be the lovely Zelanie."

She was a thin creature with dark hair that was a few degrees less lank than might be expected, more roundness in her cheeks and breasts than perhaps the average. Asa didn't think she was a beauty for the ages, and certainly not the winter dawn translated to flesh, but pretty enough and capable of smiling. Her eyes had what might or might not have been intelligence but was at least cunning. If there was royal blood in her, it was well hidden.

"What is it to you?" she asked.

"In line for the workhouse?"

"If they ever open the table and start hiring," her father said.

"Hiring? I'd have thought *buying* was the verb."

"Well, no one fucking asked you, did they?"

Asa turned to the girl, but before he could speak, a familiar voice called from the alley behind them. Josep Red staggered out, waving his good hand and grinning like he'd just found a pearl in a night pot. "Excuse me," Asa said, eyes locked on the girl's in a way that might seem meaningful. She scowled, then smiled uncertainly and turned away.

"So, Asa, you wasted spunk," Josep said as they walked a little distance from the line together. "I been looking for you."

"Flattered."

"You still in the market for news about hunters?"

Asa hoisted an eyebrow, and the old man cackled.

"Yes, I am still in that market. What have you got?"

"Two magistrate's men came down the wall last night. They're wandering in Hafner's Choke, asking people about a picture."

Asa spat, looked back at the line of men and women, the half-built pen, the girl whom Prince Steppan had decided he loved. *Can't expect me to do everything at the same time.* Asa pressed a copper coin in Josep's unscarred hand.

"How about you show me?"

The magistrate's hunters weren't dressed for subtlety. They both wore boiled-leather armor with the scales-and-axe sigil of the high council carved into the breast, and the swords at their sides would have bought food for a week to anyone with the courage to take them. They walked with a firmness that carried the right of way along with it, and they ignored most of the people on the street, accosting only the better-dressed men and women, and speaking even to them in sharp, condescending tones. Asa and Josep Red watched them for a time without being seen, and nothing that they saw made Asa think well of the men.

"Who's the picture of?" Asa asked.

"Think they'd show it? Beneath their kind, me."

"What are they asking people?"

" 'Have y'seen this man?' "

Asa's belly sank. If the Council of Nevripal had taken it into their heads to side with Steppan's enemies, things were about to become unsupportable. Josep nodded as if in agreement. Five escape plans already in place, Asa stepped smiling into the street and walked toward the hunters. Their eyes were as hard as slate and one of them put a hand on the hilt of his blade.

"Morning. Heard you strapping young men were looking for something and thought I might be of use."

"And you are?"

"Asa."

The hunters looked at each other as if unsure whether to be insulted or amused. For a tense moment, no one spoke. The one took his hand from the sword and pulled a curl of thick paper from his belt. He held it before Asa's eyes like he was pressing a scent to a hunting dog's nose. Instead of Steppan's thin nose and wide-set eyes, the inked face that looked back at him was broad and long and perfectly familiar. Asa's eyes narrowed to cover the relief.

"Chancellor *Rouse*?" Asa asked, faking incredulity.

The hunters exchanged a look that meant they had just become rather more interested in Asa than they'd been before. "You know him?"

"*Of* him. Enough to say you'd be better off searching the graveyard. He died six years ago."

"He didn't," the second hunter said. "Used a potion to feign his death and buried a servant in his place. Now we're come to pick up where they left off."

"Have you seen him?" the first asked. "Does he live here?"

"If he does, I haven't seen him. And . . . All respect, but Chancellor Rouse defeated Sarapin's army and killed seventy people with his own hands. If he were living around here, he'd be running the place by now, and we'd all be drilling in his army come mornings. At least, that's the way I've heard it."

The hunters looked at each other in disgust. "We've reason to think he's here. And if he is, we'll find him."

"Godspeed to both of you," Asa said. "I'll ask around, and if I find anything . . . Well, if I do, is there a reward?"

Fifteen minutes later, Asa was headed back to the quay. The pens were built and the overseer squatted behind his purple desk. No slaves had taken their places behind the pen's bars yet, but that would come soon enough. Zelanie and her father were nowhere to be found, and Asa had no way to know if they'd been turned down by the workhouses, if an agreement had been made, or if old Jost was holding out for a better price on his daughter's future. For the greater part of the day, the line of men and women inched forward, but those particular two didn't return. Eventually Asa gave up, spent a shaved coin in a filthy kitchen by the water, and went back to the little room carrying a burlap sack of cooked pigeons.

Steppan sat by the brazier, feeding the fire with twigs and tiny lumps of coal. The light flickered in his dark eyes as he looked up at Asa. The smoke and warmth gave the room an uncomfortable close feeling. From beyond one of the thin walls, a woman's wailing came like the mating song of a great hunting cat. A gray cloth bundle lay on Steppan's mattress. Asa dropped the feed bag and sat on the mattress beside it.

"How was your day?" Steppan asked.

"Interesting. I saw your ladylove. You're right, her father's looking to sell her."

"And?"

"And Brother Rouse down at the Temple's about to have a more interesting life. His past is sniffing at his heels again, though I don't see how that affects us. Also I thought we'd agreed *that* should stay hidden."

The prince looked at the cloth the way a mouse might eye a placid snake. "There may be a need for it."

Asa drew out a pigeon and took a thoughtful bite. The meat was on the dry end, but it was spiced with pepper and salt that forgave it. Steppan took a bird for himself in one hand and unwrapped the cloth bundle with the other. The scabbard was green enamel and as ostentatious and gaudy as everything the hunters had worn put together. Steppan drew the blade.

"So, which need was it you had in mind? Planning to go slaughter all the workhouse crews? Or maybe her father?"

"She is being sold," Steppan said, "and so I must be in a position to buy her. If I can better the price of the workhouses, I can claim her and set her free."

"I don't think you can sell it for that much. Not in our markets."

"That wasn't my plan."

Asa took another bite, then put the bird's carcass down on the mattress. Steppan looked away, caught between bravado and shame.

"Why don't you tell me what the plan is, then?" Asa said, pronouncing each word carefully.

"Everyone knows Sovereign North Bank is the haven of outlaws and thieves. I can't call it a crime to steal from the stealers. The crime lords meet in the Salt. That's what you told me. Surely there would be enough gold there to buy her freedom."

"No. That's not going to—"

"Stop it!" Steppan shouted, and when he turned, the blade turned with him. The tears in his eyes stood witness to the fact that he knew how bad the plan was. "You have been my companion and my only friend, and I will be in your debt forever, but you can't tell me to abandon her. You can't tell me not to *try.*"

"You won't help anyone dead. And there's another way."

"What?"

"I haven't thought of it yet," Asa said, and picked the pigeon back up.

Steppan's mouth opened and closed like a marionette's. The point of the blade slipped down toward the floor, and he laughed once and mirthlessly. They ate in silence while outside the sun fell and darkness crept through the filthy streets. The wailing woman's cries turned to a shouting match in a language Asa didn't know and then ended abruptly. Steppan fed the smoky little fire, went to piss out the window at the end of the hall, and then came back and collapsed onto his mattress. Asa sat up, resting against the cold and creaking wall.

The best plan, of course, was for somebody—anybody, really—to outgrow their naive illusions about love, but since that was going to be tricky to whistle up, they needed a fallback. Otherwise, Steppan really would do something desperate and florid and suicidal. The idea of buying the girl's freedom wasn't bad, but the part about how to get the coin was terrible. So perhaps there was another way. Across the tiny room, Steppan's breath slowed and deepened, his hands folded under his neck like a child's. In the dim glow, his cheeks were a lighter shadow, the curve of his lips all but lost in the darkness of his little beard. How much did the workhouses pay, anyway? Without knowing what the price would be, it was hard to think of a concrete solution. Asa thought of the hunters looking for the supposedly dead Councilor Rouse and the joke about a reward. For most of the people of Sovereign North Bank, life was pretty damned cheap.

Life was cheap, and corpses were inexpensive.

Steppan's eye flew open. "What?"

"What what?"

"You laughed."

"Did I? Well, I thought of something funny."

Steppan's smile was as much a sound as anything. "You thought of something?"

"I'll look into it in the morning while you put that thing back in hiding, eh?"

"Of course. Thank you, Asa. For everything. I don't know what I'd do without you."

Die, most likely, Asa thought.

The Temple sat beneath the city, its deepest chambers dug into the damp soil of the riverside. A great net of ropes hung suspended above the building itself, and the trash and garbage and bird's nests and dead animals that had built up on it over the course of the years blocked what sunlight struggled down through the taller structures surrounding it. Dim beams caught the dust and filth that hung in the air, and also glimmered off tilework of scarlet and gold, ancient and ruined glasswork, pathways of yellowed marble kept clean by monks and priests. The effect was often compared to being under the overhanging trees of a jungle, but Asa thought it looked more like something underwater. The ruins left beneath the waves after a vast and sludgy flood.

Torches and lamps heated the air, even at midday, and the vast central hall with the statues of seven gods smelled of sweet incense. The priests and physicians who peopled the dark halls and worshipped the gods in the dimness were an equal mixture of saints dedicated to serving the most wretched in the worst places of the world and monsters who had fouled every more pleasant nest. Sometimes—rarely—the two classes overlapped.

Asa sat in the back pew, watching the vast bulk of the priest as he made his way down the aisle. The years had grayed his hair and thickened his jowls, but anyone who looked closely would have recognized him as the man the hunters sought. When he spoke, his voice was low and rough as a landslide.

"Asa."

"Chancellor Rouse."

"That is not my name any longer," the priest said, lowering himself into the pew in front of Asa's and twisting around to look over his massive shoulder. "But you know that. And so I have to think you are saying it for effect?"

"I'm nothing if not affected. But I'm not the only one saying that name recently. I talked to a magistrate's hunter yesterday in Hafner's Choke. He had a picture of you."

Rouse pressed his lips together and heaved a sigh. "I've heard."

"Then I assume you've got some plan for removing yourself from danger."

"Perhaps. Or perhaps it is time to surrender myself to the judgment of the council."

Asa laughed once. Rouse looked injured.

"You don't think so, friend Asa?"

"I think you're as much the ice-hearted killer now as you were when you were in power, and you wear the priest's collar well because you never thought anyone less than a god had authority over you."

"True. All true."

"So you have a plan."

"Perhaps."

"Well, if you don't, I do. And the price for my help is profoundly reasonable."

Rouse was silent for a long while. The seven gods stared back at them with empty stonework eyes. Somewhere not too far away, an unseen choir lifted their dozen voices in the midday chant. Asa fought the impulse to fidget. There were stories of Chancellor Rouse slitting a man's throat and pulling the tongue out through the hole as punishment for interrupting. Chances were good it was an exaggeration, but the stakes were high if it wasn't.

"What would you have from me?" Rouse asked.

"Your help in a problem I've got. Your expertise. Nothing you haven't done before. And in return, I'll help you pull the hunter's teeth and get rid of them for you, and they don't even have to know you were involved in it."

"That sounds suspiciously reasonable."

"I can be reasonable."

"Tell me precisely what it is you have in mind," Rouse said.

Asa did, adding fewer embellishments than usual along the way. Rouse listened with an intimidating ferocity. By the end, he was laughing silently and with a violence that left the pew creaking under him.

"They will be missed," he said when he'd regained himself.

"Perhaps, but that was always going to be a problem. Be honest, you were going to kill them."

"I was."

"So they'd have been missed anyway. This way, they stop stirring up the deep mud, you aren't implicated, and we both make a little money. And if they do make their way back to the world, the danger of it falls on me. No one even knows for certain you were here at all."

The choir resolved the chant on an ambiguous harmony, as if the gods were better honored by something that stayed open and unfinished at the end.

"My way is simpler," Rouse said.

"My way doesn't kill anyone."

"Is that a good thing?"

"You've killed a lot of people, friend, and it's gotten you *here.* Not a resounding argument for the strategy."

The man who had once driven nations before his whips sat with the thought.

"Someday it will all go too far. The magistrates will come. Or the soldiers. They will burn this all to the waterline and call the world cleaner for it."

"Probably," Asa agreed. "But they aren't doing it today, so why talk about it?"

A moment later, Rouse sighed. "Let us try your way."

The rest of the day was spent preparing. Rouse's list of herbs and poisons was shorter than Asa expected and also harder to put hands to. Dried lobelia and apron grass, distilled wine and arsenic powder. Asa traded one thing for another, talked sweetly, made promises and threats, wheedled, begged, wept, and stole. By sundown, Rouse had everything he'd asked for and a bit more, and Asa felt like the rope in a pulling contest. But it was done for the moment.

Sovereign North Bank did not sleep, but it did drowse. The ruddy light of sunset deepened the shadows, reddened the towers and walkways. Fires began to glow and flicker in the windows and on the rooftops, smoke stinking of coal and wood and dried dung filling the air. Some nights, mist rose from the dark water of the Taunis and mixed with it, and Nevripal across the water faded into nothing. On those nights, Sovereign North Bank seemed to stand on the edge of an endless sea, shrouded and silent. Friends and conspirators gathered to sing or complain or plot their escape. Those without shelter begged for warmth and food or else died in the corners, unlamented. People fell in bed or fell in love, shouted and wept and danced. It was like any great city, only more so, and that was part of why Asa loved it, but only part.

Steppan wasn't in the room, and neither was his sword. He wasn't in the tiles hall where they would sometimes spend the evening playing against the old men with missing fingers and teeth. He wasn't in the alley or the common rooms. The addict who lived in the room next to theirs hadn't seen him since midday. Annoyance bit into Asa's giddiness, but not so much as to erase it entirely. And the solution to the puzzle of Prince Steppan's vanishing was perfectly clear, if only in retrospect.

Near midnight, Asa stepped onto the street beside the river that overlooked the quay. Steppan sat with his legs hanging out over the water, his gaze fixed on the pens. Where the workhouse overseer had been that morning, torches like flares lit the bars and the captives. Ten men and six women ranging from hardly out of childhood to approaching dotage huddled together, property of the workhouses now. There would be more before they shipped out. Asa had seen the pens so packed that there hardly seemed room enough to breathe. Seven guards stood or sat, laughing with one another, water and fog making their voices seem close and far away at the same time.

"We're too late," the prince said.

"How do you figure?"

"She's already sold."

Standing at the pen bars like a bird in a menagerie, Zelanie, daughter of Jost, for all the good that had done her, looked out toward them. Her gown was yellow-brown but had probably started out as pink or white. On the river, a barge hove into sight. A smuggler or a cadre of young men from the city in search of adventure. Asa's exhaustion and pleasure and anxious anticipation of what was still to come bubbled up in laughter. Steppan's expression was as stark as a slap.

"It's uncomfortable for her," Asa said, "but it's temporary. And we can't get her without going through this part."

"What?"

"Think it through," Asa said, sitting beside him. "Take her before she's sold to the workhouse, and we're stealing from her family. They live here. They know people. If they held a grudge, it could cause real problems. But if she's sold, her father's been paid. Whatever brothers or sisters or aunts needed the money already have it. When she goes lost now, it's the *workhouse* that's losing her. They can stand it better, and they're less likely to know who's behind it, and even if they do, it's a small loss to them and a small risk to us. They'll be taking a hundred people at least on their barges by the end of the week. One less they'll hardly notice, and even if they did, they come here three times a year for a week or less each time."

"You planned for this?"

Asa clapped an arm around Steppan's shoulders, grinning. The despair in the prince's eyes shifted first to disbelief, and then something like admiration. The expression was sweet as honey and intoxicating as wine to Asa, and it justified the whole day's effort.

"All this and more, my friend. I planned all this and more. But I need rest, and so do you. Tomorrow's a long day, and I'll need my wits about me. So come back to the room. I won't be able to sleep if I'm worrying where you've gotten to."

They rose together, and across the darkly turning water the girl stared out at them. Drunk with cleverness, Asa raised a hand, hailing her like a friend, and after a moment, she waved tentatively back.

Finding the hunters was easy enough. They hadn't come to be subtle. Sending a message to them was hardly more difficult. Half a dried apple was enough to buy a dozen street couriers. But until the men stepped out onto the rooftop court, Asa hadn't been sure they would come.

It was a low, gray rooftop, no larger than a peasant's bedroom would have been on the other bank of the river, but palatial by the standards of Sovereign North Bank. It huddled beneath taller buildings all around it, so that even though it was technically open to the sky, there was only a tiny square of dull blue above them. The view was mostly of walls. Drying laundry hung from gray, unglazed windows, and someone had built a dovecote across the alley below them that filled the air with alarmed coos and the stink of droppings. A squat iron brazier belched out a thin, foul smoke. A girl no more than nine years old bowed before the hunters, jabbering in the tongue of Far Coiris and pointing them on toward the table where Asa sat, waiting with three cups and a stone bowl of cider.

The men walked with the ease and grace of those accustomed to violence.

"We talked to you," the one with the paper in his belt said. "Asa, you called yourself."

"Good to be remembered. Please, sit down."

The men exchanged a glance, then sat, arranging themselves so that no one could approach unobserved.

"Seems I recall you didn't know anything."

"No one on the north bank is ever what they seem," Asa said, pouring cider from the bowl into all three cups. "I wasn't sure then what made the most sense for me. I know where the chancellor sleeps, you see. And that he's not a man who is safe to cross. I spoke with him yesterday."

The hunters both tensed. Asa gestured at the cups of cider, letting them choose first and then drinking the third almost dry to allay any fear of poison.

"And what was it you said to him?" the one with the paper asked.

"That you two were here and hunting for him. Oh, please. Don't look at me like that. As if he didn't already know! Likely, he had word of it the moment the pair of you came down the wall. I also convinced him not to kill you, and you're welcome for it. I sold him a scheme to rid himself of the pair of you at essentially no risk to him. He believes that I'm on his side."

"And yet here you sit with us."

Asa nodded. "It's a sad fallen world, filled with bastards and confidence men. I weep for it."

"What's your price?" the other hunter said, then coughed and shot an angry glance at the foul little brazier.

"Right to the point," Asa agreed. "I appreciate that. I want letters of amnesty. Two sets, and signed by the mayor."

The second hunter laughed once, but the first leaned forward. Neither one had touched the cider.

"You're asking a lot, friend Asa," the first hunter said.

"Why are we having this talk?" the second one asked. "This freak of nature knows where Rouse hides. Break a couple fingers, and we'll know too."

"But you won't be able to get him out from his protection," Asa said. "I'm not only offering information. I'm your partner now. He won't put himself in a place to be caught unless someone he thinks is his ally draws him out. You can walk the bridges and streets for the rest of your lives and not find him. Or you can do as I say and be home by nightfall."

Somewhere below them, a man's voice rose in an angry shout, and another answered it, syllable for screaming syllable. Asa took another sip of cider and waited.

"How would you draw him out?" the first hunter asked.

"Ah. An excellent question. I've already made my first contact, so he's already prone to view a note from me as legitimate. Once we've picked the right place, I'll send to him. And when he comes, I'll poison him. Nothing that would kill him, of course. But something that will take his strength and his will, at least long enough to put him in chains, yes? No fighting. No violence. Everybody wins."

The second hunter laughed, coughed, and shook his head.

"You'd poison a poisoner?" the first hunter said, fidgeting in his seat. His face was growing pale.

"I'm not saying it would be easy," Asa said. "There would have to be some sort of misdirection. A plate of honeyed dates, for instance. Something like that. A suspicious refreshment he could be wary of and avoid. There's nothing like keeping out of a trap to make a man feel safe. And then, with his guard down . . ." The second hunter coughed out another laugh, but his eyes were having trouble focusing. Asa smiled and went on. "And, of course, *I'd* take something to counteract the effects before I sat down."

"What . . ." the first hunter slurred. He stood suddenly, trying awkwardly to draw his sword.

"It was the smoke," Asa said, gesturing toward the brazier. "If you were curious."

When the hunters had collapsed, Asa brought out the lead-sealed vial Rouse had given him, straddled each sleeping man in turn, and dropped the black oil into their eyes and down their noses. The girl came close, her hands knotted together in anxiety and pleasure.

"Stay back from the fire, dear," Asa told her. "It's not good for little girls."

The hunters lay quiet and still for a long while, and then—as the chancellor and priest had said they would—each man began to tremble and shake. White foam formed at the corners of their mouths, and their eyes rolled back in their heads. Asa stripped the two men quickly to their skins and then doused the herbs in the brazier with the last of the cider. When the air cleared, the girl scuttled forward to collect the swords, belts, and armor.

"Encancú atzien," she said.

"You're welcome," Asa replied, fastening the slave chains around the hunters' necks. "Try to get a good price for them."

The line at the quay was longer. Word had spread that the work-houses had come. The desperate and the expendable came out of the overpacked, stinking buildings like juice from an orange. The hunters squatted at Asa's side like a pair of dogs. The black oil stained the whites of their eyes a greenish brown and the one who had carried the paper shook his head from time to time as if he were trying to clear it. Their nakedness seemed to cause them no discomfort, nor the black iron collars or the chains with which Asa gently encouraged them on.

The overseer at the purple table scowled when Asa's turn came, looking over the two hunters with a buyer's eye.

"What's wrong with them?"

"Bad batch of cider," Asa said. "I told them there was something growing in it, but they didn't listen. Been like this for months, and I can't take care of them anymore."

"Why the hell should I, then?"

"They're strong. Tractable."

"They're mindless."

"Hey," the second hunter said, and then seemed to lose the thought, sitting on his bare haunches.

"It might take a bit longer to train them," Asa allowed. "But they won't get bored and they won't talk back. Good teeth, good backs, and no complaints. If that's not what you're looking for, I'll find someplace else to sell 'em."

The workhouse man drummed his fingers on the purple cloth. In the pens behind him, the captives had swelled to four dozen or more. As many again stood in the snaking line behind Asa and the hunters. As the workhouse overseer hemmed and hawed, Asa caught sight of the girl, watched her work her way to the edge of the bars, pressing her body against them. She waved a little, and there was a desperate hope in the gesture.

"Twelve for the pair of them," the overseer said.

"Fifteen."

"Twelve or keep them."

"Twelve it is, then."

The overseer counted out two lines of tiny silver coins, six to a line, and Asa scooped them up. Two of the guards came to take the newly sold slaves back to the pen, and Asa made an alarmed noise.

"What?" the overseer said.

"You didn't buy the chains. These are my chains. I'll lead them back to your cage if you like, but the metal'll cost you another four."

"Keep dreaming."

Under the watchful eyes of the guards, Asa led the two hunters to the pens. Zelanie followed every motion with ravenous eyes. Her mouth hung half-open with unspoken words. Asa pretended to ignore her. At the gate to the pens, guards and captives alike stood, laughing at the naked men while their collars were removed. The magistrate's hunters seemed vaguely aware that something distasteful was happening to them, but they made no move to cover themselves and spoke no word of protest. Asa slid back, leaving both chains and men to the guards. No one had any attention to spare, except the woman. She took the black vial without any sign of surprise, hiding it in her sleeve with the practiced flicker of a pickpocket.

"Drink it at sundown and be free," Asa said, then stepped away before she could answer or ask. "Hey, those chains are mine. You can buy your own."

At the edge of the quay, Rouse leaned against a crumbling stone wall, chewing thoughtfully on a wad of tar. Asa dropped the chains in a pool at the huge priest's ankles.

"Thank you for the loan," Asa said.

"Welcome."

"Any idea how long they're going to be like that?"

"They will never be the men they were before. What does return to them will come in . . . four months. Perhaps five."

"Well, hopefully they'll enjoy their new positions. The last job they had seemed a little risky."

Rouse nodded, paused, used the nail of his pinky to dig a bit of blackness from between his teeth, which he then flicked out into the water. "We're done until tonight."

"It's not that I don't enjoy your company. But I'd best get back to my rooms before my dear friend gets word from some other place. If he thinks she's really dead, he'll likely do something dramatic and bloody. Fall on his sword or some such."

Rouse chuckled as he wrapped the chains around one thick forearm. "And to think, someday he may rule a nation."

Asa froze, then forced an easy smile. "The world's an unjust place."

"So it is," the chancellor said, rising. "So it is."

Joy radiated from the prince like heat from a fire. His smile was so wide, it seemed to creak, and he walked with his arm around Asa's shoulder as they passed through the crowded marketplace. High above them, the sky was white and featureless, and held no hint of the coming twilight. There were hours still before anything had to be done. Asa tried to share in his delight, with little success. Now that the game was almost won, the headiness that had been so rich before seemed thin and unsatisfying. The weight of Steppan's arm annoyed, and the glances that his gaiety drew held something between dismay and menace. *Not everything needs to be so damned loud.*

"Wine, my friend," Steppan half shouted. "Wine and the best food we can find. And smoke if you want it. There is nothing in the world too fine to lay at your feet today."

"Promises, always promises," Asa said.

If there was an edge to the words, Steppan missed it. Laughing, he steered them into a narrow alley of planks laid between two buildings and fifty feet above the distant ground. The old woman who claimed the place nodded at them in greeting, just as she had the night Asa had first brought Steppan there. The wine was terrible, but one of the tiny silver coins from the workhouse overseer would pay for a week's worth. Steppan lifted the clay mug in a toast.

"To Asa!" he declaimed. "Champion of love."

"God, not that! Pick something else."

"Why not that?" Steppan asked. The planks beneath their feet left gaps as wide as a thumb. Too narrow to slip through but enough to see how far the fall would be. For a moment, it seemed thick with significance.

"People love their fathers. Their sisters. People love dogs or songs or poems. If I've got to be the champion of something, make it something that doesn't change what it means every time someone says it."

Steppan laughed as if it had been a joke and drained his cup. His hair was wild and dark and glossy. If his skin had a pock on it, Asa hadn't seen it. The man was joyful and bright and full of hope. All the prince's troubles were forgotten because a girl he'd seen once at a distance probably wasn't going to die or be sent to the workhouse. It was like watching a child getting an unexpected rock of honey, and it weighted Asa's heart like lead.

"You don't understand what love is," Steppan said, wiping the back of his hand across his beard.

"And you do?"

"Love is like recognition. It's the moment when you catch sight of someone and you think *There is someone I have business with in this life. There is someone I was born to know.* Has that never happened to you?"

"It has, but I never took much comfort in it."

Steppan waved the old woman closer and held out his cup for her to refill. At this rate, he'd be snoring asleep before twilight. Which might actually be the best thing. Asa wasn't looking forward to finding a reason that Steppan couldn't come to this last part of the plot.

"Love is like a baby sleeping on its mother's breast," Steppan said.

"Inchoate and likely to piss itself?"

"Ah, you can play at being a cynic, my friend, but I've known you too long. You're a romantic at heart. You're in love with the world."

"I'd say I'm inchoate and likely to piss myself," Asa said, trying not to smile. Steppan's pleasure was simple and unfeigned and infectious.

"Fine! Fine, then love isn't like a baby. Love is like falling from a window and discovering you can fly."

"Unlikely to happen and dangerous to try."

Steppan's laughter was a howl. Asa saw the men passing below them look up, curious, and didn't feel impatient any longer. The foul mood had passed for the moment. It would come again, but for now it was gone. That was a gift.

"Love is like the burst of sweetness when you bite into a strawberry."

"Brief for you and painful for the berry."

"Ach! Love is like beautiful music played in a ruin."

"Give me a minute. No, just a minute. I'll think of something."

And the game went on with the hours and the wine. Asa tried to forget what had come before and what would come next. It was a long pleasant afternoon, just the two of them and the city beneath their feet. A golden moment that could wax and wane. By the time darkness fell, Steppan could barely walk straight. Asa had matched the prince cup for cup and felt sober as a judge. There was still work that needed doing, and a thousand things to go wrong.

Workhouse captives died all the time, of course. Usually, they had the grace to do it after they'd spent months or years behind the high gray walls, but some lucky few would die on the quay, and in those cases, the workhouse men would do the same thing they always did: fling the corpse into the river and forget it. Asa poled the little boat out just beyond the quay, tied it to a rotting stonework wall built by hands a hundred years dead, and waited. The Taunis was a dull river, predictable and deliberate as a plow horse. The children of Sovereign North Bank knew the places where wood and corpses came to rest on its banks the way in other cities they might know which corners had the sweet shops. The river stank and muttered against the side of the boat. The splash of something heavy being dropped from the quay would have been easy to miss if Asa hadn't been listening for it.

The girl's body lay facedown in the water. Her shoulders were a dim gray in the moonlight, her head a knot of ropy black. Hauling her in set the little boat tottering, but not dangerously. Her face was mottled ice white and bruise purple, her tongue swollen until it pressed out past her lips, and her eyes, open in slits, were still as stones. Asa had never seen the dead look deader.

At the shore, a little hand truck waited, and Asa was glad to have added it into the plan. Zelanie, daughter of no one any longer, was waterlogged deadweight and felt like she'd been filled with sand and lead. That the hand cart didn't have a cover was an oversight to keep in mind for next time, but it wasn't as if hauling a corpse through the lowest streets would attract much attention. Stranger things happened all the time.

Rouse waited in the tiny workshop at the back of the temple. Shelves of salt and dried herbs covered the walls and ate into what little space there was. Together, they lifted her onto the low slate table more usually employed for preparing the dead. Rouse stripped off her river-soaked clothes with a steel knife, washed the filth and river scum from her, and folded a warmed blanket of wool that covered her from toes to neck. He placed heated stones along her body, and then drew a tiny flask from the shelves and carefully placed a single crimson drop on her tongue. The chancellor grunted with satisfaction.

"She's all right?" Asa asked.

"She is as I expected her to be. After this, she should wake, not as one does from sleep, but from a wound to the head. She may wake sober, or she may be confused. Or possibly violent."

"And what do we do about that?"

"I tell you that she may be confused and violent, and you watch over her while I sleep. That is what *we* do," Rouse said, putting the flask back in its place.

After Rouse left, Asa leaned against the wall, watching the woman's face by the light of the single candle. As slowly as the stars turning in the night sky, her skin began to clear, the blackened, monstrous tongue grew smaller and retreated behind her teeth. Asa watched the changes without knowing quite what they meant. Considered for long enough, she went from pretty to plain back to pretty, and then settled into a kind of visually interesting that was in its way more compelling than beauty. It became possible to believe that a man such as Steppan might have his heart swept away by glancing at her at a fortunate moment and in the proper light. Her eyes shifted under their lids and she began to tremble like a child left too long in the cold.

When she gasped in her first real breath in hours, Asa started back like she'd shouted. Her eyes opened, bright and wild and uncomprehending, and a moment later, she laughed, deep and wild and satisfied. When she stretched, a half dozen stones fell from her blanket to the stone floor. Her gaze found Asa, and she lifted her chin, grinning like she was greeting a dear friend.

"Who are you?" she asked languorously.

"My name's Asa. We have someone in common."

"Do we?"

"Well, you don't know him, but yes."

She shook her head, blinking, and laughed again. It took a moment for her to bring her focus back, but she didn't seem fearful or prone to violence so much as drunk and happy. Asa sat at her feet.

"You saved me?"

"I did."

"Why?"

"For love."

"Of me?"

"No."

She shifted forward, wrapping herself with the blanket as an afterthought and with only partial success. Her hand found its way into Asa's, the fingers like frozen sticks. She was still very cold.

"Your friend, then?"

"Yes." The answer could have meant Steppan's love of her or Asa's love of him. Both would be true.

"You have saved me," Zelanie said softly, smiling her beatific smile.

"I did."

"Did you enjoy it?"

"Actually, yes. I like being clever, and I got to be very, very clever. So that part was nice at least."

She made a pleased hum and shifted forward. Her hair smelled of the river. Her mouth was soft and tasted of copper and dirt. When her hand slipped under Asa's clothes, the feeling of skin against skin was like pouring water on a burn. The longing to be touched—at first by Steppan but eventually by anybody—that had lain ignored so long rose up like the heat of summer. When Asa pulled back, she brought their twined fingers to her mouth.

"You're drugged."

"I am a bit, aren't I?"

"You aren't yourself."

"I'm not someone else." She lay back on the slate table, pulling them together as she did. Her hands tugged at the stays of Asa's cloak. "Anyway, how would you know who I am?"

"I'm . . . Before you do that. I may not be quite what you're expecting."

Her tongue—pink as pearls now—showed its tip between her teeth. "No? Let's find out."

A half dozen possible replies wrestled in Asa's mind—*Please stop* and *This is a terrible mistake* and *All right.* The stays came loose. Her hand moved gently. Asa's eyes closed.

"All right. Let's."

"You *bedded* her?" Steppan said. His eyes were wide, his mouth slack. His cheeks were actually gray with shock and horror.

It wasn't the only answer he could have made. Asa could think of at least a dozen others. *Did you enjoy it?* and *I'm so happy for you,* and, best wished for, *Wait for me next time.* But the prince's shock was profound and unfeigned. This was a thing he could never have imagined happening, though compared to a thousand other events in Sovereign North Bank in the last week alone, it was common as mud. All Asa's dreams and hopes vanished in that moment as if they had never been, a bubble popping. The beautiful man, desperate and noble and romantic, was a naive little boy, disgusted by anything he didn't expect. The pain was less powerful than the relief.

The cruel response floated on the back of Asa's tongue. *She's no more a virgin now than when you saw her the first time, you dunce.*

"Of course I didn't. I was joking."

"You were . . ." Steppan said, and let out a long, stuttering breath.

Color came back to his cheeks in two flaming circles of scarlet. They both laughed, but unknown to Steppan, they didn't laugh together.

"She's waiting at the Temple. The apothecary says she may be weak for a time. Days at least."

"We can bring her here," Steppan said. "Watch over her while she recovers."

Asa suppressed a grin. There was a terrible idea.

"I think not. There's another problem. One I hadn't foreseen. The priest knows who you are."

"How?" Steppan asked.

"Couldn't say. He slipped, and I pretended not to notice, but if he knows, others may also. Sovereign North Bank isn't safe for you. Not anymore. You and Zelanie have to flee, and tonight's better than morning."

Steppan's expression was solemn. He put a hand on Asa's shoulder. "Will you come with us?"

"Better that I do not. We're known companions. And in truth, my place is here."

"Then, thank you, my friend, for all you have done. I will remember you."

After Steppan left to reclaim his blade and introduce himself to his lover, Asa lit a fire in the little tin brazier. Through the thin walls, the sounds of voices filtered in as if from a thousand miles away. Someone was playing a mandolin. On the other side of the small room, the empty mattress still held the shape of Steppan's body. Asa rose, hauled it over, and stacked them. They were more comfortable that way.

Morning found Asa on the rooftops eating hot almonds from a rag pocket. To the east, the bridges of Nevripal went slowly dark as the night's torches were doused in anticipation of the dawn. Carriages lumbered down the riverside streets, the clatter of hooves and wheels barely audible across the water. One by one, the stars faded, giving way to blue. The sluggish breeze stank of coal smoke and rotting plants. Nearer in, the Salt was busy with bodies in rest or motion. The rope bridges teemed with people going from one place to another within Sovereign North Bank, as if the change of a few hundred yards would make any difference. The little city within a city didn't care, and it didn't judge, and of all its thousand aspects, that was what made Asa love it most of all.

Somewhere out there, Prince Steppan Homrey, fugitive heir of Lyria, and his beloved stranger Zelanie were likely fleeing his stepmother's assassins. Asa could only hope Zelanie was competent enough to see them through it. The sky was beautiful regardless.

Rouse's footsteps were slow, plodding, and unmistakable. He cleared his throat.

"Good morning, Chancellor."

"Friend Asa." The priest walked over and sat at Asa's side, squinting into the growing light. "I trust you're well."

"I don't know."

"No?"

Asa chuckled and held out the rag pocket. Rouse took a small handful of nuts and chewed them placidly. The poisoner unafraid of poisons after all.

"In the past few days, I have stolen a girl from the workhouses by killing her, hauling her body out of the river, and bringing her back to life; worked with an acknowledged mass murderer, no offense—"

"None taken."

"—to poison and enslave two agents of the law; and performed glorious if intoxicated sexual acts with my dearest friend's lover on a corpse table."

"Busy."

"It has occurred to me that I may not be a good person."

"I have no insight to offer on the question."

For a long moment, they were silent with their private thoughts.

"Love," Asa said, "is like a pigeon shitting over a crowd."

"How so?"

"Where it lands hasn't got much to do with who deserves it."

The priest made a deep sound in his throat and frowned. "I think you may be confusing love with a different kind of longing," he said, and Asa barked out a laugh. "You know why I've come."

"Your share of the workhouse money," Asa said, holding out a small purse. It clinked in Rouse's hand.

"You won't take offense if I count it," Rouse said.

"With me, friend? You'd be a fool not to."

Paul Cornell

British author Paul Cornell is a writer of SF and fantasy in novels, comics, and television, one of only two people to have Hugo Award nominations for all three media. His urban fantasy novel *London Falling* is out from Tor, and the sequel, *The Severed Streets,* was released in December. He's written *Doctor Who* for the BBC, and Batman and Robin for DC Comics. He's currently the writer of Marvel Comics' Wolverine. He's had short stories published in *Isaac Asimov's Science Fiction Magazine, Interzone,* and many anthologies.

The fast-paced and rather strange story that follows is one of a series of stories that Paul Cornell has been writing about the exploits of spy Jonathan Hamilton in the Great Game between nations in a nineteenth-century Europe where technology has followed a very different path from that of our own timeline, exploiting the ability to open and manipulate multidimensional folds in space—stories that read like Ruritanian romances written by Charles Stross, as Hamilton battles to prevent disaster in a flamboyantly entertaining fashion reminiscent of the adventures of James Bond, or, better, of Poul Anderson's Dominic Flandry, who may be his direct ancestor.

In this adventure, Hamilton finds himself locked in a life-or-death struggle with someone every bit as clever and dangerous as he is—himself.

A BETTER WAY TO DIE

Paul Cornell

Cliveden is one of the great houses of Greater Britain. It stands beside the Thames in Buckinghamshire, at the end of the sort of grand avenue that such places kept and made carriages fly up, when carriages were the done thing. In the extensive forests, a Grand Charles tree from the Columbian colonies has been grown into the shape of a guesthouse. The yew-tree walk leads down to a boathouse that has, painted on its ramp, dated, descending notches of where the water once rose, taken at the flood. The ramp has twice now been extended to reach the river. From the house itself, one can look out over the parterre to a 180-degree horizon of what were once flood meadows, now seamless farmland. The view of the other half of the world is that which one would expect of a hunting estate. There is a smooth, plunging hill, kept clear to present targets on the horizon, with trees either side, towards which the game can break. There are hides for beaters. There is a balcony that looks down on the yard, from which favors can be thrown and bloods scored. At certain times of the year you will hear the reports of guns, the calling of the hounds, and the sohos of those on the chase, unimpeded by fence or ditch. The gutters of the forecourt are there to catch the blood.

Hamilton often worked out of uniform, so he knew the great estates. They were where royalty risked a social life outside of their palaces, still requiring careful eyes beside them. They were where those individuals who had lost so much of their souls in the great game that they had actually changed sides were hauled. Houses like this were where such wretched people would be allowed to unburden themselves, their words helping to reset the balance that their actions had set swinging. Houses like this were also where officers like himself were interviewed following injury or failure. And finally, always finally, they were places from where such as he sometimes did not return. They were the index that ran alongside the London and abroad half of an out-of-uniform man's life, the margin in which damning notes were made. Such buildings were the physical manifestation of how these things had always been done, the plans of them a noble motto across the English countryside. Those words could be read even if your face was in the mud. Especially then. In the circumstances in which Hamilton now found himself, that thought reassured him. But still, he could not make himself ready to die.

He'd found the invitation on his breakfast table: the name of the estate and a date which was that same day. The handwriting was in the new style, which meant that no hand had been near it, that it had been spoken onto the card as if by God. He could not decide anything based upon it. Except that the confidence of this gesture indicated that, despite everything, those who had power over him still did not doubt who they were and what they could do.

He had picked it up with none of the anticipation he might once have felt, just a dull, resigned dread. This was the answer to a question he hadn't put into words. He had started to feel a deeper anger, nameless, useless, than any he had felt before. He knew what he was owed but had become increasingly sure he wouldn't receive it. The fact of his being owed it would be seen now as an impertinent gesture on his part, a burden on those who had invested elsewhere. He had one request now, he'd decided, looking at the card in his numb fingers: he would ask to be sent to contribute to some hopeless cause. But perhaps those were only to be found in the blockade now, and if they didn't want him, they especially wouldn't want him there. Still, he'd held on to that thought through dressing appropriately and packing for the country. But then even that hope had started to feel like treachery and cowardice. The condemned man must not have anything to ask of the executioner. That was the beginning of pleading.

And yet hope stayed with him. It played on him. His own balance ate at him as he prepared. A fool, he told himself, would assume he was on his way to Cliveden to be given what he was owed. To at least be thanked for all these years and given a fond farewell. He made sure he was not hoping for that.

Now he watched from the carriage as it swung down towards the avenue that led to Cliveden. He saw nobody in the grounds, not a single worker on the fields. That was extraordinary. Normally, they would be out there in numbers, waving to any carriage from their enormous harvesters and beaters and propulsion horses. Hamilton had no idea how many servants it took to maintain an estate like Cliveden, but it must be numbered in the hundreds. There would traditionally be too many, in fact, "a job for every man and several of those jobs are lounging about just in case" as some wag had put it. On the two occasions when he'd seen an officer die in such places, it had been done (in one case like an accident, in another, and that was a scene he'd take to his grave, like a suicide) in the grounds, away from the eyes of the help. You didn't need to clear them all out. But no, he stopped himself: surely this was just the larger version of what he'd seen at Keble? He was making new horrors for himself with no new evidence.

The carriage settled onto the end of the drive, and Hamilton stepped down onto the gravel. His knee spasmed and he nearly fell. Getting old. He wondered if they were watching this, and killed a thought that he didn't care. He did. He must. It had been an affectation to take a carriage, he realized, when, in moments, these days, he could have walked down a tunnel from his rooms in London. And he'd brought a valise, as if he were unwilling, should he need to dress for dinner, to return there in the same way to do so. He was silently making statements with these actions. Stubborn statements. Like he'd made, as if with the intention of ending his service, that night at Keble. This new realization angered him more than anything else had. Only fools and criminals didn't know why they did things. It seemed that he was no longer strong enough to hold that fate at bay. To arrive here as someone who bowed to the command of those other voices within one, to pain or desire or selfishness, to have allowed those threats to the balance to have grown within oneself, and to only realize it on this threshold . . . it was an invitation to the powers in this house to strike him down. And they would be right to do so.

He allowed himself to smile at the relief of that thought. *They would be right to do so.* If he could accept that, all would be well. He had brought the valise. He would not balk and desperately fly to return it, like a panicked undergraduate. If he suddenly did or said or hinted at anything not of his own volition, but that had come out of the other half of him that should be under his control, then the balance could still be restored at the cost of his life. He didn't have to worry about that.

But the thought still came to him: those with his life in their hands didn't seem to value the balance so much these days, did they?

That thought was like a far greater death that lay in wait.

If the world was tempting him into plucking at his own house of cards, it was because that was all everyone seemed to be doing now. He was hesitating on this drive, actually hesitating. He had seen his life as a house of cards.

Perhaps the world was dying too.

Perhaps everyone his age felt that.

But surely nobody had ever felt it in circumstances like these?

The carriage finally moved off. He made himself step forward, looking down at the valise now inescapably in his hand.

He found he had orders in his eyes. He wasn't to go into the house but into the forest.

He made his way down a winding path to the edge of the woods. It was overcast, but the shadows from inside the forest were slanting at impossible angles, as if somewhere in there someone was lighting a stage.

He walked into the forest.

The path took him past fallen trees, not long ago cut down, by a logger who was now absent. He stopped to listen. The sounds of nature. But no sawing, no distant echo of metal on wood, no great machines. Strange that the effect could be so complete.

He came to the edge of a clearing. Here was where the strange light was coming from. It seemed to be summer here because the light was from overhead. The air was warmer. Hamilton kept his expression steady. He walked slowly into the center, and saw the trees that shouldn't be here. He wanted to follow etiquette, but that was difficult when those one was addressing had abandoned propriety. It was as if they had grabbed the ribbon of his duty and then leapt down a well. He felt like bellowing at them. He felt awful that he felt like bellowing at them.

He addressed the tallest of the trees. "You wanted to see me, sir?"

It had been just a few weeks ago that he'd been invited to meet Turpin at Keble. His commanding officer had been a guest of the Warden, and had asked Hamilton to join him at High Table. This had seemed at the time the most natural thing in the world, Keble being where Hamilton himself had been an undergraduate. He'd driven down to Oxford as always, had the Porters fuss over the Morgan as always. He'd stopped for a moment outside the chapel, thinking about Annie, the terrible lack of her. But he could still look at the chapel and take pleasure in it. He'd been satisfied with his composure, then. At that time he'd already been on leave for several weeks. He should have realized that had been suspiciously long. And before that he'd been used for penny-ante jobs, sent on them by junior officers, not even allowed to return to the Dragoons, who were themselves on endless exercises in Scotland. He really should have understood, before it had been revealed to him, that he was being kept away from something.

It had been in the Warden's rooms at Keble that Turpin had first appeared in his life, all those years ago, had first asked him about working out of uniform. To some people, he'd said, the balance, the necessary moment-by-moment weighing and shifting of everything from military strength to personal ethics that kept war from erupting between the great nations and their colonies right across the solar system, was something felt, something in the body. This had been a couple of years before the medical theologians had got to work on how the balance actually was present in the mind. Hamilton had recognized that in himself. Turpin had already been then as Hamilton had always known him, his face a patchwork of grown skin, from where he'd had the corners knocked off him in the side streets of Kiev and the muck-filled trenches of Zimbabwe.

But on entering the Warden's rooms on this later occasion, after decades of service, Hamilton had found himself saluting a different Turpin. His features were smooth, all trace of his experience removed. Hamilton had carefully not reacted. Turpin hadn't offered any comment. "Interesting crowd this evening, Major," he'd said, nodding to indicate those assembled under the Warden's roof. Hamilton had looked. And that had been, now he looked back to it, the moment his own balance had started to slide dangerously towards collapse.

Standing beside the dress uniforms and the evening suits and the clerical collars had been a small deer.

It was not some sort of extraordinary pet. Its gaze had been following the movements of a conversation, and then it was taking part in it, its mouth forming words in a horribly human way. Hamilton had looked quickly over to where a swirl of translucent drapery had been chatting with the chaplain. Nearby, a circling pillar of . . . they had actually been continuously falling birds, or not quite birds, but the faux heraldic devices often displayed by the Foreigners whose forces were now encircling the solar system. He'd guessed that the falling was the point, rather than the . . . he'd wanted to call it a dress . . . being a celebration of the idea that the Foreigners might flock together and make their plans in great wheeling masses. The pillar held a glass of wine, supported somehow by all those shapes dropping past it. These creatures were all ladies, Hamilton had assumed. Or rather, hoped.

"It's all the rage at the Palace," said Turpin. "It's all relative this, and relative that."

Hamilton hadn't found it in him to make any sensible comment. He'd heard about such things, obviously. Enough to disdain them and move on to some other subject. That the new King had allowed, even encouraged this sort of thing, presumably to the continuing shame of Elizabeth . . . he'd stopped himself. He was thinking of the Queen, and he could not allow himself to feel so intimate with what she might or might not think of her husband.

"Not your sort of thing?" asked Turpin.

"No, sir."

Turpin paused a moment, considering, and offered a new tack. "The Bodlean is, I believe, now infinite."

"Good for it."

Turpin had nodded towards the corner. "So. What about him?"

He was indicating a young man, talking to a beautiful woman. Hamilton's first thought had been that he was familiar. Then he had realized. And had first found the anger that hadn't left him since. This was what downed Foreigner vessels had brought here. Of course it wouldn't all be used for frippery. Or perhaps now frippery had invaded war.

It had been like looking at the son he'd never had, at his own face without everything time had written on it. There was for a moment a ghost of a thought that they'd taken away from him that moment of seeing a son. That had been the first of the many ghosts.

The hair was darker. The body was thinner, more hips than shoulders. The boy had worn not uniform, but black tie, so they hadn't managed, or perhaps even wished, to get him into the regiment. The young woman the boy was talking to had nudged him, and he had looked towards Hamilton. It was the shock of running into a mirror. The eyes were the same. He hadn't known what his own expression had been in that instant, but the younger version of him had worn a smile as he made eye contact. It hadn't been in the slightest bit deferential. It wasn't attractive, either. But Hamilton had recognized it. He contained his anger, knowing that this boy would be able to read him like a book. Hamilton had had no idea that such things were now possible. This must be a very secure gathering, for the two of them to be seen together. The boy had expected this. He had been allowed that.

He had turned back to his superior officer with a raised eyebrow. "Who's the girl?"

Turpin had paused for a moment, pleasingly, taken aback by Hamilton's lack of comment about the boy. "Her name is Precious Nothing."

"Parents who like a challenge?"

"Perhaps it was a *memento mori.* She's—"

"With the College of Heralds, yes." Hamilton had seen the colors on her silk scarf, which was one hell of a place to put them.

"Well, only just about, these days. She's a senior Herald, but she's been put on probation."

"Because of him." Hamilton found the idea of a Herald being linked to such a peculiar creature as the boy utterly startling. Heralds decided what breeding was, what families and nations were. The College held the records of every family line, decided upon the details of coats of arms, were the authority on every matter of grand ceremony and inheritance. Of course, every other week now one heard rumors that the College was on the verge of dissolution or denunciation, as they tried and failed to find some new way to protest at the new manners. They seemed continually astonished that His Majesty was being advised this badly. Some of this conflict had even reached the morning plates. But it had always gone by the evening editions. To Hamilton, the idea of parts of the body public fighting each other was like the idea of a man's punching himself in the face. It was a physical blasphemy that suited this era as an index of how far it had all gone.

"You really haven't another word to say about him?" Turpin had asked, interrupting his woolgathering.

Hamilton had feigned a moment's thought. "How is he on the range?"

"Reasonable. You were only ever reasonable." He hadn't emphasized the *you*.

Then the Warden had clinked his glass with a spoon, and the ladies and the gentlemen and the *trompe l'oeil* and the small deer had gone in to dinner.

Hamilton had been relieved to find that the younger version of himself had gone to the far end of the dining table that stood on a rise at the end of the hall. In any other circumstances, it would have been comforting to be back in this place, with the smell of polish and the candlelight, but as he looked out at the tables of undergraduates, he realized that something was missing. There would normally be numerous servants moving between the rows, delivering plates of food and refilling glasses. Suddenly, he saw just such a meal appearing beside one chattering youth, something that caused the lad no surprise whatsoever. Hamilton had been seated opposite Turpin, and now he looked back to him.

"Hidden service," the senior man said. "Happens in a lot of places now. The servants move through an infinite fold, in effect an empty optional world, beside the real one. One more use for the new engines. And neater, you must admit."

Hamilton didn't feel the need to agree with such young opinions from his old mentor. He was now wondering if the man's new smoothness of face was because this was also a younger version. But no, surely not, here was still the experience, the tone of voice he was used to. Turpin had seen that look. "One of the out-of-uniform men found it for me," he said, as if he was talking about a carriage. "As soon as the great powers recognized that various of the engines that had fallen into our hands gave us access to optional worlds, outside the balance, the Palace felt it was our lot's duty to start mapping them, to find out where all these open-fold tunnels lead. Our regimental hunting parties have been going all over."

Hamilton thought he understood now why he hadn't been included in that effort. "Including another one of you?"

"Several. The original owner of this was only a Newton or so different to the original. Well, in physical terms. Where he came from, a lot of our conflicts didn't happen, hence the smoothness of face. Our lads put him in the bag, and when they got back, connected his mind to an infinite tunnel. Like using a terrier to root out a fox. Once he was out, I moved in, using the same method. Should keep me going for a bit longer."

Hamilton had found himself wondering at that statement. His balance had been thrown by the boy, and so he'd allowed himself the seditious thought because it had felt not so dangerous then, that Turpin was seeking not, as he said, an extension of his service but actually tactical advantage at Court. He was now more like those he served were. And never mind the distance that took him from his officers. "What if optional worlds start raiding us in the same way?"

"First thing we thought of. We seem to be unique, at least in all those options nearby. We're the only ones who've encountered the Foreigners. Or they may even only exist in this world. If they do start popping over, we may have to start making treaties with optional Britains rather than raiding them."

"And extending the balance into them?"

Turpin had raised his hands. Perhaps he felt this was beyond his duty or understanding.

"How can there be younger versions of people? How is there an optional world where . . . I'm . . . his age?"

"These worlds form in waves, I'm told."

"Like the waves that interfere with each other in this world to create the heights and depths of the balance?"

"Presumably." There had been that impatience with the matter of the balance once more. "Some waves are a bit behind us in time, some a bit forward."

"And there are some options where there are chatty deer and pillars of birds? Or are those just fashions anticipating such stuff?"

"A little bit of both. There's a rather large selection box, all told." Turpin had leaned forward, as if wishing Hamilton would get to the meat of it. And Hamilton had been pleased that it hadn't been him that had taken them there. "Listen, that younger you, he's the first of his kind to be brought over. He's got nobody's mind but his own. He's a whole chap, a volunteer from a world so like ours that there wasn't an iota of difference."

"Except no Foreigners?"

"Exactly."

"And no balance?"

"Yes, yes!"

Hamilton had wondered if Turpin was planning on putting his mind in the boy's skull. But he'd hardly have invited them both to a social occasion first. "If we can do all this now, and I didn't know we could—"

"I'm telling you now under a seal. You'll find, if you look, that your covers have already reacted to my tone of voice. You won't be able to tell anyone any of this." He looked suddenly chagrined at Hamilton's startled look. "Not that you *would,* of course!"

Turpin's manners seemed to have changed with his new body. That had been shocking too, a shock like one felt sometimes at things one had heard were said and done at Court. "If we can do all this now we've got their engines, why can't the Foreigners open a tunnel at the blockade, pop up in Whitehall and have at us?"

"Good question. The great powers have been pondering that. Together." Enough had been made public for Hamilton to understand that there was now a significantly greater degree of cooperation between the courts of the great powers of Europe. The arrival of the Foreigners had forced that, when the haphazard capture of the new engines in various parts of the solar system might otherwise have set the balance rocking. There, he suspected, was the hand of the deity in this. If it was anywhere. "The leading theory at the moment is that, for some reason, the Foreigners forbid, among themselves, the use of optional worlds. That it's a principle of whatever mistaken religion they practice. Optionalism is perhaps just a side effect of what they use as propulsion, but so far we've only made sense of the side effect, and none at all of the propulsion."

"Can we use it to surprise *them*?"

"Working on just that."

This was far more the sort of conversation Hamilton had been used to with his commanding officer. He had found himself regretting his earlier reactions, understanding them, regaining control of himself. Tonight, whatever else it was, was surely planned as a test of his character, and so far he had just about stumbled through. What he *felt* about anything was as beside the point now as it had always been.

Turpin had spent the rest of dinner sounding him out about the myriad aspects of the shared defense strategies being adopted by the "grand alliance" of great powers. There was some new addition to their ranks every day. Savoy, most recently. There were even rumors the Turks were going to join. Hamilton had wanted to ask where the balance was in all this. What was going to happen to it if every nation was on the same side? Was the arrival of the Foreigners and their engines, at the same time, the fatal shock, the final moment when the balance would collapse and resolve into some new social or actual reality, as experts in the matter had often hypothesized? Was that what was happening all around them now? He had always conceived of that moment as being grand, somehow, and not a matter of finding wild animals in the Warden's rooms. Or was this just some particularly ferocious swinging of the pendulum, which would resolve itself, as it always had, into a gentler motion?

But Turpin, true to his new form, hadn't mentioned the balance at all, apart from when he'd joined in the grace before the meal. Hamilton had half hoped one of the divines would strike up a debate on the subject. He had known, through the gossip of his maid, Alexandria, that all was not well among the clergy, that the next synod at York was going to be rough on His Majesty and his terrifying commonwealth of nations, but there was no sign of that here. These particular clerics were as content to swim among this stuff as that Herald had been.

All through the conversation, Hamilton had kept his gaze on his superior. He hadn't wanted to be seen craning his neck to get a look at the younger version of himself. He had continued to affect nonchalance. And hoped he was not projecting affectation. The bell had rung, the students had started to exit, and the Warden had invited his guests back to his rooms for brandy. Turpin had announced that he wanted to talk to someone and gone ahead.

As Hamilton had entered, the younger man had stepped straight to intercept him. Precious was with him. She had had an interested look on her face. Turpin had already got to the other side of the room, thank God, so there had been nobody to attempt some sort of crass introduction. But Hamilton had known his superior officer's gaze would be upon him now. He still hadn't known what was expected of him. But if this was a game, he was going to win it.

"Major," said the youth. "I can't tell you how much I've been looking forward to this moment."

"I wish I could say the same." That had come out like an insult. So he had kept his jaw firm and damn well let it stand. "Where did they find you?"

The youth had seemed unperturbed. "Oh, in some dusty corridor of what one might still call reality."

"This year's model." Hamilton couldn't help but look at Precious rather than at his younger self. She was looking back at him too. He wondered in how many ways she was comparing them.

"Most people would be full of questions," said the youth.

"It's the nature of innocence to question, the nature of duty to accept."

"And it's the nature of age to be too sure of itself." The boy had been ready to get angry if he felt he had to. He seemed very conscious of his honor. Sure he was being looked at too. Which was why Hamilton had poked him on the nose just then, to see his control, or lack of it. That rationalization, horribly, had come to Hamilton only after the fact.

Perhaps that was the point of this, to see which of them displayed the most grace? Had the boy been told what fate might await him if he failed whatever test this was? Could it be that Hamilton was, after all, being allowed to inspect his new . . . vehicle? Or was this his replacement? He couldn't let himself dwell on that possibility. Hamilton had instead turned politely to Precious. She was petite, with long red hair set off by a green evening dress that . . . yes, the influence of the optional was here too, the dress had been, or still was, a sunlit meadow. To be in her presence wasn't so much to see it as to be in the presence of it. She was used to being looked at and sought it. Her freckles didn't look girlish on her, but somehow added to the passionate seriousness of those eyes, which held an expression of tremendous interest, a challenge to the world that equaled that of her dress. She had a welcoming mouth. "So," he'd said, "where did you meet me?"

She'd smiled, but she hadn't laughed. "We were introduced at the College of Heralds. Colonel Turpin brought him to visit. But I note that *we* haven't been."

"You'll have to forgive me. I assumed we had already shared . . . a degree . . . of intimacy."

He'd wondered if she would bristle at that. But she had smiled instead of being offended. Still, it had been a forced smile. She wasn't quite on board for the anything goes of the new manners, then. Still a Herald at heart. Hamilton had found something he liked in her. Which should have come, he supposed, as no surprise.

"Why do you think," the boy asked, "that Turpin wanted us to meet?"

"Perhaps he's deciding on a suit, and wants to see both tried on." He had looked back to Precious, as if suggesting she might be doing the same thing. She'd just inclined a fine eyebrow.

The boy had stepped between them then. He had decided on both a need to bring this intangible contest into the physical world and a way to do it. "Tell me, Major," he said, "do you play cards?"

The Warden, no doubt encouraged by Turpin, had quickly warmed to the notion of a game. The select crowd, who had doubtless now realized what they were looking at when they looked between Hamilton and his younger self, had been intrigued, had talked at the top of their voices about it. He supposed, as the cards were prepared and he'd looked again at the throng, that there were clusters of people like this across Greater Britain now, in the most fashionable salons, changing their shapes and their ages and their appearances and the balance be hanged, and from now on they would all be grabbing at the novel and the extreme like they were bloody Icelandic. Perhaps the blockade had done this. Perhaps they were all starting to dance as the ship went down.

The game, someone had decided, should be clock seconds. Neither he nor the boy knew it. Which again, Hamilton supposed, was no accident. They had each taken a hand of ten from a new deck, one of a series being placed on the table. Hamilton took a glass of comfort while he was at it, a Knappogue Castle, from the Tullamore distillery, a pure pot still whiskey. Nothing served here or at High Table would be the kind of thing that the covers in his head could shrug off. That was the whole point of evenings like this. To get at the reality, that had been the thought, he supposed, back when those invited here had been interested in that. So now he was accepting a disadvantage. The boy, of course, had had to do the same, and, despite Precious's warning glance, had taken the same measure.

The idea was to form tricks of differing value by discarding cards and picking new ones from another pack. But the nature of what constituted a legal trick changed depending on the time, each ten-minute arc on the Warden's gilt bronze clock deciding the rules at that given moment. There was also a time limit of a few seconds on how long they could take to play a hand, so one couldn't just sit there waiting until the terrain became favorable. So, Hamilton had realized as they waited for nine o'clock to chime on the chapel bell, one could either hold on to cards for long-term advantage, or keep burning one's fuel steadily, playing the averages instead of waiting for some huge coup. Time and meaning in this game were freakishly interconnected. A somewhat garish intelligent projection of the rules was thrown onto the wall behind them, startling the deer. The projection had all the washes of color and blurred lines that suggested a courtier who was paying too much attention to His Majesty's aesthetic tastes. It was said that the look of the ballroom at Hampton Court now changed depending on where you were in it, often just a blur of movement, as if it were seen from a carriage. Several ladies had already fallen as a result during one of the new dances, which had all struck Hamilton as being graceless gallops where the tempo was continually changing, people might collide at any moment, and it would be hard to tell where anyone was. They had been quick to blame their own shortcomings rather than question he whose perspective made all this. And well they should, of course that was the way they had to behave, what was Hamilton thinking? He had chided himself again.

They had taken up their initial hands. The boy had made eye contact with him again. No smile now. The obvious thing would be for Hamilton to underestimate him. He would not do that. That would be to lie about himself. He had let his eyes move upwards from his seated opponent, and linger, for a moment, where they should not.

"What are you looking at?" asked the boy, without turning to look.

"Nothing," Hamilton had said, and had glanced back to his cards with a precisely calculated raise of his eyebrow.

* * *

In the first ten-minute round, Hamilton had surged ahead, his opponent failing to score while he put down some obvious, simple tricks. The boy seemed to always be waiting for something that was just one card away. Hamilton had recognized that in himself. That had been something that the service had beaten out of him.

A cheer and the Warden chiming spoon on glass had marked the end of the round, and the boy had immediately thrown down what he'd had but couldn't previously score from, putting him in the lead and generating another cheer with the flourish of it. Hamilton had wondered if there were any in this crowd who were favoring him, or if to those who came to a party dressed as a mirage, the older version of an individual would be automatically the less interesting. He'd looked again to Precious and thought he caught something in her expression. Why did he feel she wasn't quite of that opinion? She was biting her bottom lip, her eyes large with the excitement of the game. He'd turned back to the boy. "You know your fables?" he said, to conceal something that was brewing in his cards. "Slow and steady wins the race."

"Yes, the Greeks would be keen on this game." And he'd thrown down the first of a series of quick payoffs, building up a steady lead, trying to force Hamilton to bet on something that might never happen. "It's full of transformations."

"Yet hardly classical."

"What's seen as classical changes with time, just like anything else."

So he seemed to share the opinions that had made his arrival here possible. Or to be willing to join in the chorus, at least. But surely he might feel as if he were still a slave, a chattel taken by a raiding party from an invaded province? There was, after all, something of that in Hamilton himself. Hamilton had risked a glance at Turpin and decided to raise the temperature. "Shall we make it interesting?" Having heard how finely cut the boy's accent was, he had let a little Irish back into his own.

"How much?"

Hamilton had tried to remember what would have broken his bank in his twenties. Not that much less than what would now. Or was that his memory distorting time again? He didn't want to quote something that the boy would consider a trifle. Still, the value of money hadn't changed much over the years, just his concept of what sufficed. "A thousand guineas?" The onlookers made shocked noises. Hamilton had realized his mistake immediately. It looked like he was bullying the boy. Precious was shaking her head at the young man, urging him to throw in his cards. "Or, no, perhaps not, let's say—"

"A thousand guineas." The boy had been roused by that. Of course he had. Hamilton had baited him in front of his girl.

He'd have done the same at that age if Annie were here, might have done the same now. He wouldn't humiliate his younger self by backtracking now. "All right, then."

The next three rounds seemed to go by in a flash. Hamilton and the boy had barely looked up as they drew, considered, threw in, the Warden calling the scores as they did so. Aces were high or low. The order of the court cards, to gasps from a few of those assembled who under pressure revealed a more traditional turn of mind, changed too. And the Ambassador, the Horse and the Devil could sometimes raise or lower the values of the numerals in Cups, Swords, Staves, and Coins.

With eleven minutes to go, everyone had surrounded the table where Hamilton and the boy were sweating, looking to their hands and then to each other, grabbing and throwing down, faster and faster. Hamilton was considering how hard it would be for him to take a loss of a thousand. It would mean selling something, perhaps the Morgan. He could deal with that pressure because of his experience, his training. The boy would have the surety and indestructibility of youth, but he had more to lose. His life, even, if he couldn't pay, or if whatever he had here instead of a family or a regiment decided his existence wasn't worth the expenditure. Perhaps his life, at least as a mind in his own body, was dependent, even, on the larger game they were playing tonight, whatever it might be. Hamilton had put aside a twinge of conscience. That was why he'd done this, wasn't it? Not to harm the boy but to put him off his game. Or *was* that the whole of it? Then he cursed himself for losing his concentration in that second, as he saw, as he threw his hand down, that he could have kept some of those cards a moment more for much greater reward. The crowd cheered at the arrival of the last round and the last rule change. The boy was ahead, marginally. He was barely considering each hand before he threw it in, and now he didn't have to think about what might be round the corner. They had turned the last bend and were sprinting for the finish line. Hamilton decided that the only way to go was to match him for speed, glimpsing the best hand, throwing in, hoping for better, hoping to push the boy that way too. The Warden shouted the score more and more swiftly. Fumbling fingers on cards became an issue. Hamilton drew level, and had found that all he had in the final seconds was luck. It wouldn't be the first time he'd thrown himself on her mercy. He saw that he had tens of each suit, not the best hand and not the worst, and threw it down with just a moment left to play. The boy had looked at his own hand . . . and seemed to freeze. Hamilton could see his fingers trembling. Was he waiting, deliberately prolonging the misery? He himself had often been cruel, when a job had given him license to. The clock hand had thumped round the final three seconds . . . two . . . Hamilton was just a point ahead, surely the boy must have something? The boy fumbled with the cards and threw down his whole hand with a shout and the chimes of the chapel bell rang out across the room and the Warden rang his glass in unison and everyone had immediately leaned forward to see—

The boy had had nothing. He could have made nothing. And now he was staring at Hamilton, and Precious had stepped forward to defend him, her face furious, never mind that all tradition called for her to move in the opposite direction. And now, like a father, Hamilton had suddenly found he agreed.

"I'm satisfied," Hamilton had begun, "I'll just take one good bottle of—"

"Don't you dare!" bellowed the boy. "Don't you *dare*! I will pay what I owe!" And his voice had been fully Irish now, the sound that Hamilton heard often in his own thoughts and rarely in his speech. And with that the lad had leapt to his feet and marched out, without properly taking his leave or thanking his host. Precious had stared after him, outraged with the world. But she had not had the indecency in her to follow.

There had been only a brief silence before chatter had filled it.

Hamilton had looked over to the Warden, who was awkwardly closing the plate he'd used to keep the score. He didn't meet Hamilton's glance. There didn't seem to be much joy in the room at what had happened. It wasn't that this crowd had been on the younger man's side, as such. But there was a sense of something broken. It was as if these people had suddenly discovered, upon being shaken, that a lot had changed, within them and without, and they didn't know what to cheer for anymore.

Hamilton had got to his feet and taken a last sip from his glass. He had been pleased, despite everything, to find, a moment later, that Precious had joined him.

"He didn't deserve it," she said.

"No, he didn't. But *deserve* is very rarely in it."

Around them, the party had been breaking up. Farewells were being said. And now Turpin had chosen his moment to wander over. He had placed his hand on Hamilton's shoulder. Hamilton wasn't sure if he remembered his superior officer's ever touching him before. Precious had stepped quickly away.

"Bad show," Turpin had said very quietly.

"I'm sorry, sir. I assumed this was a contest."

"You didn't have to force him into a choice between bankruptcy and disgrace. I was hoping our young Herald here might be led, through her closeness to the lad, to begin a new trend in her College, to bring more of them towards His Majesty's point of view. Win or lose, she'd have felt more taken with him, having seen him prove his mettle. But now she'll be unable to see him and retain her position." Turpin had looked over to where Precious stood, her face, now she thought she was unobserved, betraying a sort of calculation, as if she was working out propriety against length of time waited before she went after the boy. Then he had looked again to Hamilton, shook his head, and gone to take leave of his host.

And, until that card on his breakfast table, that was the last Hamilton had heard from him. Hamilton had said good night to his host, left the Warden's rooms, and gone to the door of the Chapel. And he had found, in the despair that was already sinking into his stomach, that that building was now a horror to him after all.

And now he was here at Cliveden, addressing what he only knew were his superior officer, and an Equerry of the Court of Saint James's, and the Crown Secretary of Powers, because the orders in his eyes told him so. They were presumably still back in London, in Turpin's office off Horseguards Parade, or at least part of them was. They were wearing the trees, far across their nation, with no more thought than one might wear a coat.

"Good afternoon, Major." Turpin's voice came from the air around him. "I'm sorry to say . . . we have a job for you."

The sheer relief made Hamilton unable to speak for a moment. "A . . . job, sir?"

"You seem, during your encounter with him, to have fathomed the character of your younger self. Just as His Majesty wished you to." That was the Equerry. There would have been a time when the former Queen Mother would have seen to such matters herself, but now she never left her wing of the Palace, and was rumored to be . . . Hamilton found himself letting the thought breathe in his mind, his relief giving him license . . . people said she was mad now.

"I didn't realize I was acting on His Majesty's service, sir." He hoped his tone didn't convey the knowledge he was sure they both shared, that His Majesty had known as much about it as he had.

"That was of course as he wished. And he wishes to convey that you did well."

"The younger man," Turpin added, "should have dealt better with the pressure you put him under. It was the first sign of what was later revealed." He had a sound in his voice that Hamilton hadn't heard before. He was cornered, apologetic.

"The Palace offered to cover his debt to you," said the tree that was the Crown Secretary, "but, in his pride, the boy refused. We took this as a noble gesture and tried again, made it clear the offer was serious." Hamilton could imagine that whatever pressure he himself had subjected the youth to would be as nothing compared to the Palace's "making something clear."

"Then," continued Turpin, "he suddenly declared he had the funds. I asked him where he had got them. He told me he'd won at cards. But he was clearly lying. Shortly afterwards I had the pleasure of receiving a surprise visit at my office from His Grace the Earl Marischal, the Duke of Norfolk, on official business as officer of arms at the College of Heralds. He told me that a thousand guineas had gone missing from the College's account at Cuits."

He had taken exactly the right amount of money. Hamilton felt perversely annoyed at the association between the boy's amateurishness and himself. "Did Precious do that for him?" The Herald hadn't seemed capable of such foolishness. Was his younger self really that alluring? It was too tempting a thought to be true.

"Perhaps it was done with information from her, but without her knowledge," said Turpin. "His Grace also informed me that the Herald herself had gone missing. Our people inspected her rooms and found signs of a struggle, and a rather shoddy attempt to conceal those signs. The boy himself did not report when instructed."

By now Hamilton had gone beyond feeling impugned by association, and was finding it difficult to conceal his satisfaction. So their golden boy had gone rogue. "Needless to say," he said, "he hasn't paid me."

"I daresay Precious caught him with his hand in the till. An infinite fold had been opened up in her rooms some hours before our people arrived. We found traces of it. We're able to some degree to keep track of where such tunnels end up. Our quarry has fled here, to Cliveden."

"Why?"

"There is . . . a newly laid complex of fold tunnels on this estate," said the Equerry, sounding almost apologetic about his Court's fashions. "His Majesty was . . . is still . . . planning to summer here, among the optional worlds of his choosing. The College is . . . still . . . privy to such sensitive information. Your younger self, Major, is hiding in some optional version of these woods."

The Crown Secretary cleared his throat and there was silence. "His

Majesty," he said, "remains intrigued by the concept of bringing optionals into our service. He is minded to wonder if their numbers might serve against the blockade. He would need good reasons to turn aside from this policy. But he is alive to the possibility that such good reasons might be provided."

Hamilton inclined his head. He had been told all outcomes were still allowed. That if he was to bring an astonished youth out of the bushes, protesting a misunderstanding, the boy would be listened to, though possibly that conversation would take place in Cliveden's cellars. Well, then. He had a job to do. He put down his valise and opened it, then wormed his hand quickly through the multiple folds to find his Webley Collapsar and shoulder holster.

"We're keeping a watch on the boundaries," said Turpin. "We've narrowed the realities around him so he can't get out." The quality of light in the clearing changed, and Hamilton was aware that something had been done to the covers in his eyes. "We were trying these out on the boy, soon to be standard issue. It'll enable you to see all the optional worlds around you and move between them, just as he can."

Hamilton finished strapping on his holster, slipped the gun into it, and replaced his jacket. He felt what he had to do to use the new covers and did so. Suddenly, there were people in the clearing, right beside him. He went back to the previous setting, and they vanished again. He'd seen some of the laborers and farmhands, those who kept the estate going. They were, presumably, the least entertaining option for His Majesty and his friends to explore.

"Enter the folds here," said Turpin, "bring back the boy and the Herald, alive if you can." And those last three words had been delivered in a tone that privately suggested to his covers that, as far as Turpin was concerned, all Hamilton's options did indeed remain open. He hadn't seen fit to replace Hamilton's sidearm with any less deadly weapon, after all. These courtiers might not have the military knowledge to be aware of such a decision made through omission. Hamilton looked at the trees giving him orders. The question of what was owed to him because of his service had collapsed into the simplicity of that service continuing. They had all assumed, after all, that he would do his duty. His thoughts of death at their hands had become something from an optional world. He turned and headed into the forest.

"Godspeed, Major," said the Equerry.

Hamilton didn't look back. After a moment, he began to run.

He looked at the map of the estate in his head. He jogged from tree to tree, changed his eyes for a moment, was suddenly lost again. He made himself keep checking the options. He couldn't afford to let the boy take him by surprise.

Had his younger self done this dishonorable thing because the balance wasn't an idea that had been discovered in the optional worlds? That must be what His Majesty was considering, the idea that there was no army to be raised because his putative subjects from those worlds wouldn't have the required ethical fiber. Perhaps in those worlds the balance simply didn't exist, an indication that those places were less real than this world. Or perhaps the balance spread out somehow across all the worlds, perhaps that was how it endured so many shocks. Perhaps it was simply ambient and hard to fathom in his younger self's existence. He wondered what the boy, therefore, had judged himself against, in his formative years. Did this lack excuse him? It was hard to say whether or not the same rules should apply. If everything was real, if value itself was relative, what did it mean here and now to be an arms dealer, to wear a tartan, to abuse the flag, if those doing so could easily go somewhere else, where different rules applied? That might have been the boy's feeling on being made that miraculous offer of advancement, honor, the interest of a pretty woman, from somewhere aside from his own world. He had, presumably, been dragged from it in the night and had his new horizons made clear to him, over weeks, perhaps months. And if this new world included this strange custom, this desperate ideal about the preservation of order in the face of collapse, well, when in Rome . . .

But Turpin had said the boy's world was like ours in almost every detail if set a few years back along the wave. And yet they didn't have the balance. The idea that they could get along without it, that their great powers had, presumably through mere accident, in his world still preserved the status quo enough for consciousness and society . . . well, there was a subversive tidbit. No wonder Turpin felt a little vulnerable at having opened that door. No wonder he himself seemed to be leaning less and less on the balance.

Hamilton chided himself. These musings were not appropriate when in the field. He found his bearings in the forest as it stood, if anything could be said to stand on its own now. He quartered it and, moving as silently as he could, explored the territory down to the river, all the angles of the estate. He found nobody.

He used the covers in his eyes to move to the next nearest option after the servants' world. This would be one of those chosen for His Majesty's sport.

The house was much the same, with a few minor architectural differences. A flag with some sort of meaningless symbol flew over it. Hamilton didn't want to know what it meant. He quartered the ground again, and found only some old men in a uniform he didn't recognize and some young women in entertainingly little. Presumably that situation would get more extraordinary as the season arrived. He wondered if ladies would be brought here, or if they would be offered their own options of tea and mazes.

He changed his eyes again, and this time when he searched he found Columbians walking the paths, that quaint accent that reminded him of watching Shakespeare. These people, as he crouched nearby and listened to them pass, spoke with a horrid lack of care, as if there was nobody to judge them, no enemy opposing them. Some of them would know of the interest of a King in their world, some would surely not. For His Majesty to venture into any of even these carefully chosen worlds should be for him to go on safari, into territory that was not his own. And yet the choice was everything, wasn't it? These worlds must be utterly safe. Unless one of them had the boy in it.

He searched through several worlds. He kept all their meanings at bay. He considered where he would go if he were in the boy's shoes, and in so considering realized there must be something he was missing . . .

because he couldn't imagine coming here at all. He finally found, among the dozen or so options, somewhere empty. There was no house visible through the trees, the river was in a different place, the height of where he stood above sea level was different, and yet, according to the bare information about where he was on the globe that his covers insisted upon, he was in the same place. He looked around slowly, made sure he was hidden from all angles. Not only was the house gone, there were no houses on the plain, as far as he could see. And there was something . . . something extraordinary about—

"So they did send you." The voice was his own. It came from up the hillside.

Hamilton couldn't see its source. He stepped to put the trunk of a tree between it and himself. He took the Webley Collapsar from its holster.

"Where's the Herald?" he called.

"You won't find her—"

That told Hamilton she wasn't right there beside him. He dropped to his knee as he swung out from the tree, his left hand on his pistol wrist, and fired at the voice. The report and the whump of the round going off made one sound. And then there was another, a crash of branches as the boy broke cover. Hamilton leapt out and fired twice more at the sound, foliage and undergrowth compacting in instants, momentary pulses of gravity sucking at his clothes, newly focused light dazzling him like a line of new stars blossoming and then gone in a moment.

Without looking for a result, he swung back behind the tree. Then he listened.

The movement had stopped. Of course it had. He wouldn't have kept moving. He'd have lain there for a few moments, then lain there a bit longer.

He heard small movements from up the hill. With these rounds, it was likely that if the boy was still alive, he was also unwounded. He began to slowly make his way through the trees, making sure he also wasn't going to be where the boy had last placed him. As he walked, he started to wonder about his surroundings. There was indeed something very strange about this empty world. He'd sometimes heard, at parties, at Court, back when he'd been invited, the sort of people who had nothing better to do talking about the glories of nature, about some mysterious poetic energy that looking at the simplicity of it could inspire in them. Hamilton thought, and had once ill-advisedly said, that nature wasn't simple at all, that the billions of edges and details and angled surfaces in any view of it were the essence of complexity, much more so than any of the artifacts of civilization. To him, nature was cover, and all the better for its detail. Liz . . . Her Royal Highness . . . had made some joke on that occasion to cover the fact that he'd just bluntly contradicted the French ambassador.

But here was some strange feeling of glory. The trees all around him, the undergrowth he was paying such attention to as he stepped through it, it all seemed to be shouting at him. The colors seemed too bright. Was this some flaw in his covers? No. This was too complete. But it wasn't about simplicity. The objects he saw nearby, even the river glimpsed down there, they were all . . . there was more detail than he was used to. He recalled a time when he'd injured one of his corneas, the fuzziness of view in one eye, until they'd grown and fitted a new one. It was like he'd suffered from something like that all his life, and now he could see better. God, it would be good to be able to stay here. Such relief and rest would be his.

No. These were dangerous thoughts.

There was a noise ahead of him and he brought the gun up. But he swiftly saw what it was. A fox was staring at him from between two bushes. Of course, he'd been downwind of it, and it had turned to face him in that instant. Better luck than he'd ever had on the hunt. But the eyes on this thing, the sheen of its fur, the intensity of every strand, that he could see from here . . .

The fox broke the instant and ran.

Something in the world broke with it and Hamilton hit the ground hard, realizing in that moment that his eardrums were resounding and being glad they were resounding because that meant he was still alive, and he threw himself aside as the soil and leaves still fell around him and were sucked suddenly sideways, and he was rolling down the hill, crashing into cover and grabbing the soil to stop himself before the noise had died.

The boy had nearly had him. The boy had the same gun. Of course he had.

He lay there, panting. Then he lay there some more. The boy couldn't be sure he was here or he'd have fired by now. He wondered, ridiculously, for a moment, about the life of the fox. He killed the thought and started to push himself forward on his elbows. He realized, as he did so, that he wasn't injured. This might come down to a lucky shot. It was a contest of blunderbusses and balloons.

He felt, oddly, that it was apt his life should come to this. Then he killed that thought too. It would be more bloody apt if his life came to this then continued after the death of the other fellow.

"You could just stay here." That was the boy again, hard to trace where it was coming from beyond the general direction. He'd placed himself somewhere that the sound was broken, some trees close together, a rock wall.

Hamilton kept looking. "Why do you say that?"

"Don't you know where you are?"

"An optional Britain."

"Hardly, old man." The affectations he'd lost along the way. "It's not a country at all if there's nobody in it."

"I presume His Majesty has been in it. And probably found good hunting."

"As well he might. In heaven."

Hamilton grinned at the oddness of that. "How do you make that out?" It felt like the boy wanted to debate with his father. Wanted to test the bars of his cage. Perhaps he'd felt like that, at that age, but his own father's failure had meant he never felt able to, or perhaps had never felt the need. A place where there was no identity for him and no reason to do anything? More like the hell with no balance that the boy came from.

"It's more . . . real . . . than where either of us are from. And I say it's obviously heaven, because nobody got here."

Hamilton had heard the smile in his voice. "Except us. Are you sure it's not the other place?" A curious thought came to him. "Is that why you want me to stay?"

"I mean that if I went back, they wouldn't search in here. You could wait a few days, go anywhere you want."

Hamilton grimaced at that lack of meaning in the boy's life. "You think I'd abandon my duty?" He had a vision for a moment of being replaced in his life by the younger man. It felt like an invasion of himself. But also there was the frightening feel of temptation to it.

"I wouldn't dream of suggesting that, old man." He meant it too. "I mean you could take advantage of this game. They need one of us to die, so . . ."

Where had he got that idea? Turpin would have liked to see the boy hauled back as a trophy, but the Palace was decidedly lukewarm on the matter, and Hamilton couldn't see any way in which any of the interested parties would be satisfied with the boy, rather than himself, emerging from the forest. "Who told you that?"

A pause. "Are you trying to lie to me?"

"I wouldn't dream of it . . . old man. I'm just here to bring you back." The boy might assume that Hamilton had been given covers he had not, lies that could fool ears that could detect lies. Or he might know whatever he had in his head was in advance of anything Hamilton had as standard issue. But they knew each other's voices too well.

There was a sound from a direction Hamilton didn't expect. He turned, but he made himself do it with his gun lowered. There stood the boy. He had his gun lowered too. Hamilton stepped towards him. He allowed himself to make the first honest eye contact he'd had with his younger self. To see that face looking open to him was truly extraordinary, a joy that needed to be held down, a kindness worth crossing the waves that held worlds apart. He took a deep breath of an air that was indeed better than any he'd tasted. Whether or not this was heaven, he could imagine His Majesty walking in it and its giving him ideas of what should belong to him, of hunting endlessly here, with new youth for himself whenever he wished, and younger versions of every courtier and courtesan at his command. There would be, thanks to this boy, if some sort of misunderstanding could be proved, new manners forever. But that was hardly the boy's fault. And in that moment, Hamilton decided to lead him back to the clearing, and to another thing often denied to their kind: explanations.

"I was told," began the boy, "that I could only secure my place in society, in your world, by killing you. That that was why we had been brought together in . . . different contests."

Hamilton realized this was exactly what he had once himself imagined. "Who—?"

A shot exactly like his or the boy's rang out across the absolute clarity of the sky. The boy's face bloated, in a moment, his body deformed by the impact, blood and the elements of a name bursting from his mouth. The collapsar shell sucked in again and the body dropped to the ground, emptied.

She stepped forward, lowering her gun. At least she had the grace to look sad. "Miss Nothing," she said.

She was still wearing that bloody dress. She slipped her gun back inside it, hiding it again. She and Hamilton stood looking at each other for a while, until Hamilton understood that if he wanted to shoot her, she was going to let him, and angrily holstered his gun.

She immediately started back towards the house. He considered the idea of burying the boy. The absurdity of it made something catch in his throat. He marched after her and caught up. "Damn you. Damn both of us for not seeing you coming." He grabbed her by the arm to stop her. "I take it you were never truly out of favor with the College?"

She looked calmly at him. "We don't mind the idea of raiding optional worlds. We don't mind stealing new bodies for old minds. Up to a point. But we draw the line at *them* replacing *us.* We're the bloody College of Heralds, Major. Without family trees, we'd be out of business."

"And by setting up the boy to look like he was capable of theft, kidnapping, and treachery, to the point of even being a threat to His Majesty—"

"We've proven such replacements to be unreliable. They never had the balance, you see."

"And you're telling me this because—?"

She looked truly sad for him in that moment. She understood him. "Because you're going to let me get away with it."

They emerged into the clearing. As they did so, Precious immediately became the model of a trembling, rescued victim. "He was a monster!" she cried out, supporting herself on Hamilton's arm.

"Was?" asked the voice of Turpin from the trees.

Hamilton kept his expression calm. "The boy is dead now," he said.

Steven Saylor

Bestselling author Steven Saylor is one of the brightest stars in the "historical mystery" subgenre, along with authors such as Lindsey Davis, John Maddox Roberts, and the late Ellis Peters. He is the author of the long-running *Roma Sub Rosa* series, which details the adventures of Gordianus the Finder, a detective in a vividly realized Ancient Rome, in such novels as *Roman Blood, Arms of Nemesis, The Venus Throw, Catilina's Riddle, A Murder on the Appian Way, Rubicon, Last Seen in Massilia, A Mist of Prophecies, The Judgment of Caesar, The Triumph of Caesar,* and *The Seven Wonders.* Gordianus's exploits at shorter lengths have been collected in *The House of the Vestals: The Investigations of Gordianus the Finder* and *A Gladiator Dies Only Once: The Further Investigations of Gordianus the Finder.* Saylor's other books include *A Twist at the End, Have You Seen Dawn?,* and a huge non-Gordianus historical novel, *Roma: The Novel of Ancient Rome.* His most recent books are the big second volume in the *Roma* sequence, *Empire: A Novel of Ancient Rome,* and a new Gordianus novel, *Raiders of the Nile.* He lives in Berkeley, California.

Recently, as recounted in *The Seven Wonders*, Saylor has introduced a whole new series of tales that take a teenaged Gordianus to visit the Seven Wonders of the World with his traveling companion, the elderly Greek poet Antipater of Sidon. Set in the fabled city of Tyre in 91 B.C., "Ill Seen in Tyre" is a previously untold episode from the journey of the young Gordianus. As Gordianus discovers, Tyre was also the location, a hundred years before his visit, of the only known earthly adventure of two of the greatest rogues in literature, Fafhrd and the Gray Mouser (as recounted in

Fritz Leiber's 1947 novella *Adept's Gambit,* later included in the Leiber collection *Swords in the Mist*). This mulitdimensional crossing of paths in Tyre might seem a mere coincidence, but as Gordianus learns, on earth as in Nehwon, all stories and storytellers are subtly, even magically, connected.

ILL SEEN IN TYRE

Steven Saylor

"What are those curious pictures on the walls?" I said. The tavern's pretty serving girl, a voluptuous blonde, had just delivered my third cup of wine, and the pictures were looking curiouser and curiouser.

Antipater, my traveling companion and erstwhile tutor, furrowed his snowy brows and gave me that withering look I had come to know all too well during our journey. Though I was nineteen, and a man by Roman law, his look made me feel closer to nine.

"Gordianus! Can it be that you do not know the stories of Fafhrd and the Gray Mouser?"

"The gray what?"

"Mouser," he said.

I frowned. "I know what a mouse is, but what on earth is a mouser?"

Antipater sighed. "It is a term used for the common Egyptian house cat, a creature renowned for its hunting skills, particularly as regards rodents. Thus, mouser: a hunter of mice."

"Ah, well, we don't have cats in Rome, you know." I shuddered at the very thought of such a creature, with its sharp claws and vicious fangs. I had encountered a few in our travels, living on ships. Supposedly, the captains prized their ability to keep a vessel free of vermin, but I had kept my distance from these exotic creatures. Like most Romans, I found them vaguely repellent, if not downright menacing. I had been told that the Egyptians actually worshipped these furry beasts, allowing them to roam the streets and even to live in their homes. I had not yet been to Egypt, but the idea that the Egyptians lived with cats did not make me eager to visit.

Eventually, of course, Antipater and I would have to visit Egypt, for it was home to the Great Pyramid, the oldest and some said the grandest of the Wonders of the World, and it was our intent to visit all seven of those marvels. We had just come from Rhodes, home of the Colossus, and were on our way to Babylon, home of the fabled Walls and the Hanging Gardens.

At the moment—between Wonders, so to speak—we found ourselves in the port city of Tyre, which had its own long and fabled history. Tyre was perhaps most famous for the production of dye from the murex shell; every king in the world insisted on being robed in Tyrian purple. Tyre also happened to be the birthplace of Antipater, so our visit here was in some ways a homecoming for him.

Thus did my thoughts ramble as I sipped my third cup of wine. Antipater was actually ahead of me, on his fourth cup. It was uncommon for him to indulge in immoderate drinking. His abandonment of sobriety had something to do with being in his hometown. What could be more poignant than an elderly poet surrounded by childhood memories?

"Egypt, cats, mice, pyramids—but what were we talking about?" I said. "Oh, yes—the curious pictures in this place."

The tavern was called the Murex Shell. A large picture of its namesake was painted on the outside wall, and a border of clay tiles, impressed with such shells, surrounded the doorway. Inside the tavern, however, no murex shells were to be seen, and the frescoes on the walls had nothing to do with the production of purple dye. Instead, these pictures, painted on every available surface, appeared to depict the exploits of two heroes unknown to me. One was much taller and broader than the other, a brawny giant with a fiery red beard. The smaller of the two had a snub nose and wore a gray cloak with a peaked hood. Both carried swords, and in many of the pictures, wielded them with devastating results.

"What did you say they were called?" I said.

"Fafhrd—"

"Yes, I heard you say that the first time. I thought you were clearing your throat."

"Very funny, Gordianus. I repeat: Fafhrd. An exotic name, to be sure. They say he was a veritable giant and came from the far north, beyond the Ister River, beyond Dacia, beyond even the wild lands of Germania."

"But there are no lands north of Germania—are there?"

"None that any man I know has ever visited. Still, they say that's where Fafhrd came from."

"Fafhrd! Fafhrd!" I tried saying the name a few times, until a nod from Antipater indicated that I had it right. "And the other one? This so-called Gray Mouser?"

"He seems to have been a local boy, growing up on the streets of Tyre. Darker and smaller and wirier than his companion, but equally adept with a sword. Indeed, it is said that the two of them were the finest swordsmen of their day."

"And when was that?"

"Fafhrd and the Gray Mouser lived in Tyre about a hundred years ago. My grandfather met them once. According to him, they were not merely the greatest swordsmen of their day, but of all time."

"A bold claim. Why have I never heard of them?"

Antipater shrugged. "I suppose they *are* best known here in Tyre, where they made a great impression on the locals. And in Tyre, they are best remembered here, inside the four walls of the Murex Shell, where they spent a great deal of time drinking and wenching—"

"This smelly little place is a virtual shrine to them!" I laughed, looking at all the pictures on the walls.

Antipater sniffed. "Just because *you* never heard the tales of Fafhrd and the Gray Mouser, growing up in far-off Rome—"

"But Teacher, you and I have been traveling all over the Greek-speaking world for over a year—to Ephesus and Halicarnassus and Olympia, and to all those islands in the Aegean—and I don't recall ever seeing a single image or inscription about either of these fellows, anywhere. No priest ever invokes them. No poet I know of—including you!—recounts their exploits. Could it be that Fafhrd and the Gray Mouser are just local legends, known only here in Tyre?"

Antipater's grumbling was as good as an admission that I was right. But even as a callow teenager, I could imagine that the heroes of an old man's youth must be particularly dear to him, so I desisted from casting more doubt on the renown of these supposedly great swordsmen.

"It's funny," I said, "what an odd couple they make. In some of the pictures, you might think you're seeing a tall god and his dwarfish servant, and in others a diminutive sorcerer and the lumbering automaton who does his bidding."

"Very imaginative, Gordianus," said Antipater sourly. We had both emptied our cups, and he called for the serving girl to bring more wine.

"So what *are* we seeing in these pictures?" I said, striving to show more respect.

Antipater looked elsewhere and pouted for a bit, but his natural urge to play the pedagogue, along with the chance to revisit one of his boyhood fascinations, was too powerful for him to resist. "Well, since you ask . . . in that picture over there, we see their encounter with the Sidonian smugglers; and there, their legendary run-in with the Cilician pirates, and the rescue of the kidnapped Cappadocian princess. That image shows their encounter with the female Cyprian slave-dealer—how formidable she looks!—and there we see the rendezvous that turned into an ambush. And there, the Idumaean brigands come galloping out of the desert, in search of the priceless tomb-filched Egyptian jewels that no one ever saw."

"And yet, we see them in the picture."

"Artistic license, Gordianus!"

"What about that picture?" I pointed to a particularly bawdy image above the window.

"Ah, there we see pictured the night that Fafhrd and the Gray Mouser together enjoyed the lascivious favors of Laodice of Egypt, who afterwards sent a troop of Nubian eunuchs to behead them. But our heroes escaped, as you can see, taking the ebony chest of Laodice with them—which turned out to contain not only her fabulous collection of aphrodisiacs, but the very cup from which Socrates drank the hemlock."

"Fantastic!" I said. "And over on that wall—those images seem to represent a whole other set of adventures."

"Very astute of you. Yes, those images depict exploits of a more supernatural nature. Thus you see the occasion when the two swordsmen consulted the strange demon called Ningauble, which as you can see is depicted as a fat-bellied figure wearing a cloak with a shadowy hood from which protrude seven eyes on seven writhing stalks."

"How terrifying!"

"In fact, Ningauble of the Seven Eyes proved to be a friendly demon and a sage counselor. It was Ningauble who dispatched the two on their greatest journey, a trek to the east, far beyond the snowy peaks of the Lebanon Mountains. For a while they followed the legendary route of Xenophon and the Ten Thousand. Then they headed even farther into the unknown, arriving at last at the Lost City, and then at the Citadel Called Mist, where they encountered their greatest foe, an adept of truly terrifying magical powers." Antipater's eyes sparkled as he recounted the details.

I nodded, taking in the fabulous images. "And what about that picture over there? It looks as if the two are taking part in a battle. A famous battle?"

"Yes, that would be the siege of Tyre by Alexander the Great, during which the two fought valiantly to defend the city. Fafhrd is shown manning the walls and heaving stone blocks onto the besieger's ships, while the Gray Mouser is depicted underwater, filing through the anchor chains. All around them swords clash and arrows fly—"

"But Teacher, didn't you say that these two lived in Tyre a hundred years ago?"

"Yes."

"And wasn't the siege by Alexander a hundred years before that?" I smiled, because for once I actually remembered one of Antipater's history lessons.

He coughed. "Yes, that is correct."

"Then how could they possibly—?"

"Again, artistic license!" he insisted. "Or . . . it may be that Fafhrd and the Gray Mouser truly were in Tyre at events a hundred years apart."

I tried not to smirk.

"Not everything in this world is as straightforward as you hardheaded Romans would like to think," said Antipater. "It is certain that Fafhrd and the Gray Mouser were in Tyre a hundred years ago—my own grandfather attested to that fact, as do all these pictures around you—but no one knows whence they came, or where they went. There are those who believe that Fafhrd and the Gray Mouser arrived from a realm outside of ordinary time and space, a place of magic, if you will, and so it may be that they were present here in Tyre not just a hundred years ago, but also a hundred years before that."

"So why not a hundred years later? Which means . . . they might be here today!" I made an exaggerated show of peering at our fellow patrons, most of whom were quite shabby. A few cloaked figures in the tavern might have passed for the Gray Mouser, but no red-bearded giant was to be seen.

Antipater glowered, and I felt a bit ashamed of teasing him. To distract him, I pointed to the images that had started me on this discussion. They were located to either side of the door by which we had entered. "Those are the two pictures I find most curious."

Antipater raised a bristling white eyebrow. "Yes? And why is that? Describe!" Making a pupil enumerate the details of a statue or painting was a common tutorial exercise, one that Antipater had required of me often in our visits to temples and shrines—but never before in a tavern.

"Very well, Teacher. Each picture has two parts. In the first image, the one on the left, Fafhrd has a beautiful girl on his lap, a girl wearing a Cretan-revival dress that leaves her breasts entirely bare—but in the adjacent panel, it's a giant sow on his lap. Since the sow is wearing the same scanty outfit as the girl, it seems we're meant to think the girl has turned into the sow! And there, in the matching picture on the other side of the doorway, the Gray Mouser is coupled with another lovely maid, but in the next panel, she's become a giant snail. What sort of tale is that? Heroes copulating with pigs and snails! And why are such unseemly images given such prominent placement, where no one visiting the tavern could possibly miss them? What a thing to see as you're leaving, with a bellyful of wine and your head in a whirl!"

"Those pictures are especially noteworthy," said Antipater, "because the events they depict happened *right here,* in the Murex Shell."

"You must be joking! Women were transformed into pigs and snails on this very spot?"

"The fact is indisputable. My grandfather was a witness."

"Yes, I'm sure he was, but—"

"They were the victims of a curse, you see—Fafhrd and the Gray

Mouser, I mean. Any girl they embraced turned into a loathsome creature before their very eyes. It was to banish this curse that they set out on the quest that would lead them first to Ningauble of the Seven Eyes, and then, after many perils, to the Citadel Called Mist and their confrontation with the magical adept. But the story began right here, in the Murex Shell, with the tavern wench who turned into a sow. And the adept responsible for that curse had his origin here in the city of Tyre, as well. And where do you think the adept learned his sorcery?"

"I have no idea."

"From books that came from a private library right here in the city—strange volumes, collectively known by their owner as the Books of Secret Wisdom. Scrolls from many times and places, all full of esoteric knowledge to be found nowhere else. As a boy, I heard my grandfather speak of those books in a whisper, but when I asked if one could read them, he said they were far too dangerous. He told me to stick to my Homer instead."

"And a good thing you did, for like Homer, you became a poet."

"Yes, a poet of great renown; the greatest poet in the world, some say." Antipater sighed. He had many attributes, but modesty was not among them. "Ah, but what a different life I might have led, if as a boy I'd had access to the Books of Secret Wisdom! The power contained in those volumes is said to be beyond human reckoning. Not the power of the poet to entrance an audience with laughter and pathos—no, I mean the power of sorcery, able to bend the very fabric of reality!"

We had encountered a bit of magic on our journey, as in our encounter with the witch of Corinth. I shuddered at the memory and drank deeply from my cup.

Antipater finished his cup at the same time and called for more wine. I had never seen him in such a wild mood. "And now," he said, "after a lifetime away, I return to the city of my birth, a wiser man than when I left—and a craftier, more devious man, as well, I dare say. More determined. Less fearful."

"Fearful of what?"

"The Books of Secret Wisdom! Don't you understand, Gordianus? That's why we've come here to Tyre."

I frowned. "I thought Tyre was just a stop on the way between Rhodes and Babylon. That, and the place you were born, of course. It makes sense that you'd want to do a bit of reminiscing—"

"Oh, no, Gordianus, we are here for a very specific purpose. We have come to the city of Fafhrd and the Gray Mouser, the heroes of my childhood. Their adventures meant everything to me as a boy. And their greatest adventure brought them face-to-face with the magic to be found in the Books of Secret Wisdom—which I intend to possess at last! I've already taken steps toward acquiring them. By this time tomorrow—ah, but here's that pretty serving girl!"

He held his empty cup toward the girl. Was it the wine I had drunk, or was she looking more voluptuous than ever? Her smile was very friendly.

I swallowed a mouthful of wine. "By this time tomorrow . . . what?"

Antipater smiled. "You'll see. Or rather, you *won't* see!" He laughed aloud, sounding so strange that I hurriedly gulped down the whole cup of wine.

The next morning, in the upstairs room we had taken at the Murex Shell, I woke with a terrible hangover. Worse than the pounding in my head was the nattering of Antipater, who seemed completely unaffected by the wine he had consumed the night before.

"Up, up, Gordianus! We are in Tyre and must make the most of our brief stay here."

"Brief?" I groaned and covered my head with a pillow. "I thought we might stay here for a while . . . in this nice, quiet room—"

"Ha! Once I achieve my intention, we will leave Tyre at once. So let us play tourist while we can." He yanked the pillow away and practically kicked me out of bed.

An hour later, with some food in my belly and fresh sea air filling my lungs, I set out with Antipater for a tour of the city. Tyre was not as grand as some of the places we had seen in our travels, but it was one of the oldest cities we had visited and full of history. It was seafarers from

Tyre who first sailed beyond the Pillars of Hercules (known to them by his Phoenician name, Melkart); it was Queen Dido of Tyre who founded the city of Carthage, which once rivaled Rome. Carthage was no more, but Tyre still stood, though changed forever by the conquest of Alexander the Great.

"Alexander found the city an island, and left it a peninsula," said Antipater. By winding streets we had arrived at the highest point of the city, from which Antipater pointed to the massive earth-and-stone causeway that connected the erstwhile island on which we stood to the mainland. "Alexander besieged the island fortress not just by sea but also by land, building that mole out to the island so that he could bring up huge battering rams. Seven months it took him to bring Tyre to its knees, but in the end he succeeded, and marked his conquest with a celebration over there, in the ancient Temple of Melkart. Thus did Tyre become part of the Greek-speaking world, and has been so ever since, sometimes under the sway of the Seleucids, sometimes under the Ptolemies of Egypt. But forty years ago, Tyre regained her independence and began to issue her own coinage again—the famous shekel of Tyre. Once more, she is a proud and independent city-state, and may remain so—if she can elude the clutches of Rome." This was not the first time Antipater had expressed a degree of anti-Roman sentiment.

By winding streets we descended to the city's waterfront, which teemed with activity. Tyre is blessed with two natural harbors, one to the north and one to the south, and both were filled with ships. The wharves were crowded with busy sailors and merchants overseeing the slaves who loaded and unloaded cargoes. The waterfront taverns were doing a brisk business (including the Murex Shell, which was off the northern harbor). Away from the waterfront, in paved enclosures, dyers went about the work of spreading wet green cloth. According to Antipater, the hot sunlight would turn the purple to green.

"How can that be?" I said. "It sounds like magic."

"Does it? Yes, I suppose it does. But we shall come back later, and you'll see that it's a fact." He smiled. "One way or another, you shall see some magic done this day!"

I looked at him sidelong. "Teacher, what are you talking about?"

"Last night, after I put you to bed, I went back downstairs and made contact with the fellow I'd been hoping to meet."

"What fellow?"

"The man who knows the man who currently owns the Books of Secret Wisdom. We are to meet him tonight in the Murex Shell."

"And then what?"

"You'll see. Or *not* see!"

My memory was muddled by wine, but I vaguely recalled Antipater uttering a similar turn of phrase the previous night. What was my old tutor up to?

We continued our tour of the city, which was actually quite small and easily traversed on foot. Having so little land to build on, the Tyrians built *up,* and in the central part of the island the tightly packed residential tenements were five or six or even seven stories tall. This made Tyre an even taller city than Rome, and many of the narrow, winding streets were quite dark, even at midday. The areas more open to the sun were largely occupied by the dye manufactories, and in those neighborhoods the air was the foulest I had ever smelled in a city. This had something to do with the various solutions and compounds involved in the production of the purple dye, which emitted powerful odors.

To get a bit of sunlight and fresh air, we took a stroll on Alexander's causeway, but Antipater declined to walk all the way to the mainland. I could see that a considerable town had grown up along the shore, but Antipater assured me there was nothing of interest to see in the drab suburbs of the mainland. Instead we turned back and made our way to the Temple of Melkart. The place was musty and dark and smelled of mildew, but it did contain an eternal flame (not unlike the hearth of Vesta back in Rome), as well as some remarkable statues and paintings of the god I knew as Hercules, who was Tyre's most venerated deity.

On our way back to the Murex Shell, we stopped at the square where the dyers had earlier spread their cloth, and I was amazed to see that the green had indeed turned to purple as it dried.

"Like magic!" I whispered.

Antipater only smiled and nodded.

* * *

That night at the Murex Shell, in a small private room off the tavern, we dined on a salad of octopus and hearts of palm followed by fish stew, served by the same pretty blonde who had brought our wine the night before. Her name, I learned, was Galatea.

I discovered why Antipater had gone to the expense of paying for the private room when a stranger appeared in the doorway.

The man wore a dark blue tunic cinched by a broad leather belt. From the belt hung a scabbard with a dagger, the hilt of which was inlaid with ivory circled with a band of tiny rubies. The tunic was long enough to cover the man's knees but left bare his muscular, darkly tanned arms, both of which sported elaborately chased-silver armbands and bracelets. Around his neck gleamed a tangle of silver necklaces hung with pendants of carnelian and lapis, and from his ears hung thick rings of silver so heavy they had stretched his earlobes. His hair was long and unkempt, mostly black but with a few strands of silver, and his jaw was covered with several days' growth of beard. His creased, darkly weathered features made it hard to determine his age; I could only be sure that he was quite a bit older than I and quite a bit younger than Antipater.

Antipater, who had just finished his stew, looked up and raised his eyebrows. "Are you . . . ?"

"My name is Kerynis. I believe we have an appointment."

Antipater kept his eyes on the man and pushed the bowl aside, clearing the table before him. "Indeed we do. Have you brought . . . ?"

Slung over his shoulder, the man carried a satchel that bulged with leather cylinders. He removed one of the cylinders, from which he extracted a scroll of raggedy brown papyrus.

"It looks very old," said Antipater.

"So it is," said Kerynis. "With a document such as this, older is better. The later the copy, the more likely that errors have crept in, and that can be . . . dangerous . . . as I'm sure you can imagine. Get the smallest detail wrong, and—poof!—you've turned yourself into a cabbage."

Antipater laughed, sounding a bit nervous. "Indeed, yes, I can imagine. So old . . . and so delicate."

"Handle it with care."

"I may touch it?" said Antipater.

"You may. But until you've purchased it, treat it as the rare and valuable object it is."

"Of course!" Eagerly but carefully, Antipater took the scroll from Kerynis and unrolled it on the table. It was so worn that it lay flat without being weighted.

I rose from my chair and looked over his shoulder. The Greek letters were in some archaic style I did not recognize and so badly faded that the text was almost impossible for me to read, but Antipater seemed able to make sense of it. I watched him run his finger from line to line, muttering to himself as he read.

"Fantastic! 'Transformation of male to female' . . . 'How to kill with a gaze' . . . 'Temporary ability to understand the speech of birds' . . . 'How to control the dreams of a sleeper' . . . 'Revivification of the dead' . . . Marvelous!"

"What is this, Teacher?" I said, glancing up at Kerynis. The man stood with his arms folded, watching Antipater's reaction with a look of wry amusement.

"This document is a précis, or list of contents, of the Books of Secret Wisdom," said Antipater. "Extraordinary! If even half of these formulas work . . ."

"Such a collection would be of incalculable value," said Kerynis, finishing Antipater's thought. He laughed. "And so you may wonder: why am I willing to sell it?" He patted the satchel. "Here's the fact: a lot of these books are rubbish, plain and simple. You make up the witch's brew exactly as it's written, following the recipe to the tiniest degree, but instead of growing two heads, you just get indigestion. But I ask you: who wants two heads anyway?" Again he laughed. "And some of the volumes are pure nonsense. All the stuff about Chaldean stargazing—even if you could tell the future by reading the stars, who'd want to? Life is too dull as it is. I prefer to be surprised. As for the book of Hebrew proverbs, those I can take or leave." He shrugged.

"It sounds like you've done quite a bit of reading in these books," said Antipater.

"Indeed I have. Don't let my appearance fool you. I know what you think when you look at me: pirate. What other sort of man walks around wearing all that jewelry, ready to hock it all at a moment's notice in case he has to get out of town fast? But in fact, my father was a scholar at the Library of Alexandria, and I grew up among books. I could recite Hesiod before I was toilet-trained—'Some days are like a stepmother, but others like a mother.'" He laughed. "My life's taken a few twists and turns since then, but I know the value of the written word."

"So you're telling me the Books of Secret Wisdom are worthless?" Antipater looked crestfallen.

"I didn't say that, my friend." Kerynis patted the satchel and glanced down at the tightly packed leather cylinders. "Among these books are some works of true genius. The problem is separating the wheat from the chaff. You could do that using trial and error, but that could take a lifetime—or shorten your lifetime, if you make a mistake."

"A mistake?"

Kerynis nodded. "You'll find a lot of love spells in these books. That's what most people are interested in and willing to pay money for. Now, me, I've never had a problem reeling in just about any pretty fish I took a fancy to, but for some people, I understand this can be a problem. So in these scrolls you'll find a lot of spells for that, and a lot of potions. But let's say that some rich toad hires you to make up one of these potions and administer it to the pretty girl or boy he has his eye on, and the potion works well enough—at first—but turns out to be poisonous." He whistled and blew out his cheeks. "You've never seen anybody madder than a paying customer who's found himself in bed with a corpse, no matter how pretty, and thinks it's *your* fault. Believe me, I know. I've been there."

"So you *have* used these books?" said Antipater. "You've tested them?"

"In bits and pieces. But I haven't devoted my life to it, which is what a man would have to do to make sense of it all. Candidly? It's just not worth my time. I don't need sorcery. I prefer direct action if you know what I mean. If I see something I want, I take it. I don't need to use mind control or to make myself invisible."

"Invisible?" Antipater whispered. "Is there really such a formula? The man I spoke to last night indicated . . ."

"Yes, that was my confederate. He knows a little of what's in these books, but not much."

"But he *did* mention invisibility."

"Oh, yes. And he conveyed to me your particular interest in that area. So I went to the trouble of looking up that particular passage . . ." Kerynis rummaged about in the satchel for a while, cursing when he couldn't seem to find what he was looking for. "Oh wait, here it is!"

From an especially battered leather cylinder, he extracted an especially tattered piece of papyrus.

"May I see it?" said Antipater, with a quaver in his voice.

"Careful! It's ready to fall to pieces. You can see where a corner fell off yesterday when I was making up the formula."

"You actually *made* a potion of invisibility?"

"Oh, yes. And not for the first time. But it's not easy! Some of the ingredients are almost impossible to find, and you have to mix them just so." Kerynis reached deeper into his satchel and drew out a small vial made of dark green glass with a cork stopper.

"Is that it?" Antipater asked.

"The real thing," said Kerynis with a smile. "I brewed it myself, last night."

"But how . . . ?"

Kerynis nodded at the scroll. "Read the instructions."

Antipater pored over the piece of papyrus and began to read aloud. " 'Take the left foot of the creature called a chameleon—' "

"The *left* foot, notice," said Kerynis. "Front or back doesn't make a difference, but do *not* use a right foot. I've made that mistake, and the result is not pretty. Go on."

" 'Add an equal measure of the herb called chameleon'—what is that?"

Kerynis shrugged. "It grows hereabouts. Down in Egypt, too."

Antipater nodded. " 'Roast in a furnace until brown but not blackened, then pulverize and mix with an unguent made of . . .' " He read silently for a while and nodded. "Yes, this recipe is simple enough. 'Decant into a glass container.' "

"Glass, not metal!" said Kerynis. "Any kind of metal will make it go bad right away."

"Ah! Good to know." Antipater turned back to the scroll. "'Kept stoppered, this concoction will retain its efficacy indefinitely. Allows the user to go about in a throng unseen. Ingest only the smallest dose on first use, and larger doses thereafter as needed.'"

Kerynis nodded. "You have to take larger and larger doses to make it work. I've done it so many times, now I'd have to swallow this whole vial to make myself invisible, and even then you'd probably still be able to see me in bright light. But if you've never used it before, a couple of drops on the tongue should do the trick, as least for a few minutes."

"Fantastic!"said Antipater. "Are you saying I can try it?"

"Of course."

"Here and now?"

"Why not? But I should warn you, it may make you feel a bit strange."

"Strange?"

"Woozy. A little odd. Light-headed. Not drunk, exactly. It can be slightly unpleasant, but that's the price you pay."

Antipater frowned. "But otherwise it's safe?"

Kerynis spread his arms. "Look at me. Still alive, and with all my senses."

Antipater picked up the vial and pulled out the stopper. He held it to his nose and then thrust it away, replacing the stopper. "That smell! It's vile."

Kerynis smirked. "I never said it tasted good."

I could stay silent no longer. "Teacher, are you sure you want to do this?"

"As a matter of fact, Gordianus, I've wanted to do this since I was a boy. I never dreamed I would have the chance."Antipater stared at the vial for a long moment. "I'm going to do it! Then we'll sit here until it takes effect, and you, my boy, will tell me how well it works."

Kerynis shook his head. "That's probably not going to work. As a test, I mean."

"Why not?" said Antipater.

"Am I right that the two of you are traveling together?"

"Yes."

"And you have been for quite some time?"

"For over a year."

"Seeing each other pretty much every day?"

"Yes."

"Then your young friend here will be able to see you despite the effect of the potion."

"What are you saying?"

"It has to do with something called 'rays of visibility.' There's an explanation of how it works, in one of the other volumes. I can't claim to understand the details, but it's sort of like seeing the afterimage of a thing you've been staring at, even when you close your eyes. A person who sees you every day, whose eyes have been attuned to your rays of visibility, will still see you even though others can't."

Antipater frowned. "That rather puts a limit on the potion's practical use."

Kerynis shrugged. "It means a man can't make himself invisible and sneak past his wife, that's true. But the same man can go out in a crowd of strangers and not be seen."

Antipater nodded thoughtfully. "So if I use the potion and venture out into the common room, no one there will be able to see me?"

"Correct."

"What about Galatea, the serving girl?" I said. "She's seen Antipater lots of times over the last couple of days."

"That's not long enough to absorb his rays of visibility. That can take months."

"I'm ready!" Antipater moved to unstop the bottle again, but Kerynis gripped his hand.

"Not quite yet. Let's make sure we're in agreement first. Did you bring the sum that was talked about?"

Antipater patted the pouch inside his tunic, producing a muffled clinking sound, then pulled out a small but bulging moneybag. "All here. You can count it if you want."

"I intend to. And all in Tyrian shekels? I don't want foreign coins."

"It's just as your man requested."

Kerynis nodded. "Put the money on the table. And next to that, I'll put the Books of Secret Wisdom." He lugged the satchel onto the table. "The books for the money. That's the deal."

"Understood," said Antipater. "Now let's get on with it."

I had never seen Antipater so eager. I watched as he unstoppered the vial, carefully poured a couple of drops of the oily brown unguent onto the back of his hand, then touched his tongue to the drops. "Like that?" he said, peering at Kerynis.

"That should do it. It may be a few minutes before you feel the effects. Have a look at the books while you're waiting. And I'll count the money."

Antipater rummaged through the satchel. Attached to each of the leather cylinders was a tag that identified the title or author of the scroll inside. Meanwhile, Kerynis opened the moneybag and poured the coins onto the table, then began arranging them in little piles. I gasped at the amount of silver Antipater was ready to hand over. How had he come up with so much money?

Kerynis saw my reaction. He held up one of the coins so that it caught the light of the lamps. "The silver shekel of Tyre! Is there anything prettier? Handsome Melkart in profile on one side, and on the other, a proud eagle clutching a palm branch. Who'd want a bunch of smelly old books when he could have these instead? But to each his own, I say. So if my little collection of books is worth it to you, I'm happy to make the trade."

Suddenly Antipater dropped the leather cylinder he was holding and sat bolt upright. Kerynis looked at him and nodded. "There, it's beginning to take effect. You're a little hazy around the edges already."

"Yes, I feel it," whispered Antipater. "A warm sensation—not unpleasant—but decidedly *different* . . ."

I squinted at him. "I'm not seeing a change."

"Nor will you, young man," said Kerynis. "Just as I explained. By Melkart, would you look at him fade away! It amazes me, every time."

"Has it happened?" said Antipater, rising from his chair. "Am I invisible?" He moved toward the door.

Kerynis continued to stare at the spot where Antipater had been sitting. "Go into the common room if you like. See how the people there react. But remember, it'll last only a few minutes."

When Antipater pushed open the door to leave the room, Kerynis gave a start and uttered a mild curse. He shook his head and laughed. "I told myself I wouldn't be startled, but invisible people make you jump."

"I should go with him." I began to get up.

Kerynis waved me back. "Let the old man have his fun."

I looked at the piles of silver coins on the table, and the cylinders full of scrolls, and decided not to leave the room after all. There were three exits from the room, one leading to the common room, one to the kitchen, and another leading somewhere else. If no one stayed to watch him, what was to stop Kerynis from absconding with the money *and* the books?

He held up one of the coins and whistled. "Would you look at that! A Melkart without a nose."

"What are you talking about?"

"These are very rare, my young friend. Apparently, something broke on the original mold, and on some coins, Melkart has no nose. Once they saw the problem, they stopped making them, so you don't see these very often."

"Are they valuable?"

He snorted. "No more valuable than any other shekel of the same weight. If anything, less valuable. Who wants a Melkart with no nose in his coin purse?"

While he continued to fondle the coins, doting over them like a boy with toy soldiers, I took a closer look at the so-called Books of Secret Wisdom. I chanced to pull out a scroll that gave instructions for changing men into women, and vice versa. This was a subject with which I had some acquaintance, having witnessed such an alleged transformation at the sacred spring of Salmacis in Halicarnassus. I was scanning the text to see if it mentioned Salmacis, when I realized that Kerynis had leaned forward, bringing his head close to mine, and was reading the text upside down.

"Interested in becoming a girl?" he said, flashing an ingratiating smile. "Perhaps just for the night?"

I cleared my throat. "Not with the likes of you around."

He laughed. "Come, come, young Roman—you are Roman, aren't you? There's no mistaking the accent. What do you have against me? I'm just an honest fellow trying to make an honest transaction."

"I see. And how did you come to possess these Books of Secret Wisdom?"

"Ah, now that is none of your business. But I can assure you that they are absolutely authentic. Do you think I'd try to cheat a distinguished fellow like your traveling companion? He's a lot older and wiser than you, my young friend, and he seems to trust me."

I glowered at him, trying to think of a response, then gave a start as the door opened and Antipater stepped back inside, grinning from ear to ear.

Kerynis heard the noise and looked toward the doorway. He stared blankly for a moment, then squinted. "Ah, yes, it's starting to wear off. I can vaguely see your outline. How did it go?"

"Fantastic!" declared Antipater. "I was completely invisible. No one could see me at all. It made me feel quite . . . naughty. I couldn't resist playing a few tricks on people."

"What sort of tricks?" I said, dismayed at the thought of my old tutor behaving like a schoolboy.

"Never mind, Gordianus." Antipater straightened his shoulders, as if to shrug off his puerile behavior. "The important thing is that the formula *works.* The implications are astounding. The value of such a tool for military purposes, or for espionage—a man could change the course of history!"

"But, Teacher, do you not recall the lesson of Icarus? If men were meant to fly, the gods would have given us wings. And if we were meant to be invisible—"

"You must try it yourself!" said Antipater, thrusting the vial toward me.

"What?"

"Yes, give it a try," said Kerynis.

I stared at the vial for a long moment, then took it from Antipater. I pulled out the stopper and took a whiff. As Antipater had said, the smell was vile.

"Go on," said Antipater. "Two drops on the back of your hand."

Kerynis cocked his head. "You're young and strong. Maybe you should try three drops."

I took a deep breath, then carefully poured three drops of the unguent onto my hand. After a final moment of hesitation, I licked it up. The taste was horrible.

For what seemed a long time, they stared at me in silence. At last I began to feel a warm sensation in the pit of my stomach, spreading to my chest and limbs. My head felt light. The room took on a faint glow.

Kerynis smiled and nodded. "Ah, it's beginning to work."

Antipater frowned. "I see no change."

"Nor will you, as I explained. How do you feel, young Roman?"

I swallowed. "Strange . . . but not in a bad way." I looked at the hand from which I had lapped the drops. "I can still see myself."

"Of course you can," said Kerynis. "It's the rays of visibility. You see yourself every day, so you're not susceptible to your own invisibility." Though I had slowly and quietly risen from my chair and walked across the room, he continued to gaze at the place where I had been sitting.

"Try it!" whispered Antipater. "Step into the common room and see what happens. I'll come with you."

"No, Teacher, stay here," I said, looking at the money on the table and the bag of books, and at Kerynis, whom I still didn't trust.

"Very well." Antipater gladly took a seat and began looking through the cylinders.

Feeling the strange effects of the potion, I ventured into the common room. A dozen or so patrons were scattered about the small tavern, drinking wine and gambling. I walked from one side of the room to the other, treading as silently as I could. To be sure, no one seemed to see me. I conducted a few simple experiments, such as clapping my hands in front of a drunken stranger's face, only to see him start back in surprise.

Galatea passed by, carrying a pitcher full of wine. I walked alongside her, openly staring at her lovely face and golden hair and at the upper portion of her white breasts, which were suggestively framed by the bosom of her dress. Oh, to have lived a century before, in the days of Fafhrd and the Gray Mouser, when the Cretan revival was in vogue and women wore garments that exposed their breasts completely!

I followed her on her rounds, and watched her flirt shamelessly with every man in the establishment. Feeling an irrational stab of jealousy, I couldn't resist putting my lips close to her ear and whispering, "Boo!"

The poor girl gave such a start that she sloshed wine from the pitcher all over the front of her dress. Some of the wine landed on her breasts. The men who witnessed her apparent clumsiness hooted and laughed. One of them shouted, "Here, Galatea, let me lick that off for you!"

I saw her blush and felt a bit ashamed of myself. But when she turned and hurried down a narrow hallway, I followed. As she stepped into a little room, I slipped behind her and barely avoided being struck by the door.

The cluttered, windowless little room was dimly lit by a single lamp. It was apparently the room where she slept, for there was a narrow bed, a chair, and an open trunk full of clothes and other items. While I stood very still and watched, Galatea pulled the wine-spattered dress over her head and stood before me completely naked.

It had been a while since I had seen a naked woman. Through the winter months, while we stayed on Rhodes, I had enjoyed the intimate companionship of Vindovix the Gaul, but that was not the same thing. Unafraid of being seen, I openly stared. This way and that she turned in the amber light, so that I had a view of her from every angle. Galatea was like a statue of Venus, endowed with sleek white limbs, enticing hips and buttocks, and breasts that changed from one shape to another as she stooped, turned, and stood, each shape more provocative than the last.

When she pulled another dress from the trunk, I couldn't contain my groan of disappointment.

Galatea whirled about and looked directly at me. "Is someone there?"

I held my breath.

She frowned, then went on about her business, turning her back to me as she pulled the new dress over her head. But by the time she turned to face me again, the potion of invisibility seemed to have waned, for she started back and raised her arms as if to defend herself.

"What are you—? How did you—?" She seemed at a loss for words, as any girl would be if a man suddenly materialized from nowhere in a closed room.

I, too, was speechless, but only for a moment. "I think it was my fault that you spilled the wine," I finally said.

She frowned. "Don't be silly. I was clumsy, that's all. But where did you come from?"

"Does that matter?"

Galatea cracked a smile. "Ah, yes, I recognize you now. You're the young Roman traveling with the old man. I . . . couldn't quite see you at first. It must be the dim light. Even so . . . how did you . . . ?"

"I'm sorry you spilled the wine."

"The dress is ruined." She sighed.

"I'll buy you another."

"That's very sweet of you. But I must get back to work now, or else those drunken louts will climb over the counter and start serving themselves." She moved toward the door, sidling past me so close that we touched, front to front. From that brief, brushing contact, I think she must have perceived the effect she had on me, for she glanced downward, then flashed a knowing smile and gave me a quick kiss on the lips before she pushed the door open and left me standing alone in the little room.

By the time I returned to the private dining room, Antipater and Kerynis had settled their transaction. The coins were no longer in sight, and the satchel full of scrolls was on the floor beside Antipater.

"How did it go?" said Kerynis.

"Yes, Gordianus, did you do something naughty?" I must have blushed, for Antipater laughed and shook his head. "By Hercules, I think you *did* do something naughty."

Kerynis also seemed richly amused and took advantage of my consternation to give me a swat on the backside. After a few words of farewell, he was gone, leaving the books and taking the shekels with him.

That night, in our room, long after midnight, Antipater pored over his newly acquired scrolls, refilling the lamps with oil whenever they burned low. Occasionally he muttered to himself or uttered an exclamation of amazement. "Imagine that!" he would say, or "Astonishing! Can such a thing be possible?"

While Antipater read, I could think of nothing except Galatea. I lay on my narrow bed, wearing only my loincloth and covered by a sheet. From the open window came the sounds of the waterfront at night—waves gently lapping the piers, and the quiet creaking of ships—but these did nothing to calm me. My eyes were shut but I was fully awake. An idea occurred to me.

"Teacher, what became of the vial?"

"The what?"

"The vial with the potion."

"It's here in the satchel, along with the scrolls. Why do you ask?"

"No reason."

He turned his gaze from the scroll in his lap and looked at me sidelong. "Do you have some need to be invisible tonight?"

"Of course not!"

He hummed skeptically, then returned his full attention to the scroll.

I tossed and turned. Sleep would not come.

In my imagination, I was certain that Galatea slept in the nude, without even a sheet to cover her. Try as I might, I could think of nothing else.

At some point the room grew dim, as the lamps burned low and Antipater did not refill them. He nodded, and his grip loosened, so that the scroll on his lap unfurled and rolled down his legs and onto the floor. Antipater began to snore.

Very quietly I rose from the bed. I started to put on my tunic, then realized I had no need for it. Nor did I need the loincloth I was wearing. An invisible man had no need for clothes! With the thrill that only a nineteen-year-old can feel at simply being naked, I stripped off the loincloth and luxuriated in the cool sea breeze from the window.

Moving stealthily, I found the vial, unstoppered it, and ingested a few drops. Moments later, I felt it take effect.

Downstairs, all was quiet. The empty common room was closed for the night. In the darkness I navigated the narrow hallway to Galatea's room.

The door was not locked. Very quietly, I unlatched the handle, pushed the door open, and stepped inside.

A small lamp set atop the trunk burned very low. I had been wrong about at least one thing: Galatea slept with a sheet over her. No glimmer of flesh was revealed by the lamp's slanting amber glow, only a jumbled linen landscape of ridges and shadows.

Next to the lamp, something shone brightly. It was a silver coin. Drawn by its glitter, I leaned over the trunk and took a closer look.

It was a shekel of Tyre, but not just any shekel. The profile of Melkart had no nose.

What were the chances that I should see not one, but two of these rare coins in a single day?

I took a closer look. Almost certainly, this was the very coin that Kerynis had shown me. How had Galatea come to have it—unless Kerynis had given it to her? And why would any man give a silver coin of such value to a mere serving girl—unless she had performed a service far more valuable than pouring wine?

To how many others in the tavern that night had Kerynis paid a silver shekel, in return for their flawless performances? He could have given a shekel to every man there and still have plenty left over.

I heard a sleepy sigh. I turned and stood at the foot of the bed. Suddenly angry at having been made a fool, I clutched the nearest corner of the sheet and yanked it from the bed.

I had been right about one thing: Galatea slept in the nude. The play of the soft amber light across her recumbent form sent a stab of longing through me despite my anger.

But she was not alone.

Next to her was Kerynis, equally naked. The two of them stirred, sleepily clutching for the sheet that had been so rudely taken from them.

A new thought occurred to me, running counter to the first: what if Kerynis had paid Galatea the shekel for the pleasure of her company, and not for going along with the pretense that two traveling fools were temporarily invisible? If that were true, my flash of anger was unjustified, and the potion *did* work—in which case, neither of them could see me standing before them, completely naked.

An instant later, I was disabused of this notion by Kerynis himself. Groggy from wine and who could say what other pleasures, he scooted to one side of the bed and managed to make a bit of room between himself and Galatea, then patted the empty spot.

"Come to join us, you studly Roman? The three of us can reenact the amorous encounter of Fafhrd and the Gray Mouser and Queen Laodice!"

Galatea laughed, looked at me through narrow eyes, and flashed a sleepy smile. She joined Kerynis in patting the empty spot.

The two of them could see me, after all.

"But Teacher, I don't understand why you're won't take legal action. Doesn't Tyre have magistrates? Call the scoundrel into a court of law and demand that he return the money to you in exchange for all these worthless books!"

The first light of morning had been seeping from the open window when I woke Antipater and told him what I had discovered. Now bright, slanting sunlight shone on the masts in the harbor, and still we were arguing.

"No, no, Gordianus. I won't do it. The money is his now, and the books are mine, and that's the end of it."

"It's not right," I said. "You were taken advantage of. He made fools of us both."

Antipater raised a snowy brow. "Is it seemly, to call your old tutor a fool?"

"That's not what I mean, and you know it." I paced the room. "Whenever I think of it, my face burns hot."

"Think of what?"

"How they must all have been laughing at us, behind our backs. That whole roomful of men, paid off by Kerynis to go along with his charade. We thought we were fooling them, walking around invisible, but they were fooling us! Because they could see us the whole time!"

"Consider the acting skills required for such a performance," said Antipater thoughtfully. "It's quite remarkable that none of them burst into laughter."

"Well, I'm sure they're laughing at us now. And they'll laugh every time they tell the story. When I think of it—"

"Then my advice, Gordianus, is that you do *not* think of it."

I drew a sharp breath. "If I could have stolen the money back from Kerynis, I would have. But I had no weapon on me . . ." The fact that I had not even had clothes, much less a weapon, when I encountered Kerynis, I had not revealed to Antipater. It seemed best to leave out certain details of my nocturnal encounter.

"But there was no theft in the first place, Gordianus. What law was broken?"

"Kerynis defrauded you!"

"About the potion, yes. But I wasn't paying him for the potion; I was paying him for the Books of Secret Wisdom."

"And what makes you think those aren't frauds as well? Useless forgeries, utter gibberish—"

"Because last night I had the chance to closely examine them. I have no doubt: these are indeed the Books of Secret Wisdom spoken of in the legends of Fafhrd and the Gray Mouser."

"But the invisibility potion was useless. We both felt a little giddy, but it didn't make us invisible."

"True, that batch of potion was useless; but it does *not* follow that the recipe itself is useless. Kerynis was at fault, not the scroll. The fellow was probably too lazy to go searching for all the proper ingredients to make a genuine batch. For one thing, I think he's mistaken when it comes to identifying this so-called chameleon herb. I suspect it's a plant not native to these parts at all—and it may take quite a bit of further research to determine exactly what plant the text refers to."

"But, Teacher, what makes you think these Books of Secret Wisdom are any less fraudulent than the man who sold them to you?"

For a moment Antipater appeared to be taken aback, then he gave me a stony look. "I believe in the Books of Secret Wisdom, Gordianus, because I believe in the legends, and the legends affirm that the magic in these scrolls does exist—if we can but interpret their wisdom correctly."

I took a deep breath. There was no arguing with a man's faith in the legends of his childhood.

"So, Gordianus—where is our friend Kerynis now?"

"He left the tavern at first light, taking his loot with him. But we could still track him down—"

"No, no, no!" Antipater was adamant. "I *am* glad that you happened to encounter him and that you got the truth out of him, about the useless potion. I trust that neither of you was harmed during the interchange? You didn't come to blows?"

"No. No violence, no physical contact . . . of that sort."

He responded to this ambiguous addendum with a blank look but let it pass. "And I'm sorry that you had to face such a disappointment when you went to the girl's room. Not only did you realize that she had taken part in deceiving us, but you discovered her in the arms of another man. Alas! Another had plucked the fruit before you. I take it that Kerynis turned tail and ran at once after you got the truth out of him?"

I shifted uneasily from foot to foot. "Not exactly."

"Ah. So you extracted the truth from him, then left him there, in bed with the girl?"

"No, I saw him get dressed and leave the room. Eventually."

Antipater frowned. "I can't be sure when I fell asleep, but I've been thinking you went to the girl's room shortly before dawn, and returned very shortly thereafter, at first light. Or . . . did you go to her room earlier than that? Just how long were the three of you in that girl's room—and what kept you so long?" He watched me fidget and raised an eyebrow. "Well, never mind. It's none of my business. Just as my acquisition of these books, and the price I paid for them, is none of yours. Agreed?"

After a long pause, I nodded. "Agreed."

"Then we shall never speak of it again."

That day we hired a small team of mules and made other arrangements for the next leg of our journey, and the day after that we left Tyre and headed for Babylon.

As the mules carried us up the well-worn road toward the Lebanon Mountains, we were both quiet and pensive. How, I wondered, could a man such as Antipater, ordinarily so wise, have been such a fool as to let himself be deceived by the likes of Kerynis? And why was he so certain of the value of the Books of Secret Wisdom, which had turned out to be useless? This lapse in prudence had something to do with returning to his hometown, I thought. Half-forgotten dreams of boyhood heroes had stirred the naive child inside him and laid waste to his hard-earned wisdom.

As for any lapse in judgment on my part, I could only plead that I was nineteen and susceptible to persuasion, far from home and in the midst of a long journey. The places I visited and the people I met continually surprised me, and I continually surprised myself.

At last, Antipater spoke. "On our first night in the Murex Shell, Gordianus, you remarked that nowhere else in our travels have you encountered the legends of Fafhrd and the Gray Mouser, and you asked why that was so. I have given that question considerable thought. Why have two figures of such remarkable interest been so scanted by the annalists and historians, so overlooked by philosophers, poets, and priests? I think it may be that they were, to put it bluntly, too disreputable. They were too stubbornly independent to give allegiance to a single city and thus become subject matter for a civic epic. They were too often involved with demons and sorcerers to appeal to the staid philosopher and too shifty to please the sober historian. In short, they were rogues, and rogues have no place in the lists of kings and demigods and heroes. It may be that no poet shall ever write of them, alas!"

For a long while we were both quiet, as the road grew steeper and the mules trudged onward.

"I wonder . . ."

"Yes, Gordianus?"

"Do you think that someday a poet will write of *our* adventures, Teacher?"

Antipater smiled ruefully. "Alas, I doubt if I'll live long enough to do so." Typically, at the mention of the word "poet," Antipater thought immediately and only of himself.

"Perhaps I'll do it," I said.

"You, Gordianus? But you're not a poet. And your Greek is barbaric!"

"Must every poem be in Greek?"

"Any poem worth reading." Antipater was showing his anti-Roman sentiment again.

"I wonder, Teacher, would this poem show us as heroes or scoundrels, as wise men or fools? Or as rogues?"

"Ha! I should think the rogue in our latest encounter would be your bedmate Kerynis!" Antipater saw the chagrin on my face and laughed aloud. "Can a man not be all those things at once, as were Fafhrd and the Gray Mouser? That's what makes them so fascinating. Some men are one thing on the surface and another underneath. The true poet shows not just the exterior of his subject, but all the contradictions within, and lets the reader draw his own conclusions."

I looked at my snowy-haired tutor and smiled, feeling a great affection for him. "I shall remember that, Teacher, when it's time to write my memoirs."

Garth Nix

New York Times bestselling Australian writer Garth Nix worked as a book publicist, editor, marketing consultant, public-relations man, and literary agent before launching the bestselling *Old Kingdom* series, which consists of *Sabriel, Lirael: Daughter of the Clayr, Abhorsen,* and *The Creature in the Case.* His other books include the *Seventh Tower* series, consisting of *The Fall, Castle, Aenir, Above the Veil, Into Battle,* and *The Violet Keystone,* the *Keys to the Kingdom* series, consisting of *Mister Monday, Grim Tuesday, Drowned Wednesday, Sir Thursday, Lady Friday, Superior Saturday,* and *Lord Sunday,* as well as stand-alone novels such as *The Ragwitch* and *Shade's Children.* His short fiction has been collected in *Across the Wall: Tales of the Old Kingdom and Beyond.* His most recent books are two novels written with Sean Williams, *Troubletwisters: The Mystery* and *Troubletwisters: The Monster,* a new stand-alone novel, *A Confusion of Princes,* and a new collection, *Sir Hereward and Mister Fitz: Three Adventures.* Born in Melbourne, he now lives in Sydney, Australia.

Nix has written a popular series detailing the adventures of Sir Hereward, a roving knight, and his companion Mister Fitz, a millennia-old sorcerer who happens to be an enchanted puppet. Here Sir Hereward and Mister Fitz reluctantly undertake a spot of housebreaking, only to find everything they were *not* looking for, including some very deadly surprises.

A CARGO OF IVORIES

Garth Nix

"We should have purchased the monkey," whispered Sir Hereward, as he balanced precariously on the ridge of the tiled roof, which was shining bright under the moon and had become extremely slippery, the result of the squall of needle-sharp rain that had just blown through and over the erstwhile knight and his puppet-sorcerer companion, Mister Fitz.

Neither looked the part of knight or sorcerer this night. Sir Hereward was garbed in the soot-stained leather vest and breeches of a chimney sweep, the latter cut short at the knee, with a coil of rope over his shoulder and a dagger at his belt rather than a sword; and Mister Fitz had assumed the disguise of a sweep's boy by putting a ragged and filthy hood over his pumpkin-shaped papier-mâché head and child-sized leather gauntlets on his wooden hands.

"The monkey was insufficiently trained, and its mind not well formed enough for the impressing of sorcerous commands," Fitz whispered back.

"It stole my purse easily enough," countered Sir Hereward. "If we had bought it, then it would be here, and I wouldn't be wet and cold and—"

"The matter is moot, as we did not purchase the monkey, and furthermore we have arrived at our point of ingress."

Sir Hereward glanced ahead at the huge brick chimney stack that protruded six or seven feet from the roof. Halfway up the stack, a thin ribbon of gold had been affixed to the brickwork, the metal etched with many malevolent-looking runes and sorcerous writings.

"The monkey could have jumped straight to the top of the stack and avoided those curses," said Sir Hereward. He shuffled forward a pace or two, wincing as his bare feet found a sharp edge to the copper that sheathed the ridge.

"Jumping to the top would not avoid them," said Mister Fitz. His piercing blue eyes reflected brightly in the moonlight as he studied the gold ribbon. "The architect-sorcerer who made this place was well versed in her art."

"I trust you can counter the spells?" asked Sir Hereward.

"It were best to leave them in place but render them less efficacious," replied the puppet sorcerer. He rummaged in the pouch at his belt as he spoke, withdrawing a number of long pieces of onionskin paper that were heavily inscribed with runes, written in an ink the color of dried blood, in close lines.

"Less efficacious?" asked Sir Hereward. "In exactly what proportion? Those are death curses, are they not?"

"Indeed," said Fitz. He licked the roof with his long, blue, fabriclike tongue, picking up the moisture he would need in lieu of the saliva his mouth did not make, moistened one of the pieces of paper, and carefully pasted it over the gold ribbon, pressing it hard against the brickwork of the chimney. The runes in the gold began to glow hotly, before being soothed and quietened by the counterspells on the paper. "They will now merely cause a pang, an ache, or something of that order."

"There are many degrees and varieties of ache," said Sir Hereward gloomily. But he took the coil of rope off his shoulder and pressed the catch on the grapnel that extended its three barbed arms. "Shall I fix this in place now?"

"Not yet," said the puppet, who was peering closely at the lip of the chimney. He took another paper, wet it in the same manner, and stuck it over the cornice. "A clever mage. There were hidden spells upon the top bricks. But I believe it is now safe enough to proceed. Are you confident of the plan?"

"If everything is as we have been told, and as you have scried," said Sir Hereward. "Which, of course, is almost certainly not the case. But I do not think Montaul suspects our coming, which is something."

The house whose ensorcelled roof they were perched upon belonged to the aforementioned Montaul, commonly known as "Flatpurse"—not because of his poverty but because of his vast riches, which he denied existed and did not easily spend. He had drawn the attention of Sir

Hereward and Mister Fitz, who were only house-robbers upon occasion, because two days previously he had secretly taken delivery of a cargo of ivory figurines, seventy-four finger-high carvings that represented the godlets of the far kingdom of Asantra-Lurre. Possibly unbeknownst to Montaul, fourteen of the figurines were not merely representations of godlets but energistic anchors that secured the actual deities to this mortal plane and could be used to summon them into renewed existence. As the said godlets were all proscribed for various reasons, usually their inimical nature, the destruction of the ivories had long been sought by the Council of the Treaty for the Safety of the World, the possibly mythical, often thought defunct, and generally surprising sisterhood that Sir Hereward had been born into, his male gender a surprise that had not been allowed to interfere with his usefulness. Mister Fitz, on the other hand, was both male and female, or neither, or whichever he wished to be, and had served the Council in various roles almost since its establishment by a number of now mostly vanished polities several millennia gone.

In other places, or perhaps other times, it would not have been necessary for Sir Hereward and Mister Fitz to climb over the rooftops and make entry into Montaul's house through a death-charm-warded chimney. But the city of Kwakrosh was far from any of the Council's traditional allies who might exert some influence or force. Here, Montaul was not only a councillor and a colonel of the city's trained bands, he also reluctantly but wisely paid good, fine-minted money to a great number of judges, advocates, watchmen, and thief-takers to ensure that if any criminal activity was going on, it would be done *by* him rather than *to* him or to his exceedingly valuable property.

Hence the rooftop in the rain and the descent down the chimney.

Sir Hereward gritted his teeth as he lifted one leg over the papered charms to straddle the chimney stack, expecting something like a dagger strike to the groin, this being the kind of thing Mister Fitz might call an ache. But there was only a faint tingle, reminiscent of the sensation usually called pins and needles, that came from sitting too long in one spot.

Fastening the grapple to the lip of the chimney, he let the rope down as slowly and quietly as he could, till it hung slack. If the plans they had bribed the chimney-tax inspector to provide were accurate, the rope should now be hanging a foot or so above the top of the open hearth. Close enough to drop easily but hidden from view.

"Considering the quantity of Alastran wine you drank last night, I think we should take a moment to recapitulate the plan," said Mister Fitz quietly. "I go first, to take care of any additional sorcerous defenses. You follow on the count of eight . . ."

"Ten. I thought we agreed ten," whispered Sir Hereward. "What if there is something that takes you more than a moment to dispel? I don't want to blunder into a death spell or skin separator or the like."

"Very well. You follow upon the count of ten. We emerge in the Great Hall, likely deserted—"

"Hmmpf," said Hereward, which was not exactly disagreement but a certain hedging of bets.

"Likely deserted due to Montaul's parsimony, apart from the hounds who have free range of the interior," continued Mister Fitz. "If they are present, we throw the soporific bone I prepared earlier . . . I trust you have that somewhere easy to reach?"

Sir Hereward indicated the left leg of his breeches, where there was an unusually large bulge that extended almost to his knee, marking the position of the segmented bone that Mister Fitz had imbued with a sleeping spell for dogs. The bone itself was jointed in quarters, to allow each of the four lurchers, grippers, alaunts, or whatever breed of guard dog there was inside to tear off and secure its own portion. The merest lick would then send them to sleep. Fortunately, the soporific bone only worked on dogs, so it was safe to handle. Mister Fitz knew many variations for other species, though when he prepared it for humans, the spell was normally emplaced in confectionary or sweetmeats, unless intended for cannibals such as the terrible inhabitants of the ruined city of Coradon.

"We turn right, along the hall, up the steps, and through the inner door to the countinghouse," said Mister Fitz. "Scrying suggests that this inner way is not locked when Montaul is in residence, he likes to come and go, but in any case I have two remaining curiosities, which should suffice to pick the lock if it proves necessary."

"We grab the ivories, open the main door of the countinghouse from the inside, go across the courtyard, fight the gate guards who won't be expecting us, go out the night postern, and run away," picked up Hereward. "Simple, elegant, straightforward."

"I would not describe it as elegant," said Mister Fitz. "However, it should serve the purpose. Shall we proceed?"

"Please do," said Sir Hereward, inclining his head as if acknowledging someone of importance at a ball or court levee.

Mister Fitz gripped the rope with both gauntleted hands and began to climb down the rope headfirst, his blue-pupiled eyes staring down into the sooty darkness.

Hereward counted to twelve before he followed. His movements were not as fluid as the puppet's, but he climbed with a spare efficiency, the technique learned years before as a supernumerary aboard the pirate chaser *Termagant Biter* returning to him without conscious thought.

The chimney, though rarely used, in accordance with Montaul's cheeseparing ways that begrudged the purchase of any fuel, was still caked with soot. Though Hereward tried to keep to the rope and only touch the side with his feet, he swung a few times on the way down, and his back and elbows dislodged a considerable quantity of choking, black dust. Much of it blew up as well as sinking down, so that by the time he gently lowered himself down next to Mister Fitz, they were both entirely blackened, their chimney-sweep disguises much enhanced.

The Hall was not only empty, but very dark. Montaul did not approve of candles or lanterns in rooms where he was not present. Mister Fitz could see perfectly well, but Sir Hereward had to depend upon his ears alone, and he didn't like what he was hearing. A wet, slobbery snuffling that sounded likely to precede the crunch of large teeth, and it was much closer than he deemed secure. It also did not sound particularly like a dog. It was louder and just . . . different.

"Hand me the bone," said Mister Fitz, who seemed calm enough, though this was little indication of the seriousness of the situation. Mister Fitz was always calm.

"What is it?" whispered Sir Hereward, moving very slowly to pull the soporific bone out of his trousers. He moved slowly because he was deeply concerned that a sudden movement might hasten the transition from slobbering noises to crunching ones, with his hand or arm featuring as the source of the crunching.

"A basilisk," said Mister Fitz. "It's licking my glove right now."

"A basilisk!" hissed Sir Hereward, instinctively screwing his eyes tight at the very mention of the petrifying beast. "Will the bone work on a basilisk?"

"We shall see," replied Mister Fitz. Hereward felt the puppet take the bone and a second later the slobbering noise increased, followed by the hideous crunching sounds he had feared. Almost immediately they then ceased and were punctuated by a very loud thud, a strong vibration through the floor, and the cessation of the munching and crunching.

"Remind me to amend my treatise on soporific bones," said Mister Fitz. "I thought there was a slim chance it would prove efficacious, as Plontarl's Index states there was dog in the original hybrid made by Kexil-Ungard when it created the first basilisks. A gaze-hound, perhaps, though there is clearly a preponderance of reptile in the creature—"

"Is there?" asked Sir Hereward, with no small degree of sarcasm apparent in his voice. "Given I can't see a thing, I must trust to your opinion. Could we perhaps continue? With a little light?"

"Indeed," replied Mister Fitz.

The puppet did not resort to an esoteric needle for something as simple as shedding a little light. Instead Sir Hereward noticed two faint blue sparks appear, as if a copperized wick had been lit. Slowly they grew brighter as Fitz increased the luminosity of his eyes, an old trick of his that had more than once proven to be of great value, most famously when the hasty reading of a map at midnight had resulted in Hereward's leading a rear guard to safety, rather than certain defeat and a lingering death, since the enemy in question were devotees of Pozalk-Nimphenes, a god whose concept of prisoners of war was indistinguishable from that of food, so anyone captured was invariably fed into its insatiable but toothless maw, expiring days later in the god's otherworldly stomach or whatever organ processed things so devoured.

Fitz did not make his eyes shine very brightly, so Hereward squinted as he poked his head out of the hearth and looked around the hall. The basilisk was a dark shape on the floor just beyond the bronze firedogs. As far as he could tell from its silhouette, it looked entirely like an ugly lizard, which is what he had always thought they were, albeit ones with the power to mesmerize their prey into statuelike stillness.

"Why would there be a basilisk here?" asked Sir Hereward as he slowly looked around the room. "Unless there is some trap to set lights going, it would be entirely wasted in the dark."

"I do not think it is an intentional inhabitant of the house," said Mister Fitz.

"There is something else near the door to the countinghouse," said Hereward. He could make out a silhouette that at first he had thought some very large piece of furniture, but it was moving slightly, suggesting breathing. "The door behind it is ajar. Can you see what it is?"

The puppet edged out next to him, holding Hereward's knee for a moment as he leaned around the marmorealized foot of a moklek, the shorn and domesticated cousins of the wild mammoth. This hollowed-out foot served to hold several pokers and other useful fireplace implements, including a six-tined toasting fork.

"Yes . . . I can," said Mister Fitz. "Curious."

"What is it, if you don't mind?"

"A pygmy moklek. An albino, I should think. Which is surprising, but also presents us with an opportunity."

"A basilisk and an albino pygmy moklek were most definitely not part of the plan," said Sir Hereward. "Nor do I consider the presence of said creatures to be an 'opportunity.' That moklek is lying in front of the door. Does it have tusks?"

"Short tusks jeweled at the tips," confirmed Mister Fitz. "It is asleep."

"Even a moklek can lose its temper, and even short tusks can disembowel," said Sir Hereward. "The jewels might even help. The question is, how did it get here?"

"The 'why' may also be relevant," suggested Mister Fitz, his tone educational. He had never really given up his early role as Sir Hereward's nurse and tutor.

"Lord Arveg, whose house lies adjacent to the perimeter wall here, has a private menagerie . . ." mused Sir Hereward, after a moment's thought. "If breaches were made in the west wall of his house, and then the eastern wall of this . . . but there has been no explosion, no petard blast . . ."

"Stone may be dissolved by sorcery," said Mister Fitz. "Animals transported energistically through solid matter. Sound may be dulled, or sent elsewhere, via a number of magical instruments."

"Someone else is after the ivories," concluded Sir Hereward. He drew his dagger, turning it so the light from Fitz's eyes did not reflect from the bright steel blade. "Presumably a sorcerer."

"Or someone equipped with sorcerous apparatus," agreed Mister Fitz. He reached inside his sooty robe and withdrew an energistic needle from some hidden interior pocket, holding it tightly inside his gloved fist so that its shocking light could not escape, nor the energies within curdle Sir Hereward's mind or vision. "They might also have a different aim in mind, apart from the ivories. Montaul has many riches, and many enemies. In any case, it is doubly unfortunate, for use of sorcery may . . . wake something in one of the ivories. They tremble on the verge of immanence at the best of times. We had best hurry."

Sir Hereward nodded, stepped out of the fireplace, and began to walk cautiously towards the door out to the countinghouse, his bare feet silent on the flagstones. Mister Fitz rustled at his side, the light of his eyes like a hooded lantern in a mine, illuminating the way just enough for safe movement while creating shadows at every side that hinted at terrible things.

"Are you sure the moklek is asleep?" whispered Hereward as they drew closer.

"No, I think it is merely resting," said Mister Fitz. "Don't tread on its tail."

As they ascended the four steps to the door to the countinghouse, skirting the pygmy moklek, it suddenly stood up, turned about very daintily on the spot, and made a plaintive whuffling noise with its trunk.

Sir Hereward stopped in midstep and tightened his grip on his dagger. It was fine Trevizond steel, and very sharp, but whether he could punch it through the weak spot in a moklek's head above and between its eyes was very much a moot question. Particularly if it had to be done while trying not to be disemboweled.

"There, there," said Mister Fitz, reaching out to stroke the trunk that came questing out to them. "All will be well."

"Are you talking to me or the moklek?" whispered Sir Hereward.

"Both," said Mister Fitz. "It is a youngster, and scared. There, there. All will be well. Say hello to the moklek, Hereward."

"Hello," said Sir Hereward. He reached out gingerly with his left hand and joined Mister Fitz in gently stroking the moklek's trunk.

"You had better come with us," said Mister Fitz. "Follow along."

The moklek made a soft trumpeting noise and took a step forward. Sir Hereward hastily jumped up a step and bent down to whisper in Mister Fitz's ear.

"Why are we bringing the moklek? You didn't want a monkey. Surely a moklek is no better?"

"It is a very smart moklek," said Mister Fitz. "As opposed to a particularly stupid monkey. And it may prove useful. As I said, its presence provides an opportunity. One that may be lost if we don't procure the ivories quickly."

Sir Hereward sighed, hefted his dagger, and sidled through the open doorway and along a short corridor into the countinghouse proper. He had expected this large chamber to also be dark, but it was filled with moonlight, courtesy of a large, ragged round hole in the eastern wall where something sorcerous or immensely acidic had melted through a three-foot thickness of good red brick.

The person presumably responsible for this absence of wall was in the middle of the room, opening drawers in Montaul's trading desk, a massive piece of powerful but ugly furniture that had dozens of drawers in great columns of polished mahogany on the left and right of the actual writing surface, a slab of Perridel marble characteristically veined with gold.

She whirled around as Hereward took another step though he thought he'd been extremely stealthy, and, in the next instant, he had to parry away not one but two thrown daggers, which flew clattering to the wall and the floor. She followed that up by jumping to the desk and then to the ceiling, running along it upside down by virtue of Ikithan spider-slippers, dropping on Hereward from above in a move that he fortunately recognized as the vertical shearing scissor-leg attack of the long-defunct but still influential warrior nuns of the Red Morn Convent, and so was able to adopt the countermove of swaying aside and delivering two quick punches to the head as she descended. One of the punches was with the pommel of his dagger, and so particularly efficacious. The thief, as she must be, dropped to the floor long enough for Sir Hereward to press a knee on her back and place the point of his dagger in the nape of her neck, angled so that it would strike through to the brain with little effort.

"Move and you die," he rasped. "Also, we are not guards, but visitors like yourself, so there is no profit in employing any unusual stratagem or sorcery you may be considering."

"You are trespassers, then," said the woman coolly. She was dressed in thieves' garb, entirely in dark grey, a single suit of it like a cold-weather undergarment, complete with a padded hood. Even prone, she was clearly tall and lightly built, but as evident from her jumping, made of corded muscle and sinew.

"As are you," said Sir Hereward. "What are you looking for?"

"Trespassing against the guild, I mean," said the woman impatiently. "I have bought the license to steal here. But if you release me and go now, I will not take you to the Thief-Mother's court for the doubtless inevitable separation of thumbs from hands."

"Ah, a *professional* thief," said Mister Fitz. "We are not, however, here to rob Montaul. We are reclaiming stolen property."

"Oh," said the woman. "You are agents, then?"

Sir Hereward grew still and his grip on his dagger tightened, ready to drive it home. A human's brain was so less well protected than a moklek's as he knew well. It would be an easy and quick death. Not that his and Mister Fitz's occupation was necessarily secret, it was simply that only their enemies tended to know who they were.

"Agents?" asked Sir Hereward, his voice flat and dull.

"Of the Barcan Insurance? Or the Association of Wealth Protection?"

"Insurance agents," said Mister Fitz. "Yes . . . but from far away. We have been tracking a stolen cargo for some considerable time. Now we believe it has arrived here."

"Then we can come to an agreement," said the thief. "My name is Tira, Thief of the Seventh Circle of the Guild of Thieves in Kwakrosh, Lesemb, and Navilanaganishom. Who might you be?"

"I am Sir Hereward," said Hereward, though he did not ease off with his knee or remove his dagger. "My companion is known as Mister Fitz. Where are the guards from the courtyard outside, before we get to talking about agreements?"

"Asleep," said Tira. "I sprinkled Nighty Dust down on them from my shadow-stilts, as they gathered to gossip about tomorrow's battlemount races."

"And the wall here, was it dissolved with a spray of Argill's Discontinuance of Stone, or something else?" asked Mister Fitz.

"Argill's," confirmed Tira. "And the wall of Arveg's menagerie across the courtyard, though I must confess that was an error. The mixture was stronger than I thought and the wind came up. But the creatures are docile, I presume made to be that way. There is nothing to fear from them."

"You have invested considerable coin to enter here, on stilts and dust and dissolving," said Mister Fitz. "You seek some particular treasure?"

"Montaul is known as a very warm man," said Tira.

"Please answer the question," said Sir Hereward.

"The new ivories," she said, after a moment's pause. "The guild has a buyer for them. But I guess that's what you are after, too, is it not, arriving so soon on their heels?"

"Yes," said Sir Hereward. "But not all of them. Only fourteen are . . . covered by our contract. You can have the others. Agreed?"

"Agreed," said Tira.

Hereward removed his dagger, leaned back, and stood up. Tira rolled over and looked up at him. Her hood was drawn close about her face, and though her skin was dark, her nose and cheekbones had also been painted with a grey stuff almost the same color as her curious garment, to dull any shine. As far as Hereward could tell, she seemed fair, or as fair as could be without facial scars, and she looked younger than he had expected. Her eyes were hidden behind a strip of a dark red gauzy cloth loose-woven with hundreds of tiny holes, allowing her to see while offering some protection against such things as a basilisk's gaze, unless it got nose to nose, by which time its petrifying properties would be of the least concern. The fact she was wearing it suggested that she had not spoken the truth about dissolving the wall to the menagerie by accident.

"I could have got free, you know," she said.

"Doubtless," agreed Sir Hereward politely, though he thought quite the opposite. "Where are the ivories?"

"Not here," said Tira. "Or so I had just discovered when you came."

Sir Hereward looked around the room. Apart from Montaul's trading desk with its drawers askew, there were three lesser perching desks for his clerks, a cabinet whose doors were open to show the papers and parchments piled within, and a great chest with its padlock awry and its lid back. Mister Fitz was already inside the chest, rummaging around.

"Nothing of consequence," said the puppet. "A fallen coin or two in the corners. I should say it was emptied in some hurry. Hereward, go and see if Montaul is in his rooms upstairs."

Hereward nodded and ran up the circular stair in the corner, returning a scant minute later with a shake of his head.

"Chamber's empty. Like a monk's cell up there, thin blanket and all. But our watchers . . . they were supposed to blow their screech-whistles if anyone left, damn them!"

"Oh," said Tira. She made a motion with her fingers, indicating the sprinkling of dust. "They were *your* watchers . . ."

Mister Fitz jumped out of the chest and went to the door that led out to the gatehouse, his back bent from the waist, his round head close to the ground. At the door itself, he sniffed the ground, dust swirling around his papier-mâché nose, though its carefully molded nostrils did not inflate.

"One of the godlets has begun to manifest," he said shortly. "Some hours ago, I judge. We must presume it now controls Montaul's actions and follow before it can fully emerge upon this plane and ease the way of its fellows from the pantheon of ivories."

"Godlet?" asked Tira. "What godlet?"

"The ivories are not simply treasure," said Hereward, as he went to the door and unbarred it, using only his left hand, the dagger ready in his right. "At least the fourteen we seek. Did you make the gate guards sleep as well as those in the western court?"

"No," said Tira. She retrieved her thrown knives and went to stand by the knight, Mister Fitz bringing up the rear, his sorcerous needle still hidden in his gauntleted hand.

"You would think they would enter," said Sir Hereward, "given the noise within. Moklek and basilisk, and all your rummaging about. Ready?"

"They are not valiant, nor young," said Tira, readying her knives to throw. "Go!"

Sir Hereward pulled the door back. Tira stood with knives poised, then slowly lowered them. Sir Hereward moved past her, and looked down at the two desiccated bodies that lay on the steps. They were more vaguely human-shaped parcels of dust wrapped in mail than bodies, their swords lying next to withered hand-and-arm bones that would have not disgraced some revenant a thousand years dead.

"It needed life to stabilize its presence," said Mister Fitz, bending down to sniff again at the bodies of the guards. "They were convenient."

"Do you know which one it is?" asked Sir Hereward. There were fourteen ivories, and fourteen godlets, but of that number, one was far more to be feared than any of the rest.

"No," answered Mister Fitz. "It has left no obvious signs or declarations, and we cannot spare the time to take a sample of whatever essence it may have excreted."

"I like not this talk," said Tira. "If I had not seen these two, I might think you sought to scare me from my rightful theft."

"You need not come with us, lady," said Sir Hereward over his shoulder as he ran to the gate, ignoring the small night postern they had planned to use, for it would not be broad enough to permit the moklek's passage. Mister Fitz ran after him but jumped to one of the torch brackets above, and peered through an arrow slit, taking care not to draw too close to another ensorcelled band of gold set there to slay any child, monkey, or ensorcelled rat that might otherwise be able to creep inside.

Behind them, the pygmy moklek gingerly investigated the wizened bodies with its trunk, gave a snort of disgust, and trotted after the knight, thief, and puppet.

"I am no lady," said Tira, as she helped Sir Hereward lift the bar of the gate. "I am a Thief of the Sixth Circle of the Guild of Thieves in Kwakrosh, Lesemb, and Navilanaganishom!"

"I thought you said the Seventh Circle," said Sir Hereward.

"When I return with the ivories," said Tira. "I merely anticipated my elevation. In truth, I did not expect any complications with godlets."

Mister Fitz dropped down as they opened the postern.

"There is some commotion by the harborside," he said. "It will be the godlet. Quickly!"

Montaul's house lay on a low hill directly above the harbor, so that he could watch the arrival and departure of his ships, the foundation of his riches. A cobbled road ran down to the long, semicircular quay where four ships were tied up at the jetties that thrust out from the quay like fingers from a hand. A few other vessels were some distance away, bulky trading cogs lying at anchor under the shelter of the mole, a long breakwater of great stones that protected the harbor from wind and wave, with a hexagonal fort at its seaward end, built to protect the port against pirates and naval foes. The fort could fire forge-heated red-hot shot from the cannons on its walls, and explosive bombs the size of a puncheon from the great mortar that squatted in the center of the fort like a fat spider in a hole. Except that, as with many other civic buildings in Kwakrosh, it was somewhat neglected, and only fully manned in time of obvious threat, the good worthies of the town council not wanting to recognize that by that point it would be too late.

Sir Hereward, Mister Fitz, Tira, and the pygmy moklek ran down the harbor road, fleet shadows in the night. The moon lit the street in stark relief, casting silver shadows and reflecting off the puddles left by the earlier rainstorm, illuminating the drunks asleep in the doorways of the warehouses closer to the quay—drunks who upon inspection in the morning would be found to be no more than husks within their layers of rags.

"It must be after a ship," called out Sir Hereward. "But the wind is against the mole and the tide on the flood, no ship can leave harbor tonight."

"Not under sail," answered Mister Fitz. He pointed ahead to the most distant jetty, where there was the sound of screaming, suddenly cut short, and a yellow lantern winked out. Behind it, the dim outline of a long but relatively low ship with only a single stubby mast could be seen.

"The hexareme?" asked Sir Hereward, sidestepping a particularly deep-looking puddle in an area of missing cobbles. He referred to the state ship of Kwakrosh, a relic of the past, that was rowed out once a year for the Grand Mayor to perform the ritual throwing of the flotsam, a floating basket of spices, wine, cloth, smoked herring, and a very small amount of silver currency. This was then fought over by all the bum-boaters, fisherfolk, and semiaquatic layabouts of the harbor in joyous anarchy, a mark of respect for the ancient days when the town had been no more than a village of wreckers.

"But it has no rowers, no crew," said Tira, who ran easily at Sir Hereward's side.

"If the godlet is strong enough, it will bend the oars by energistic means," said Mister Fitz. "I am heartened by this."

"You are heartened?" asked Sir Hereward. "If it is strong enough to row a hexareme of sixty benches against this wind and tide, it is too strong by my measure!"

"It indicates a certain stupidity, a singleness of purpose," said Mister Fitz. "It wants to return to Asantra-Lurre, not knowing or caring that the kingdom is no more, and a thousand leagues distant besides."

"What is *it*?" asked Tira. "Do you mean Montaul?"

"Montaul lives no more, save as a vessel for the godlet," said Mister Fitz.

They reached the quay as he spoke, cobbles giving way to the smooth planks of the boardwalk. Two watchmen in the livery of the town guard stared at them nervously, their lantern-adorned halberds held high over the starched and dehydrated body of one of their companions, her arms frozen in the act of trying to fend off some horror that had come upon her.

"Who . . . who goes there?" stuttered one of them.

"Friends," called out Sir Hereward easily as he ran past, momentarily forgetting he was covered from head to toe in soot, was barefoot, had a dagger bare in his hand, and was accompanied by a sorcerous puppet, an obvious thief, and an albino pygmy moklek.

"Oh good," said the watchman nervously to their backs. He raised his voice to add, "Uh, pass, friends."

Up ahead, there was a great squeal of long-unused timber moving against bronze, and the splash of water as the hexareme's starboard oars all came out at once, the port side being up against the jetty.

"We must board before it shoves off," said Sir Hereward, increasing his pace, bare feet pounding across quayside to jetty. The hexareme's oars were tumbled together for the moment, but were already lifting and shifting, energistic tendrils of bright violet visible through the oar ports as the godlet sought to properly organize the rowing benches, like a team of octopi sorting toothpicks.

"Do we *want* to be on board with whatever is doing that?" asked Tira.

"The godlet's mind and power is bent upon moving the ship," said Mister Fitz, who had jumped to Sir Hereward's shoulder as the sprint became too fast for his short legs. "While it is focused upon that task, we have a better chance of dispatching it to whence it came."

"Almost there!" panted Sir Hereward. He jumped to the gangway and ran up it even as the starboard oars dug deep and the hexareme groaned and moved diagonally away from the jetty, mooring ropes at stern and bow singing as they stretched taut. There was a great crash as the gangway fell, the pygmy moklek jumping the last few feet, the deck resounding like an enormous drum as it landed.

"Why is that moklek still following us?" asked Sir Hereward, who had narrowly avoided being crushed by the pachyderm's leap.

"I asked her to," said Mister Fitz. "As I said, she could be very useful. Time for the declaration. We have a few minutes now, I doubt the godlet is aware of our presence, it being fixated on a swift exit from the harbor."

The starboard oars sank in and pushed again. The mooring ropes snapped with cracks like gunshots, and the hexareme wallowed far enough away from the jetty for the portside oars to come out, again propelled by energistic tendrils.

Sir Hereward and Mister Fitz reached into pocket and pouch and brought out silk armbands, which they slipped over their arms, above the elbow. Sorcerous symbols began to shine upon the cloth, brighter than the moon. Then man and puppet spoke together:

"In the name of the Council of the Treaty for the Safety of the World, acting under the authority granted by the Three Empires, the Seven Kingdoms, the Palatine Regency, the Jessar Republic, and the Forty Lesser Realms, we declare ourselves agents of the Council. We identify the godlet manifested . . . uh . . ."

Sir Hereward paused and looked at Mister Fitz, who carried on, the man echoing the puppet's words a moment later.

"Aboard this vessel as an unknown, but listed entity under the Treaty, as proven by its dire actions upon innocents. Consequently, the said godlet and all those who assist it are deemed to be enemies of the World and the Council authorizes us to pursue any and all actions necessary to banish, repel, or exterminate the said godlet."

"You're not insurance agents," said Tira. Her hood had come slightly unstuck in the race to the ship and slipped backwards, showing more of her face. She looked even younger than she had previously.

"You could say we are," replied Mister Fitz. "After a fashion."

"In any case, you'll get your share of the ivories," said Hereward, thinking he correctly judged the fleeting expression that crossed Tira's eyes and flattened her mouth. "Presuming we survive."

The ship lurched sternwards as the oars on both sides moved in unison, a clumsy, lurching progress that made the deck tilt one way and then the other, with every part of the old ship groaning and screeching in turn.

"We won't get far like this," said Sir Hereward. "I doubt this tub has been out in anything but a dead calm for years, and going in the right direction at that. Where is the godlet? And what's to stop its sucking the life out of us as we approach?"

"It is underneath us," said Mister Fitz. "In the center of the ship, on the middle deck. As long as it keeps rowing, it will have no energy to spare for dehydrative assaults."

"And if it stops rowing?" asked Tira.

"The ship will probably sink," said Sir Hereward, who didn't like the feel of the deck under his feet. The planks were shifting sideways, the hull clearly lacked rigidity, and it was already down a foot or more at the stern, not so much piercing the small harbor waves as plowing into them. "It is moot whether it will turn turtle as soon as we pass the mole, or be driven under stern first."

"We must get the ivories before then," said Mister Fitz. "If the ship does sink, the godlet will realize that it can simply walk on the floor of the sea. For the moment, it is still imprinted with Montaul's view of the world and his human limitations."

"Is it weak enough for you to banish it with your needle?" asked Sir Hereward. "We distract it, while you get close enough?"

"I fear not," said Mister Fitz. "Rather we must secure the ivory figurine that anchors it, bring it up here, and have Moonray Pallidskin Helterskelter III step on it."

Sir Hereward followed the flick of the puppet's eyeballs to the left, indicating their animal companion.

"You mean the moklek?"

"It is one sure means of destruction for such things," said Mister Fitz. "To be trodden on by an albino moklek. That is why I said it was an opportunity. Considerably more convenient than our original plan to take the ivories to the fire pools of Shundalar, and cheaper than committing them to the priests of the Infallible Index to be stored without hope of retrieval. Though it would be even better if our friend here had silver shoes, that speeds the process—"

"How you do know her name?" interrupted Sir Hereward.

"It is carved on her right tusk," said the puppet. "That is her pedigree name. But there is a name on her left tusk, which I suspect she prefers. Rosie."

The moklek raised her trunk and gave a short, soft trumpet. Almost as if in answer, a red rocket suddenly shot up from the fort on the mole, followed by two cannon blasts.

"Not so swift on the alarm," said Sir Hereward, eyeing the rocket's trajectory with professional interest. When not engaged directly in the elimination of inimical godlets, he was a mercenary officer of artillery. "And their powder is damp. That rocket should have gone twice as high."

"Even with damp powder, the idiots in the fort might hit us if they decide to shoot," said Tira. "It is close enough."

"So how *do* we get to the ivories?" asked Sir Hereward, grabbing at a rail and wincing as the oars sank again to drive the ship backwards, and a particularly nasty groan came from the timbers below, the vessel shivering down its whole length as it was propelled too fast into the swell. They were already a good hundred yards out from the quay and heading into brisker waters away from the protection of the mole. "I presume it keeps them close, and even if the thing is rowing for dear life, I don't fancy just strolling in on a desiccating inimical godlet."

"I suggest you and Tira climb over the sides and go in through the oar ports on the deck above it—"

"There are huge *oars* going up and down in those ports," interrupted Tira. "We would be crushed."

"It has already broken a number of oars, or they were broken before, so there are empty ports," said Mister Fitz. "Choose carefully, climb down, swing in. I will cast a nimbus on your weapons that will allow them to engage the energistic tendrils of the godlet. As you hack and slash them away from the oars, it will disrupt the rowing, and the entity will have to fight back. While it is distracted fighting you on the upper deck, I will sneak in on the middle deck where it lies, gather the ivories, and bring them up here, where Rosie will stomp on them."

"The fourteen ivories you mentioned," said Tira. "Not the others."

"Indeed," said Mister Fitz, who did not lie but did not always tell the truth.

"So there will be a few inches of rotten worm-eaten oak between us and the main presence of the godlet?" mused Sir Hereward. "That is better than I feared. Do you wish to take the port or starboard side, Tira?"

"Neither," said the thief. "But having come this far, and waiting a year already for my Fifth Circle testing—"

"Fifth Circle?" asked Sir Hereward. "At this rate we will discover you were only apprenticed yesterday."

"Fifth, Sixth, Seventh, a haul such as these ivories will grant me rapid advancement," said Tira nonchalantly. "I will take the port side."

"Hold out your weapons and look away," said Mister Fitz.

They did so. The sorcerous needle flared, a flash of light illuminating the deck as if lightning had struck the stumpy mast above them. When they looked back, the needle was once again closed in Fitz's hand, and the blades of dagger and knives glowed with shimmering blue light, like a Wintertide pudding in burning brandy, only somewhat more impressive.

"A word of advice," said Sir Hereward to Tira. "Ikithan spider silk does not stick when subjected to seawater."

Tira looked surprised, but quickly schooled her face, and stripped the slippers from her feet. The nails of her big toes were clad in bronze, darkened at the tips with some kind of poison.

"Watch the oars through at least two strokes before you choose your port," added Sir Hereward. "Make sure you won't be caught by those forr'ard or behind."

Tira nodded. She looked scared, and Hereward thought he heard her suppress a whimper.

"You're really just an apprentice, aren't you?" asked Sir Hereward suddenly. "How old are you?"

Tira shrugged, then nodded her head again.

"Fifteen," she whispered. "And a half."

"Gods help us," muttered Sir Hereward, from the lofty height of his twenty-five years. "Stay here with the moklek. Please."

Hereward turned away from her and so did not see the smile that so briefly flickered across her face. He looked over the side, his head jerking back in momentary startlement at how low the hexareme was in the water, so low that the bottom tier of oar ports was only a handsbreadth above the sea, with the taller waves slopping in. If there had been any hope the ship would weather a turn past the protective mole, it was now extinguished.

It was the matter of only a few seconds to find a suitable gap, where no oars extended. He briefly considered holding the dagger with its energistic flames in his teeth but instead put it through his belt, climbed swiftly over the side, and, wasting no time, went feetfirst through the port below.

It was brighter belowdecks than above, the moonbeams through the ports faint beside the bright violet light of the energistic tendrils that worked the oars, tendrils that came up like a great trunk from below, through the gridded hatch in the lane between the empty benches, and then broke into branches extending to every oar.

Sir Hereward slashed at the closest tendril, severing it from the oar, and had to duck and dodge as the iron-shod shaft kicked up. He stayed low, crawling forward to hack at the next tendril, with similar results, and this time that oar crossed with the one in front, with a rending and splintering that spread along the deck as the oars in motion tangled with those suddenly stopped. The hexareme yawed broadside to the wind, and almost immediately listed to port, the lowest oar ports two decks below now fully submerged, water cascading in with unstoppable force.

Sir Hereward felt the list and heard the fateful gurgling. Leaping back from a tendril that came questing for him, not for an oar, he cut it in two and retreated to the port where he'd come in.

"Fitz!" he roared, in full sea captain's shout. "Do you have them?"

More tendrils came towards him, from both sides and in the front, and many more were giving up their useless, broken oars and reorienting themselves to attack. Hereward cut and slashed at them while he hung half-out of the port. His bare foot touched the crest of a wave, and he felt the hexareme shudder with every wave. It was sinking, and sinking fast.

"Fitz! Do you have them?"

"Yes! Come up!"

The puppet's thin, reedy voice came clear and high through the bass groans of breaking timber and the drowning gurgles of the ship. Sir Hereward hacked at a tendril that was trying to grasp him by the throat, threw the dagger at another that almost had his ankle, and exited through the port faster than the monkey he had almost bought earlier had disappeared with his purse when demonstrating its abilities.

He was none too soon. The sea poured in under him as he climbed, and there was already water washing halfway up the main deck, which was inclined at an angle of some twenty degrees, perhaps halfway to turning over. Rosie the albino pygmy moklek was leaning against the mainmast, one foot raised, and Mister Fitz was placing a wooden case with a bronze handle and reinforced edges under that foot. The case containing the ivories.

Then the puppet was suddenly caught up in a glowing net of bright *blue* energistic spiracules and dragged away from the case, which was snatched up by Tira. Letting the netted puppet roll down the deck, she sprang to the port gunwale, the case in her right hand.

Sir Hereward swarmed up the slanted deck on all fours. Tira held up the case, smiled at him, and shouted, "Asantra-Lurre may no longer be, but we Asantrans live on!"

She turned to dive into the sea, just as Hereward drew his short, three-barreled pepperbox pistol from the secret pocket under his vest, cocked it, and shot her in one swift motion. Only two barrels fired, but at least one ball struck the thief, low on her right arm above the wrist. Blood and fragments of bone sprayed out. Tira dropped the case and fell over the side, her scream of anguish cut short by the green wave that caught her.

The case slid down toward Hereward. He bent and grabbed it, swinging it over to the moklek even as lurid violet tendrils broke out through the deck in a dozen places and shot towards him, and a hulking, vaguely man-shaped mass of sickening energies erupted from the aft companionway, its inhuman voice shrieking in some incomprehensible language that hurt Hereward's ears. The godlet staggered along the deck, and its furthermost tendrils reached with snakelike speed to grip Hereward around the bare ankles, his skin sizzling from the touch till he let himself slide down the deck to plunge into the great wash of sea that was roiling about above the already-submerged gunwales.

As he fell, Sir Hereward cried out: "Crush the case, Rosie! Crush the case!"

The pygmy moklek trumpeted in response and brought her foot down on the case. It splintered, but did not break. A wave crashed in, sending Hereward, struggling amidst tendrils, back up towards the mast. The wash caught the case and threatened to push it away, till Rosie gripped the handle with her trunk. The godlet, or that portion of it within the remnant body of Montaul, staggered towards the ivories, reaching out, only to be seized by an energistic lash, white as lightning, that emanated from a needle in the hand of Mister Fitz, who had escaped the blue net and was now some ten feet up the mainmast backstay.

"Crush—" Sir Hereward called again, but a tendril closed around his throat, and his shout was curtailed, the breath stopped from his lungs. He tried to prize the noose open, but his fingers burned and could get no purchase, and more and more tendrils were wrapping themselves around every part of his body, squeezing and tugging, so that he was as like to be torn apart as strangled, or even drowned, as in their viciousness the tendrils kept shoving him underwater.

Rosie the moklek, her broad rear wedged against the mainmast, did not need to be told again. She raised her foot and brought it down with all her strength, smashing the lid of the case. Treading down, she ground the case and all the ivories within to dust, continuing to stomp and crush till there was nothing left larger than a tiny splinter.

The energistic tendrils grew flaccid and shrank back from Hereward, who crawled coughing and spluttering up the slanted deck, emerging from the froth of broken water just in time to see the tendrils withdraw into the corpse of Montaul. There, they dimmed to become small lights that flickered within the cadaver's eyes, mouth, and open ribs. Then there was a dull pop, a sudden rush of air against the wind, and the lights went out. The remnants of Montaul fell to the deck and were whisked away by the roiling sea, for the hexareme had now settled so far that only a small part of its deck was above the surface.

"Abandon ship!" called out Hereward weakly. "She's foundering!"

Mister Fitz nodded, but instead of jumping to the sea from the backstay, he climbed up it, and then swung down on a rope to Rosie's back, where he perched easily atop her head. The moklek raised her trunk, ready for use as a breathing tube, shifted away from the mast, and plunged into the sea.

Hereward swam to them. Seeing that Rosie was at home even in the sea, and her broad back, though smaller than a regular moklek's, offered considerable room, he pulled himself aboard with a little help from Mister Fitz. Though the moklek's back offered only inches of freeboard, Rosie floated with the waves, and wind and tide were already carrying them back to the quay, aided by her four strong legs paddling vigorously below.

"Well shot," said Mister Fitz. "Somewhat making up for your misjudgment of the woman, though I should have come to expect that."

"She fooled you too," said Sir Hereward, grimacing as he felt his burned throat. "You, to be caught like a novice in an Ikithan net."

"True," mused the puppet. "It was fortunate she did not have one resistant to seawater. But I suspected her from the first, for she had too much sorcerous gear for any thief of Kwakrosh, even she be the Thief-Mother herself."

"Then why did you not—" said Sir Hereward hotly before a great crack sounded behind them, and man and puppet turned to see a gout of flame leap up from the fortress on the mole.

"Mortar bomb," said Sir Hereward, watching fuse sparks trail across the sky. "They are poor aimers . . . if you have a needle left, Fitz . . ."

"None to hand," said the puppet. "My sewing desk is back at the inn."

"Or perhaps their aim is good," said Sir Hereward, as the spark trail plummeted towards the almost-completely-submerged hulk of the hexareme, only its stumpy mast now visible above the white tops of the waves, a hundred yards behind them. "But if the fuse is too long, the bomb will be drowned . . ."

A yellow-red flash lit the sky, followed a moment later by the shock of force through the water, and a moment later still by a great boom. As Hereward blinked to clear the flash from his eyes, he saw that there was no longer a mast or any other indication of the hexareme.

"I thought they were shooting at us," he said.

"Perhaps they were," said Mister Fitz.

"In any case, it will take them some time to load another bomb," said Sir Hereward, looking back again. "We will be ashore before then. It is a sad end for a famous vessel. One of the last surviving hexaremes of Ashagah, I believe. It will be difficult to explain to the worthies of the town, who I perceive are amongst the notable force gathering on the quay as our reception."

"Perhaps not so difficult, should we provide a suitable scapegoat," said Mister Fitz. He stood up on Rosie's head, held on to Hereward's shoulder, and pointed ahead.

Tira the thief, or priestess, or whatever she was, was floating on her back ahead of them, feebly kicking her legs. As the moklek drew closer, Hereward reached out and half slid her, half dragged her onto Rosie's back.

"Curse you," she whispered. "May Pixalten-Qockril send—"

Mister Fitz leaned across and pressed one wooden finger against the middle of her forehead, his gauntlets being long since swept away. Tira stopped talking, her eyes rolled back, and Hereward had to turn her head so her mouth and nose weren't in the water.

"And we have money for bribes," continued Mister Fitz. He reached to his arm and pulled off the brassard, the letters fading. "All will be well."

"So I suppose," said Sir Hereward. He took off his own armband, slapped his hand lightly on the moklek's back, and added, "We have much to thank you for, Rosie."

"Indeed, she is a princess amongst mokleks," said Mister Fitz. "Quite literally, albinism is a mark of the royal line."

"Hexareme of Ashagah and mokleks," said Hereward thoughtfully. "It reminds me of a poem. Let me see . . .

Hexareme of Ashagah
From far-off Panas
Drumming down the sea-lanes
In search of easy prey
Seeking a cargo of ivories, gold and mokleks . . .

"Bah!" protested Mister Fitz. "That is doggerel, a murder of the original poem. If you must recite, Hereward, you should do honor to the poet, not commit a crime!"

"It is a later translation, true, but nonetheless I stand by it!" protested Sir Hereward. "You and your heart of cypress have no feeling for verse!"

The moklek trumpeted, spraying them with a little seawater. A wave lifted her, and the east wind blew against Hereward's back, taking them shorewards, knight and puppet bickering all the way.

Walter Jon Williams

Walter Jon Williams was born in Minnesota and now lives near Albuquerque, New Mexico. His short fiction has appeared frequently in *Asimov's Science Fiction*, as well as in *The Magazine of Fantasy and Science Fiction, Lightspeed, Subterranean,* and in other markets, and has been gathered in the collections *Facets* and *Frankensteins and Foreign Devils.* His novels include *Ambassador of Progress, Knight Moves, Hardwired, The Crown Jewels, Voice of the Whirlwind, House of Shards, Days of Atonement, Aristoi, Metropolitan, Rock of Ages, City on Fire,* as well as a huge disaster thriller, *The Rift,* and a *Star Wars* novel, *Destiny's Way,* and three novels in his acclaimed Modern Space Opera epic, "Dread Empire's Fall," *Dread Empire's Fall: The Praxis, Dread Empire's Fall: The Sundering,* and *Dread Empire's Fall: Conventions of War.* His most recent books are the novels *Implied Spaces, This Is Not a Game, Deep State,* and *The Fourth Wall,* the chapbook novella *The Boolean Gate,* and a new collection, *The Green Leopard Plague and Other Stories.* He won a long-overdue Nebula Award in 2001 for his story "Daddy's World," and took another Nebula in 2004 with his story "The Green Leopard Plague."

In the sly story that follows, a movie star (Sean Makin, the comically self-absorbed narrator of Walter's novel *The Fourth Wall)* becomes involved in an intricate real-life plot that proves to be even more outlandish than that of a Hollywood movie, and more dangerous for everyone involved.

DIAMONDS FROM TEQUILA

Walter Jon Williams

"No," says Ossley. "No. Really. You can make diamonds out of tequila."

"Sell enough tequila," says Yunakov, "and you can buy all the diamonds you want."

"That's not what I mean," says Ossley.

We're sitting in Yunakov's room at the resort, with the breeze roaring through the windows and doors and sweeping our cannabis smoke out to sea. In one corner of the room a 3D printer hums through its routine, and in another corner is a curved wet bar with two stools and about fifteen half-empty bottles of liquor. Six or eight of us are sitting around a blocky wooden coffee table on which is perched a large clear plastic bong that Ossley had printed out on the first day of principal photography.

The movie is called *Desperation Reef.* Yunakov is the prop master, and Ossley is his assistant. The others in the room are members of the crew: a couple gaffers, a wardrobe assistant, a set dresser, and somebody's cousin named Chip.

I'm the star of the picture. In fact I'm a very big star, and the producers are spending a couple hundred million dollars to make me a bigger one; but I'm not so big a star that I can't hang with the crew.

I want the crew to like me because they can make me look good. And besides, they have the best dank on the set.

We're in Mexico, but we're not smoking Mexican bud. Buying dank in Mexico is hazardous, largely because the dealer would likely turn you in to the cops, who in turn would put you in jail, then confiscate the weed and sell it back to the dealer. Plus of course there would be the embarrassment of having a major Hollywood guy busted in Mexico, with all the outcry and bribes that would involve.

No, this is 420 grown in California, where it's pretty much legal, and smuggled to Mexico, where it isn't, in boxes of film equipment. All of which is fine with me because California has the best of everything, including the best herb.

In fact I'm less than thrilled to be in a foreign country, where people speak a foreign language and have foreign customs and serve Mexican food that isn't as good as the Mexican food I can get in L.A. But still, I'm a big international star, so even though I'm in a foreign country, everyone is treating me very well; and that's better than being treated as a washed-up has-been in California, which is also within my experience.

We watch as Chip—the person who is somebody's cousin—sparks the bong's bowl and inhales a truly heroic amount of smoke, a binger big enough to keep him cross-eyed for hours . . . After an appreciative pause, Ossley says, "No, really. You have to heat the tequila up to eight hundred degrees centigrade, after which nanoscale diamonds will precipitate onto trays of silicon or steel. There are, like, industrial applications."

"You're just making this shit up," says Yunakov, but by that point someone's looked up the answer on their phone and discovered that the story is true, or at least true on the Internet. Which is not always the same thing.

At which time the 3D printer, which has been humming away in its corner, makes a final mechanical whine and then dies. Ossley half crawls across the tile floor to the machine and removes an object that looks like a thick-walled laboratory beaker. It isn't entirely transparent: there seem to be yellowish layers made of slightly different materials.

"Okay," he says. "Here's my latest project."

Ossley is a short man, five-four or -five, and thin. His hair hangs in tight corkscrew curls over his ears. Black-rimmed glasses magnify his eyes into vast staring Rorschach blotches, and five o'clock shadow darkens his jawline. He wears tank tops and cargo shorts bulging with tools, cables, and electronics.

Since he's established his credibility by building James Bong with his machine, we pay attention to what follows. He goes behind the bar, produces an unlabeled bottle of wine, unscrews the cap, and pours out a glass. The wine is a deep blood red, so dark it's almost purple.

"Okay," he says. "Some friends of mine have a Central Coast winery, and they sent me this stuff to practice on. It's your basic cabernet. The cab is only a couple weeks old, just old enough that fermentation has stopped. It's been racked once, so I've filtered it to take out any remaining sediment, but otherwise it's pretty raw."

He passes it around and we all take a sample. When it's my turn I take a whiff, and it doesn't smell like much of anything. I sip, and as the wine flows over my tongue I can feel my taste buds try to actually crawl away from the stuff like victims crawling from the site of a toxic spill. I swallow it only because spitting on the floor would be rude. I pass it on.

"Two things would turn this into an acceptable wine," Ossley says from behind the bar. "Time and aging in oak barrels. Oak is perfect for wine, and hardly any winemaker uses anything else. Oak allows oxygen to enter the wine, and oxygenation speeds the other processes that go on between oak and wine. Which have to do with hydro-hydrolysable tannins and phenols and terpenes and fur-furfurals." The cannabis makes him stumble on the technical terms.

He holds up the beaker. "I've designed this to do in a few minutes what aging in oak does in months. So let's see if it works."

Ossley puts the beaker down on the bar, then pours the wine into it. He glances at us over the bar. "The reaction can be a little, ah, splattery." He finds a plate and puts it over the top of his beaker.

"Now we wait twenty minutes or so."

We go back to enjoying our evening. The bong makes another round, and I chase my hit with a beer.

Normally I wouldn't get this chewed when I know I'll be working the next day, but in fact I have no dialogue to learn for the next day's shoot. All my scenes will be underwater, and I won't have to talk.

Desperation Reef concerns my character's attempt to salvage a sunken submarine, an effort made problematic by the fact that the sub is one used by a Mexican drug cartel to smuggle narcotics to the States. The sub went down with 200 million dollars' worth of cocaine on board, making it a desirable target for my character, a commercial diver with a serious coke habit. Unfortunately the cartel wants its drugs back, and of course the Coast Guard and DEA are also in the action.

My character Hank isn't a good guy, particularly. He starts as angry and addicted, but over the course of the film, he finds love and inspiration with Anna, the sister of one of the sailors who went down with the sub. In the climax, when cartel heavies come calling, he trades his coke spoon for a Heckler & Koch submachine gun and takes care of business.

What happens in the denouement is kind of up in the air. As it stands, the movie has two endings, by two different writers. In the first, the original, Hank raises and sells the cocaine, and he and Anna head off into the sunset many millions of dollars the richer.

In the second ending, Hank learns the important moral lesson that Drugs are Bad, he turns the coke over to the DEA, and he walks away with nothing.

The first ending, which everyone likes, makes a lot more sense in terms of Hank's character. The second ending, which no one at all likes, is an act of cowardice on the part of the producers, who are afraid of being accused of making a movie promoting drug use.

Last I've been told, we're going to film both endings, and the producers will decide during editing which ending will end up on the final film. Since film producers are notorious cowards, I figure I know which ending will end up on the picture.

Unless I make a stand or something. I could just refuse to film the second ending, or I could blow every take.

But then I'm a coward, too, so that probably won't happen.

"Right, then," Ossley says. He's back behind the bar, peering at his beaker with his huge magnified eyes. "I think the reaction's over." He gets a glass and jams it in the ice bucket, then pours the contents of the beaker into the glass. From the way he handles the beaker I can see it's hot.

The wine has changed color. It's a lot brighter shade of red.

Ossley puts a thermometer into the glass and waits till the wine reaches room temperature. Then he takes the glass from the ice bucket, and he walks from behind the bar and hands the glass to me.

"Here you go, Sean," he says. "Taste it and let me know what you think."

The outside of the glass is slippery with melted ice. I look at it with a degree of alarm. "Do I really want to drink your chemistry experiment?" I ask.

"It won't hurtcha." Ossley raises the glass to his nose, takes a whiff, and then a hearty swallow. "Give it a try."

I take the glass dubiously. I recall that, in the past, people have tried to kill me. People I didn't even *know,* and all for reasons I didn't have a clue about.

"You realize," I say, "that if you poison me, the whole production shuts down and you're out of a job?"

Ossley gives me a purse-lipped, superior look. "This is actually Version Six point One of the container," Ossley says. "I've drunk from all of them. There's nothing in there that will harm you. Not in these quantities, anyway."

I hold the glass beneath my nose and give a whiff. I'm surprised. Unlike the earlier sample, this sure as hell *smells* like wine. Ossley grins.

"See?" he says. "That's vanillin you're smelling. And some lactones that give it a kinda oakey scent."

Yunakov, the prop master, gives me a wink. "It's wine, dude," he says. "I've been drinking Ossley's product all week. It's fine."

I cautiously draw a small amount of the liquid across my tongue. It tastes more or less like red table wine. Not brilliant, but perfectly acceptable.

"Not bad," I say. "Much improved." I pass the glass to the set dresser to my right.

"See?" Ossley says. "It normally takes *months* to produce a wine of that quality, and my reactant did it in twenty minutes. Imagine what would happen to the wine industry if every winery could produce *grand cru* in twenty minutes?"

The set dresser sips, then smacks her lips critically. "This is hardly *grand cru,*" she says.

"It's early days," Ossley says. "In another couple years, I'll be serving up something that you won't be able to tell from Haut-Brion."

She raises an eyebrow. "How do you account for *terroir*?" she asks.

Ossley laughs. "*Terroir* isn't a mystical thing. *Terroir* doesn't happen because your ancestors wore wooden shoes and prayed to Saint Valery. It's just chemistry. Give me a chemical analysis, and I can probably duplicate the result."

There follows an earnest discussion on *terroir* and *debourbage* and *encépagement,* and I return to my beer. I like my plonk just fine, but I'm not fanatic enough about wine to care about the fiddly details.

The bong goes round one more time, and then I decide it's time to go to bed. Yunakov's room is on the ground floor of the resort, so I leave by hopping over the balcony rail onto the walk beyond, and then I lope over toward my cabana.

The sea glitters in starlight. Tropical flowers sway pale in the breeze. The beach is an opalescent shimmer.

If I close my eyes, I can almost imagine that I'm back in paradise, which is to say Southern California.

I turn the corner and jump as I hear a shriek. It's one of the hotel waiters carrying a room-service tray. The bottles and dishes give a leap, and I lunge to get them all settled before something crashes. Eventually the waiter and I get everything sorted out.

"I'm sorry, Mr. Makin," the waiter says. "I didn't see you coming."

The resort is in Quintana Roo, so the waiter is Mayan and maybe five feet tall, with a broad face and beaky nose and an anxious smile. I look down at him.

"That's all right," I say. "Have a good evening."

I'm not entirely unused to hearing people scream when I turn up unexpectedly, which is why I'm an unlikely movie star.

I was a cute, big-headed kid actor when I was young, and when all America invited me into their living rooms as the star of the sitcom *Family Tree.* But when I grew, I grew tall, and my head kept growing after my body stopped. It's a condition called pedomorphosis—my head is freakishly large, and my features have retained the proportions of an infant, with a snub nose, a vast forehead, and unusually large eyes.

At the moment I look even more sinister than is usual for me since for my morally ambiguous part I've shaved my balding head and have grown a goatee. I look like someone you really *don't* want to see looming around the corner on a dark night.

My appearance explains why my career collapsed after I stopped being cute, and why I struggled to find work for more than a decade until I was rescued by an unlikely savior—a game designer named Dagmar Shaw, who employed me as the star of a production called *Escape to Earth* that was broadcast over the Internet. I played Roheen, who was sort of an alien and sort of an angel. *Escape to Earth* was an enormous hit, and so was the sequel. I'm in negotiation with Dagmar now for more Roheen projects, but in the meantime I'm trying to expand my celebrity by starring in a feature.

My freakish face guarantees that I'll never be the star of a romantic comedy, and also that I can be accepted fairly readily as a villain—during the years I was scuffling for work, I played heavies more than anything else. So in *Desperation Reef,* I'm playing a villainous character who finds redemption and turns into a good guy.

Even if I nail the part, even if I'm absolutely brilliant, it's still unclear whether people will pay to see my weird head blown up to the size of a theater screen. After all, my only successes have been in smaller formats.

Thinking about these uncertainties, I walk to my cabana. It's a white-plastered building with a tall, peaked Mayan roof of palm-leaf thatch, all oozing local color. I open the door, and I see that Loni Rowe has arrived before me. She's hunched in an armchair drinking some of my orange juice and thumbing text into her handheld, but when she sees me arrive, she puts her phone away and stands.

"Hi," she says. "There was a camera drone overhead, so I thought I'd come to your cabana and give them something to write about."

She's a pale redhead who hides from the sun, and when she's on-screen she has to slather on the makeup to hide all her freckles. She has large brilliant teeth accentuated by a minor overbite, and a lush figure that has won her admirers all over the world. There's a popular poster of Loni that's sold millions, and it's hard to picture the room of any adolescent American male without a view of Loni's cleavage in it somewhere.

Loni is an ambitious young actress, and she has a part in the movie as the mistress of a drug lord. She's also my girlfriend—or actually, my

Official Tabloid Girlfriend, good for headlines guaranteed to keep our names in the public eye.

Even though our affaire is mostly for publicity purposes, we have in fact had sex now and then. The teenagers who go to sleep every night staring at Loni's poster will be disappointed to learn the experience was pleasant enough, but nothing special. There is no passion in our relationship because both of us are far more passionate about our careers. But Loni and I are friends, even given that we're using each other, and I imagine we'll remain friends even after we've both gone on to other tabloid romances.

Loni, you will remember, is the hottie who stole me from my previous tabloid girlfriend, Ella Swift. Ella is a much bigger star than Loni, and snagging me was quite a coup for Loni. It boosted her profile enormously.

Both tabloid romances were dreamed up by my agent, Bruce Kravitz of PanCosmos Talent Associates back in Beverly Hills. *Desperation Reef* is a near-complete PCTA package—Bruce represents most of the talent and the writer who drafted the first script—a script I've never seen from a writer I've never met—as well as the other writer who rewrote the script and created the first ending, and the *other* other writer who wrote the second ending, the one that everyone hates but which will probably be used anyway.

Bruce also represents Ella Swift, and he put us together as tabloid lovers to generate headlines for us during a period when neither of us had anything in the theaters to remind viewers that we existed. For reasons best known to herself, Ella wanted to conceal the fact that she is a lesbian and in the middle of a passionate relationship with her hairdresser.

I have no idea why Ella wants to stay in the closet because to me the thought of her with other women makes her even more exotic and interesting; but I had no one else in my life right then and played along. So we were seen at premieres, parties, charity events, and the odd Lakers game, and I slept at her Malibu house two or three nights a week—in a guest bedroom, while she shared the master suite with the hairdresser.

Then Ella went off to South Africa to make *Kimberley,* about the diamond trade, and Loni, who is at the stage of her career when any publicity at all is good for her, agreed to become the other woman who broke Ella's heart.

The triangle produced a massive number of Bruce-generated headlines, in which Ella wept to her friends, or broke down on the set of *Kimberley,* or flew to the States to beg me to come back to her. Some weeks the tabloids dutifully reported that Loni and I were fighting on the set or had broken up; some weeks we were about to announce our engagement. Sometimes she'd catch me talking on the phone to Ella and be furious, and sometimes I secretly flew off to Africa to be with Ella.

I was always happy to see myself in the headlines, even if the stories weren't remotely true.

If you're in the news, it means people care. I *like* it when people care. Seeing my name on the front page of the tabloids warms my heart.

But there are a few disadvantages to becoming such a tabloid celebrity, including the camera-carrying drone aircraft that paparazzi send buzzing over our living and work spaces. These are illegal, at least in the States, but you can't arrest a drone; and if you can find and arrest the operator, all you have is a man with a controller, and you can't prove that he's done anything with his controller that's against the law.

To me, the drones are cheating. As far as I'm concerned, the tabloids are supposed to report the stories our publicists give them, not start their own air force and find out stuff on their own.

Still, Loni had known what to do when the report came of a drone camera-bombing the hotel. She'd gone from her room to my cabana, as if for a rendezvous, and made certain that the *Tale,* or the *Weekly Damage,* or whoever, had their next story. *Loni's Secret Night Visits to Sean,* or something.

"Is the drone still up?" I ask.

Loni looks at her handheld and checks the report filed by our nighttime security staff. "Apparently not," she says. "The coast is clear."

I walk up to her and help myself to a sip of her orange juice.

"You can stay if you like," I say.

She offers a little apologetic smile. "I'll go back to my room, if that's okay. I need a few more hours on social media tonight."

The aspiring star must network, or so it seems. "Have fun," I tell her, and finish her orange juice as she heads for the door.

Exit, texting. Apparently I'm sleeping alone tonight.

Next morning I'm underwater, in scuba gear, doing about a zillion reaction shots. With the camera close on my face, I mime surprise, anger, determination, desperation, and duress. I swim across the frame left to right. I swim right to left. I go up and down. I crouch behind coral heads while imaginary bad guys swim overhead. I handle underwater salvage apparatus with apparent competence.

The director, an Englishman named Hadley, sits in a kind of tent on a converted barge and gives me instructions through underwater speakers. He's not even getting his feet wet; all he's doing is watching video monitors and sipping a macchiato made by his personal barista.

"Too small," he says. "Make it bigger."

"Too big," he says. "Make it smaller."

I hate the underwater stuff. We all do. I tried to convince the producers that we could do this all on green screen, but they didn't believe me.

I'm done by twelve thirty, but the better part of four hours in the water has me exhausted, and the diver's mask has scored a red circle around my nose and eyes. I'm lucky that everything was filmed at shallow depth, where there's ample natural light, and I don't have to go through decompression.

A powerboat takes me back to the hotel, and on the way I decide to stop by Loni Rowe's room. I'd seen the call sheets that morning and noted that the shooting schedule's changed and I've got a scene with Loni the next day. I want to talk to her about it—I'm thinking of giving her some of my lines actually, because they're too on the nose, as they say, for my character but would be okay for her.

She's got a ground-floor suite in one wing of the hotel, with a patio looking out on the beach, and on the patio is some lawn furniture where a bathing suit and some towels are drying in the breeze. The bathing suit is big enough to cover her whole body, like a wet suit, and aids the pale redhead in hiding from the sun. There's a cardboard sign by the door with Loni's name, L. ROWE, so that people from the production staff won't wake someone else by accident.

I notice that the sliding glass door is cracked—a bird probably hit it, I think, a gull or something—and then I knock on the doorframe, open the door, and step into the air-conditioned interior.

Loni lies dead on the tiles. There's not a lot of doubt about her status, because her head is a bloody mess. Her pink sundress is spattered with a deeper shade of red, deeper even than the red of her hair. A broken coffee cup lies on the floor next to her in a puddle of mocha liquid. There's a cloying scent in the air that wraps itself around my senses.

I look around wildly to see if there's anyone else in the room, particularly anyone with a weapon. There isn't.

My heart pounds in my throat, and my pulse is so loud in my ears that I can no longer hear the breeze, the ocean waves, or my own thoughts. I'm not a complete stranger to dead bodies, but if I'm going to face death, I need more preparation.

I back out of the room and try to remember if I touched anything. As I back onto the porch I get a tissue out of my pocket, and I scrub the door handle. Then I shut the sliding glass door, and suddenly all the glass in the doorframe falls out and crashes to the ground in a huge pile of glittering rainbow shards. The sound is louder than the cry of a guilty conscience.

Again I look around wildly, but no one seems to be paying attention. I scuttle to my cabana, and then I do the obvious thing for someone in my position.

I call my agent.

"So Loni's been shot?" Bruce says.

"Shot? I guess." My gut clenches, and I bend over my dinette in a sudden agonizing spasm. "I don't know how she was killed," I say. "I only know she's dead."

"But you didn't kill her."

"No."

He ticks off the next question on his mental list.

"Do you have an alibi?"

I try to think. Thinking is hard, because my mind keeps whirling, and my guts are in a turmoil, and I keep seeing Loni's body crumpled on the floor in her pink sundress.

"I was on the underwater set all morning," I say.

"So you're fine," Bruce says. There's a tone of self-congratulation in his voice, in the logical way he's handling the crisis. "You're in the clear."

"Bruce," I say, "these aren't the Beverly Hills police we have down here. These aren't kid-gloves kind of police. They might just pin this on me because I'm handy."

"That's why you only talk with one of our lawyers present," Bruce says. "I'll have someone on his way to you in a few minutes, along with a Mexican colleague."

The gut spasm passes. I straighten. The panic begins to fade.

"Sean," Bruce says, "do you think this might have been aimed at you? Because of, you know, what happened."

What happened a couple years ago, when a surprising number of people were trying to screw up my comeback by killing me.

Bruce's question sends a wave of paranoia jittering along my nerves, but then I consider the timeline of events.

"I don't see how," I say.

Because really, all those bad times are behind me, those times when I was traveling with bodyguards and hiding in hotel rooms and complete strangers were trying to stick me with kitchen knives.

I'm a big star now. People love me. Nobody wants me dead now except for maybe a few spoilsports.

"It's all good, Sean," Bruce says. "You're absolutely in the clear. And we'll make sure you don't have any problems."

"Okay. Okay." A sense of well-being descends on me. Bruce Kravitz is an absolute wizard at conjuring up that sense of well-being. It's how he gets things done and how he makes people happy.

"Now," Bruce says, "you should tell somebody about the body."

The paranoia returns. "Not the police!" I say.

"No," Bruce says. "Absolutely not the police, you're right. Are any of the producers on the premises?"

"I don't know."

"I'll start calling and I'll find out. Just sit tight and remember that you're devastated."

"Of *course* I'm devastated!" I say.

"I mean," Bruce says firmly, "remember that you and Loni were supposed to be an item. It's your *girlfriend* that was killed, Sean, your *lover.* You'll have to be ready to play that."

"Right." In my panic and terror I'd sort of forgotten that everything the public knew about me and Loni was a complete fabrication.

"Can you do that, Sean? Can you play that part?" Bruce sounds like he wants reassurance, so I reassure him.

"Of course I can play that," I say. "I liked Loni. I found the body. It won't be hard."

"Good. Now I'm going to make some calls, and I'll call you right back."

Once again Bruce's voice conjures up that amazing sense of well-being. I thank him and hang up and sit down on a couch, and wait for what happens next.

What happens next is Tom King, the line producer. On a set, the line producer is the person who keeps everything running, who controls the budget and supervises the production—a job that requires the financial acumen of JP Morgan and the relentless tenacity of a TV cop. He's experienced with big productions like this one, and the horrific, complex troubles they can cause.

He's knocking on my door just as my phone rings, Bruce telling me he's on his way. I open the door and let him in.

Tom King is a burly, balding man of fifty. He wears a white cotton shirt and Dockers, and he holds his phone in his hand. There's an odd little triangular patch of hair on his philtrum, hair his razor had missed that morning.

He has intelligent blue eyes that are looking at me warily through black-rimmed spectacles, as if I might explode if not handled carefully.

"Bruce tells me there's a problem," he says.

"The problem is that Loni is dead," I say a little sharply. Because this isn't some small issue in catering or shooting schedules that needs to be smoothed out; there's an actual dead body lying in one of the rooms, and Tom seems to be regarding it less as a violent crime than as a tactical problem.

His blue eyes flicker. "Can you show me?" he asks.

"Why don't you go and look for yourself?" Because I have no desire to see Loni dead again.

"I only know what Bruce told me," he says. He is still regarding me warily, as if he's suspecting me of hallucinating.

Unhinged speculation whirls through my mind. Maybe he's used to actors going off the rails and hallucinating dead bodies. Maybe this happens to him all the time.

"Please," he says.

"I'm not going inside," I say.

"Okay. You don't have to go in."

We walk back to Loni's patio. Her towels are still fluttering in the breeze. Tom steps onto the patio and shades his eyes with his hand to look inside. I stand a good fifteen feet away, where I won't be in danger of seeing anyone dead.

"The door glass is shattered," Tom says.

"I did that. The glass broke when I shut the door."

He looks at the pile of glass and frowns. "I'm sure the code requires safety glass," he says. Which is a line-producer sort of thing to say.

He gives me a look over his shoulder, seems about to say something, then decides against it. I know what he's thinking: *You broke the glass when you were fleeing the scene of your crime.*

Fuck him, I think.

He opens the door carefully and steps inside, and I hear a sudden intake of breath. I step onto the patio, feeling the cool breath of air-conditioning escaping through the door, and as my eyes adjust to the shade I see Tom bent over Loni's body. He's touching her leg. He straightens, still looking down at the corpse.

"She's cold," he says. "She's been here a while."

Which lets me off the hook, as he well knows. He straightens and looks at me.

"Sean, I'm sorry," he says.

"What happened?" I ask. "Do you have any idea?"

Now that he's actually in the room, he doesn't want to look at the body. I don't want to look at it, either. We stare at each other instead. And then I glance past his shoulder, and I see the bullet hole in the wall behind him.

"Look," I say, pointing.

Tom steps to the wall and examines the bullet hole. My mind is starting to recover from its shock, and I'm able to process a few of the facts.

"The bullet went through the glass door," I say, "and it hit Loni, and then it kept on going into the next room."

He looks at the hole, and he nods, and then at the same instant the same horrifying thought occurs to the both of us. He spins around, his blue eyes wide.

"Who's in the next room?" he asks.

We sprint clean around the building. I'm out of breath by the time I come to the room on the other side from Loni's, with its neat cardboard sign, E. COUSTEAU.

"Emeline," I pant. She's one of the set dressers, a French-Canadian from Montreal. I jump onto her patio, and the sliding glass door is open, so I just walk in.

"Emeline!" I call. No answer. There's a faint, sweet smell in the air.

At least there's no body on the floor. But I find the bullet hole easily enough, and looking from the hole to the door, it's clear that the bullet punched through the wall and flew out through the open door.

"What's back there?" I ask, waving an arm.

"Swimming pool, and tennis courts beyond," Tom says. "And if a bullet hit anyone out there, we'd know about it by now."

"Emeline!" I call again, and I check the bedroom, but she's not in. I return to find Tom standing pensively in the front room, staring down at one of Ossley's printed bongs sitting on the table, next to a bag of bud, which explains the cannabis scent in the air. Thoughtfully, Tom confiscates both.

"I don't think we want the police finding this," he says.

"Check."

He looks at me. "If you've got anything in your place, you'd better make it disappear."

"I'm clean," I say. "I never travel with anything that could get me busted."

That's what the *crew* is for, for heaven's sake.

"I'm going to have to call people," Tom says. "You should go back to your cabana. And expect the police."

"Bruce says he has a lawyer on the way."

"Police will probably get here first." He frowns at me. "Do you have any idea who'd want to kill Loni?"

"No. No one at all."

"You and she were, you know, seeing each other," he says. "She didn't mention anyone?"

By now the shock is over and I'm getting pissed off. "She did not tell me she was being stalked by a killer, no," I say. "Oddly, that did not come up."

He's a little surprised by my vehemence.

"Okay," he says. "I believe you. But maybe you should go to your room now."

Which I do. But not before a sense begins to come over me that I've been through all this before.

The fact is that people around me keep getting killed. I don't have ill intentions to anyone; it just seems to work out that they die. When I look into my past, I see a lot of blood there.

I've only killed one person myself. Well, two. But nobody knows about one of them. And I had no animosity in either case.

I don't get up in the morning thinking, "Well, who will I kill today?" I don't intend harm to anybody. I never have.

I'd hoped all that was behind me. But now Loni's been murdered by an unknown party for unknown reasons, and it's all beginning to seem horribly familiar.

By the time the police interview me, late at night, reliving my old memories has me emotionally exhausted and discouraged and depressed, and I don't have to act at all in order to seem like Loni's stunned, grieving boyfriend. It's only the knowledge that if I misstep, I might be blamed for everything that keeps me from lurching in the direction of the nearest tequila bottle and drowning in it.

The police interview goes better than I expected. Turns out that the production rates the best—very quickly the local cops are supplanted by the PFM, the Policía Federal Ministerial, who are the top investigators in the country. I'm interviewed by a very polite man in a neat gray civilian suit with excellent English skills. His name is Sandovál. He offers his condolences on my loss and records the interview on a very new recorder with a transcription function, which displays a written version of the interview on a nine-inch screen. The problem is that it keeps transcribing the English words as whatever Spanish words seem phonetically close, and the result is complete gibberish. He doesn't know how to turn on the English function, if there is one, but he assures me that the audio recording will be all right.

He sort of looks like Charlton Heston in *Touch of Evil,* and I have a moment of grim amusement as I remember Heston's character trying to get his radio-bugging device working in that film.

Sandovál has two assistants, an older white-haired man, well dressed, who sits quietly and listens without speaking. He might be the senior officer, but I think he might not be talking because his English isn't very good. And there's another man, thick-necked and blond, in hiking boots and some kind of faded blue bush-ranger jacket with lots of pockets. He looks American, but he doesn't talk either, so I can't tell.

No lawyers have shown up, but Tom King sits in on the interview as moral support, and confirms my story as I tell it.

It goes well enough until I mention that after I found the body I contacted Tom. Sandovál's eyebrows go up.

"You didn't call the police?" he asks.

"I don't know *how* to call the police in Mexico," I said. "I don't have the emergency number. I thought someone else might know."

If Sandovál finds this implausible, he doesn't say so. I finish my story, and Sandovál asks a few follow-up questions, and then he offers his sympathies again and leaves.

Speaking as someone who's been interrogated by police any number of times, I am sure this interview is about as good as they get.

After, I have no trouble sleeping. In the morning, I'm awakened by the assistant director bringing me breakfast. This is not normally part of her job, but she's offering condolences and also trying to find out if I'm functional and can carry on with the production.

I assure her that I'm okay. I ask her what's going on, and she tells me the police are still around, taking measurements and interviewing everyone. The news of Loni's death leaked, of course, and half a dozen paparazzi drones are circling the hotel, while extra police have been deployed to keep intruders off the premises.

In fact, because she speaks Spanish and overheard some of the cops yelling at one another, she knows a lot about the investigation. Apparently the local police bungled everything before the PFM got here.

"They cut out pieces of the drywall where the bullet went through," she burbles. "Both in Loni's apartment and in Emeline's. They put them in evidence bags, but they forgot to label them, and now they don't know which is which. And so many cops came into Loni's apartment to have their pictures taken that all the evidence there, like the blood spatter, is useless . . ." Her eyes grow big as she realizes that Loni's presumed lover is perhaps not the best recipient of this news. She puts her hands over her mouth.

"Oh gosh, Sean, I'm sorry," she says. "I shouldn't have said any of that!"

"They wanted their pictures taken with a *corpse*?" I demand. I'm sickened.

I can see the whole thing. Cops in uniforms tramping around, posing with the body, the famous scandalous Hollywood star . . .

Though, on second thought, maybe that's how Loni would have wanted it.

The assistant director scurries away, but she isn't the last person to bring me food. Apparently it's customary to bring food to someone in mourning, even if that person doesn't need it—after all, I'm the star of the production, and normally I get three catered meals a day, plus healthy snacks—and now my refrigerator's filling up with fruit bowls, soups, boxes of chocolate, six-packs of yogurt, cakes, bags of nuts, and a gluten-free pizza.

Plus there are lots and lots of flowers, including a perfectly giant bouquet from my agent.

The only person who doesn't express condolences is Mila Cortés, the beautiful Venezuelan who plays my character's girlfriend, Anna. Mila is a complete prima donna. She's too good for the resort hotel that's housing everyone else on the production, and she's staying on a yacht berthed in Playa del Carmen, north of here. I only see her when we have a scene together, and the rest of the time she ignores me.

Worse than ignores, actually. In fact she's repulsed by my appearance and is offended to her soul that she has to share the universe with someone as strange-looking as me. I've been strange-looking for a long time now, and people with Mila's attitude stand out from the others quite easily.

Still, most everyone else cares, and despite the ridiculous superabundance of flowers and food, I'm genuinely touched by everyone's concern. They expect me to be torn with grief, and so powerful is the force of their belief that I find myself genuinely grief-stricken. Sometimes my voice chokes and dies in midsentence. Tears come to my eyes. I'm in awe of my ability to embody the character of a devastated lover.

When one of the sound techs, a really beautiful California blonde named Tracee, offers to help me forget Loni, I tell her I'm too broken up to respond. So we make an appointment for late that night.

The lawyers turn up around midmorning and I have to go through the story again, which depresses me even more.

Around noon the claustrophobia gets to me, so I decide to pay a visit to the director, Hadley. I put on a pair of shades and a stolid expression and go out into the sunlight, and suddenly the air is full of whirring as camera drones zoom in for close-ups.

Being in the tabloids always makes me feel happy and wanted, so I force myself to don the required attitude of moody bereavement and shuffle along with my hands in my pockets.

I find Hadley talking to Sandovál by the pool. Another Mexican cop is talking to Chip, the man who's cousin to somebody on the set. There's a line of people to be interviewed, so obviously this will go on for a while.

People keep walking up to me to offer condolences. The advantage of being out of doors is that I can escape them. I thank them and move on, as if I had somewhere to go.

I end up on the beach, alone on the brilliant white sand staring out at the water. I figure it'll make a great picture on the cover of the *Weekly Dish,* or some other such publication.

The ocean is a perfect turquoise blue, with surf breaking over the reef a hundred yards offshore. There are police standing around on the beach, guarding the sand or something, but they're polite enough not to approach.

I breathe in the iodine scent of the sea.

"Hi," someone says. "You doin' okay?"

I turn and see that it's the blond cop who was present at my interview the night before, the man I thought might be American. He's still in his blue bush jacket, and he's wearing Ray-Bans, like Gregory Peck in that movie about some war or other. His voice is a sort of tidewater North Carolina.

"Who are you, anyway?" I ask.

He scans the sky for any drone that might be able to read his lips.

"Special Agent Sellers," he said. "DEA."

I blink in deep surprise. "You think Loni got killed in some kind of drug crime?"

"No." He shakes his head. "I'm just tagging along with the PFM. I'm here on another matter."

A cool warning throbs through my veins. If he's after drugs, there are plenty of them on the set. And I, for one, could not pass a urine test right now.

"Another matter?" I ask. "What's that?"

He takes out a handheld and turns it on. The display is washed out in the sunlight, so he says, "Can we move to the shade?" We find some palms and stand under them, where the drones won't be able to spy on us, and he thumbs through different pictures until he finds the one he wants. He shows it to me.

"Do you know this man?"

I push my shades up onto my forehead and look at the photograph. A feeling of recognition passes through me, and I look closer.

It's Ossley, the assistant prop guy with the fondness for chemical experiments, though in the photo he's got a shaved head and a goatee. It's the blurry eyes behind the thick glasses that give him away, that and the rather superior expression.

"What's his name?" I ask.

"Oliver Ramirez," Sellers says. "Goes by Ollie."

I say nothing.

"You look like you recognized him," Sellers probes.

"He looks like a barista I know," I say. "Works in a coffee shop in Sherman Oaks." I slide my shades down to cover my eyes and look at Sellers with what I hope is an expression of innocence. "I don't know whether his name is Ollie or not."

I'm not about to finger someone who could implicate me as a drug user, especially if the drug is more or less legal where I live.

So far as I know, Ossley's chemical experiments haven't actually hurt anybody. And for obvious reasons I'm not a big fan of my country's archaic, punitive drug laws.

I decide to change the subject.

"Do you have any idea about—" I pause, as if overcome by emotion. "About what happened to Loni?"

Sellers looks out to sea. "Nobody really knows anything yet," he says. "But there's a theory the whole thing was an accident."

I don't have to counterfeit surprise. My jaw drops open of its own accord.

Sellers understands my confusion. "See, the shot came from the water," he says. He waves a hand out to sea. "The shooter must have been in a boat some distance away, on the other side of the reef, otherwise someone would have seen him. And the police are having a hard time figuring out how the killer managed an uncannily accurate rifle shot from out to sea, in a boat that was bobbing up and down, through a glass door and into a darkened room that would have been damn near impossible to see into. And because nobody can find a motive, they're thinking that maybe it was an accidental discharge . . ."

He falls silent when he sees my reaction.

"That's wrong," I say. "That's not what happened."

"Yes?" he says, suddenly very interested. "How do you know?"

Because what happens around me aren't accidents, I'm on the edge of saying. *What happens around me is murder.*

But I don't say that because my phone rings right at that instant, and it's my agent, so I have to pick up.

"Thanks for the flowers," I say.

"Are things okay?" Bruce asks.

"More or less."

"The lawyers seemed to think everything was all right."

Other than Loni's still being dead, I think.

"I'm glad they think so," I say. I'm not being very candid, since there's a DEA agent listening from less than three feet away.

There's a pause, and then Bruce goes on with the next item on his checklist.

"Have you talked to Loni's parents?" he asks. "This morning they heard about Loni's death from the news. I'm sure they'd appreciate a more personal touch."

"Oh Jesus Christ!" Because normally I'd just have my assistant send a card, you know? But I'm supposed to be Loni's boyfriend, so now I'm nearly family, and I'll probably have to spend ages on the phone faking pathos to a couple of strangers.

"I don't even know their names," I say.

"Kevin's texting you all that." Kevin being Bruce's assistant. "Are you okay otherwise?"

"I'm holding up," I say.

My phone gives a chime as the text arrives.

"I'll call them right away," I say. Because that will give me an excuse to get away from Special Agent Sellers.

Which I do. I go back to my cabana and make the phone call, which is gruesome and produces anxiety and depression in equal amounts, and then I go looking for Ossley.

Ossley's room isn't even in the hotel, it's on the ground floor of some annex tucked between the main hotel and the highway. In fact I think the annex may be an older, shabbier hotel that the bigger hotel acquired. When I knock, it's not Ossley who calls from inside the room, but a woman.

"This is Sean," I say. "Is Ossley in?"

The door opens and I see Emeline Cousteau, the set dresser whose suite was punctured by the bullet. She's tall and dark-haired, with an open face that reminds me of Karen Allen, except without the freckles. She's barefoot and wears a fiesta top that leaves her shoulders bare.

"Hi, Sean, come in," she says. "I'm so sorry about Loni."

"Yeah. Me too."

Ossley's place is small, an ordinary hotel room, and has two beds and a little desk. The drapes are drawn, the room is dark and stuffy, and the air smells of mildew from the shower. Ossley is sitting at the desk working on a computer and drinking from a soda can.

I sit on the bed that hasn't been used. Ossley tells me how sorry he is about Loni. His eyes are impossible to read behind the thick glasses.

"There's a DEA agent here along with the Mexican police," I say. "They're looking for a guy named Ollie Ramirez."

You can't say my dart doesn't hit home. Ossley turns spastic in about half a nanosecond. He knocks his keyboard to the floor, his soda can jumps across the desk, and his glasses sag down his nose.

"Peace, brother," I tell him. "I didn't rat you out." Though of course that was no guarantee someone else wouldn't.

Ossley picks up his keyboard, then puts his head in his hands. "What am I going to do?" he cries, to no one in particular.

Emeline walks over to him and puts hands on his shoulders. She massages his stringy muscles and bends over him to whisper into his ear.

"Don't worry, baby. You'll be all right."

As I watch the two, comprehension strikes me like a sandbag dropped on my chest. I think my heart actually stops beating for a while. I gape for a few seconds as I try to jigsaw my thoughts together, and I raise a hand to point at Ossley.

"They were shooting at *you,*" I say. "You were in Emeline's room, and the bullet missed and went through the wall and killed Loni." And then punched a hole in her door and vanished out to sea.

I remember glass on Loni's patio when I walked to her door yesterday morning. The glass had blown *outward,* which would have been a clue as to which direction the bullet was headed, except that all the glass fell out of the door right afterwards and lay in heaps everywhere, and I'd forgotten about all that till now.

Maybe if you looked closely at the bullet hole in the wall, the actual trajectory might have been more clear, but all I remembered were neat little holes. No one was paying much attention to the wall, not with a body lying right there, an obvious target for a seaborne sniper.

Ossley and Emeline stare at me as if I've just uncovered the great secret that will send their souls screaming all the way to Hell. Which I have, maybe.

"We were—y'know—together," Ossley says. "And I lowered my head to, um—and anyway, the bullet went right over my head."

"We hid for a while," says Emeline. "And then we ran away."

I look at Ossley. "What chemical experiments have you been doing," I say, "to get both the DEA and a sniper after you?"

Ossley flaps a hand at me. "Well," he said. "You know."

Somehow I keep a hold on my patience. "No," I say, "I don't."

Emeline looks up at me. "You know," she said. "Like with the wine."

I nod. "He's making a reactor vessel—"

"Reactant," Ossley corrects.

"You're going to print drugs," I tell him.

He shakes his shaggy head. "I just lay down the precursor chemicals," he says. "They're like prodrugs in nature—they'll produce drugs once they've finished reacting with the vessel."

"The vessel," I say, "which you also print."

"Yeah."

"*Which* drugs?" I ask.

He gives a hapless shrug. "The opiates are easier," he says. "I mean, they're all closely related, you just decide how many acetyl groups or whatever you want to tag onto morphine . . ."

"Oxy?" I ask. "Dilaudid? Heroin?"

"Diacetylmorphine hydrochloride," Ossley says. "But that's not . . ." He shrugs, nods, and concedes the point. "Well yeah, it *is* heroin, yeah."

"And how much of this stuff have you made?"

He seems surprised by the question. "Um," he says. "None. My gear isn't good enough. If you're aiming at producing drugs, your printer needs to be really precise, and you have to control temperature and humidity and light really well. I've never been able to afford a printer that good. And even if I get one, I'll have to run tons of experiments before I can produce anything like a pharmaceutical-grade product."

"So why is the DEA . . . ?"

"I put some stuff on the Internet."

I nod. "Of *course* you did," I snarl. "Because the conventions of social media *demand* that you announce your growing criminality on an electronic forum searchable by law enforcement. What else could you possibly do?"

He spreads his hands in a helpless gesture. "The narcs showed up. They started talking about 'criminal conspiracy to distribute narcotics.' I decided it was time to leave town, so I cashed in the Ramirez identity and created a new one."

"You had a backup identity just lying around."

"I printed it. And then I got a job here because I know some people."

At this point I am beyond surprise, so I just nod. Ossley gives a superior grin. "I named myself after the greatest drug dealer of all time."

I'm blank. "There's a famous drug dealer named Ossley?"

"Owsley. Augustus Owsley Stanley. He practically created the Psychedelic Sixties. Made millions of tabs of acid back when it was still legal."

I rub my forehead. "I really don't care what your grandparents got up to," I say. "I'm just trying to figure out what I'm going to do with you."

Ossley's alarm is clear even behind his thick glasses. He and Emeline exchange looks.

"You can't tell the cops," he says. "I mean, everything I did was just theoretical."

"Someone," I say, "is *shooting* at you. Another innocent person could get hit." I looked up at him. "Maybe you should just disappear."

Ossley and Emeline exchange looks again. "We thought about it," he says. "But shit, we're sitting right here in the middle of this huge police presence. I figure we're safer here than outside."

"Tell that to Loni," I say.

There is a long silence. "Look," he says finally. "Nobody's going to shoot with all these cops around. It's just not going to happen."

"No?" I point at the drapes drawn over his window. "Then why don't you open your drapes? Stand out on your patio and drink a beer?"

Ossley licks his lips. He looks desperate. Emeline, who is still standing behind him, gives his shoulders a little push.

"Tell him about the paradigm shift," she says.

"I—"

She pushes him again. "*Tell* him," she insists.

His eyes blink behind the thick glasses. "Well, see, it's a shift in how everything's going to be manufactured, right? Little 3D printers in kiosks and garages, making all the tools you need."

"Including drugs," I say.

"Right. Most of the stuff now that they need big factories and assembly lines to create." He licks his lips again. "But see, if you can make—or someone in your *village* can make—stuff that used to need a factory, then nobody's going to need that factory, right?"

"So," I say, "factories go out of business."

"*Drug* factories," says Ossley. "Because once the formula gets out, people can make their medication on their own. Not just the illegal stuff, but everything else—statins for cholesterol, beta-blockers for hypertension, triterpenoids for kidney disease, antibiotics for infection . . ."

"It's a *paradigm shift,*" Emeline says. She's desperate to be understood.

"So drug companies go crash," I say. "I get it."

"Not just drug companies," Ossley says. "But the whole mechanism by which drugs are distributed, or, um, *not* distributed. Suppressed." He gives a desperate little laugh. "See, the DEA's job becomes *impossible* if *anyone* can make the drugs they want." He grins. "It's a new world. Prohibition will go away because there will be too many ways around it."

"That's why the DEA wants to put Ossley away!" Emeline cries. "He's not breaking the law, he's threatening their *jobs.*"

I try to put my mind around what Emeline is trying to tell me. "You're saying it was the DEA who tried to shoot you?" I say.

"No," Ossley says, just as Emeline shouts *"Of course!"* They glare at each other for a minute, and then Ossley turns back to me.

"See, it's not just the cops who are out of business," he says. "It's the *criminals.*"

"Ah," I say. Because right now there are elaborate networks that take coca or opium poppies or whatever, and refine the raw vegetable matter down to powerful alkaloids, and smuggle that stuff across borders, and then cut it and break it into small packages and distribute it around neighborhoods . . . and of course there are a lot of really hard men with guns whose job it is to make sure that business is successful and protected from competition.

Whole organizations, reaping billions of dollars in profit, for whom violence is a *first* response, and every member of which will have to go back to shining shoes, planting beans, or working at the convenience store if Ossley perfects his technology.

"You'll put the cartels out of business," I say.

"Couldn't happen to a nicer bunch of people, yeah?" he says.

"And in the meantime they're trying to kill you."

"I still think it's the damn cops," Emeline says. "How would the cartels even know you're here?"

I don't have an answer for that, or for much of anything else. I stand.

"Better print a new identity and plan your escape," I say. "You can't stay here much longer."

He chews on that while I leave.

I'm sitting in my cabana that afternoon when Hadley, the director, comes to see me. He doesn't bring me food.

"Jesus Christ, we're in such fucking trouble," he says.

I'm almost grateful that he's not oozing sympathy. He wanders over to one of the baskets of fruit I've been given and starts popping grapes into his mouth.

Hadley is bearded and blond and twitchy, with a full range of nervous tics probably acquired during the course of helming a series of huge, complex films, where a single mistake on his part, or on the part of practically anyone else connected with the production, could result in a couple hundred million dollars disappearing just as surely as if it had been doused with gasoline and set on fire. He's devoted to his films with a formidable single-mindedness that's just slightly inhuman.

"We've still got Loni's two big scenes," he says. "Completion-bond company thinks we can just cut them and nobody will notice."

A completion bond is the film's insurance, who guarantee that in the event of some catastrophe that threatens the production, either the film will be completed or the backers will be repaid their investment. On a big production like this, specialists from the completion-bond company are on the set a lot, mostly auditing the various departments. But though they'd obviously prefer that the film be made and they don't have to pay anyone back, they don't guarantee that the film will be any *good*—and they might well be within their rights to insist that the film do without an important subplot and two important scenes. All they care about is whether the movie's in the can, preferably on time and under budget.

You can imagine my delight in the prospect of my first big feature being a hacked-up, incoherent mess.

"I've got to argue them out of it," Hadley says. He's pulled a pineapple out of the fruit basket and is absently tugging on the leaves at the top. But he's too weak to actually yank any of them out, so he loses his patience and slams the pineapple back into the basket.

"Somebody made me a casserole," I said. "It's in the fridge. Why don't you beat that up instead?"

Hadley looks at me. "You've got to help, mate."

"Damn right I will." I lead with my ace. "I'll call Bruce Kravitz."

He puts a finger to his nose. "Brilliant."

Hadley isn't a Kravitz client—all PanCosmos directors capable of handling such a big, complicated production are off on other projects—so he doesn't have access to the biggest cannon in the industry. But I do.

I call Bruce right then, and he understands the equation right away: crappy film => declining careers for PanCosmos clients.

"I'll start calling around," he says.

I'm telling the good news to Hadley when Tom King, the line producer, strides in.

"Thought you'd better know," he tells Hadley. "The cops have been running background checks on everyone connected with the production, and they've come across a problem."

I feel my shoulders tense as I anticipate the news that Ossley is about to be arrested, but that isn't what Tom is telling us.

"It's the trucking company we've hired to move our gear around on location. It's a cartel front."

Hadley and I both stare.

"It really *is* the fucking narcos?" Hadley says.

"The trucking company's owned by one Antonio Germán Contreras.

His brother Juan Germán Contreras is one of the leaders of the Tricolor Cartel, which controls narcotics trafficking in the Gulf Coast."

"Fuck me all standing!" Hadley says.

Tom's blue eyes are relentless. "The Tricolors are badasses," he says, "even as cartels go. They've killed thousands of people to get where they are."

Hadley clutches his head and looks at me. "What the fuck do we *do*? If we fire them, they'll kill us. If we *don't* fire them, they'll kill us anyway."

Tom turns to me. "Sean," he says, "do you have *any* idea why the cartel and Loni are connected?"

"I don't think they are," I say, truthfully enough. I give the subject some desperate consideration. "Does the cartel have rivals?" I ask. "Maybe it was a warning to the Tricolors from some other cartel."

Tom sees the implications of this immediately. He turns to Hadley. "That's our excuse to fire them. We'll say that their presence is making the production more likely to be attacked."

"And then they'll *kill* us!" Hadley says. He paces around in a frantic little circle. He is literally gnashing his teeth.

Tom gives this some more thought. "Maybe we'll have to pay them anyway."

"Completion-bond company isn't going to go for that!" Hadley says.

"We'll talk about it." Tom turns to me. His blue eyes grow concerned. "Sean," he says, "how are you doing?"

"Okay, I guess." An honest self-evaluation would be something like, "I'm really tired of having to pretend to be this grieving lover," but I don't think that's in the cards.

"Because we're all going to be under pressure to finish the film," Tom says. "I want you to know that you can take as long as you think necessary to return to the set." There is a groan from Hadley at this idea. Tom's eyes flick to the director, then back to me. "But it would be a good thing to know—"

"I'm ready to work," I say.

I can sense deep relief behind the concerned blue eyes. "Are you sure? Because—"

"Yes," I say. "I really want to get out of here and get back on location. It's the best thing for me."

This makes them very happy. They leave together to assemble a revised shooting schedule, leaving me alone in my cabana amid the smell of fruit baskets and flower arrangements.

Two seconds after they roll the sliding door shut, my phone rings. I look at it and see that it's Dagmar.

Oh damn. More trouble.

"I'm on vacation," Dagmar says. "I'm in the Virgin Islands with my husband and my daughter. My first vacation in years that wasn't marked by riots, murder, and the collapse of society. And you couldn't stay out of trouble for two lousy weeks, could you?"

"I'm not in trouble," I point out. "I had nothing to do with this one."

"You've lied to me before," she says, "when people were trying to kill you."

Well, I admit to myself, *that's fair.*

It has to be conceded that my relationship with Dagmar Shaw is imperfect. She's the woman who rescued me from obscurity and made me a star by casting me in *Escape to Earth* and its sequel, and for that I'm grateful—but on the other hand she's controlling and devious and driven and far too smart, and she's got an agenda that's far beyond mine.

I want to be a big star and have millions of people love me. This strikes me as a modest and understandable ambition.

Dagmar, by contrast, is basically a genius supervillain who wants to take over the world.

"I'm sending you bodyguards," she tells me. "You need looking after."

I have a hard time summoning up the moral courage to resist Dagmar. The fact is that she knows a lot more about me than I'd like. She knows where the bodies are buried—or actually *body,* singular, not that this makes it any better from my perspective.

"Yeah, okay," I say. I've lived in a circle of bodyguards before—at times it was annoying, but most of the time it was like having servants with guns. They have to do what you tell them, and there's the extra bonus in that they keep the bad people away.

"One more thing," she says. "It's your job to make sure the guards are charged to *your* production. Not to my company."

I consider this.

"I can probably manage that." Hiring bodyguards for me would probably count as due diligence, considering both the shooting and my own past.

"And by the way," she says, "I'm very sorry about Loni Rowe."

"Most people would have led with that," I point out.

"Most people," she says, "don't know she wasn't your real girlfriend."

It never occurs to me to ask Dagmar how she knows this. She has her sources, some of them uncanny.

"Keep out of trouble, now," she says. "Don't interrupt my vacation again."

"I'll do my best," I say, and she hangs up.

It's at that point that my nerves give a snarling leap as big, booming gunshots ring out over the compound. I dive behind the sofa.

Bodyguards, I think, might not be such a bad idea.

It turns out to be the Mexican police who are shooting. They've warned the tabloid reporters that the airspace above the hotel is to be treated as a crime scene, and that the drones should be recalled, but the reporters as usual ignored the warnings. Except this is Quintana Roo, not Beverly Hills, and the PFM okayed the use of shotguns to knock the drones from the skies. In addition, any stranger caught with a radio controller is dragged from his vehicle, beaten silly, and tossed in jail.

I stay indoors while the skeet shooting goes on, and falling birdshot rattles down the palm-leaf roof and rains onto the patio. In no time at all, the airspace over the hotel is free of clutter, which makes it easier for Tracee, the sound tech, to slip into my cabana after nightfall. She thinks she's comforting me after Loni's death, but in fact she's easing my anxieties about a lot of things that I couldn't explain to her if I tried.

Next day, new call sheets appear, and we find out that production will resume the following day. My bodyguards, four of them, arrive in Cancun on the same flight as Mrs. Trevanian, the agent from the completion-bond company. The bodyguards are the gents carrying weapons, but Trevanian is the one who can kill the movie by cutting all of Loni's scenes and turning the story into nonsense. She's a sinister figure in a navy blue suit, with a determined way of walking that sends a cold warning shuddering up my back. She looks as if she already knows what she's willing to pay for and what she's not.

That afternoon there's a memorial for Loni. We all get together in one of the producer's cabanas and take turns talking about how wonderful she was, and all the while I know Mrs. Trevanian is deciding my future in another room. I have a hard time finding anything to say at the memorial. Other people are effusive, chattering on about their happy memories of Loni; but I'm just depressed, struck dumb with grief at the knowledge that Mrs. Trevanian is going to destroy my chances of being a movie star.

I drag myself away from the memorial as soon as I decently can, and I try to learn my next day's lines while in a frenzy of anxiety.

Tom comes to tell me after dinner that the meeting didn't go well. Mrs. Trevanian insisted that it was not necessary to replace Loni but only to cut all her scenes. When Hadley shrieked, tore at his facial hair, and cried that without those scenes the film would be incoherent, Mrs. Trevanian said that *Desperation Reef* was an action blockbuster and that action blockbusters didn't *have* to make sense. "Haven't you seen the *Transformers* films?" she asked.

I sink deep into my sofa and restrain a whimper of despair. My visions of superstardom are being shot down, just like the spy drones, and I know they're not coming back. This movie is going to crash, and afterwards, nobody's going to spend another couple hundred million dollars on someone as certifiably freaky-looking as I am.

My only choice will be to go on working for Dagmar until she gets tired of me, and then I'll be back on the beach, a nobody, like I was three years ago.

"This whole thing will have been for nothing," I moan. "Loni will have died for nothing."

"Yeah well," Tom says, "what can we do?"

"Raise more money?" I say.

He gives me a skeptical look. "It's a little late for that," he says.

"Seriously," I say. "How much would it cost to shoot all Loni's scenes with another actress? We don't have to hire a big star or anything—just some competent, reliable . . ."

Tom is trying to be kind. "Who else has Loni's sex appeal? Who else looks as good in a bikini? The character's a femme fatale."

"California is *full* of girls who look good in bikinis," I point out, truthfully enough.

Tom goes into his tablet computer and scrolls through figures. "Not counting Loni's paycheck," he says, "reshooting all Loni's scenes will cost ten million dollars."

I stare at him. Loni's only in a few scenes. "Ten million dollars for—"

"Most of it's for the cigarette-boat chase," he says.

Oh Christ, I'd forgotten about the cigarette-boat chase, mainly because I hadn't shot my part of it yet. Loni had already shot her half, and after I shot my bit, the two parts would be edited together, along with many, many expensive shots, already in the can, involving stunt doubles, explosions, and gunfire, to make it seem as if I had barely managed to evade murder by Loni and a group of cartel gunmen, all of whom get blown up in a flaming crash that cost a fortune in special effects.

"Look," I point out, "if we don't shoot the rest of the boat chase, we'll save millions of dollars. Just put those millions of dollars into hiring a new actress, find some cheap substitute for the boat chase, and reshooting Loni's scenes."

Tom looks at me blankly. "I made that suggestion. Trevanian turned it down flat. It's absolutely not approved."

"But the money's *already in the budget*!"

"Not anymore, it isn't!"

The cords on Tom's neck are standing out. There's despair in his tone. He's already been through this argument.

For a desperate moment I consider putting up the money myself. With my savings and investments, and of course the cash sitting in the Caymans, I might just pull it off.

But no, that's insane. Motion pictures are the worst investments *in the world.* Worse than investing in brand-new factories for buggy whips and antimacassars and snoods. Hollywood has a way of making people's money disappear.

And even if no one tried to steal my money outright, even if everyone on the picture did his best, all it would take was a screwup in *one* department to make the movie a flop. The studio could demand a catastrophically bad reedit or bungle a last-second transfer into 3D, the composer doing the score could have a tin ear, the trailers could suck, the publicity department could be at war with the producers and sabotage the promotion, and all my money would disappear.

In which case, I'd be out of work *and* broke.

I lean back in the sofa and try not to snivel. "We're fucked."

"Hadley's on the verge of shooting himself," Tom says.

"Better if he shot Mrs. Trevanian."

"Well," Tom says, "we can always hope for a last-minute backer with a big check."

I reach for my phone. "I'll call Bruce."

Bruce's phone goes straight to voice mail. It's annoying that he has other clients and a personal life, but I suppose it's only to be expected.

I put the phone away. "I'll try again later."

Tom is looking back out the door, where one of my guards is pacing around.

"Where did the guards come from?" he asks.

"You're paying for them," I tell him. "It's your due diligence. Even Mrs. Trevanian would agree."

"Fuck!" he yells. But that's the only objection he makes.

I go over my lines one more time, and then I hear a shotgun boom out as another tabloid drone makes a run at the hotel. I give up. No one's come to console me in a long time, thank God, and so I decide it's time to stroll over to my bar and open a bottle of reposado. A couple of shots down, and I realize how to raise the money to make the movie as it ought to be made.

I knock on Ossley's door and receive a muffled, paranoid query in response. I tell him it's me, and he cracks the door open to make sure I'm not lying. When he sees my two bodyguards, he assumes they're assassins and panics, but I jam my shoe into the door, lean close, and speak in a low voice.

"Look," I say, "I can get you off the hook."

He lets me into the room. My guards take up stations outside, on either side of the door. Emeline isn't there, and without her the place has a look of despair, its only light a laptop computer running its screen saver, and a forsaken room-service meal slowly composting on the dresser.

I take the room's single chair, leaving Ossley to sit on the bed, where I had sat that morning.

"I see that your curtains are still drawn," I say.

"Be careful walking in front of them," he says. "You might get silhouetted."

I look at the curtains with more respect. "I'll do that," I say. And then I turn to him.

"Look," I say, "they found people from the Tricolor Cartel working on the production." He winces. "They're going to keep coming after you," I assure him, "so what we need to do is make you harmless."

I'm hoping for a glimmer of hope to shine in his eyes, but what I get instead is a glimmer of suspicion.

"How do you plan to pull *that* off?" he says.

"We sell your process to the cartel."

He considers this with what seems to be impatience. His lips curls. *You cretin,* is what the lips seem to say.

"I see two problems," he says. "First, what stops them from just killing me instead of giving me money?"

"You need to have insurance. You need to have the process documented, and in the hands of people you can trust to release it if anything should happen to you."

His sneer grows. "People like you?"

"No," I say. "I don't want anything to do with it. I wouldn't understand it anyway."

"You sure don't," he says. "Because you didn't even get what I told you earlier—*there is no process.* I haven't printed any drugs, all I've done is *theory.* And all my theories are available *right on the Internet,* in forums devoted to additive manufacturing. There's nothing to sell!"

I give this some consideration. "Well," I tell him, "we could *say* that you've got a complete process. And then get money for not telling anyone about it."

Ossley jumps off the bed and paces about, waving his arms. "Tell a bunch of violent criminals I have a process that doesn't exist? And expect them to pay me to suppress it?"

"Well," I say, "yeah."

"That's crazy!" he says.

I'm on the verge of agreeing with him: yeah, it's not my most brilliant idea. But then he goes on.

"You don't know me at all!" he proclaims. "If there's one thing I believe in, it's *freedom*!"

I'm not sure what any of this has to do with freedom, but then Ossley goes on to tell me.

"I'm not interested in making money from my ideas!" he says. "I'm not interested in *patents* and *copyrights* and *trademarks*!" He practically spits the words. "All that gets in the way of freedom to use the technology, and the technology's what's important! The tech's gotta be free—free to all the people who want to use it, without some asswipe standing there with his hand out collecting the toll!"

"Even if it kills you?" I ask.

A gleam of absolute certainty shimmers through Ossley's thick glasses. "If I die," he says, "the technology's going to happen anyway! *Someone* will figure out how to do it! People are going to print drugs in their homes! It's as inevitable as people connecting their computers to phone lines and creating the Internet!"

"Yeah," I say, "and whoever figures out the answer is going to get a ton of money."

He looks down at me from the absolute heights of moral superiority. "This information needs to be free," he says. "And I'm the one to free it."

It occurs to me that the last thing I need tonight is to put up with a lecture from some sneering, megalomaniac geek. I remind myself that I'm very tall and that I look like a Klingon and that I'm a murderer, and that I could just stand up right now, pick up Ossley, throw him down on the ground, and tell him that he's going to do what I tell him, or I'll kick his stupid fucking head in.

But I don't do that. I'm not really that guy.

Instead I leave, pick up my bodyguards, and return to my cabana, where I study my lines until it's time to go to bed. I get a call from Tracee, the sound tech, but I tell her that I'm too upset to see her.

Have sex with someone three times, it's dangerously near a relationship. So I decide not to see her again.

"I want it bigger," Hadley tells me. "I need you to fucking *act,* here, Sean."

When Hadley is actually being a director—when he's in his little shed or tent, surrounded by video monitors, and communicating with his minions through a headset or a loudspeaker—he's not the grimacing, twitching, half-hysterical character he is the rest of the time. When he's directing, Hadley is in his element. He's authoritative, decisive, and he tells you what he wants.

Though of course he's still a prat.

Still, I could use some direction about now. I'd rather it come from a director who's actually on the set, and knows how to talk to actors, instead of some Jehovah-wannabe off in a little room by himself with his barista, a macchiato, and a Napoleon complex, but I'll take what I can get.

Fact is, I'm beyond depressed. Mrs. Trevanian has killed the movie, the movie will kill my career, and the point of finishing the film at all has begun to elude me.

I know that I should be the living embodiment of the Three Ps

(Prompt, Perky, and Professional, if you want to know) and that I should give the part everything I've got because I should be happy simply to be working; but now I'm wondering what the reward for any of that will be. I've been a hardworking professional all my life—I've even *killed people*—and annoying characters like Mrs. Trevanian and anonymous Tricolor snipers still won't let my happy place alone.

Suddenly I'm wondering why I'm even bothering trying to play the lead in a feature. I've never played the hero in a movie. And working in movies and television requires different styles of acting.

TV stars are cool. Even if their characters are less than admirable, they come across as somehow sympathetic, maybe even neighborly. They are, after all, people you invite into your home every week. If you don't like them, you won't watch them.

Movie stars, by contrast, are *hot.* They have to blaze so fiercely that they fill a screen forty feet high and demand the attention of a crowded theater.

That's why very few TV stars have graduated successfully to features. It requires not only different skills but a different personality. You have to go from amiable to commanding.

Likewise, some movie stars are simply too big for television. Jack Nicholson is riveting on-screen, but you wouldn't want him in your living room week after week. The television simply couldn't contain his personality.

I *think* I'm doing well in the feature. Everyone tells me I'm great—but then they would whether I was any good or not. I could sit through the dailies and find out for myself, but I've always been too insecure to watch dailies.

But now I'm having a hard time seeing the point.

I get through it somehow, and Hadley pronounces himself satisfied with whatever energy I've been able to summon. I go back to my cabana for a shower and supper, and then—thank God—my guards tell me that the prop master Yunakov is at the door.

He's inviting me to a party in his suite by way of consoling me for my loss. I'm so eager to get out of the depressing flower-filled environment that I jump at the chance.

It's much the same as the party the other night, except that Ossley is in hiding and there's no sign of cannabis, not least because a pair of Mexican police have joined the fun. These are uniformed state police who are here to guard us and to keep order, as opposed to the plainclothes PFM who are actually investigating Loni's murder. I assume the two police are off duty, because they're slamming down cognac as if they've never had expensive, imported Napoleon brandy before. Both of them are Mayans around five feet tall.

I look at the pistols they're carrying on their belts—and the two Heckler & Koch submachine guns they've propped in a corner, along with a shotgun for shooting at drones—and a scheme begins to drift across my brain on featherlight feet.

I decide that the cops are going to be my friends.

I top up their glasses. I talk to them both, and ask them about their lives. Hector has the better English skills, but Octavio is far more expressive, communicating through expansive gestures, tone of voice, and a natural talent for mimicry. I ask if he's ever thought of being an actor.

They're pretty flattered that a big Hollywood star is taking an interest in them. They tell big exciting police stories that, though they may be true, I suspect didn't happen to them but to someone else.

When the party breaks up, I take Hector and Octavio for a walk, me swaying along with a couple tipsy guys shouldering automatic weapons nearly as long as they are. They let me march along with the shotgun. I take them to the little hotel annex where Ossley is holed up, and I carefully count the number of sliding-glass patio doors until I come to Ossley's room.

I offer to pay them a thousand dollars apiece if they'll shoot at that door sometime tomorrow afternoon, when I'm scheduled to be on the set. I tell them I want them to aim high, so no one will be hurt.

They're sufficiently hammered that they don't see anything terribly wrong in my request, and a thousand dollars is, after all, about three times their monthly salary. Though Hector is a little puzzled. "But why?" he asks.

"Publicity," I tell them with a wink, and that seems to satisfy him.

"Okay," Hector says. "But we need another five hundred."

"What for?"

"To pay the sergeant to make the evidence disappear."

I'm hardly sober during this conversation, but next morning I remember enough of what I'd said to stock up on some cash. We are in a part of Quintana Roo filled with Americans and American dollars, and getting a few thousand from the bank is no problem. After which I head off to my makeup call.

We're shooting another underwater scene. I'm scheduled to be on the set for six hours, but there are a raft of technical problems, more than the usual amount of chaos, a distinct lack of cooperation on the part of the ocean, the sun, and the clouds, and so many retakes that I'm working for nearly twelve long hours, much of it in the ocean. It's nearly ten o'clock by the time I'm out of makeup and back at the cabana.

My guards go into my cabana ahead of me to make certain there are no assassins lurking therein, and to their surprise discover Ossley and Emeline hiding in my spare bedroom. I affect more astonishment than I actually feel and ask Ossley what they're doing here.

"Umm," he says. "Can we talk privately?"

My guards make sure he's not carrying anything pointy, then slip out to guard the gardens.

I sit in a chair beneath a vase filled with fading mourning blossoms. "What can I do for you?" I ask.

Ossley doesn't look good. He's unshaven, he's shambling, and his hands keep roaming over his body as if to make sure it's all still there.

"They took another shot at him today!" Emeline says in complete outrage.

I look at Ossley. "I ran for it before the police got there," he says.

I conceal my inner dance of delight. "Sorry about all that," I tell him, "but you can't hide here, you know. I don't want anyone in my place who will be drawing fire."

Emeline looks at Ossley. "Tell him," she says. "Tell him what you're thinking."

He gives a little twitch. "I've been thinking about what we talked about the other night."

I put on my Klingon mien and look at him seriously. "Maybe you'd better remind me. Because what I most remember is you lecturing me about freedom."

It's Emeline who's responsible for his change of heart, Emeline and of course the bullets Hector fired through Ossley's patio door. When all is said and done, I've won. And I see no damn reason why I shouldn't rub his superior little nose in it.

After I finish talking to Ossley and Emeline, I decide to let him stay in the spare room overnight, then hide him somewhere else the next day. After which I take a little walk, find Hector and Octavio, and make them and their unknown sergeant as happy as I am.

Hollywood stardom opens a lot of doors. Which is why it doesn't take nearly as much effort to get an interview with Juan Germán Contreras as you might think. I go through his brother, who owns the trucking company, and when I finally get the word that he'll see me, I bring presents. A very expensive bottle of small-batch bourbon, plus Ossley's 3D printer, the beaker he'd shown me at the party, and a container of Ossley's rotgut cabernet.

The actual meeting is all very last-second. I get some GPS coordinates texted to me and drive to the location with my bodyguards. This turns out to be a half-completed Burger King overlooking the ocean, with the waves breaking white over the reef, and waiting for me there is the brother, Antonio. We're required to put our cell phones in a plastic bag hidden on the construction site because cops can follow our phones' GPS. We follow Antonio's Chevy Tahoe off into the jungle, where we go through several gates guarded by some very large, well-armed Mexicans, and then to a modest-sized bungalow with a tile roof, a house identical to about a million homes in California.

My guards aren't happy about any of this, but I'm the boss, and they sort of have to do what I tell them. They're warned to stay in the car. Antonio's guards help me carry my gear into the house, and there I meet the man of the hour.

I'm all dressed up like the Pope of Greenwich Village. Gray tropical suit, red tie, wingtips. My goatee has been trimmed, and my head re-shaved. I'm hoping I look like a Klingon mafioso.

I suppose I should ask forgiveness for pointing out again that I happen to look sinister in a very freakish way. I terrify small children. I scare room-service waiters I meet by chance at night.

Plus during my wilderness years, when I was struggling, if I worked at all, I played a heavy. I'm very good at projecting menace when I need to.

Juan is so menacing in real life that he doesn't have to act scary. He also didn't put on a tie. He's a trim man of around forty, dressed casually in a cotton peasant shirt, drawstring pants, and sandals. I've done my research, and I know that the most wanted man in Mexico is a former high-ranking officer in the PFM who went over to the Dark Side. He maintains what can only be described as a paramilitary bearing, and he seems to bear a reserved curiosity about what brings me here.

He smiles whitely and shakes my hand. I present him with the bourbon, and he offers me a seat on a chair so grandly carved and painted with Mesoamerican designs that it should really be sitting in a museum of folk art.

He and his brother Antonio take their seats. "I understand there has been violence on your production," Juan says.

"I'm afraid so," I tell him.

"I regret to say that I can't help you," he says. "The police have surrounded your company with their own people, and they and I—" He waves a hand ambiguously. "We do not work together."

He thinks I've come to him for protection. Instead I plan to take his money—but first, I think, a little flattery.

"I'm impressed," I say. "You speak extremely good English."

He lets the compliment pass without changing expression. "I used to work with your Drug Enforcement Agency," he says. "When I was with the police."

I think about asking him if he knows Special Agent Sellers, and then decide against it.

"My children and I enjoyed *Escape to Earth,*" he says. "We watched it together."

My heart warms as I picture this charming domestic scene, Juan and his children absorbed in the drama while the chieftain's followers go about on their murderous errands, smuggling, stabbing, shooting, and cutting off heads.

"Thank you," I say. "Those projects were very special."

We chat a bit about the picture business, and the current production here in Mexico. He expresses condolences on Loni's death. He seems to know all about *Desperation Reef,* and appears moderately amused by the story line. I'm pleased that he doesn't seem to want to cut my head off.

"I wonder," I say, "if you know Ollie Ramirez."

He looks blank.

"He's a kind of inventor," I say. "He's the person that the assassins have been trying to kill."

He seems surprised. "It was not Loni Rowe?" he says.

"Loni's death was accidental," I tell him, though I'm confident he knows that already. "May I demonstrate something?"

I go through the wine demonstration, just as Ossley had performed it in Yunakov's suite. I let Juan taste the dreadful young wine, then put the cabernet in Ossley's container, let the reaction take place, chill the result to room temperature, and hand it to him. His brows rise as he tastes the result.

"This is only one of Ollie's inventions," I say. "Some of the others you can find online." I give him a look. "If you look at some of these sites, you can see that he's working on using this technology to print drugs."

A shadow passes over Juan's eyes. I try not to shiver. He's no longer the courteous host, not entirely, but the lord of a criminal empire. Very calculating, very hard. All the warmth in the room is gone.

If my career as a major Hollywood action star weren't at stake, I wouldn't want to be within a thousand miles of him.

"Your Mr. Ramirez wants to sell me this technology?" he says.

"No," I say. "That would be too dangerous." He lifts his head in a kind of query, his eyes like stone. "Once this technology is known to exist," I point out, "you can't possibly control it. All people will need to fabricate drugs is a printer and some precursor chemicals and some instructions from the Internet. People in the States would make their own drugs and could sell them cheaper than you could."

Juan regards me as a young child might regard a housefly, just before he pulls off its wings.

"May I ask," he says, "where your interest lies in all this?"

I've been on my feet demonstrating the technology. I return to the folk-art armchair and sit, looking at Juan evenly, at his own level.

"I'm trying to get Ollie Ramirez out of trouble," I say. "Someone's trying to kill him, and it simply isn't necessary."

He looks at me, unblinking. Because I've done my research, I know that his organization has killed maybe twenty thousand people in just the last few years. Not just killed, but tortured, mutilated, dismembered, blown up, and burned alive.

But I've killed too. It's not something in which I take any particular pride, but it's public knowledge, and if Juan has done his research, he knows this. Maybe on that account I'm entitled to a little of his respect.

"Killing Ollie right now would be a mistake," I say. "As soon as he realized someone was after him, he made sure that other people had custody of his research. People he could trust. A lawyer in one place, a friend in another. So if anything were to happen to Ollie, the information would be made public."

Which is true enough. Though what Bruce Kravitz, in his office high in the PanCosmos Building, made of the PDF file in his in-box could only be conjectured.

Juan's face seems carved of stone. "Do you know any of these friends of Ramirez?" he asks.

"No. I don't want to know their names, and I don't understand the technology. I'm an actor, not a scientist."

And maybe, therefore, I won't be tortured for information that I don't have.

"And what does Ramirez want?" Juan asks.

"Fair value for his discoveries." I take out a piece of paper, and put it on the table between us.

I've done some calculations based on what I've been able to find out about Juan's business. Each year, he makes a profit of around $6 billion on income of 20 billion. He has something like 150,000 people who work for him in one capacity or another, not counting the corrupt officials he has on his payroll.

"In order to make certain that Ollie's discoveries never see the light of day," I say, "he asks for $25 million. That's $25 million *each year.*"

That figure doesn't seem unreasonable. One of the difficulties of Juan's business is finding places to put all the money he makes. Sometimes it just stacks up in garages or spare rooms. When cartel honchos are arrested, sometimes they're found with $100 million or more, all in cash, just piled in some room because they can't find a place for it.

"You can make this investment or not," I say. "You know your own business best." I nod at the piece of paper. "That's an account in the Cayman Islands," I say. "If the money appears there, we'll know that you find Ollie a good investment, and he'll find some other line of research that has nothing to do with you or your business."

Juan looks at the paper but doesn't touch it. The Cayman account is mine, as it happens, an attempt at tax avoidance by yours truly. Some of the money behind *Desperation Reef* is French, and some Japanese, and at Bruce Kravitz's suggestion I stashed most of my pay in an offshore account. The money's never been in the States, and I won't have to pay taxes on it till I bring it home.

"There's only one point I should make," I add. "This technology . . . it's going to happen sooner or later. Someone's going to duplicate Ollie's research, and then—" I shrug. "Then you stop paying. You'll have bought some years."

Juan's look is unreadable. "If this printing technology should break free," he says, "how do I know it's not Ramirez behind it?"

I wave a hand. "You have resources," I tell him. "You'll find out. Besides, it's not like any of these people can keep a secret—my guess is that whoever does it will be bragging in every online forum he can find."

Juan looks at his brother, and his brother looks back. Then Juan turns to me.

"I don't know this Ramirez," he says. "But what you say is interesting. I understand why someone is shooting at him."

I rise from my Mesoamerican chair. "I've taken up enough of your time," I say.

And then I shake hands with the Germán Contreras brothers and leave, carrying the printer. I'd leave it as a gift, but it belongs to the property department.

I'm modestly surprised at my own survival, and so are my bodyguards. By the time I get back to the hotel, I'm convinced the whole trip was deranged, and that the Germáns were sitting back in their bungalow knocking back bourbon and laughing at their idiot visitor.

Which is why I'm surprised when, the next day, I check my bank balance and find that $25 million has been deposited to the Cayman account. In cash, no less, which means that Juan not only had the money sitting in the Caymans, but was able to get someone to physically carry the money from his stash to my bank.

I go to Cancun, where Ossley's hiding in a hotel under yet another alias, and I tell him the money has arrived. In another day or two, he'll fly to Cayman, where he'll open a bank account, and I can transfer his share of the money.

"If you go back into the drug business," I tell him, "I'll kill you myself."

He should devote himself to his wine project, I tell him. Stay away from anything illegal.

I leave my cabana after supper and take a stroll through the hotel grounds. I avoid the beach or ocean views, since I spend my working day on one or in the other. I'm looking in a vague way for a gathering where I can relax, but Yunakov isn't in his room, and so I wander up to the open-walled bar by the pool and order myself a Negro Modelo.

When my eyes adjust to the murk in the bar, I see Special Agent Sellers standing in a corner, trying to communicate with the green-and-red talking parrot the bar has installed on a perch. Sellers is still wearing his Jungle Jim outfit. I stroll over with my beer in hand and take a look at the parrot.

"Got him to confess yet?" I say.

Sellers glances at me, then gives a little start—yes, I am indeed a disturbing and ominous figure to find looming over one's shoulder—and then he turns to me.

"The parrot's not talking," he says. "I think he wants his lawyer."

"Motherfucker!" the parrot shrieks. His vocabulary seems to have been strongly influenced by drunken American tourists.

"Obviously a hard case," I point out. "Why don't you take a break and have a drink?"

He joins me at the bar and orders a vodka tonic.

"Did you ever find that man you were looking for?" I ask.

"He kept dodging the interview. Then someone shot into his room and he split."

"You were looking for the props guy?" I ask in feigned surprise. He nods. "Do you know who shot at him?" I ask.

"That's confidential," he says, which I figure means he has no clue.

I decide to change the subject. "Any progress on who killed Loni?" I ask.

He looks a little uncertain whether or not he should be sharing any news, but then he decides to let his vodka tonic do the talking.

"Remember when I said it might have been an accident?" he says.

I nod.

"There was some problem with the evidence at first," Sellers says, "but it got straightened out, and now it looks as if the shot was fired from the land. Maybe at someone on the tennis courts, from someone hiding in the jungle across the highway. And it punched through the wall and killed Loni purely by mistake."

It isn't hard to look shocked. I'd thought I was really clever working that one out all by myself.

"I've been thinking and thinking," I say. "And I couldn't imagine why anyone would—" I succeed in summoning a tear to my eye. "And now you say it really was an accident!" I blurt.

He nods in what is probably meant to be a comforting way. "That's how the physical evidence lines up," he says. "I said before that it could be random, but you disagreed."

"I don't know what I think anymore," I say. I think about putting a quaver in my voice but decide against it. I don't want to overact when my audience is only three feet away.

I sip my sweet, dark beer. Sellers says nothing. "Motherfucker!" says the parrot.

There's a stir, and then a half dozen film crew come into the bar. They've obviously just come in from dinner somewhere, and among them I recognize Chip, the man who is here because he's somebody's cousin. And for some reason a memory of Juan rises to my mind. *I don't know this Ramirez. But what you say is interesting. I understand why somebody's shooting at him.*

It suddenly occurs to me that maybe Juan was telling the truth.

I nod toward the group. "Do you know the tall one there?" I ask. "The blond?"

"I was there when he was interviewed," Sellers says.

"He's not part of the crew," I say.

"He's here on vacation," Sellers says. "He's related to, ah, I think it was the assistant greenskeeper."

I consider Chip from the vantage point of the bar. "Do you know what he does for a living?" I ask.

Sellers pulls out his handheld and pages through his files. Which is probably something he wouldn't do if he hadn't had more than a couple vodka and tonics.

"He works for Porter-Bakker Pharmaceuticals," he says. "In marketing."

It's like an explosion in my mind, only in reverse. All the smoke and flame and debris fly together, the bits assembling to form a complete whole.

"Okay," I say. "That's interesting."

It turns out that Chip is a golfer, and goes out most days to one of the many courses in Cancun. I watch him when he comes back from one of his trips, his golf bag slung over his shoulder. He walks into his suite, and he immediately realizes that someone has broken into his rooms and scattered his belongings everywhere. He drops his bag and runs to the settee in his front room, and pulls out a long box from underneath. He looks relieved to discover it's still there.

"Right," I say. "Let's go."

I and my four bodyguards leave my cabana, where I'm watching Chip's antics on video, and then stroll across the compound to Chip's suite. Two guards precede me through the open door.

"Hold on there, cowboy," I say. "We've got to talk."

Chip spins around, his face alight with what I believe is called a "guilty countenance." He stares as my guards approach him.

"What do you have in the box there?" I ask, and then—because he looks as if he's going to attempt desperate resistance—I add, "No point in fighting. A video record of this is already on a server in New Zealand."

Which is true. My guards and I broke into Chip's suite earlier in the day, put video cameras everywhere, then tossed his belongings all over the room all under the assumption that he would lead us to the box hiding under the settee—which of course we had discovered in the course of our search.

My guards, I am pleased to remark, seem to be brigands only slightly disguised in tropical suits. They would probably have taken Chip to sea and drowned him if I'd asked.

One of my guards takes the box from Chip's nerveless fingers. I look at the box with all my Klingon intensity.

"What do you want?" says Chip. His face is stony.

"Let's go outside and talk." Away from any recording devices.

My guards pat Chip down for weapons, and then we all stroll to the pool, where Chip and I sit at a wrought-iron table. The sun dazzles on the water. There is the scent of chlorine. One of my guards adjusts the table's red-and-yellow umbrella to keep us in the shade, and then the guards withdraw out of earshot.

I look at Chip, still using my Klingon face. "Let's open the conversation by agreeing that you're an idiot," I begin.

"You don't know what you're talking about," he says.

"Okay," I say. "Let's make sure we're on the same page. Because from what I can see, you came here to kill Ollie Ramirez, only you missed him and killed a *movie star.* Which brings heat and publicity down on this whole production, making it difficult to complete your mission, and so you while away your time playing *golf.* And you did this in *Mexico,* where the authorities won't even *need* to open that box, and find there a rifle covered with your fingerprints, to beat a confession out of you and throw you in jail, which you will very likely not survive because it's going to be full of violent cartel killers who will torture you to death simply for the fun of hearing you scream."

There is a moment of appalled silence, and then Chip summons the fortitude to ask a question.

"Why would I kill this Ollie Ramirez?"

I sigh. "On behalf of Porter-Bakker Pharmaceuticals, who've clearly made up their minds that Ollie's discoveries are a threat to their bottom line. I looked them up—last year they made a profit of 6.3 billion on income of 49 billion. They could hardly keep *that* up if people could print their own prescriptions in their basement." I give a contemptuous laugh. "They're *also* idiots, by the way."

Chip just glares at me. I reach into my pocket and take out a piece of paper. A piece of paper very similar to that which I'd given Juan only a few days before.

"If you don't want your rifle given to the PFM, along with a suitably edited copy of the video, I want $50 million sent to this account. By tomorrow. And another 50 mil. every year, on the anniversary of Loni's death, to guarantee that Ollie Ramirez won't continue his researches."

He stares. His lips move but nothing comes out. He's beyond speech.

"That may seem like a lot to you and me," I say, "but on profits of 6.3 billion, it's not so much. Plus, of course, there's the matter of evading all the investigations, bad publicity, and the collapse of your company's stock. Along with jail for everyone concerned."

I lean back in my chair and consider the possibilities. "Of course," I say, "your superiors may decide that their most sensible action now is to kill *you.* So I suggest you stay in your room, under guard, until the money is delivered." I smile. "And since I don't trust you or your company in the least, the evidence will be hidden, and released automatically if anything unfortunate should happen to me."

I stand. My bodyguards look in my direction. Chip hasn't said anything in a long time.

"Maybe now," I say, "you should go find a phone or something."

Chip goes back to his room, and one of my guards goes in with him. And as for me, I think I shall raise a magic editing wand, perform a cinematic dissolve from this scene by the pool, and go straight to the happy ending.

Porter-Bakker Pharmaceuticals paid up. Some of their lower-level executives resigned, but by that point I wasn't very interested because I was busy rescuing my movie. I shelled out 10 million in cash, received executive producer credit and a percentage of the gross, and Bruce Kravitz provided Loni's replacement, a fine actress named Karen Wilkes. She didn't fill a bikini as well as Loni but added a kind of crazed evil to the part of the gangster's girlfriend that made the role memorable. The wicked Mrs. Trevanian was foiled and gathered up her cloak of evil and went back to Los Angeles.

I didn't split the Porter-Bakker money with Ossley. After all, he was *already* being paid not to continue his drug research.

So everything ends really well for me. It's unfortunate that justice wasn't meted out to Loni's killer, but even if Chip went to jail, it wouldn't bring Loni back. And of course I'm sorry that Loni had to die—but if she *had* to die, at least it was in a way that got me both publicity and a fortune. And a good movie, which is nothing to sneeze at.

Of course, *I* didn't die. Which is always a plus.

And the best part comes later, in a meeting with Hadley and Tom King. We're in Hadley's cabana, eating seafood tacos, drinking iced caramel macchiatos made by his barista, and hashing out the shooting schedule. We're trying to work out how and where we're shooting the ending.

I finish a taco and lick my fingers.

"And by the way," I tell Tom, "I'm not going to shoot that second chickenshit ending, the one where I give the drugs to the cops instead of selling them and living happily ever after. That's just not my character. My character keeps the money."

Hadley looks up at me in alarm. "Sean," he says, "the producers *want* that chickenshit ending."

"*I'm* the producer now," I tell him, and flash him my Klingon look.

He wabbles and waffles, but in the end caves in.

What choice does he have? I'm the man who saved his picture. I'm the boy who made money from tragedy, happiness from misery, diamonds from tequila.

Desperation Reef is going to be a hit. I know this because Loni's getting killed gave it the sort of publicity that the studio would have paid hundreds of millions of dollars for. All the people who have seen the tabloid headlines or who watch the entertainment news will want to be part of the story—part of *my* story.

They will pay money to be closer to me. And I will let them. I will accept their love, and their love will make me happy, and in return I will give them everything I have. I will give them brilliant things.

I will give them diamonds.

Phyllis Eisenstein

Phyllis Eisenstein's short fiction has appeared in *The Magazine of Fantasy & Science Fiction, Asimov's, Analog, Amazing,* and elsewhere. She's probably best known for her series of fantasy stories about the adventures of Alaric the Minstrel, born with the strange ability to teleport, which were later melded into two novels, *Born to Exile* and *In the Red Lord's Reach*. Her other books include the two novels in the *Book of Elementals* series, *Sorcerer's Son* and *The Crystal Palace,* as well as stand-alone novels *Shadow of Earth* and *In the Hands of Glory*. Some of her short fiction, including stories written with husband Alex Eisenstein, has been collected in *Night Lives: Nine Stories of the Dark Fantastic.* Holding a degree in anthropology from the University of Illinois at Chicago, for twenty years she was a member of the faculty of Columbia College, where she taught creative writing, also editing two volumes of *Spec-Lit,* a softcover anthology showcasing SF by her students. She now works as a copy editor in a major ad agency, and still lives, with her husband, in her birthplace, Chicago.

Here, in the first new Alaric story in decades, the minstrel sets off in a caravan headed deep into the trackless desert, where evil spirits howl in the night and mirages are commonplace—but, as it turns out, not all dangers are illusionary, by any means.

THE CARAVAN TO NOWHERE

Phyllis Eisenstein

The dark-eyed man wore long, sun-faded robes and a thick, dirty-white wrapping about his head like most of the other men gathered in the tavern that night, but Alaric realized quickly that he was not one of them. They were all talkers, drinkers, men who laughed easily, who pulled willing women onto their knees and lifted their tankards with any excuse, bellowing at each other and the landlord across the trestle tables. They were men who spent carelessly, and Alaric's songs had already gained him some benefit from their drunken generosity.

But the dark-eyed man sat quietly in his corner, nursing a single goblet of wine and watching the crowd. The hand that raised the goblet was roughened with work, the forearms, bared by flaring, turned-back sleeves, tanned and sinewy. A hardworking man, Alaric thought, stopping at the only tavern in a town on the fringe of the Western Desert with purpose in his eyes.

This evening, Alaric sang bawdy songs to the raucous room, his clear, carrying voice rising above the din in rhymes to make the drinkers laugh and choruses to make them join in the music. His lute was barely audible, and often he scarcely bothered to pluck the strings, but none of his listeners seemed to care. Young though he was, his trove of songs was well tested in scores of taverns just like this one, and he knew their effect. But the dark-eyed man never laughed or joined the choruses, and Alaric understood he was waiting for something.

Meandering through the room, still singing while nodding his thanks for the coppers dropped into the open deerskin pouch at his belt, he came at last to the dark-eyed man's small table. And there, on the wood whose finish was scarred by the spillage of countless goblets of wine, lay a silver coin. The dark-eyed man lowered his gaze to it as Alaric approached and then looked up into the young minstrel's face.

"You are a traveler," said the man, and his deep voice easily pierced the clamor of the room—a leader's voice.

Alaric inclined his head and pitched his own voice high for clarity. "Say minstrel and mean traveler. We minstrels spend our lives seeking the stuff of new songs."

"You sing well," said the dark-eyed man. "You could find a place in some rich house. A king's house, even, I think."

Alaric looked at the silver coin. He kept a few like it inside his shirt, but not many, not enough to tempt a thief. He had been a thief himself often enough, in the long ago, and he could always be one again, using the power he had been born with—the power to move from one place to another in the blink of an eye. Still, he preferred earning silver with his songs. He stretched his right hand out toward the coin without touching it, two fingers brushing the table lightly beside it. "I've had my share of rich houses. Even kings' houses. But the horizon draws me." He raised his eyes. "I would see what lies beyond it."

The dark-eyed man smiled with one side of his mouth. "I was young once, like you, and I wondered what lay beyond the horizon. Now I am older and I have been there, and still I make the journey from time to time. But you knew that, didn't you? You know who I am."

Alaric pulled his hand back and strummed his lute. "The landlord told me something of the man who takes a caravan across the great desert every year. Your name, he said, is Piros."

The man narrowed his dark eyes. "And did he tell you that Piros is seeking adventurers for the trek?"

Alaric shook his head. "He said that you're seeking men to work your camels. And that it is a hard crossing, where fate sometimes decrees death. Though I guessed that much without the telling." He lifted a shoulder in a small shrug. "Sadly, I know nothing at all about camels."

Piros pushed the coin closer to Alaric's side of the table. "I have listened to you this evening, and watched you. The nights are long and dull on the great desert, even to men weary with a full day of riding. And there is much silent time for them to fill with squabbles over nothing. Songs could make that time pass more easily." He straightened in his chair then. "Take my coin as one of many acquired in this place, and likely we will never meet again. Or take it as first payment for your songs on our journey, if that pleases you better. And the camel lore will come along the way, I promise."

Alaric picked up the coin then and turned it over between his fingers. "You have spoken to the landlord, too, I imagine."

The dark-eyed man nodded. "You have been here eight days, and he would have you stay. Not that such a place needs a minstrel to draw custom, but he sees you at least half as an entertainment for himself. And you make friends easily, Alaric minstrel. Of course that would be necessary, in your trade, as it is in mine. But my brother thinks you would do well on the journey, and I have always trusted his judgment."

"Your brother?"

Piros tapped his goblet with one finger. "Has the resemblance faded so much with the years?"

Alaric glanced over his shoulder at the landlord. He saw it now, though the caravan leader was older and more weathered.

"Well, minstrel," said the dark-eyed man, "by tomorrow, every man in this room will have spent his last copper and asked for a place in the caravan. Will you join the ones I choose?"

Alaric flipped the coin into the air. "They say there's a lost city in the great desert. They say there's a hidden treasure trove, too."

Piros smiled that half smile again. "You've been listening to drunken fancies."

"And they say that on the other side of the great desert is a land of wonders."

"Ah, that depends on what one has seen before."

Alaric tucked the coin into his pouch. "I have seen wonders before now, Piros, and I would see more." He offered his hand to seal the bargain. "I will come with you."

The dark-eyed man ignored the hand. "There is one more thing, minstrel."

Alaric pulled his hand back and spread it over the strings of his lute. "Yes?"

"I have a son. He is somewhat of your age, a bit younger perhaps, and he has made this journey with me before. But do not think that he speaks for me. You are in my employ, not his. Do I make myself clear?"

Alaric looked down at his lute and plucked a single string. "Will the other men understand the same?"

"Every one of them."

Alaric nodded. "Then it shall be as you wish, Master Piros."

"Piros," the man said. "Only Piros. Be in the courtyard and ready to leave at daybreak."

Alaric sang for the rest of the evening, while he wondered what kind of son required such a warning.

In the gray of dawn twilight, the tavern's courtyard already bustled with men binding casks and rope-wound bundles to the backs of more camels than Alaric could easily count. The camels were kneeling, enduring their growing burdens with an occasional hoarse bellow, like a poorly greased axle laboring beneath a heavy cart. Alaric recognized most of the men from the previous night and wondered how they could work so vigorously with the headaches they must have from their drinking. Several of them grinned at him as he walked past in search of their master.

Piros was at the western extremity of the courtyard, closest to the start of the journey, and beside him stood a youth in robes brighter and newer than his own, with a headwrap of dark-dyed green and a face that marked him likely to be Piros's son. He had his father's stance, too, his straight back and squared shoulders. But where Piros gestured now and then with peremptory economy or called a word or a name, the youth stood silent, arms crossed over his chest, seeming to pay little attention to the activity around him.

Alaric caught the caravan master's eye. "Good morrow."

"Indeed," said the man. "It's a good day to go west." He looked Alaric up and down, his eyes lingering at the plaited straw hat that Alaric had made with his own hands and then sweeping down the dark tunic and trews to the sturdy boots, no longer new but still serviceable. "Is this how you think to cross the great desert?"

The minstrel carried the rest of his meager belongings in a knapsack, with the lute slung over it. He had traveled a long time so lightly, both by foot and in his own special way. "It is what I have," he said.

Piros turned his attention back to the camels. "This is my son Rudd," he said, though he made no gesture toward the youth. "He will find you desert robes for the journey."

Alaric glanced at the young man, who showed no reaction, as if he had not heard his father's words.

"Rudd," said his father, and then more sharply, "Rudd!"

The youth blinked several times and frowned. "Father?"

Again, Piros did not look at him. "Go ask your uncle for traveling robes for the minstrel."

Rudd peered at Alaric, seeming to notice him for the first time. His mouth turned down sullenly. "Can't he ask for himself?"

"Go," said Piros. "Make yourself useful."

The young man's lips tightened for a moment, and then the sullen expression faded away, and his eyes seemed to lose their focus. "I could be useful," he said in a listless tone, "if you'd allow it."

"Do as I say."

Shoulders less square and back less straight than before, Rudd turned toward the tavern. But with almost his first step, he swayed like a drunken man, and Alaric caught his arm to keep him from falling. The youth looked Alaric straight in the face then, and he shook off the assistance and kept going.

"I'll follow," Alaric said to Piros.

"As you will. For now." The caravan leader gestured sharply to a nearby cluster of men, though Alaric could see from the cant of his head that he was still watching his son.

At the tavern's entrance, Rudd opened the door only wide enough to slip through, closing it hard behind him. By the time Alaric reached it and stepped inside, the youth had vanished into the dim interior, and the only movement visible was a pair of dogs at the far end of the room, squabbling over some crusts of bread and rinds of cheese that were the only remnants of the previous night's activities. Alaric called out for both Rudd and the landlord, but there was no answer, and long moments passed before they finally emerged from a rear chamber, Rudd bearing a bundle of cloth on his shoulder, his uncle following close behind to keep the trailing edges of fabric from dragging on the wine-sticky floor. As the youth stopped to cuff aside one of the dogs and snatch up the crust it had been gnawing, the bundle slid away from him, and the landlord caught it deftly, leaving his nephew to give his whole attention to tearing at the stale bread like a starveling cur.

The cloth was a three-part garment—ankle-length robe, loose pantaloons, and headwrap, all the color of pale sand. Alaric stripped off his own clothes, donned the desert gear, and packed his discards in his knapsack. The landlord helped him with the long, scarflike headwrap, which tucked intricately into itself, leaving a tail to loop about his neck and hang down his back. That, said the landlord, would be his mask when the sand blew.

Alaric shouldered the knapsack, the lute strapped tight against it, and gestured at the youth, who had done with his crust and was sitting on a table, methodically kicking at the dogs, which were nosing at his legs in spite of the kicks.

"They know," said the landlord, nodding toward his nephew. His voice was very low. "Dogs always know. And they always forgive."

Alaric looked at the landlord's face and saw sadness there. "What do you mean?"

"Can't you see it?"

Alaric frowned. "I see . . . a number of things. But perhaps not what you speak of."

"Ah," said the landlord. "Piros has not told you."

Alaric looked back at Rudd. "He said not to obey his son."

The landlord was silent for a long moment, and then he said, "Yes, that's good advice." He hitched a leg up on the table beside him and nodded toward his nephew. "Once he thought I was his brother who died at birth."

The door to the tavern swung open, and Piros stood there, a dark shape with the brightening sun behind him. "Are you ready?"

"Yes," said the minstrel.

"Rudd," called the landlord.

The youth made no reply. His back was to the others.

"Rudd!" said his father, and when there was still no answer, he strode to his son's side and took him by the elbow. "Time to begin the journey."

Rudd blinked a few times then, as if waking from some reverie, and dropped to his feet, swaying a little. His father did not release his arm as they walked through the door. Without looking back, Piros gestured for Alaric to follow.

The landlord shook his head. "He still hopes for a grandchild."

"Is there a woman?" asked Alaric. They walked side by side across the room.

"What woman would want that?" said the landlord.

Alaric shrugged. He held his straw hat in one hand; it had not fit in the knapsack. Now he gave it to the landlord. "Take this as my thanks for the garments."

The man turned it over, one way and then the other, and finally set it on his head at a jaunty angle.

Outside, the men of the caravan had already mounted their camels except for one, who held the leads of two kneeling animals. At Piros's gesture, he helped Alaric to the long, narrow seat atop the smaller of the pair. It was an odd perch though not uncomfortable, well padded and with a thick hoop at the front for holding on and another behind, a handhold for a second rider. With large panniers behind his legs, a bulky sack lashed in the other seat, and a waterskin at his knee, Alaric felt secure enough as the camel lurched erect, though the ground seemed oddly far away.

The man watched Alaric for a moment before handing up the reins and mounting his own steed. "I am Hanio," he said. "Piros has given you into my care. Call out to me if you have any difficulty."

"My thanks," said Alaric. "I hope to avoid difficulty."

"She is a placid creature. Just hold tight, and she will follow the others."

At that moment, the line of camels began to move forward, and the placid creature needed no urging to move into place with its fellows. Hanio followed.

The camel's gait was different from that of a horse, but not at all unpleasant, and Alaric soon found himself adjusting to it. Under Hanio's tutelage, he learned to guide the animal, and he also learned that calling it by name—Folero—would cause it to swivel its head about on the long neck and look at him with all evidence of curiosity. Sometimes it would even nibble at his knee with its great soft lips. He would treat it like a horse then, with a pat on the neck and praise.

Piros occasionally led at the front of the caravan. But more often he ranged all along it, speaking to riders, checking the security of their lashings, now and then pulling an animal to the side to readjust its burden. Alaric could almost always see him, atop an especially tall camel. Rudd was rarely nearby; he occupied a place far forward, his bobbing head marked by the deep green headwrap.

The heat of the day increased steadily though it was not so great, Alaric knew, as it would be later in the year, and not so great for a man riding as it would be if he were walking on the sun-baked desert floor. The horizon was a line in the far distance, the great flat plain upon which they moved showing few landmarks once the tavern fell behind them, just an occasional cairn of stones to indicate the trail. For most of the day, clumps of coarse grass and low bushes were the only visible vegetation; now and then a camel would turn aside to nibble at the grass, but its rider would quickly bring it back to the column. Folero seemed to disdain such sampling and walked steadily onward. By day's end, the novelty of riding a new kind of steed had begun to wear thin, and Alaric was glad enough to dismount and hand his camel over to Hanio for care.

He could have crossed the desert far more swiftly in his own special way, flitting from horizon to horizon in one heartbeat after another, following a path laid out by the limits of his vision, but ordinary travel enabled him to question his companions about their destination and so arrive as not quite a stranger to the land. And for that purpose, that evening by the largest fire of several, after the camels had been unloaded and tethered to stakes driven into the ground, and after he and the riders had supped well of the provisions that Piros had packed for them and he had entertained the group with a dozen bawdy songs, he struck up conversations with various of the men, asking with a youth's curiosity of the people and cities that lay beyond the desert. He was a trifle surprised at their answers, which were limited to the pleasures of a single town, a handful of inns, and a small population of women willing to slake their appetites and take their silver. To a man, they confessed they had not ventured beyond but were instead eager to unload the goods they had brought along, pack up whatever their employer had traded for them, and come back home with their pay.

"Is the place so dull that no one cares to see it?" Alaric said to Piros.

"These are careful men," the caravan master replied, "for all that they did not seem so at my brother's establishment. The customs on the far side of the desert are different, the very language is odd, and the men prefer the familiar."

"And yourself?" said Alaric.

"I am a trifle more daring. One does not become a successful merchant without being so." He did not look at the minstrel as he spoke but kept his eyes on his son, as he had since the fires were first kindled. The youth sat with a cluster of men who were speaking together with some animation, occasionally laughing, though young Rudd never did. Rather, he stared into the flames, as if he saw something there so fascinating that he could not tear his attention away. Alaric saw nothing there but burning camel dung.

Alaric nodded toward the youth, though he was not certain Piros noticed the gesture. "I suppose you would want your son to learn of that other place."

Piros did not answer for a long moment, and then he murmured, "I think he knows enough of it already." He stood up. "Time to pitch the tents. Hanio will find you a place."

At Piros's signal, the men swiftly unpacked an array of low tents and set them up, flooring them with patterned carpets and settling themselves, six men to a tent, with sacks of trade goods for their pillows. Alaric wrapped himself in his own thin blanket and lay down near Hanio. The night cooled swiftly, but the warmth of six bodies made the tent comfortable enough.

Morning twilight came soon, and after a meal of bread not quite stale and cheese hard but tasty enough, the camels were loaded once more, the riders mounted, and the caravan moved on. Again, Hanio rode behind Alaric, until the minstrel dropped back purposely to ride beside him.

Hanio barely glanced in his direction. He wore the trailing edge of his sun-bleached headwrap draped loosely about his throat, and above it his nose was sharp, hawklike, his face weather-worn. He seemed of an age with Piros.

"Have you worked with Piros for long?" Alaric asked him.

The man's gaze did not waver from the line of camels ahead. "Some years."

"Then you must know a great deal about his business."

Hanio made no reply to that.

"I've been wondering," said Alaric, "what are we trading to the far side of the desert that is worth this yearly journey?"

"Various goods," said Hanio, and as if he knew that Alaric was about to ask for greater detail, he added, "Fine woolens and leathers, metal-work, lace, dried herbs. And we will stop for salt halfway across—the purest salt in the world. They pay especially well for that."

"Pure salt would be valued back there, too." Alaric tilted his head to indicate the land from which they had come.

"We will stop at the mines again on the way back."

"The mines?"

Hanio nodded.

"I did not know that salt came from mines."

"You are young, minstrel. There may be many things you don't know."

"And I look forward to learning them in my travels," said Alaric. "But tell me, good Hanio, if the mines are halfway across the desert, why don't the folk of the west send caravans to fetch their own salt?"

Hanio curled his lip. It was not a smile. He shook his head. "They fear the desert too much."

Alaric straightened his back and sat tall on Folero. He looked all around, and aside from the plodding camels, he saw nothing but a flat landscape to the horizon. If there were animals in this part of the desert, they had fled or were hiding underground. If there were men, they had not attempted to approach within human vision. At Hanio's knee was a heavy sword in a tooled scabbard, and most of the other riders also had weapons, short swords and long, bows, slings, and lances twice the length of a man's arm. The caravan seemed ready for whatever fate might deliver.

"What do they fear?" he asked.

"At night, sometimes, one can hear the desert moaning," Hanio replied. "Evil spirits, they say, coming out of the lost city to steal men's souls. You will hear them when we reach the dunes." He gestured vaguely ahead.

"Ah," said Alaric. "The lost city. I've heard a tale or two of that. Have you been there?"

Hanio snorted. "It would hardly be lost if men could visit it."

"Then it's nothing more than travelers' fancies?"

"Well," said Hanio. He turned his head at last and looked at Alaric hard. "Sometimes one sees it from afar, and there are towers and domes and walls, all white as ash. But if one tries to approach, it retreats steadily and eventually vanishes altogether. It is a phantom city, a fitting residence for evil spirits." He paused for a pair of heartbeats. "Men have died chasing after it. I have no desire to die."

"Nor I," murmured the minstrel, but he could not help wondering if it could be caught by his own special brand of travel. What he said, though, was, "How much farther to the salt mines?"

"Are you restless already, minstrel?" said Hanio.

Alaric shook his head. "I just like to know what to expect."

Hanio laughed softly. "So do we all. Ask again in eighteen days, and there will be an answer." He looked away again. "You do well on Folero. Perhaps there is no need for me to watch the two of you so closely."

"As you will, good Hanio."

The man nodded and urged his mount up the line, to where Alaric could see Piros riding beside Rudd. He did not return until the caravan stopped for the night at a grove of trees that had appeared as a smudge on the horizon and grown steadily as the sun descended behind it. There was a pond at the heart of the grove, its banks tamped hard by many feet, and the riders filled waterskins and teakettles before they allowed their camels to encircle it and drink. The shade of the trees was pleasant, and as fires were kindled and supper prepared, Alaric sang of the northern wastes, of the snow and ice, as strange to the caravaneers as the desert would have been to the nomads who rode their deer among the glaciers. And the men around him marveled that such ice-bound places could actually exist.

That night, in the desert tent, he dreamed of the North, and when he woke deep in the darkness, he almost wanted to return there, to see the only people who cared whether he lived or died. He could have done so in an instant. But he knew that the caravaneers were unlikely to think well of someone who could show a witch's power and vanish as surely as that phantom city vanished, and so he turned over and went back to sleep instead. Another time, he told himself, as he had so often before.

The next day, a faint undulation became visible at the horizon, and word sped down the line of riders that they would reach the dunes in no more than two days. The caravan began bending southward and arrived at another grove of trees, this time surrounding a well, late in the day. The men spent considerable time raising water, one bucket after another, for the evening meal and the camels. None but the camels drank the water before it was boiled; the men even filled their waterskins with the heated water. Alaric did not attempt to taste the raw liquid after Hanio told him it would affect his bowels adversely. The trees of the grove offered dates, which several of the men climbed after, and Alaric was glad to eat the handful that was his allotted share, as a change from cheese and the remnants of stale bread.

In the morning, the men brought out flour and, with boiled water, shaped flat loaves to set on rocks heating in their fires. The results were not what Alaric was accustomed to, but they were delicious nonetheless, and he felt well fortified for the day. The dunes were clear to see in the distance, great rolling hills of sand, and the caravan bent ever southward to skirt the worst of them. Even so, by day's end they had left the flat desert behind and were moving on less secure footing. That night there was no grove of trees, no pond or well, though there was still plenty of bread from the morning's baking and plenty of water in every man's bag. The camels seemed unperturbed by the lack of available drink and fodder, and several caravaneers assured him that the animals' humps were storage for both.

"Remarkable creatures," he murmured, trying to think how that information would fit into the array of songs that he knew would come out of this journey. Lying down that night, on a bed made softer by the sand, he lulled himself to sleep trying various rhymes for "hump."

In deep darkness, he woke to the sound of moaning—a chorus of moaning at a dozen pitches, as of a crowd of men laboring to move some gigantic stone far beyond their combined strength, or the same crowd lamenting the deaths of countless loved ones. None of the other men in his tent seemed to have been awakened by it, or at least they did not move in response.

Alaric stripped off his blanket and crawled out of the tent. A brisk wind had sprung up, and moonlight showed the sand eddying here and there. After a few moments, he thought the moaning seemed to rise and fall with the wind. The fires had all been banked for the night, and two men were sitting by the largest of them, keeping watch as someone did every night. One man lifted a hand toward Alaric. The minstrel skirted a pair of tents to join them.

"How does anyone sleep through that noise?" he said.

The men grinned, and one of them said, "It's just the desert." And then he looked past Alaric and stood up.

Alaric turned and saw a figure beside one of the tents he had passed. The headwrap was gone, and the dark hair revealed stuck out in wild spikes, but as the person approached, Alaric recognized Rudd.

"Will you sit here with us?" said the man who had stood. He held a hand out to Rudd. "We'll pour you some tea." His companion was already reaching for the kettle that rested on the embers.

Rudd stopped a few strides away. "They're calling us. We must go."

"We'll go at first light."

"We must go now," said Rudd. "Load the camels."

The man crossed the small space between them and laid his arm across Rudd's shoulders. "The others need their rest. There's a long journey ahead yet."

Rudd shook his head. "Not long."

"Still, we should all arrive refreshed." He stretched his other hand out toward the fire, and his companion pressed a cup of tea into it. "Here," he said, offering it to Rudd. "A few sips against the chill, and then lie down and try to sleep a little more. You'd be a poor visitor if you dozed off astride your camel and broke your head in a fall."

"The sand is soft," Rudd murmured. He took the cup and gulped once, twice. Then he pointed to Alaric. "You can hear the music in their call. Come with me and play your lute for them."

"Tomorrow," whispered the man who stood beside him.

Rudd spilled the remainder of his tea into the fire and tossed the cup into the darkness before letting himself be turned and walked back toward his tent.

Alaric looked at the man with the kettle. He was pouring another cup, and he offered it to Alaric, who accepted the warm metal gratefully.

"Was he sleepwalking?" the minstrel asked.

"Some might call it that." The man filled a cup for himself and set the kettle down.

"He's done this before?"

The man nodded. "It's one of the reasons there's a watch. Piros would have our hides if anything happened to the boy." He drank a little of his tea.

"What if he had walked the other way, away from the fire?"

"He never does that. The fire draws him like a moth."

"But still . . ."

"As I said, there's a watch."

Alaric stayed by the fire for a time, and eventually the other man returned. Then, yawning, the minstrel went back to his own tent.

Morning seemed to come very quickly.

The sun was high, the day's journey near half-done, when Piros, who had ranged up and down the line of camels as usual, fell in beside Alaric.

"I see Folero continues to treat you well," he said.

"We seem to suit each other." Alaric leaned far forward to pat the animal's neck. "Piros," he said, "I woke last night and heard the desert singing."

Piros looked at him sidelong. "I suppose a minstrel might call it that."

"Your son heard it, too."

"Ah," said Piros. "It was one of those nights."

"Who did he think was calling?"

Piros shook his head. "The boy sometimes has wild fancies. I advise you not to credit them." He rose a little in his seat, as if looking at something ahead. "Sing of the North again tonight, minstrel. It makes a welcome change." He kicked his mount then and swerved out of the line to trot forward. Parts of a camel's burden had cascaded to the sand, and the whole caravan halted while it was lashed in place once more.

Later in the day, Alaric got his first glimpse of the phantom city.

At least it looked something like a city, far off on the southern horizon, blurred with distance, its towers and walls wavering shapes in the desert sunlight, with silver water all around them. As he stared, his mouth open in wonder, he could hear the men behind him laughing. The laughter stopped abruptly as a camel broke away from the line and began galloping toward them, its rider—his green headwrap unmistakable—urging it with sharp blows from a rod. He passed Alaric, shouting, "Come with me," and then swerved southward, out into the desert. Four other riders burst from the caravan to follow him, and the pursuit moved considerably before they caught up and formed a tight cluster about him, preventing him from going farther. Alaric could make out Rudd's wild arm movements; he appeared to be striking at the other men with the rod. The thin sounds of their voices reached Alaric, but he could not make out any words.

Piros moved out of the line, though he did not make any attempt to join the group surrounding his son. Alaric pulled up beside him as the caravan marched onward, leaving them behind.

"He told me to come with him," said the minstrel.

"You can see what good that would have done you," said Piros, barely glancing at him. He waved a hand toward the caravan. "Go along with the rest."

"A minstrel is always looking for new stories to sing," said Alaric. "I think there's one here."

"Not a good one," Piros muttered.

Alaric pointed toward the southern horizon. "The city alone is worth a song." But as he watched the riders turn back toward the caravan, the distant image wavered and smeared and flattened until it was nothing but a sheet of silver water. "Is even the water real?" he wondered.

"Not even that," said Piros.

"It must be attractive to men less well supplied than we are."

Piros shook his head very slightly. "No matter how far you follow, no matter how swiftly, it will always be beyond your reach. When I was young and traveled the desert with my own father, I learned that." He leaned forward, forearms on his thighs. "There was a time when my son knew it as well."

The riders returned, one of the pursuers gripping the reins of Rudd's mount. As Rudd passed his father, he scowled, and said, "It's your fault they wouldn't wait."

Piros made no reply. He only pointed toward the retreating caravan and turned his mount to bring up the rear as the group hurried to rejoin it. Folero did not require any command from Alaric to match pace with the other camels, and the minstrel found himself clinging to the hoops before and behind him to retain his seat.

That night, after supper was done and some of the men of the caravan had gathered to listen to Alaric sing, Rudd pushed his way to the front of the group and sat almost at the minstrel's feet. He did not join in the raucous choruses, but he nodded his head slightly in time to the music and occasionally smiled, though Alaric was not quite sure it was at the songs. As the night deepened and the listeners gradually drifted away, he stayed until Alaric finally set the lute aside, and only then did he allow a pair of his father's men to escort him to his tent. Afterward, Alaric settled by one of the smaller fires, where Piros was discussing their route with the men who had been in the fore of the caravan. He waited until the conversation ebbed to nothing and the other men sought their tents. The night watch was at a larger fire some distance away, and so he and Piros found themselves alone.

"It must be a hard thing for you," said Alaric, "to have such a son."

Piros watched the low flames for a few heartbeats. "Most of the men know how to deal with him. Otherwise, I would have lost him long since."

Alaric picked up a ladle that had been used to stir porridge for the evening meal, and, reversing it, he poked at the fire. The embers flared into dancing life for a moment, the warmth pleasant against the night's chill. "Has he always been like this?"

Again, Piros was silent for a long moment. Then he said, "Not always. I thought he would take my place someday. He was a good rider. He learned to race early and bested most of the men in this caravan. But that was before."

"Before . . . ?"

The caravan master sighed. "I suppose I'm a little surprised that none of the others has told you. That they've all kept their oath."

Alaric waited.

"I'd ask for your oath, too, but I can't believe you'd give it or intend it. Not after hearing your songs. Do people recognize themselves when you sing?"

Alaric smiled a little. "I'd be a fool to put too much truth in my songs. I care a great deal for my skin."

Piros selected some fragments of dried camel dung from a pile not far from his hip and fed them to the fire. In a moment, it flared up. "I thought that might be the case."

Alaric leaned an elbow on his knee. "People can recognize themselves in any story, whether it's about them or not. I'll give you my oath that no one else will recognize you. Or your son. And whatever song I sing of this journey will be far away, where no one will even know your name."

Piros shrugged. "I don't know why it matters to me. But it does." He looked at Alaric sidelong. "And yet, there is a part of me, a vain, greedy part, that wants to hear what you'll make of our story. That wants the immortality you offer. At my age, I think that's the only sort of immortality I'll ever have." He glanced over his shoulder toward the tent where his son slept. "Not grandchildren, that's certain."

Alaric reached for the kettle that rested amid the flames. There was a bit of liquid in the bottom, and he poured himself half a cup of the strong desert tea. "I make no guarantee of immortality."

Piros took the kettle from him and filled his own cup. "Don't be modest, minstrel. You already have songs that are older than the two of us together."

"Tell me your tale, then. Or tell me the version you want me to hear."

"Not . . . the truth?"

"No one ever tells the truth about himself. We tell what we want others to judge, for good or ill. And when I have heard your tale, perhaps I will make something more of it." He blew on his tea to cool it before taking a sip. "Perhaps I will sing of our visit to the sky-touching towers of the lost city. Does it have a name?"

Piros swallowed a mouthful of his own tea. "I've heard it called Haven," he murmured.

"A fine, romantic name," observed Alaric.

"And what do you think we would find there?"

Alaric smiled just a little. "Our hearts' desires, of course. Isn't that what we're all seeking?"

Piros rolled his cup between his hands. "Perhaps that's why it always retreats beyond our reach." Again, he glanced toward his son's tent. "He blames me for that. He blames me for most things."

"I've heard that isn't uncommon among sons," Alaric said.

Piros looked down into his cup for a moment, as if he could read something in its contents. "If I had never taken him to the caves . . . perhaps our tale would be very different."

"The caves?"

Piros nodded slowly. "Some would say it was fated to happen, because of the kind of boy he was. Headstrong. Of limited obedience. If his mother were alive, she would despise me for not beating it out of him. She believed very much in beatings."

"So you were the soft one."

"For all the good it did, yes." He took another small sip of his tea. "He was twelve summers old when she died. Afterward, I kept him by my side. Except for the trip to the caves. That waited until he was sixteen." He shook his head. "I should have let it go longer. But he wanted to know. He was curious in those days." He finished his tea, set the cup down by his thigh, and leaned forward with elbows on his knees, fingers interlaced. For a moment, he pressed his chin to his fingers, and then he straightened his back once more and sighed. "I warned him. But in the end he did as he pleased. You've seen the result."

"The caves are . . . dangerous?"

"Deadly dangerous," said Piros. "The vapors that rise within them are poisonous. But something highly coveted by the people who live on the far side of the desert grows there. And so there is profit to be made in conveying it to them. My father did it, and his father, and before him there was the merchant who passed the trade to my family."

"But if the caves are poisonous," said Alaric, "how is this substance obtained?"

"The people who live nearby know the secret of harvesting it without dying."

"Then it's a plant of some kind."

Piros shrugged. "It might be a moss, or it might be a mineral incrustation. No one quite seems to know. It's not easy to study something that exists in a poisonous mist."

"So . . . Rudd was poisoned."

Piros shook his head. "That would be a much simpler fate." He took a deep breath and seemed to squint at something far beyond the fire, though there was nothing to see but the dark and starry sky. "I knew I would have to tell you when I asked you to join us, but now it seems more difficult than I expected. Still . . ." He looked at Alaric sidelong. "When we reach the salt mines, there will be another journey of two days, for just a few of us. Myself. Hanio. And Rudd, because he will refuse to stay behind.

"Our destination will be the caves, and we will return with a considerable quantity of a certain powder, which will be in my charge, although Rudd will be given small amounts from time to time. Under its influence, and knowing we have renewed our supply of it, he may urge you to try it. As you value your life, do not." He sighed heavily. "He will praise it. He will tell you it will make you feel like a king. One would think he would not, that he would wish to keep as much of it as he could for himself, but under its influence, men tend not to consider the future. For the sake of your own future, do not accept it. Believe me when I tell you this. You will think you are gaining the world, but you will be losing yourself."

"I have no desire to do that," said Alaric.

Piros sighed again. "What man would not want to feel like a king?"

Alaric allowed himself a ghost of a smile. "I've observed a few kings. It's not as enviable a life as one might think."

Piros glanced at him. "On the far side of the desert, they pay well for it. They call it the Powder of Desire."

"An interesting name."

"It's a fine grind, blue-gray in color, and not unlike thyme, but with an even sharper scent and a more pungent taste. It goes well with fowl."

"You've tried it?"

Piros looked back to the fire. "I was young and foolish, and there was a wager. I have not wagered since. Rudd has shown me what I might have become."

Alaric nodded slowly. "I take your warning. But I do wonder . . . why not withhold it from him? Surely its power fades with time."

The caravan master's interlaced fingers tightened until the cords stood out on the backs of his hands. "On the far side of the desert . . . I saw a man accustomed to it die for its lack. It was a long, slow, painful death." He closed his eyes and bent his head. "Shall I lose even the shadow of my son?"

Alaric glanced toward the tent where Rudd slept. There was a man at the entrance, rolled in a blanket, his head pillowed on a camel saddle. Alaric knew there was another at the rear. "It's a sad tale," he said at last. "But it needs more shaping before it can be a song." He avoided saying that it needed an end.

"Well," said Piros, "we have a long journey yet. Plenty of time for shaping." With one hand against the sandy ground, he pushed himself to his feet.

The next day, just past midmorning, the phantom city became visible again. And this time, Alaric was riding only a short distance behind

Rudd, and he could see that Hanio held the reins of the young man's mount, and two other men rode close beside him. As before, the city wavered and shifted at the horizon, its many towers now relatively distinct, now merging into a broad blur. Toward evening, the whole mass seemed to rise into the air, and empty sky was visible beneath it. Clouds, Alaric thought, though that was a difficult surmise to accept while the rest of the sky was a featureless blue save for the brilliant smear of the sun.

The next dozen days passed with little to mark them apart. Each morning, fresh bread was baked and shared out before the men mounted their camels and the long line of burdened animals began to move westward. Each day, the caravan moved westward, sometimes crossing hard-packed desert pavement, sometimes skirting more dunes and wading through sand ankle deep on a man, and the distant spectral city almost always accompanied them, far to the south. Each evening, they stopped at a well whose water was potable only after boiling, and there might be scattered scrub grass around the well, though the camels ensured that it did not survive their presence. And when the tents were pitched, the fires kindled, and the remnants of the morning bread consumed along with dried fruit, almost equally dry cheese, and sometimes a few portions of preserved meat that required soaking in hot water to keep it from being nearly as tough as leather, Alaric swung the lute into his arms and played and sang until only the night watch remained. And every night, Rudd sat almost at Alaric's feet and listened and smiled and nodded a little and said nothing.

Then, on one day that promised to be like so many others, a dark smudge appeared on the horizon and grew, with the caravan's approach, to be a broad grove of trees surrounding a shimmering sheet of water that was no illusion. To one side of the water, nestled among the trees, was a village of a dozen huts, and scattered around it were men, women, and children tending vegetable gardens and even a small flock of goats. Alaric could scarcely believe his eyes. In the middle of the desert, where nothing but a few lonely wells reminded a traveler that men sometimes passed this way, here were settled human beings with homes neatly made and, in the open space framed by those homes, finely crafted chairs and tables set atop gorgeously loomed carpets—furniture and floor coverings worthy of a royal house.

The camels, Folero included, were picketed at one side of the water, their leads looped through ring-tipped metal spikes driven deep into the trunks of the trees, to keep them away from the gardens. The men of the caravan pitched their tents and set their fires nearby, Alaric thought for much the same reason. Piros handed his own mount off to Hanio and strode to the heart of the carpets, and as he reached that place, a man in white robes, with a gold chain about his neck and a diadem at his brow, came out of one of the houses to meet him, and other villagers, less opulently arrayed, left off their gardening to draw close to the man who was obviously their prince.

Alaric saw bowing and broad gestures exchanged between the visitor and the prince, and after some moments of conversation, Piros waved to him to draw near. Alaric approached and bowed deeply to the man in white robes.

"This is our minstrel," said Piros. "He will entertain us tonight."

The prince smiled. "And if he pleases me, there will be a reward for him." He glanced at Piros. "But what of the nights you are gone? Will he stay here? And perhaps even after?"

"That shall be as he wishes," said Piros.

"If he is as skilled as you say, I will hope he does."

They all bowed then, and Alaric followed Piros's lead in backing away until they reached the edge of the carpets, where the caravan master turned and raised an arm toward the men who waited nearest among the camels. At that signal, they began unloading sacks from a score of animals.

Alaric trailed Piros to the largest fire, where the men tending it poured tea for both of them. Piros drank his while he watched the camels being stripped of their burdens, the men shouldering the sacks, carrying them to the carpets, and piling them high. The prince was still there, and now he held chalk and slate and was evidently tallying the delivery.

Finally, unable to keep silent any longer, Alaric said, "You weren't suggesting that I might want to stay here when the caravan moves on, were you?"

Piros did not look at him. "As I said, that will be your choice. It's a soft life here, except when the sandstorms blow. Still, the people have managed to recover from every storm. The food is good. We'll be eating fresh goat meat during our stay, and taking dried with us for the rest of the journey. And most of those sacks are filled with grain, for fresh bread; they'll have more than enough for the year. A minstrel could do worse than sing for such a prince."

"I think not," said Alaric.

Piros smiled thinly. "He'll offer you gold. I'm sure of it."

Alaric shook his head. "I've had gold. It attracts thieves. I prefer to travel. Or are you tired of me, good Piros, that you would unload me like those sacks of grain?"

Piros looked at him then. "He may offer you the Powder to keep you. As the lord of the caves it comes from, he has quite a large personal supply of it."

"Has he? Then perhaps I won't eat his food after all. Is the Powder how he's grown rich?"

"Among other ways," said Piros. "There are the furnishings, which command high prices on both sides of the desert. And there is the salt." He gestured toward the north. "The mines are some distance yonder, though no one here will say exactly where or how far. They gathered it in last year's grain sacks, and it waits for us at a storage area half a day's journey from here. A party of my men will fetch it tomorrow, while I am elsewhere. If you care for hard work, you can go with them."

"And you," said Alaric, "will be . . . elsewhere."

Piros shifted his gaze to the prince, who was nodding as the last of the grain sacks was set at his feet. Piros echoed the nod, and Alaric could not tell whether it was directed at him or just in satisfaction at the stage of his transactions with the prince. "Perhaps you'll want to come with me," the caravan master said. "We'll return in four or five days."

"With the Powder." It was not a question.

Piros crossed his arms over his chest. "A man comes to know his fellows in the desert."

Alaric smiled. "As do traveling companions anywhere." He was thinking of the Arctic wastes, deserts of another kind, but deserts nonetheless, and the people he had known there.

"You have courage, minstrel," said Piros.

Alaric shook his head. "Less than you think, good Piros. But I have considerable curiosity, and that sometimes masquerades as courage."

Piros glanced toward the camels, the fires. "As I told you, my son will be coming along. He'll need watching. He likes your songs. They may keep him from running after the city."

"Why not leave him behind? Your men seem good at the watching."

"I have the Powder that he requires, at least enough until we reach the source," said Piros. "There is only one of them I can trust with it, and he'll be coming with us." He looked hard at Alaric. "I think I have your measure, minstrel. There will be no special reward for the journey, but I doubt that you care."

"A good song is reward enough for me."

Piros nodded again. "Hanio and I know how to find the place. It isn't easy to read the signs in the desert. Especially for a novice. Wander off and you could be lost forever."

"I'm a careful traveler, and I've rarely been lost," said Alaric. He was reluctant to say "never," though it was true enough. The map he carried in his mind, of every place he had ever been or seen, had always served his special power well. "And I'm good at following other people."

"Very well," said Piros. "In the morning, when the salt party goes north, we'll go south."

"Toward the phantom city."

"Yes. That, too, should please my son."

That night, the village hosted them well, with fresh meat and vegetables for the whole caravan and praise for Alaric's music. The prince did not offer him any gold, but Alaric did not expect it after a single night of entertainment. In the morning, a large group of men and camels was told off for the salt; one of the villagers would be their guide, though Piros told Alaric he had no doubt that his men could find the usual storage place by themselves. Piros, Hanio, and Rudd started south on their own mounts, with Alaric, Folero, and four riderless camels heavy-laden with food and water following behind. In the evening, they camped in a place as desolate as any Alaric had seen on the journey. It had no source of water, but of course they had brought their own, and they brewed tea and shared out some of that morning's bread for their supper. Afterward, the minstrel sang a newly crafted song about the moaning dunes, with a repeated chorus that made two of his companions nod in time to it although not Rudd, who only sat by the fire and looked southward into the darkness, as if there were something there to see.

The next day they rode onward and camped and ate, and Alaric sang again. The day after, a slight rise in the landscape became visible ahead—not dunes, but a line of modest hillocks stretching southwestward. Half a day's journey brought the travelers to them and to a tight cluster of seven huts, well made but smaller than the ones in the prince's settlement, at their feet. There was water, too, but Piros cautioned that it was not drinkable, even after boiling, and at close range Alaric could see that it had a disagreeable yellowish color; even the camels disdained it.

Half a dozen men came out of the huts to greet them. They were gaunt men, the bones clearly visible in their faces, their eyes sunken and rimmed with dark, their hands and forearms skeletal where they showed at the ends of their sleeves, their desert robes hanging loose on their bodies as if the men had once been more substantial. Their leader, the tallest of the group, bowed low to Piros and escorted him into one of the huts while the others began to unload the pack camels. Alaric lent a hand, shouldering goatskin bags that had been filled at the village pond and slung over the camels in pairs linked by thick rope.

The gaunt men delivered water to six huts; the rest of the supplies went into the one that stood closest to a communal fire pit. Shortly after everything had been distributed, Piros and the tall man emerged from their meeting.

"There's more harvesting to be done," Piros told his companions, "and so we'll be here a full day tomorrow while they finish."

Hanio nodded. He had brought a live young goat from the village, carried at his knee in a mesh bag, and now he slaughtered it with a single quick stroke of his knife, skinned it neatly, cleaned out its innards, and spitted the carcass to roast over the fire while the gaunt men put the organ meats to stew in a large pot, wasting nothing.

During the cooking, a pair of the gaunt men took small, empty sacks from the supply hut, climbed the rise beyond their tiny village, and descended behind it till they were no longer visible. They were gone for some time, and when they returned, their sacks were slung over their shoulders, full of something heavy and shapeless, and another pair went out along the same path, again with empty sacks, again returning later with sacks filled. The gaunt men continued this, pair by pair, turn and turn about, while Hanio secured the full sacks on the camels and Piros brought other full sacks from several of the huts and did the same.

At one point, Rudd, who had been sitting cross-legged by the fire pit, watching their dinner roast, stood and climbed the rise himself, and Hanio left off his camel loading and went after him. After a few moments, Alaric followed, two dozen paces behind, and from the top he could see the phantom city on the southern horizon and Rudd descending the southern slope toward it, Hanio at his elbow. Hanio was saying something that Alaric could not make out, but his tone seemed soft and persuasive, and finally he caught Rudd's arm and stopped him and looked to be urging him to turn back. Piros joined Alaric on the rise, but he made no attempt to go after his son. Hanio turned the youth around at last, and Piros gave a small nod before returning to the fire.

Alaric sang that night, of a long and perilous search for treasure. It was an old song he had learned far away, but it seemed appropriate. He carved his own serving of goat meat from the carcass, and it was delicious; at Piros's small signal, he did not taste the organ meats, which smelled strongly of what might or might not have been thyme, and neither Piros nor Hanio ate any either. Whether Rudd did or not, Alaric did not see. After the meal, Piros set up a tent for his group, and they all crawled in to share warmth against the cool of the desert night. Alaric woke once, when one of the others—not Rudd, who slept nearest him—went out, presumably to answer nature's call, but he had no need for it himself and so went back to sleep.

In the morning, they baked a little bread on fire-pit-heated stones and broke their fast with that and cold goat meat. Afterward, Hanio suggested that Alaric might want to see what he could of the gathering of the Powder, to satisfy some of the curiosity that had brought him to the desert.

"Is it allowed?" said Alaric.

"Yes, but there's little to see," said Piros.

Rudd, who had been bent over his food, looked up at that. "I'd like to see it."

"You've seen it before," said his father. "It is no different now."

"I want to see it," Rudd said loudly. He stood up and tossed his half-eaten meal aside, then he turned and began climbing the rise.

Piros looked to Hanio. "Go along with him, and don't let him take too much of the fresh."

"I may need a bit of help," said Hanio.

Rudd looked over his shoulder at his father. "Don't you want to come along, Father? To keep me under your eye?"

Piros glanced at Alaric but said nothing.

"I'll go," said the minstrel. He caught up with Rudd. "You can explain the harvesting to me."

"Father understands it better," Rudd said, and there was a sullen tone in his voice, and a sullen look on his face. "But he's afraid of it. Aren't you, Father?"

Piros looked at him with slitted eyes. "As you should be," he said. "Look what it's done to the harvesters." To Alaric, he said, "They die before their time even though they don't inhale the poison. So many years of exposure takes its toll."

"Perhaps I don't want to see it," said Alaric, and he took a step back down the slope.

"Stand well away from the opening," said Piros. "You'll be safe there. The smell that emanates from it is enough to warn men from approaching too close."

"Afraid of a smell," said Rudd.

"What kind of smell?" said Alaric.

"You won't mistake it for perfume," said Piros. "Or for thyme."

Alaric hesitated for another moment. Still, Hanio was going along, and he seemed healthy enough. Curiosity finally won out over doubt, and Alaric nodded to Rudd and Hanio, and the three of them climbed to the top of the rise. There, they followed the crests of the line of hillocks westward for a hundred paces, two hundred. To their right, the phantom city wavered on the southern horizon, and Rudd glanced at it often, though he did not attempt to run toward it, Alaric thought, because Hanio had a tight hold on his arm. A sheet of water—or something that looked like water—stretched outward from the city, and it looked real enough except that its margins shifted constantly, like liquid in a basin carried through a jostling tavern crowd.

"Tell me about the harvesting," Alaric said.

Rudd made no reply, and finally Hanio said, "They hold their breath. There's no more to it than that. No one would want to breathe that stench anyway."

"They gather it while holding their breath?" said Alaric.

"There is no other way," replied Hanio. "Through long practice, they become very good at holding their breath. Those who are less good at it are never selected for the work. Or they die."

"This does not sound like a very attractive sort of work," said the minstrel. "An early death or perhaps an even earlier one. What kind of man would choose it?"

"There is no choosing," said Hanio. "The prince commands, and they obey. Of course, the harvesters use as much of the Powder as they like, so there are compensations."

Alaric smelled his destination before he saw it, and it was as repellent as Piros had promised, a strong scent of rot, like offal left too long in the sun. He paused for a moment, letting Hanio and Rudd draw farther ahead and begin to scramble down the southern slope. He watched them turn and disappear under an overhanging shelf of rock. After a long moment, he took two more steps in that direction and then stopped again, uncertainty warring once more with his curiosity. A feeling of unease was building in him, and no matter how many times he told himself that if Hanio felt it was safe enough, he should, he still hesitated.

Then, one of the gaunt men was leaping up the slope toward him, and he heard Hanio shouting something, though he could not make out the words. He stepped sideways, and the gaunt man brushed past him, sprinting back the way they had come.

Hanio leaned out from under the rocky overhang and shouted again, waving urgently for Alaric to join him. The minstrel looked down the south-facing slope. What was happening, he wondered, that Hanio and the second gaunt man could not deal with? How did they think he could help?

The sounds of running made him turn. Piros and all five of the remaining gaunt men were rushing across the ridge of hillocks.

"What has the stupid boy done?" shouted Piros. But he pounded past Alaric without waiting for an answer.

The last two gaunt men clutched at Alaric's arms and dragged him along with them, and he stumbled, half losing his footing as the three of them plunged down the slope.

Under the overhang, at the back of the shallow space created by that shelf of rock, the slope of the hillside was nearly vertical, forming a wall a little more than the height of a man, and set into that wall was a massive wooden door. Rudd lay almost at the foot of that door, and Hanio knelt beside him, cradling him like a child.

"What's happened?" said Piros, bending over his son.

And suddenly, all in a few quick heartbeats, one of the gaunt men flung the wooden door open, revealing the darkness of a cave beyond, and as the odor of rot rushed out, ten times more powerful than before, and as Alaric stopped his own breath against it, three of the gaunt men laid hands on Piros, lifted him high, and heaved him through the doorway while the others swept the minstrel off his feet with strength he could not counter and threw him in as well. What breath Alaric had was knocked away as he fell hard on Piros. And then the wooden door slammed shut and daylight vanished.

In the pitch-blackness, Alaric clutched the caravan master's body against his own, and in one more heartbeat they were both in the North, and the stench of rot was blowing away on the crisp, clean Northern wind.

Alaric let go of Piros and rolled to his knees, coughing and taking great gasping breaths. The air was cold, and he shivered at the contrast to the heat of the desert, though for the North, at this time of year, the day was mild. He was almost afraid to look at Piros. He hadn't given any real thought—any real will—to the use of his power; there hadn't been time. Had he taken Piros's entire body with him, or would there just be a piece of him, like part of a butchered carcass?

A soft moan drew his eyes. Piros propped himself up on his elbows and coughed. He was whole, and not only that, but he and Alaric were lying on a broad pallet of rock. Alaric realized that his power had taken not just Piros but also a goodly chunk of the cave floor. And on that floor lay an age-discolored human skeleton, ribs cracked, limb bones scattered—Alaric thought he and Piros must have struck it when they fell—and among those bones were incrustations of something that might have been tiny crystals or might have been mold, blue-gray in color. There were smears of that blue-gray on one of Alaric's sleeves, and as he climbed to his feet he dusted them off against the other sleeve, careful not to let any of it touch his skin, careful not to inhale any of it. He guessed at what it must be.

Piros was sitting up and looking around with wide-eyed wariness at the hardy Northern grass that spread outward from the rock pallet beneath him, at the bushes and stunted trees scattered across the rolling landscape, and the distant, white-capped mountains beyond. He frowned up at Alaric. "Is this the land of the dead?"

Alaric shook his head. "No, we've evaded that. This is just the North."

The caravan master rolled to his knees and crawled to the edge of the rock slab, laying his hands on the chill Northern soil and digging his fingers into it for just a moment. Then he pushed himself to his feet. "How did we come here?" he whispered. He looked at Alaric again. "You did this."

Alaric said nothing.

Piros turned entirely about. "This is far," he murmured, and he clutched his desert robes close against the chill. Then he bowed deeply to Alaric. "What would you have of me, my lord?"

Alaric caught his breath sharply. That was not a reaction he had expected. Fear of his witch's power, yes, and its likely cousin hate. But reverence? "I want nothing, good Piros, except your friendship."

"I owe you my life," said Piros. "That is not a debt easily repaid."

Alaric shook his head. "I saved myself. It was just as easy to take you along."

"You could have left me to die."

"I am not that kind of man," said Alaric.

Piros's eyes narrowed. "Are you a man? Or are you some sort of magical spirit?"

"A man."

"And yet . . ."

"It's an ability I was born with. I try not to use it where others can observe. It frightens them." He looked hard at Piros. "But you are not frightened."

"I have seen many things in my life," said Piros, "and I have never found fear to be useful. Can you take me back? Not to the cave, but outside."

"I can take you back to the gaunt men's camp or to the village by the pond or to your brother's inn."

"To the hill above the cave?"

"Yes, that, too."

"I must know who commanded this. And I must see to my son and Hanio if they aren't dead already."

"The harvesters outnumber us," said Alaric.

"They do," said Piros, "but we have the advantage of surprise this time." He shook his head. "This is not their doing alone. Their prince would never allow them to kill me unless someone else was ready to take over the trade, and with a more advantageous offer. The question is . . . who?"

"You suspect . . . ?"

Piros's mouth made a tight, grim line. "Someone who came with us to the source of the Powder, to make sure the deed was done. And to kill you, as well, to leave no credible witness."

"Two possibilities," murmured Alaric.

"Indeed," said Piros. "Take me back, minstrel. I need the truth."

"A little distance from the cave," said Alaric. "Just out of sight."

Piros nodded.

"Very well," said the minstrel. "Come into the circle of my arms."

They embraced each other, and a heartbeat later they were in the desert once more, on the north slope of the ridge they had followed to the cave. The ridge stood above their heads, but they both dropped to the ground anyway, and Piros crawled to the top, his head and body low. He peered over the rise and then signaled Alaric to join him.

The overhang that marked the cave was only a dozen long, slantwise strides away, and three of the gaunt men were visible around it.

"Do you have a knife?" whispered Piros.

Alaric shook his head. He did, but it was in his knapsack back at the gaunt men's camp.

"Take this one." Piros pulled a long blade from his sleeve and held it out, hilt first.

"I don't kill people," whispered the minstrel.

"All I want is the threat. Ghosts with knives. Do you think they'll stand against that?"

Alaric took the knife. Piros pulled two others from his sleeves. Alaric wondered how many more he carried.

"Follow me," said the caravan master, and he sprang to his feet, leaped over the rise, and sprinted down the other side, shouting, "Murderers! Murderers!"

Alaric gripped the knife tightly and ran after him.

The three gaunt men looked up and began to scream—sharp, high-pitched screams, like wounded dogs. They clutched one another like terrified children, and then the other three came out from the overhang and began to scream, too.

By then, Piros had reached them. "Down!" he shouted. "Down like the curs you are, with your faces to the ground! Pour dust and stones on your heads and beg me not to give you the justice you deserve!" He waved his knives, and Alaric stopped a few paces behind him and began to wave his own blade in a manner he hoped was menacing enough.

The gaunt men crouched low, scrabbling at the ground with clawed and shaking fingers and dashing what they scraped up over their heads, screaming all the while.

"Silence!" roared the caravan master.

The screaming fell abruptly to whimpers punctuated by choking coughs.

"Who gave the order?" demanded Piros, and he kicked the nearest bowed head once, twice. When there was no response, he slashed at the man's shoulder with the tip of one knife, ripping both the cloth and the skin beneath, and blood began to stain the man's robe. "Answer!" Piros shouted.

The wounded man clutched at his shoulder and groaned.

"Your man," said one of the others. "It was your man."

"Hanio," said another. "He said if we did it, we could go back to the village. Back to our families!"

"He said they would welcome us," said yet another. "Someone else would have to harvest the Powder!"

Piros strode past the crouching cluster of men, and they made no attempt to stop him; they only followed him with their eyes. Alaric gave them a wider berth, wondering how long their terror would keep them from guessing that he and Piros were not spirits.

Hanio was waiting under the overhang, his back against the door that sealed the cave. He, too, had a pair of knives, long, wicked blades. "So there's another way out," he said. "And the poison is a lie."

Piros shook his head. "You killed us."

"I think not," said Hanio, and he kicked a stone toward Piros. It struck the caravan master's soft boot where it showed beneath the hem of his robe. "You're still flesh and blood."

Piros frowned. "Where is my son?"

"Gone," said Hanio. He gestured southward with the tip of one knife. "Where he always wanted to go."

Piros did not take his eyes from the man. "Did he know what you were planning?"

"Of course he did. You think he liked the prison you made of his life?"

Alaric could see Piros's grip on his knives tighten, the knuckles white with the strain. "I would have given it all to you someday," he said. "Not to him."

"Someday, twenty years from now," said Hanio. "And till then I would have to endure his madness. I've had enough. I've long since had enough."

Piros eased to one side of the rock shelter, till the wall was at his shoulder. "So this is where we are."

"Two against one," said Hanio.

"Seven against two," said Piros. "You set the odds yourself."

Hanio shook his head. "They think you're dead. They've run away."

Piros did not look back toward the cowering gaunt men, but Alaric could not help glancing that way. They were indeed gone. "We seem to be alone," he said.

Piros nodded. "Tell me if they come back. Otherwise, this is between Hanio and me." He took a single step toward Hanio. "Which of the others is for you?"

"All of them," said Hanio, "when I return without you." He raised one of his knives to waist height and kept the other at his hip.

Piros sprang, knocking Hanio's knives aside with his own, and then both men were hard against the wooden door for a moment before they dropped to the ground in a tangle of desert robes, Hanio on top. Alaric realized he was holding his breath, ready to flee in his own way but uncertain enough to stay another moment, and another.

Then Piros pushed Hanio aside and staggered to his feet. The blade in his left hand was bloody to the hilt, and there was a spreading stain of the same color at Hanio's belly. Piros wiped the bloody knife on the hem of Hanio's robe and slipped both of his blades back into his sleeves. Silently, Alaric passed him the knife he had loaned out, and that, too, went into one of his sleeves. "We'll let the villagers bury him," said Piros. "Or perhaps they'll just leave him out in the heat to dry. Now for my son." He started back up the rise.

Alaric followed. "What will you do to him?" he said.

At the top, Piros turned and looked southward, and Alaric stood beside him and did the same. The phantom city was there, as so often before, and between it and them, barely visible against the pale desert floor, was a tiny figure topped by a dark headwrap.

"I wonder how much fresh Powder they gave him," said Piros. "It's stronger fresh. He probably sees alabaster towers and gardens of flowers in full bloom where we see shapes that could as easily be clouds. And perhaps even boats on the water." He took a deep, heavy breath. "That's what I saw. And it frightened me enough that I never tried the Powder again."

"We can fetch him back," said Alaric.

"We can," said Piros. "But I had no need of Hanio to tell me that the boy knew. Else they would have tossed him into the cave along with us. Hanio was ever a careful man. A good subordinate who never left anything to chance. If he killed you to leave no witness, he would not have spared Rudd."

"You can't be sure of that," said Alaric. "Hanio could have been lying to gain an advantage in the fight. He might have trusted the Powder to befuddle the boy's mind." He squinted against the sun, gauging the distance. It would be an easy enough journey with his special power, and if he seized the boy quickly enough, while he was too surprised to struggle, the return would be easy, too. "Piros," he said, "he's your son."

Piros laughed softly, ruefully. "He's the Powder's son. And I, too, have had enough of managing his prison." He took another deep breath and then turned away from the south, the city, his son. "Let him have his heart's desire." He started down the north slope, toward the gaunt men's cluster of huts.

Alaric trotted after him. "Piros . . ."

The caravan master kept walking. "Isn't this a good enough end to your song, minstrel?"

"A perfect end for a song," said Alaric. "But not for a man's life. Will you let him die out there because the Powder is twisting his mind?"

"If you go after him," said Piros, "he will become your charge. Is that what you want?"

Alaric swallowed hard. "Piros . . . I can't let him die."

Piros shook his head. "I didn't take you for a fool, minstrel, but it seems you are."

A heartbeat later, Alaric was walking south a few paces behind Piros's son. "Rudd!" he shouted.

The youth barely glanced over his shoulder. He seemed unsurprised to see Alaric.

"Come back," said the minstrel. "There's nothing out there. There's no city."

"You listened to my father too much," said Rudd. "He knew there was a city, but it frightened him, and so he denied it."

"It's an illusion," said Alaric. "A trick of the desert. I've seen it nearly every day, and it always disappears eventually."

"It won't disappear for me." He sped up his pace, as if to catch it before it vanished.

Alaric stopped and let the space between himself and Rudd increase. The city was there, ahead, tantalizingly indistinct, but still there. Piros had said it was an illusion, and Alaric had accepted that, but what if it was something else? What if there *was* a city—some sort of city—out there? What if Rudd was the one who was right? He gauged its distance and leaped toward it in his own special way, a leap the equivalent of a man walking half a day across the desert. When he looked back, he could no longer see Rudd, but ahead, the city remained as far off as before. Another leap. Two. Three. At the tenth, the city was gone, though the sheet of water that had surrounded it still spread enticingly across the desert in the distance. A few more leaps showed the water continuing to recede.

Illusions, all illusions. Now he knew for certain, and he felt disappointed as well as a trifle embarrassed that he had let himself think otherwise even for a short time. He returned to the spot he had left, now a few score paces behind Rudd, and he ran to catch up with the boy.

"Still here?" said Rudd.

"I'll walk with you," Alaric said, "and when the city disappears, we'll go back."

"Go back to what?" said Rudd. "Hanio runs the caravan now; he won't want me there." He glanced at Alaric. "Yes, I know my father is dead, and so are you. You're an illusion, but here you are. Why should I believe in you and not the city?"

Alaric did not try to answer that. Instead, he said, "I'm here to take you back to the land of the living. To your uncle's inn, if you wish."

Rudd fumbled at a fold in his robe and brought out a leather pouch such as might hold coins. But when he dipped his fingers into it, they came out with a pinch of gray powder that he licked away. "I am in the land of the living," he said. "And the city will welcome me."

"Rudd . . ."

The boy held the pouch out toward Alaric. "Can the dead enjoy the Powder?"

Alaric shook his head.

"That's a shame," said Rudd. "There's plenty of Powder in the city." He closed the pouch and tucked it away.

"There's plenty of Powder in the caravan," said Alaric. "Come back to it with me." He caught at Rudd's arm just above the elbow.

Rudd stopped abruptly and stared at the hand gripping his arm. "No illusion at all," he murmured. He jerked his arm free and pushed the minstrel away. Then he took a few steps back, pulled a knife from his sleeve, and thrust it toward Alaric.

Alaric skipped sideways, fighting his instinct to vanish.

"So you can die twice," said Rudd, and he lunged forward.

An instant later, Alaric found himself in the North. At his feet was the pallet of stone with its scattered human bones. He took a deep breath and leaped back to a spot a dozen paces behind the boy. "Rudd!" he shouted. "The city doesn't want you. It sent me to keep you away!"

The boy twisted around. "Liar!" he shouted, and he waved the knife. "It's always wanted me!" Then he turned back to the south and resumed his march.

"Rudd!"

The boy did not respond this time.

"Rudd," Alaric said more softly. And he watched for a long time while the boy's figure dwindled in the distance and the phantom city beckoned beyond him, unreachable. When he had become no more than a dot in the broad desert landscape, Alaric returned to the gaunt men's cluster of huts.

Piros was there alone with the camels, inspecting the lashings of the many bags of Powder. He looked up as Alaric approached. "He wouldn't come?"

Alaric shook his head.

"I didn't think he would." He patted the neck of the camel beside him. "We'll leave now. We've been gone long enough."

Alaric looked to his left and right. "The harvesters?"

"Run off," said Piros. "Perhaps back to their prince, with some story about our magic, if they dare. He'll lay it off to the Powder, I'd guess. Or perhaps they're just out in the desert, waiting for us to go. No matter. We don't need them anymore. We have enough of the Powder for this trip. And I'd wager they'll have forgotten it all by this time next year."

"And you and I?"

"Back to the village to resume our journey. Pack up a bit of that goat meat for tomorrow."

Alaric tore some scraps from the bones and wrapped them in a sack that had formerly held bread. He tucked the sack into some netting on Folero's side. By the time he finished, Piros was atop his own camel.

"How many of the others know, do you think?" Alaric said as Folero knelt to let him mount.

"It doesn't matter," said Piros. "They'll follow the one who comes back." His lip curled, but there was no humor in the expression. "Do you think this is the first time someone tried to kill me?"

Alaric frowned.

"It's a rich trade," said Piros. "And the men are paid well at the end. But sometimes someone wants to be paid even better. Before today, Hanio was the one who took my side. I thought . . . Well, no matter what I thought. Folero is waiting for you."

Alaric mounted, and the camel lurched to its feet with the odd combination of awkwardness and grace that Alaric had become accustomed to. "You're leaving your son out there," he said. "Perhaps the two of us could persuade him together."

"I have no son," said Piros. He tugged at his camel's lead, and the animal began to amble northward. The others, linked to it by a line of ropes, began to move in its wake. He looked back at Alaric and gestured for him to follow. "But that might be mended, given time."

As he rode at the rear of the miniature caravan, Alaric could not help thinking that Piros was not speaking of taking a new young wife.

All the next day, as they moved northward, every time the minstrel looked back, he saw the phantom city on the horizon, beckoning, but he stayed with Piros and tried not to think of the boy who had answered its call but would never reach it. The song was already shaping itself in his mind, a poignant tale, fit for long winter nights by a blazing fire far, far away from the desert. Someday, he might be able to sing it without wondering what else he could have done to change its ending.

Lisa Tuttle

Lisa Tuttle made her first sale in 1972 to the anthology *Clarion II,* after having attended the Clarion workshop, and by 1974 had won the John W. Campbell Award for Best New Writer of the Year. She has gone on to become one of the most respected writers of her generation, winning the Nebula Award in 1981 for her story "The Bone Flute"—which, in a still-controversial move, she refused to accept—and was nominated for the Arthur C. Clarke Award in 1993 for her novel *Lost Futures.* Her other books include a novel in collaboration with George R. R. Martin, *Windhaven,* the solo novels *Familiar Spirit, Gabriel, The Pillow Friend, The Mysteries,* and *The Silver Bough,* as well as several books for children, the nonfiction works *Heroines* and *Encyclopedia of Feminism,* and, as editor, *Skin of the Soul: New Horror Stories by Women.* Her copious short work has been collected in *A Nest of Nightmares, A Spaceship Built of Stone, Memories of the Body: Tales of Desire and Transformation, Ghosts and Other Lovers,* and *My Pathology.* Born in Texas, she moved to Great Britain in 1981, and now lives with her family in Scotland.

Here a proper young nineteenth-century gentlewoman who is acting in the unlikely role of "Watson" to an eccentric Sherlock Holmes–like figure must delve into the mystery of a woman who is both missing and not missing, and dead but not dead.

THE CURIOUS AFFAIR OF THE DEAD WIVES

Lisa Tuttle

The calling card rested dead center in the gleaming silver salver on the credence in the hall. I saw it the moment I entered, but the thrill I felt at the prospect of a client was tinged with anxiety because I should have to deal with this person on my own. Where was Mr. Jesperson?

We had grown bored, waiting indoors day after day for something to happen, and had gone our separate ways that morning without agreeing upon a time for return. It was, I knew, unfair of me to feel annoyed—it was not his fault. I could use his absence as an opportunity to prove myself an equal—or more than equal—partner.

Miss Alcinda Travers was the name on the card. I wondered how long the lady had been cooling her heels, and if the sight of a female detective would please her, but most of all I wondered if she had brought the genuine, challenging mystery we had been longing for. I checked my appearance in the gilt-framed mirror on the wall, tucked back a strand of hair that had escaped from the coil at the back of my neck, and adjusted my waist. My costume was sadly old and shabby, but if it was unfashionable, at least it might be seen as businesslike. I looked, I decided, neat, composed, and serious; I could only hope that I would satisfy Miss Travers's expectations.

Moving the card to the "quarter past" position to signal that I was with the client, I went into the room that served as both parlor and office, and was startled to discover a child waiting there alone.

She was masquerading as an adult, in an expensive, ill-fitting pink silk dress with an excess of flounces, and a hat that was simply absurd, but the serious, anguished look on her face convinced me that her visit was no joke, so I pretended to have been taken in by her deception and spoke to the adult she wished to seem. After introducing myself to Miss Travers, and apologizing for keeping her waiting, I asked her business.

"I want you to find my sister."

"Her age?"

"Seventeen and three-quarters."

"Name?"

"Alcinda Travers."

I raised my eyebrows. "I thought that was *your* name?"

She flushed. I heard a faint rustling sound and saw it came from her clutching at a brown-paper parcel in her lap. "No. I'm sorry. I should have said . . . I . . . I wasn't expecting to be asked, and I don't—I didn't—that is, I had one of Cinda's cards, and I didn't think it would matter—"

"It doesn't matter at all, my dear," I said gently. "I am simply trying to establish the facts. If your sister is Alcinda, you are—?"

"Felicity Travers. Alcinda is—was—*is* my half sister, actually, but she has been more like a mother to me. I can't believe she's gone. I never imagined she would leave me. I can't believe it, still, even though it has been a month. A whole month!" Twisting her hands, she bit her lip and fell silent.

I shifted in my chair. "She went missing a month ago?"

"Not *missing.* Well, not exactly. But it was a month ago that it happened. That she . . . she . . . she didn't wake up one morning. Nobody could understand why. It was completely unexpected. She wasn't ill. She was never ill. And she was so happy. Excited, I should say. She had a secret, something was about to happen, some sort of adventure, but she wouldn't tell me what; she said she would explain everything later—'afterwards'—but afterwards it was too late, because in the morning, in the morning . . ." She shook her head helplessly. "She never woke up."

I waited for a moment before prompting: "Your sister died in the night?"

She stared at me, outraged. "She is not dead!"

"I beg your pardon. When you said she did not wake . . . What happened next?"

"The doctor was called, of course, but not even he could find a pulse. He said it must have been her heart, some weakness like the one that killed her mother although we had never seen a sign of it. But he said she was dead, so it must be true. Even I believed it."

Some people know how to tell stories; others must have them dragged out of them in bits. “And when did you realize that she was not dead?”

“When I saw her last week.”

“Last . . . week? But she had seemed to be dead for a whole month?”

She nodded. I found that I was massaging my temples in just the way I used to see my mother do when my sister was attempting to justify some outrageous scheme.

“What happened *after* the doctor said she was dead and *before* you saw her again?”

She shrugged. “Why, just what you might expect. A lot of crying. We were all terribly sad. Friends and relations came to the house the next day and brought us food no one wanted to eat. I sat with her in the parlor all night, thinking that she *must* wake up; she could not really be dead. She didn’t even look dead, just like she was sleeping. But no matter how I chafed her hands and whispered her name, she just lay there, perfectly still, and in the morning, they took her away and buried her.”

“She was buried? You are quite certain of that?”

“I didn’t see it if that’s what you mean. I wasn’t allowed to attend the funeral. But my father was there, and he wouldn’t lie. I have seen her grave although my stepmother did not wish it; she wanted to forbid me going to the cemetery after what happened to Cinda.”

“What happened to Cinda?”

She looked cross. “I just *told* you.”

“I mean, how was that connected to visiting the cemetery?”

“It wasn’t. That’s just the way our stepmother thinks. If you can call it thinking. Cinda went to visit her mother’s grave practically every day in the months before she died, so maybe that’s why she died? It’s crazy, that’s all, and if she had stopped my going there, I would never have seen Alcinda.”

I felt my heart sink. Once, I would have found her story of great interest, but not now.

“You saw your sister last week, in the cemetery where she was buried?”

She nodded vigorously.

"I suppose she wore a veil?"

"Yes!"

"Yet, although you could not see her face, you were quite certain of her identity?"

More nodding.

"She was standing above her grave?"

"No. By her mother's grave—that's where she always went. I had brought some flowers to put on it because I thought that would please Cinda, if she knew, more than my putting flowers on *her* grave."

"It didn't occur to you, that the figure you saw could be a ghost?"

"Of course. That's why I didn't dare speak to her, or go closer, because ghosts never let you touch them. It was only when I saw the man that I knew she was really there. That she must be alive."

"What man?"

"Why, the man who took her away! I don't know who he was, but I can show you just what he looked like." She ripped open the brown paper to reveal a square black book that she opened and handed across to me.

I looked at a pencil portrait of a heavily bearded fellow with narrow, squinting eyes and a snub nose. It was not a flattering likeness, but there was a spark of life to it that made me think it true.

"You drew this from memory?"

"Gosh, no, not me! Alcinda did it. That was her book, and she kept it very close. She used to show us her drawings, but not recently, not what she was drawing or writing in that book. I never saw it until after—after she was gone."

"But it was the man you saw?"

"It was him. I saw him as clearly as I see you now, and I was nearly as close. He walked up to Alcinda, and said, 'Mrs. Merle!' Then he said something else that I couldn't understand—I don't think it was English—and he took hold of her arm, and she didn't resist."

She took a deep breath. "You can't touch a ghost. So, unless *he* was a ghost as well, she must be alive. I ran after them, but just as I was about to catch up, he turned round and looked at me." She clasped her hands beneath her chin and drew her shoulders in, hunching down in the chair. "He *glared* at me in the most horrible way, I can't tell you how horrible it was! And he said—his voice was soft and gentle, but that made it worse—he said, 'Go away, little girl. Don't bother me unless you are ready to die.'"

She shuddered. "So I ran away! He frightened me so."

"He meant to. How did the woman respond?"

"Not at all. She was like a sleepwalker. I don't think she even knew I was there."

"How well did you see her?"

"I know it was Alcinda," she said stubbornly. "It absolutely, positively was! Isn't there someone *you* know so well that you can recognize them from a distance, in the dark, without a word spoken? It was her. I know it. My sister is alive, and he's got her."

Tears shone in her blue eyes. "Oh, why did I have to run away! I am such a rotten coward! I should have followed them, seen where he took her, but I let him frighten me."

"You were quite right to flee," I said firmly. "It would be horribly dangerous—and utterly foolish—for a lone girl to try to pit herself against a grown man, especially one who spoke to her like that."

"You must help me find her. Please, say you will, Miss Lane!"

I felt strangely torn. It was absurd, her story, and it made no difference that she obviously believed what she said. She must be fantasizing. And yet—

"Have you told anyone else? Did you tell your father?"

She nodded, looked wretched. "He thinks my brain has been affected by grief, and now he agrees with his wife that visiting the cemetery has such a bad effect, I'm forbidden to go there." Her shoulders slumped. "*You* believe me, don't you? I swear it's all true. You must take this case. Jesperson and Lane are probably the only people in London clever enough to figure it out."

For a moment I was distracted by the question of where this child had heard of our fledgling business, but I did not ask because it could not possibly matter. She was a child, she was grieving, she could not accept the reality of her loss. There was no case. I was about to tell her so, when she spoke again.

"There is another clue. In the book." She nodded at Alcinda's drawing book, still in my hands. "Towards the back, my sister wrote a few pages I can't read. It might be Latin, or some other language. I'm sure it's important."

I found the pages. They were not in Latin. Although I could make no sense out of the jumble of letters and symbols, I knew Mr. Jesperson would enjoy the challenge; codes and ciphers were meat and drink to him. I realized then that although I did not believe we would find Alcinda Travers alive, I had decided we must help her little sister, somehow.

"Let me be honest with you," I said. "I do not think your sister is alive somewhere, and I do not want to encourage you in false hopes. But there does seem to be some mystery connected with her death, and it may have to do with the man you met in the cemetery. My partner, Mr. Jesperson, should be able to decipher these notes left behind by your sister, and the picture should enable us to uncover the man's identity. After that, we may discuss whether or not there is anything to be investigated."

Despite all that I had said to discourage her hope, she was positively glowing with it now as she thanked me.

I asked a few pertinent questions—the location of the cemetery, the identity of the physician who had made the official verdict of death, whether Alcinda had any suitors, and how best to contact my young client if we needed more information or had news to impart.

"Our address is inside the front cover of Alcinda's book," she said. "Our telephone number, too, although my stepmother would find it awfully suspicious if someone she didn't know wrote or telephoned to me—I will come back here."

"If you come tomorrow afternoon, you can meet Mr. Jesperson," I told her.

Very late in the day, a messenger arrived with a note from Mr. Jesperson, written on headed notepaper from his club, informing Mrs. Jesperson and me that he had been invited to dine and we should not wait for him.

Women are generally responsible for all the cooking and planning of meals in private households, but I have never known any to bother about "proper meals" without a man around. Left to ourselves, we glory in "feasting"—standing at the kitchen table, or wrapped in blankets before the fire—on whatever wild assortment we can forage from the larder, or delight in a "nursery tea" of soft-boiled eggs with bread and butter; or dine on tea and cakes, or apples and cheese, while reading.

It required no discussion for us to agree that soup, beef, potatoes, and all should be held over for the following day, and bread and cheese would satisfy us.

"We can have the apple tart—easy enough to make another tomorrow," Mrs. Jesperson said. "Shall we eat in here, or . . . ?"

"If you don't mind," I said, "I'll take a plate to my room."

"As you wish, Miss Lane."

Although I felt sorry for it, a certain chill had come between us. "Call me Edith," she had urged, more than once, but as I had not responded with a matching invitation, she must still call me "Miss Lane," while I, to avoid giving further offense, hardly knew how to address her.

Mrs. Jesperson was an excellent woman, capable, kind, and intelligent. She might not have the brilliance of her son, but she was no fool, and I should have been grateful for her friendship. Having taken me in, knowing nothing about me, she continued to provide room and board without asking, or getting, anything in return. Of course, she did this to please her son. Many mothers must find themselves in a similar situation, forced to coexist with an unsympathetic younger woman, but our situation was rather different.

Jasper and I had come together through mutual liking and respect, with a view to business, but as we'd yet to see a ha'penny's profit, our detective agency was more like an expensive hobby. This fine front bedroom, which might have been rented to a paying lodger, was mine gratis, and all my meals provided, even my laundry done, by the woman who kept us all on her own meager inheritance.

Being dependent had never made me happy. I longed to prove that Mrs. Jesperson's investment had been a wise one; I did not know how much longer I could stay here without earning my keep. Jasper did not see the problem—for him, there was no problem. Edith Jesperson was his mother, after all, and he'd never known life without her capable, comforting support behind him. He was young, male, and utterly confident that any investment in his talents would be repaid a thousand-fold—in time.

Time, I must give it time. I reminded myself that we had been in partnership for a mere six weeks, and then I settled down to my supper and the absorbing company of a book about the adventures of an intrepid lady traveler in Lapland.

When I went downstairs in the morning, I found that Jesperson was ahead of me, behind the big desk, already at work.

"You're up early," I began, before reading the story in his wilted collar, stained cuffs, and faint golden stubble on his chin. "Or shall I say late? When did you get in?"

He gave me a vague look. "Oh, a few hours ago, I suppose."

"What has kept you so absorbed?"

"Why, what do you suppose? You left it for me to decipher." I saw he had been at work on Alcinda's drawing book.

"You have managed it?"

"It was not too difficult, but as my head was none too clear when I began, I made some false starts. But once I'd cracked it—what an intriguing story! I can hardly wait to hear the rest of the case—some mystery, I presume, surrounding the young lady's sudden demise and disappearance of her body?"

I stared, then slowly shook my head. "Sudden demise, yes, but the body was buried. Some weeks after, her sister saw what at first she took for a ghost in the graveyard." I recounted the story as efficiently as I could, referring him to the pencil sketch.

He gave it a long, hard look. "Mr. S, I presume." He rose then and handed me his notes. "You may like to read Miss Travers's account while I make myself more presentable. It is—odd. You are ready to go out?"

I nodded uncertainly. "Yes, but where—?"

"To the cemetery, of course."

(What follows is J. J.'s transcription)

To be reunited with my beloved mother is all I have ever wanted—to feel her presence and know she is close to me. When I was a little child, I used to talk to her every night. After rote prayers to a God I could not imagine, I turned more eagerly to share my hopes, fears, and experiences with my beloved Mama. I used to think that she answered my questions by responding to me in dreams, or leaving hidden messages in daily life, things that to others would appear meaningless, that only I would notice and understand.

As I grew older, I lost my faith, yet never managed to give up the belief that Mama, wherever she may be, is still watching over me. But it is hard to only believe, to take it on trust, never to *know.* Never to know, that is, until it is too late, and I, too, am dead. Until that time, my conversations with her would remain one-sided, and I would continue to be haunted by the fear that I was only talking to myself—that no one was listening—that there was no one to hear my questions and confessions because there is no survival of physical death, no spirit independent of the body.

I don't *want* to believe that. I am, perhaps, too intellectual, too modern, for my own comfort! How lovely it would be to sink into the warm comfort of established religion . . .

Some part of me does still believe. I think that when I die, I will be reunited with Mama. But if I die when I am wrinkled and toothless and wandering in my wits, like that old crone we see sometimes at the back of the church, mumbling away to herself and disrupting the services with her laughter . . . why, I might not even know my own mother, or she know me—horrible!!

I don't want that. I want death on my own terms.

I know what I am about to do is not without danger. I admit, I am frightened, but now that Mr. S has shown me what is possible, I must see for myself.

The Ancient Egyptians had their guides to the afterlife, and the Buddhist Masters in the High Himalayas also—many cultures have found it worthwhile to instruct the living and prepare them for the life to come, but our own "civilized" society prefers to pretend that death cannot be known except once, finally, at the end of life. Mr. S has told me that death does not have to be the country from which no traveler returns; he has gone there and returned himself, more than once, and has agreed—at last!—to share his knowledge with me.

He is a strange man. I appreciate his wisdom in the ways of the afterlife, and am ever so grateful that he has agreed to help me, but he makes me uneasy. Sometimes, when he looks at me, I feel he wants something, that he expects that I understand what he wants from me, but then, just as I think he might try to make love to me—instead, he remarks on my youth and innocence, and advises me to wait a few years before embarking on this great adventure.

So perhaps I have misinterpreted those looks. But it is too late, far too late, for him to stop me. He has told me what must be done and provided me with the means, and I mean to do it tonight.

He would be cross if he knew I was writing this—even so carefully hidden—for I promised not to say a word to anyone, about him, or about the plan we have agreed. And I have told no one, although the temptation to share it with Felicity was strong. But she is still a child. She might tell Father.

I write this to say that I am going to die tonight, but my death will not be—is not meant to be—forever. I have no wish to be a suicide. I want my second death, the real one, to be only after many, many years of living. This first death is an exploration, a way of learning the truth.

If it goes wrong, I am deeply sorry, but that is a risk I must take. Felicity, if you have deciphered these words, let me tell you that I love you dearly and if it is permitted to me, I shall continue to watch over you from another plane, as I feel my own mother watches over me. I hope you will understand, and forgive me, if I have gone, a bit too soon, to a better place. We will meet again.

The cemetery was quite new—Alcinda's mother must have been one of the first to be interred there—and when we arrived at the unassuming gates that led into the Park Grove Cemetery, we saw at once that, unlike the larger modern graveyards of London, it had not been designed as a destination for visitors who might wish to spend a quiet hour of reflection, but for the sole purpose of storing dead bodies underground.

In my childhood, I had played in the local churchyard, and I remembered family excursions to Highgate Cemetery, where my uncle and aunt and a grandfather were buried. I had imagined Alcinda's visits to her mother's grave taking place in a similar setting, watched over by solemn stone angels and women in classical draperies, surrounded by weeping willows and mournful, ivy-clad trees. I expected mausoleums and family enclosures, statues, tombstones decorated with curious symbols, all that attractive paraphernalia of mourning that so often appeals to girls of a certain age and disposition.

But this modern cemetery, despite its evocative name, had few trees, no groves, and was nothing like my idea of a park. We saw not a single statue or decorative monument, and the gravestones were uniformly plain. With the graves laid out on strict gridlines, the effect was strict and utilitarian, reminding me of a school dormitory or a military barracks. My contemporaries may mock the sentimental, elaborate rituals of mourning that we grew up with, and one might well argue that the dead care not where their bones are stored, but the Park Grove Cemetery was like a glimpse into a well-organized but brutally impersonal future, offering nothing to comfort the living. There was little reason, one would have thought, to ever visit this place after the funeral, which made Alcinda's obsession seem all the stranger.

"I see now why there were no sketches of crumbling, ivy-shrouded tombstones or statues in Miss Travers's drawing book," said Jesperson as we strolled along one straight dull path after another.

"But not why she bothered to bring her book and pencils along at all."

"Surely the secretive Mr. S did not allow her to sketch him from life."

I agreed it was more likely that she had drawn him from memory.

"Let us see if there is a caretaker here, who might recognize his face," he said, and we turned back towards the entrance, where we had noticed a tidy little gatehouse.

At that moment, the rain, which had been threatening for so long, finally burst free of the heavy grey clouds above our heads, and we arrived not as the sober, mournful visitors we had hoped to appear, but out of breath, disheveled, and damp.

A small, spry, bald little man in hairy tweeds opened the door almost as soon as Jesperson's knuckles collided with its outside surface. He was eager to welcome us inside, all the while making so many apologies for the rain that it might have been his personal responsibility that it had fallen.

"Please, ma'am, sit by the fire, it'll warm you up nicely and you'll be dry in no time," he said, directing me to a chintz-covered armchair nearest the hearth. The room was small, and oversupplied with chairs.

Pouring us cups of tea—he had just brewed a fresh pot, he would not take no for an answer—he continued to express his regrets about the weather and assured us we were welcome to stay as long as we liked.

Jesperson managed to insert a question into our host's hospitable flow: "I assume you are the caretaker—or should we call you the guard?"

"Why, bless you, sir, I am both of those, and more: caretaker, watchman, guard, head gardener, gravedigger, spare mourner, and guide, should a guide be needed," he said proudly. "Eric Bailey at your service. If you want to know anything about Park Grove Cemetery—past, present, or future—I'm the man to ask. Or perhaps you'd like to take away one of our informative brochures, to read at your leisure?"

"Thank you—most kind—" murmured Jesperson, putting out his hand for the little booklet but distracted by something on the wall.

Following his gaze, I saw a system of bells with numbers and letters beneath each one, reminiscent of something I had seen in large houses for summoning servants, although I could not think how that would serve in a graveyard.

"If you was thinking to purchase a plot, I'm happy to answer your questions, but I don't handle that side of the business, so I'd have to refer you to—"

"No, no," said Jesperson. "We are here on behalf of a young lady who, while paying a visit to one of the graves—Rather than go into the whole story, let me simply say that she lost an item and believes that a man she encountered may be of help."

Mr. Bailey did not look entirely convinced by this flimsy concoction, and I wished we had spent more effort in creating a plausible excuse for our questions. "An *hitem*? What sort of an hitem? If anything was lost here, I'd be the one to find it, you may be certain. I go over the grounds every—"

"We'd like to speak to this gentleman," Jesperson said, abandoning his story and opening the drawing book. "Do you recognize him?"

It was immediately clear that Mr. Bailey did. "Why, I should say I do! Although I don't suppose Mr. Smurl would be gratified by the likeness—quite sinister, he looks there, and I'm sure I've never seen him with such an expression in life!" Then he frowned and looked at us suspiciously. "'Ere! Your friend wasn't meaning to imply Mr. Smurl might have taken her 'hitem'?"

"Certainly not," Jesperson said quickly. "I hope you did not mistake me—I meant to cast no aspersions—but if we could find him . . . she would be most grateful, and we, on her behalf . . ."

Unexpectedly, the caretaker chuckled. His suspicions had vanished, and he seemed genuinely amused. "The young lady would like to see Mr. Smurl again, I suppose! Yes, I should not be surprised! And did she drop her 'ankerchief in his path, to tempt him? Ooh la la! I have seen it all before, too many times . . ." He shook his head, and then composed his face into seriousness. "You had better tell your young friend that Mr. Smurl is a 'appily married man."

Jesperson frowned and shook his head. "From the picture, he does not strike me as a ladies' man. Is Mr. Smurl a frequent visitor to the cemetery?"

"Why, I should say he is! He's my guv'nor! One of the founders and chief stockholders in Park Grove Cemetery, not to mention being a long-established, well-respected undertaker, and an important member of the local community." He shifted about in his seat, picked up a card from a stack on the table, and—Jesperson's hands being occupied with the drawing book—gave it to me.

Smurl & Snigg
Undertakers of Quality since 1879
121 The High Street
Sydenham

Remembering Felicity had said that the man in the cemetery had addressed her sister as "Mrs. Merle"—I felt the chill touch of horror as I understood.

Mrs. Smurl.

I was on my feet almost before I knew it. "We have to go," I said. "At once."

My partner did not question my urgency; he had made the same connection, although he managed to maintain a polite demeanor and thank our host even as I charged out the door, back into the rain, the thought of Alcinda's probable fate burning inside me.

But what could I do? I had no idea where to find her. I paced up and down, my thoughts in an uproar, my garments getting wetter, until Jesperson hailed a cab and gently but firmly handed me inside. *"Courage, ma brave,"* he murmured, close to my ear, and somehow this worked like a dash of smelling salts to clear my head.

"We mustn't let Smurl know we are on to him," I said. "I will pretend to have a . . . some elderly, distant relation near the end of life, and make inquiries about his services. Perhaps, I don't know, perhaps I can find out where he lives. You, meanwhile, must keep watch, I think, and follow him when he leaves. See if he goes home—or anywhere else—for his dinner, or at the end of the day. How does that sound?"

"Like a sensible course of action."

The journey to the funeral parlor on the high street took little more than five minutes; we could easily have walked it, and saved the fare, although, as the rain was falling even more heavily now, I considered the benefits of arriving only a trifle damp rather than thoroughly sodden and uncomfortable. After paying the driver, my partner walked off briskly to wait until he should see me emerge.

My heart was beating a little too fast for comfort when I opened the door. A bell tinkled as I entered, and then I was greeted by a voice nearly as high and sweet.

"Welcome. Do come in, my dear, and tell me how we may be of service."

The woman who came towards me with her hands outstretched as if ready to take some burden from me was, I estimated, in her early thirties; decorously attired in lavender silk, brown hair neatly coiffed, plain-featured except for a pair of melting and expressive dark eyes.

"I should like to speak with Mr. Smurl, if you please."

Clasping her hands (since I had neither taken nor filled them), she made a *moue* of regret and shook her head. "I am afraid he's not available for personal consultation at all today—or tomorrow. He is a very busy man, our Mr. Smurl! Perhaps I might be of service? I am Miss Hyacinth Snigg, the daughter of Mr. Edgar Snigg, who is also unavailable at the moment, but you must not let that concern you in the least. I am fully informed about all aspects of the business, and can answer any questions, and am well qualified to give advice. Will you take a seat?" She gestured to a small couch covered in dark red plush.

"No, thank you; you're very kind, but I would particularly like to speak to Mr. Smurl."

The polished, professional sorrow of her expression gave way to a different, more genuine feeling. "Perhaps you do not understand. I am not a *receptionist,* but a full partner in this firm, which has been my entire career for almost ten years now."

"My dear Miss Snigg!" Now *I* was annoyed—with myself. "You misunderstand me. I meant no disrespect. If I wished to make arrangements for a funeral, or to take advice on that subject, I should be more than happy to take your advice."

She frowned a little. "You have not come here to discuss funeral arrangements?"

I bit my lip. "Not exactly. That is . . . The matter is complicated and quite urgent. I really must speak to Mr. Smurl. He is the only one who can help me with this matter. I don't mind waiting. If he could see me for just a few minutes, I could explain."

She set her chin. "If you can explain it to Mr. Smurl in a few minutes, pray take as long as you like to explain it to *me.* I am not slow-witted, and if it is truly a matter of *business,* I should be able to help."

Fiction at short notice was never my specialty. As my silence continued, I could feel her mood hardening still more against me. It seemed unfair that she should think me one of those women who denigrate their own sex and will only discuss business matters with a man; I wished I had not stated so plainly that I had not come to discuss funeral arrangements, but I could see no way out of it now.

"My business with Mr. Smurl is of a personal nature," I said.

Her eyes glittered. "Indeed? Then you had better approach him outside of business hours—why not call at his home? Or write to him?"

"I do not have his home address."

"Surely you do not expect me to give it to you."

"That would be most kind of you."

She snorted—a word she would certainly take objection to, but accurate. "I will do nothing to encourage your delusions. You are not the first female person to imagine she might have business of a *personal nature* with Mr. Smurl."

"I don't know what you mean," I said, giving her my iciest glare.

"Oh, I think you do, Miss . . . ?"

When I did not respond, she sniffed. "It is *Miss,* I presume?"

"You make quite a few presumptions," I replied, still frostily. "I am sorry if you feel I have misled you. That was never my intention. I have come here in the hope of having a quiet word with Mr. Smurl with regard to his wife."

I saw that I had surprised her. "His wife?"

"Yes." It was a shot in the dark, but I could think of nothing better. "Are you acquainted with Mrs. Smurl?"

"Certainly." She drew herself up. "I told you, I have been with the firm for in excess of ten years, and our families have long been friends. I know both ladies."

Goodness knows what she made of the shock that registered on my face at this, but she hastened to amplify: "I mean, of course, both Mr. Albert's mother and his wife."

"I suppose his marriage is quite recent?"

She frowned. "Why should you suppose that? Mr. Smurl has been married perhaps a dozen years. If you claim to know her . . ."

I saw that I had not won her over in the least. "I never claimed to know her. I said my business with Mr. Smurl concerned his wife—yet perhaps I was wrong, as I was unaware there was another lady in his household bearing the same name; the 'Mrs. Smurl' I have been delegated to find may have been his mother. I came here on behalf of the Travers family. You may recall a recent funeral—"

"Oh, the poor young lady! Of course I remember. How could I forget? She was so young and beautiful, and her death so sudden and inexplicable! So terribly, terribly sad!" Her eyes were moist, her whole aspect again as soft and yearning as when I had first seen her. "But what business could her family have with *Mrs.* Smurl?"

"I had assumed they might have met her here, or at the funeral."

"Oh, no, that is quite impossible. Neither lady has ever had anything to do with the business."

"Maybe, in passing . . . ?"

"No. There must be some mistake. Possibly, although I introduced myself quite clearly, I am the lady she was thinking of? If you will tell me the message, I can . . ."

"There was no mistake. If she was not at the funeral, then perhaps Mrs. Travers met her elsewhere—"

"Utterly impossible."

We glared at each other. I said, "I find it remarkable that you are so certain."

"Mr. Smurl does not entertain visitors—and never does business—in his home. Both his mother and his wife are in poor health, and have scarcely set foot out of doors in recent years. Nor do they receive. So unless Mrs. Travers is a doctor or a priest, she has not met either lady."

I saw I should have to back down. "Forgive me. Perhaps, after all, she was thinking of you. She was so deeply moved by the genuine kindness she received . . ." Seeing that she looked mollified, I took another chance. "But I won't feel I have done my duty unless I have a word with Mr. Smurl. Could I not call back later today? Will he not be in at all?"

I saw training and business instincts—and perhaps the thought of what Mr. Smurl might say—battling her desire to be rid of me. "He always calls in just before he goes home for his di—luncheon. Between half past twelve and one o'clock."

I thanked her, effusively and insincerely, saying I would return. "Might you ask him to wait for me? At least until one o'clock?"

It had occurred to me there might be another way of learning Mr. Smurl's home address, and when I met Mr. Jesperson outside, I proposed we should go to the nearest post office to look in the local directory. Smurl was such an unusual surname, we were unlikely to be misled, and, indeed, apart from the business listing for Smurl and Snigg, the local directory revealed only one: Smurl, Albert E. A glance at a map of the area enabled Jesperson to locate his street almost exactly halfway between the funeral parlor and the cemetery.

I looked at the clock on the wall. "We still have nearly two hours before he may go home," I said. "Thank goodness the rain is off."

We set off at a brisk walk. The area was unknown to me, but I knew I could trust in Jesperson's sense of direction, and his memory: even a quick look at a map was enough to fix it in his mind.

Although I knew it was pointless to try to plan a rescue before we had set eyes on the prison, I could not help speculating on her situation. Did he keep her locked in an attic or allow her some limited freedom? Were his wife and mother aware of her presence? Did he use her as a servant, nursemaid, perhaps, to the two invalids, or did he, as his mode of address suggested, consider her his wife? Wife and slave and prisoner—unfortunately, those terms need not necessarily be exclusive.

"She may even be a willing prisoner," said Jesperson.

His words made me shudder, and I had to disagree. "You saw the portrait—did that look like a lover to you?"

"Not to me, but recall Mr. Bailey's remarks—and Miss Snigg's. A certain class of female must find him irresistible."

"Not Alcinda! You read what she wrote—she hated the idea that he might try to make love to her."

"And who do you suppose she was trying to convince? Herself? But please, let us not quarrel! I only wish you to bear in mind the possibility that the lady may not thank us; may even refuse to be rescued."

I understood. I am not entirely ignorant of what may be done in the name of love. The heart has its reasons, and so on. Even if Miss Travers had not lost her heart to her abductor, she might, like many before her, choose to stay and suffer his attentions, rather than return and find herself disgraced, "ruined" in the eyes of a world that values women as if they were soft fruit. "But we must give her the chance."

"Of course."

I took his arm, and, as we walked along together, I mused aloud on how the kidnapping had been managed. Of course, Miss Travers must have agreed to drink some potion, but how had he been so certain he could steal her away from her own funeral? Did he have confederates? Perhaps the doctor who signed the death certificate, or trusted employees who would help him make the switch to an empty coffin and ensure Miss Travers was not buried alive . . .

"Of course she was buried alive," said Jesperson.

I flinched, my fingers tightening on his arm, and he looked down into my face, surprised. "Surely you noticed the alarm bell system in Bailey's quarters?"

"I thought . . . they might alert him to intruders. Protection against body-snatchers, perhaps?"

"How should the dead summon their protectors? I admit, I did not understand until I read the brochure given me by Mr. Bailey." He quoted the paragraph he'd found so enlightening:

"'Security coffins, made to Mr. Smurl's own original design (patent pending), are available for a very reasonable additional charge. The in-built alarm system will alert the on-site security guard (always listening, night and day) within moments of revival, in the unfortunate event of a burial having been premature. In such an event, the coffin is designed to keep its inhabitant alive and comfortable, with more than sufficient air to breathe until disinterment may be effected, which will be done with the utmost dispatch to minimize discomfort and eliminate all worries.'"

"My goodness," I murmured, feeling weak at the knees. I had to fight the impulse to take great, gasping gulps of air.

He squeezed my arm. "We may hope that she remained in a state of unconsciousness throughout and never suffered a moment's fear. Since Smurl knew that she was not dead, there would be no reason to make her ring for help . . . unless, of course, he simply wished to test his system . . . Forgive me," he said, contrite. "Ah, here we are."

We had arrived at a long, curving, quiet street where the substantial houses were set well back from the road in their own gardens.

"Which house is it?"

"Just over there, I think. Can you make out a number on that gatepost? The one overhung with laburnum?"

Although I had no idea what a laburnum might be, I saw the bush-draped gatepost, and as we approached, the number 14 was revealed through a veil of leaves.

Mr. Jesperson opened the gate and ushered me through, indicating that I should precede him up the narrow path to the front door. My mind was quite blank. I stood to one side and let my partner knock on the door. We waited. He knocked again. Prickles of anxiety and frustration ran through me as the seconds dragged by. We could hear nothing moving within, not even surreptitious movements, footsteps, or the quiet closing of an interior door, and yet, somehow, the heavy silence did not suggest an empty house.

The door, of course, was locked.

Jesperson reached towards his inside jacket pocket, then checked himself and paused to survey the area immediately around the door. I followed his eyes along the lintel, to the plain doormat, and then to a rather sickly plant, possibly some sort of citrus tree, in a terra-cotta tub to the right side of the door. Stepping towards it, he bent down and lifted the tub, felt beneath it and, grinning with satisfaction, flourished a key.

It was a large, old-fashioned key of the sort that may be used from either side, to lock someone out, or in. When Jesperson turned it, I heard the smooth, heavy movement of tumblers, and then the door was open to us. And, a moment later, we both stood in a dark entrance hall with a high ceiling, walls covered in dark green and cream-figured paper, seeing a staircase ahead, and dark, varnished doors, uncompromisingly shut, in the walls on either side.

"Mrs. Smurl," called my partner, making me jump. His voice, so loud, seemed more of an intrusion than our entrance had been. "Mrs. Smurl? Please don't be alarmed. We mean you no harm. I hope you won't mind, but we've taken the liberty of letting ourselves in."

I held my breath when he fell silent, and heard something. Meeting his eyes, I saw he had heard it too. A sound too small and faint to identify, it came from behind the door on the right.

When the door was opened, we saw a room filled with women: all seated, silent and motionless as life-sized dolls.

"I beg your pardon," Jesperson began, but his words fell like stones into the stillness, and he did not continue.

There were six of them, in total, spaced around the parlor like the members of a religious order or ladies' sewing circle, unexpectedly frozen by a spell like the one that guarded the castle of the Sleeping Beauty. If they slept, it was with eyes wide open but presumably unseeing. I could tell they were living creatures, neither wax figures nor corpses, by the very slight movements caused by their slow breathing and the occasional blink of an eye.

We crept quietly farther in without a word, although it seemed unlikely that even more violent movements would disturb this unnatural, eerie calm. Examining them more closely, I began to see them as individuals, not the identical dolls they had first seemed. There were slight variations in the colors of the otherwise uniformly simple but well-made silk gowns they all wore, and the same was true of their hair color: chiefly mouselike shades of brown or beige or grey. The sisterlike similarity of their faces was most likely due to the same blank lack of expression on every one, as if they wore copies of the same mask. I was unable to decide if any of them should be described as plain or beautiful.

Two of them stood out from the others; one because she was clearly much older than the rest, white-haired and slightly hunchbacked; the other for her youth and golden hair.

This must be Alcinda, I thought, and could not resist saying her name aloud.

The response was slow in coming but unmistakable. She turned her head in my direction.

I felt Mr. Jesperson stiffen beside me. I gasped. "Alcinda? Can you hear me?"

Her eyes remained blank and inward-looking, and she made no further movement.

"I wonder if there is a magic word we are missing, or if we simply must engage their attention," said Jesperson. Speaking in a normal, conversational tone, he went on, "Dear ladies, I should be most obliged if you could enlighten us as to the subject of your most skillful, yet puzzling, *tableau vivant.*"

"Certainly it can be nothing in the Bible, or what is popularly conceived of as history," I said. "Perhaps—a ladies' Bible study group? Or, no—I have it. A modern Methodist, English harem, as they await the return of their lord and master." It had started off as a joke, until I noticed the one chair that was not occupied in the room: a large, battered but comfortable-looking leather armchair, reserved, one must suppose, for the patriarch of this meek little tribe.

"I prefer my *tableau* rather more *vivant,*" said Jesperson. "Come, come, ladies! You are neglecting your duties. You might show a bit of hospitality to your guests."

"What has he *done* to them?" I murmured, and picked up one of Alcinda's hands. It was cool and remained as limp and unresponsive as a dead fish no matter how I chafed and squeezed it. I was unable to find her pulse; after a few seconds of trying, I let the hand flop back into her lap. "What sort of drug would induce a state like this?"

My partner shook his head. "I think it is more likely the result of hypnosis, possibly facilitated by some sedative draft."

"A drug should wear off in time. How can we wake them from hypnosis?"

"I'm afraid we may need Smurl for that."

As he pronounced the name, I was aware of a subterranean rustling, like a shiver running through the room. This gave me an idea, and I said, loudly, "Mrs. Smurl!"

Nothing happened right away. Later, it occurred to me that the pause between my speaking and their response was the sort of delay one might get if sound were to be slowed, forced to pass through some medium much denser than air, and then the listener must interpret the spoken syllables separately before putting them together and translating them from one language to another. After two or three seconds, when I had stopped expecting anything, five women turned their heads towards me, like pale, blind sunflowers—all responding to the call of their name, all of them "Mrs. Smurl"—all, save Alcinda.

It was an eerie moment. Under the force of that massed, unseeing gaze, I felt a quiver of fear, imagining this power yoked by one man.

"Mrs. Smurl, if you can hear me, please rise."

Nothing happened, although we waited a whole minute.

I exchanged a look with my friend: perhaps a man's voice would produce the desired result? "Mrs. Smurl," he said, low and deliberate. "Mrs. Smurl, nod your head to show you hear me."

None of them moved a muscle.

"There may be some key word to release them from trance; or perhaps he has trained them to respond only to *his* voice."

That seemed horribly likely to me, as surely no man mad enough to establish such a household would risk relinquishing control of it to anyone else.

Yet Alcinda had not responded to the summons of "Mrs. Smurl." So I tried again:

"Alcinda. Please stand up."

I held my breath. She stood up.

Jesperson and I looked at each other, and I knew we were thinking the same thing, that there was nothing to stop us walking out with Alcinda. Once away from Smurl, no longer drugged, she might return to normal; if not, there must be doctors, or specialists in hypnosis . . .

But we could not make the others follow us, and, knowing that Smurl was likely to return very soon, how could we leave them? It was an impossible dilemma.

"Take her to Gower Street," Jesperson said decisively.

"You're not staying here alone."

"Would that I could," he said dryly, with a tilt of his head to our silent audience.

"I won't let you."

He stared at me, half-affronted, half-amused. "And how do you mean to stop me, Miss Lane? Would you drag me out by the ear?"

"Please." I stared at him, wishing I could make him see it as I did. "It's too dangerous—"

"You think I am no match for a middle-aged undertaker? Do me some credit. A danger to women he may be, but—"

Seeing that I had offended his pride, I tried to explain. "He's nothing in himself, and of course you're not afraid of a few weak women, but imagine if a word from him should transform them into Maenads. Someone without fear can do the most terrible things, and if he has made himself their god—!"

I knew, by the puzzled impatience of his expression, that he did not share my mental image of these silent, soberly dressed ladies turned to howling, blood-maddened creatures who would tear a man apart with their bare hands and feast on his bloody flesh.

"Dear Miss Lane," he said gently. "Trust me. We cannot abandon—"

"If you mean to stay, I shall go from here straight to the police."

The creaking of a chair, the silken rustle of a skirt, made me turn my head in time to see that one of the statues had come to life. It was a woman in a brown dress, bending over her neighbor in grey, speaking words too low for me to distinguish.

"Mrs. Smurl?" The woman straightened. No longer a colorless, lifeless statue, she had changed into an unfriendly-looking individual with snapping dark eyes, a strong jaw, and a belligerently thrust chin. Two brown corkscrew curls bobbed over her ears—a girlish touch that did nothing to make her look a day under eight-and-thirty.

"Who are you?" she asked. "What is the meaning of this intrusion? How dare you enter uninvited?" Despite a ring of righteous anger, she kept her voice low and well modulated as her eyes darted quickly between Mr. Jesperson and myself.

"I do beg your pardon," he said insincerely. "However, after knocking for some time with no effect, I felt we had no choice—"

The ringlets quivered. "You *broke in*?"

"Not at all." He flourished the key, and her eyes widened with shock.

"But—how—Where—"

"Where do you think? When Mr. Smurl heard we were concerned about Miss Travers, naturally—"

"Who is Miss Travers?"

Jesperson indicated the young lady in question. Alcinda gave no sign that she had heard, still staring blankly in my general direction.

Mrs. Smurl gave a small hiss of displeasure, and said coldly, "The young lady is no concern of yours."

"But she is. Her family wish her home."

"*This* is her home. *We* are her family."

He raised a skeptical eyebrow. "I might be more inclined to believe that assertion if it came from the lady herself."

"She cannot speak to you."

"That I can see. But who is stopping her?"

"Mr. Smurl does not wish it."

"Mr. Smurl, I feel certain, would not wish to be arrested and charged with false imprisonment and other crimes."

"You dare to threaten . . . ?" Her voice was hardly more than a whisper. Her lips had thinned almost to invisibility.

"I do," said Jesperson, sounding jolly. "Bigamy is another charge he may face, although I suspect most of his marriages have been recognized nowhere beyond these four walls. Despite the saying that an Englishman's home is his castle, there are still some things he may not do even there with impunity. Why should you try to defend him? You cannot be happy to share your husband with other women; women he has stolen from their families and forced into submission—"

Her pale face grew flushed. "How dare you! Mr. Smurl is a good man, a perfect gentleman. He would never use force against a woman—he has never made any of us do anything against our will."

"You call this their will?" He gestured at the silent, motionless women.

"You know nothing of us. It's for their own good. It makes the day go by more pleasantly."

"Drugged and dreaming? Yes, I daresay the denizens of an opium den reason so. But why should life as the wife of your 'perfect gentleman' require such an escape?"

As he went on speaking, my nervousness increased. How long had we been here? What if Smurl was made suspicious when he heard someone had been asking about his wife and was even now on his way home?

Looking at the agitated little woman—I am small, but she was smaller still—I said, "You may justify that man and your life as you like, but we've come for Miss Travers and mean to take her home."

"There is no Miss—"

"Alcinda," I said sharply, and managed to draw her closer. Getting her to move on her own would be a slow business; I again addressed the angry woman:

"Can you wake her?"

"Why should I?"

"If she wants to stay, let her tell us so, and we will leave."

She stared at me. "You would go away without her?"

"Of course. We would not take her against her will." I wasn't sure if I was telling the truth.

Mr. Jesperson said, "I assure you, if the young lady says she prefers to stay, we will let her remain. Otherwise we shall escort her to wherever she wishes."

"And let her spread her lies about our husband? No. She would make too much trouble for us." Turning away, she began to mutter, rousing the mesmerized figures one by one. By the last, my ears sufficiently habituated to her voice, I managed to understand that she was repeating a simple Latin phrase attached to each woman's Christian name, and heard her command, "*Carpe diem,* Violet."

So that was Smurl's "Open Sesame" that unlocked their imprisonment. Their slow responses, confused reactions, and sleepy demeanor made me think we were in no immediate danger, although I did not rule out the possibility that a few more words from the first woman might turn them into an army of Furies. As jailers may have a "trusty" amongst their prisoners, so it seemed that Smurl had given this first wife power over the others. It could be only with her collusion that he had managed to gather his collection of "dead" women; had she spoken out, he might now be in prison and most of these women still safely in the bosom of their real families. This was her fault as surely as his, I thought, a furious contempt against her growing in my breast. Maybe I wasn't being fair to her, maybe he had spent years breaking down her spirit, forcing her to become his abject slave, but she did not look enslaved to me, standing there with a smug little smirk on her face, aware that she'd increased her odds of winning against us . . .

"*Carpe Diem,* Alcinda," said Mr. Jesperson.

The girl's eyes popped open. She looked like a startled doll, then confusion and resentment and fear battled for the upper hand in her expression.

"We're here to help you," I said quickly. "Tell me, would you like to come away from here?"

"Dear God," she cried fervently. "Yes!"

"Alcinda!" barked the Mrs.-Smurl-in-charge. *"Dormite!"*

Although my sisters and I were not allowed to study Latin, because of some notion that dead languages might damage the weaker female brain, we heard odds and ends of it from my father while we were growing up, and that particular command was one he'd often directed at one or another of us at the end of a long and tiring day.

She froze, as in a game of statues, but the utter blankness of Alcinda's expression had nothing playful about it.

"Violet," I said sharply, and when I was rewarded by a look of surprise from the pale, wan creature in beige, I said, *"Dormite."* It worked. Unfortunately, I knew no one else's name.

"I suppose you think you're very clever," said Mrs. Smurl.

"Not really. You wake her, we wake Alcinda, and so on, and so forth. What a waste of time. I'm sure you wouldn't like Mr. Smurl to find us here . . ."

"*You* would like it even less, I think," she said with a malicious smile.

I felt a quiver of apprehension, wondering if she might actually want to keep us here until he returned.

Jesperson, meanwhile, had roused Alcinda, and, his manner cool, informed Mrs. Smurl that we were taking her away. "And if either of you ladies would care to join us?" With a charming smile, he looked at the two women flanking Mrs. Smurl. They responded as if to a lewd suggestion, shrinking back, shaking their heads; the slightly plumper one in grey even shut her eyes.

"We are happy as we are," said Mrs. Smurl, putting an arm around the waist of the trembling lady in grey.

"Not all of you," I said, offering my hand to Alcinda, who gripped it hard.

"Ungrateful minx!" Mrs. Smurl glared, and her anger gleamed a moment like a razor blade catching the light, then vanished into the darkness of her shrug, as she seemed to relax. "Very well. You may go, if you wish, Alcinda, but you can never return. There will be no forgiveness. And if you should even think of betraying us—"

Beside me, I felt her shudder as she shook her head.

The woman continued: "But if you should try, Mr. Smurl will have his revenge. There is no escaping him, you know, no matter how far you go, no matter what happens to him in this life, his power over you will not be diminished."

"I won't say anything, Martha. I promised him I would not, and I keep my promises, even though he did not keep his. I've told him so many times: I do not love him. I do not want to be married to him."

"He has done nothing wrong. Albert is a good man. He has never forced you, has he? You admit it? Yes, I see you do; you must bow before the truth. I know, you know, you were a mistake, his little weakness, but it wasn't the end of the world, was it? It was not. You would soon learn how to be happy. And it could still be all right, you know, if only . . ."

Although I did not realize, the dull repetition of her voice was having an effect. Fortunately, Jesperson was alert to the danger, and quick to pick up the key Alcinda had provided.

"Martha, *dormite*!" he cried, and his voice felt like a splash of water, shocking me awake.

Martha Smurl flinched; but after a brief flash of anger, her eyes were as guarded, and alert, as ever. The magic words did not work on her. "How dare you?" She drew herself up, looking daggers. "How dare you break into my home, intrude upon my peace and quiet, refuse to give *your* name, and then take liberties with mine? You presume to give orders that a woman should accept only from her husband.

"Get out of here," she said, in a low and dangerous voice. "Go now."

I was halfway to the door with Alcinda before I realized that Jesperson had not budged.

"One more thing, before I go," he said. "I want to make it clear, if anyone else wishes to leave, she has my promise of protection."

"*Our* protection," I put in, so no one would think she must trade one master for another.

"It is not wanted," replied Mrs. Smurl.

"With respect, madam, I should prefer to hear from each individual lady, however well qualified you may feel to speak for her."

There was a brief, silent struggle between them, but then she gave in and woke her sisters. It turned out to be as unnecessary as she had implied: except for the old woman, Mary, who was too bewildered to understand, each of the others proclaimed her love for Mr. Smurl and expressed her desire to stay there. However the wide world might judge them, they all felt themselves to be his loving wives. While Violet was still passionately declaring that she could never leave her beloved Albert, no matter what might happen, the old woman stood up and wandered away and out of the room.

Martha Smurl gave a hiss of annoyance. "She'll *never* settle now, and I shall have to spend all my time chasing after her, and Mr. Smurl will be so cross if dinner is late—"

"Never mind, dear," said Violet, sounding anxious. "I'll go and tend to Mother Mary—you can get on with the cooking."

So we left them. What else could we do? We would have to be content with the rescue of Alcinda for our happy ending. After all, we had not been asked to do more.

The house where Alcinda had grown up and her family still lived was scarcely two miles away, on the other side of the cemetery, but she would not go there. Pressing her about it only made her more anxious, so we suggested that she come back to Gower Street with us. At least for the time being, it seemed wise to remove her from the chance of another encounter with Mr. Smurl.

We made our way to the train station and were soon comfortably settled with the whole of a carriage to ourselves. With no need to worry about being overheard, I raised the subject of a visit to Scotland Yard.

Her eyes widened. "Why?"

"As Mr. Smurl is so well regarded in his neighborhood, it might be better to avoid the local police. And considering the seriousness of his crimes—"

Tears filled her eyes, threatened to spill. "Crimes?" she whispered. "Oh, no, no, never!"

Although I thought she might be frightened of the revenge Mrs. Smurl had suggested, I had little patience. "He kidnapped you," I pointed out. "That is a very serious crime."

"But I agreed to it!"

"You agreed to become his prisoner? I think not. If you were happy there, we can take you back." I regretted my cruel words when I saw her shudder.

"No. Please. I don't want that. And I am grateful—oh! How grateful you may never know! It's true—he betrayed my trust. He had his own reason for wanting me dead to the world; I was so caught up in my own plans, I did not realize. I expected to go home again a day or two after I was buried, and—" She stopped, as I was unable to repress a cry of horror. "What?"

"Do you mean to say . . . you knew you would be buried alive? You *agreed* to it?"

"Of course. Mr. Smurl explained the operation of his safety coffins to me and—well—as I was so determined to have the experience of death, how could I be satisfied unless I was pronounced dead and buried? Anything less would be hardly more than sleep. I wanted to be dead to the world, to know the quiet of the grave—it was the only way." She spoke with simple conviction, but it was like hearing a hymn of praise to some ancient and long-forgotten god. I had found the notes in her sketchbook peculiar enough, but I was struck now even more forcibly by the distance between her way of thinking and my own. We might have belonged to two different races, indoctrinated into different belief systems. It seemed to me there was something almost inhuman about her.

It left me speechless, but Jesperson's face was alight with curiosity as he asked, "Weren't you frightened?"

"Oh, yes! Certainly! Terrified!" She gave a nervous laugh and no longer looked like anything but a pretty, modern, ordinary girl. "Never so frightened in all my . . . But then that was part of it, don't you see? Who would not be frightened to die?"

He nodded. "You wanted to meet Death, like the boy in the fairy tale—and for Mr. Smurl, I presume, it was to be an unrivaled opportunity to advertise the worth of his wares?"

She looked as if he had made the most astounding of deductions, like Sherlock Holmes laying out the entire course of a man's career after a glance at his hat. "Yes! Exactly! How very clever of you! Of course, people would say it was terribly wrong of him if they knew, but it wasn't like that, you see! Not a real crime—certainly not a crime against *me.* I begged him—I practically made him do it! And I was never in any danger, for he knew it would work—"

"Having already used the same plan at least three times before," I interjected. "On those poor women. Surely you won't tell me they were all just like you, eager to taste death? Or help him prove the worth of his invention?"

She grimaced. "No, of course not. Their reasons . . . They did it for love. That's all. They were so crazy in love with Albert Smurl that they'd do anything he asked, agree to any crazy scheme that would allow them to live with him."

"Afterwards, when they found they weren't the only one, they still felt the same?"

"You heard them. They are strange, sad creatures, I agree! Love is a peculiar, powerful force, don't you think, Miss Lane?" The look she gave me was disconcerting, a sudden connection that was the more unexpected after my earlier feeling about her.

"It does make some people act like fools," I said.

"Albert Smurl is one of them." She sighed. "He fell in love with me—I never invited his affection!—and then he was unable to resist temptation; especially, I suppose, as all his experience with women suggested that I was bound to return his feelings, that I would fall in love with him soon enough . . ." She gave me a pleading look. "He was always kind to me. I can't blame him for loving me, Miss Lane, I truly cannot. What he did was wrong, certainly, but I am not blameless. I gave him my full cooperation, and now that I am free, I should like to say that is the end. I will not bring charges against the man."

She sounded very sure—not like someone forced to act against her will by a canny hypnotist—but I am no expert on these matters. Still, we could discuss the matter of criminal charges later. We had other things to talk about.

As the train carried us ever farther from Smurl's territory, the physical distance made it possible to raise the question of when and how Miss Travers might return to her own home, and for her to consider it without alarm. She told us that she did not know why, but the very act of moving towards her own street had made her heart pound uncomfortably hard and her breath come more shallowly: she seemed to be afraid of something she could not name.

Jesperson said, "I suspect Smurl planted a suggestion in your mind while you were in his thrall, to keep you from returning to your family in the event that you managed to escape. You would not know why but would simply feel an aversion to going to your old address."

She looked distressed. "How dreadful! Does that mean I can never go home again? What if my family should move to another house? Could I go to them there?"

Jesperson smiled. "Hypnotic suggestions can be countered—especially once you are aware of them. I can teach you a simple technique, or, if you prefer, with your permission, I can easily rid you of the problems he created. I have studied the arts of hypnosis . . ."

Was there no end to his talents?

Although I thought I would not be so eager to allow yet another strange man access to my mind, there is something so *likeable* about Jasper Jesperson—and he is so obviously trustworthy—that I was not surprised that Miss Travers expressed her gratitude for the offer.

"But when I do go home," she said hesitantly, "whatever shall I tell them? They all think I am dead. How can I possibly explain? What story can I tell?"

"You must tell them the truth," I said at once. "However improbable, however unlikely . . . the truth has a force that cannot be denied; much greater than any fiction you attempt to contrive."

"But . . . then I should have to mention . . . his name."

I wondered if her reluctance was entirely due to another posthypnotic command. There was certainly much to inhibit any well-bred young girl from admitting to abduction by a serial bigamist. She was undoubtedly sensible of the social consequences that would follow once her story became public. She might claim—it might even be true—that he had treated her with scrupulous courtesy, as a guest in his home, but still she would be regarded with suspicion, as "damaged goods" ruined forever in the marriage market. Society puts a heavy burden on its females. Some carry that burden without noticing, some are able to shrug it off, others manage to adapt in some way or another to the lot imposed upon them. I did not know Alcinda well enough to know if she would think her "taste of death" had been worth the lasting suspicion.

"You will have to bring Mr. Smurl into it. I don't see any other way . . . After all, he has invented the device that allowed you to be released from your premature grave."

"But no one would believe you had been entombed for weeks," Jesperson added. "Not looking as well as you do."

She flushed a little, and smiled up at him from under her lashes, although I perceived nothing flirtatious in his manner.

He went on: "You must have been rescued soon after the burial, although it was kept quiet. Perhaps Mr. Smurl's wife—just the one, mind you; those other ladies must be her unwed sisters—tenderly nursed you back to health. They did not alert your family through fear that at any moment you would expire, and their reluctance to arouse false hopes."

"Yes, yes," she said eagerly. "That might do! I think that might be believed. It is close enough to what happened—we might say that only in the last few days have I been back to normal, truly well enough to risk going out . . . We might say that I awoke while my nurse slept, and did not recognize my surroundings and took fright . . ." She frowned, and her gaze turned inward; I saw her lips move as she rehearsed her careful lies.

We arrived at 203-A to be greeted by the most welcome smells of cooking. Without knowing when we might arrive, Mrs. Jesperson had made the best possible use of the beef, cooking it slowly in a large pot with onions, carrots, parsnips, turnips, and potatoes, producing a dish that could be reheated, as well as being substantial enough to feed a crowd.

We dined heartily on the *ragout* (so she called what, in my childhood home, had been simply stew) along with lightly steamed cabbage and a loaf of fresh, crusty bread. Afterwards there was cheese and apple pie with cream.

It was the first meal of the day for Jasper and me, and our guest demonstrated an appetite that matched ours, so that we scarcely said a word beyond "pass the salt" or "may I have more bread, please" until we were finished and, replete, sank back in our chairs to recover while Mrs. Jesperson went to put the kettle on.

Just then there was a knock at the street door. Jasper went to answer, and moments later, Felicity all but flew into the room.

"Is it true? You have found her? Oh, Cinda! My Cinda!"

Alcinda nearly overturned her chair in her haste to rise, and in an instant they were hugging each other and weeping with joy.

"But how? How did you know?" Pulling away from her younger sister a moment, Alcinda looked from her to us, bewildered.

I explained that Felicity was our client. "Surely you wondered how we had come to find you?" I did not find it strange that she had not asked, with so many other things to think about.

But she surprised me. "No. I felt certain it was Mama's doing."

"Your stepmother?"

She shook her head, smiling uncertainly. "I mean my own dear, departed mother. Departed from this plane, but not utterly gone. I know that now, because while I was . . . dead . . . I found her again." She sighed. "I know you find it strange that I don't feel angry and *vengeful* towards Mr. Smurl for what he did to me, but I can't. This is not, as you may think, that I am afraid of him, or that I am under compulsion, but, truly, because I am grateful. Yes, really grateful for what he did, for the great gift he gave me. Perhaps I would feel differently if I had been kept there much longer, pressured to become another wife, but in that time the good still seemed to me to outweigh the bad. Every time he 'put me under' he enabled me to escape to another place—and my mother was there. I would have happily stayed there with her forever, but she told me I must go back, I was too young and still had a life to live. She said I must escape." She frowned and looked uncertain. "I know that I tried. I have a feeling I did manage to get away from the house, once, but then Mr. Smurl found me and brought me back . . ." She shrugged off the incomplete memory. "I don't know exactly what happened, but she said not to worry, she would send someone to save me." She smiled at us. "And then you came."

"Your Mama sent *me,*" said Felicity. "She came to me in a dream. It was a true dream—I knew it all along." She smiled triumphantly, then added, "It was after I saw you in the cemetery that I had the dream."

Felicity explained that Alcinda *had* somehow managed to get away, and described what she had seen. But when she repeated Smurl's words to her, Alcinda exclaimed that it *could not* be true; she would not believe he would ever say such a thing, especially not to a child!

"Are you certain, my dear, that *that* was not a dream?"

Felicity glowered. "Of course it was not! I know very well when I am awake. But Papa would not believe me, either, even though he did not know it was Mr. Smurl I had met, and I did not know what to do, how to find you again and save you from that horrible beast."

She carried on speaking over her sister's objection. "I wished Mr. Sherlock Holmes was not just in stories, because if he was real, I could write him a letter. I thought he would surely recognize that I was telling the truth! That night I dreamt that he *was* real and that I had decided to visit him, so I took the train all by myself, up to London, and set off to find Baker Street. I was standing on a street corner, looking at a map that I couldn't quite read, when a kind lady offered her help. She looked just like the picture on the wall above Alcinda's bed, so I knew at once who she was. I almost said, 'Aren't you dead?' but then I thought that would be rude, so I thanked her and said I was looking for the great detective, at 221-B Baker Street. She told me that the address I wanted was actually 203-A Gower Street, and then she walked with me, all the way—it was the most extraordinarily *detailed* dream!—and she showed me the door. It was *your* door," she said, nodding at us, "but in the dream it was different. You really only have a number on the door. In the dream, there was a brass plate on it with the names Jesperson and Lane. When I woke up, I remembered those names, as well as the address, and I knew that *this* was where I had to come—although it was a very long way from Sydenham. And expensive."

"I did wonder how you came to find us," I said.

"Did you know my mother, when she was alive?" asked Alcinda, obviously puzzling over the question. "Before she was Mrs. Eugene Travers, she was Maria Lessingham."

Jesperson, who would have been a mere child at the time of Mrs. Travers's death, said mildly, "I never had the pleasure."

The name Lessingham provoked no more recognition in me than Travers had, but, before I said as much, I thought of the past few years in which I had spent so many hours in darkened rooms, in the company of men and women who claimed the ability to commune with the dead and act as conductors for their spirits. Many, if not most, were frauds, but I could not dismiss them all, even if I had sometimes speculated whether thought-reading, or telepathy, might not provide a more accurate explanation of their powers than the claims made by spiritualists. Maria was a common enough name; while I could be certain I had never met Alcinda's mother in the flesh, I could not so easily dismiss the possibility that her spirit had encountered mine at some séance . . .

For a moment, recalling the excitement of my early explorations in psychical research, I wondered how I could have let myself be distracted from the great question of what becomes of us after death by smaller concerns, and I realized, too, that Alcinda Travers and I were not as different as I had thought. Perhaps, a few years ago, I would also have found Mr. Smurl's strange proposal too tempting to refuse?

Mrs. Jesperson returned bearing a tea tray. For her son, she had prepared a small silver pot of very strong coffee (to revive his sleep-deprived brain), and for the rest of us there was a light and fragrant Chinese tea served in beautiful little blue-and-white china bowls.

Gulping down her tea without ceremony, Felicity was eager to go back home at once. Alcinda explained her concerns, and that Mr. Jesperson had offered his help. "Perhaps, if it is not too great an imposition for me to stay here overnight . . ."

Felicity interrupted her sister: "Why can't Mr. Jesperson do it *now*?"

"Certainly I can, if it suits you," said he, and drained the last of his coffee.

Alcinda was soon settled in the most comfortable chair, with Jesperson perched beside her on a stool.

"Would you like us to leave?" I asked.

"No, no. So long as Miss Alcinda is happy."

"I am," she said. "I do not wish to be parted from Felicity so soon!"

"You would like to go home with her?"

"Oh, yes!"

It occurred to me that the inhibition about returning was already gone, but Jesperson continued:

"I would like for you to envision the place, a very specific place, that means home to you."

"My own bedroom," she said promptly. "It is the smallest and the highest in the house, but I chose it for my own."

"Think of it in as much detail as you can."

"Oh, that's easy. My little worktable and chair are beneath the dormer window. My bed is against the wall behind it. There are shiny brass knobs on the bedstead, and a patchwork quilt on the bed that I made with my two best friends. Over the bed is my favorite portrait of my mother. I look at it every day and night. I used to talk to it."

"Focus on it. See it in as much detail as you can—you don't have to speak aloud; just observe it for yourself."

She closed her eyes.

"As you look at it, think of how happy you are to be back home again, how comfortable it makes you feel, to be in that room, looking at your mother's face. You can see the love she felt for you in your mother's face. She is the person who loved you the most, and has always kept you safe. There is nowhere else you would rather be; nowhere else you feel so warm, and protected, and loved, and safe. You are in your room, safe and happy, warm and well."

He went on like that for some minutes more, in a voice so compelling and soporific that at one point I dozed off and dreamt I was in that room myself, a room I had never seen but felt was my own true home, looking at a picture of my own mother with a relaxed feeling of comfortable well-being that was very far from the reality of our relationship.

When he talked her—*us*—back to our present surroundings, I knew he had been successful. Without mumbo jumbo, his ordinary magic had worked. Most unexpectedly, it had worked on *me;* I felt as refreshed and relaxed as my partner told Alcinda she now felt.

Although Felicity and Alcinda said there was no need for us to accompany them all the way back to Sydenham, Jesperson insisted. What if Smurl should be lurking outside their home, with an accomplice, ready to seize his escaped prisoner? Perhaps Miss Travers might like to reconsider. We could go to Scotland Yard before we left London . . .

But she was adamant that she would bring no charges against Mr. Smurl and begged us to respect her decision.

We walked to the Holborn Viaduct Station, and from there bought tickets to Sydenham. It was just as well, really, that we had come, because although Felicity had a return ticket, she did not have quite enough money to buy a single for Alcinda. I wondered, as Jesperson dug into his pocket to pay for one first-class single and two returns, if we would *ever* make any money from the curious cases we took on.

Leaving the two sisters outside their house—they preferred to be alone with their family—I felt that we were being gently pushed out of the story; whatever explanation Alcinda had come up with would not feature the names of Jesperson and Lane. But if that was their decision, what right had we to argue? Sometimes good deeds must be their own reward.

No one was waiting for them with evil intent. The street was quiet; a few birds singing in the trees. After we had seen them go safely inside, my partner and I set off, without discussion, for Smurl's house.

It was evening by the time we arrived; the streetlamps were not yet lit, but most of the houses along the street now had warmly glowing windows, hinting at comfort within—except for Smurl's. But someone was ahead of us, someone had pushed open the gate beside the laburnum bush, and was making his way, steps a trifle hesitant, towards the front door.

The figure looked familiar. In a moment, I recognized the cemetery's caretaker, Eric Bailey.

We continued to approach the house, walking more slowly to observe him. He rapped several times upon the door: the sound carried clearly through the quiet air. We heard him call out to Mr. Smurl, identifying himself, but received no response. By this time, we were just outside the gate, so we were able to watch him try the door handle, and then bend to inspect the keyhole.

When he straightened, his manner had changed. I wondered if he had seen something through the keyhole that worried him. He rubbed his chin and fidgeted nervously, turning around on the spot. At this point, Mr. Jesperson opened the gate, and we walked through.

Giving a start of surprise, the man called out an uncertain greeting.

"Good evening," said Jesperson, touching his hat. "We meet again, Mr. Bailey!"

Recognizing us, he relaxed a little. "Why, fancy! Have you come to call on Mr. Smurl?"

"Indeed. That brochure you gave me was very interesting. I thought I should like to hear more about his famous security coffin, from the inventor himself."

He could not have looked more astonished if my friend had said he'd an invitation from Saint Peter to discuss his place in Heaven. "You don't mean to say Mr. Smurl invited you here, to his house?"

"Why, is that so unusual?"

"Never heard of such a thing! Never for business, and not for anything else since his wife took ill—four, five, maybe six years now? I felt a bit strange coming here myself, but didn't know what else to do. They haven't seen him in the parlor since he left just before one. I expected him at three o'clock, but when he didn't show up, didn't think too much about it. He likes to show his face at the graveside, but I thought something must have come up. They told me he missed two meetings, and never a note, never a word of explanation—well, that's not like him. He went home for his dinner at one o'clock; I thought, if his wife had taken a turn for the worse . . ." He mentally pulled himself back, looked sharply at Mr. Jesperson. "You had an appointment? You say he invited you here, to his own private abode, to talk business?"

"No, I did not say that. I decided to call by, on the chance. But I take it he is not at home."

He's on the run, I thought. Packed up his remaining "wives" and headed for the Continent to hide out. Or maybe they were in Southampton, planning to sail to America, where he might hope to be met with open arms by the polygamous Mormons.

Eric Bailey shook his head unhappily. "The door is locked from the inside."

"Perhaps his wife is not inclined to admit anyone before her husband returns."

"Mrs. Smurl is an invalid. He has told me so often enough. She could not come downstairs to let him in—or to lock the door."

"There must be another way out," I said. "A back door, into the garden."

There was a high wall and a locked gate barring access to the back garden, but this, of course, was small obstacle to a long-legged, strong, and agile young man. While we waited for Jesperson to come back and tell us, as I expected, that the house was empty, our quarry flown, Mr. Bailey and I looked at each other and then awkwardly away, finding nothing to say. A very long minute or so went by before we heard him coming back over the wall.

In the gloom, his face was ghostly.

"I think, Mr. Bailey, you had better go for the police," he said.

* * *

On the side of the house, as he told us, there were French doors that served as the dining-room window. Looking in, he had glimpsed what he described as a tableaux of death. Although many details were obscured by darkness, the positions of the bodies—fallen across the table, collapsed in chairs, or in a contorted position on the floor—suggested they had all died quite suddenly and horribly.

"Bodies?" squeaked the guardian of the cemetery in horror. "But whose?"

"One man, five women," he replied shortly. "Although I am certain they are all past saving, nevertheless—what is the quickest way to the local police station?"

We went with him but, as strangers to Mr. Smurl, were not detained. We learned the results of the police investigation only after they were made public and, although we did not agree with their conclusion, it seemed neither necessary nor wise to tell them so.

Albert Smurl was a respected local figure with many influential friends. The official verdict was "accidental death" caused by the ingestion of an arsenic-laced soup. There was never the slightest suggestion of murder—except amongst low-minded gossips. It could only be an accident. Mr. Smurl's mother was known to be wandering in her wits. Perhaps, trying to be helpful, she had put what she thought was salt into the soup prepared by her daughter-in-law. "Who keeps arsenic in the kitchen?" was not a question anyone felt like asking.

The questions that were asked largely concerned the identities of the three unknown women who had been dining with the Smurls. From their closeness in age and genteel dress it was thought they were more likely friends of Mrs. Smurl than servants or impecunious relations. There was evidence within the house to show that they had probably been living there for some weeks or months at least.

Newspapers cooperated with the police in requesting that anyone with missing female relatives of the right age should come forward. The postmortem photographs of the nameless victims were too unpleasant to be published but might be inspected at the local police station. I don't know how many people came forward, but if anyone ever said,

"Why, if I didn't know she had died three years ago, I should say that was a picture of my neighbor's daughter!" that news was not reported, and the identities of those three women remained a mystery to the police and public.

From the moment that Jesperson reported everyone in the house was dead, I felt relief that we had managed to rescue Alcinda, and sorrow for the other five women. I felt certain that Mr. Smurl was their murderer. It is, sadly, not unknown for men today to behave like savage kings of the past who insisted on taking their wives, concubines, and servants with them on departing this life. It struck me as just the sort of thing a horrible man like Smurl would do, to take his victims with him, when he killed himself to avoid having to face justice for his crimes.

I was forced to change my mind upon learning that the Christian name of Mrs. Albert Smurl was Violet.

Who was Martha?

After a search, I believe we found her false grave in Park Grove Cemetery. Her name, two years ago, at the time of her supposed death, was Martha Boyd Elliott, and she was married to Channing Elliott, a man who described her as his "dearly beloved wife, taken too soon" and had the words FOREVER IN MY HEART carved below her name and dates. This should not make any difference. The same horrible crimes were committed against the same people. Nothing has changed, but after this knowledge, I have to consider if someone can be a victim and a villain at the same time.

Although I am not certain if I ask myself that question in regard to Martha Boyd Elliott or Albert E. Smurl.

Certain phrases haunt me. I keep hearing Alcinda's soft, sweet voice saying "I can't blame him" and "He couldn't help himself," but also I remember a policeman who muttered, "Poison is a woman's weapon."

Neil Gaiman

One of the hottest stars in science fiction, fantasy, and horror today, Neil Gaiman has won four Hugo Awards, two Nebula Awards, one World Fantasy Award, six Locus Awards, four Stoker Awards, three Geffens, two Mythopoeic Fantasy Awards, and a Newbery Medal. Gaiman first came to wide public attention as the creator of the graphic-novel series *The Sandman,* still one of the most acclaimed graphic-novel series of all time. Gaiman remains a superstar in the graphic-novel field; his graphic novels include *Breakthrough, Death Talks About Life, Legend of the Green Flame, The Last Temptation, Only the End of the World Again, Mirrormask,* and a slew of books in collaboration with Dave McKean, including *Black Orchid, Violent Cases, Signal to Noise, The Tragical Comedy or Comical Tragedy of Mr. Punch, The Wolves in the Walls,* and *The Day I Swapped My Dad for Two Goldfish.*

In recent years he's enjoyed equal success in the science-fiction and fantasy fields as well, with his bestselling novel *American Gods* winning the 2002 Hugo, Nebula, and Bram Stoker Awards, *Coraline* winning both Hugo and Nebula in 2003, and his story "A Study in Emerald" winning the Hugo in 2004. His novel *The Graveyard Book* won the Hugo, the Newbery Medal, and the Carnegie Medal in 2009. He also won the World Fantasy Award for his story with Charles Vess, "A Midsummer Night's Dream," and won the International Horror Critics Guild Award for his collection *Angels & Visitations: A Miscellany.* Gaiman's other novels include *Good Omens* (written with Terry Pratchett), *Neverwhere, Stardust,* and *Anansi Boys.* In addition to *Angels & Visitations,* his short fiction has been collected in *Smoke & Mirrors: Short Fictions & Illusions, Adventures in the Dream Trade,* and *Fragile Things.* A movie based on his novel *Stardust* was in theaters worldwide in 2007, and an animated movie based on *Coraline* was in theaters in 2009. His most recent books include a picture book with Adam Rex, *Chu's Day,* his first new novel for adults in many years, *The Ocean at the End of the Lane,* a time-traveling romp for all ages, *Fortunately, the Milk,* and, as editor, the anthology *Unnatural Creatures.*

Here he takes us deep into the surreal world of London Below, the setting for his famous novel *Neverwhere,* for an adventure that demonstrates that sometimes the clothes make the man—quite literally.

HOW THE MARQUIS GOT HIS COAT BACK

Neil Gaiman

It was beautiful. It was remarkable. It was unique. It was the reason that the Marquis de Carabas was chained to a pole in the middle of a circular room, far, far underground, while the water level rose slowly higher and higher. It had thirty pockets, seven of which were obvious, nineteen of which were hidden, and four of which were more or less impossible to find—even, on occasion, for the Marquis himself.

He had (we shall return to the pole, and the room, and the rising water, in due course) once been given—although "given" might be considered an unfortunate, if justified, exaggeration—a magnifying glass by Victoria herself. It was a marvelous piece of work: ornate, gilt, with a chain and tiny cherubs and gargoyles, and the lens had the unusual property of rendering transparent anything you looked at through it. The Marquis did not know where Victoria had originally obtained the magnifying glass, before he pilfered it from her, to make up for a payment he felt was not entirely what had been agreed—after all, there was only one Elephant, and obtaining the Elephant's diary had not been easy, nor had escaping the Elephant and Castle once it had been obtained. The Marquis had slipped Victoria's magnifying glass into one of the four pockets that practically weren't there at all and had never been able to find it again.

In addition to its unusual pockets, it had magnificent sleeves, an imposing collar, and a slit up the back. It was made of some kind of leather, it was the color of a wet street at midnight, and, more important than any of these things, it had style.

There are people who will tell you that clothes make the man, and mostly they are wrong. However, it would be true to say that when the boy who would become the Marquis put that coat on for the very first time, and stared at himself in the looking glass, he stood up straighter, and his posture changed, because he knew, seeing his reflection, that the sort of person who wore a coat like that was no mere youth, no simple sneak thief and favor-trader. The boy wearing the coat, which was, back then, too large for him, had smiled, looking at his reflection, and remembered an illustration from a book he had seen, of a miller's cat standing on its two hind legs. A jaunty cat wearing a fine coat and big, proud boots. And he named himself.

A coat like that, he knew, was the kind of coat that could only be worn by the Marquis de Carabas. He was never sure, not then and not later, how you pronounced Marquis de Carabas. Some days he said it one way, some days the other.

The water level had reached his knees, and he thought, *This would never have happened if I still had my coat.*

It was the market day after the worst week of the Marquis de Carabas's life and things did not seem to be getting any better. Still, he was no longer dead, and his cut throat was healing rapidly. There was even a rasp in his throat he found quite attractive. Those were definite upsides.

There were just as definite downsides to being dead, or at least, to having been recently dead, and missing his coat was the worst of them.

The sewer folk were not helpful.

"You sold my corpse," said the Marquis. "These things happen. You also sold my possessions. I want them back. I'll pay."

Dunnikin of the Sewer Folk shrugged. "Sold them," he said. "Just like we sold you. Can't go getting things back that you sold. Not good business."

"We are talking," said the Marquis de Carabas, "about my coat. And I fully intend to have it back."

Dunnikin shrugged.

"To whom did you sell it?" asked the Marquis.

The Sewer dweller said nothing at all. He acted as if he had not even heard the question.

"I can get you perfumes," said the Marquis, masking his irritability with all the blandness he could muster. "Glorious, magnificent, odiferous perfumes. You know you want them."

Dunnikin stared, stony-faced, at the Marquis. Then he drew his finger across his throat. As gestures went, the Marquis reflected, it was in appalling taste. Still, it had the desired effect. He stopped asking questions: there would be no answers from this direction.

The Marquis walked over to the food court. That night, the Floating Market was being held in the Tate Gallery. The food court was in the Pre-Raphaelite Room, and had already been mostly packed away. There were almost no stalls left: just a sad-looking little man selling some kind of sausage, and, in the corner, beneath a Burne-Jones painting of ladies in diaphanous robes walking downstairs, there were some Mushroom People, with some stools, tables, and a grill. The Marquis had once eaten one of the sad-looking man's sausages, and he had a firm policy of never intentionally making the same mistake twice, so he walked to the Mushroom People's stall.

There were three of the Mushroom People looking after the stall, two young men and a young woman. They smelled damp. They wore old duffel coats and army-surplus jackets, and they peered out from beneath their shaggy hair as if the light hurt their eyes.

"What are you selling?" he asked.

"The Mushroom. The Mushroom on toast. Raw the Mushroom."

"I'll have some of the Mushroom on toast," he said, and one of the Mushroom People—a thin, pale young woman with the complexion of day-old porridge—cut a slice off a puffball fungus the size of a tree stump. "And I want it cooked properly all the way through," he told her.

"Be brave. Eat it raw," said the woman. "Join us."

"I have already had dealings with the Mushroom," said the Marquis. "We came to an understanding."

The woman put the slice of white puffball under the portable grill.

One of the young men, tall, with hunched shoulders, in a duffel coat that smelled like old cellars, edged over to the Marquis and poured him a glass of mushroom tea. He leaned forward, and the Marquis could see the tiny crop of pale mushrooms splashed like pimples over his cheek.

The Mushroom person said, "You're de Carabas? The fixer?"

The Marquis did not think of himself as a fixer. He said, "I am."

"I hear you're looking for your coat. I was there when the Sewer Folk sold it. Start of the last Market it was. On Belfast. I saw who bought it."

The hair on the back of the Marquis' neck pricked up. "And what would you want for the information?"

The Mushroom's young man licked his lips with a lichenous tongue. "There's a girl I like as won't give me the time of day."

"A Mushroom girl?"

"Would I were so lucky. If we were as one both in love and in the body of the Mushroom, I wouldn't have nothing to worry about. No. She's one of the Raven's Court. But she eats here sometimes. And we talk. Just like you and I are talking now."

The Marquis did not smile in pity and he did not wince. He barely raised an eyebrow. "And yet she does not return your ardor. How strange. What do you want me to do about it?"

The young man reached one grey hand into the pocket of his long duffel coat. He pulled out an envelope inside a clear plastic sandwich bag.

"I wrote her a letter. More of a poem, you might say, although I'm not much of a poet. To tell her how I feels about her. But I don't know that she'd read it if I gived it to her. Then I saw you, and I thought, if it was you as was to give it to her, with all your fine words and your fancy flourishes . . ." He trailed off.

"You thought she would read it and then be more inclined to listen to your suit."

The young man looked down at his duffel coat with a puzzled expression. "I've not got a suit," he said. "Only what I've got on."

The Marquis tried not to sigh. The Mushroom woman put a cracked plastic plate down in front of him, with a steaming slice of grilled the Mushroom on it.

He poked at the Mushroom experimentally, making sure that it was cooked all the way through, and there were no active spores. You could never be too careful, and the Marquis considered himself much too selfish for symbiosis.

It was good. He chewed and swallowed, though the food hurt his throat.

"So all you want is for me to make sure she reads your missive of yearning?"

"You mean my letter? My poem?"

"I do."

"Well, yes. And I want you to be there with her, to make sure she doesn't put it away unread, and I want you to bring her answer back to me." The Marquis looked at the young man. It was true that he had tiny mushrooms sprouting from his neck and cheeks, and his hair was heavy and unwashed, and there was a general smell about him of abandoned places, but it was also true that through his thick fringe his eyes were pale blue and intense, and that he was tall and not unattractive. The Marquis imagined him washed and cleaned up and somewhat less fungal, and approved. "I put the letter in the sandwich bag," said the young man, "so it doesn't get wet on the way."

"Very wise. Now, tell me: who bought my coat?"

"Not yet, Mister Jumps-the-Gun. You haven't asked about my true love. Her name is Drusilla. You'll know her because she is the most beautiful woman in all of the Raven's Court."

"Beauty is traditionally in the eye of the beholder. Give me more to go on."

"I told you. Her name's Drusilla. There's only one. And she has a big red birthmark on the back of her hand that looks like a star."

"It seems an unlikely love pairing. One of the Mushroom's folk, in love with a lady of the Raven's Court. What makes you think she'll give up her life for your damp cellars and fungoid joys?"

The Mushroom youth shrugged. "She'll love me," he said, "once she's read my poem." He twisted the stem of a tiny parasol mushroom growing on his right cheek and, when it fell to the table, he picked it up and continued to twist it between his fingers. "We're on?"

"We're on."

"The cove as bought your coat," said the Mushroom youth, "carried a stick."

"Lots of people carry sticks," said de Carabas.

"This one had a crook on the end," said the Mushroom youth. "Looked a bit like a frog, he did. Short one. Bit fat. Hair the color of gravel. Needed a coat and took a shine to yours." He popped the parasol mushroom into his mouth.

"Useful information. I shall certainly pass your ardor and felicitations on to the fair Drusilla," said the Marquis de Carabas, with a cheer that he most definitely did not feel.

De Carabas reached across the table and took the sandwich bag with the envelope in it from the young man's fingers. He slipped it into one of the pockets sewn inside his shirt.

And then he walked away, thinking about a man holding a crook.

The Marquis de Carabas wore a blanket as a substitute for his coat. He wore it swathed about him like Hell's own poncho. It did not make him happy. He wished he had his coat. *Fine feathers do not make fine birds,* whispered a voice at the back of his mind, something someone had said to him when he was a boy: he suspected that it was his brother's voice, and he did his best to forget it had ever spoken.

A crook: the man who had taken his coat from the Sewer people had been carrying a crook.

He pondered.

The Marquis de Carabas liked being who he was, and when he took risks he liked them to be calculated risks, and he was someone who double- and triple-checked his calculations.

He checked his calculations for the fourth time.

The Marquis de Carabas did not trust people. It was bad for business and it could set an unfortunate precedent. He did not trust his friends or his occasional lovers, and he certainly never trusted his employers. He reserved the entirety of his trust for the Marquis de Carabas, an imposing figure in an imposing coat, able to outtalk, outthink, and outplan anybody.

There were only two sorts of people who carried crooks: bishops and shepherds.

In Bishopsgate, the crooks were decorative, nonfunctional, purely symbolic. And the bishops had no need of coats. They had robes, after all, nice, white, bishopy robes.

The Marquis was not scared of the bishops. He knew that the Sewer Folk were not scared of bishops. The inhabitants of Shepherd's Bush were another matter entirely. Even in his coat, and at the best of times, at the peak of health and with a small army at his beck and call, the Marquis would not have wanted to encounter the shepherds.

He toyed with the idea of visiting Bishopsgate, of spending a pleasant handful of days establishing that his coat was not there.

And then he sighed dramatically, and went to the Guide's Pen, and looked for a bonded guide who might be persuaded to take him to Shepherd's Bush.

His guide was quite remarkably short, with fair hair cut close. The Marquis had first thought she was in her teens, until, after traveling with her for half a day, he had decided she was in her twenties. He had talked to half a dozen guides before he found her. Her name was Knibbs, and she had seemed confident, and he needed confidence. He told her the two places he was going, as they walked out of the Guide's Pen.

"So where do you want to go first, then?" she asked. "Shepherd's Bush, or Raven's Court?"

"The visit to Raven's Court is a formality: it is merely to deliver a letter. To someone named Drusilla."

"A love letter?"

"I believe so. Why do you ask?"

"I have heard that the fair Drusilla is most wickedly beautiful, and she has the unfortunate habit of reshaping those who displease her into birds of prey. You must love her very much, to be writing letters to her."

"I am afraid I have never encountered the young lady," said the Marquis. "The letter is not from me. And it doesn't matter which we visit first."

"You know," said Knibbs thoughtfully, "just in case something dreadfully unfortunate happens to you when you get to the shepherds, we should probably do Raven's Court first. So the fair Drusilla gets her letter. I'm not saying that something horrible will happen to you, mind. Just that it's better to be safe than, y'know, dead."

The Marquis de Carabas looked down at his blanketed shape. He was uncertain. Had he been wearing his coat, he knew, he would not have been uncertain: he would have known exactly what to do. He looked at the girl and he mustered the most convincing grin he could. "Raven's Court it is, then," he said.

Knibbs had nodded, and set off on the path, and the Marquis had followed her.

The paths of London Below are not the paths of London Above: they rely to no little extent on things like belief and opinion and tradition as much as they rely upon the realities of maps.

De Carabas and Knibbs were two tiny figures walking through a high, vaulted tunnel carved from old, white stone. Their footsteps echoed.

"You're de Carabas, aren't you?" said Knibbs. "You're famous. You know how to get places. What exactly do you need a guide for?"

"Two heads are better than one," he told her. "So are two sets of eyes."

"You used to have a posh coat, didn't you?" she said.

"I did. Yes."

"What happened to it?"

He said nothing. Then he said, "I've changed my mind. We're going to Shepherd's Bush first."

"Fair enough," said his guide. "Easy to take you one place as another. I'll wait for you outside the shepherds' trading post, mind."

"Very wise, girl."

"My name's Knibbs," she said. "Not girl. Do you want to know why I became a guide? It's an interesting story."

"Not particularly," said the Marquis de Carabas. He was not feeling particularly talkative, and the guide was being well recompensed for her trouble. "Why don't we try to move in silence?"

Knibbs nodded and said nothing as they reached the end of the tunnel, nothing as they clambered down some metal rungs set in the side of a wall. It was not until they had reached the banks of the Mortlake, the vast underground Lake of the Dead, and she was lighting a candle on the shore to summon the boatman, that she spoke again.

Knibbs said, "The thing about being a proper guide is that you're bonded. So people know you won't steer them wrong."

The Marquis only grunted. He was wondering what to tell the shepherds at the trading post, trying out alternate routes through possibility and through probability. He had nothing that the shepherds would want, that was the trouble.

"You lead them wrong, you'll never work as a guide again," said Knibbs, cheerfully. "That's why we're bonded."

"I know," said the Marquis. She was a most irritating guide, he thought. Two heads were only better than one if the other head kept its mouth shut and did not start telling him things he already knew.

"I got bonded," she said, "in Bond Street." She tapped the little chain around her wrist.

"I don't see the ferryman," said the Marquis.

"He'll be here soon enough. You keep an eye out for him in that direction, and halloo when you sees him. I'll keep looking over here. One way or another, we'll spot him."

They stared out over the dark water of the Tyburn. Knibbs began to talk again. "Before I was a guide, when I was just little, my people trained me up for this. They said it was the only way that honor could ever be satisfied."

The Marquis turned to face her. She held the candle in front of her at eye level. *Everything is off here,* thought the Marquis, and he realized he should have been listening to her from the beginning. *Everything is wrong.* He said, "Who are your people, Knibbs? Where do you come from?"

"Somewhere you ain't welcome anymore," said the girl. "I was born and bred to give my fealty and loyalty to the Elephant and the Castle."

Something hard struck him on the back of the head then, hit him like a hammerblow, and lightning pulsed in the darkness of his mind as he crumpled to the floor.

* * *

The Marquis de Carabas could not move his arms. They were, he realized, tied behind him. He was lying on his side.

He had been unconscious. If the people who did this to him thought him unconscious still, then he would do nothing to disabuse them of the idea, he decided. He let his eyes slit open the merest crack, to sneak a glance at the world.

A deep, grinding voice said, "Oh, don't be silly, de Carabas. I don't believe you're still out. I've got big ears. I can hear your heart beat. Open your eyes properly, you weasel. Face me like a man."

The Marquis recognized the voice and hoped he was mistaken. He opened his eyes. He was staring at legs, human legs with bare feet. The toes were squat and pushed together. The legs and feet were the color of teak. He knew those legs. He had not been mistaken.

His mind bifurcated: a small part of it berated him for his inattention and his foolishness. Knibbs had *told* him, by the Temple and the Arch: he just had not listened to her. But even as he raged at his own foolishness, the rest of his mind took over, forced a smile, and said, "Why, this is indeed an honor. You really didn't have to arrange to meet me like this. Why, the merest inkling that Your Prominence might have had even the teeniest desire to see me would have—"

"Sent you scurrying off in the other direction as fast as your spindly little legs could carry you," said the person with the teak-colored legs. He reached over with his trunk, which was long and flexible, and a greenish blue color, and which hung to his ankles, and he pushed the Marquis onto his back.

The Marquis began rubbing his bound wrists slowly against the concrete beneath them while he said, "Not at all. Quite the opposite. Words cannot actually describe how much pleasure I take in your pachydermic presence. Might I suggest that you untie me and allow me to greet you, man to . . . man to elephant?"

"I don't think so, given all the trouble I've been through to make this happen," said the other. He had the head of a greenish grey elephant. His tusks were sharp and stained reddish brown at the tips. "You know, I swore when I found out what you had done that I would make you scream and beg for mercy. And I swore I'd say no, to giving you mercy, when you begged for it."

"You could say yes, instead," said the Marquis.

"I couldn't say yes. Hospitality abused," said the Elephant. "I never forget."

The Marquis had been commissioned to bring Victoria the Elephant's diary, when he and the world had been much younger. The Elephant ran his fiefdom arrogantly, sometimes viciously and with no tenderness or humor, and the Marquis had thought that the Elephant was stupid. He had even believed that there was no way that the Elephant would correctly identify his role in the disappearance of the diary. It had been a long time ago, though, when the Marquis was young and foolish.

"This whole spending years training up a guide to betray me just on the off chance I'd come along and hire her," said the Marquis. "Isn't that a bit of an overreaction?"

"Not if you know me," said the Elephant. "If you know me, it's pretty mild. I did lots of other things to find you too."

The Marquis tried to sit up. The Elephant pushed him back to the floor with one bare foot. "Beg for mercy," said the Elephant.

That one was easy. "Mercy!" said the Marquis. "I beg! I plead! Show me mercy—the finest of all gifts. It befits you, mighty Elephant, as lord of your own demesne, to be merciful to one who is not even fit to wipe the dust from your excellent toes . . ."

"Did you know," said the Elephant, "that everything you say sounds sarcastic?"

"I didn't. I apologize. I meant every single word of it."

"Scream," said the Elephant.

The Marquis de Carabas screamed very loudly and very long. It is hard to scream when your throat has been recently cut, but he screamed as hard and piteously as he could.

"You even scream sarcastically," said the Elephant.

There was a large black cast-iron pipe jutting out from the wall. A wheel in the side of the pipe allowed whatever came out of the pipe to be turned on and turned off. The Elephant hauled on it with powerful arms, and a trickle of dark sludge came out, followed by a spurt of water.

"Drainage overflow," said the Elephant. "Now. Thing is, I do my homework. You keep your life well hidden, de Carabas. You have done all these years, since you and I first crossed paths. No point in even trying anything as long as you had your life elsewhere. I've had people all over London Below: people you've eaten with, people you've slept with or laughed with or wound up naked in the clock tower of Big Ben with, but there was never any point in taking it further, not as long as your life was still carefully tucked out of harm's way. Until last week, when the word under the street was that your life was out of its box. And that was when I put the word out, that I'd give the freedom of the Castle to the first person to let me see . . ."

". . . See me scream for mercy," said de Carabas. "You said."

"You interrupted me," said the Elephant mildly. "I was going to say, I was going to give the freedom of the Castle to the first person to let me see your dead body."

He pulled the wheel the rest of the way and the spurt of water became a gush.

"I ought to warn you. There is," said de Carabas, "a curse on the hand of anyone who kills me."

"I'll take the curse," said the Elephant. "Although you're probably making it up. You'll like the next bit. The room fills with water, and then you drown. Then I let the water out, and I come in, and I laugh a lot." He made a trumpeting noise that might, de Carabas reflected, have been a laugh, if you were an elephant.

The Elephant stepped out of de Carabas's line of sight.

The Marquis heard a door bang. He was lying in a puddle. He writhed and wriggled, then got to his feet. He looked down: there was a metal cuff around his ankle, which was chained to a metal pole in the center of the room.

He wished he were wearing his coat: there were blades in his coat; there were picklocks; there were buttons that were nowhere nearly as innocent and buttonlike as they appeared to be. He rubbed the rope that bound his wrists against the metal pole, hoping to make it fray, feeling the skin of his wrists and palms rubbing off even as the rope absorbed the water and tightened about him. The water level continued to rise: already it was up to his waist.

De Carabas looked about the circular chamber. All he had to do was free himself from the bonds that tied his wrists—obviously by loosening the pole to which he was bound—and then he would open the cuff around his ankle, turn off the water, get out of the room, avoid a revenge-driven Elephant and any of his assorted thugs, and get away.

He tugged on the pole. It didn't move. He tugged on it harder. It didn't move some more.

He slumped against the pole, and he thought about death, a true, final death, and he thought about his coat.

A voice whispered in his ear. It said, "Quiet!"

Something tugged at his wrists, and his bonds fell away. It was only as life came back into his wrists that he realized how tightly he had been bound. He turned around.

He said, "What?"

The face that met his was as familiar as his own. The smile was devastating, the eyes were guileless and adventuresome.

"Ankle," said the man, with a new smile that was even more devastating than the previous one.

The Marquis de Carabas was not devastated. He raised his leg, and the man reached down, did something with a piece of wire, and removed the leg cuff.

"I heard you were having a spot of bother," said the man. His skin was as dark as the Marquis' own. He was less than an inch taller than de Carabas, but he held himself as if he were easily taller than anyone he was ever likely to meet.

"No. No bother. I'm fine," said the Marquis.

"You aren't. I just rescued you."

De Carabas ignored this. "Where's the Elephant?"

"On the other side of that door, with a number of the people working for him. The doors lock automatically when the hall is filled with water. He needed to be certain that he wouldn't be trapped in here with you. It was what I was counting on."

"Counting on?"

"Of course. I'd been following them for several hours. Ever since I heard that you'd gone off with one of the Elephant's plants. I thought, bad move, I thought. He'll be needing a hand with that."

"You *heard* . . . ?"

"Look," said the man who looked a little like the Marquis de Carabas, only he was taller, and perhaps some people—not the Marquis, obviously—might have thought him just a hair better-looking, "you don't think I was going to let anything happen to my little brother, did you?"

They were up to their waists in water. "I was fine," said de Carabas. "I had it all under control."

The man walked over to the far end of the room. He knelt down, fumbled in the water, then, from his backpack, he produced something that looked like a short crowbar. He pushed one end of it beneath the surface of the water. "Get ready," he said. "I think this should be our quickest way out of here."

The Marquis was still flexing his pins-and-needles cramping fingers, trying to rub life back into them. "What is it?" he said, trying to sound unimpressed.

The man said, "There we go," and pulled up a large square of metal. "It's the drain." De Carabas did not have a chance to protest, as his brother picked him up and dropped him down a hole in the floor.

Probably, thought de Carabas, *there are rides like this at funfairs.* He could imagine them. Upworlders might pay good money to take this ride if they were certain they would survive it.

He crashed through pipes, swept along by the flow of water, always heading down and deeper. He was not certain he was going to survive it, and he was not having fun.

The Marquis' body was bruised and battered as he rode the water down the pipe. He tumbled out, facedown, onto a large metal grate, which seemed scarcely able to hold his weight. He crawled off the grate onto the rock floor beside it, and he shivered.

There was an unlikely sort of a noise, and it was immediately followed by his brother, who shot out of the pipe and landed on his feet, as if he'd been practicing. He smiled. "Fun, eh?"

"Not really," said the Marquis de Carabas. And then he had to ask. "Were you just going '*Whee!*'?"

"Of course! Weren't you?" asked his brother.

De Carabas got to his feet, unsteadily. He said only, "What are you calling yourself these days?"

"Still the same. I don't change."

"It's not your real name, Peregrine," said de Carabas.

"It'll do. It marks my territory and my intentions. You're still calling yourself a Marquis, then?" said Peregrine.

"I am, because I say I am," said the Marquis. He looked, he was sure, like a drowned thing, and sounded, he was certain, unconvincing. He felt small and foolish.

"Your choice. Anyway, I'm off. You don't need me anymore. Stay out of trouble. You don't actually have to thank me." His brother meant it, of course. That was what stung the hardest.

The Marquis de Carabas hated himself. He hadn't wanted to say it, but now it had to be said. "Thank you, Peregrine."

"Oh!" said Peregrine. "Your coat. Word on the street is, it wound up in Shepherd's Bush. That's all I know. So. Advice. Mean this most sincerely. I know you don't like advice. But, the coat? Let it go. Forget about it. Just get a new coat. Honest."

"Well then," said the Marquis.

"Well," said Peregrine, and he grinned and shook himself like a dog, spraying water everywhere, before he slipped into the shadows and was gone.

The Marquis de Carabas stood and dripped balefully.

He had a little time before the Elephant discovered the lack of water in the room, and the lack of a body, and came looking for him.

He checked his shirt pocket: the sandwich bag was there, and the envelope appeared safe and dry inside it.

He wondered, for a moment, about something that had bothered him since the Market. Why would the Mushroom lad use him, de Carabas, to send a letter to the fair Drusilla? And what kind of letter could persuade a member of the Raven's Court, and one with a star on her hand at that, to give up her life at the court and love one of the Mushroom People?

A suspicion occurred to him. It was not a comfortable idea, but it was swept aside by more immediate problems.

He could hide: lie low for a while. It would pass. But there was the coat to think about. He had been rescued—rescued!—by his brother, something that would never have happened under normal circumstances. He could get a new coat. Of course he could. But it would not be *his* coat.

A shepherd had his coat.

The Marquis de Carabas always had a plan, and he always had a fallback plan; and beneath these plans he always had a real plan, one that he would not even let himself know about, for when the original plan and the fallback plan had both gone south.

Now, it pained him to admit to himself, he had no plan. He did not even have a normal, boring, obvious plan that he could abandon as soon as things got tricky. He just had a *want,* and it drove him as their need for food or love or safety drove those the Marquis considered lesser men.

He was planless. He just wanted his coat back.

The Marquis de Carabas began walking. He had an envelope containing a love poem in his pocket, he was wrapped in a damp blanket, and he hated his brother for rescuing him.

When you create yourself from scratch you need a model of some kind, something to aim towards or head away from—all the things you want to be, or intentionally not be.

The Marquis had known whom he had wanted not to be, when he was a boy. He had definitely not wanted to be like Peregrine. He had not wanted to be like anyone at all. He had, instead, wanted to be elegant, elusive, brilliant and, above all things, he had wanted to be unique.

Just like Peregrine.

* * *

The thing was, he had been told by a former shepherd on the run, whom he had helped across the Tyburn River to freedom, and to a short but happy life as a camp entertainer for the Roman Legion who waited there, beside the river, for orders that would never come, that the shepherds never *made* you do anything. They just took your natural impulses and desires and they pushed them, reinforced them, so you acted quite naturally, only you acted in the ways that they wanted.

He remembered that, and then he forgot it, because he was scared of being alone.

The Marquis had not known until just this moment quite how scared he was of being alone, and was surprised by how happy he was to see several other people walking in the same direction as he was.

"I'm glad you're here," one of them called.

"I'm glad you're here," called another.

"I'm glad I'm here too," said de Carabas. Where was he going? Where were they going? So good that they were all traveling the same way together. There was safety in numbers.

"It's good to be together," said a thin white woman, with a happy sort of a sigh. And it was.

"It's good to be together," said the Marquis.

"Indeed it is. It's good to be together," said his neighbor on the other side. There was something familiar about this person. He had huge ears, like fans, and a nose like a thick, grey-green snake. The Marquis began to wonder if he had ever met this person before, and was trying to remember exactly where, when he was tapped gently on the shoulder by a man holding a large stick with a curved end.

"We never want to fall out of step, do we?" said the man, reasonably, and the Marquis thought *Of course we don't,* and he sped up a little, so he was back in step once more.

"That's good. Out of step is out of mind," said the man with the stick, and he moved on.

"Out of step is out of mind," said the Marquis aloud, wondering how he could have missed knowing something so obvious, so basic. There was a tiny part of him, somewhere distant, that wondered what that actually meant.

They reached the place they were going, and it was good to be among friends.

Time passed strangely in that place, but soon enough the Marquis and his friend with the grey-green face and the long nose were given a job to do, a real job, and it was this: they disposed of those members of the flock who could no longer move or serve, once anything that might be of use had been removed and reused. They removed the last of what was left, hair and tallow fat and all, then they dragged it to the pit, and dropped the remnants in. The shifts were long and tiring, and the work was messy, but the two of them did it together and they stayed in step.

They had been working proudly together for several days when the Marquis noticed an irritant. Someone appeared to be trying to attract his attention.

"I followed you," whispered the stranger. "I know you didn't want me to. But, well, needs must."

The Marquis did not know what the stranger was talking about.

"I've got an escape plan, as soon as I can wake you up," said the stranger. "Please wake up."

The Marquis was awake. Again, he found he did not know what the stranger was talking about. Why did the man think he was asleep? The Marquis would have said something, but he had to work. He pondered this, while dismembering the next former member of the flock, until he decided there was something he could say, to explain why the stranger was irritating him. He said it aloud. "It's good to work," said the Marquis.

His friend, with the long, flexible nose, and the huge ears, nodded his head at this.

They worked. After a while his friend hauled what was left of some former members of the flock over to the pit, and pushed them in. The pit went down a long way.

The Marquis tried to ignore the stranger, who was now standing behind him. He was quite put out when he felt something slapped over his mouth, and his hands being bound together behind his back. He was not certain what he was meant to do. It made him feel quite out of step with the flock, and he would have complained, would have called out to his friend, but his lips were now stuck together and he was unable to do more than make ineffectual noises.

"It's me," whispered the voice from behind him urgently. "Peregrine. Your brother. You've been captured by the shepherds. We have to get you out of here." And then: "Uh-uh."

A noise in the air, like something barking. It came closer: a high yip-yipping that turned suddenly into a triumphant howl, and was answered by matching howls from around them.

A voice barked, "Where's your flockmate?"

A low, elephantine voice rumbled, "He went over there. With the other one."

"Other one?"

The Marquis hoped they would come and find him and sort this all out. There was obviously some sort of mistake going on. He wanted to be in step with the flock, and now he was out of step, an unwilling victim. He wanted to work.

"Lud's gate!" muttered Peregrine. And then they were surrounded by shapes of people who were not exactly people: they were sharp of face and dressed in furs. They spoke excitedly to one another.

The people untied the Marquis' hands, although they left the tape on his face. He did not mind. He had nothing to say.

The Marquis was relieved it was all over and looked forward to getting back to work, but to his slight puzzlement, he, his kidnapper, and his friend with the huge, long, flexible nose were walked away from the pit, along a causeway, and eventually, into a honeycomb of little rooms, each room filled with people toiling away in step.

Up some narrow stairs. One of their escorts, dressed in rough furs, scratched at a door. A voice called "Enter!" and the Marquis felt a thrill that was almost sexual. That voice. That was the voice of someone the Marquis had spent his whole life wanting to please. (His whole life went back, what? A week? Two weeks?)

"A stray lamb," said one of the escorts. "And his predator. Also his flockmate."

The room was large, and hung with oil paintings: landscapes, mostly, stained with age and smoke and dust. "Why?" said the man, sitting at a desk in the back of the room. He did not turn around. "Why do you bother me with this nonsense?"

"Because," said a voice, and the Marquis recognized it as that of his would-be kidnapper, "you gave orders that if ever I were to be apprehended within the bounds of the Shepherd's Bush, I was to be brought to you to dispose of personally."

The man pushed his chair back and got up. He walked towards them, stepping into the light. There was a wooden crook propped against the wall, and he picked it up as he passed. For several long moments he looked at them.

"Peregrine?" he said at last, and the Marquis thrilled at his voice. "I had heard that you had gone into retirement. Become a monk or something. I never dreamed you'd dare to come back."

(Something very big was filling the Marquis' head. Something was filling his heart and his mind. It was something enormous, something he could almost touch.)

The shepherd reached out a hand and ripped the tape from the Marquis' mouth. The Marquis knew he should have been overjoyed by this, should have been thrilled to get attention from this man.

"And now I see . . . who would have thought it?" The shepherd's voice was deep and resonant. "He is here already. And already one of ours? The Marquis de Carabas. You know, Peregrine, I had been looking forward to ripping out your tongue, to grinding your fingers away while you watched, but think how much more delightful it would be if the last thing you ever saw was your own brother, one of our flock, as the instrument of your doom."

(An enormous thing filled the Marquis' head.)

The shepherd was plump, well fed, and excellently dressed. He had sandy-grey-colored hair and a harassed expression. He wore a remarkable coat, even if it was somewhat tight on him. The coat was the color of a wet street at midnight.

The enormous thing filling his head, the Marquis realized, was rage. It was rage, and it burned through the Marquis like a forest fire, devouring everything in its path with a red flame.

The coat. It was elegant. It was beautiful. It was so close that he could have reached out and touched it.

And it was unquestionably *his.*

The Marquis de Carabas did nothing to indicate that he had woken up. That would be a mistake. He thought, and he thought fast. And what he thought had nothing to do with the room he was in. The Marquis had only one advantage over the shepherd and his dogs: he knew he was awake and in control of his thoughts, and they did not.

He hypothesized. He tested his hypothesis in his head. And then he acted.

"Excuse me," he said blandly, "but I'm afraid I do need to be getting along. Can we hurry this up? I'm late for something that's frightfully important."

The shepherd leaned on his crook. He did not appear to be concerned by this. He said only, "You've left the flock, de Carabas."

"It would appear so," said the Marquis. "Hello, Peregrine. Wonderful to see you looking so sprightly. And the Elephant. How delightful. The gang's all here." He turned his attention back to the shepherd. "Wonderful meeting you, delightful to spend a little time as one of your little band of serious thinkers. But I really must be tootling off now. Important diplomatic mission. Letter to deliver. You know how it is."

Peregrine said, "My brother, I'm not sure that you understand the gravity of the situation here . . ."

The Marquis, who understood the gravity of the situation perfectly, said, "I'm sure these nice people"—he gestured to the shepherd and to the three fur-clad, sharp-faced, sheepdog people who were standing about them—"will let me head out of here, leaving you behind. It's you they want, not me. And I have something extremely important to deliver."

Peregrine said, "I can handle this."

"You have to be quiet now," said the shepherd. He took the strip of tape he had removed from the Marquis' mouth and pressed it down over Peregrine's.

The shepherd was shorter than the Marquis and fatter, and the magnificent coat looked faintly ridiculous on him. "Something important to deliver?" asked the shepherd, brushing dust from his fingers. "What exactly are we talking about here?"

"I am afraid I cannot possibly tell you that," said the Marquis. "You are, after all, not the intended recipient of this particular diplomatic communiqué."

"Why not? What's it say? Who's it for?"

The Marquis shrugged. His coat was so close that he could have reached out and stroked it. "Only the threat of death could force me even to show it to you," he said reluctantly.

"Well, that's easy. I threaten you with death. That's in addition to the death sentence you're already under as an apostate member of the flock. And as for Laughing Boy here"—the shepherd gestured with his crook towards Peregrine, who was not laughing—"he's tried to steal a member of the flock. That's a death sentence too, in addition to everything else we're planning to do to him."

The shepherd looked at the Elephant. "And, I know I should have asked before, but what in the Auld Witch's name is this?"

"I am a loyal member of the flock," said the Elephant humbly, in his deep voice, and the Marquis wondered if he had sounded so soulless and flat when he had been part of the flock. "I have remained loyal and in step even when this one did not."

"And the flock is grateful for all your hard work," said the shepherd. He reached out a hand and touched the sharp tip of one elephantine tusk experimentally. "I've never seen anything like you before, and if I never see another one again, it'll be too soon. Probably best if you die too."

The Elephant's ears twitched. "But I am of the flock . . ."

The shepherd looked up into the Elephant's huge face. "Better safe than sorry," he said. Then, to the Marquis: "Well? Where is this important letter?"

The Marquis de Carabas said, "It is inside my shirt. I must repeat that it is the most significant document that I have ever been charged to deliver. I must ask you not to look at it. For your own safety."

The shepherd tugged at the front of the Marquis' shirt. The buttons flew, and rattled off the walls onto the floor. The letter, in its sandwich bag, was in the pocket inside the shirt.

"This is most unfortunate. I trust you will read it aloud to us before we die," said the Marquis. "But whether or not you read it to us, I can promise that Peregrine and I will be holding our breath. Won't we, Peregrine?"

The shepherd opened the sandwich bag, then he looked at the envelope. He ripped it open and pulled a sheet of discolored paper from inside it. Dust came from the envelope as the paper came out. The dust hung in the still air in that dim room.

"'My darling beautiful Drusilla,'" read the shepherd aloud. "'While I know that you do not presently feel about me as I feel about you . . .' what *is* this nonsense?"

The Marquis said nothing. He did not even smile. He was, as he had stated, holding his breath; he was hoping that Peregrine had listened to him; and he was counting, because at that moment counting seemed like the best possible thing that he could do to distract himself from needing to breathe. He would soon need to breathe.

35 . . . 36 . . . 37 . . .

He wondered how long mushroom spores remained in the air.

43 . . . 44 . . . 45 . . . 46 . . .

The shepherd had stopped speaking.

The Marquis took a step backwards, fearing a knife in his ribs or teeth in his throat from the rough-furred guard-dog men, but there was nothing. He walked backwards, away from the dog-men, and the Elephant.

He saw that Peregrine was also walking backwards.

His lungs hurt. His heart was pounding in his temples, pounding almost loudly enough to drown out the thin ringing noise in his ears.

Only when the Marquis' back was against a bookcase on the wall and he was as far as he could possibly get from the envelope, he allowed himself to take a deep breath. He heard Peregrine breathe in too.

There was a stretching noise. Peregrine opened his mouth wide, and the tape dropped to the ground. "What," asked Peregrine, "was all that about?"

"Our way out of this room, and our way out of Shepherd's Bush, if I am not mistaken," said de Carabas. "As I so rarely am. Would you mind unbinding my wrists?"

He felt Peregrine's hands on his bound hands, and then the bindings fell away.

There was a low rumbling. "I'm going to kill somebody," said the Elephant. "As soon as I figure out who."

"Whoa, dear heart," said the Marquis, rubbing his hands together. "You mean *whom.*" The shepherd and the sheepdogs were taking awkward, experimental steps towards the door. "And I can assure you that you aren't going to kill anybody, not as long as you want to get home to the Castle safely."

The Elephant's trunk swished irritably. "I'm definitely going to kill *you.*"

The Marquis grinned. "You are going to force me to say *pshaw,*" he said. "Or *fiddlesticks.* Until now I have never had the slightest moment of yearning to say *fiddlesticks.* But I can feel it right now welling up inside me—"

"What, by the Temple and the Arch, has got into you?" asked the Elephant.

"Wrong question. But I shall ask the right question on your behalf. The question is actually what *hasn't* got into the three of us—it hasn't got into Peregrine and me because we were holding our breath, and it hasn't got into you because, I don't know, probably because you're an elephant, with nice thick skin, more likely because you were breathing through your trunk, which is down at ground level—and what did get into our captors. And the answer is, what hasn't got into us are the selfsame spores that have got into our portly shepherd and his pseudocanine companions."

"Spores of the Mushroom?" asked Peregrine. "The Mushroom People's the Mushroom?"

"Indeed. That selfsame Mushroom," agreed the Marquis.

"Blimming Heck," said the Elephant.

"Which is why," de Carabas told the Elephant, "if you attempt to kill me, or to kill Peregrine, you will not only fail but you will doom us all. Whereas if you shut up and we all do our best to look as if we are still part of the flock, then we have a chance. The spores will be threading their way into their brains now. And any moment now the Mushroom will begin calling them home."

A shepherd walked implacably. He held a wooden crook. Three men followed him. One of those men had the head of an elephant; one was tall and ridiculously handsome; and the last of the flock wore a most magnificent coat. It fit him perfectly, and it was the color of a wet street at night.

The flock were followed by guard dogs, who moved as if they were ready to walk through fire to get wherever they believed that they were going.

It was not unusual in Shepherd's Bush to see a shepherd and part of his flock moving from place to place, accompanied by several of the fiercest sheepdogs (who were human, or had been once). So when they saw a shepherd and three sheepdogs apparently leading three members of the flock away from Shepherd's Bush, none of the greater flock paid them any mind. The members of the flock who saw them simply did the same things they had always done, as members of the flock, and if they were aware that the influence of the shepherds had waned a little, then they patiently waited for another shepherd to come and to take care of them and to keep them safe from predators and from the world. It was a scary thing to be alone, after all.

Nobody noticed as they crossed the bounds of Shepherd's Bush, and still they kept on walking.

The seven of them reached the banks of the Kilburn, where they stopped, and the former shepherd and the three shaggy dog-men strode out into the water.

There was, the Marquis knew, nothing in the four men's heads at that moment but a need to get to the Mushroom, to taste its flesh once more, to let it live inside them, to serve it, and to serve it well. In exchange, the Mushroom would fix all the things about themselves that they hated: it would make their interior lives much happier and more interesting.

"Should've let me kill 'em," said the Elephant as the former shepherd and sheepdogs waded away.

"No point," said the Marquis. "Not even for revenge. The people who captured us don't exist any longer."

The Elephant flapped his ears hard, then scratched them vigorously. "Talking about revenge, who the hell did you steal my diary for anyway?" he asked.

"Victoria," admitted de Carabas.

"Not actually on my list of potential thieves. She's a deep one," said the Elephant, after a moment.

"I'll not argue with that," said the Marquis. "Also, she failed to pay me the entire amount agreed. I wound up obtaining my own *lagniappe* to make up the deficit."

He reached a dark hand into the inside of his coat. His fingers found the obvious pockets, and the less obvious, and then to his surprise, the least obvious of all. He reached inside it and pulled out a magnifying glass on a chain. "It was Victoria's," he said. "I believe you can use it to see through solid things. Perhaps this could be considered a small payment against my debt to you . . . ?"

The Elephant took something out of its own pocket—the Marquis could not see what it was—and squinted at it through the magnifying glass. Then the Elephant made a noise halfway between a delighted snort and a trumpet of satisfaction. "Oh fine, very fine," it said. It pocketed both of the objects. Then it said, "I suppose that saving my life outranks stealing my diary. And while I wouldn't have needed saving if I hadn't followed you down the drain, further recriminations are pointless. Consider your life your own once more."

"I look forward to visiting you in the Castle someday," said the Marquis.

"Don't push your luck, mate," said the Elephant, with an irritable swish of his trunk.

"I won't," said the Marquis, resisting the urge to point out that pushing his luck was the only way he had made it this far. He looked around and realized that Peregrine had slipped mysteriously and irritatingly away into the shadows, once more, without so much as a good-bye.

The Marquis hated it when people did that.

He made a small, courtly bow to the Elephant, and the Marquis' coat, his glorious coat, caught the bow, amplified it, made it perfect, and made it the kind of bow that only the Marquis de Carabas could ever possibly make. Whoever he was.

The next Floating Market was being held in Derry and Tom's Roof Garden. There had been no Derry and Tom's since 1973, but time and space and London Below had their own uncomfortable agreement, and the roof garden was younger and more innocent than it is today. The folk from London Above (they were young, and in an intense discussion, and they had stacked heels and paisley tops and bell-bottom flares, the men and the women) ignored the folk from London Below entirely.

The Marquis de Carabas strode through the roof garden as if he owned the place, walking swiftly until he reached the food court. He passed a tiny woman selling curling cheese sandwiches from a wheelbarrow piled high with the things, a curry stall, a short man with a huge glass bowl of pale white blind fish and a toasting fork, until, finally, he reached the stall that was selling the Mushroom.

"Slice of the Mushroom, well grilled, please," said the Marquis de Carabas.

The man who took his order was shorter than he was and still somewhat stouter. He had sandy, receding hair and a harried expression.

"Coming right up," said the man. "Anything else?"

"No, that's all." And then, curiously, the Marquis asked, "Do you remember me?"

"I am afraid not," said the Mushroom man. "But I must say, that is a most beautiful coat."

"Thank you," said the Marquis de Carabas. He looked around. "Where is the young fellow who used to work here?"

"Ah. That is a most curious story, sir," said the man. He did not yet smell of damp although there was a small encrustation of mushrooms on the side of his neck. "Somebody told the fair Drusilla, of the Court of the Raven, that our Vince had had designs upon her, and had—you may not credit it, but I am assured that it is so—apparently sent her a letter filled with spores with the intention of making her his bride in the Mushroom."

The Marquis raised an eyebrow quizzically, although he found none of this surprising. He had, after all, told Drusilla himself, and had even shown her the original letter. "Did she take well to the news?"

"I do not believe that she did, sir. I do not believe that she did. She and several of her sisters were waiting for Vince, and they all caught up with us on our way to the Market. She told him they had matters to discuss, of an intimate nature. He seemed delighted by this news, and went off with her to find out what these matters were. I have been waiting for him to arrive at the Market and come and work all evening, but I no longer believe he will be coming." Then the man said a little wistfully, "That is a very fine coat. It seems to me that I might have had one like it in a former life."

"I do not doubt it," said the Marquis de Carabas, satisfied with what he had heard, cutting into his grilled slice of the Mushroom, "but this particular coat is most definitely mine."

As he made his way out of the Market, he passed a clump of people descending the stairs and he paused and nodded at a young woman of uncommon grace. She had the long orange hair and the flattened profile of a Pre-Raphaelite beauty, and there was a birthmark in the shape of a five-pointed star on the back of one hand. Her other hand was stroking the head of a large, rumpled owl, which glared uncomfortably out at the world with eyes that were, unusually for such a bird, of an intense, pale blue.

The Marquis nodded at her, and she glanced awkwardly at him, then she looked away in the manner of someone who was now beginning to realize that she owed the Marquis a favor.

He nodded at her amiably, and continued to descend.

Drusilla hurried after him. She looked as if she had something she wanted to say.

The Marquis de Carabas reached the foot of the stairs ahead of her. He stopped for a moment, and he thought about people, and about things, and about how hard it is to do anything for the first time. And then, clad in his fine coat, he slipped mysteriously, even irritatingly, into the shadows, without so much as a good-bye, and he was gone.

Connie Willis

Connie Willis lives with her husband in Greeley, Colorado. She first attracted attention as a writer in the late seventies with a number of stories for the now-defunct magazine *Galileo,* and went on to establish herself as one of the most popular and critically acclaimed writers of the 1980s. In 1983, she won two Nebula Awards, one for her novelette "Fire Watch," and one for her short story "A Letter from the Clearys"; a few months later, "Fire Watch" went on to win her a Hugo Award as well. In 1989, her novella *The Last of the Winnebagos* won both the Nebula and the Hugo, and she won another Nebula in 1990 for her novelette "At the Rialto." In 1993, her landmark novel *Doomsday Book* won both the Nebula Award and the Hugo Award, as did her short story "Even the Queen." She won another Hugo in 1994 for her story "Death on the Nile," another in 1997 for her story "The Soul Selects Her Own Society," another in 1999 for her novel *To Say Nothing of the Dog,* another for her novella *The Winds of Marble Arch* in 2000, another in 2006 for her novella *Inside Job,* and yet *another* in 2008 for her novella *All Seated on the Ground*—capped off in 2011 by her most recent book, the massive two-volume novel *Blackout/All Clear,* winning *both* the Nebula and the Hugo Awards. In 2009 she was voted into The Science Fiction Hall of Fame, and in 2011, she received the SFWA Grand Master Award. All of which makes her the most honored writer in the history of science fiction, and the only person ever to win *two* Nebulas and *two* Hugos in the same year. Her other books include the novels *Water Witch, Light Raid,* and *Promised Land,* all written in collaboration with Cynthia Felice, *Lincoln's Dreams, Bellwether, Uncharted Territory, Remake,* and *Passage,* and, as editor, the anthologies *The New Hugo Winners, Volume III, Nebula Awards 33,* and (with Sheila Williams), *A Woman's*

Liberation: A Choice of Futures by and About Women. Her short fiction has been gathered in the collections *Fire Watch, Impossible Things,* and *Miracle and Other Christmas Stories.* Coming up is a huge retrospective collection, *The Best of Connie Willis.*

In the fast, funny, and furious story that follows, she takes us out for a night at the movies that turns out to be a lot trickier and more complicated than just buying a ticket.

NOW SHOWING

Connie Willis

"A charming, lighthearted comedy!"
—*Entertainment Daily*

The Saturday before Christmas break, Zara came into my dorm room and asked me if I wanted to go to the movies with her and Kett at the Cinedrome.

"What's playing?" I asked.

"I don't know," she said, shrugging. "Lots of stuff," which meant the point of going wasn't to see a movie at all. Big surprise.

"No, thanks," I said and went back to typing my econ paper.

"Oh, come on, Lindsay, it'll be fun," she said, flopping down on my bed. "*X-Force* is playing, and *The Twelve Days of Christmas* and the reboot of *Twilight.* The Drome's got a hundred movies. There must be *something* you want to see. How about *Christmas Caper*? Didn't you want to see that?"

Yes, I thought. At least I had eight months ago when I'd seen the preview. But things had changed since then.

"I can't," I said. "I've got to study."

"We've *all* got to study," Zara said. "But it's *Christmas.* The Drome will be all decorated and everybody will be there."

"Exactly, which means the light rail will be packed and security will take *forever.*"

"Is this about Jack?"

"Jack?" I said, wondering if I could get away with, "Jack who?"

Better not. This was Zara. I said instead, "Why would my not going to the Drome with you have anything to do with Jack Weaver?"

"It's . . . I don't know," she stammered, "it's just that you've been so . . . grim since he left, and you two used to watch a lot of movies together."

That was an understatement. Jack was the only guy I'd ever met who liked movies as much as I did, and all kinds, not just comic-book-hero and slasher films. He'd loved everything from Bollywood to romcoms like *French Kiss* to black-and-whites like *The Shop Around the Corner* and *Captain Blood,* and we'd gone to dozens of them at the Drome and streamed hundreds more in the semester we'd been together. Correction, semester minus one week.

Zara was still talking. "And you haven't gone to the Drome once since—"

"Since you talked me into going with you to see *Monsoon Gate,*" I said, "and then when we got there you wanted to eat and talk to guys, and I never did get to see it."

"That won't happen this time. Kett and I promise we'll go to the movie. Come on, it'll be good for you. There'll be tons of guys there. Remember that Sig Tau who said he liked you? Noah? *He* might be there. Come on. *Please* come with us. This is our last chance. We won't be able to go next weekend because of finals, and then we'll be gone on break."

And nobody at home would want to see *Christmas Caper.* If I suggested going to the movies, my sister would insist on us going to *A Despicable Me Noel* with her kids, and we'd end up spending the whole afternoon in the arcade playing Minion Mash and buying *Madagascar* stuffed giraffes and *Ice Age* Icees. By the time I got back to school, *Christmas Caper* would be gone. And it wasn't like Jack would magically show up and take me like he'd promised. If I wanted to see it on the big screen, I needed to do it now.

"Okay," I said. "But I'm not going with you to meet guys. I'm going because I really want to see *Christmas Caper.* Understood?"

"Yeah, sure," she said, getting out her phone and punching keys. "I'll just text Kett and—"

"I mean it," I said. "You have to promise me you won't get sidetracked like last time, that we'll actually go to the movie."

"I promise," she said. "No guys and no eating till afterward."

"And no shopping," I said. I had missed *Monsoon Gate* because Zara was trying on Polly Pepper shoes in *The Devil Wears Prada* boutique. "Promise me."

Zara sighed. "Fine. I promise. Cross my heart."

"A sweet romantic comedy with lots of action!"
—*popcorn.com*

Zara's promise meant about as much as the ones Jack had made me. Zara began texting the second we arrived, and we weren't even through the preliminary bag and phone check at the Drome before Kett said, "The NWU guys behind me in line just asked me to ask you if we want to go see the cast of *The Bourne Dynasty.* They're holo-skyping over at the Universal booth."

Zara looked hopefully at me. "We could go to the 12:10 instead of the ten o'clock."

"Or the 2:20," Kett said.

"No," I said.

"Sorry," Zara said to the guys. "We promised Lindsay we'd go to *Christmas Caper* with her first," and they promptly began hitting on the girls behind them.

"I don't see why we couldn't have gone to a later showing," Kett said, pouting, as we went through the explosives check.

"Because after the holo-skyping was over, they'd have wanted to play Skyfall or go eat at Harold and Kumar's White Castle, and we'd have missed the 2:20 *and* the 4:30," I said, and as soon as we made it through the body- and retinal-scans and into the Drome, I headed straight for the tickets kiosks, ignoring the barrage of previews and holograms and ads and elves passing out coupons for free cookies and video games and schedules of today's autographing sessions.

"I thought you were going to get the tickets online before we left," Zara said.

"I tried," I said, "but it's playing a special limited engagement, so you have to get them here." I dragged my finger down the list of movies—*Ripper 2, X-Force, The House on Zombie Hill, The Queen's Consort, Switching Gears, Just When You Thought You Were Over Him . . .*

Honestly, you'd think with a hundred movies, they'd put them in alphabetical order. *Lethal Rampage, The Twelve Days of Christmas, Texas Chainsaw Massacre—The Musical, A Star-Crossed Season, Back to Back to the Future, Wicked—*

Here it was. *Christmas Caper.* I tapped the tickets button and "3" and swiped my card.

"Unavailable," the screen said. "Tickets must be purchased at ticket counter," which meant we had to get in line, one of the worst things about going to the Drome.

You'd think as huge as it is and as many people as it has to cope with, they'd have Disneyverse-style back-and-forth lines, but they only use those to line people up for showings. The tickets lines snaked single file all the way back through the Drome's football-field-sized lobby, the *Hunger Games* paintball stadium, the No Reservations food court, Wetaworks' Last Homely House, the virtual-reality terrace, and half a mile of souvenir shops and boutiques.

It took us twenty minutes just to find the end, and in the process we nearly lost Kett twice, once at Pretty in Pink—"Oh, my God! They have stilettos in fifty shades of gray!"—and again when she saw that Hope Floats, Shakes, and Cones was selling cranberry malts.

Zara and I dragged her out of both and into the end of the line, which was getting longer by the minute. "We're never going to get into the movie," Kett grumbled.

"Yes, we will," I said confidently, though I wasn't sure. There were so many people in line, though most of them were little kids, who were obviously going to *The Little Goose Girl* or The Muppets' *It's a Wonderful Life* or *Dora the Explorer Does Duluth.* The adults around us who I asked were all going to *A Tudor Affair* or *Return to the Best Exotic Marigold Hotel,* and everybody else was wearing an *Ironman 8* T-shirt. "We'll definitely get in."

"We'd better," Kett said. "Why are you so set on seeing this *Christmas Caper,* anyway? I never heard of it. Is it a romcom?"

"No," I said, "more like a romantic spy adventure. Like *Charade.* Or *The Thirty-Nine Steps.*"

"I haven't seen previews for either of those," she said, looking up at the schedule board above us. "Are they still playing?"

"No." I should have known better than to mention an old movie. In this day of reboots and remakes nobody watches anything older than last week. Except Jack. He'd even liked silents.

"You know, the kind of movie where the heroine gets accidentally caught up in a crime," I said, "or some kind of conspiracy, and the hero's a spy, like in *Jumpin' Jack Flash,* or a reporter, or a detective who's pretending to be a criminal, like in *How to Steal a Million,* or he's a scoundrel—"

"A scoundrel?" Kett said blankly.

"A rebel," I said, "a rake, a rogue, like Michael Douglas in *Romancing the Stone,* or Errol Flynn—"

"I haven't seen previews for those either," she said. "Is *Arrow Flin* still playing?"

"No," I said. "A scoundrel's a guy who's cocky and doesn't care about rules or laws—"

"Oh, you mean a slimewad," Kett said.

"*No,* a scoundrel's funny and sexy and charming," I said, trying desperately to think of a movie recent enough that she might have seen it. "Like Ironman. Or Jack Sparrow."

"Or Jack Weaver," Zara said.

"No," I said, "*not* like Jack Weaver. In the first place—"

"Who's Jack Weaver?" Kett asked.

"This guy Lindsay used to be in love with," Zara said.

"I was not in—"

"Wait," Kett said. "Is that the guy who put a whole bunch of ducks in the dean's office last year?"

"Geese," I said.

"Wow!" Kett said, impressed. "You went with him?"

"Briefly," I said. "Before I found out he was—"

"A scoundrel?" Zara put in.

"No," I said. "A slimewad. Who got himself thrown out of Hanover. The week before he was supposed to graduate."

"He didn't actually get thrown out," Zara explained to Kett. "He took off before they could expel him."

"Or press criminal charges," I said.

"That's too bad," Kett said. "He sounds totally *depraved*! I'd have liked to meet him."

"You might get your chance," Zara said in an odd voice. "Look!" She pointed toward the lobby.

And there, leaning against a pillar with his hands in his pockets, looking up at the movie schedule, was Jack Weaver.

> "Exciting fun! Sets your pulse racing!"
> —*USA Today*

"It *is* him, isn't it?" Zara asked.

"Yes," I said grimly.

"I wonder what he's doing here."

"As if you didn't know," I said. No wonder she'd been so insistent I come with them. She and Jack had cooked up a—

"Oh, my God!" Kett cried. "Is *that* the guy you were talking about? The—what did you call him?"

"Wanker," I said.

"Scoundrel," Zara said.

"Right, the scoundrel. You didn't tell me he was so hot! I mean, he's positively scorching!"

"Shh," I said, but it was too late. Jack had already looked over and seen us.

"Zara," I said, "if you set this up, I'm never speaking to you again!"

"I didn't, I swear," she said, which didn't mean anything, but two things made me inclined to believe her. One was that even though this looked suspiciously like a movie "meet cute," the expression on Zara's face had been completely stricken, the reason for which became apparent a few seconds later when a trio of Sig Taus, including Noah, sauntered up way too casually.

"Wow!" Noah said. "I had no idea you three were coming to the Drome today, too."

Except for Zara's texting you fifteen times while we were in the security lines, I thought. But at least their being here would keep Jack from coming over to talk to me.

If he even wanted to. Because the other reason I thought Zara didn't have anything to do with Jack's being here had been the look on *his* face. He'd looked not just surprised to see me here, but dismayed. Which meant I was right—he wasn't a scoundrel, he was a slimewad. And probably here with some other girl.

"I'm especially surprised to see *you* here, Lindsay," Noah, who would never make it as an actor even in the *Twilight* movies, said. "What are you doing at the Drome?"

"The three of us," I said, emphasizing the word "three," "are going to a movie."

"Oh," he said, frowning at Zara, who gave him a "go on" look. "We were just going to get something to eat at the Mos Eisley Cantina, and we wondered if you'd like to come with us."

"Oh, I *love* the Cantina," Kett cooed.

"I'll buy you a Darth Vader daiquiri," Noah said to me.

"Lindsay prefers Pimm's Cups," Zara said. "Don't you?"

I glanced toward the lobby, hoping against hope Jack hadn't heard that.

He wasn't there. He wasn't at the end of the line either, or at the ticket machines. Good, he'd gone off to meet his new girlfriend. I hoped she hated movies.

Noah was saying, "What the hell's a Pimm's Cup?"

"It's a drink from a movie," I said. *My favorite drink,* I added silently. Or at least it used to be. The drink Jack had made me after we'd watched *Ghost Town* and Téa Leoni had said it was *her* favorite drink.

"We could have lunch and *then* go to the movie, couldn't we, Lindsay?" Kett asked, looking adoringly at Noah. "I just got a text coupon for Breakfast at Tiffany's breakfast bar."

"No," I said.

Zara gave Noah another nudging look, and he said, "Maybe we could go with you. What are you going to?"

"Christmas Caper," Kett said.

"I never heard of it," Noah said.

"It's a spy adventure," Kett explained. "A *romantic* spy adventure."

Noah made a face. "Are you kidding me? I *hate* romcoms. How about we all go see *Lethal Rampage* instead?"

"No," I said.

"Maybe we could meet you at the Cantina after the movie," Zara suggested.

"Yeah, I don't know," Noah mumbled, looking at the other guys. "We're pretty hungry. Listen, I'll text you," he said, and the three of them wandered off.

"I can't believe you did that," Zara said. "I was just trying to help you forget about—"

"That Noah guy was scorching," Kett said, looking after him, and sighed. "This better be some movie."

"It is," Jack said at my elbow. "Hi."

"What are you doing here?" I demanded.

"Going to the movies," he said. "What else?" He leaned toward me. "Traitor," he said in my ear. "You promised you'd go to *Christmas Caper* with me."

"You weren't here," I said coldly.

"Yeah, about that," he said. "Sorry. Something came up. I—"

"Is it really a good movie?" Kett asked, sidling over to him. "Lindsay didn't tell us what it was about. All she said was that there was a scoundrel in it."

"Scoundrel," Jack said, raising an eyebrow at me. "I like the sound of that."

"How do you like the sound of 'loser'?" I said. "Or 'slimewad'?"

He ignored me. "Actually," he said to Kett, "he's an undercover agent working on a case, and it's classified, so he can't tell the heroine about it or why he had to leave town—"

"Nice try," I said, and to Kett, "What it's *really* about is this creep who tells the heroine a bunch of lies, does something staggeringly stupid, and then goes off without a *word*—"

"Why don't you come with us, Jack?" Kett interrupted, looking up at him hungrily. "I'm Kett, by the way. I'm friends with Lindsay, but she didn't tell me you were so—"

Zara pushed between them. "Kett and I actually wanted to go play drone tag with these Pi Kappas, Jack," she said. "We—"

"*What* Pi Kappas?" Kett demanded.

Zara ignored her. "We were just going to the movie with Lindsay to keep her company, but now that you're here, you could take her."

"I'd love to," Jack said, frowning, "but unfortunately I can't."

"He has to put a flock of geese a-laying in the theater where *The Twelve Days of Christmas* is showing," I said. "Or is it partridges this time, Jack?"

"Swans a-swimming," he said, grinning. "I've got eight of them in my pocket."

"Really?" Kett said, as if it was actually possible to get *anything* through security, let alone a flock of swans.

"That would be so *depraved*!" she purred. "What you did to the dean's office was so amazing! You definitely should come with us to *Christmas Caper*!"

"I have no intention of going anywhere with Jack," I said.

"Then I will." Kett tucked her arm cozily in his. "The two of us can go see it."

"Yeah, well, I'm sure that would be fun," Jack said, disentangling himself from her like she was barbed wire, "but it's not gonna happen. We can't get in. It's sold-out."

"It *is* not," I said, pointing up at the schedule board. "Look."

"Not right now maybe, but trust me, it will be by the time you get to the front of the line."

"You're kidding," Zara said. "After we've stood in line all this time?"

"And told Noah we couldn't go to the Cantina with him," Kett added.

"It's *not* going to be sold-out," I said confidently.

"Wrong," Jack said, pointing at the board, where NO TICKETS AVAILABLE had begun flashing next to *Christmas Caper.*

"An engrossing mystery . . ."
—*flickers.com*

"Oh, no," Zara said. "What do we do now?"

"We could go see *A Star-Crossed Season,*" Kett said to Jack. "It's supposed to be really good. Or *The Diary.*"

"We're not going to either one," I said. "Just because the 12:10 of *Christmas Caper*'s sold-out doesn't mean the other showings are. We can still get tickets to the 2:20."

"And wait around for another two *hours*?" Kett wailed.

"Why don't we get lunch first and then get the tickets?" Zara said. "We could go to Chocolat—"

"No," I said. "This is not going to turn into another *Monsoon Gate.* We are staying right here till we get our tickets."

"How about you stay in line, Lindsay, and we go and bring you back something?" Kett suggested.

"No," I said. "You promised you'd go with me."

"Yeah, and you promised you'd go with *me,* Lindsay," Jack said.

"You stood me up."

"I did not," he said. "I'm here, aren't I? And anyway, Kevin Kline stood up Meg Ryan in *French Kiss.* Michael Douglas stood up Kathleen Turner in *Romancing the Stone.* Indiana Jones left Marion tied up in the bad guys' tent. Admit it, that's what scoundrels do."

"Yes, well, but they don't throw their entire future away on some stupid prank."

"You mean the geese? That wasn't a prank."

"Oh, really? Then what was it?"

"I can see you two have a lot of stuff to discuss," Zara said. "We don't want to get in the way. We'll catch up with you later. Text me." And before I could protest, she and Kett had vanished into the crowd.

I turned to Jack. "I'm still not going with you to see it."

"True," he said, looking over at the ticket counter. "You're not going to get in to the 2:20 either."

"I suppose now you're going to tell me it'll be sold-out, too?"

"No, they usually don't use that one twice," he said. "This time it'll be something more subtle. Free tickets to a Special Christmas Showing of *The Shop Around the Corner* or a personal appearance by the new

Hulk. Or, since you like scoundrels, of the new Han Solo." He grinned. "Or me."

"I do *not* like scoundrels," I said. "Not anymore. And what do you mean, 'they don't use that one twice'?"

He shook his head disapprovingly. "*That's* not your line. You're supposed to say, 'I happen to like nice men,' and then I say, '*I'm* a nice man.'" He leaned toward me. "And then *you* say—"

"This is not *The Empire Strikes Back,*" I snapped, backing away from him. "And you are not Han Solo."

"True," he said. "I'm more like Peter O'Toole in *How to Steal a Million.* Or Douglas Fairbanks in *The Mask of Zorro.*"

"Or Bradley Cooper in *The World's Biggest Liar,*" I said. "Why did you say I'm not going to get in to the 2:20 either? Have you done something to the theater?"

"Nope, not a thing. I swear." He held up his right hand.

"Yes, well, your word isn't exactly trustworthy, is it?"

"Actually, it is. It's just that . . . Never mind. I promise you I didn't have anything to do with the 12:10 being sold-out."

"Then why were you so sure it was going to be?"

"Long story. Which I can't tell you here," he said, looking around. "What say we go somewhere quiet and I'll explain everything?"

"Including where you've been for the past eight months? And what possessed you to put those geese in the dean's office?"

"No," he said. "Sorry, I can't until—"

"Until what? Until you've done the same thing here?" I lowered my voice. "Seriously, Jack, you could get in a *lot* of trouble. The Dromes have really heavy security—"

"I *knew* it," he said delightedly. "You're still crazy about me. 'So what say we go discuss this over a nice cozy lunch,' as Peter said to Audrey in *How to Steal a Million.* There's a little place over on Pixar Boulevard called Gusteau's—"

"I am not going anywhere with you," I said. "I am going to the 2:20 showing of *Christmas Caper.* By myself."

"That's what you think," he said.

"Watch the sparks fly between these two!"
—*The Web Critic*

Jack had sauntered off before I could demand to know what "That's what you think" meant, and I couldn't go after him to ask for fear of losing my place in line, so I spent the rest of the wait to get tickets worrying that the 2:20 would be sold-out, too, though there were only a couple of dozen people left ahead of me, they were all going to something else, and the schedule boards were still showing tickets were available.

But there were three other lines, and the ticket seller on mine apparently had the brain of a character in *Dumb and Really Really Dumb.* It took him forever to make change and/or swipe people's cards and then shove their tickets at them. It was a good thing I wasn't trying to get a ticket for the 1:10. I'd never have made it.

It was half past before I even got close to the ticket counter, and then the guy three people ahead of me couldn't make up his mind whether to see *Zombie Prom* or *Avatar 4.* He and his girlfriend spent a good ten minutes trying to decide, and then his card wouldn't swipe and they had to use his girlfriend's, and *she* had to search through her entire bag to find it, digging out handfuls of stuff for him to hold while she looked and standing there to put it all back after they'd finally gotten the tickets.

This is exactly what Jack was talking about, I thought. What if they were doing it purposely to keep me from getting in?

Don't be ridiculous, I told myself. *You're seeing conspiracies where they don't exist.* But I still looked anxiously up at the schedule board as I came up to the counter, afraid the NO TICKETS AVAILABLE would blink on at the last minute.

It didn't, and when I said, "One adult for the 2:20 showing of *Christmas Caper,*" the ticket seller nodded, swiped my card without incident, handed me my ticket, and told me to enjoy the show.

"I will," I said determinedly and started toward the entrance of the theater complex.

Halfway there, Jack suddenly reappeared and fell in step with me. "Well?" he said.

"They weren't sold-out, and I didn't have any trouble getting a ticket. See?" I said, showing it to him.

He wasn't impressed. "Yeah, and in *Romancing the Stone,* they found the diamond," he said, "and Whoopi Goldberg got Jumpin' Jack Flash an exit contact, and look what happened."

"What is that supposed to mean?"

"It means you're not in the theater yet, and if you don't make it by 2:20, they won't let you in."

That was true—it was part of the Drome's security precautions not to let anyone in to a movie after it had started—but it was only 1:30. I told Jack that.

"Yeah, but the line to get in could be really long, or the line to buy popcorn."

"I'm not buying popcorn. And there isn't any line to get in," I said, pointing over at the usher standing all alone in the entrance to the theaters.

"At the moment," he said. "You're not there yet. A horde of middle-aged women could show up for the new *Fifty Shades of Grey* before you get over to the usher. And even if you do make it into the theater, the film could break—"

"The Drome doesn't use film. It's all digital."

"Exactly, which means something could go wrong with the digital feed. It could be contaminated by a virus, or the server could crash. Or something could trigger the TSA's alarms and send the whole Drome into lockdown."

"Like setting geese loose in a theater?" I said. "What are you up to, Jack?"

"I told you, *I'm* not up to anything. I'm just saying you might not get in. In fact, I'm almost certain you won't. And if you don't, I'll be at Gusteau's."

"Nothing is going to happen," I said and started across the remaining half of the lobby toward the entrance and the usher.

The lobby was getting more crowded by the minute with gaggles of excited children and texting teenagers and families arguing about where to go first. I pushed past and around them, hoping a line wouldn't suddenly collect in front of the usher and prove Jack right, but the usher was still standing there alone, leaning on the ticket stand and looking bored.

I handed him my ticket.

He handed it back. "You can't go in yet. The movie's not over. Excuse me," he said, and reached around me to take the tickets of two eight-year-old boys who'd come up behind me.

He tore their tickets in half and handed them back. "Theater 76. Up the stairs to the third floor and turn right."

The boys went in. I said, "Can't I go in and wait in the hall outside the theater till it lets out?"

He shook his head. "It's against security regulations. I can't let anybody in till the movie gets out."

"Which is when?"

"I'll check," he said, and consulted the schedule. "1:55." Ten minutes from now. "If you don't want to wait—"

"I do." I moved over against the wall, out of the way.

"Sorry, you can't stand there," a manager said, coming up. "That's where the line for *Dr. Who: The Movie* has to go." He began busily cordoning off the space.

I moved to the other wall, but a bunch of little girls and their parents were already lining up there to get in to see *The Little Goose Girl,* and the sole bench near the door was occupied by a mother vainly trying to talk her two daughters into relinquishing their virtual-reality glasses. Shrieking was involved. And kicking.

I was going to have to wait out the ten minutes in the lobby. *Hopefully Jack's gone off to Gusteau's,* I thought, but he hadn't. He was standing just outside the entrance with his hands in his pockets and an "I told you so" smile on his face. "What happened?" he asked.

"Nothing happened," I said, walking past him. "The 12:10's not out yet."

"So you decided to have that talk with me after all. Great," he said, taking hold of my arm and propelling me through the lobby toward Pixar Boulevard. "We can go to Gusteau's and you can tell me what excuse the usher gave you for not letting you in and why they wouldn't let you wait there in the entryway."

"I don't have any intention of telling you *anything,*" I said, wrenching my arm free of him. "Why should I? You didn't tell *me* you were planning to get yourself expelled a week before you were supposed to graduate."

"Yeah, about that," he said, frowning. "I wasn't actually going to graduate—"

"Of course not," I said disgustedly. "Why am I not surprised? Was that why you broke into the dean's office, because you were flunking out and you were trying to change your grades?"

"No," he said. "The fact is, I wasn't actually—"

"You weren't what?"

"I can't tell you," he said. "It's classified."

"Classified!" I said. "That's it. I'm not listening to any more of your paranoid fantasies. I am going to go stand over by the entrance until this movie gets out," I said, pointing, "and then I am going inside, and if you try to follow me, I'll report you to security."

I fought my way back to the entryway through a mob of cloaked and hairy-footed Hobbits who were obviously on their way to *The Return of Frodo,* a bunch of old ladies going to see a special Nostalgia Showing of *Sex and the City,* and the mazelike line for *Dr. Who,* which now extended ten yards out into the lobby. By the time I made it to where I intended to wait, there was no longer any reason to. It was already two o'clock.

I went over to the usher and handed him my ticket.

He shook his head. "You can't go in yet."

"But you said the 12:10 got out at 1:55."

"It did, but you can't go in till the crew finishes cleaning."

"Which will be when?"

He shrugged. "I don't know. Some guy threw up all over. It's going to take them at least twenty minutes to clean it up." He handed me back my ticket. "Why don't you go get something to eat? Or do some Christmas shopping? They're having a sale on Inception sleep masks over at the Sleepless in Seattle shop."

And Jack will be standing right outside of it, smirking, I thought. "No, thanks," I said, and squeezed past the *Dr. Who* and *Little Goose Girl* lines to the bench, hoping the mother and girls had gone.

They had, but the bench was now completely taken up by a passionately kissing and practically horizontal couple. I edged past them to stand by the wall, but by the time I made it, the couple had reached the R-rated stage and was rapidly approaching NC-17. I braced myself for Jack and another round of conspiracy theories and went back out into the lobby again.

> "A gift for holiday moviegoers!"
> —*silverscreen.com*

Jack wasn't there. But he—and Zara and Kett—were the only ones who weren't in the lobby. It was crammed to bursting with people checking their coats and buying tickets and refreshments and staring up at the previews and schedule boards. I found myself alternately jostled and smushed by the crowds going into and coming out of the theater complex and by kids mobbing the Christmas characters who meandered through, tossing candy canes and distributing Coming Attractions flyers. Alvin the Chipmunk gave me a chit for a free mince pie at Sweeney Todd's snack bar, and a frighteningly friendly Grinch presented me with a coupon for half off a *Twelve Dancing Princesses* T-shirt at the Disney Pavilion.

I'd no sooner handed it off to a NewGoth girl and read a text on my phone, telling me I'd won a free ticket to a special Encore Presentation of *Ghost Town,* than I was nearly run down by an enormous Transformer stomping through the crowd, flailing his huge metal arms and nearly bumping his head against the lobby ceiling. I partly dived and was partly pushed out of its way by the crowd as it scattered and ended up on the opposite side of the lobby.

The crowd surged back toward the Transformer, snapping pictures on their cell phones, jockeying for position to have their photos taken with it, their backs forming an impenetrable wall. There was no way I was getting through that, at least till the Transformer left.

It didn't matter—it was still fifteen minutes till they'd be finished cleaning. I turned to look for a place I could wait without being run down. *Not* Gusteau's—I had no desire to hear Jack say "I told you so." And not Sweeney Todd's. It was too far away.

I needed someplace close so I could start back the second the crowd dwindled or the moment I saw the cleaning crew give the usher the high sign, and someplace with a short line, but finding one was practically impossible. Zombie Juice was even more mobbed than the lobby. *Stargate*'s Starbucks, which was advertising Mistletoe Mochas, had a line merging over into Zombie Juice, and the Transformer had apparently been passing out coupons for a Transformer Tea because Tea and Sympathy, usually a safe bet, was jammed, too.

And I was definitely not going to the Cantina even though at this point I could have used a drink. But Jack had obviously sent that text, which meant he was waiting in the Cantina to get me drunk and tell me more conspiracy theories. I was *not* going there.

That left a hot cocoa at the Polar Express, which was just off the lobby and whose line only had two people in it, but even then it took forever. The guy at the counter wanted a gingerbread clove latte, which the barista didn't know how to make, so he had to give her step-by-step instructions, and then the teenager behind him couldn't get her swipe card to work.

I looked back out at the lobby. The Transformer was gone, but now the zeppelin from *The Steampunk League* was floating above the ticket machines, throwing down gift cards on a converging crowd. If I didn't go soon, the lobby would be even more jammed than it had been with the Transformer.

I decided I'd better bag the cocoa and head back, and I started for the door. And collided with the gingerbread guy, who was bringing his latte back for having insufficient whipped cream and who managed to spill the entire drink down my front.

Customers converged with napkins and commiserations, and the barista insisted on my waiting while she fetched a wet rag. "That's okay," I said. "I'm kind of in a hurry. I have a movie I need to get to."

"It'll just take a sec," she said, running back to the counter. "You can't go all wet like that."

"I'm fine," I said and started for the door.

The gingerbread man grabbed my arm. "I insist on buying you a drink to apologize," he said. "What would you like?"

"Nothing, really," I said. "I need to go—" and the barista came over with the rag and began swabbing me down.

"That's not necessary. Really," I said, brushing her away.

"You're not going to sue the Polar Express, are you?" she asked tearfully.

Yes, I thought, *if I miss this movie because of you.* "No, of course not," I said. "I'm fine. No harm done."

"Oh, good," she said. "If you'll hang on just a minute, I'll get you a coupon for a free scone the next time you come."

"I don't want—"

"At least let me pay for the cleaners," the guy said, getting out his phone. "If you'll give me your e-mail address—"

"On second thought," I said, "I think I would like that drink. A peppermint chai," and when he started for the counter, I darted out of the Polar Express, into the protective cover of the crowd, and into the lobby.

It was even more crowded than it had been with the Transformer. I pushed into the scrum and started across, and it was a good thing I hadn't gotten my cocoa. I had to bull my way through with both hands, prying couples apart and slipping between them, pushing aside excited kids in bright blue *A Smurf Hanukkah* T-shirts and teenagers staring up at *House on Zombie Hill* previews.

It was like swimming through molasses, and it seemed to take hours to get to a place where I could finally see the usher. There was a line in front of him now, but it wasn't the *Dr. Who* or the *Little Goose Girl* people, who were still waiting in their mazelike lines. I needed to get over to him before those movies got out, or I'd never get in to *Christmas*—

Someone grabbed me by my arm. *Please don't let it be the Gingerbread Man,* I thought as I was yanked back into the center of the crowd.

It wasn't. It was Santa Claus, with a microphone and a phalanx of reindeer. "What do you want for Christmas, little girl?" he asked, sticking the mike in my face.

"To get over there," I said, pointing.

"Ho ho ho," he said. "How would you like a nice pair of tickets to the 3:25 showing of *The Claus Chronicles*?"

"No, thank you," I said. "I'm going to see *Christmas Caper.*"

"What?" he said. "You don't want to see Santa's own movie?"

He turned to his reindeer. "Did you hear that, Prancer?" he said, loudly enough for the entire lobby to hear. "We have a problem here. I think I need to check my naughty-and-nice list, Blitzen." The list was duly produced, Santa put on a pair of spectacles, and he ran a very slow finger down it while I looked longingly over at the entrance to the theaters, where the line in front of the usher was growing longer by the minute.

"Here she is," Santa finally announced. "Yes, definitely naughty. And what do we give naughty children for Christmas, Vixen?"

"Coal!" the crowd shouted.

Santa reached into his sack and produced a lump of licorice. "Shall I give this to her or shall we give her another chance? After all, it is Christmas."

"Coal!" the crowd bellowed, and Santa had to ask them two more times to persuade them to offer me the tickets again, which this time I had the sense to take.

"And here's a ticket to the 2:30 showing of *The Twelve Days of Christmas* for being such a good sport," he said. "*Merry* Christmas, ho ho ho," and I was finally free.

I shot over to the entrance, where the line in front of the usher had miraculously disappeared, and handed the usher my ticket. "Sorry," he said, handing it back.

"They're *still* cleaning?" I asked incredulously.

"No, but you're late. It's 2:22. The 2:20's already started."

"But they do previews for the first fifteen minutes—"

"Sorry. It's theater policy. No one's allowed in after the start time. I think you can still get tickets to the 4:30."

I don't, I thought, *and I know who's responsible.*

"Do you want me to check and see if there are still tickets available?" he asked.

"No, that's okay. Never mind," I said and went out, across the lobby, and into the wilds of the Drome to find Jack.

"A great movie! Don't miss it!"
—*Time Out Magazine*

I'd expected Gusteau's to be a bar somewhere near the dance clubs and Rick's from *Casablanca,* but it wasn't, and after consulting two maps and a Drome guide dressed as Frosty the Snowman, I found it in the depths of Munchkinland, sandwiched between the *Monsters, Inc.* ball pool and the *Despicable Me* moon drop, both of which were filled with toddlers emitting ear-slashing shrieks of joy and/or terror.

The restaurant was a replica of the French bistro in *Ratatouille,* with rats on the wallpaper and the tables. Jack was seated at a table at the back. "Hi," he shouted over the din from the ball pool. "Didn't get back in, huh?"

"No," I said grimly.

"Sit down. Would you like something to drink? Gusteau's is G-rated, so I can't offer you a Pimm's Cup, but I can get you a mouse mocha."

"No, thank you," I said, ignoring his invitation to sit down. "I want to know what you're up to and why you saw to it I didn't—"

"Hey, what happened to you?" he interrupted, pointing at my still-wet top. "Don't tell me you collided with Hugh Grant carrying an orange juice, like in *Notting Hill*?"

"No," I said through gritted teeth, "a gingerbread latte—"

"And they wouldn't let you in because of the Drome's dress code?"

"*No,* they wouldn't let me in because the movie had already started. Because a guy with a gingerbread latte and Santa Claus kept me from getting back from the Polar Express in time, as you well know. You're the one who put them up to it. This is just another one of your adolescent pranks, isn't it?"

"I told you, that wasn't a prank."

"Then, what was it?"

"It . . . you remember when we watched *Oceans 17,* and there's a break-in at the casino? Cops, sirens, helicopters, the whole nine yards? But that's just a diversion, and the real crime is taking place over at the bank?"

"You're saying the geese were a diversion?"

"Yeah. Just like Santa Claus. What did he do to delay you?"

"You know perfectly well what he did. You hired him to do it so I wouldn't get in and I'd have to go with you. But it won't work. I have no intention of seeing *Christmas Caper* with you."

"Good," he said, "because you're not going to. Not today, anyway."

"Why not? What did you do?"

"Nothing. I'm not the one responsible for any of this."

"Really?" I said sarcastically. "And who is?"

"If you'll sit down, I'll tell you. I'll also tell you why the 12:10 was sold out, why *The Steampunk League* sent its zeppelin over when it did, and why you couldn't buy tickets to *Christmas Caper* online."

"How did you know that?"

"Lucky guess. The ticket machines wouldn't let you buy them either, would they?"

"No," I said and sat down. "Why not?"

"I need to know something first. What were you doing at the Polar Express? When I left you, you were handing the usher your ticket."

"He wouldn't let me in. Some guy threw up in the theater."

"Ah, yes, good old vomit. Works every time. But why didn't you just wait there in the entryway?"

I told him about the *Dr. Who* and *Goose Girl* lines and the bench people.

"Did anything else happen while you were waiting? Anybody send you a text telling you you'd won free tickets to something?"

"Yes." I told him about the Encore Presentation of *Ghost Town.* "Which you can't tell me you didn't put them up to. Who else would know *Ghost Town* was one of my favorite movies?"

"Who, indeed?" he said. "When we were in line, you said, 'This isn't going to turn into another *Monsoon Gate.*' I take it you didn't get in to that movie either. Why not? Did the same thing happen?"

"No," I said. I told him about Zara trying on shoes and us missing the six o'clock showing. "And then she got a tweet saying there was going to be a special preview of *Bachelorette Party*—"

"Which, let me guess, was a movie she really wanted to see?"

"Yes," I said. "So we decided to go to the ten o'clock, but when we checked its running time, it didn't get out till—"

"After the last light rail back to Hanover," he said, nodding. "Are you sure you don't want something to drink? A rat root beer? A vermin vanilla coke?"

"No. Why are we here anyway?" I asked, looking around. "Surely there's someplace we could go to that we wouldn't have to shout."

"This and the Tunnel of Love are the only areas not under surveillance. We could go do that."

I had been in the Tunnel of Love with Jack before. "No," I said.

"I heard they've got some new features that are really romantic—Anne Hathaway dying of consumption, Keira Knightley being hit by a train, Edward and Bella catching fire on their wedding night and burning to a crisp—"

"We are *not* going in the Tunnel of Love," I said. "What do you mean, these are the only areas not under surveillance?"

"I mean, there's no need to distract kids from going to see *Ice Age 22,*" he said. "Kids *invented* the short attention span. You, on the other hand, have been remarkably single-minded, hence the vomit. And the Gingerbread Man."

"You're saying the *Drome* was the one trying to keep me from seeing *Christmas Caper*?"

"Yup."

"But why?"

"Okay, so you know how this all started, that after the *Batman* and Metrolux and *Hobbit III* massacres, movie attendance totally tanked, and they had to come up with some way to get the public back, so they turned the theaters into fortresses where people felt safe bringing their kids and sending their teenagers. But to do that, they had to introduce all kinds of security—metal detectors, full-body scans, explosives sniffers, and that meant people were standing in line for an hour and forty-five minutes to see a two-hour movie, which only made attendance drop off more. Who wants to stand in a line when you can stay home and stream movies on your ninety-inch screen? They had to come up with something new, something really spectacular—"

"The moviedromes," I said.

"Yup. Turn going to the movies into an all-day full-surround entertainment experience—"

"Like Disneyverse."

He nodded. "Or IKEA. Show *lots* of movies. A hundred instead of the multiplexes' twenty. And add lots of razzle-dazzle: 4-D, IMAX, interactives, Hollywood-style premieres, celebrity appearances, plus theme restaurants and shops and rides and dance clubs and Wii arcades. None of which was really new."

"But I thought you said—"

"Movie theaters have never made their money off the movies they showed. They were just a sideline, a way to get the public into the theater and buy popcorn and jujubes at outrageous prices. The Dromes just expanded on the concept, to the point that the movies have become less and less important. Did you know 53 percent of the people who go to a Drome never see a movie at all?"

"I can believe it," I said, thinking of Kett and Zara.

"And that's not an accident. In the two hours a movie takes to watch, you could be spending way more than the price of a ticket *and* refreshments. And if they can get you to see a later showing, you'll eat lunch *and* dinner here—and stick around to play glittertag afterward. The longer you're at the Drome—"

"The more I spend."

He nodded. "So the Drome does everything it can to see that happens."

"You expect me to believe the Drome orchestrated all that—the tickets and the vomit and the text and the sold-out sign—just to get me to buy more souvenirs?"

"No. You know that old movie we watched where the guy's investigating what looks like a simple train accident and then it turns out it *wasn't* an accident?"

"I Love Trouble," I said promptly. "With Nick Nolte and Julia Roberts. She was a reporter—"

"And he was a scoundrel," Jack said, grinning. "Who, as I recall, Julia really liked."

"What's your point?"

"My point is, that the train accident was just the tip of the iceberg. And so is *Christmas Caper.* I think there's a whole vast conspiracy—"

"To keep me from seeing a *movie*?"

"Not you. Anyone. And not just *Christmas Caper. The Pimmsleys of Parson's Court,* too, and *Just When You Thought You Were Over Him,* and *Switching Gears,* and possibly a couple of others."

"Why?"

"Because they can't afford to let the public find out what's going on. Remember the things I told you the Dromes used to attract people—lots of razzle-dazzle and merchandise, and lots of movies?"

"Yes."

"Well, that's the problem. The old multiplexes had fifteen screens to fill. The Dromes have a hundred."

"But they show some movies in more than one theater."

"Right, and in 3-D, 4-D, and Wii versions, plus there are tons of sequels and remakes and reboots—"

"And Encore Presentations—"

"And rereleases and film festivals and *Harry Potter* marathons and sneak previews, but even if you add in foreign films and Bollywood and bad remakes of British romantic comedies and crummy remakes of all three, it's still a hell of a lot of screens to fill. Especially when most people are only interested in seeing *The Return of Frodo.* Do you remember when we went to see *Gaudy Night* and we were the only two people in the theater?"

"Yes—"

"It's like Baskin-Robbins. They advertise thirty-one flavors, but who the hell ever orders raisin or lemon custard? Those could actually be vanilla with a little food coloring added for all anybody knows. And so could half the Dromes' movies."

"So you're saying *Christmas Caper* doesn't exist?"

"I think that's a very real possibility."

"But that's ridiculous. You and I saw a trailer for it. There was a preview on the overheads while we were in line."

"Which was three minutes long and could have been filmed in a day."

"But why would they advertise it if it doesn't exist?"

"Because otherwise somebody—like me, for instance—might get suspicious."

"But there's no way they could get away with—"

"Sure there is. Most people want to see the latest blockbuster, and with a minor nudge—like a sold-out sign—you can talk 95 percent of the rest of them into seeing something else. Or having lunch at Babette's Feast."

"And the other 5 percent?"

"You just saw it."

"But movies sell out, especially at Christmastime—"

"And people throw up and accidentally spill drinks and get picked up by fraternity guys and can't go to the 10:20 showing because it gets out after the last light-rail train home. But the last showing of every movie I named gets out after the last scheduled light rail, and I've tried to get into *Switching Gears* for the last five days and haven't made it. What time is it?"

"Four o'clock."

"Come on," he said, grabbing my hand and pulling me up. "We've gotta get going if we're going to make it to *Christmas Caper.*"

> "Exciting, suspenseful, and unbelievably romantic!"
> —*Front Row*

"But I thought you said it doesn't exist," I said as he dragged me out of Gusteau's.

"It doesn't. Come on." He led me through Hogwarts and Neverneverland and down an aisle of shops selling *Toy Story* and *The Great Oz* and *Son of Lion King* souvenirs.

"This isn't the way to the theater complex," I protested.

"We've got some shopping to do first," he said, leading me into the Disney Princess Boutique.

"Shopping? Why?"

"Because we can't afford to have Management notice us, and the surest way to draw attention to yourself in a Drome is by not spending money," he said, riffling through a rack of *Tangled* T-shirts.

"Besides," he said, moving to another rack, this one full of *Snow White and the Seven Dwarfs* hoodies, "this is a big date. You should have something special to wear. Something the usher hasn't seen." He flipped through the entire rack and then one of *Twelve Dancing Princesses* tutus, pulling them out and then hanging them back up.

"What are you looking for?" I asked.

"I told you. Something special," he said, searching through yet another rack. "And something that doesn't make you smell like Mrs. Claus's kitchen. Ah, here we go," he said, pulling out a yellow *Dora and Diego Do the Himalayas* T-shirt, with Diego pointing his trademark camera at Dora and the monkey, who were standing atop Mt. Everest. "Just the ticket."

"I am not wearing—" I began, but he'd already thrust it and a bright pink *Little Goose Girl* baseball cap into my hands.

"Tell the clerk to deactivate the tags so you can wear them now," he said, "and then go in the dressing room, take off your top, and put the shirt on. I'll be in the store next door." He gave me a push in the paydesk's direction. "And no questions."

I did as he said, pulling my top off over my head—he was right, it did reek of gingerbread—and putting the T-shirt on over my singlet.

It was too tight, which I suspected was part of the plan, and looked even worse on me than it had on the hanger. "You could have at least had me get something cute," I told him when I found him in the shop next door, trying on *Risky Business* sunglasses.

"No, I couldn't," he said. "What'd you do with your top?"

"I put it in the bag," I said.

"Good. Come on," he said, taking it from me and steering me out of the shop, back toward Gusteau's, to a recycler. He dropped the bag in.

"I liked that top," I protested.

"Shh, do you want to go to this movie or not?" he said, leading me through a maze of balloon artists and tattoo laser techs and kiddie rides and candy stores to the lobby.

He stopped just short of it. "Okay, I want you to go over to the kiosk and buy a ticket to *Dragonwar.*"

"*Dragonwar?* But I thought we were going to—"

"We are. You buy a ticket to *Dragonwar* and then—"

"One ticket? Not two?"

"Definitely not two. We're going in separately."

"What if the machine tells me I have to buy it at the ticket counter?"

"It won't," he said. "Once you're inside—"

"Or what if they say I can't go in yet?"

"They won't do that either," he said. "Once you're inside, go to the concessions stand and buy a large popcorn and a large 7-Up with two straws, and go down to Theater 17."

"Theater 17? But *Dragonwar*'s playing at Theater 24."

"We're not going to *Dragonwar.* Or to *Au Revoir, Mon Fou,* which is what's showing in Theater 17. You're not going into any theater. You're just going to stand in the doorway of 17. I'll meet you there in a couple of minutes."

"And you promise we'll see *Christmas Caper*?"

"I promise I'll *take* you to *Christmas Caper.* Large popcorn," he ordered. "Large 7-Up. *Not* Coke." He jammed the *Goose Girl* cap down over my eyes. "Theater 17," he repeated, and took off through the crowd.

> "Based on a true story . . . but you won't believe it!"
> —*At the Movies*

He was right. No one got in my way or spilled a felony frappe on me or stopped me to give me a free pass to *You're Under Arrest,* and the usher didn't even glance at me as he tore my ticket in half. "Theater 24," he said, and motioned to the right. "End of the hall," and turned his attention to a trio of thirteen-year-olds, and I went down the plush-carpeted hall.

There was no sign of Jack, but he could be hiding in one of the recessed entrances to the theater or past the point halfway down where the hall took a turn to the right.

He wasn't. I stood outside Theater 17 for longer than a couple of minutes and then walked slowly down to 24, where *Dragonwar* was playing, but he wasn't there either.

He got caught trying to sneak in, and they threw him out, I thought, walking back to Theater 17 and planting myself in the recessed doorway.

I waited some more.

Still no sign of Jack, or of anyone else, except a kid who shot out of Theater 30 and down to the restroom, banging its door loudly behind him. I waited some more. I would have gotten my phone out to see what time it was, but between the giant 7-Up I was cradling in my left arm and the enormous bag of popcorn, there was no way I could manage it.

A door slammed farther down the hall, and I looked up eagerly, but it was just the kid, racing back to 30, obviously determined not to miss a second more than necessary of his movie. I wondered what it was that was so riveting. I moved down the hall a little so I could see the marquee above the door.

Lethal Rampage. And next door to it, on the marquee above Theater 28, *Christmas Caper.*

"The cast is terrific!"
—*Goin' Hollywood*

That *rat*! Jack had told me it didn't exist, and yet here it was. And all those problems I'd had, all those people who'd gotten in my way, weren't Drome employees hired to keep me out. They were just moviegoers like me, and the things that had happened were nothing more than coincidences. There *was* no conspiracy.

When are you going to learn you can't trust a word he says? I thought, and if he'd been there, I'd have taken great pleasure in dumping the 7-Up—and the popcorn—over his head and stomping out.

But he'd apparently gotten himself caught and thrown out of the

Drome. If he'd ever intended to come. And I was left, quite literally, holding the bag. And now that I thought about it, Nick Nolte had done the same thing to Julia Roberts in *I Love Trouble*—sending her on what else?—a wild-goose chase. With real geese.

I'll kill him when I find him, I thought, and started back toward the entrance, fuming, and then stopped and looked back at Theater 28. I had come to the Drome to see *Christmas Caper,* and it was right here, with the 4:30 showing due to start at any minute. And it would serve Jack right if I saw it without him.

I walked back to the turn and peeked around the corner to make sure no one—especially not somebody on the staff—was coming and would catch me going into a different movie than the one I had the ticket for, and then hurried over to Theater 28 and pulled the door open. That was no mean feat given the popcorn and the 7-Up, but I managed to get it open far enough to hold it with my hip while I sidled through.

It was pitch-dark inside. The door shut behind me, and I stood there in the blackness, waiting for my eyes to adjust. They didn't, even though there should be *some* light from the movie screen, or, if the previews hadn't started yet, from the overhead lights. And weren't these hallways supposed to have strip lighting in case they had to evacuate the theater?

This one obviously didn't, and I couldn't see *anything.* I stood there in the darkness, listening. The previews had definitely started. I could hear crashes and clangs and ominous music. It must be a preview for one of those shot-totally-at-night movies like *The Dark Knight Rises* or the *Alien* reboot, and that was why I couldn't see, and in a minute, when a different preview came on, there'd be enough light to find my way by. But though the sounds changed to laughter and the muffled murmur of voices, the corridor remained coal-mine black.

I was going to have to feel my way along the passage, but I didn't have a free hand to hold on to the wall with. Or to fish out my phone with so I could use its lit screen as a flashlight.

This is all Jack's fault, I thought, stooping to set down the 7-Up so I could get my phone out of my pocket. I flipped it open and held it out in front of me. And no wonder the passage was so dark. It went a few more feet and then turned sharply to the left in a kind of dogleg. If I'd kept going, I'd have run face-first into a wall.

That's a lawsuit waiting to happen, I thought, trying to figure out a way to hold on to my phone and the 7-Up. There wasn't one—the cup was too big around—but if I could just make it past the dogleg, there should be some light from the screen to see by. I put my phone back in my pocket, felt for the cup, picked it up, and started down the passage again, counting the steps to the wall.

"Four . . . five . . ." I whispered. "Six, sev—"

And was grabbed abruptly from behind by a hand around my waist. I yelped, but a second hand was already over my mouth, and Jack's voice was in my ear. "Shh. In here," he whispered and pulled me, impossibly, right through the wall.

"A winner! You'll be glad you came!"
—*Variety Online*

Amazingly, I hadn't dropped the 7-Up *or* the bag of popcorn. "What do you think you're doing?" I said, wrestling free of him.

"Shh!" he whispered. "These walls aren't soundproof. Did you spill any of the popcorn?"

"Of course I spilled the popcorn," I said. "You scared me half to death!"

"Shh. Look, you can yell at me all you want," he whispered, "but not till the next chase scene. And don't take out your cell phone. I don't want the light to give us away. Stay here," he ordered, and I heard the swish of a door's opening and closing softly, and then nothing but the sounds of pandemonium coming through the left-hand wall.

It sounded similar to what I'd heard before and had thought was from the previews for *Christmas Caper,* but it was clearly coming from the theater next door, which meant it was *Lethal Rampage.*

I couldn't see anything at all, let alone enough to make out my surroundings, but this had to be the corridor leading to *Christmas Caper* because I could hear a voice intoning, "Coming this Valentine's Day!" through the other wall.

Good, the previews were still playing. I hadn't missed the start of the movie. I would have time to tell Jack what I thought of him for grabbing me like that and still make it into the theater in time for the opening credits. If I could find it in the darkness, which was still absolute.

Jack was back. I heard him shut the door. "Luckily, you only spilled a couple of handfuls," he said over the crash of explosions from *Lethal Rampage.* "Which I ate. What took you so long? I was afraid the usher had spotted you, and I was going to have to come back out and rescue you."

"Where *was* I?" I said angrily. "I was standing outside Theater 17 just like you told me to. You *lied* to me—"

"Nobody saw you go in the door to 28, did they?"

"Don't change the subject. You—"

"Did they?" He grabbed my arm, jostling the popcorn.

"No," I said, only half listening. In between deafening explosions, the announcer on the *Christmas Caper* side of the wall was saying muffledly, "And now for our feature presentation."

"Look," I said. "I'd love to stand here in the dark and fight with you, but *I* intend to see *Christmas Caper.* So if you'll please let go of my arm, the movie's about to start."

"No, it's not," he said. He squeezed my arm. "Hang on," he said, let go, and moved away from me, and I could hear him doing something, though I couldn't tell what, and then the wall I was facing lit up with the beam from a penlight.

From what I could see in its dim light, we were in a narrow passage just like the one outside, with carpet on the floor and the walls and no strip lighting, but it was long and straight and ended in a wall, not in the entrance to the theater. There was no sign of the door Jack had just come through though it had to be in that wall because Jack had taken off his jacket and laid it against the bottom of it.

"To keep any stray light from seeping out," he explained over the racket.

"What *is* this place?" I said. "Where *are* we?"

"Shh," he said, putting a finger to his lips and whispering. "Kissing scene coming up," and he must have been telling the truth because the gunfire and explosions were suddenly replaced by the strains of violins.

He took the popcorn and 7-Up cup from me, tiptoed halfway down the corridor, stooped and set them on the floor and then stood up again, listening with his finger to his lips. And apparently the lethal rampagers were back, because the romantic violins cut off abruptly, replaced by a blast of trumpets, lots of drumming, and the sound of revving engines and squealing tires.

"Chase scene," Jack said, coming back over to me. "Time to go to work."

"You said you were going to tell me what this place is. Where's the theater?"

"I'll tell you everything, I swear. After we do this. Take off your shirt."

"*What?*"

"Your shirt. Take it off."

"You never change, do you?"

"Wrong line," he said. "You're supposed to say, 'Are you sure we're planning the same sort of crime?' and I say—"

"This is not *How to Steal a Million,*" I said.

"You're right," he said. "It's more like *Jumpin' Jack Flash.* Or *I Love Trouble.* Take it off. And hurry. We don't have much time."

"I have no intention of taking off any—"

"Calm down. It's for the photos. Of this passage and the one outside," he said, and when I still stood there, my arms crossed, "The camera the boy on your shirt is holding isn't just a picture. There's a digital-strip camera embedded in it."

And that was why he'd riffled through all those shirts in the Disney Princess boutique. He'd been looking for one with a camera. "Why can't you just use the camera in your phone?"

"When they scan them in the security line, they check your info against the police and FBI databases."

"Which you're in because of the geese," I said. "That's why you wanted me to come with you, so I could smuggle in your camera for you."

"Of course. That's what scoundrels do. They use the girl to smuggle the necklace through customs or to get the news story or to get them out of East Germany—"

"This is *not* a movie!"

"You're right about that. Which is why I've got to get those pictures. So, do you want to give me that shirt or do you want me to take the camera off of it while you're wearing it?"

"Fine," I said, pulled the T-shirt off over my head, handed it to him, and stood there fuming in my singlet while he turned the shirt inside out, peeled off the digital-strip camera, and handed the T-shirt back to me. I pulled it on while he snapped pictures of the passage, motioning me out of the way so he could get a shot of the long wall behind me.

He snapped the end wall he'd dragged me through and the one at the other end, and then came back to me and listened a moment. "I'll be right back," he said, switched off the penlight, plunging us in darkness, and went out into the passage again.

He was gone for what seemed like forever. I put my ear to the door, but all I could hear were detonations and screams from the *Lethal Rampage* side and disgustingly perky music from the other. I listened intently, afraid the din would subside any minute, but it didn't, though on the *Rampage* side I could hear, over the crashing, the sound of muffled voices.

Please don't let that be the usher or Drome security, I thought, *demanding to know what Jack was doing in here,* but it must not have been because the door was opening again, and I had to back away hastily as Jack came in and shut it behind him.

"Can you find my jacket?" he whispered, and I felt around for it in vain, and then pulled my shirt off again and handed it to him to put against the door.

"Thanks," he whispered and, after a few seconds, switched on the penlight again.

"Did you get the pictures?"

He waved the digital strip at me. "Yeah."

"Good. You *lied* to me."

"No, I didn't. Besides, Jimmy Stewart lied to Margaret Sullavan,

Peter O'Toole lied to Audrey Hepburn, Cary *Grant* lied to Audrey Hepburn. It's what scoundrels do."

"That's no excuse. You promised you'd take me to *Christmas Caper.*"

"And I did," he said. "This is it." He waved his arm to show the passage. "Welcome to Theater 28."

"This isn't a theater," I said.

"You're right," he said. "Come on." He grabbed my hand, led me down to where he'd set the popcorn and 7-Up. "Have a seat, and I'll explain everything. Come on, sit down."

I sat down on the floor, my back against the carpeted wall, my arms folded belligerently across my chest, and he sat down across from me. "That passage outside splits in two and goes into the theaters on either side," he said. "If I hadn't reached out and pulled you in here, you'd have turned and followed that dogleg into Theater 30 and *Lethal Rampage.*

"And if you'd turned the other way, you'd have ended up in Theater 26"—he jerked his thumb toward the wall behind him—"where *Make Way for Ducklings* is now showing, a fact you wouldn't have discovered until you'd sat through fifteen minutes of previews, at which point you'd have thought you'd somehow gotten in the wrong theater, and go tell the usher, who'd tell you he was sorry, but you'd missed the start of *Christmas Caper* and he couldn't let you in, but that there might still be tickets available for the seven o'clock. A neat trick, huh?"

"But why—?"

"They have to have a last line of defense in case a determined fan makes it past all the other firewalls. That hardly ever happens, but occasionally somebody does what you just did—can't get in, buys a ticket for another movie, and then tries to sneak in to what they originally wanted to see."

"Why don't they just *not* put up a marquee for it?"

"They tried that, which is what made us suspicious in the first place, so they had to come up with an alternative plan. Which you see before you."

"Us?" I asked.

"Oops, I almost forgot," he said, scrambling to his feet and going to retrieve his jacket. He put it on, came back, and began searching through its pockets.

"Now what are you doing?" I asked.

"Trying to get this made before *Lethal Rampage* hits another quiet stretch." He frowned at the red Coca-Cola cup. "You *did* get 7-Up, didn't you? Not Coke?"

"I got 7-Up." I handed it over to him. "You're not making a stink bomb out of that, are you?" I asked as he pulled out a flask and poured a brown liquid into it.

"No," he said, patting his pockets some more and pulling out a *Terminator 12* commemorative glass and then a baggie full of lemon slices.

He poured half the 7-Up-and-brown-liquid-and-ice mixture into the *Terminator* glass, added a lemon slice and a sprig of mint from his breast pocket, reached inside his jacket, pulled out a stalk of rhubarb with a flourish, stuck it in the glass, stirred the mixture with it, and handed it to me. "Your Pimm's Cup, madam," he said.

"Just like the ones you made the night we watched *Ghost Town,*" I said, smiling.

"Well, not just like them. These are made with rum, which was all Tom Cruise's Cocktail Bar had. And when I made the *Ghost Town* ones, I was trying to get you into bed."

"And what are you trying to do this time? Get me drunk so I'll agree to help you do something else illegal?"

"No," he said, sitting down next to me. "Not right now, anyway," which wasn't exactly a reassuring answer.

"I got the photos," he went on, "which is what I came for, and, thanks to you and that awful Dora T-shirt"—he raised his Coke cup to me—"I'm a lot less likely to get caught smuggling them out. But it's still too risky to do any more investigating till I've gotten them safely off the premises." He took a leisurely sip of his drink.

"Then, shouldn't we be going?" I asked.

"We can't. Not till *Lethal Rampage* is over and we can blend in with the audience as it leaves. So relax. Drink your Pimm's Cup, have some popcorn. We've got—" He stopped and listened to the din coming through the wall for a moment, "an hour and forty-six minutes to kill. Enough time to—"

"Tell me what's going on, like you promised you would. Or are you going to tell me that's classified, too?"

"As a matter of fact, it is," he said. "And you've already seen what *they're* doing—covering up movies that don't exist."

"But why? Most people don't even *care* about the movies part."

"Oh, but they do. They think they've got a hundred to choose from, and that's what makes them come all the way out here on the light rail and stand in security lines forever. Do you think they'd do that just to buy a bag of popcorn and an overpriced Avengers mug? How long do you think Baskin-Robbins would stay in business if they only had three flavors, even if they were the most popular ones? Look at your friends. They may have spent today shopping and eating and—"

"Picking up guys."

"And picking up guys, but if somebody asked them tomorrow what they did, they'd say they went to the movies, and they'd believe it. The Drome's not selling popcorn, it's selling an *illusion,* an idea—a giant screen with magical images on it, your girlfriend sitting beside you in the dark, romance, adventure, mystery . . ."

"But I still don't understand. Okay, they have to maintain the illusion, but it's not as if they don't have *any* movies. You said there were only four or five movies here that didn't exist, and they already show some movies on more than one screen. Why not just show *X-Force* and *The Return of Frodo* in one more theater instead of making movies up?"

"Because they're already showing *X-Force* in six theaters as it is, and Starstruck just announced they're building a chain of 250-screen Superdromes. Besides, I don't think the moviegoing public's the only people they're trying to fool."

"What do you mean?"

"I mean, if you're a film company, this could really work to your advantage. If your movie's behind schedule, nobody gets fined or fired for missing the release date. You release it anyway, and then, when it's finished, you put out the DVD and stream it, and nobody's the wiser. Which, by the way, is what happened to *Monsoon Gate* and what I think probably happened to *Christmas Caper.* You can't release a Christmas movie in February. It's got to come out in December or you'll lose your shirt. Figuratively speaking."

"Which means it might show up on the Net in a few months," I said.

"Yeah, and if it does, I'll watch it with you, I promise."

"Do you think that's what happened to the other movies?"

"No. *The Ripper Files* never came out, and neither did *Mission to Antares* or *By the Skin of Our Teeth.* And why spend millions making a movie when you can do a three-minute trailer instead, pay the Dromes to block people from seeing it, and pocket the difference? The shareholders wouldn't even have to know."

"Which would make it fraud."

"It's already fraud," he said. "And false advertising. There are laws against selling products that don't exist."

"Which is why they don't sell the tickets online," I said. "But if they're criminals, isn't what you're doing dangerous?"

"Not if they don't know I'm doing it. Which is why," he said, his voice dropping to a whisper, "we need to sit here quietly, eat our popcorn"—he scooted closer to me—"and watch the movie."

"What's it about?" I whispered.

"This guy who's investigating a conspiracy when who should turn up but his old girlfriend. It's the last thing he needs. He's trying to stay invisible—"

Which explains why he looked so dismayed when he saw me, I thought, a weight lifting from me.

"And he knows he should probably get out of there before she blows his cover, but she already thinks he's a—"

"Scoundrel?"

"I was going to say 'wanker.'"

"Scoundrel," I said firmly, "and besides, he needs her to help him smuggle something in past the guards, like Kevin Kline in *French Kiss.*"

"Exactly," he said. "Plus, he's got some stuff to tell her, so he recruits her to help him, and in the course of their investigations, he convinces her to forgive him, like Olivia de Havilland forgives Errol Flynn and Julia Roberts forgives Nick Nolte and Whoopi Goldberg forgives—"

"Jack. Because that's what scoundrels' girlfriends do."

"Exactly," he said. "Which is why you should—"

"Shh," I said.

"What is it?" he whispered.

"Kissing scene coming up," I said, and switched off the penlight.

"The most fun you can have at the movies!"
—*moviefone.com*

"How long does *Lethal Rampage* run?" I asked him a considerable time later. "That sounds like Final Scene music to me."

He raised himself up on one elbow, said, "It is," and went back to nuzzling my neck.

"But don't we have to be out of here before it ends?"

"Yeah, but you're forgetting, it's a Hollywood Blockbuster. Remember when we saw the reboot of *Speed,* how we kept thinking it was over and it wasn't? Or *The Return of the King*? That had like seven endings. *Lethal Rampage* has got at least three more climaxes to go."

"Oh, good," I murmured, snuggling into his shoulder, but a moment later he sat up, reached for his jacket, pulled a phone out of it, and flipped it open.

"I thought you didn't have a phone," I said, sitting up.

"Not one I wanted to get caught with photos on," he said, looking at its screen. "Change of plans. There's something I've got to go take care of." He began buttoning his shirt. "Wait till the next explosion and then slip out into the passage and wait for *Lethal Rampage* to get out. And don't leave anything behind."

I nodded.

"When you get out to the lobby, go over to one of the cafés, *not* the Polar Express, order a drink, text your friends, and then wait at least a few minutes before you try to leave, and you should be fine."

He pulled me to my feet. "Look, I can't tweet or call you—it might be traced—so it may be a while before I can get in touch. All I've proved so far is that there's a blocked-off passageway between theaters and some suspicious activity. I still have to prove the movies don't exist, which I'll have to do in Hollywood." He hesitated. "I feel bad about leaving you here like this."

"But Peter O'Toole left Audrey Hepburn in a closet and Kevin Kline left Meg Ryan in Paris without a passport," I said, following him down to the far end of the passage. "And now I suppose I'm supposed to say, 'It's okay. Go,' and you kiss me good-bye, and I stand in the doorway like Olivia, looking longingly after you with my tresses blowing in a wind that smells like the sea?"

"Exactly. Except in this case it smells more like rancid popcorn oil," he said, "and we can't afford to leave the door open. It lets in too much light. But I can definitely manage the kiss."

He did. "See?" he said. "You do like scoundrels."

"I happen to like nice men," I said. "How are you going to get out of the Drome without security's catching you?"

"I'll be fine," he said. "Look, if you get in trouble—"

"I won't. Go."

He kissed me again, opened the wall, and went through it, only to appear again almost instantly. "By the way," he said, "about the geese and the graduating thing. Remember in *How to Steal a Million* where Peter O'Toole tells Audrey Hepburn he's not a burglar, that he's actually a security expert 'with advanced degrees in art history and chemistry and a diploma, with distinction, from London University in advanced criminology'? "

"Yes," I said. "I suppose now you're going to tell me you have an advanced degree from London University?"

"No, Yale. In consumer fraud," he said and was gone, leaving me to hurriedly gather up all the telltale trash by the less-than-helpful light of my cell-phone screen, get out into the passage, shutting the door soundlessly behind me, and over to the corridor that led to the theater next door, and wait for the movie to let out.

"A movie experience that leaves you wanting more!
An enthusiastic thumbs-up!"
—*rogerebert.net*

He'd been right about *Lethal Rampage.* It went on for another twenty minutes, giving me time to make sure the door was completely shut with no seams showing, check again for stray popcorn, and then lean against the corridor wall, listening to a whole symphony of crashes, bangs, and explosions before the lights came up, people started trickling out, and I had to somehow merge with them without being noticed.

It was easier than I'd thought. They were all too intent on switching their cell phones back on and complaining about the movie to pay any attention to me.

Lethal Rampage had apparently been just as awful as it had sounded through the wall. "I couldn't believe how lame the plot was," a twelve-year-old boy said, and his friend nodded. "I *hated* the ending."

Me, too, I thought, wistfully.

I eased in behind them and followed them down the passage, eavesdropping on their conversation so I could talk about the movie in case anybody asked me about it.

Like the ticket-taker, who I still had to get past. I wondered if he'd remember I'd been going to *Dragonwar,* not *Lethal Rampage.* Maybe I should go back to Theater 17 and go out with the *Dragonwar* audience.

But if it had already let out, I'd have to go out past the ticket-taker alone, ensuring he'd notice me. And what if somebody on staff saw me going back and concluded I was sneaking into a second movie? I'd better stick with this crowd.

I stopped just inside the door, loitering by the trash can till a group of high-school kids came by, and then hastily tossed my popcorn sack and Coke cup and attached myself to them. And it was a good thing because there was a cleaning crew lurking just outside the door with their dustpans and garbage bags, and for all their slouching against the wall, waiting for the theater to empty out, they looked unnaturally alert.

I stuck close to the high-schoolers as we passed them, bending over my phone and pretending to text like they were doing and stayed with them as we merged with the audience from *Pirates of the Caribbean 9,* which had just gotten out.

From the sound of things, *Pirates* hadn't been any better than *Lethal Rampage,* and it occurred to me that I'd had a better time than any of them even though I hadn't seen a movie.

The conclusion of that thought was swept away by a bunch of people pouring down from the upstairs theaters, and it was all I could do to keep my footing as the whole mass of people surged past the ticket-taker and out into the only-slightly-less-crowded lobby, which I was relieved to see wasn't full of security guards and blaring sirens. Jack must have gotten safely away.

But just in case he was still in the Drome somewhere, I needed to do what I could to keep them from getting suspicious.

Which meant detaching myself from the high-schoolers and getting in line to get tickets for the next showing of *Christmas Caper.* If I were still trying to see it, I obviously didn't know it didn't exist.

The high-schoolers were trying to decide which restaurant to go to. "While you make up your minds, I'm going to go get a funnel cake," I said to the nearest of them, who didn't even look up from her smartphone, and went to check the time of the next showing, which should be at 6:40.

It wasn't. It was at seven thirty, and the one after that was at ten. I stared at the board for a long minute, contemplating what that meant, and then went to try to find the end of the ticket line.

It was ten times longer than it had been when we'd first arrived, snaking all the way back to the Death Star Diner, and it was barely moving. It was a good thing I wasn't trying to actually get in. I wouldn't make it even halfway to the front before the last light-rail train home.

I wondered how long I needed to stand here. Jack had said it wasn't safe to use his phone, but he might have been able to borrow someone else's and send me a text from it, so I turned on my phone and looked at my messages.

There weren't any from him, but there were four from Zara, all of them asking, "Where r u?" except the last one, which said, "Assume ur not ansring means u finally got in 2 *Xmas Cpr.* How was it?"

I needed to text her back, but not till I was far enough along the line that it wouldn't look like I'd just gotten into it. I didn't want her wondering what I'd been doing all this time—she was way too quick to draw connections to Jack. So I switched off my phone and then stood there, periodically inching forward, and thinking about Zara's text. "How was it?" she'd asked.

Great, I thought, and remembered those boys complaining about *Lethal Rampage* and my thinking I'd had a much better time at the movies than they had.

And how did I know that wasn't what *I'd* just experienced—an afternoon at the movies? That I hadn't just been participating in a romantic spy adventure concocted by Jack, who knew how much I wanted to believe he'd had a good reason for going off without saying a word to me and who'd heard me complain countless times about going to a movie with Zara and Kett and ending up not getting to see it?

There could have been lots of reasons that that passage was there. It could've been a shortcut between theaters for the projectionist, or some sort of required evacuation route in case of fire that Jack had appropriated for his own private Tunnel of Love. He could have bribed the usher to tell me I couldn't get in and to put *Christmas Caper* up on Theater 28's marquee after the audience for *Make Way for Ducklings* was inside. And the other stuff—the vomit and the spilled gingerbread latte and Santa—could all have been coincidences, and Jack had simply made them sound like a conspiracy.

Don't be ridiculous, I told myself. *Do you honestly think he'd go to that much trouble just to get you into bed?*

Of course he would. Look how much trouble he went to just to play a practical joke on the dean. And the whole thing had been just like the plot of *How to Steal a Million* or *I Love Trouble,* complete with spies, slapstick, a sparring couple forced together into a small confined space, and a hero who was lying to the heroine.

And believing it was a scam made a lot more sense than believing that some vast Hollywood conspiracy lay behind this decorated-for-Christmas Cinedrome.

There isn't any conspiracy, I thought. *You've been had, that's all. Again.* Christmas Caper *is showing right now in Theater 56 or 79 or 100. And Jack is off plotting some other practical joke—or the seduction of some other gullible girl—while I stand here in this stupid line trying to protect him from a danger that never existed.*

I looked back at the end of the line, which I was only a dozen people away from. I still couldn't text Zara, but for a completely different reason now—she couldn't *ever* find out what an idiot I'd been.

So I continued to stand there, thinking about how easy it would have been for Jack to bribe somebody on the staff to put a NO TICKETS AVAILABLE sign on the schedule board, just like he'd bribed some farmer to lend him those geese. And to pay somebody to block me on my way across the lobby. And thinking how, when I found *Christmas Caper* was sold-out, I should just have gone to see *A Star-Crossed Season* instead.

Three Hanover freshmen leaned over the barrier to talk to the girls ahead of me in line. "What are you going to?" one of them asked.

"We haven't decided," one of the girls said. "We were thinking maybe *Saw 7.* Or *A Star-Crossed Season.*"

"Don't!" the trio shouted, and the middle one said, "We just saw it. It was beyond boring!"

> "Well worth the trip!"
>
> —*comingsoon.com*

I waited another ten minutes, during which I moved forward about a foot and then called Zara.

"Where have you *been*?" she asked. "I've been texting and texting you."

"You have?" I said. "I haven't gotten them. I think there's something wrong with my phone."

"So where are you now?"

"Where do you think? In line."

"In *line*?" she said. "You mean you still haven't seen *Christmas Card*?"

"Caper," I corrected her. "No, not yet. All three afternoon showings sold out before I got to the front of the line, so I'm trying to get a ticket to the seven o'clock."

"Where are you exactly?" she asked.

I told her.

"I'll be right there," she said, which I doubted. It would take her at least twenty minutes to disentangle herself and Kett from the guys, and then on the way here they'd be delayed by the dress Zoe Deschanel wore in *Son of Elf* or some other guys, and by that time I'd hopefully be far enough forward in the line to make it look like I'd been in line since the 12:10.

But she showed up almost immediately and alone. "This is all the farther you've gotten?" she said. "What happened to Jack?"

"I have no idea," I said. "Where's Kett?"

Zara rolled her eyes. "She texted Noah and they went off to the Dirty Dancing Club. Did he tell you where he's been all these months?"

"Who? Noah?"

"Very funny," Zara said. "No. *Jack.*"

"No. In jail, probably."

"It's too bad," Zara said, shaking her head sadly. "I was hoping you might get back together. I mean, I know he's kind of a . . ."

Scoundrel, I thought.

". . . wanker," Zara said. "But he's so scorching!"

That he is, I thought. "What are you going to do now?" I asked her, to change the subject.

"I don't know," she said, sighing. "This trip's been a complete bust. I didn't meet anybody even lukewarm, and I couldn't find anything for my family for Christmas. I suppose I should go over to the Pretty Woman store and see if they have anything my mom would like, but I think maybe I'll just go see *Christmas Caper* with you. When did you say the next showing was?"

"Seven."

She checked the time on her phone. "It's already 6:30," she said, looking at her phone and then up at the line ahead of us. "We'll never make it."

"When's the showing after that?" I asked her, but before she could look it up, Kett came up, looking annoyed.

"What happened to Noah?" Zara asked her.

"He's at the first-aid station," she said.

"The first-aid—?"

"He had a bloody nose. He said he wanted to take me dancing, but it turned out it was because he wanted to enter me in the wet T-shirt contest, the slimewad," she said. "So what's going on?"

"Lindsay's still trying to get in to see *Christmas Caper,*" Zara said.

"You mean, you haven't managed to see it *yet*?" Kett asked. "Geez, how long have you been standing in line?"

"Forever," Zara said, studying her phone. "And she's definitely not going to get in to see the seven o'clock. This is showing it as sold-out." She scrolled down. "And the next showing isn't till ten"—she scrolled some more—"which doesn't get out till after the last train to Hanover leaves, so that one won't work either."

"Geez," Kett said. "You spent all this time standing in line for a movie you don't even get to see. Was it worth it spending the whole day on it?"

Oh, yes, I thought. Because, lies or not, bill of goods or not, it was still the best afternoon at the movies I'd had in a long time. Much better than if I'd gone to see *A Star-Crossed Season.* Or *Lethal Rampage.* And *much* better than wandering around looking at Black Widow boots and Silver Linings Playbook leotards like Zara, or dealing with creeps, like Kett had. Unlike theirs, my afternoon had been great. It had had everything—adventure, suspense, romance, explosions, danger, snappy dialogue, kissing scenes. The perfect Saturday afternoon at the movies.

Except for the ending.

But it might not be over yet—Jack had after all promised me he'd watch *Christmas Caper* with me if it ended up being streamed. And right before the end of *Jumpin' Jack Flash,* Jack had left Whoopi Goldberg sitting waiting for him in a restaurant. Michael Douglas had left Kathleen Turner standing abandoned on a parapet. Han Solo had left Princess Leia on the rebel moon. And they'd all showed up again, just like they'd said.

Of course Jack had also told me he'd graduated from Yale and was investigating a huge, far-reaching conspiracy, and that putting those geese in the dean's office hadn't been a prank. But not everything he'd told me was a lie. He'd said he loved movies, and that was true. Nobody who didn't love them could have engineered such a perfect one.

And even if he'd made up everything else, even if he was every bit the scoundrel I was afraid he was and I never saw him again, it had still been a terrific afternoon at the movies.

"Well?" Kett was saying. "*Was* it? I mean, you didn't get to *do* anything."

"Or have anything to eat," I said, getting out of line. "Let's go get some sushi or something. How late is Nemo's open?"

"I'll see," Kett said, getting out her phone. "I think it stays open till—Oh, my God!"

"What?" Zara asked. "That slimewad Noah didn't text you something obscene, did he?"

"No," Kett said, scrolling down through her phone-number list. "You won't believe this." She tapped a number and put the phone up to her ear. "Hi," she said into it. "I got your text. What happened? . . . You're kidding! . . . Oh, my God! . . . Are you sure? Which channel?"

Oh, no, I thought, even though I'd decided he'd concocted the whole thing, *they've arrested Jack. They caught him with the camera strip.*

"Oh, my God, *what*?" Zara said.

"Hang on," Kett said to whoever was on the other end, and pressed the phone to her chest. "We should have stayed home," she said to us. "We missed all the excitement."

Jack went back to the campus to leave me a message, I thought, *and the campus police caught him.*

"What excitement?" Zara asked. "*Tell* us."

"Margo says there are all these TV-camera crews and squad cars with flashing lights around the admin building, and a few minutes ago Dr. Baker told her the dean's been arrested."

"The *dean*?" I said.

"For what?" Zara asked.

"I don't know," Kett said. She texted like mad for a minute, and then said, "Margo says it has something to do with taking federal loan money for students who don't exist. It's apparently all over the news," and Zara began swiping through screens to find the coverage.

"The dean says it's all a big mistake," Kett said, "but apparently the FBI's consumer-fraud division's been investigating him for months, and they've got all kinds of evidence."

I'll bet they do, I thought, thinking of Jack's saying he had to go, that something had come up, and of what a good idea geese had been. In all the chaos—and mess—nobody would have even thought to check the dean's office to see if anything was missing.

"There are?" Kett was saying. She put her hand over her phone. "Margo says the place has been crawling with scorching FBI agents."

"Here it is," Zara said, holding her phone so I could see the screen, which showed the quad full of police officers and FBI agents, and reporters trying to get a shot of the dean as he was perp-walked down the steps and over to a squad car. There was no sign of Jack.

"Are they still there?" Kett said and then glumly, "Oh." She turned to us. "She says there's no point in our coming home. It's all over. I can't believe we missed it."

"Especially the FBI agents," Zara said teasingly.

"Right," Kett said. She sighed. "Instead, I got felt up by a slimewad."

"And I still don't have a present for my mother," Zara said. She turned to me. "And you didn't get to see your movie, after I *promised* you would."

"It doesn't matter."

"We could go to the 9:30," Zara said, "and leave before it's over. That way you could at least see part of it."

"And miss the ending?" I said, thinking of *Romancing the Stone,* where Michael Douglas comes back when Kathleen Turner least expects it, and of *French Kiss,* where Meg Ryan's already on the plane, and of *Jumpin' Jack Flash,* where he finally shows up in the very last scene and is every bit as wonderful as she thought he was.

"No, that's okay," I said, trying hard not to smile. "I'll watch it when it comes out on the Net."

Patrick Rothfuss

New York Times bestseller Patrick Rothfuss gained great popularity and critical acclaim with the publication of his debut novel, *The Name of the Wind.* The second novel in the series, *The Wise Man's Fear,* was greeted with similar success and acclaim all over the world. Patrick's other projects include a darkly humorous children's book, *The Adventures of the Princess and Mr. Whiffle,* and Worldbuilders, a geek-centered charity that has raised more than $2 million for Heifer International since he founded it in 2008. (Worldbuilders.org)

Here he takes us to the iconic Waystone Inn to follow a typical day in the life of one of the *Kingkiller Chronicle*'s most popular characters, the mysterious Bast, ostensibly an errand boy, who is much more than he seems to be—a day in which Bast learns many lessons, and teaches a few as well.

THE LIGHTNING TREE

Patrick Rothfuss

Morning: The Narrow Road

Bast almost made it out the back door of the Waystone Inn.

He actually *had* made it outside, both feet were over the threshold and the door was almost entirely eased shut behind him before he heard his master's voice.

Bast paused, hand on the latch. He frowned at the door, hardly a handspan from being closed. He hadn't made any noise. He knew it. He was familiar with all the silent pieces of the inn, which floorboards sighed beneath a foot, which windows stuck . . .

The back door's hinges creaked sometimes, depending on their mood, but that was easy to work around. Bast shifted his grip on the latch, lifted up so that the door's weight didn't hang so heavy, then eased it slowly closed. No creak. The swinging door was softer than a sigh.

Bast stood upright and grinned. His face was sweet and sly and wild. He looked like a naughty child who had managed to steal the moon and eat it. His smile was like the last sliver of remaining moon, sharp and white and dangerous.

"Bast!" The call came again, louder this time. Nothing so crass as a shout, his master would never stoop to bellowing. But when he wanted to be heard, his baritone would not be stopped by anything so insubstantial as an oaken door. His voice carried like a horn, and Bast felt his name tug at him like a hand around his heart.

Bast sighed, then opened the door lightly and strode back inside. He was dark and tall and lovely. When he walked he looked like he was dancing. "Yes, Reshi?" he called.

After a moment the innkeeper stepped into the kitchen; he wore a clean white apron and his hair was red. Other than that, he was painfully unremarkable. His face held the doughy placidness of bored innkeepers everywhere. Despite the early hour, he looked tired.

He handed Bast a leather book. "You almost forgot this," he said without a hint of sarcasm.

Bast took the book and made a show of looking surprised. "Oh! Thank you, Reshi!"

The innkeeper shrugged and his mouth made the shape of a smile. "No bother, Bast. While you're out on your errands, would you mind picking up some eggs?"

Bast nodded, tucking the book under his arm. "Anything else?" he asked dutifully.

"Maybe some carrots too. I'm thinking we'll do stew tonight. It's Felling, so we'll need to be ready for a crowd." His mouth turned up slightly at one corner as he said this.

The innkeeper started to turn away, then stopped. "Oh. The Williams boy stopped by last night, looking for you. Didn't leave any sort of message." He raised an eyebrow at Bast. The look said more than it said.

"I haven't the slightest idea what he wants," Bast said.

The innkeeper made a noncommittal noise and turned back toward the common room.

Before he'd taken three steps Bast was already out the door and running through the early morning sunlight.

By the time Bast arrived, there were already two children waiting. They played on the huge greystone that lay half-fallen at the bottom of the hill, climbing up the tilting side of it, then jumping down into the tall grass.

Knowing they were watching, Bast took his time climbing the tiny hill. At the top stood what the children called the lightning tree, though these days it was little more than a branchless trunk barely taller than a man. All the bark had long since fallen away, and the sun had bleached the wood as white as bone. All except the very top, where even after all these years the wood was charred a jagged black.

Bast touched the trunk with his fingertips and made a slow circuit of the tree. He went deasil, the same direction as the turning sun. The proper way for making. Then he turned and switched hands, making three slow circles widdershins. That turning was against the world. It was the way of breaking. Back and forth he went, as if the tree were a bobbin and he was winding and unwinding.

Finally he sat with his back against the tree and set the book on a nearby stone. The sun shone on the gold gilt letters, *Celum Tinture.* Then he amused himself by tossing stones into the nearby stream that cut into the low slope of the hill opposite the greystone.

After a minute, a round little blond boy trudged up the hill. He was the baker's youngest son, Brann. He smelled of sweat and fresh bread and . . . something else. Something out of place.

The boy's slow approach had an air of ritual about it. He crested the small hill and stood there for a moment quietly, the only noise coming from the other two children playing below.

Finally Bast turned to look the boy over. He was no more than eight or nine, well dressed, and plumper than most of the other town's children. He carried a wad of white cloth in his hand.

The boy swallowed nervously. "I need a lie."

Bast nodded. "What sort of lie?"

The boy gingerly opened his hand, revealing the wad of cloth to be a makeshift bandage, spattered with bright red. It stuck to his hand slightly. Bast nodded; that was what he'd smelled before.

"I was playing with my mum's knives," Brann said.

Bast examined the cut. It ran shallow along the meat near the thumb. Nothing serious. "Hurt much?"

"Nothing like the birching I'll get if she finds out I was messing with her knives."

Bast nodded sympathetically. "You clean the knife and put it back?"

Brann nodded.

Bast tapped his lips thoughtfully. "You thought you saw a big black rat. It scared you. You threw a knife at it and cut yourself. Yesterday one of the other children told you a story about rats chewing off soldiers' ears and toes while they slept. It gave you nightmares."

Brann gave a shudder. "Who told me the story?"

Bast shrugged. "Pick someone you don't like."

The boy grinned viciously.

Bast began to tick off things on his fingers. "Get some blood on the knife before you throw it." He pointed at the cloth the boy had wrapped his hand in. "Get rid of that too. The blood is dry, obviously old. Can you work up a good cry?"

The boy shook his head, seeming a little embarrassed by the fact.

"Put some salt in your eyes. Get all snotty and teary before you run to them. Howl and blubber. Then when they're asking you about your hand, tell your mum you're sorry if you broke her knife."

Brann listened, nodding slowly at first, then faster. He smiled. "That's good." He looked around nervously. "What do I owe you?"

"Any secrets?" Bast asked.

The baker's boy thought for a minute. "Old Lant's tupping the Widow Creel . . ." he said hopefully.

Bast waved his hand. "For years. Everyone knows." Bast rubbed his nose, then said, "Can you bring me two sweet buns later today?"

Brann nodded.

"That's a good start," Bast said. "What have you got in your pockets?"

The boy dug around and held up both his hands. He had two iron shims, a flat greenish stone, a bird skull, a tangle of string, and a bit of chalk.

Bast claimed the string. Then, careful not to touch the shims, he took the greenish stone between two fingers and arched an eyebrow at the boy.

After a moment's hesitation, the boy nodded.

Bast put the stone in his pocket.

"What if I get a birching anyway?" Brann asked.

Bast shrugged. "That's your business. You wanted a lie. I gave you a good one. If you want me to get you out of trouble, that's something else entirely."

The baker's boy looked disappointed, but he nodded and headed down the hill.

Next up the hill was a slightly older boy in tattered homespun. One of the Alard boys, Kale. He had a split lip and a crust of blood around one nostril. He was as furious as only a boy of ten can be. His expression was a thunderstorm.

"I caught my brother kissing Gretta behind the old mill!" he said as soon as he crested the hill, not waiting for Bast to ask. "He knew I was sweet on her!"

Bast spread his hands helplessly, shrugging.

"Revenge," the boy spat.

"Public revenge?" Bast asked. "Or secret revenge?"

The boy touched his split lip with his tongue. "Secret revenge," he said in a low voice.

"How much revenge?" Bast asked.

The boy thought for a bit, then held up his hands about two feet apart. "This much."

"Hmmm," Bast said. "How much on a scale from mouse to bull?"

The boy rubbed his nose for a while. "About a cat's worth," he said. "Maybe a dog's worth. Not like Crazy Martin's dog, though. Like the Bentons' dogs."

Bast nodded and tilted his head back in a thoughtful way. "Okay," he said. "Piss in his shoes."

The boy looked skeptical. "That don't sound like a whole dog's worth of revenge."

Bast shook his head. "You piss in a cup and hide it. Let it sit for a day or two. Then one night when he's put his shoes by the fire, pour the piss on his shoes. Don't make a puddle, just get them damp. In the morning they'll be dry and probably won't even smell too much . . ."

"What's the point?" the boy interrupted angrily. "That's not a flea's worth of revenge!"

Bast held up a pacifying hand. "When his feet get sweaty, he'll start to smell like piss," Bast said calmly. "If he steps in a puddle, he'll smell like piss. When he walks in the snow, he'll smell like piss. It will be hard for him to figure out exactly where it's coming from, but everyone will know your brother is the one that reeks." Bast grinned at the boy. "I'm guessing your Gretta isn't going to want to kiss the boy who can't stop pissing himself."

Raw admiration spread across the young boy's face like sunrise in the mountains. "That's the most bastardly thing I've ever heard," he said, awestruck.

Bast tried to look modest and failed. "Have you got anything for me?"

"I found a wild beehive," the boy said.

"That will do for a start," Bast said. "Where?"

"It's off past the Orissons'. Past Littlecreek." The boy squatted and drew a map in the dirt. "You see?"

Bast nodded. "Anything else?"

"Well . . . I know where Crazy Martin keeps his still . . ."

Bast raised his eyebrows at that. "Really?"

The boy drew another map and gave some directions. Then he stood and dusted off his knees. "We square?"

Bast scuffed his foot in the dirt, destroying the map. "We're square."

The boy dusted off his knees. "I've got a message too. Rike wants to see you."

Bast shook his head firmly. "He knows the rules. Tell him no."

"I already told him," the boy said with a comically exaggerated shrug. "But I'll tell him again if I see him . . ."

There were no more children waiting after Kale, so Bast tucked the leather book under his arm and went on a long, rambling stroll. He found some wild raspberries and ate them. He took a drink from the Ostlar's well.

Eventually Bast climbed to the top of a nearby bluff where he gave a great stretch before tucking the leather-bound copy of *Celum Tinture* into a spreading hawthorn tree where a wide branch made a cozy nook against the trunk.

He looked up at the sky then, clear and bright. No clouds. Not much wind. Warm but not hot. Hadn't rained for a solid span. It wasn't a market day. Hours before noon on Felling . . .

Bast's brow furrowed a bit, as if performing some complex calculation. Then he nodded to himself.

Then Bast headed back down the bluff, past Old Lant's place and around the brambles that bordered the Alard farm. When he came to

Littlecreek he cut some reeds and idly whittled at them with a small bright knife. Then he brought the string out of his pocket and bound them together, fashioning a tidy set of shepherd's pipes.

He blew across the top of them and cocked his head to listen to their sweet discord. His bright knife trimmed some more, and he blew again. This time the tune was closer, which made the discord far more grating.

Bast's knife flicked again, once, twice, thrice. Then he put it away and brought the pipes closer to his face. He breathed in through his nose, smelling the wet green of them. Then he licked the fresh-cut tops of the reeds, the flicker of his tongue a sudden, startling red.

Then he drew a breath and blew against the pipes. This time the sound was bright as moonlight, lively as a leaping fish, sweet as stolen fruit. Smiling, Bast headed off into the Bentons' back hills, and it wasn't long before he heard the low, mindless bleat of distant sheep.

A minute later, Bast came over the crest of a hill and saw two dozen fat, daft sheep cropping grass in the green valley below. It was shadowy here and secluded. The lack of recent rain meant the grazing was better here. The steep sides of the valley meant the sheep weren't prone to straying and didn't need much looking after.

A young woman sat in the shade of a spreading elm that overlooked the valley. She had taken off her shoes and bonnet. Her long, thick hair was the color of ripe wheat.

Bast began playing then. A dangerous tune. It was sweet and bright and slow and sly.

The shepherdess perked up at the sound of it, or so it seemed at first. She lifted her head, excited . . . but no. She didn't look in his direction at all. She was merely climbing to her feet to have a stretch, rising high up onto her toes, hands twining over her head.

Still apparently unaware she was being serenaded, the young woman picked up a nearby blanket, spread it beneath the tree, and sat back down. It was a little odd, as she'd been sitting there before without the blanket. Perhaps she'd just grown chilly.

Bast continued to play as he walked down the slope of the valley toward her. He did not hurry, and the music he made was sweet and playful and languorous all at once.

The shepherdess showed no sign of noticing the music or Bast himself. In fact she looked away from him, toward the far end of the little valley, as if curious what the sheep might be doing there. When she turned her head, it exposed the lovely line of her neck from her perfect shell-like ear, down to the gentle swell of breast that showed above her bodice.

Eyes intent on the young woman, Bast stepped on a loose stone and stumbled awkwardly down the hill. He blew one hard, squawking note, then dropped a few more from his song as he threw out one arm wildly to catch his balance.

The shepherdess laughed then, but she was pointedly looking at the other end of the valley. Perhaps the sheep had done something humorous. Yes. That was surely it. They could be funny animals at times.

Even so, one can only look at sheep for so long. She sighed and relaxed, leaning back against the sloping trunk of the tree. The motion accidentally pulled the hem of her skirt up slightly past her knee. Her calves were round and tan and covered with the lightest down of honey-colored hair.

Bast continued down the hill. His steps delicate and graceful. He looked like a stalking cat. He looked like he was dancing.

Apparently satisfied the sheep were safe, the shepherdess sighed again, closed her eyes, and lay her head against the trunk of the tree. Her face tilted up to catch the sun. She seemed about to sleep, but for all her sighing her breath seemed to be coming rather quickly. And when she shifted restlessly to make herself more comfortable, one hand fell in such a way that it accidentally drew the hem of her dress even farther up until it showed a pale expanse of thigh.

It is hard to grin while playing shepherd's pipes. Somehow Bast managed it.

The sun was climbing the sky when Bast returned to the lightning tree, pleasantly sweaty and in a state of mild dishevel. There were no children waiting near the greystones this time, which suited him perfectly.

He did a quick circle of the tree again when he reached the top of the hill, once in each direction to ensure his small workings were still in place. Then he slumped down at the foot of the tree and leaned against the trunk. Less than a minute later his eyes were closed and he was snoring slightly.

After the better part of an hour, the near-silent sound of footsteps roused him. He gave a great stretch and spied a thin boy with freckles and clothes that were slightly past the point where they might merely be called well-worn.

"Kostrel!" Bast said happily. "How's the road to Tinuë?"

"Seems sunny enough to me today," the boy said as he came to the top of the hill. "And I found a lovely secret by the roadside. Something I thought you might be interested in."

"Ah," Bast said. "Come have a seat, then. What sort of secret did you stumble on?"

Kostrel sat cross-legged on the grass nearby. "I know where Emberlee takes her bath."

Bast raised a half-interested eyebrow. "Is that so?"

Kostrel grinned. "You faker. Don't pretend you don't care."

"Of course I care," Bast said. "She's the sixth prettiest girl in town, after all."

"Sixth?" the boy said, indignant. "She's the second prettiest and you know it."

"Perhaps fourth," Bast conceded. "After Ania."

"Ania's legs are skinny as a chicken's," Kostrel observed calmly.

Bast smiled at the boy. "To each his own. But yes. I am interested. What would you like in trade? An answer, a favor, a secret?"

"I want a favor *and* information," the boy said with a small smirk. His dark eyes were sharp in his lean face. "I want good answers to three questions. And it's worth it. Because Emberlee is the third prettiest girl in town."

Bast opened his mouth as if he were going to protest, then shrugged and smiled. "No favor. But I'll give you three answers on a subject named beforehand," he countered. "Any subject except that of my employer, whose trust in me I cannot in good conscience betray."

Kostrel nodded in agreement. "Three *full* answers," he said. "With no equivocating or bullshittery."

Bast nodded. "So long as the questions are focused and specific. No *'tell me everything you know about'* nonsense."

"That wouldn't be a question," Kostrel pointed out.

"Exactly," Bast said. "And you agree not to tell anyone else where Emberlee is having her bath?" Kostrel scowled at that, and Bast laughed. "You little cocker, you would have sold it twenty times, wouldn't you?"

The boy shrugged easily, not denying it, and not embarrassed either. "It's valuable information."

Bast chuckled. "Three full, earnest answers on a single subject with the understanding that I'm the only one you've told."

"You are," the boy said sullenly. "I came here first."

"And with the understanding that you won't tell Emberlee anyone knows." Kostrel looked so offended at this that Bast didn't bother waiting for him to agree. "And with the understanding that you won't show up yourself."

The dark-eyed boy spat a couple words that surprised Bast more than his earlier use of "equivocating."

"Fine," Kostrel growled. "But if you don't know the answer to my question, I get to ask another."

Bast thought about it for a moment, then nodded.

"And if I pick a subject you don't know much about, I get to choose another."

Another nod. "That's fair."

"And you loan me another book," the boy said, his dark eyes glaring. "And a copper penny. And you have to describe her breasts to me."

Bast threw back his head and laughed. "Done."

They shook on the deal, the boy's thin hand as delicate as a bird's wing.

Bast leaned against the lightning tree, yawning and rubbing the back of his neck. "So. What's your subject?"

Kostrel's grim look lifted a little then, and he grinned excitedly. "I want to know about the Fae."

It says a great deal that Bast finished his great yawp of a yawn as if nothing were the matter. It is quite hard to yawn and stretch when your belly feels like you've swallowed a lump of bitter iron and your mouth has gone suddenly dry.

But Bast was something of a professional dissembler, so he yawned and stretched, and even went so far as to scratch himself under one arm lazily.

"Well?" the boy asked impatiently. "Do you know enough about them?"

"A fair amount," Bast said, doing a much better job of looking modest this time. "More than most folk, I imagine."

Kostrel leaned forward, his thin face intent. "I thought you might. You aren't from around here. You *know* things. You've seen what's really out there in the world."

"Some of it," Bast admitted. He looked up at the sun. "Ask your questions, then. I have to be somewhere come noon."

The boy nodded seriously, then looked down at the grass in front of himself for a moment, thinking. "What are they like?"

Bast blinked for a moment, taken aback. Then he laughed helplessly and threw up his hands. "Merciful Tehlu. Do you have any idea how crazy that question is? They're not like anything. They're like themselves."

Kostrel looked indignant. "Don't you try to shim me!" he said, leveling a finger at Bast. "I said no bullshittery!"

"I'm not. Honest I'm not." Bast raised his hands defensively. "It's just an impossible question to answer is all. What would you say if I asked you what *people* were like? How could you answer that? There are so many kinds of people, and they're all different."

"So it's a big question," Kostrel said. "Give me a big answer."

"It's not just big," Bast said. "It would fill a book."

The boy gave a profoundly unsympathetic shrug.

Bast scowled. "It could be argued that your question is neither focused nor specific."

Kostrel raised an eyebrow. "So we're arguing now? I thought we were trading information? Fully and freely. If you asked me where Emberlee was going for her bath, and I said, 'In a stream' you'd feel like I'd measured you some pretty short corn, wouldn't you?"

Bast sighed. "Fair enough. But if I told you every rumor and snippet I'd ever heard, this would take a span of days. Most of it would be useless, and some probably wouldn't even be true because it's just from stories that I've heard."

Kostrel frowned, but before he could protest, Bast held up a hand. "Here's what I'll do. Despite the unfocused nature of your question, I'll give you an answer that covers the rough shape of things and . . ." Bast hesitated. ". . . one true secret on the subject. Okay?"

"Two secrets," Kostrel said, his dark eyes glittering with excitement.

"Fair enough." Bast took a deep breath. "When you say fae, you're talking about anything that lives in the Fae. That includes a lot of things that are . . . just creatures. Like animals. Here you have dogs and squirrels and bears. In the Fae, they have raum and dennerlings and . . ."

"And trow?"

Bast nodded. "And trow. They're real."

"And dragons?"

Bast shook his head. "Not that I've ever heard. Not anymore . . ."

Kostrel looked disappointed. "What about the fair folk? Like faerie tinkers and such?" The boy narrowed his eyes. "Mind you, this isn't a new question, merely an attempt to focus your ongoing answer."

Bast laughed helplessly. "Lord and lady. *Ongoing?* Was your mother scared by an azzie when she was pregnant? Where do you get that kind of talk?"

"I stay awake in church." Kostrel shrugged. "And sometimes Abbe Leodin lets me read his books. What do they look like?"

"Like regular people," Bast said.

"Like you and me?" the boy asked.

Bast fought back a smile. "Just like you or me. You wouldn't hardly notice if they passed you on the street. But there are others. Some of them are . . . They're different. More powerful."

"Like Varsa never-dead?"

"Some," Bast conceded. "But some are powerful in other ways. Like the mayor is powerful. Or like a moneylender." Bast's expression went sour. "Many of those . . . they're not good to be around. They like to trick people. Play with them. Hurt them."

Some of the excitement bled out of Kostrel at this. "They sound like demons."

Bast hesitated, then nodded a reluctant agreement. "Some are very much like demons," he admitted. "Or so close as it makes no difference."

"Are some of them like angels too?" the boy asked.

"It's nice to think that," Bast said. "I hope so."

"Where do they come from?"

Bast cocked his head. "That's your second question, then?" he asked. "I'm guessing it must be, as it's got nothing to do with what the Fae are *like* . . ."

Kostrel grimaced, seeming a little embarrassed, though Bast couldn't tell if he was ashamed he'd gotten carried away with his questions, or ashamed he'd been caught trying to get a free answer. "Sorry," he said. "Is it true that a faerie can never lie?"

"Some can't," Bast said. "Some don't like to. Some are happy to lie but wouldn't ever go back on a promise or break their word." He shrugged. "Others lie quite well, and do so at every opportunity."

Kostrel began to ask something else, but Bast cleared his throat. "You have to admit," he said. "That's a pretty good answer. I even gave you a few free questions, to help with the focus of things, as it were."

Kostrel gave a slightly sullen nod.

"Here's your first secret." Bast held up a single finger. "Most of the Fae don't come to this world. They don't like it. It rubs all rough against them, like wearing a burlap shirt. But when they do come, they like some places better than others. They like wild places. Secret places. Strange places. There are many types of fae, many courts and houses. And all of them are ruled according to their own desires . . ."

Bast continued in a tone of soft conspiracy. "But something that appeals to all the fae are places with connections to the raw, true things that shape the world. Places that are touched with fire and stone. Places that are close to water and air. When all four come together . . ."

Bast paused to see if the boy would interject something here. But

Kostrel's face had lost the sharp cunning it had held before. He looked like a child again, mouth slightly agape, his eyes wide with wonder.

"Second secret," Bast said. "The fae folk look nearly like we do, but not *exactly*. Most have something about them that makes them different. Their eyes. Their ears. The color of their hair or skin. Sometimes they're taller than normal, or shorter, or stronger, or more beautiful."

"Like Felurian."

"Yes, yes," Bast said testily. "Like Felurian. But any of the Fae who have the skill to travel here will have craft enough to hide those things." He leaned back, nodding to himself. "That is a type of magic all the fair folk share."

Bast threw the final comment out like a fisherman casting a lure.

Kostrel closed his mouth and swallowed hard. He didn't fight the line. Didn't even know that he'd been hooked. "What sort of magic can they do?"

Bast rolled his eyes dramatically. "Oh come now, that's another whole book's worth of question."

"Well, maybe you should just *write* a book, then," Kostrel said flatly. "Then you can lend it to me and kill two birds with one stone."

The comment seemed to catch Bast off his stride. "Write a book?"

"That's what people do when they know every damn thing, isn't it?" Kostrel said sarcastically. "They write it down so they can show off."

Bast looked thoughtful for a moment, then shook his head as if to clear it. "Okay. Here's the bones of what I know. They don't think of it as magic. They'd never use that term. They'll talk of art or craft. They talk of seeming or shaping."

He looked up at the sun and pursed his lips. "But if they were being frank, and they are rarely frank, mind you, they would tell you almost everything they do is either glammourie or grammarie. Glammourie is the art of making something seem. Grammarie is the craft of making something be."

Bast rushed ahead before the boy could interrupt. "Glammourie is easier. They can make a thing seem other than it is. They could make a white shirt seem like it was blue. Or a torn shirt seem like it was whole. Most of the folk have at least a scrap of this art. Enough to hide themselves from mortal eyes. If their hair was all of silver-white, their glammourie could make it look as black as night."

Kostrel's face was lost in wonder yet again. But it was not the gormless, gaping wonder of before. It was a thoughtful wonder. A clever wonder, curious and hungry. It was the sort of wonder that would steer a boy toward a question that started with a *how.*

Bast could see the shape of these things moving in the boy's dark eyes. His damn clever eyes. Too clever by half. Soon those vague wonderings would start to crystallize into questions like *"How do they make their glammourie?"* or, even worse, *"How might a young boy break it?"*

And what then, with a question like that hanging in the air? Nothing good would come of it. To break a promise fairly made and lie outright was retrograde to his desire. Even worse to do it in this place. Far easier to tell the truth, then make sure something happened to the boy . . .

But honestly, he liked the boy. He wasn't dull or easy. He wasn't mean or low. He pushed back. He was funny and grim and hungry and more alive than any three other people in the town all put together. He was bright as broken glass and sharp enough to cut himself. And Bast too, apparently.

Bast rubbed his face. This never used to happen. He had never been in conflict with his own desire before he came here. He hated it. It was so simply singular before. Want and have. See and take. Run and chase. Thirst and slake. And if he were thwarted in pursuit of his desire . . . what of it? That was simply the way of things. The desire itself was still his, it was still pure.

It wasn't like that now. Now his desires grew complicated. They constantly conflicted with each other. He felt endlessly turned against himself. Nothing was simple anymore, he was pulled so many ways . . .

"Bast?" Kostrel said, his head cocked to the side, concern plain on his face. "Are you okay?" he asked. "What's the matter?"

Bast smiled an honest smile. He was a curious boy. Of course. That was the way. That was the narrow road between desires. "I was just thinking. Grammarie is much harder to explain. I can't say I understand it all that well myself."

"Just do your best," Kostrel said kindly. "Whatever you tell me will be more than I know."

No, he couldn't kill this boy. That would be too hard a thing.

"Grammarie is changing a thing," Bast said, making an inarticulate gesture. "Making it into something different than what it is."

"Like turning lead into gold?" Kostrel asked. "Is that how they make faerie gold?"

Bast made a point of smiling at the question. "Good guess, but that's glammourie. It's easy, but it doesn't last. That's why people who take faerie gold end up with pockets full of stones or acorns in the morning."

"Could they turn gravel into gold?" Kostrel asked. "If they really wanted to?"

"It's not that sort of change," Bast said, though he still smiled and nodded at the question. "That's too big. Grammarie is about . . . shifting. It's about making something into more of what it already is."

Kostrel's face twisted with confusion.

Bast took a deep breath and let it out through his nose. "Let me try something else. What have you got in your pockets?"

Kostrel rummaged about and held out his hands. There was a brass button, a scrap of paper, a stub of pencil, a small folding knife . . . and a stone with a hole in it. Of course.

Bast slowly passed his hand over the collection of oddments, eventually stopping above the knife. It wasn't particularly fine or fancy, just a piece of smooth wood the size of a finger with a groove where a short, hinged blade was tucked away.

Bast picked it up delicately between two fingers and set it down on the ground between them. "What's this?"

Kostrel stuffed the rest of his belongings into his pocket. "It's my knife."

"That's it?" Bast asked.

The boy's eyes narrowed suspiciously. "What else could it be?"

Bast brought out his own knife. It was a little larger, and instead of wood, it was carved from a piece of antler, polished and beautiful. Bast opened it, and the bright blade shone in the sun.

He laid his knife next to the boy's. "Would you trade your knife for mine?"

Kostrel eyed the knife jealously. But even so, there wasn't a hint of hesitation before he shook his head.

"Why not?"

"Because it's mine," the boy said, his face clouding over.

"Mine's better," Bast said matter-of-factly.

Kostrel reached out and picked up his knife, closing his hand around it possessively. His face was sullen as a storm. "My da gave me this," he said. "Before he took the king's coin and went to be a soldier and save us from the rebels." He looked up at Bast, as if daring him to say a single word contrary to that.

Bast didn't look away from him, just nodded seriously. "So it's more than just a knife," he said. "It's special to you."

Still clutching the knife, Kostrel nodded, blinking rapidly.

"For you, it's the best knife."

Another nod.

"It's more important than other knives. And that's not just a *seeming,*" Bast said. "It's something the knife *is.*"

There was a flicker of understanding in Kostrel's eyes.

Bast nodded. "That's grammarie. Now imagine if someone could take a knife and make it be more of what a knife is. Make it into the best knife. Not just for them, but for *anyone.*" Bast picked up his own knife and closed it. "If they were really skilled, they could do it with something other than a knife. They could make a fire that was more of what a fire is. Hungrier. Hotter. Someone truly powerful could do even more. They could take a shadow . . ." He trailed off gently, leaving an open space in the empty air.

Kostrel drew a breath and leapt to fill it with a question. "Like Felurian!" he said. "Is that what she did to make Kvothe's shadow cloak?"

Bast nodded seriously, glad for the question, hating that it had to be *that* question. "It seems likely to me. What does a shadow do? It conceals, it protects. Kvothe's cloak of shadows does the same, but more."

Kostrel was nodding along in understanding, and Bast pushed on quickly, eager to leave this particular subject behind. "Think of Felurian herself . . ."

The boy grinned, he seemed to have no trouble doing that.

"A woman can be a thing of beauty," Bast said slowly. "She can be a focus of desire. Felurian is that. Like the knife. The most beautiful. The focus of the most desire. For everyone . . ." Bast let his statement trail off gently yet again.

Kostrel's eyes were far away, obviously giving the matter his full deliberation. Bast gave him time for it, and after a moment another question bubbled out of the boy. "Couldn't it be merely glammourie?" he asked.

"Ah," said Bast, smiling. "But what is the difference between *being* beautiful and *seeming* beautiful?"

"Well . . ." Kostrel stalled for a moment, then rallied. "One is real and the other isn't." He sounded certain, but it wasn't reflected in his expression. "One would be fake. You could tell the difference, couldn't you?"

Bast let the question sail by. It was close, but not quite. "What's the difference between a shirt that *looks* white and a shirt that *is* white?" he countered.

"A woman isn't the same as a shirt," Kostrel said with vast disdain. "You'd know if you touched her. If she looked all soft and rosy like Emberlee, but her hair felt like a horse's tail, you'd know it wasn't real."

"Glammourie isn't just for fooling eyes," Bast said. "It's for everything. Faerie gold feels heavy. And a glamoured pig would smell like roses when you kissed it."

Kostrel reeled visibly at that. The shift from Emberlee to a glamoured pig obviously left him feeling more than slightly appalled. Bast waited a moment for him to recover.

"Wouldn't it be harder to glamour a pig?" he asked at last.

"You're clever," Bast said encouragingly. "You're exactly right. And glamouring a pretty girl to be *more* pretty wouldn't be much work at all. It's like putting icing on a cake."

Kostrel rubbed his cheek thoughtfully. "Can you use glammourie and grammarie at the same time?"

Bast was more genuinely impressed this time. "That's what I've heard."

Kostrel nodded to himself. "That's what Felurian must do," he said. "Like cream on icing on cake."

"I think so," Bast said. "The one I met . . ." He stopped abruptly, his mouth snapped shut.

"You've met one of the Fae?"

Bast grinned like a beartrap. "Yes."

This time Kostrel felt the hook and line both. But it was too late. "You bastard!"

"I am," Bast admitted happily.

"You tricked me into asking that."

"I did," Bast said. "It was a question related to this subject, and I answered it fully and without equivocation."

Kostrel got to his feet and stormed off, only to come back a moment later. "Give me my penny," he demanded.

Bast reached into his pocket and pulled out a copper penny. "Where does Emberlee take her bath?"

Kostrel glowered furiously, then said, "Out past Oldstone bridge, up toward the hills about half a mile. There's a little hollow with an elm tree."

"And when?"

"After lunch on the Boggan farm. After she finishes the washing up and hangs the laundry."

Bast tossed him the penny, still grinning like mad.

"I hope your dick falls off," the boy said venomously before stomping back down the hill.

Bast couldn't help but laugh. He tried to do it quietly to spare the boy's feelings but didn't meet with much success.

Kostrel turned at the bottom of the hill and shouted, "And you still owe me a book!"

Bast stopped laughing then as something jogged loose in his memory. He panicked for a moment when he realized *Celum Tinture* wasn't in its usual spot.

Then he remembered leaving the book in the tree on top of the bluff and relaxed. The clear sky showed no sign of rain. It was safe enough. Besides, it was nearly noon, perhaps a little past. So he turned and hurried down the hill, not wanting to be late.

Bast sprinted most of the way to the little dell, and by the time he arrived he was sweating like a hard-run horse. His shirt stuck to him unpleasantly, so as he walked down the sloping bank to the water, he pulled it off and used it to mop the sweat from his face.

A long, flat jut of stone pushed out into Littlecreek there, forming one side of a calm pool where the stream turned back on itself. A stand of willow trees overhung the water, making it private and shady. The shoreline was overgrown with thick bushes, and the water was smooth and calm and clear.

Bare-chested, Bast walked out onto the rough jut of stone. Dressed, his face and hands made him look rather lean, but shirtless his wide shoulders were surprising, more what you might expect to see on a field hand, rather than a shiftless sort that did little more than lounge around an empty inn all day.

Once he was out of the shadow of the willows, Bast knelt to dunk his shirt in the pool. Then he wrung it over his head, shivering a bit at the chill of it. He rubbed his chest and arms briskly, shaking drops of water from his face.

He set the shirt aside, grabbed the lip of stone at the edge of the pool, then took a deep breath and dunked his head. The motion made the muscles across his back and shoulders flex. A moment later he pulled his head out, gasping slightly and shaking water from his hair.

Bast stood then, slicking back his hair with both hands. Water streamed down his chest, making runnels in the dark hair, trailing down across the flat plane of his stomach.

He shook himself off a bit, then stepped over to a dark niche made by a jagged shelf of overhanging rock. He felt around for a moment before pulling out a knob of butter-colored soap.

He knelt at the edge of the water again, dunking his shirt several times, then scrubbing it with the soap. It took a while, as he had no washing board, and he obviously didn't want to chafe his shirt against the rough stones. He soaped and rinsed the shirt several times, wringing it out with his hands, making the muscles in his arms and shoulders tense and twine. He did a thorough job, though by the time he was finished, he was completely soaked and spattered with lather.

Bast spread his shirt out on a sunny stone to dry. He started to undo his pants, then stopped and tipped his head on one side, trying to jog loose water from his ear.

It might be because of the water in his ear that Bast didn't hear the excited twittering coming from the bushes that grew along the shore. A sound that could, conceivably, be sparrows chattering among the branches. A flock of sparrows. Several flocks, perhaps.

And if Bast didn't see the bushes moving either? Or note that in among the hanging foliage of the willow branches there were colors normally not found in trees? Sometimes a pale pink, sometimes blushing red. Sometimes an ill-considered yellow or a cornflower blue. And while it's true that dresses might come in those colors . . . well . . . so did birds. Finches and jays. And besides, it was fairly common knowledge among the young women of the town that the dark young man who worked at the inn was woefully nearsighted.

The sparrows twittered in the bushes as Bast worked at the drawstring of his pants again. The knot apparently giving him some trouble. He fumbled with it for a while, then grew frustrated and gave a great, catlike stretch, arms arching over his head, his body bending like a bow.

Finally he managed to work the knot loose and shuck free of his pants. He wore nothing underneath. He tossed them aside and from the willow came a squawk of the sort that could have come from a larger bird. A heron perhaps. Or a crow. And if a branch shook violently at the same time, well, perhaps a bird had leaned too far from its branch and nearly fell. It certainly stood to reason that some birds were more clumsy than others. And besides, at the time Bast was looking the other way.

Bast dove into the water then, splashing like a boy and gasping at the cold. After a few minutes he moved to a shallower portion of the pool where the water rose to barely reach his narrow waist.

Beneath the water, a careful observer might note the young man's legs looked somewhat . . . odd. But it was shady there, and everyone knows that water bends light strangely, making things look other than they are. And besides, birds are not the most careful of observers, especially when their attention is focused elsewhere.

An hour or so later, slightly damp and smelling of sweet honeysuckle soap, Bast climbed the bluff where he was fairly certain that he'd left his master's book. It was the third bluff he'd climbed in the last half hour.

When he reached the top, Bast relaxed at the sight of a hawthorn tree. Walking closer, he saw it was the right tree, the nook right where he remembered. But the book was gone. A quick circle of the tree showed that it hadn't fallen to the ground.

Then the wind stirred and Bast saw something white. He felt a sudden chill, fearing it was a page torn free from the book. Few things angered his master like a mistreated book.

But no. Reaching up, Bast didn't feel paper. It was a smooth stretch of birch bark. He pulled it down and saw the letters crudely scratched into the side.

I ned ta tawk ta ewe. Ets emportant.
Rike

Afternoon: Birds and Bees

With no idea of where he might find Rike, Bast made his way back to the lightning tree. He had just settled down in his usual place when a young girl came into the clearing.

She didn't stop at the greystone and instead trudged straight up the side of the hill. She was younger than the others, six or seven. She wore a bright blue dress and had deep purple ribbons twining through her carefully curled hair.

She had never come to the lightning tree before, but Bast had seen her. Even if he hadn't, he could have guessed by her fine clothes and the smell of rosewater that she was Viette, the mayor's youngest daughter.

She climbed the low hill slowly, carrying something furry in the crook of her arm. When she reached the top of the hill she stood, slightly fidgety, but still waiting.

Bast eyed her quietly for a moment. "Do you know the rules?" he asked.

She stood, purple ribbons in her hair. She was obviously slightly scared, but her lower lip stuck out, defiant. She nodded.

"What are they?"

The young girl licked her lips and began to recite in a singsong voice. "No one taller than the stone." She pointed to the fallen greystone at the foot of the hill. "Come to blacktree, come alone." She put her finger to her lips, miming a shushing noise.

"Tell no—"

"Hold on," Bast interrupted. "You say the last two lines while touching the tree."

The girl blanched a bit at this but stepped forward and put her hand against the sun-bleached wood of the long-dead tree.

The girl cleared her throat again, then paused, her lips moving silently as she ran through the beginning of the poem until she found her place again. "Tell no adult what's been said, lest the lightning strike you dead."

When she spoke the last word, Viette gasped and jerked her hand back, as if something had burned or bitten her fingers. Her eyes went wide as she looked down at her fingertips and saw they were an untouched, healthy pink. Bast hid a smile behind his hand.

"Very well, then," Bast said. "You know the rules. I keep your secrets and you keep mine. I can answer questions or help you solve a problem." He sat down again, his back against the tree, bringing him to eye level with the girl. "What do you want?"

She held out the tiny puff of white fur she carried in the crook of her arm. It mewled. "Is this a magic kitten?" she asked.

Bast took the kitten in his hand and looked it over. It was a sleepy thing, almost entirely white. One eye was blue, the other green. "It is, actually," he said, slightly surprised. "At least a little." He handed it back.

She nodded seriously. "I want to call her Princess Icing Bun."

Bast simply stared at her, nonplussed. "Okay."

The girl scowled at him. "I don't know if she's a girl or a boy!"

"Oh," Bast said. He held out his hand, took the kitten, then petted it and handed it back. "It's a girl."

The mayor's daughter narrowed her eyes at him. "Are you fibbing?"

Bast blinked at the girl, then laughed. "Why would you believe me the first time and not the second?" he asked.

"I could *tell* she was a magic kitten," Viette said, rolling her eyes in exasperation. "I just wanted to make sure. But she's not wearing a dress. She doesn't have any ribbons or bows. How can you tell if she's a girl?"

Bast opened his mouth. Then closed it again. This was not some farmer's child. She had a governess and a whole closetful of clothes. She didn't spend her time around sheep and pigs and goats. She'd never seen a lamb born. She had an older sister, but no brothers . . .

He hesitated; he'd rather not lie. Not here. But he hadn't promised to answer her question, hadn't made any sort of agreement at all with her. That made things easier. A great deal easier than having an angry mayor visit the Waystone, demanding to know why his daughter suddenly knew the word "penis."

"I tickle the kitten's tummy," Bast said easily. "And if it winks at me, I know it's a girl."

This satisfied Viette, and she nodded gravely. "How can I get my father to let me keep it?"

"You've already asked him nicely?"

She nodded. "Daddy hates cats."

"Begged and cried?"

Nod.

"Screamed and thrown a fit?"

She rolled her eyes and gave an exasperated sigh. "I've *tried* all that, or I wouldn't be here."

Bast thought for a moment. "Okay. First, you have to get some food that will keep good for a couple days. Biscuits. Sausage. Apples. Hide it in your room where nobody will find it. Not even your governess. Not even the maid. Do you have a place like that?"

The little girl nodded.

"Then go ask your daddy one more time. Be gentle and polite. If he still says no, don't be angry. Just tell him that you love the kitten. Say if you can't have her, you're afraid you'll be so sad you'll die."

"He'll still say no," the little girl said.

Bast shrugged. "Probably. Here's the second part. Tonight, pick at your dinner. Don't eat it. Not even the dessert." The little girl started to say something, but Bast held up a hand. "If anyone asks you, just say you're not hungry. Don't mention the kitten. When you're alone in your room tonight, eat some of the food you've hidden."

The little girl looked thoughtful.

Bast continued. "Tomorrow, don't get out of bed. Say you're too tired. Don't eat your breakfast. Don't eat your lunch. You can drink a little water, but just sips. Just lie in bed. When they ask what's the matter—"

She brightened. "I say I want my kitten!"

Bast shook his head, his expression grim. "No. That will spoil it. Just say you're tired. If they leave you alone, you can eat, but be careful. If they catch you, you'll never get your kitten."

The girl was listening intently now, her brow furrowed in concentration.

"By dinner they'll be worried. They'll offer you more food. Your favorites. Keep saying you're not hungry. You're just tired. Just lie there. Don't talk. Do that all day long."

"Can I get up to pee?"

Bast nodded. "But remember to act tired. No playing. The next day, they'll be scared. They'll bring in a doctor. They'll try to feed you broth. They'll try everything. At some point your father will be there, and he'll ask you what's the matter."

Bast grinned at her. "That's when you start to cry. No howling. Don't blubber. Just tears. Just lie there and cry. Then say you miss your kitten so much. You miss your kitten so much you don't want to be alive anymore."

The little girl thought about it for a long minute, petting her kitten absentmindedly with one hand. Finally she nodded. "Okay." She turned to go.

"Hold on now!" Bast said quickly. "I gave you what you wanted. You owe me now."

The little girl turned around, her expression an odd mix of surprise and anxious embarrassment. "I didn't bring any money," she said, not meeting his eye.

"Not money," Bast said. "I gave you two answers and a way to get your kitten. You owe me three things. You pay with gifts and favors. You pay in secrets . . ."

She thought for a moment. "Daddy hides his strongbox key inside the mantel clock."

Bast nodded approvingly. "That's one."

The little girl looked up into the sky, still petting her kitten. "I saw Mama kissing the maid once."

Bast raised an eyebrow at that. "That's two . . ."

The girl put her finger in her ear and wiggled it. "That's all, I think."

"How about a favor, then?" Bast said. "I need you to fetch me two dozen daisies with long stems. And a blue ribbon. And two armfuls of gemlings."

Viette's face puckered in confusion. "What's a gemling?"

"Flowers," Bast said, looking puzzled himself. "Maybe you call them balsams? They grow wild all over around here," he said, making a wide gesture with both hands.

"Do you mean geraniums?" she asked.

Bast shook his head. "No. They've got loose petals, and they're about this big." He made a circle with his thumb and middle finger. "They're yellow and orange and red . . ."

The girl stared at him blankly.

"Widow Creel keeps them in her window box," Bast continued. "When you touch the seedpods, they pop . . ."

Viette's face lit up. "Oh! You mean *touch-me-nots,*" she said, her tone more than slightly patronizing. "I can bring you a bunch of those. That's *easy.*" She turned to run down the hill.

Bast called out before she'd taken six steps. "Wait!" When she spun around, he asked her, "What do you say if somebody asks you who you're picking flowers for?"

She rolled her eyes again. "I tell them it's none of their tupping business," she said. "Because my daddy is the mayor."

After Viette left, a high whistle made Bast look down the hill toward the greystone. There were no children waiting there.

The whistle came again, and Bast stood, stretching long and hard. It would have surprised most of the young women in town how easily he spotted the figure standing in the shadow of the trees at the edge of the clearing nearly two hundred feet away.

Bast sauntered down the hill, across the grassy field, and into the shadow of the trees. There was an older boy there with smudgy face and a pug nose. He was perhaps twelve and his shirt and pants were both too small for him, showing too much dirty wrist at the cuff and bare ankle below. He was barefoot and had a slightly sour smell about him.

"Rike." Bast's voice held none of the friendly, bantering tone he'd used with the town's other children. "How's the road to Tinuë?"

"It's a long damn way," the boy said bitterly, not meeting Bast's eye. "We live in the ass of nowhere."

"I see you have my book," Bast said.

The boy held it out. "I wann't tryin' to steal it," he muttered quickly. "I just needed to talk to you."

Bast took the book silently.

"I didn't break the rules," the boy said. "I didn't even come into the clearing. But I need help. I'll pay for it."

"You lied to me, Rike," Bast said, his voice grim.

"And din't I pay for that?" the boy demanded angrily, looking up for the first time. "Din't I pay for it ten times over? Ent my life shit enough without having more shit piled on top of it?"

"And it's all beside the point because you're too old now," Bast said flatly.

"I aren't either!" The boy stomped a foot then struggled and took a deep breath, visibly forcing his temper back under control. "Tam is older'n me and he can still come to the tree! I'm just taller'n him!"

"Those are the rules," Bast said.

"It's a shite rule!" the boy shouted, his hands making angry fists. "And you're a shite little bastard who deserves more of the belt than he gets!"

There was a silence then, broken only by the boy's ragged breathing. Rike's eyes were on the ground, fists clenched at his sides; he was shaking.

Bast's eyes narrowed ever so slightly.

The boy's voice was rough. "Just one," Rike said. "Just one favor just this once. It's a big one. But I'll pay. I'll pay triple."

Bast drew a deep breath and let it out as a sigh. "Rike, I—"

"Please, Bast?" He was still shaking, but Bast realized the boy's voice wasn't angry anymore. "Please?" Eyes still on the ground, he took a hesitant step forward. "Just . . . please?" His hand reached out and just hung there aimlessly, as if he didn't know what to do with it. Finally he caught hold of Bast's shirtsleeve and tugged it once, feebly, before letting his hand fall back to his side.

"I just can't fix this on my own." Rike looked up, eyes full of tears. His face was twisted in a knot of anger and fear. A boy too young to keep from crying, but still old enough so that he couldn't help but hate himself for doing it.

"I need you to get rid of my da," he said in a broken voice. "I can't figure a way. I could stick him while he's asleep, but my ma would find out. He drinks and hits at her. And she cries all the time and then he hits her more."

Rike was looking at the ground again, the words pouring out of him in a gush. "I could get him when he's drunk somewhere, but he's so big. I couldn't move him. They'd find the body and then the azzie would get me. I couldn't look my ma in the eye then. Not if she knew. I can't think what that would do to her, if she knew I was the sort of person that would kill his own da."

He looked up then, his face furious, eyes red with weeping. "I would, though. I'd kill him. You just got to tell me how."

There was a moment of quiet.

"Okay," Bast said.

They went down to the stream where they could have a drink and Rike could wash his face and collect himself a little bit. When the boy's face was cleaner, Bast noted not all the smudginess was dirt. It was easy to make the mistake, as the summer sun had tanned him a rich nut brown. Even after he was clean it was hard to tell they were the faint remains of bruises.

But rumor or no, Bast's eyes were sharp. Cheek and jaw. A darkness all around one skinny wrist. And when he bent to take a drink from the stream, Bast glimpsed the boy's back . . .

"So," Bast said as they sat beside the stream. "What exactly do you want? Do you want to kill him, or do you just want to have him gone?"

"If he was just gone, I'd never sleep again for worry he'd come slouching back," Rike said, then was quiet for a bit. "He went gone two span once." He gave a faint smile. "That was a good time, just me and my ma. It was like my birthday every day when I woke up and he wasn't there. I never knew my ma could sing . . ."

The boy went quiet again. "I thought he'd fallen somewhere drunk and finally broke his neck. But he'd just traded off a year of furs for drinking money. He'd just been in his trapping shack, all stupor-drunk for half a month, not hardly more than a mile away."

The boy shook his head, more firmly this time. "No, if he goes, he won't stay away."

"I can figure out the how," Bast said. "That's what I do. But you need to tell me what you really want."

Rike sat for a long while, jaw clenching and unclenching. "Gone," he said at last. The word seemed to catch in his throat. "So long as he stays gone forever. If you can really do it."

"I can do it," Bast said.

Rike looked at his hands for a long time. "Gone, then. I'd kill him. But that sort of thing ent right. I don't want to be that sort of man. A fellow shouldn't ought to kill his da."

"I could do it for you," Bast said easily.

Rike sat for a while, then shook his head. "It's the same thing, innit? Either way it's me. And if it were me, it would be more honest if I did it with my hands rather than do it with my mouth."

Bast nodded. "Right, then, Gone forever."

"And soon," Rike said.

Bast sighed and looked up at the sun. He already had things to do today. The turning wheels of his desire did not come grinding to a halt because some farmer drank too much. Emberlee would be taking her bath soon. He was supposed to get carrots . . .

He didn't owe the boy a thing either. Quite the opposite. The boy had lied to him. Broken his promise. And while Bast had settled that account so firmly that no other child in town would ever dream of crossing him like that again . . . it was still galling to remember. The thought of helping him now, despite that, it was quite the opposite of his desire.

"It *has* to be soon," Rike said. "He's getting worse. I can run off, but Ma can't. And little Bip can't neither. And . . ."

"Fine, fine . . ." Bast cut him off, waving his hands. "Soon."

Rike swallowed. "What's this going to cost me?" he asked, anxious.

"A lot," Bast said grimly. "We're not talking about ribbons and buttons here. Think how much you want this. Think how big it is." He met the boy's eye and didn't look away. "Three times that is what you owe me. Plus some for soon." He stared hard at the boy. "Think hard on that."

Rike was a little pale now, but he nodded without looking away. "You can have what you like of mine," he said. "But nothin' of Ma's. She ent got much that my da hasn't already drank away."

"We'll work it out," Bast said. "But it'll be nothing of hers. I promise."

Rike took a deep breath, then gave a sharp nod. "Okay. Where do we start?"

Bast pointed at the stream. "Find a river stone with a hole in it and bring it to me."

Rike gave Bast an odd look. "Yeh want a faerie stone?"

"Faerie stone," Bast said with such scathing mockery that Rike flushed with embarrassment. "You're too old for that nonsense." Bast gave the boy a look. "Do you want my help or not?" he asked.

"I do," Rike said in a small voice.

"Then I want a river stone." Bast pointed back at the stream. "You have to be the one to find it," he said. "It can't be anyone else. And you need to find it dry on the shore."

Rike nodded.

"Right, then." Bast clapped his hands twice. "Off you go."

Rike left and Bast returned to the lightning tree. No children were waiting to talk to him, so he idled the time away. He skipped stones in the nearby stream and flipped through *Celum Tinture,* glancing at some of the illustrations. Calcification. Titration. Sublimation.

Brann, happily unbirched with one hand bandaged, brought him two sweet buns wrapped in a white handkerchief. Bast ate the first and set the second aside.

Viette brought armloads of flowers and a fine blue ribbon. Bast wove the daisies into a crown, threading the ribbon through the stems.

Then, looking up at the sun, he saw that it was nearly time. Bast removed his shirt and filled it with the wealth of yellow and red touch-me-nots Viette had brought him. He added the handkerchief and crown, then fetched a stick and made a bindle so he could carry the lot more easily.

He headed out past the Oldstone bridge, then up toward the hills and around a bluff until he found the place Kostrel had described. It was cleverly hidden away, and the stream curved and eddied into a lovely little pool perfect for a private bath.

Bast sat behind some bushes, and after nearly half an hour of waiting he had fallen into a doze. The sharp crackle of a twig and a scrap of an idle song roused him, and he peered down to see a young woman making her careful way down the steep hillside to the water's edge.

Moving silently, Bast scurried upstream, carrying his bundle. Two minutes later he was kneeling on the grassy waterside with the pile of flowers beside him.

He picked up a yellow blossom and breathed on it gently. As his breath brushed the petals, its color faded and changed into a delicate blue. He dropped it and the current carried it slowly downstream.

Bast gathered up a handful of posies, red and orange, and breathed on them again. They too shifted and changed until they were a pale and vibrant blue. He scattered them onto the surface of the stream. He did this twice more until there were no flowers left.

Then, picking up the handkerchief and daisy crown, he sprinted back downstream to the cozy little hollow with the elm. He'd moved quickly enough that Emberlee was just coming to the edge of the water.

Softly, silently, he crept up to the spreading elm. Even with one hand carrying the handkerchief and crown, he went up the side as nimbly as a squirrel.

Bast lay along a low branch, sheltered by leaves, breathing fast but not hard. Emberlee was removing her stockings and setting them carefully on a nearby hedge. Her hair was a burnished golden red, falling in lazy curls. Her face was sweet and round, a lovely shade of pale and pink.

Bast grinned as he watched her look around, first left, then right. Then she began to unlace her bodice. Her dress was a pale cornflower blue, edged with yellow, and when she spread it on the hedge, it flared and splayed out like the wing of a great bird. Perhaps some fantastic combination of a finch and a jay.

Dressed only in her white shift, Emberlee looked around again: left, then right. Then she shimmied free of it, a fascinating motion. She tossed the shift aside and stood there, naked as the moon. Her creamy skin was amazing with freckle. Her hips wide and lovely. The tips of her breasts were brushed with the palest of pink.

She scampered into the water. Making a series of small, dismayed cries at the chill of it. They were, on consideration, not really similar to a raven's at all. Though they could, perhaps, be slightly like a heron's.

Emberlee washed herself a bit, splashing and shivering. She soaped herself, dunked her head in the river, and came up gasping. Wet, her hair became the color of ripe cherries.

It was then that the first of the blue touch-me-nots arrived, drifting on the water. She glanced at it curiously as it floated by and began to lather soap into her hair.

More flowers followed. They came downstream and made circles around her, caught in the slow eddy of the pool. She looked at them, amazed. Then sieved a double handful from the water and brought them to her face, drawing a deep breath to smell them.

She laughed delightedly and dunked under the surface, coming up in the middle of the flowers; the water sluiced her pale skin, running over her naked breasts. Blossoms clung to her, as if reluctant to let go.

That was when Bast fell out of the tree.

There was a brief, mad scrabbling of fingers against bark, a bit of a yelp, then he hit the ground like a sack of suet. He lay on his back in the grass and let out a low, miserable groan.

He heard a splashing, and then Emberlee appeared above him. She held her white shift in front of her. Bast looked up from where he lay in the tall grass.

He'd been lucky to land on that patch of springy turf, cushioned with tall green grass. A few feet to one side, and he'd have broken himself against the rocks. Five feet the other way and he would have been wallowing in mud.

Emberlee knelt beside him, her skin pale, her hair dark. One posy clung to her neck—it was the same color as her eyes, a pale and vibrant blue.

"Oh," Bast said happily as he gazed up at her. His eyes were slightly dazed. "You're so much lovelier than I'd imagined."

He lifted a hand as if to brush her cheek, only to find it holding the crown and knotted handkerchief. "Ahh," he said, remembering. "I've brought you some daisies too. And a sweet bun."

"Thank you," she said, taking the daisy crown with both hands. She had to let go of her shift to do this. It fell lightly to the grass.

Bast blinked, momentarily at a loss for words.

Emberlee tilted her head to look at the crown; the ribbon was a striking cornflower blue, but it was nothing near as lovely as her eyes. She lifted it with both hands and settled it proudly on her head. Her arms still raised, she drew a slow breath.

Bast's eyes slipped from her crown.

She smiled at him indulgently.

Bast drew a breath to speak, then stopped and drew another through his nose. Honeysuckle.

"Did you steal my soap?" he asked incredulously.

Emberlee laughed and kissed him.

A good while later, Bast took the long way back to the lightning tree, making a wide loop up into the hills north of town. Things were rockier up that way, no ground flat enough to plant, the terrain too treacherous for grazing.

Even with the boy's directions, it took Bast a while to find Martin's still. He had to give the crazy old bastard credit, though. Between the brambles, rockslides, and fallen trees, there wasn't a chance he would have stumbled onto it accidentally, tucked back into a shallow cave in a scrubby little box valley.

The still wasn't some slipshod contraption bunged together out of old pots and twisted wire either. It was a work of art. There were barrels and basins and great spirals of copper tube. A great copper kettle twice the size of a washbin, and a smolder-stove for warming it. A wooden trough ran all along the ceiling, and only after following it outside did Bast realize Martin collected rainwater and brought it inside to fill his cooling barrels.

Looking it over, Bast had the sudden urge to flip through *Celum Tinture* and learn what all the different pieces of the still were called, what they were for. Only then did he realize he'd left the book back at the lightning tree.

So instead Bast rooted around until he found a box filled with a mad miscellany of containers: two dozen bottles of all sorts, clay jugs, old canning jars . . . A dozen of them were full. None of them were labeled in any way.

Bast lifted out a tall bottle that had obviously once held wine. He pulled the cork, sniffed it gingerly, then took a careful sip. His face bloomed into a sunrise of delight. He'd half expected turpentine, but this was . . . well . . . he wasn't sure entirely. He took another drink. There was something of apples about it, and . . . barley?

Bast took a third drink, grinning. Whatever you care to call it, it was lovely. Smooth and strong and just a little sweet. Martin might be mad as a badger, but he clearly knew his liquor.

It was better than an hour before Bast made it back to the lightning tree. Rike hadn't returned, but *Celum Tinture* was sitting there unharmed. For the first time he could remember, he was glad to see the book. He flipped it open to the chapter on distillation and read for half an hour, nodding to himself at various points. It was called a condensate coil. He'd thought it looked important.

Eventually he closed the book and sighed. There were a few clouds rolling in, and no good could come of leaving the book unattended again. His luck wouldn't last forever, and he shuddered to think what would happen if the wind tumbled the book into the grass and tore the pages. If there was a sudden rain . . .

So Bast wandered back to the Waystone Inn and slipped silently through the back door. Stepping carefully, he opened a cupboard and tucked the book inside. He made his silent way halfway back to the door before he heard footsteps behind him.

"Ah, Bast," the innkeeper said. "Have you brought the carrots?"

Bast froze, caught awkwardly midsneak. He straightened up and brushed self-consciously at his clothes. "I . . . I haven't quite got round to that yet, Reshi."

The innkeeper gave a deep sigh. "I don't ask a . . ." He stopped and sniffed, then eyed the dark-haired man narrowly. "Are you drunk, Bast?"

Bast looked affronted. "Reshi!"

The innkeeper rolled his eyes. "Fine then, have you been drinking?"

"I've been *investigating,*" Bast said, emphasizing the word. "Did you know Crazy Martin runs a still?"

"I didn't," the innkeeper said, his tone making it clear he didn't find this information to be particularly thrilling. "And Martin isn't crazy. He just has a handful of unfortunately strong affect compulsions. And a touch of tabard madness from when he was a soldier."

"Well, yes . . ." Bast said slowly. "I know, because he set his dog on me and when I climbed a tree to get away, he tried to chop the tree down. But also, aside from those things, he's crazy too, Reshi. Really, really crazy."

"Bast." The innkeeper gave him a chiding look.

"I'm not saying he's bad, Reshi. I'm not even saying I don't like him. But trust me. I know crazy. His head isn't put together like a normal person's."

The innkeeper gave an agreeable if slightly impatient nod. "Noted."

Bast opened his mouth, then looked slightly confused. "What were we talking about?"

"Your advanced state of investigation," the innkeeper said, glancing out the window. "Despite the fact that it is barely three bells."

"Ah. Right!" Bast said excitedly. "I know Martin's been running a tab for the better part of a year now. And I know you've had trouble settling up because he doesn't have any money."

"He doesn't *use* money," the innkeeper corrected gently.

"Same difference, Reshi." Bast sighed. "And it doesn't change the fact that we don't need another sack of barley. The pantry is choking on barley. But since he runs a still . . ."

The innkeeper was already shaking his head. "No, Bast," he said. "I won't go poisoning my customers with hillwine. You have no idea what ends up in that stuff . . ."

"But I *do* know, Reshi," Bast said plaintively. "Ethel acetates and methans. And tinleach. There's none of that."

The innkeeper blinked, obviously taken aback. "Did . . . Have you actually been reading *Celum Tinture*?"

"I did, Reshi." Bast beamed. "For the betterment of my education and my desire to not poison folk. I tasted some, Reshi, and I can say with some authority that Martin is not making hillwine. It's lovely stuff. It's halfway to Rhis, and that's not something I say lightly."

The innkeeper stroked his upper lip thoughtfully. "Where did you get some to taste?" he asked.

"I traded for it," Bast said, easily skirting the edges of the truth. "I was thinking," Bast continued. "Not only would it give Martin a chance to settle his tab, but it would help us get some new stock in. That's harder, the roads as bad as they are . . ."

The innkeeper held up both hands helplessly. "I'm already convinced, Bast."

Bast grinned happily.

"Honestly, I would have done it merely to celebrate you reading your lesson for once. But it will be nice for Martin too. It will give him an excuse to come by more often. It will be good for him."

Bast's smile faded a bit.

If the innkeeper noticed, he didn't comment on it. "I'll send a boy round to Martin's and ask him to come by with a couple bottles."

"Get five or six," Bast said. "It's getting cold at night. Winter's coming."

The innkeeper smiled. "I'm sure Martin will be flattered."

Bast paled at that. "By all the gorse *no,* Reshi," he said, waving his hands in front of himself and taking a step backwards. "Don't tell him I'll be drinking it. He hates me."

The innkeeper hid a smile behind his hand.

"It's not funny, Reshi," Bast said angrily. "He throws rocks at me."

"Not for months," the innkeeper pointed out. "Martin has been perfectly cordial to you the last several times he's stopped by for a visit."

"Because there aren't any rocks inside the inn," Bast said.

"Be fair, Bast," the innkeeper continued. "He's been civil for almost a year. Polite even. Remember he apologized to you two months back? Have you heard of Martin ever apologizing to anyone else in town? Ever?"

"No," Bast said sulkily.

The innkeeper nodded. "That's a big gesture for him. He's turning a new leaf."

"I know," Bast muttered, moving toward the back door. "But if he's here when I get home tonight, I'm eating dinner in the kitchen."

* * *

Rike caught up with Bast before he even made it to the clearing, let alone the lightning tree.

"I've got it," the boy said, holding up his hand triumphantly. The entire lower half of his body was dripping wet.

"What, already?" Bast asked.

The boy nodded and flourished the stone between two fingers. It was flat and smooth and round, slightly bigger than a copper penny. "What now?"

Bast stroked his chin for a moment, as if trying to remember. "Now we need a needle. But it has to be borrowed from a house where no men live."

Rike looked thoughtful for a moment, then brightened. "I can get one from Aunt Sellie!"

Bast fought the urge to curse. He'd forgotten about Sellie. "That will do . . ." he said reluctantly, "but it will work best if the needle comes from a house with a lot of women living in it. The more women the better."

Rike looked up for another moment. "Widow Creel, then. She's got a daughter."

"She's got a boy too," Bast pointed out. "A house where no men *or boys* live."

"But where a lot of girls live . . ." Rike said. He had to think about it for a long while. "Old Nan don't like me none," he said. "But I reckon she'd give me a pin."

"A needle," Bast stressed. "And you have to borrow it. You can't steal it or buy it. She has to lend it to you."

Bast had half expected the boy to grouse about the particulars, about the fact that Old Nan lived all the way off on the other side of town, about as far west as you could go and still be considered part of the town. It would take him half an hour to get there, and even then, Old Nan might not be home.

But Rike didn't so much as sigh. He just nodded seriously, turned, and took off at a sprint, bare feet flying.

Bast continued to the lightning tree, but when he came to the clearing he saw an entire tangle of children playing on the greystone, doubtless waiting for him. Four of them.

Watching them from the shadow of the trees at the edge of the clearing, Bast hesitated, then glanced up at the sun before slipping back into the woods. He had other fish to fry.

The Williams farm wasn't a farm in any proper sense. Not for decades. The fields had gone fallow so long ago that they were barely recognizable as such, spotted with brambles and sapling trees. The tall barn had fallen into disrepair and half the roof gaped open to the sky.

Walking up the long path through the fields, Bast turned a corner and saw Rike's house. It told a different story than the barn. It was small but tidy. The shingles needed some repair, but other than that, it looked well loved and tended-to. Yellow curtains were blowing out the kitchen window, and there was a flower box spilling over with fox fiddle and marigold.

There was a pen with a trio of goats on one side of the house, and a large well-tended garden on the other. It was fenced thickly with lashed-together sticks, but Bast could see straight lines of flourishing greenery inside. Carrots. He still needed carrots.

Craning his neck a bit, Bast saw several large, square boxes behind the house. He took a few more steps to the side and eyed them before he realized they were beehives.

Just then there was a great storm of barking and two giant black, floppy-eared dogs came bounding from the house toward Bast, baying for all they were worth. When they came close enough, Bast got down on one knee and wrestled with them playfully, scratching their ears and the ruff of their necks.

After a few minutes of this, Bast continued to the house, the dogs weaving back and forth in front of him before they spotted some sort of animal and tore off into the underbrush. He knocked politely at the front door, though after all the barking his presence could hardly be a surprise.

The door opened a couple of inches, and for a moment all Bast could see was a slender slice of darkness. Then the door opened a little wider, revealing Rike's mother. She was tall, and her curling brown hair was springing loose from the braid that hung down her back.

She swung the door fully open, holding a tiny, half-naked baby in the curve of her arm. Its round face was pressed into her breast and it was sucking busily, making small grunting noises.

Glancing down, Bast smiled warmly.

The woman looked fondly down at her child, then favored Bast with a tired smile. "Hello Bast, what can I do for you?"

"Ah. Well," he said awkwardly, pulling his gaze up to meet her eye. "I was wondering, ma'am. That is, Mrs. Williams—"

"Nettie is fine, Bast," she said indulgently. More than a few of the townfolk considered Bast somewhat simple in the head, a fact that Bast didn't mind in the least.

"Nettie," Bast said, smiling his most ingratiating smile.

There was a pause, and she leaned against the doorframe. A little girl peeked out from around the woman's faded blue skirt, nothing more than a pair of serious dark eyes.

Bast smiled at the girl, who disappeared back behind her mother.

Nettie looked at Bast expectantly. Finally she prompted, "You were wondering . . ."

"Oh, yes," Bast said. "I was wondering if your husband happened to be about."

"I'm afraid not," she said. "Jessom's off checking his traps."

"Ah," Bast said, disappointed. "Will he be back anytime soon? I'd be happy to wait . . ."

She shook her head. "I'm sorry. He'll do his lines then spend the night skinning and drying up in his shack." She nodded vaguely toward the northern hills.

"Ah," Bast said again.

Nestled snugly in her mother's arm, the baby drew a deep breath, then sighed it out blissfully, going quiet and limp. Nettie looked down, then up at Bast, holding a finger to her lips.

Bast nodded and stepped back from the doorway, watching as Nettie stepped inside, deftly detached the sleeping baby from her nipple with her free hand, then carefully tucked the child into a small wooden cradle on the floor. The dark-eyed girl emerged from behind her mother and went to peer down at the baby.

"Call me if she starts to fuss," Nettie said softly. The little girl nodded seriously, sat down on a nearby chair, and began to gently rock the cradle with her foot.

Nettie stepped outside, closing the door behind her. She walked the few steps necessary to join Bast, rearranging her bodice unselfconsciously. In the sunlight Bast noticed her high cheekbones and generous mouth. Even so, she was more tired than pretty, her dark eyes heavy with worry.

The tall woman crossed her arms over her chest. "What's the trouble, then?" she asked wearily.

Bast looked confused. "No trouble," he said. "I was wondering if your husband had any work."

Nettie uncrossed her arms, looking surprised. "Oh."

"There isn't much for me to do at the inn," Bast said a little sheepishly. "I thought your husband might need an extra hand."

Nettie looked around, eyes brushing over the old barn. Her mouth tugging down at the corners. "He traps and hunts for the most part these days," she said. "Keeps him busy, but not so much that he'd need help, I imagine." She looked back to Bast. "At least he's never made mention of wanting any."

"How about yourself?" Bast asked, giving his most charming smile. "Is there anything around the place you could use a hand with?"

Nettie smiled at Bast indulgently. It was only a small smile, but it stripped ten years and half a world of worry off her face, making her practically shine with loveliness. "There isn't much to do," she said apologetically. "Only three goats, and my boy minds them."

"Firewood?" Bast asked. "I'm not afraid to work up a sweat. And it has to be hard getting by with your gentleman gone for days on end . . ." He grinned at her hopefully.

"And we just haven't got the money for help, I'm afraid," Nettie said.

"I just want some carrots," Bast said.

Nettie looked at him for a minute, then burst out laughing. "Carrots," she said, rubbing at her face. "How many carrots?"

"Maybe . . . six?" Bast asked, not sounding very sure of his answer at all.

She laughed again, shaking her head a little. "Okay. You can split some wood." She pointed to the chopping block that stood in back of the house. "I'll come get you when you've done six carrots' worth."

Bast set to work eagerly, and soon the yard was full of the crisp, healthy sound of splitting wood. The sun was still strong in the sky, and after just a few minutes Bast was covered in a sheen of sweat. He carelessly peeled away his shirt and hung it on the nearby garden fence.

There was something different about the way he split the wood. Nothing dramatic. In fact he split wood the same way everyone did: you set the log upright, you swing the axe, you split the wood. There isn't much room to extemporize.

But still, there was a difference in the way he did it. When he set the log upright, he moved intently. Then he would stand for a tiny moment, perfectly still. Then came the swing. It was a fluid thing. The placement of his feet, the play of the long muscles in his arms . . .

There was nothing exaggerated. Nothing like a flourish. Even so, when he brought the axe up and over in a perfect arc, there was a grace to it. The sharp cough the wood made as it split, the sudden way the halves went tumbling to the ground. He made it all look somehow . . . well . . . *dashing.*

He worked a hard half hour, at which time Nettie came out of the house, carrying a glass of water and a handful of fat carrots with the loose greens still attached. "I'm sure that's at least six carrots' worth of work," she said, smiling at him.

Bast took the glass of water, drank half of it, then bent over and poured the rest over his head. He shook himself off a bit, then stood back up, his dark hair curling and clinging to his face. "Are you sure there's nothing else you could use a hand with?" he asked, giving her an easy grin. His eyes were dark and smiling and bluer than the sky.

Nettie shook her head. Her hair was out of her braid now, and when she looked down, the loose curls of it fell partly across her face. "I can't think of anything," she said.

"I'm a dab hand with honey too," Bast said, hoisting the axe to rest against his naked shoulder.

She looked a little puzzled at that until Bast nodded toward the wooden hives scattered through the overgrown field. "Oh," she said, as if remembering a half-forgotten dream. "I used to do candles and honey. But we lost a few hives to that bad winter three years back. Then one to nits. Then there was that wet spring and three more went down with the chalk before we even knew." She shrugged. "Early this summer we sold one to the Hestles so we'd have money for the levy . . ."

She shook her head again, as if she'd been daydreaming. She shrugged and turned back to look at Bast. "Do you know about bees?"

"A fair bit," Bast said softly. "They aren't hard to handle. They just need patience and gentleness." He casually swung the axe so it stuck in the nearby stump. "They're the same as everything else, really. They just want to know they're safe."

Nettie was looking out at the field, nodding along with Bast's words unconsciously. "There's only the two left," she said. "Enough for a few candles. A little honey. Not much. Hardly worth the bother, really."

"Oh come now," Bast said gently. "A little sweetness is all any of us have sometimes. It's always worth it. Even if it takes some work."

Nettie turned to look at him. She met his eyes now. Not speaking, but not looking away either. Her eyes were like an open door.

Bast smiled, gentle and patient, his voice was warm and sweet as honey. He held out his hand. "Come with me," he said. "I have something to show you."

The sun was starting to sink toward the western trees by the time Bast returned to the lightning tree. He was limping slightly, and he had dirt in his hair, but he seemed to be in good spirits.

There were two children at the bottom of the hill, sitting on the greystone and swinging their feet as if it were a huge stone bench. Bast didn't even have time to sit down before they came up the hill together.

It was Wilk, a serious boy of ten with shaggy blond hair. At his side was his little sister Pem, half his age with three times the mouth.

The boy nodded at Bast as he came to the top of the hill, then he looked down. "You hurt your hand," he said.

Bast looked down at his hand and was surprised to see a few dark streaks of blood dripping down the side of it. He brought out his handkerchief and daubed at it.

"What happened?" little Pem asked him.

"I was attacked by a bear," he lied nonchalantly.

The boy nodded, giving no indication of whether or not he believed it was true. "I need a riddle that will stump Tessa," the boy said. "A good one."

"You smell like Granda," Pem chirruped as she came up to stand beside her brother.

Wilk ignored her. Bast did the same.

"Okay," said Bast. "I need a favor, I'll trade you. A favor for a riddle."

"You smell like Granda when he's been at his medicine," Pem clarified.

"It has to be a good one, though," Wilk stressed. "A stumper."

"Show me something that's never been seen before and will never be seen again," Bast said.

"Hmmm . . ." Wilk said, looking thoughtful.

"Granda says he feels loads better with his medicine," Pem said, louder, plainly irritated at being ignored. "But Mum says it's not medicine. She says he's on the bottle. And Granda says he feels loads better, so it's medicine by dammit." She looked back and forth between Bast and Wilk, as if daring them to scold her.

Neither of them did. She looked a little crestfallen.

"That is a good one," Wilk admitted at last. "What's the answer?"

Bast gave a slow grin. "What will you trade me for it?"

Wilk cocked his head on one side. "I already said. A favor."

"I traded you the riddle for a favor," Bast said easily. "But now you're asking for the answer . . ."

Wilk looked confused for half a moment, then his face went red and angry. He drew a deep breath as if he were going to shout. Then seemed to think better of it and stormed down the hill, stomping his feet.

His sister watched him go, then turned back to Bast. "Your shirt is ripped," she said disapprovingly. "And you've got grass stains on your pants. Your mam is going to give you a hiding."

"No, she won't," Bast said smugly. "Because I'm all grown, and I can do whatever I want with my pants. I could light them on fire and I wouldn't get in any trouble at all."

The little girl stared at him with smoldering envy.

Wilk stomped back up the hill. "Fine," he said sullenly.

"My favor first," Bast said. He handed the boy a small bottle with a cork in the top. "I need you to fill this up with water that's been caught midair."

"What?" Wilk said.

"Naturally falling water," Bast said. "You can't dip it out of a barrel or a stream. You have to catch it while it's still in the air."

"Water falls out of a pump when you pump it . . ." Wilk said without any real hope in his voice.

"*Naturally* falling water," Bast said again, stressing the first word. "It's no good if someone just stands on a chair and pours it out of a bucket."

"What do you need it for?" Pem asked in her little piping voice.

"What will you trade me for the answer to that question?" Bast said.

The little girl went pale and slapped one hand across her mouth.

"It might not rain for *days,*" Wilk said.

Pem gave a gusty sigh. "It doesn't have to be rain," his sister said, her voice dripping with condescension. "You could just go to the waterfall by Littlecliff and fill the bottle there."

Wilk blinked.

Bast grinned at her. "You're a clever girl."

She rolled her eyes. "Everybody says that . . ."

Bast brought out something from his pocket and held it. It was a green cornhusk wrapped around a daub of sticky honeycomb. The little girl's eyes lit up when she saw it.

"I also need twenty-one perfect acorns," he said. "No holes, with all their little hats intact. If you gather them for me over by the waterfall, I'll give you this."

She nodded eagerly. Then both she and her brother hurried down the hill.

Bast went back down to the pool by the spreading willow and took another bath. It wasn't his usual bathing time, so there were no birds waiting, and as a result the bath was much more matter-of-fact than before.

He quickly rinsed himself clean of sweat and honey and he daubed a bit at his clothes too, scrubbing to get rid of the grass stains and the smell of whiskey. The cold water stung the cuts on his knuckles a bit, but they were nothing serious and would mend well enough on their own.

Naked and dripping, he pulled himself from the pool and found a dark rock, hot from the long day of sun. He draped his clothes over it and let them bake dry while he shook his hair dry and stripped the water from his arms and chest with his hands.

Then he made his way back to the lightning tree, picked a long piece of grass to chew on, and almost immediately fell asleep in the golden afternoon sunlight.

Evening: Lessons

Hours later, the evening shadows stretched to cover Bast, and he shivered himself awake.

He sat up, rubbing his face and looking around blearily. The sun was just beginning to brush the tops of the western trees. Wilk and Pem hadn't returned, but that was hardly a surprise. He ate the piece of honeycomb he'd promised Pem, licking his fingers slowly. Then he chewed the wax idly and watched a pair of hawks turn lazy circles in the sky.

Eventually he heard a whistle from the trees. He got to his feet and stretched, his body bending like a bow. Then he sprinted down the hill . . . except, in the fading light it didn't quite look like a sprint.

If he were a boy of ten, it would have looked like skipping. But he was no boy. If he were a goat, it would have looked like he were prancing. But he was no goat. A man headed down the hill that quickly, it would have looked like he were running.

But there was something odd about Bast's motion in the fading light. Something hard to describe. He almost looked like he were . . . what? Frolicking? Dancing?

Small matter. Suffice to say that he quickly made his way to the edge of the clearing where Rike stood in the growing dark beneath the trees.

"I've got it," the boy said triumphantly. He held up his hand, but the needle was invisible in the dark.

"You borrowed it?" Bast asked. "Not traded or bargained for it?"

Rike nodded.

"Okay," Bast said. "Follow me."

The two of them walked over to the greystone, Rike following wordlessly when Bast climbed up one side of the half-fallen stone. The sunlight was still strong there, and both of them had plenty of space to stand on the broad back of the tilted greystone. Rike looked around anxiously, as if worried someone might see him.

"Let's see the stone," Bast said.

Rike dug into his pocket and held it out to Bast.

Bast pulled his hand back suddenly, as if the boy had tried to hand him a glowing coal. "Don't be stupid," he snapped. "It's not for me. The charm is only going to work for one person. Do you want that to be me?"

The boy brought his hand back and eyed the stone. "What do you mean, one person?"

"It's the way of charms," Bast said. "They only work for one person at a time." Seeing the boy's confusion written plainly on his face, Bast sighed. "You know how some girls make come-hither charms, hoping to catch a boy's eye?"

Rike nodded, blushing a little.

"This is the opposite," Bast said. "It's a go-thither charm. You're going to prick your finger, get a drop of your blood on it, and that will seal it. It will make things go away."

Rike looked down at the stone. "What sort of things?" he said.

"Anything that wants to hurt you," Bast said easily. "You can just keep it in your pocket, or you can get a piece of cord—"

"It will make my da leave?" Rike interrupted.

Bast frowned. "That's what I said. You're his blood. So it will push him away more strongly than anything else. You'll probably want to hang it around your neck so—"

"What about a bear?" Rike asked, looking at the stone thoughtfully. "Would it make a bear leave me alone?"

Bast made a back-and-forth motion with his hand. "Wild things are different," he said. "They're possessed of pure desire. They don't want to *hurt* you. They usually want food or safety. A bear would—"

"Can I give it to my mum?" Rike interrupted again, looking up at Bast. His dark eyes serious.

". . . want to protect its terr . . . What?" Bast stumbled to a halt.

"My mum should have it," Rike said. "What if I was off away with the charm and my da came back?"

"He's going farther away than that," Bast said, his voice thick with certainty. "It's not like he'll be hiding around the corner at the smithy . . ."

Rike's face was set now, his pug nose making him seem all the more stubborn. He shook his head. "She should have it. She's important. She has to take care of Tess and little Bip."

"It will work just fine—"

"It's got to be for HER!" Rike shouted, his hand making a fist around the stone. "You said it could be for one person, so you make it be for her!"

Bast scowled at the boy darkly. "I don't like your tone," he said grimly. "You asked me to make your da go away. And that's what I'm doing . . ."

"But what if it's not enough?" Rike's face was red.

"It will be," Bast said, absentmindedly rubbing his thumb across the knuckles of his hand. "He'll go far away. You have my word—"

"NO!" Rike said, his face flushed and angry. "What if sending *him* isn't enough? What if I grow up like my da? I get so . . ." His voice choked off, and his eyes started to leak tears. "I'm not good. I know it.

I know better than anyone. Like you said. I got his blood in me. She needs to be safe from me. If I grow up twisted up and bad, she needs the charm to . . . she needs something to make me go a—"

Rike clenched his teeth, unable to continue.

Bast reached out and took hold of the boy's shoulder. He was stiff and rigid as a plank of wood, but Bast gathered him in and put his arms around his shoulders. Gently, because he had seen the boy's back. They stood there for a long moment, Rike stiff and tight as a bowstring, trembling like a sail tight against the wind.

"Rike," Bast said softly. "You're a good boy. Do you know that?"

The boy bent then, sagged against Bast and seemed like he would break himself apart with sobbing. His face was pressed into Bast's stomach and he said something, but it was muffled and disjointed. Bast made a soft crooning sound of the sort you'd use to calm a horse or soothe a hive of restless bees.

The storm passed, and Rike stepped quickly away and scrubbed at his face roughly with his sleeve. The sky was just starting to tinge red with sunset.

"Right," Bast said. "It's time. We'll make it for your mother. You'll have to give it to her. River stone works best if it's given as a gift."

Rike nodded, not looking up. "What if she won't wear it?" he asked quietly.

Bast blinked, confused. "She'll wear it because you gave it to her," he said.

"What if she doesn't?" he asked.

Bast opened his mouth, then hesitated and closed it again. He looked up and saw the first of twilight's stars emerge. He looked down at the boy. He sighed. He wasn't good at this.

So much was so easy. Glamour was second nature. It was just making folk see what they wanted to see. Fooling folk was simple as singing. Tricking folk and telling lies, it was like breathing.

But this? Convincing someone of the truth that they were too twisted to see? How could you even begin?

It was baffling. These creatures. They were fraught and frayed in their desire. A snake would never poison itself, but these folk made an art of it. They wrapped themselves in fears and wept at being blind. It was infuriating. It was enough to break a heart.

So Bast took the easy way. "It's part of the magic," he lied. "When you give it to her, you have to tell her that you made it for her because you love her."

The boy looked uncomfortable, as if he were trying to swallow a stone.

"It's essential for the magic," Bast said firmly. "And then, if you want to make the magic stronger, you need to tell her every day. Once in the morning and once at night."

The boy nodded, a determined look on his face. "Okay. I can do that."

"Right, then," Bast said. "Sit down here. Prick your finger."

Rike did just that. He jabbed his stubby finger and let a bead of blood well up then fall onto the stone.

"Good," Bast said, sitting down across from the boy. "Now give me the needle."

Rike handed over the needle. "But you said it just needed—"

"Don't tell me what I said," Bast groused. "Hold the stone flat so that the hole faces up."

Rike did.

"Hold it steady," Bast said, and pricked his own finger. A slow bead of blood grew. "Don't move."

Rike braced the stone with his other hand.

Bast turned his finger, and the drop of blood hung in the air for a moment before falling straight through the hole to strike the greystone underneath.

There was no sound. No stirring in the air. No distant thunder. If anything, it seemed there was a half second of perfect brick-heavy silence in the air. But it was probably nothing more than a brief pause in the wind.

"Is that it?" Rike asked after a moment, clearly expecting something more.

"Yup," Bast said, licking the blood from his finger with a red, red tongue. Then he worked his mouth a little and spat out the wax he had been chewing. He rolled it between his fingers and handed it to the boy. "Rub this into the stone, then take it to the top of the highest hill you can find. Stay there until the last of the sunset fades, and then give it to her tonight."

Rike's eyes darted around the horizon, looking for a good hill. Then he leapt from the stone and sprinted off.

Bast was halfway back to the Waystone Inn when he realized he had no idea where his carrots were.

When Bast came in the back door, he could smell bread and beer and simmering stew. Looking around the kitchen he saw crumbs on the breadboard and the lid was off the kettle. Dinner had already been served.

Stepping softly, he peered through the door into the common room. The usual folk sat hunched at the bar, there was Old Cob and Graham, scraping their bowls. The smith's prentice was running bread along the inside of his bowl, then stuffing it into his mouth a piece at time. Jake spread butter on the last slice of bread, and Shep knocked his empty mug politely against the bar, the hollow sound a question in itself.

Bast bustled through the doorway with a fresh bowl of stew for the smith's prentice as the innkeeper poured Shep more beer. Collecting the empty bowl, Bast disappeared back into the kitchen, then he came back with another loaf of bread half-sliced and steaming.

"Guess what I caught wind of today?" Old Cob said with the grin of a man who knew he had the freshest news at the table.

"What's that?" the boy asked around half a mouthful of stew.

Cob reached out and took the heel of the bread, a right he claimed as the oldest person there, despite the fact that he wasn't actually the oldest, and the fact that nobody else much cared for the heel. Bast suspected he took it because he was proud he still had so many teeth left.

Cob grinned. "Guess," he said to the boy, then slowly slathered his bread with butter and took a big bite.

"I reckon it's something about Jessom Williams," Jake said blithely.

Old Cob glared at him, his mouth full of bread and butter.

"What I heard," Jake drawled slowly, smiling as Old Cob tried furiously to chew his mouth clear, "was that Jessom was out running his traplines and he got jumped by a cougar. Then while he was legging it away, he lost track of hisself and went right over Littlecliff. Busted himself up something fierce."

Old Cob finally managed to swallow. "You're thick as a post, Jacob Walker. That ain't what happened at all. He fell off Littlecliff, but there weren't a cougar. Cougar ain't going to attack a full-grown man."

"It will if he's all smelling of blood," Jake insisted. "Which Jessom was, on account of the fact that he was baggin' up all his game."

There was a muttering of agreement at this, which obviously irritated Old Cob. "It weren't a cougar," he insisted. "He was drunk off his feet. That's what I heard. Stumbling-lost drunk. That's the only sense of it. 'Cause Littlecliff ent nowhere near his trapline. Unless you think a cougar chased him for almost a mile . . ."

Old Cob sat back in his chair then, smug as a judge. Everyone knew Jessom was a bit of a drinker. And while Littlecliff wasn't really a mile from the Williams's land, it was too far to be chased by a cougar.

Jake glared venomously at Old Cob, but before he could say anything Graham chimed in. "I heard it was drink too. A couple kids found him while they were playing by the falls. They thought he was dead, and ran to fetch the constable. But he was just head-struck and drunk as a lord. There was all manner of broken glass too. He was cut up some."

Old Cob threw his hands up in the air. "Well, ain't that wonderful!" he said, scowling back and forth between Graham and Jake. "Any other parts of my story you'd like to tell afore I'm finished?"

Graham looked taken aback. "I thought you were—"

"I wasn't finished," Cob said, as if talking to a simpleton. "I was reelin' it out slow. I swear. What you folk don't know about tellin' stories would fit into a book."

A tense silence settled among the friends.

"I got some news too," the smith's prentice said almost shyly. He sat slightly hunched at the bar, as if embarrassed at being a head taller than everyone else and twice as broad across the shoulders. "If'n nobody else has heard it, that is."

Shep spoke up. "Go on, boy. You don't have to ask. Those two just been gnawing on each other for years. They don't mean anything by it."

"Well, I was doing shoes," the prentice said, "when Crazy Martin came in." The boy shook his head in amazement and took a long drink of beer. "I ain't only seen him a few times in town, and I forgot how big he is. I don't have to look up to see him. But I still think he's biggern me. And today he looked even bigger still 'cause he was furious. He was spittin' nails. I swear. He looked like someone had tied two angry bulls together and made them wear a shirt!" The boy laughed the easy laugh of someone who's had a little more beer than he's used to.

There was a pause. "What's the news, then?" Shep said gently, giving him a nudge.

"Oh!" the smith's prentice said. "He came asking Master Ferris if he had enough copper to mend a big kettle." The prentice spread his long arms out wide, one hand almost smacking Shep in the face.

"Apparently someone found Martin's still." The smith's prentice leaned forward, wobbling slightly, and said in hushed voice, "Stole a bunch of his drink and wrecked up the place a bit."

The boy leaned back in his chair and crossed his arms proudly across his chest, confident of a story well told.

But there was none of the buzz that normally accompanied a piece of good gossip. He took another drink of beer, and slowly began to look confused.

"Tehlu anyway," Graham said, his face gone pale. "Martin'll kill him."

"What?" the prentice said. "Who?"

"Jessom, you tit," Jake snapped. He tried to cuff the boy on the back of his head and had to settle for his shoulder instead. "The fellow who got skunk drunk in the middle of the day and fell off a cliff carrying a bunch of bottles?"

"I thought it was a cougar," Old Cob said spitefully.

"He'll wish it was ten cougars when Martin gets him," Jake said grimly.

"What?" The smith's prentice laughed. "Crazy Martin? He's addled, sure, but he ain't *mean.* A couple span ago he cornered me and talked bollocks about barley for two hours." He laughed again. "About how it was healthful. How wheat would ruin a man. How money was dirty. How it chained you to the earth or some nonsense."

The prentice dropped his voice and hunched his shoulders a bit, widening his eyes and doing a passable Crazy Martin impression. "*You know?*" he said, making his voice rough and darting his eyes around. "*Yeah. You know. You hear what I'm sayin?*"

The prentice laughed again, rocking back on his stool. He had obviously had a little more beer than was good for him. "People think they have to be afraid of big folk, but they don't. I've never hit a man in my life."

Everyone just stared at him. Their eyes were deadly earnest.

"Martin killed one of Ensal's dogs for growling at him," Shep said. "Right in the middle of market. Threw a shovel like it was a spear. Then gave it a kicking."

"Nearly killed that last priest," Graham said. "The one before Abbe Leodin. Nobody knows why. Fellow went up to Martin's house. That evening Martin brought him to town in a wheelbarrow and left him in front of the church." He looked at the smith's prentice. "That was before your time, though. Makes sense you wouldn't know."

"Punched a tinker once," Jake said.

"*Punched a tinker?*" the innkeeper burst out, incredulous.

"Reshi," Bast said gently. "Martin is fucking *crazy.*"

Jake nodded. "Even the levy man doesn't go up to Martin's place."

Cob looked like he was going to call Jake out again, then decided to take a gentler tone. "Well, yes," he said. "True enough. But that's 'cause Martin pulled his full rail in the king's army. Eight years."

"And came back mad as a frothing dog," Shep said.

Old Cob was already off his stool and halfway to the door. "Enough talk. We got to let Jessom know. If he can get out of town until Martin cools down a bit . . ."

"So . . . when he's dead?" Jake said sharply. "Remember when he threw a horse through the window of the old inn because the barman wouldn't give him another beer?"

"A *tinker*?" the innkeeper repeated, sounding no less shocked than before.

Silence descended at the sound of footsteps on the landing. Everyone eyed the door and went still as stone, except for Bast, who slowly edged toward the doorway to the kitchen.

Everyone breathed a huge sigh of relief when the door opened to reveal the tall, slim shape of Carter. He closed the door behind him, not noticing the tension in the room. "Guess who's standing a round of bottle whiskey for everyone tonight?" he called out cheerfully, then stopped where he stood, confused by the roomful of grim expressions.

Old Cob started to walk to the door again, motioning for his friend to follow. "Come on, Carter, we'll explain on the way. We've got to find Jessom double quick."

"You'll have a long ride to find him," Carter said. "I drove him all the way to Baden this afternoon."

Everyone in the room seemed to relax. "That's why you're so late," Graham said, his voice thick with relief. He slumped back onto his stool and tapped the bar hard with a knuckle. Bast drew him another beer.

Carter frowned. "Not so late as all that," he groused. "I'd like to see you make it all the way to Baden and back in this time, that's more'n forty miles . . ."

Old Cob put a hand on the man's shoulder. "Nah. It ain't like that," he said, steering his friend toward the bar. "We were just a little spooked. You probably saved that damn fool Jessom's life by getting him out of town." He squinted at him. "Though I've told you, you shouldn't be out on the road by yourself these days . . ."

The innkeeper fetched Carter a bowl while Bast went outside to tend to his horse. While he ate, his friends told him the day's gossip in dribs and drabs.

"Well, that explains it," Carter said. "Jessom showed up reeking like a rummy and looking like he'd been beat by twelve different demons. Paid me to drive him to the Iron Hall, and he took the king's coin right there." Carter took a drink of beer. "Then paid me to take him to Baden straight off. Didn't want to stop off at his house for his clothes or anything."

"Not much need for that," Shep said. "They'll dress and feed him in the king's army."

Graham let out a huge sigh. "That was a near miss. Can you imagine what would happen if the azzie came for Martin?"

Everyone was silent for a moment, imagining the trouble that would come if an officer of the Crown's Law was assaulted here in town.

The smith's prentice looked around at him. "What about Jessom's family?" he asked, plainly worried. "Will Martin come after them?"

The men at the bar shook their heads in concert. "Martin is crazy," Old Cob said. "But he's not that sort. Not to go after a woman or her wee ones."

"I heard he punched the tinker because he was making some advances on young Jenna," Graham said.

"There's truth to that," Old Cob said softly. "I saw it."

Everyone in the room turned to look at him, surprised. They'd known Cob all their lives and had heard all his stories. Even the most boring of them had been trotted out three or four times over the long years. The thought that he might have held something back was . . . well . . . it was almost unthinkable.

"He was getting all handsy with young Jenna," Cob said, not looking up from his beer. "And she was younger still back then, mind you." He paused for a moment, then sighed. "But I was still old, and . . . well . . . I knew that tinker would give me a hiding if I tried to stop him. I could see that plain enough on his face." The old man sighed again. "I ain't proud of that."

Cob looked up with a vicious little grin. "Then Martin came round the corner," he said. "This was off behind the old Cooper's place, remember? And Martin looked at the fellow, and at Jenna, who wasn't crying or nothing, but she obviously wasn't happy either. And the tinker has hold of her wrist . . ."

Cob shook his head. "When he hit him. It was like a hammer hitting a ham. Knocked him right out into the street. Ten feet, give or take. Then Martin eyed Jenna, who was crying just a bit then. More surprised than anything. And Martin stuck the boot in him. Just once. Not as hard as he could either. I could tell he was just settling up accounts in his head. Like he was a moneylender shimming up one side of his scale."

"That fellow wasn't any kind of proper tinker," Jake said. "I remember him."

"And I heard things about that priest," Graham added.

A few of the others nodded wordlessly.

"What if Jessom comes back?" the smith's prentice asked. "I heard some folk get drunk and take the coin, then turn all cowardly and jump the rail when they sober up."

Everyone seemed to consider that. It wasn't a hard thought for any of them. A band of the king's guard had come through town only last month and posted a notice, announcing a reward for deserters.

"Tehlu anyway," Shep said grimly into his nearly empty mug. "Wouldn't that be a great royal pisser of a mess?"

"Jessom's not coming back," Bast said dismissively. His voice had such a note of certainty that everyone turned to eye him curiously.

Bast tore off a piece of bread and put it in his mouth before he realized he was the center of attention. He swallowed awkwardly and made a broad gesture with both hands. "What?" he asked them, laughing. "Would you come back, knowing Martin was waiting?"

There was a chorus of negative grunts and shaken heads.

"You have to be a special kind of stupid to wreck up Martin's still," Old Cob said.

"Maybe eight years will be enough for Martin to cool down a bit," Shep said.

"Not likely," Jake said.

Later, after the customers were gone, Bast and the innkeeper sat down in the kitchen, making their own dinner from the remainder of the stew and half a loaf of bread.

"So what did you learn today, Bast?" the innkeeper asked.

Bast grinned widely. "Today, Reshi, I found out where Emberlee takes her bath!"

The innkeeper cocked his head thoughtfully. "Emberlee? The Alards' daughter?"

"Emberlee Ashton!" Bast threw his arms up into the air and made an exasperated noise. "She's only the third prettiest girl in twenty miles, Reshi!"

"Ah," the innkeeper said, an honest smile flickering across his face for the first time that day. "You'll have to point her out to me."

Bast grinned. "I'll take you there tomorrow," he said eagerly. "I don't know if she takes a bath every day, but it's worth the gamble. She's sweet as cream and broad of beam." His smile grew to wicked proportions. "She's a milkmaid, Reshi," he said the last with heavy emphasis. "A *milkmaid.*"

The innkeeper shook his head, even as his own smile spread helplessly across his face. Finally he broke into a chuckle and held up his hand. "You can point her out to me sometime when she has her clothes on," he said pointedly. "That will do nicely."

Bast gave a disapproving sigh. "It would do you a world of good to get out a bit, Reshi."

The innkeeper shrugged. "It's possible," he said as he poked idly at his stew.

They ate in silence for a long while. Bast tried to think of something to say.

"I did get the carrots, Reshi," Bast said as he finished his stew and ladled the rest of it out of the kettle.

"Better late than never, I suppose," the innkeeper said, his voice listless and grey. "We'll use them tomorrow."

Bast shifted in his seat, embarrassed. "I'm afraid I lost them afterwards," he said sheepishly.

This wrung another tired smile from the innkeeper. "Don't worry yourself over it, Bast." His eyes narrowed then, focusing on the hand that held Bast's spoon. "What happened to your hand?"

Bast looked down at the knuckles of his right hand; they weren't bloody anymore, but they were skinned rather badly.

"I fell out of a tree," Bast said. Not lying, but not answering the question either. It was better not to lie outright. Even weary and dull, his master was not an easy man to fool.

"You should be more careful, Bast," the innkeeper said, prodding listlessly at his food. "And with as little as there is to do around here, it would be nice if you spent a little more time on your studies."

"I learned loads of things today, Reshi," Bast protested.

The innkeeper sat up, looking more attentive. "Really?" he said. "Impress me then."

Bast thought for a moment. "Nettie Williams found a wild hive of bees today," he said. "And she managed to catch the queen . . ."

George R. R. Martin

Hugo, Nebula, and World Fantasy Award–winner George R. R. Martin, *New York Times* bestselling author of the landmark *A Song of Ice and Fire* fantasy series, has been called "the American Tolkien."

Born in Bayonne, New Jersey, George R. R. Martin made his first sale in 1971, and soon established himself as one of the most popular SF writers of the seventies. He quickly became a mainstay of the Ben Bova *Analog* with stories such as "With Morning Comes Mistfall," "And Seven Times Never Kill Man," "The Second Kind of Loneliness," "The Storms of Windhaven" (in collaboration with Lisa Tuttle, and later expanded by them into the novel *Windhaven*), "Override," and others, although he also sold to *Amazing, Fantastic, Galaxy, Orbit,* and other markets. One of his *Analog* stories, the striking novella *A Song for Lya,* won him his first Hugo Award, in 1974.

By the end of the seventies, he had reached the height of his influence as a science-fiction writer and was producing his best work in that category with stories such as the famous "Sandkings," his best-known story, which won both the Nebula and the Hugo in 1980 (he'd later win another Nebula in 1985 for his story "Portraits of His Children"), "The Way of Cross and Dragon," which won a Hugo Award in the same year (making Martin the first author ever to receive two Hugo Awards for fiction in the same year), "Bitterblooms," "The Stone City," "Starlady," and others. These stories would be collected in *Sandkings,* one of the strongest collections of the period. By now, he had mostly moved away from *Analog* although he would have a long sequence of stories about the droll interstellar adventures of Haviland Tuf (later collected in *Tuf Voyaging*) running throughout the eighties in the Stanley Schmidt *Analog,* as well as a few strong individual pieces such as the novella *Nightflyers*—most of his major work of the late seventies and early eighties, though, would appear in *Omni*. The late seventies and the eighties also saw the publication of his memorable novel *Dying of the Light*, his only solo SF novel, while his stories were collected in *A Song for Lya*, *Sandkings*, *Songs of Stars and Shadows*, *Songs the Dead Men Sing*, *Nightflyers*, and *Portraits of His Children*. By the beginning of the eighties, he'd moved away from SF and into the horror genre, publishing the big horror novel *Fevre Dream*, and winning the Bram Stoker Award for his horror story "The Pear-Shaped Man" and the World Fantasy Award for his werewolf novella *The Skin Trade*. By the end of that decade, though, the crash of the horror market and the commercial failure of his ambitious horror novel *Armageddon Rag* had driven him out of the print world and to a successful career in television instead, where for more than a decade he worked as story editor or producer on such shows as the new *Twilight Zone* and *Beauty and the Beast*.

After years away, Martin made a triumphant return to the print world in 1996 with the publication of the immensely successful fantasy novel *A Game of Thrones*, the start of his *Song of Ice and Fire* sequence. A freestanding novella taken from that work, *Blood of the Dragon*, won Martin another Hugo Award in 1997. Further books in the *Song of Ice and Fire* series—*A Clash of Kings*, *A Storm of Swords*, *A Feast for Crows*, and *A Dance with Dragons*—have made it one of the most popular, acclaimed, and bestselling series in all of modern fantasy. Recently, the books were made into an HBO TV series, *Game of Thrones*, which has become one of the most popular and acclaimed shows on television, and made Martin a recognizable figure well outside of the usual genre boundaries, even inspiring a satirical version of him on *Saturday Night Live*. Martin's most recent books are the latest in the *A Song of Ice and Fire* series, *A Dance with Dragons*; *Dreamsongs*, a massive two-volume retrospective collection spanning the entire spectrum of his career; *Starlady and Fast-Friend*, a novel written in collaboration with Gardner Dozois and Daniel

Abraham, *Hunter's Run,* and, as editor, several anthologies edited in collaboration with Gardner Dozois, including *Warriors, Songs of the Dying Earth, Songs of Love and Death, Down These Strange Streets,* and *Dangerous Women,* as well as several new volumes in his long-running *Wild Cards* anthology series, *Wild Cards: Busted Flush* and *Wild Cards: Inside Straight.* In 2012, Martin was given the Life Achievement Award by the World Fantasy Convention. *A World of Ice and Fire,* a comprehensive history of Westeros and the lands beyond—for which this story is the source material—will be released in fall of 2014.

Here he takes us to the turbulent land of Westeros, home to his Ice and Fire series, for the story of that swashbuckling rogue Daemon Targaryen, the Prince who never became a King—although his ambition to become one would plunge the entire world into war.

THE ROGUE PRINCE,
or,
A KING'S BROTHER

a consideration of the early life, adventures, misdeeds, and marriages of Prince Daemon Targaryen, as set down by Archmaester Gyldayn of the Citadel of Oldtown

here transcribed by George R. R. Martin

He was the grandson of a king, the brother of a king, husband to a queen. Two of his sons and three of his grandsons would sit the Iron Throne, but the only crown that Daemon Targaryen ever wore was the crown of the Stepstones, a meager realm he made himself with blood and steel and dragonfire, and soon abandoned.

Over the centuries, House Targaryen has produced both great men and monsters. Prince Daemon was both. In his day there was not a man so admired, so beloved, and so reviled in all Westeros. He was made of light and darkness in equal parts. To some he was a hero, to others the blackest of villains. No true understanding of that most tragic bloodletting known as the Dance of the Dragons is possible without a consideration of the crucial role played before and during the conflict by this rogue prince.

The seeds of the great conflict were sown during the last years in the long reign of the Old King, Jaehaerys I Targaryen. Of Jaehaerys himself, little need be said here, save that after the passing of his beloved wife, Good Queen Alysanne, and his son Baelon, Prince of Dragonstone—Hand of the King, and heir apparent to the Iron Throne—His Grace was but a shell of the man that he had been.

With Prince Baelon lost to him, the Old King had to turn elsewhere for a partner in his labors. As his new Hand, he called upon Ser Otto

Hightower, younger brother to Lord Hightower of Oldtown. Ser Otto brought his wife and children to court with him, and served King Jaehaerys faithfully for the years remaining to him. As the king's strength and wits began to fail, he was oft confined to bed. Ser Otto's fifteen-year-old daughter, Alicent, became his constant companion, fetching His Grace his meals, reading to him, helping him to bathe and dress himself. The Old King sometimes mistook her for one of his daughters, calling her by their names; near the end, he grew certain she was his daughter Saera, returned to him from beyond the narrow sea.

In the year 103 AC King Jaehaerys I Targaryen died in his bed as Lady Alicent was reading to him from Septon Barth's *Unnatural History.* His Grace was nine-and-sixty years of age, and had reigned over the Seven Kingdoms since coming to the Iron Throne at the age of fourteen. His remains were burned in the Dragonpit, his ashes interred with Good Queen Alysanne's beneath the Red Keep. All of Westeros mourned. Even in Dorne, where his writ had not extended, men wept and women tore their garments.

In accordance with his own wishes, and the decision of the Great Council of 101, his grandson Viserys succeeded him, mounting the Iron Throne as King Viserys I Targaryen. At the time of his ascent, King Viserys was twenty-six years old. He had been married for a decade to a cousin, Lady Aemma of House Arryn, herself a granddaughter of the Old King and Good Queen Alysanne through her mother, the late Princess Daella (d. 82 AC). Lady Aemma had suffered several miscarriages and the death of one son in the cradle, but she had also given birth to a healthy daughter, Rhaenyra (born 97 AC). The new king and his queen both doted on the girl, their only living child.

Viserys I Targaryen had a generous, amiable nature and was well loved by his lords and smallfolk alike. The reign of the Young King, as the commons called him upon his ascent, would be peaceful and prosperous. His Grace's openhandedness was legendary, and the Red Keep became a place of song and splendor. King Viserys and Queen Aemma hosted many a feast and tourney, and lavished gold, offices, and honors on their many favorites.

At the center of the merriment, cherished and adored by all, was

Princess Rhaenyra, the little girl the court singers soon dubbed the Realm's Delight. Though only six when her father came to the Iron Throne, Rhaenyra was a precocious child, bright and bold and beautiful as only one of dragon's blood can be beautiful. At the age of seven, she became a dragonrider, taking to the sky atop the young dragon she named Syrax, after a goddess of old Valyria. At eight, like many another highborn girl, the princess was placed into service as a cupbearer . . . but for her own father, the king. At table, at tourney, and at court, King Viserys thereafter was seldom seen without his daughter by his side.

Meanwhile, the tedium of rule was left largely to the king's small council and his Hand. Ser Otto Hightower had continued in that office, serving the grandson as he had the father; an able man, all agreed, though many found him proud, brusque, and haughty. The longer he served, the more imperious Ser Otto became, it was said, and many great lords and princes came to resent his manner and envy him his access to the Iron Throne.

The greatest of his rivals was our rogue prince: Daemon Targaryen, the king's ambitious, impetuous younger brother.

As charming as he was hot-tempered, Prince Daemon had earned his knight's spurs at six-and-ten, and had been given Dark Sister by the Old King himself in recognition of his prowess. Though he had wed the Lady of Runestone in 97 AC, during the Old King's reign, the marriage had not been a success. Prince Daemon found the Vale of Arryn boring ("In the Vale, the men fuck sheep," he wrote. "You cannot fault them. Their sheep are prettier than their women."), and soon developed a mislike of his lady wife, whom he called "my bronze bitch," after the runic bronze armor worn by the lords of House Royce. Upon the accession of his brother to the Iron Throne, the prince petitioned to have his marriage set aside. Viserys denied the request but did allow Daemon to return to court, where he sat on the small council, serving as master of coin from 103–104, and master of laws for half a year in 104.

Governance bored this warrior prince, however. He did better when King Viserys made him commander of the City Watch. Finding the watchmen ill armed and clad in oddments and rags, Daemon equipped each man with dirk, short sword, and cudgel, armored them in black ringmail (with breastplates for the officers), and gave them long golden cloaks that they might wear with pride. Ever since, the men of the City Watch have been known as gold cloaks.

Prince Daemon took eagerly to the work of the gold cloaks, and oft prowled the alleys of King's Landing with his men. That he made the city more orderly no man could doubt, but his discipline was a brutal one. He delighted in cutting off the hands of pickpockets, gelding rapists, and slitting the noses of thieves, and slew three men in street brawls during his first year as commander. Before long, the prince was well-known in all the low places of King's Landing. He became a familiar sight in winesinks (where he drank for free) and gambling pits (where he always left with more coin than when he entered). Though he sampled countless whores in the city's brothels, and was said to have an especial fondness for deflowering maidens, a certain Lysene dancing girl soon became his favorite. Mysaria was the name she went by, though her rivals and enemies called her Misery, the White Worm.

As King Viserys had no living son, Daemon regarded himself as the rightful heir to the Iron Throne and coveted the title Prince of Dragonstone, which His Grace refused to grant him . . . but by the end of year 105 AC, he was known to his friends as the Prince of the City and to the smallfolk as Lord Flea Bottom. Though the king did not wish Daemon to succeed him, he remained fond of his younger brother and was quick to forgive his many offenses.

Princess Rhaenyra was also enamored of her uncle, for Daemon was ever attentive to her. Whenever he crossed the narrow sea upon his dragon, he brought her back some exotic gift on his return. King Viserys never claimed another dragon after Balerion's death, nor did he have much taste for the joust, the hunt, or swordplay, whereas Prince Daemon excelled in these spheres and seemed all that his brother was not: lean and hard, a renowned warrior, dashing, daring, more than a little dangerous.

Though the origins of their enmity are much disputed, all men agree that Ser Otto Hightower, the King's Hand, took a great mislike to the king's brother. (The king's fool Mushroom asserts that the quarrel began when Prince Daemon deflowered Ser Otto's young daughter

Alicent, the future queen, but this scurrilous tale is unsupported by any other source.) It was Ser Otto who had convinced Viserys to remove Prince Daemon as master of coin, and then as master of laws—actions he soon came to regret. As commander of the City Watch, with two thousand men under his command, Daemon waxed more powerful than ever.

"On no account can Prince Daemon be allowed to ascend to the Iron Throne," the Hand wrote his brother, Lord of Oldtown. "He would be a second Maegor the Cruel, or worse." It was Ser Otto's wish (then) that Princess Rhaenyra succeed her father. "Better the Realm's Delight than Lord Flea Bottom," he wrote. Nor was he alone in his opinion. Yet his party faced a formidable hurdle. If the precedent set by the Great Council of 101 was followed, a male claimant must prevail over a female. In the absence of a trueborn son, the king's brother would come before the king's daughter, as Baelon had come before Rhaenys in 92 AC.

As for the king's own views, all the chronicles agree that King Viserys hated dissension. Though far from blind to his brother's flaws, he cherished his memories of the free-spirited, adventurous boy that Daemon had been. His daughter was his life's great joy, he oft said, but a brother is a brother. Time and time again he strove to make peace between Prince Daemon and Ser Otto, but the enmity between the two men roiled endlessly beneath the false smiles they wore at court. When pressed upon the matter, King Viserys would only say that he was certain his queen would soon present him with a son. And in 105 AC, he announced to the court and small council that Queen Aemma was once again with child.

During that same fateful year, Ser Criston Cole was appointed to the Kingsguard to fill the place created by the death of the legendary Ser Ryam Redwyne. Born the son of a steward in service to Lord Dondarrion of Blackhaven, Ser Criston was a comely young knight of three-and-twenty years. He first came to the attention of the court when he won the melee held at Maidenpool in honor of King Viserys's accession. In the final moments of the fight, Ser Criston knocked Dark Sister from Prince Daemon's hand with his morningstar, to the delight of His

Grace and the fury of the prince. Afterward, he gave the seven-year-old Princess Rhaenyra the victor's laurel, and begged for her favor to wear in the joust. In the lists, he defeated Prince Daemon once again, and unhorsed both of the celebrated Cargyll twins, Ser Arryk and Ser Erryk of the Kingsguard, before falling to Lord Lymond Mallister.

With his pale green eyes, coal-black hair, and easy charm, Cole soon became a favorite of all the ladies at court . . . not the least amongst them Rhaenyra Targaryen herself. So smitten was she by the charms of the man she called "my white knight" that Rhaenyra begged her father to name Ser Criston her own personal shield and protector. His Grace indulged her in this, as in so much else. Thereafter Ser Criston always wore her favor in the lists and became a fixture at her side during feasts and frolics.

Not long after Ser Criston donned his white cloak, King Viserys invited Lyonel Strong, Lord of Harrenhal, to join the small council as master of laws. A big man, burly and balding, Lord Strong enjoyed a formidable reputation as a battler. Those who did not know him oft took him for a brute, mistaking his silences and slowness of speech for stupidity. This was far from the truth. Lord Lyonel had studied at the Citadel as a youth, earning six links of his chain before deciding that a maester's life was not for him. He was literate and learned, his knowledge of the laws of the Seven Kingdoms exhaustive. Thrice-wed and thrice a widower, the Lord of Harrenhal brought two maiden daughters and two sons to court with him. The girls became handmaids to Princess Rhaenyra, whilst their elder brother, Ser Harwin Strong, called Breakbones, was made a captain in the gold cloaks. The younger boy, Larys the Clubfoot, joined the king's confessors.

Thus did matters stand in King's Landing late in the year 105 AC, when Queen Aemma was brought to bed in Maegor's Holdfast, and died whilst giving birth to the son that Viserys Targaryen had desired for so long. The boy (named Baelon, after the king's father) survived her only by a day, leaving king and court bereft . . . save perhaps for Prince Daemon, who was observed in a brothel on the Street of Silk, making drunken japes with his highborn cronies about the "heir for a day." When word of this got back to the king (legend says that it was the whore sitting in Daemon's lap who informed on him, but evidence suggests it was actually one of his drinking companions, a captain in the gold cloaks eager for advancement), Viserys became livid. His Grace had finally had a surfeit of this ungrateful brother and his ambitions.

Once his mourning had run its course, the king moved swiftly to resolve the long-simmering issue of the succession. Disregarding the precedents set by King Jaehaerys in 92 and the Great Council in 101, King Viserys I declared his daughter Rhaenyra to be his rightful heir, and named her Princess of Dragonstone. In a lavish ceremony at King's Landing, hundreds of lords did obeisance to Rhaenyra as she sat at her father's feet at the base of the Iron Throne, swearing to honor and defend her right of succession.

Prince Daemon was not amongst them, however. Furious at the king's decree, the prince quit King's Landing, resigning from the City Watch. He went first to Dragonstone, taking his paramour Mysaria with him upon the back of his dragon Caraxes, the lean red beast the smallfolk called the Blood Wyrm. There he remained for half a year, during which time he got Mysaria with child.

When he learned that his concubine was pregnant, Prince Daemon presented her with a dragon's egg, but in this he went too far. King Viserys commanded him to return the egg and return to his lawful wife or else be attainted as a traitor. The prince obeyed, though with ill grace, dispatching Mysaria (eggless) back to Lys, whilst he himself flew to Runestone in the Vale and the unwelcome company of his "bronze bitch." But Mysaria lost her child during a storm on the narrow sea. When word reached Prince Daemon he spoke no word of grief, but his heart hardened against the king his brother. Thereafter he spoke of King Viserys only with disdain and began to brood day and night on the succession.

Though Princess Rhaenyra had been proclaimed her father's successor, there were many in the realm who still hoped that Viserys might father a male heir, for the Young King was not yet thirty. Grand Maester Runciter was the first to urge His Grace to remarry, even suggesting a suitable choice: the Lady Laena Velaryon, who had just turned twelve. A fiery young maiden, freshly flowered, Lady Laena had inherited the beauty of a true Targaryen from her mother Rhaenys and a bold, adventurous spirit from her father the Sea Snake. As he had loved to sail, Laena loved to fly, and had claimed for her own no less a mount than mighty Vhagar, the oldest and largest of the Targaryen dragons since the passing of the Black Dread in 94 AC. By taking the girl to wife, the king could heal the rift that had grown up between the Iron Throne and Driftmark, Runciter pointed out. And Laena would surely make a splendid queen.

Viserys I Targaryen was not the strongest-willed of kings, it must be said; always amiable and anxious to please, he relied greatly on the counsel of the men around him and did as they bid more oft than not. In this instance, however, His Grace had his own notion, and no amount of argument would sway him from his course. He would marry again, yes . . . but not to a twelve-year-old girl, and not for reasons of state. Another woman had caught his eye. He announced his intention to wed Lady Alicent of House Hightower, the clever and lovely eighteen-year-old daughter of the King's Hand, the girl who had read to King Jaehaerys as he lay dying.

The Hightowers of Oldtown were an ancient and noble family, of impeccable lineage; there could be no possible objection to the king's choice of bride. Even so, there were those who murmured that the Hand had risen above himself, that he had brought his daughter to court with this in mind. A few cast doubt on Lady Alicent's virtue, suggesting she had given her maidenhead to Prince Daemon and later welcomed King Viserys into her bed as well, even before Queen Aemma's death. In the Vale, Prince Daemon reportedly whipped the serving man who brought the news to him within an inch of his life. Nor was the Sea Snake pleased. House Velaryon had been passed over once again, his daughter Laena scorned just as his son Laenor had been scorned by the Great Council in 101, and his wife by the Old King back in 92 AC. (Lady Laena herself seemed untroubled. "Her ladyship shows far more interest in flying than in boys," her maester observed.)

When King Viserys took Alicent Hightower to wife in 106 AC, House Velaryon was notable for its absence. Princess Rhaenyra poured for her stepmother at the feast, and Queen Alicent kissed her and named her "daughter." The princess was amongst the women who disrobed the king and delivered him to the bedchamber of his bride. Laughter and love ruled the Red Keep that night . . . whilst across Blackwater Bay, Lord Corlys the Sea Snake welcomed the king's brother Prince Daemon to a war council. The prince had suffered all he could stand of the Vale of Arryn, Runestone, and his lady wife. "Dark Sister was made for nobler tasks than slaughtering sheep," he is reported to have told the Lord of the Tides. "She has a thirst for blood." But it was not rebellion that the rogue prince had in mind; he saw another path to power.

The Stepstones, the chain of rocky islands between Dorne and the Disputed Lands of Essos, had long been a haunt of outlaws, exiles, wreckers, and pirates. In themselves the isles were of little worth, but placed as they were, they controlled the sea-lanes to and from the narrow sea, and merchant ships passing through those waters were oft made the prey of their inhabitants. Still, for centuries such depredations had remained no more than a nuisance.

Ten years earlier, however, the Free Cities of Lys, Myr, and Tyrosh had put aside their ancient enmities to make common cause in a war against Volantis. After defeating the Volantenes, the three victorious cities had entered into an "eternal alliance" and formed a strong new power: the Triarchy, better known in Westeros as the Kingdom of the Three Daughters, or, more rudely, the Three Whores (this "kingdom" was without a king, being governed by a council of thirty-three magisters). Once Volantis withdrew from the Disputed Lands, the Three Daughters had turned their gaze westward. Their armies swept over the Stepstones under the command of the Myrish prince-admiral, Craghas Drahar, who earned the sobriquet Craghas Crabfeeder by staking out hundreds of pirates on the wet sands, to drown beneath the rising tide.

The annexation of the Stepstones by the Triarchy at first met with approval from the lords of Westeros. Order had replaced chaos, and if the Three Daughters demanded a toll of any ship passing through their waters, that seemed a small price to pay.

The avarice of Craghas Crabfeeder and his partners in conquest soon turned feelings against them, however; the toll was raised again, and yet again, soon becoming so ruinous that merchants who had once paid gladly now sought to slip past the galleys of the Triarchy as once they had the pirates. Drahar and his Lysene and Tyroshi coadmirals seemed to be vying with one another to see who could demonstrate the greatest avarice. The Lyseni became especially loathed, for they claimed more than coin from passing ships, taking off women, girls, and comely young boys to serve in their pleasure gardens and pillow houses. (Amongst those thus enslaved was Lady Johanna Swann, a fifteen-year-old niece of the Lord of Stonehelm. When her infamously niggardly uncle refused to pay the ransom, she was sold to a pillow house, where she rose to become the celebrated courtesan known as the Black Swan, and ruler of Lys in all but name. Alas, her tale, however fascinating, has no bearing upon our present history.)

Of all the lords of Westeros, none suffered so much from these practices as Corlys Velaryon, Lord of the Tides, whose fleets had made him as wealthy and powerful as any man in the Seven Kingdoms. The Sea Snake was determined to put an end to the Triarchy's rule over the Stepstones, and in Daemon Targaryen he found a willing partner, eager for the gold and glory that victory in war would bring him. Shunning the king's wedding, they laid their plans in High Tide on the isle Driftmark. Lord Velaryon would command the fleet, Prince Daemon the army. They would be greatly outnumbered by the forces of the Three Daughters . . . but the prince would also bring to battle his dragon Caraxes, the Blood Wyrm, and his fires.

The fighting began in 106 AC. Prince Daemon had little difficulty assembling an army of landless adventurers and second sons, and won many victories during the first two years of the conflict. In 108 AC, when at last he came face-to-face with Craghas Crabfeeder, he slew him single-handed and cut off his head with Dark Sister.

King Viserys, doubtless pleased to be rid of his troublesome brother, supported his efforts with regular infusions of gold, and by 109 AC Daemon Targaryen and his army of sellswords and cutthroats controlled all but two of the islands, and the Sea Snake's fleets had taken firm control of the waters between. During this brief moment of victory, Prince Daemon declared himself King of the Stepstones and the Narrow Sea, and Lord Corlys placed a crown upon his head . . . but their "kingdom" was far from secure. The next year, the Kingdom of the Three Daughters dispatched a fresh invasion force under the command of a devious Tyroshi captain named Racallio Ryndoon, surely one of the most curious and flamboyant rogues in the annals of history, and Dorne joined the war in alliance with the Triarchy. Fighting resumed.

King Viserys and his court remained unperturbed. "Let Daemon play at war," His Grace is reported to have said. "It keeps him out of trouble." Viserys was a man of peace, and during these years King's Landing was an endless round of feasts, balls, and tourneys, where mummers and singers heralded the birth of each new Targaryen princeling. Queen Alicent had soon proved to be as fertile as she was pretty. In 107 AC, she bore the king a healthy son, naming him Aegon, after the Conqueror. Two years later, she produced a daughter for the king, Helaena; in 110 AC, she bore His Grace a second son, Aemond, who was said to be half the size of his elder brother but twice as fierce.

Yet Princess Rhaenyra continued to sit at the foot of the Iron Throne when her father held court, and His Grace began bringing her to meetings of the small council as well. Though many lords and knights sought her favor, the princess had eyes only for Ser Criston Cole, her gallant young sworn shield. "Ser Criston protects the princess from her enemies, but who protects the princess from Ser Criston?" Queen Alicent asked one day at court.

The amity between Her Grace and her stepdaughter had proved short-lived, for both Rhaenyra and Alicent aspired to be the first lady of the realm . . . and though the queen had given the king not one but two male heirs, Viserys had done nothing to change the order of succession. The Princess of Dragonstone remained his heir, with half the lords of Westeros sworn to defend her rights. Those who asked, "What of the ruling of the Great Council of 101?" found their words falling on deaf ears. The matter had been decided, so far as King Viserys was concerned; it was not an issue His Grace cared to revisit.

Still, questions persisted, not the least from Queen Alicent herself. Loudest amongst her supporters was her father, Ser Otto Hightower, Hand of the King. Pushed too far on the matter, in 109 AC King Viserys stripped Ser Otto of his chain of office and named in his place the taciturn Lord of Harrenhal, Lyonel Strong. "This Hand will not hector me," His Grace proclaimed.

Even after Ser Otto had returned to Oldtown, a "queen's party" still existed at court, a group of powerful lords friendly to Queen Alicent and supportive of the rights of her sons. Against them was pitted the "party of the princess." King Viserys loved both his wife and daughter and hated conflict and contention. He strove all his days to keep the peace between his women and to please both with gifts and gold and honors. So long as he lived and ruled and kept the balance, the feasts and tourneys continued as before, and peace prevailed throughout the realm . . . though there were some, sharp-eyed, who observed the dragons of one party snapping and spitting flame at the dragons of the other party whenever they chanced to pass near each other.

In 111 AC, a great tourney was held at King's Landing on the fifth anniversary of the king's marriage to Queen Alicent. At the opening feast, the queen wore a green gown, whilst the princess dressed dramatically in Targaryen red and black. Note was taken, and thereafter it became the custom to refer to "greens" and "blacks" when talking of the queen's party and the party of the princess, respectively. In the tourney itself, the blacks had much the better of it when Ser Criston Cole, wearing Princess Rhaenyra's favor, unhorsed all of the queen's champions, including two of her cousins and her youngest brother, Ser Gwayne Hightower.

Yet one was there who wore neither green nor black but rather gold and silver. Prince Daemon had at last returned to court. Wearing a crown and styling himself King of the Narrow Sea, he appeared unannounced in the skies above King's Landing on his dragon, circling thrice above the tourney grounds . . . but when at last he came to earth, he knelt before his brother and offered up his crown as a token of his love and fealty. Viserys returned the crown and kissed Daemon on both cheeks, welcoming him home, and the lords and commons sent up a thunderous cheer as the sons of Prince Baelon Targaryen were reconciled. Amongst those cheering loudest was Princess Rhaenyra, who was thrilled at the return of her favorite uncle, and begged him to stay a while.

Prince Daemon did remain at King's Landing for half a year, and even resumed his seat on the small council, but neither age nor exile had changed his nature. Daemon soon took up again with old companions from the gold cloaks and returned to the establishments along the Street of Silk where he had been such a valued patron. Though he treated Queen Alicent with all the courtesy due her station, there was no warmth between them, and men said that the prince was notably cool toward her children, especially his nephews Aegon and Aemond, whose birth had pushed him still lower in the order of succession.

Princess Rhaenyra was a different matter. Daemon spent long hours in her company, enthralling her with tales of his journeys and battles. He gave her pearls and silks and books and a jade tiara said once to have belonged to the Empress of Leng, read poems to her, dined with her, hawked with her, sailed with her, entertained her by making mock of the greens at court, the "lickspittles" fawning over Queen Alicent and her children. He praised her beauty, declaring her to be the fairest maid in all the Seven Kingdoms. Uncle and niece began to fly together almost daily, racing Syrax against Caraxes to Dragonstone and back.

Here our sources diverge. Grand Maester Runciter says only that the brothers quarreled again, and Prince Daemon departed King's Landing to return to the Stepstones and his wars. Of the cause of the quarrel, he does not speak. Others assert that it was at Queen Alicent's urging that Viserys sent Daemon away. But Septon Eustace and Mushroom tell another tale . . . or rather, two such tales. Eustace, the less salacious of the two, writes that Prince Daemon seduced his niece the princess and claimed her maidenhood. When the lovers were discovered abed together and brought before the king, Rhaenyra insisted she was in love with her uncle and pleaded with her father for leave to marry him. King Viserys would not hear of it, however, and reminded his daughter that Prince Daemon already had a wife. In his wroth, he confined his daughter to her chambers, told his brother to depart, and commanded both of them never to speak of what had happened.

The tale as told by Mushroom is far more depraved. According to the dwarf, it was Ser Criston Cole that the princess yearned for, not Prince Daemon, but Ser Criston was a true knight, noble and chaste and mindful of his vows, and though he was in her company day and night, he had never so much as kissed her, nor even said he loved her. "When he looks at you, he sees the little girl you were, not the woman you've become," Daemon told his niece, "but I can teach you how to make him see you as a woman."

He began by giving her kissing lessons, Mushroom claims. From there the prince went on to show his niece how best to touch a man to bring him pleasure—an exercise that sometimes involved Mushroom himself and his alleged enormous member. Daemon taught the girl to disrobe enticingly, suckled at her teats to make them more sensitive, and flew with her on dragonback to lonely rocks in Blackwater Bay, where they could disport naked unobserved and the princess could practice the art of pleasuring a man with her mouth. At night he would smuggle her from her rooms dressed as a page boy and take her to brothels on the Street of Silk, where the princess could observe men and women in the act of love, and learn the "womanly arts" from the harlots of King's Landing.

Just how long these lessons continued Mushroom does not say, but unlike Septon Eustace, he insists that Princess Rhaenyra remained a maiden, for she wished to preserve her innocence as a gift for her beloved. But when at last she approached her "white knight," using all she had learned, Ser Criston was horrified and spurned her. The whole tale soon came out, in no small part thanks to Mushroom himself. King Viserys at first refused to believe a word of it until Prince Daemon himself confirmed that the tale was true. "Give the girl to me to wife," he purportedly told his brother. "Who else would take her now?" Instead King Viserys sent him into exile, never to return to the Seven Kingdoms on pain of death. (Lord Strong, the King's Hand, argued that the prince should be put to death immediately as a traitor, but Septon Eustace reminded His Grace that no man is as accursed as the kinslayer.)

Of the aftermath, these things are certain. Daemon Targaryen returned to the Stepstones and resumed his struggle for those barren storm-swept rocks. Grand Maester Runciter and Ser Harrold Westerling, Lord Commander of the Kingsguard, both died in 112 AC. Ser Criston Cole was named the Lord Commander of the Kingsguard in

Ser Harrold's place, and the archmaesters of the Citadel sent Maester Mellos to the Red Keep to take up the grand maester's chain and duties. Elsewise, King's Landing returned to its customary tranquility for the best part of two years . . . until 113 AC, when Princess Rhaenyra turned sixteen, took possession of Dragonstone as her own seat, and married.

Long before any man had reason to doubt her innocence, the question of selecting a suitable consort for Rhaenyra had been of concern to King Viserys and his council. Great lords and dashing knights fluttered around her like moths around a flame, vying for her favor. When Rhaenyra visited the Trident in 112, the sons of Lord Bracken and Lord Blackwood fought a duel over her, and a younger son of House Frey made so bold as to ask openly for her hand (Fool Frey, he was called thereafter). In the west, Ser Jason Lannister and his twin Ser Tyland vied for her during a feast at Casterly Rock. The sons of Lord Tully of Riverrun, Lord Tyrell of Highgarden, Lord Oakheart of Old Oak, and Lord Tarly of Horn Hill paid court to the princess, as did the Hand's eldest son, Ser Harwin Strong. Breakbones, as he was called, was heir to Harrenhal and said to be the strongest man in the Seven Kingdoms. Viserys even talked of wedding Rhaenyra to the Prince of Dorne, as a way of bringing the Dornish into the realm.

Queen Alicent had her own candidate: her eldest son, Prince Aegon, Rhaenyra's half brother. But Aegon was a boy, the princess ten years his elder. Moreover, the two half siblings had never gotten on well. "All the more reason to bind them together in marriage," the queen argued. Viserys did not agree. "The boy is Alicent's own blood," he told Lord Strong. "She wants him on the throne."

The best choice, king and small council finally agreed, would be Rhaenyra's cousin, Laenor Velaryon. Though the Great Council of 101 had ruled against his claim, the Velaryon boy remained a grandson of Prince Aemon Targaryen of hallowed memory, and a great-grandson of the Old King himself, with dragon blood on both sides of his lineage. Such a match would unite and strengthen the royal bloodline and regain the Iron Throne the friendship of the Sea Snake with his powerful fleet. One objection was raised: Laenor Velaryon was now nineteen years of age yet had never shown any interest in women. Instead he surrounded himself with handsome squires of his own age and was said to prefer their company. But Grand Maester Mellos dismissed this concern out of hand. "What of it?" he is supposed to have said. "I am not fond of fish, but when fish is served, I eat it." Thus was the match decided.

King and council had neglected to consult the princess, however, and Rhaenyra proved to be very much her father's daughter, with her own notions about whom she wished to wed. The princess knew much and more about Laenor Velaryon and had no wish to be his bride. "My half brothers would be more to his taste," she told the king (the princess always took care to refer to Queen Alicent's sons as half brothers, never as brothers). And though His Grace reasoned with her, pleaded with her, shouted at her, and called her an ungrateful daughter, no words of his could budge her . . . until the king brought up the question of succession. What a king had done, a king could undo, Viserys pointed out. She would wed as he commanded, or he would make her half brother Aegon his heir in place of her. At this the princess's will gave way. Septon Eustace says she fell to her father's knees and begged for his forgiveness, Mushroom that she spat in her father's face. Both agree that in the end she consented to be married.

And here again our sources differ. That night, Septon Eustace reports, Ser Criston Cole slipped into the princess's bedchamber to confess his love for her. He told Rhaenyra that he had a ship waiting on the bay and begged her to flee with him across the narrow sea. They would be wed in Pentos or Tyrosh or Old Volantis, where her father's writ did not run, and no one would care that he had betrayed his vows as a member of the Kingsguard. His prowess with sword and morningstar was such that he did not doubt he could find some merchant prince to take him into service. But Rhaenyra refused him. She was the blood of the dragon, she reminded him, and meant for more than to live out her life as the wife of a common sellsword. And if he could set aside his Kingsguard vows, why would marriage vows mean any more to him?

Mushroom tells a very different tale. In his version, it was Princess Rhaenyra who went to Ser Criston, not him to her. She found him alone in White Sword Tower, barred the door, and slipped off her cloak to reveal her nakedness underneath. "I saved my maidenhead for you," she told him. "Take it now, as proof of my love. It will mean little and less to my betrothed, and perhaps when he learns that I am not chaste he will refuse me."

Yet for all her beauty, her entreaties fell on deaf ears, for Ser Criston was a man of honor and true to his vows. Scorned and furious, the princess donned her cloak and swept out into the night . . . where she chanced to meet Ser Harwin Strong, returning from a night of revelry in the stews of the city. Breakbones had long desired the princess and had none of Ser Criston's scruples. Thus it was he who took Rhaenyra's innocence, shedding her maiden's blood upon the sword of his manhood . . . according to Mushroom, who claims to have found them in bed at break of day.

However it happened, from that day forward the love that Ser Criston Cole had borne for Rhaenyra Targaryen turned to loathing, and the man who had hitherto been the princess's constant companion and champion became the most bitter of her foes.

Not long thereafter, Rhaenyra set sail for Driftmark, accompanied by her handmaids (two of them the daughters of the Hand and sisters to Ser Harwin), the fool Mushroom, and her new champion, Breakbones himself. In 114 AC, Rhaenyra Targaryen, Princess of Dragonstone, took to husband Ser Laenor Velaryon (knighted a fortnight before the wedding, since it was deemed necessary the prince consort be a knight). The bride was seventeen, the groom twenty, and all agreed that they made a handsome couple. The wedding was celebrated with seven days of feasts and jousting. Amongst the competitors were Queen Alicent's siblings, five Sworn Brothers of the Kingsguard, Breakbones, and the groom's favorite, Ser Joffrey Lonmouth, known as the Knight of Kisses. When Rhaenyra bestowed her garter on Ser Harwin, her new husband laughed and gave one of his own to Ser Joffrey.

Ser Criston Cole turned to Queen Alicent instead. Her Grace was pleased to grant him her favor. Wearing her token, the young Lord Commander of the Kingsguard defeated all challengers, fighting in a black fury. He left Breakbones with a broken collarbone and a shattered elbow (prompting Mushroom to name him Brokenbones thereafter), but it was the Knight of Kisses who felt the fullest measure of his wroth. Cole's favorite weapon was the morningstar, and the blows he rained down on Ser Laenor's champion cracked his helm and left him senseless in the mud. Borne bloody from the field, Ser Joffrey died without recovering consciousness six days later. Mushroom tells us that Ser Laenor spent every hour of those days at his bedside and wept bitterly when he died.

King Viserys was most wroth as well; a joyous celebration had become the occasion of grief and recrimination. It was said that Queen Alicent did not share his displeasure, however; soon after, she asked that Ser Criston Cole be made her personal protector. The coolness between the king's wife and the king's daughter was plain for all to see; even envoys from the Free Cities made note of it, in letters sent back to Pentos, Braavos, and Old Volantis.

Ser Laenor returned to Driftmark thereafter, leaving many to wonder if his marriage had ever been consummated. The princess remained at court, surrounded by her friends and admirers. Ser Criston Cole was not amongst them, having gone over entirely to the queen's party, the greens, but the massive and redoubtable Breakbones (or Brokenbones, as Mushroom had it) filled his place, becoming the foremost of the blacks, ever at Rhaenyra's side at feast and ball and hunt. Her husband raised no objections. Ser Laenor preferred the comforts of High Tide, where he soon found a new favorite in a household knight named Ser Qarl Correy.

Thereafter, though he joined his wife for important court events where his presence was expected, Ser Laenor spent most of his days apart from the princess. Septon Eustace says they shared a bed no more than a dozen times. Mushroom concurs, but adds that Qarl Correy oft shared that bed as well; it aroused the princess to watch the men disporting with each other, he tells us, and from time to time the two would include her in their pleasures. Yet Mushroom contradicts himself, for elsewhere he claims that the princess would leave her husband with his lover on such nights and seek her own solace in the arms of Harwin Strong.

Whatever the truth of these tales, it was soon announced that the princess was with child. Born in the waning days of 114 AC, the boy was a large, strapping lad, with brown hair, brown eyes, and a pug nose (Ser Laenor had the aquiline nose, silver-white hair, and purple eyes that bespoke his Valyrian blood). Laenor's wish to name the child Joffrey was overruled by his father, Lord Corlys. Instead the child was given a traditional Velaryon name: Jacaerys (friends and brothers would call him Jace).

The court was still rejoicing over the birth of the princess's child when her stepmother, Queen Alicent, also went into labor, delivering Viserys his third son, Daeron . . . whose coloring, unlike that of Jace, testified to his dragon blood. By royal command, the infants Jacaerys Velaryon and Daeron Targaryen shared a wet nurse until weaned. It was said that the king hoped to prevent any enmity between the two boys by raising them as milk brothers.

If so, his hopes proved to be sadly forlorn.

A year later, in 115 AC, there came a tragic mishap, of the sort that shapes the destiny of kingdoms: the "bronze bitch" of Runestone, Lady Rhea Royce, fell from her horse whilst hawking and cracked her skull upon a stone. She lingered for nine days before finally feeling well enough to leave her bed . . . only to collapse and die within an hour of rising. A raven was duly sent to Storm's End, and Lord Baratheon dispatched a messenger by ship to Bloodstone, where Prince Daemon was still struggling to defend his meager kingdom against the men of the Triarchy and their Dornish allies. Daemon flew at once for the Vale. "To put my wife to rest," he said, though more like it was in the hopes of laying claim to her lands, castles, and incomes. In that he failed; Runestone passed instead to Lady Rhea's nephew, and when Daemon made appeal to the Eyrie, not only was his claim dismissed, but Lady Jeyne warned him that his presence in the Vale was unwelcome.

Flying back to the Stepstones afterward, Prince Daemon landed at Driftmark to make a courtesy call upon his erstwhile partner in conquest, the Sea Snake, and the Princess Rhaenys. High Tide was one of the few places in the Seven Kingdoms where the king's brother could be confident he would not be turned away. There his eye fell upon Lord

Corlys's daughter Laena, a maid of two-and-twenty, tall, slender, and surpassingly lovely (even Mushroom was taken with her beauty, writing that she "was almost as pretty as her brother"), with a great mane of silver-gold ringlets that fell down past her waist. Laena had been betrothed from the age of twelve to a son of the Sealord of Braavos . . . but the father had died before they could be wed, and the son soon proved a wastrel and a fool, squandering his family's wealth and power before turning up on Driftmark. Lacking a graceful means to rid himself of the embarrassment, but unwilling to proceed with the marriage, Lord Corlys had repeatedly postponed the wedding.

Prince Daemon fell in love with Laena, the singers would have us believe. Men of a more cynical bent believe the prince saw her as a way to check his own descent. Once seen as his brother's heir, he had fallen far down in the line of succession, and neither the greens nor the blacks had a place for him . . . but House Velaryon was powerful enough to defy both parties with impunity. Weary of the Stepstones, and free at last of his "bronze bitch," Daemon Targaryen asked Lord Corlys for his daughter's hand in marriage.

The exiled Braavosi betrothed remained an impediment, but not for long; Daemon mocked him to his face so savagely the boy had no choice but to call him to defend his words with steel. Armed with Dark Sister, the prince made short work of his rival, and wed Lady Laena Velaryon a fortnight later, abandoning his hardscrabble kingdom on the Stepstones. (Five other men followed him as Kings of the Narrow Sea, until the brief and bloody history of that savage sellsword "kingdom" ended for good and all.)

Prince Daemon knew that his brother would not be pleased when he heard of his new marriage. Prudently, the prince and his new bride took themselves far from Westeros soon after the wedding, crossing the narrow sea on their dragons. Some said they flew to Valyria, in defiance of the curse that hung over that smoking wasteland, to search out the secrets of the dragonlords of the old Freehold. The truth was less romantic. Prince Daemon and Lady Laena flew first to Pentos, where they were feted by the city's prince. The Pentoshi feared the growing power of the Triarchy to the south and saw Daemon as a valuable ally against the Three Daughters. From there, the prince and his bride crossed to Old Volantis, where they enjoyed a similar warm welcome. Then they flew up the Rhoyne, to Qohor and Norvos. In those cities, far removed from the woes of Westeros and the power of the Triarchy, their welcome was less rapturous. Everywhere they went, however, huge crowds turned out for a glimpse of Vhagar and Caraxes.

The dragonriders were once again in Pentos when Lady Laena learned she was with child. Eschewing further flight, Prince Daemon and his wife settled in a manse outside the city walls as guests of a Pentoshi magister, until such time as the babe was born.

Meanwhile, back in Westeros, Princess Rhaenyra had given birth to a second son late in the year 115 AC. The child was named Lucerys (Luke for short). Septon Eustace tells us that both Ser Laenor and Ser Harwin were at Rhaenyra's bedside for his birth. Like his brother Jace, Luke had brown eyes and a healthy head of brown hair, rather than the silver-gilt hair of Targaryen princelings, but he was a large and lusty lad, and King Viserys was delighted with him when the child was presented at court. These feelings were not shared by his queen. "Do keep trying," Queen Alicent told Ser Laenor. "Soon or late, you may get one who looks like you." And the rivalry between the greens and blacks grew deeper, finally reaching the point where the queen and the princess could scarce suffer each other's presence. Thereafter Queen Alicent kept to the Red Keep of King's Landing, whilst the princess spent her days on Dragonstone with her champion, Ser Harwin Strong. Her husband, Ser Laenor, was said to visit "frequently."

In 116 AC, in the Free City of Pentos, Lady Laena gave birth to twin daughters, Daemon Targaryen's first trueborn children. The prince named the girls Baela (after his father) and Rhaena (after her mother). When they were half a year old, the girls and their mother sailed to Driftmark, whilst Daemon flew ahead with both dragons. From High Tide, he sent a raven to King's Landing, informing the king of the birth of his nieces and begging leave to present the girls at court to receive a royal blessing. Though his Hand and small council argued heatedly against it, Viserys consented, for the king still loved the brother who had been the companion of his youth. "Daemon is a father now," he told Grand Maester Mellos. "He will have changed." Thus were the sons of Baelon Targaryen reconciled for the second time.

In 117 AC, on Dragonstone, Princess Rhaenyra bore yet another son. Ser Laenor was at last permitted to name a child after his fallen friend, Ser Joffrey Lonmouth. Joffrey Velaryon was as big and red-faced and healthy as his brothers, but like them he had brown hair, brown eyes, and features that some at court called common. The whispering began again. Amongst the greens, it was an article of faith that the father of Rhaenyra's sons was not her husband, Laenor, but her champion, Harwin Strong.

Whatever the truth of these allegations, there was never any doubt that King Viserys still meant for his daughter to follow him upon the Iron Throne, and her sons to follow her in turn. By royal decree, each of the Velaryon boys was presented with a dragon's egg whilst in the cradle. Those who doubted the paternity of Rhaenyra's sons whispered that the eggs would never hatch, but the birth in turn of three young dragons gave the lie to their words. The hatchlings were named Vermax, Arrax, and Tyraxes. And Septon Eustace tells us that His Grace sat Jace upon his knee atop the Iron Throne as he was holding court, and was heard to say, "One day this will be your seat, lad."

Childbirth exacted a toll on the princess; the weight that Rhaenyra gained during her pregnancies never entirely left her, and by the time the youngest boy was born, she had grown stout and thick of waist, the beauty of her girlhood a fading memory, though she was but twenty years of age. According to Mushroom, this only served to deepen her resentment of her stepmother, Queen Alicent, who remained slender and graceful at almost twice her age.

The sins of the fathers are oft visited on the sons, wise men have said; and so it is for the sins of mothers as well. The enmity between Queen Alicent and Princess Rhaenyra was passed on to their sons, and the queen's three boys, the Princes Aegon, Aemond, and Daeron, grew to be bitter rivals of their Velaryon nephews, resentful of them for having stolen what they regarded as their birthright: the Iron Throne itself. Though all six boys attended the same feasts, balls, and revels, and sometimes trained together in the yard under the same master-at-arms and studied under the same maesters, this enforced closeness only served to feed their mutual mislike rather than binding them together as brothers.

Whilst Princess Rhaenyra misliked her stepmother, Queen Alicent, she became fond and more than fond of her good-sister Lady Laena. With Driftmark and Dragonstone so close, Daemon and Laena oft visited with the princess, and her with them. Many a time they flew together on their dragons, and the princess's she-dragon Syrax produced several clutches of eggs. In 118 AC, with the blessing of King Viserys, Rhaenyra announced the betrothal of her two eldest sons to the daughters of Prince Daemon and Lady Laena. Jacaerys was four and Lucerys three, the girls two. And in 119 AC, when Laena found she was with child again, Rhaenyra flew to Driftmark to attend her during the birth.

And so it was that the princess was at her good-sister's side on the third day of that accursed year 120 AC, the Year of the Red Spring. A day and a night of labor left Laena Velaryon pale and weak, but finally she gave birth to the son Prince Daemon had so long desired—but the babe was twisted and malformed, and died within the hour. Nor did his mother long survive him. Her grueling labor had drained all of Lady Laena's strength, and grief weakened her still further, making her helpless before the onset of childbed fever.

As her condition steadily worsened, despite the best efforts of Driftmark's young maester, Prince Daemon flew to Dragonstone and brought back Princess Rhaenyra's own maester, an older and more experienced man renowned for his skills as a healer. Sadly, Maester Gerardys came too late. After three days of delirium, Lady Laena passed from this mortal coil. She was but twenty-seven. During her final hour, it is said, Lady Laena rose from her bed and made her way from her room, intent on reaching Vhagar that she might fly one last time before she died. Her strength failed her on the tower steps, however, and it was there she collapsed and died. Her husband, Prince Daemon, carried her back to her bed. Afterward, Princess Rhaenyra sat vigil with him over Lady Laena's corpse and comforted him in his grief.

Lady Laena's death was the first tragedy of 120 AC, but it would not be the last. For this was to be the year when many of the long-simmering tensions and jealousies that had plagued the Seven Kingdoms finally came to a boil, a year when many and more would have reason to wail and grieve and rend their garments . . . though none more than the Sea Snake, Lord Corlys Velaryon, and his noble wife, Princess Rhaenys, she who might have been a queen.

The Lord of the Tides and his lady were still in mourning for their beloved daughter when the Stranger came again, to carry off their son. Ser Laenor Velaryon, husband to the Princess Rhaenyra and the putative father of her children, was slain whilst attending a fair in Spicetown, stabbed to death by his friend and companion Ser Qarl Correy. The two men had been quarreling loudly before blades were drawn, merchants at the fair told Lord Velaryon when he came to collect his son's body. Correy had fled by then, wounding several men who tried to hinder him. Some claimed a ship had been waiting for him offshore. He was never seen again.

The circumstances of the murder remain a mystery to this day. Grand Maester Mellos writes only that Ser Laenor was killed by one of his own household knights after a quarrel. Septon Eustace provides us with the killer's name, and declares jealousy the motive for the slaying; Laenor Velaryon had grown weary of Ser Qarl's companionship and grown enamored of a new favorite, a handsome young squire of six-and-ten. Mushroom, as always, favors the most sinister theory, suggesting that Prince Daemon paid Qarl Correy to dispose of Princess Rhaenyra's husband, arranged for a ship to carry him away, then cut his throat and fed him to the sea. A household knight of relatively low birth, Correy was known to have a lord's tastes and a peasant's purse, and was given to extravagant wagering besides, which lends a certain credence to the fool's version of events. Yet there was no shred of proof, then or now, though the Sea Snake offered a reward of ten thousand golden dragons for any man who could lead him to Ser Qarl Correy or deliver the killer to a father's vengeance.

Even this was not the end of the tragedies that would mark that dreadful year. The next occurred at High Tide after Ser Laenor's funeral, when king and court made the journey to Driftmark for the funeral pyre, many on the back of their dragons. (So many dragons were present that Septon Eustace wrote that Driftmark had become the new Valyria.)

The cruelty of children is known to all. Prince Aegon Targaryen was thirteen, Princess Helaena twelve, Prince Aemond ten, and Prince Daeron six. Both Aegon and Helaena were dragonriders. Helaena now flew Dreamfyre, the she-dragon who had once carried Rhaena, Maegor the Cruel's "black bride," whilst her brother Aegon's young Sunfyre was said to be the most beautiful dragon ever seen upon the earth. Even Prince Daeron had a dragon, a beautiful blue she-dragon named Tessarion, though he had yet to ride. Only the middle son, Prince Aemond, remained dragonless, but His Grace had hopes of rectifying that, and had put forward the notion that perhaps the court might sojourn at Dragonstone after the funerals. A wealth of dragon's eggs could be found beneath the Dragonmont, and several young hatchlings as well. Prince Aemond could have his choice "if the lad is bold enough."

Even at ten, Aemond Targaryen did not lack for boldness. The king's gibe stung, and he resolved not to wait for Dragonstone. What did he want with some puny hatchling, or some stupid egg?

Right there at High Tide was a dragon worthy of him: Vhagar, the oldest, largest, most terrible dragon in the world.

Even for a son of House Targaryen, there are always dangers in approaching a strange dragon, particularly an old, bad-tempered dragon who has recently lost her rider. His father and mother would never allow him to go near Vhagar, Aemond knew. So he made certain they did not know, sliding from his bed at dawn whilst they still slept and stealing down to the great outer yard where Vhagar and the other dragons were fed and stabled. The prince had hoped to mount Vhagar in secrecy, but as he crept up to the dragon a boy's voice rang out: "You stay away from her!"

The voice belonged to the youngest of his half nephews, Joffrey Velaryon, a boy of three. Always an early riser, Joff had sneaked down from his bed to see his own young dragon, Tyraxes. Afraid that the boy would raise the alarm, Prince Aemond slapped him, shouted at him to be quiet, then shoved him backward into a pile of dragon droppings. As

Joff began to bawl, Aemond raced to Vhagar and clambered up onto her back. Later he would say that he was so afraid of being caught that he forgot to be frightened of being burned to death and eaten.

Call it boldness, call it madness, call it fortune or the will of the gods or the caprice of dragons. Who can know the mind of such a beast? We do know this: Vhagar roared, lurched to her feet, shook violently . . . then snapped her chains and flew. And the boy prince Aemond Targaryen became a dragonrider, circling twice around the towers of High Tide before coming down again.

But when he landed, Rhaenyra's sons were waiting for him.

Joffrey had run for his brothers when Aemond took to the sky, and both Jace and Luke had come to his call. The Velaryon princelings were younger—Jace was six, Luke five, Joff three—but there were three of them, and they had armed themselves with wooden swords from the training yard. Now they fell on him with a fury. Aemond fought back, breaking Luke's nose with a punch, then wrenching the sword from Joff's hands and cracking it across the back of Jace's head, driving him to his knees. As the younger boys scrambled back away from him, bloody and bruised, the prince began to mock them, calling them the Strongs. Jace was old enough to grasp the insult. He flew at Aemond again, but the older boy began pummeling him savagely . . . until Luke, coming to the rescue of his brother, drew his dagger and slashed Aemond's face, taking out his right eye. By the time the stableboys arrived to pull apart the combatants, the prince was writhing on the ground, howling in pain, and Vhagar was roaring as well.

Afterward, King Viserys tried to make a peace, requiring each of the boys to tender a formal apology to his rivals on the other side, but these courtesies did not appease their mothers. Queen Alicent demanded that one of Lucerys's eyes be put out for the eye he had cost Aemond. Rhaenyra would have none of that, but insisted that Prince Aemond should be questioned "sharply" until he revealed where he had heard her sons called "Strongs." To so name them, of course, was tantamount to saying they were bastards, with no rights of succession . . . and that she herself was guilty of high treason. When pressed by the king, Prince

Aemond said it was his brother Aegon who had told him they were Strongs, and Prince Aegon said only, "*Everyone* knows. Just look at them."

King Viserys finally put an end to the questioning, declaring he would hear no more. No eyes would be put out, he decreed . . . but should anyone—"man or woman or child, noble or common or royal"—mock his grandsons as "Strongs" again, their tongues would be pulled out with hot pincers. His Grace further commanded his wife and daughter to kiss and exchange vows of love and affection, but their false smiles and empty words deceived no one but the king. As for the boys, Prince Aemond said later that he lost an eye and gained a dragon that day, and counted it a fair exchange.

To prevent further conflict, and put an end to these "vile rumors and base calumnies," King Viserys further decreed that Queen Alicent and her sons would return with him to court, whilst Princess Rhaenyra confined herself to Dragonstone with her sons. Henceforth Ser Erryk Cargyll of the Kingsguard would serve as her sworn shield, whilst Breakbones returned to Harrenhal.

These rulings pleased no one, Septon Eustace writes. Mushroom demurs: one man at least was thrilled by the decrees, for Dragonstone and Driftmark lay quite close to each other, and this proximity would allow Daemon Targaryen ample opportunity to comfort his niece, Princess Rhaenyra, unbeknownst to the king.

Though Viserys I would reign for nine more years, the bloody seeds of the Dance of the Dragons had already been planted, and 120 AC was the year when they began to sprout.

Next to perish were the elder Strongs. Lyonel Strong, Lord of Harrenhal and Hand of the King, accompanied his son and heir Ser Harwin on his return to the great, half-ruined castle on the lakeshore. Shortly after their arrival, a fire broke out in the tower where they were sleeping, and both father and son were killed, along with three of their retainers and a dozen servants. The cause of the fire was never determined. Some put it down to simple mischance, whilst others muttered that Black Harren's seat was cursed, and brought only doom to any man who held it. Many suspected the blaze was set intentionally. Mushroom suggests that the Sea Snake was behind it, as an act of vengeance against the man who had cuckolded his son. Septon Eustace, more plausibly, suspects Prince Daemon, removing a rival for Princess Rhaenyra's affections. Other have put forth the notion that Larys Clubfoot might have been responsible; with his father and elder brother dead, Larys Strong became the Lord of Harrenhal.

The most disturbing possibility was advanced by none other than Grand Maester Mellos, who muses that the king himself might have given the command. If Viserys had come to accept that the rumors about the parentage of Rhaenyra's children were true, he might have wished to remove the man who had dishonored his daughter lest he reveal the bastardy of her sons. Were that so, Lyonel Strong's death was an unfortunate accident, for his lordship's decision to see his son back to Harrenhal had been unforeseen.

Lord Strong had been the King's Hand, and Viserys had come to rely upon his strength and counsel. His Grace had reached the age of three-and-forty, and had grown quite stout. He no longer had a young man's vigor and was afflicted by gout, aching joints, back pain, and a tightness in the chest that came and went and oft left him red-faced and short of breath. The governance of the realm was a daunting task; the king needed a strong, capable Hand to shoulder some of his burdens. Briefly he considered sending for Princess Rhaenyra. Who better to rule with him than the daughter he meant to succeed him on the Iron Throne? But that would have meant bringing the princess and her sons back to King's Landing, where more conflict with the queen and her own brood would have been inevitable. He considered his brother as well, until he recalled Prince Daemon's previous stints on the small council. Grand Maester Mellos suggested bringing in some younger man, and put forward several names, but His Grace chose familiarity, and recalled to court Ser Otto Hightower, the queen's father, who had filled the office before for both Viserys and the Old King.

Yet hardly had Ser Otto arrived at the Red Keep to take up the Handship than word reached court that Princess Rhaenyra had remarried, taking to husband her uncle, Daemon Targaryen. The princess was twenty-three, Prince Daemon thirty-nine.

King, court, and commons were all outraged by the news. Neither Daemon's wife nor Rhaenyra's husband had been dead even half a year; to wed again so soon was an insult to their memory, His Grace declared angrily. The marriage had been performed on Dragonstone, suddenly and secretly. Septon Eustace claims that Rhaenyra knew that her father would never approve of the match, so she wed in haste to make certain he could not prevent the marriage. Mushroom puts forward a different reason: The princess was once again with child, and did not wish to birth a bastard.

And thus that dreadful year 120 AC ended as it had begun, with a woman laboring in childbirth. Princess Rhaenyra's pregnancy had a happier outcome than Lady Laena's had. As the year waned, she brought forth a small but robust son, a pale princeling with dark purple eyes and pale silvery hair. She named him Aegon. Prince Daemon had at last a living son of his own blood . . . and this new prince, unlike his three half brothers, was plainly a *Targaryen*.

In King's Landing, Queen Alicent grew most wroth when she learned the babe had been named Aegon, taking it for a slight against her own Aegon . . . which it most certainly was. (Hereafter, we will refer to Queen Alicent's son as Aegon the Elder and Princess Rhaenyra's son as Aegon the Younger.)

By all rights, the year 122 AC should have been a joyous one for House Targaryen. Princess Rhaenyra took to the birthing bed once more, and gave her uncle Daemon a second son, named Viserys after his grandsire. The child was smaller and less robust than his brother Aegon and his Velaryon half brothers, but proved to be a most precocious child . . . though, somewhat ominously, the dragon's egg placed in his cradle never hatched. The greens took that for an ill omen and were not shy about saying as much.

Later that same year, King's Landing celebrated a wedding as well. Following the ancient tradition of House Targaryen, King Viserys wed his son Aegon the Elder to his daughter Helaena. The groom was fifteen years of age, a lazy and somewhat sulky boy, Septon Eustace tells us, but possessed of more than healthy appetites, a glutton at table, given to swilling ale and strongwine and pinching and fondling any serving girl who strayed within his reach. The bride, his sister, was but thirteen. Though plumper and less striking than most Targaryens, Helaena was a pleasant, happy girl, and all agreed she would make a fine mother.

And so she did, and quickly. Barely a year later, in 123 AC, the fourteen-year-old princess gave birth to twins, a boy she named Jaehaerys and a girl called Jaehaera. Prince Aegon had heirs of his own now, the greens at court proclaimed happily. A dragon's egg was placed in the cradle of each child, and two hatchlings soon came forth. Yet all was not well with these new twins. Jaehaera was tiny and slow to grow. She did not cry, she did not smile, she did none of the things a babe was meant to do. Her brother, whilst larger and more robust, was also less perfect than was expected of a Targaryen princeling, boasting six fingers on his left hand, and six toes upon each foot.

A wife and children did little to curb the carnal appetites of Prince Aegon the Elder, who fathered two bastard children the same year as his trueborn twins: a boy on a girl whose maidenhood he bought on the Street of Silk, and a girl by one of his mother's maidservants. And in 127 AC, Princess Helaena gave birth to his second son, who was given a dragon's egg and the name Maelor.

Queen Alicent's other sons had been growing older as well. Prince Aemond, despite the loss of his eye, had become a proficient and dangerous swordsman under the tutelage of Ser Criston Cole but remained a wild and willful child, hot-tempered and unforgiving. His little brother Prince Daeron was the most popular of the queen's sons, as clever as he was courteous, and most comely as well. When he turned twelve in 126 AC, Daeron was sent to Oldtown to serve as cupbearer and squire to Lord Hightower.

That same year, across Blackwater Bay, the Sea Snake was stricken by a sudden fever. As he took to his bed, surrounded by maesters, the issue arose as to who should succeed him as Lord of the Tides and Master of Driftmark should the sickness claim him. With his trueborn children dead, by law his lands and titles should pass to his grandson Jacaerys . . . but since Jace would presumably ascend the Iron Throne after his mother, Princess Rhaenyra urged her good-father to name instead her second son, Lucerys. Lord Corlys also had half a dozen nephews, however, and the eldest of them, Ser Vaemond Velaryon, protested that the inheritance by rights should pass to him . . . on the grounds that Rhaenyra's sons were bastards sired by Harwin Strong. The princess was not slow in answering this charge. She dispatched Prince Daemon to seize Ser Vaemond, had his head removed, and fed his carcass to her dragon.

Even this did not end the matter, however. Ser Vaemond's younger brothers fled to King's Landing with his wife and sons, there to cry for justice and place their claims before the king and queen. King Viserys had grown extremely fat and red of face, and scarce had the strength to mount the steps to the Iron Throne. His Grace heard them out in a stony silence, then ordered their tongues removed, every one. "You were warned," he declared, as they were being dragged away. "I will hear no more of these lies."

Yet as he was descending, His Grace stumbled and reached out to right himself, and sliced his left hand open to the bone on a jagged blade protruding from the throne. Though Grand Maester Mellos washed the cut out with boiled wine and bound up the hand with strips of linen soaked in healing ointments, fever soon followed, and many feared the king might die. Only the arrival of Princess Rhaenyra from Dragonstone turned the tide, for with her came her own healer, Maester Gerardys, who acted swiftly to remove two fingers from His Grace's hand to save his life.

Though much weakened by his ordeal, King Viserys soon resumed the rule. To celebrate his recovery, a feast was held on the first day of 127 AC. The princess and the queen were both commanded to attend, with all their children. In a show of amity, each woman wore the other's color and many declarations of love were made, to the king's great pleasure. Prince Daemon raised a cup to Ser Otto Hightower, and thanked him for his leal service as Hand and Ser Otto in turn spoke of the prince's courage, whilst Alicent's children and Rhaenyra's greeted one another with kisses and broke bread together at table. Or so the court chronicles record.

Yet late in the evening, after King Viserys had departed (for His Grace still tired easily), Mushroom tells us that Aemond One-Eye rose to toast his Velaryon cousins, speaking in mock admiration of their brown hair, brown eyes . . . and strength. "I have never known anyone so strong as my sweet cousins," he ended. "So let us drain our cups to these three strong boys." Still later, the fool reports, Aegon the Elder took offense when Jacaerys asked his wife, Helaena, for a dance. Angry words were exchanged, and the two princes might have come to blows if not for the intervention of the Kingsguard. Whether King Viserys was ever informed of these incidents we do not know, but Princess Rhaenyra and her sons returned to their own seat on Dragonstone the next morning.

After the loss of his fingers, Viserys I never sat upon the Iron Throne again. Thereafter he shunned the throne room, preferring to hold court in his solar, and later in his bedchamber, surrounded by maesters, septons, and his faithful fool Mushroom, the only man who could still make him laugh (says Mushroom). His Grace did recover some of his old vigor when Grand Maester Mellos passed away and was replaced by Grand Maester Gerardys, whose potions and tinctures proved more efficacious than the leechings Mellos had preferred. But such recoveries proved short-lived, and gout, chest pains, and shortness of breath continued to trouble the king. His health failing, Viserys left ever more of the governance of the realm to his Hand and small council.

As the Seven Kingdoms welcomed the 129th year after Aegon's Conquest with bonfires, feasts, and bacchanals, King Viserys I Targaryen was growing ever weaker. His chest pains had grown so severe that he could no longer climb a flight of steps and had to be carried about the Red Keep in a chair. By the second moon of the year, His Grace had lost all appetite and was ruling the realm from his bed . . . when he felt strong enough to rule at all. On Dragonstone, meanwhile, Princess Rhaenyra was once again great with child. She too took to her bed, with her husband the rogue prince ever at her side.

On the third day of the third moon of 129 AC, Princess Helaena brought her three children to visit with the king in his chambers. The twins Jaehaerys and Jaehaera were six years old, their brother Maelor only two. His Grace gave the babe a pearl ring off his finger to play with, and told the twins the story of how their great-great-grandsire and namesake Jaehaerys the Old King had flown his dragon north to the Wall to defeat a vast host of wildlings, giants, and wargs. The children listened attentively. Afterward the king sent them away, pleading weariness. Then Viserys of House Targaryen, the First of His Name, King of the Andals, the Rhoynar, and the First Men, Lord of the Seven Kingdoms and Protector of the Realm, closed his eyes and went to sleep.

He never woke. His Grace was fifty-two years of age and had reigned over most of Westeros for twenty-six years.

The tale of Prince Daemon Targaryen's bold deeds, black crimes, and heroic death in the carnage that followed are well known to all, so we shall end our story here.

After this the storm broke, and the dragons danced and died.

Story copyrights

About the Editors

George R. R. Martin is the #1 *New York Times* bestselling author of many novels, including the acclaimed series A Song of Ice and Fire—*A Game of Thrones, A Clash of Kings, A Storm of Swords, A Feast for Crows,* and *A Dance with Dragons.* As a writer-producer, he has worked on *The Twilight Zone, Beauty and the Beast,* and various feature films and pilots that were never made. He lives with the lovely Parris in Santa Fe, New Mexico.

Gardner Dozois has won fifteen Hugo Awards and thirty-two Locus Awards for his editing work, plus two Nebula Awards for his own writing. He was the editor of *Asimov's Science Fiction* for twenty years, and is the author or editor of over a hundred books, including *The Year's Best Science Fiction.*